THE EPIMETHEUS TRIAL
BOOK TWO
INTO ANTIQUITY

I0584829

E. A. SETSER

"Into Antiquity"

Book Two of "The Epimetheus Trial"

©   Copyright 2016 Social Detriment Publishing

Cover Art by Angela McNeese

Editing by Brendan Bird

The Epimetheus Trial

Elder Blood

Into Antiquity

To Tavin

For not letting me give up on this.

Prologue

Years of history smudged away

By regret spiked with hatred

A monster born in captivity

Freed against their will

The landscape purged

Within and without

Cover the tracks

Ruin the beast

Even the greatest flood

Cannot wash the past away

A river of deceit carved the land

Though as the stream of lies is dammed

Truth will bleed through the cracks in the façade

1

Chapter 1

Leaning back in his executive leather throne, Spril thumbed through a stack of papers propped on his thigh. Behind him, the urban landscape stretched toward every horizon. It had, somewhat paradoxically, reverted and evolved since he first claimed this office.

He paused to study a packet more intently. With a knowing smile, he laid the papers aside and reached for his intercom.

"Chief Negotiator Phylus?" he called.

"Brigadier General Elite Spril?" Phylus answered with mock formality, "Come on, man. We're on a closed channel, and I used to change your diapers. Drop the formality."

"Hey, I did not climb up to this post to ignore protocol," Spril scoffed, "And neither did you."

"I used to wipe your ass, Spril," Phylus deflected, "I think it's okay if we work on a names-only basis here."

"Fine then," Spril sighed, "I have an assignment for you."

"Let's hear it, buddy."

"We're due to send foreign aid to Berinin," Spril answered, ignoring the flippant casualness of his colleague.

"That time again already, is it?" Phylus mused, digging in one of his desk drawers.

"Sneaked up on me, as well," Spril agreed, "Remember, this is our last contracted donation, so let's make the most of it. Show them we haven't forgotten what Chieftain Sage Galo did for us. Get with Chief Treasurer Biroe and have him allocate as much as we can stand to spare."

"I'll get right on it."

"I'd also rather not simply mail the money as we usually do."

"That's delicate cargo. I'll work with EshCal to coordinate guards and couriers."

"Half of that won't be necessary. You've been requested as transporter."

"Are you serious?" Phylus guffawed, trying to mask his excitement, "Who issued the request?"

"The only person even I can't pull rank on," Spril smirked.

"Of course she did. I'll have a word with her."

"Naturally. Well, call me when Biroe has our figures, please."

Phylus cut the line, shaking his head. A trip to Berinin, even a business trip, would be a welcome reprieve from the marble and tile scenery of ArcNos's Platinum Hall, but the circumstances left him wary. Although Biroe worked directly across the hall, he paged him on his desk intercom.

"Biroe!" he opened, "Phylus here. Are you in the middle of anything urgent?"

"That's Chief Treasurer Biroe to you," Biroe teased, "My plate's pretty empty over here, actually. What did you need?"

"Fifth anniversary of the attack on Masnethege."

"Say no more, my friend."

Biroe cut the transmission at that, having already gleaned what Phylus expected of him. Despite his ignorance at the time, he had helped fund the development of the Triad Titan and the subsequent assault on Masnethege. He had thus come to hold himself partially accountable. His first encounter with Galo amplified this guilt, despite the fact that it ended with his car in shambles.

In fact, Galo, Eytea, and Sinkua had kindled within him a sense of empowerment unlike any he had ever known. For this, he sought to both extend his gratitude and atone for his wrongdoing, regardless of his past ignorance.

Sidestepping the looming financial crisis brought on by the last administration had been a delicate balancing act. The Avatars of Fate had fed most public services to the war machine, also taking a sizable helping for themselves. Admittedly, the wanton destruction brought on by the Subtransit Resistance had padded the bill. Biroe assuaged his guilt by telling himself that it had been for nobler ends. He often worried that only he had considered the economic impact, even though most of his current staff had lived and worked in the Subtransit.

In no particular order, he paged each member of his committee to request budget reports. They collaborated regularly, but each specialized in a particular sector of the economy. Many landed their positions in the treaty and merger, but Biroe had personally selected the head of the infrastructure budget.

KalChi had been his colleague since his university days. Biroe had long respected her talent and thus found her perfect for this particularly demanding position. Anxious despite his authority, he paged her last.

"K-KalChi?" he stammered, "This is Chief Treasurer Biroe. Do you have a moment?"

"Of course, sir. What do you need?" KalChi answered mellowly.

"We're compiling the fifth donation to Masnethege. You know, the situation with ArcNos and the Triad Titan?"

"Yes, I remember," she muttered, "Those damn mechs ruined me and a lot of my colleagues."

"I'm sorry, I just…"

"Not your fault, sir. Anyway, you were saying?"

"Right then," Biroe fumbled, "I need our projected infrastructure budget for the next thirteen months."

"You need to know what we can spare without biting our own asses, right?" KalChi deduced, "How about I do you one better and just tell you what we can siphon from infrastructure?"

"That would be fantastic, KalChi. Thank you."

"I'll have it to you as quickly as possible."

Phylus navigated the maze of cubicles, searching for a familiar skullcap hung upon a corner. He felt a twinge of guilt for having not memorized the route to her cubicle, but most bore so little personalization that the rows looked all but identical. He hurried his gait as he spotted her cubicle, stepping softly on the noise-dampening carpet.

"What do you think you're doing?" he whispered hoarsely.

"Working?" Vielle called back, turning her chair, "Why? What do you think I'm doing?"

"Overstepping your bounds. Just because I got you this Junior Consultant position, doesn't mean…"

"Oh come on, you know my sociology degree got me this job" she argued, raising her voice slightly.

"It helped me talk your boss into taking a chance on you, but she flat out said that she was doing me a favor," Phylus scolded, "Like I said, you are overstepping your bounds. You know Spril can't say no to you."

"If you're worried about people thinking he's playing favorites, just say so."

"It's not that. Everyone plays favorites, and anyone who bitches about it has never been anyone's favorite."

"Then what is this about? I have work to do, because apparently, I still need to prove myself."

"And I have work to do, too. Don't ask Spril to send me on business trips without checking with me first. Don't ask me why, but he finds it pretty easy to say no to me if it means not saying no to you."

"Dad. Calm down," Vielle smiled, "I've got it under control. You'll see what I mean when you get back to your office. Plus I got my leave approved before I even asked Spril about it."

"This discussion is not over," Phylus ordered.

"Dad!" she protested, "My phone is ringing. I'm sorry, but we'll have to pick this up later, okay?"

Phylus nodded authoritatively and shuffled out of the cubicle maze exit. Even with his deserved title of Chief Negotiator, his daughter could still weasel her way out of nigh any trouble. He often wondered how she had yet to coax out the truth about her mother.

Upon returning to his office, he found a memo posted on his desk. Two of his associates had offered to take over his workload during his trip, the dates left blank since the itinerary had not yet been finalized. Still wanting the last word, he headed for Brigadier Elite EshCal's office at the other end of the Platinum Hall.

"EshCal?" he called as he knocked, "I need to speak with you."

"What do you need?" she answered as she opened the door shortly thereafter, "I'm rather busy, so please be quick about it. Got new Green Rookies this week, and I need to decide who's going to train whom."

"I'm taking the last donation to Berinin. Vielle has been assigned to accompany me."

"I suppose she made that happen," EshCal mused.

"Naturally."

"Do you want me to find someone to work guard duty with her?"

"Either that or get me a good shotgun and sidearm if you're too pressed for time."

"I'm putting a soldier on that boat with you," she insisted, unaware of Phylus's bait even as she bit it, "One with cannon and melee training."

Phylus nodded and returned to his office. He poured himself a cup of coffee, only for his intercom to interrupt his first sip.

"Chief Negotiator Phylus," Spril ordered, "Parliament assembles in fifteen minutes. Compile your case files, and I'll meet you there."

"Right. Of course," Phylus agreed, wincing as he swigged his coffee, "I'll be right there."

Since his ascension to Brigadier General Elite and the restoration of Parliamentary order, Spril had been working to diminish his own authority. The position historically placed military leadership as a top priority, and he believed that this should not qualify him to rule on non-military affairs such as education and healthcare.

HarEin had worked toward such ends, but he had failed to garner the necessary support before the Avatars of Fate had overthrown Parliament. In fact, many believed that standard had made ArcNos vulnerable to their invasion. Once they coaxed the remaining Parliamentary Chairs off the fence though, Spril and his compatriots could implement a new standard.

A vast circular room housed the Parliamentary hall, a table lining the perimeter about two meters from the wall. Intervallic hinged platforms perforated the table, allowing access to the central dais. Spril stood atop the dais, surrounded by Parliamentary Representatives, when EshCal and SenRas entered the room. They joined Phylus and Biroe along the wall.

"If we are to remain relevant in the modern world," Spril insisted, "This is the only way forward. After what CreSam and the Avatars of Fate brought upon Ouristihra on behalf of our nation . . ."

"There you go again, bringing up the Avatars of Fate!" a comparatively young Representative argued, "It's been five years. We can't keep blaming them."

"The floor does not recognize Representative LenSom," Spril countered, "As I was saying, we have made considerable progress toward smudging away the nearly indelible stain on our international reputation, but..."

"What? Why not? You afraid of the truth?" LenSom taunted, "Maybe you've gotten too big for your post."

"No. The floor does not recognize Representative LenSom because Representative LenSom is speaking out of turn."

"I'll speak whenever I want to. This country needs blokes like me to keep the bourgeoisie like you in check."

"LenSom!" EshCal shouted from the fringes, "Shut. Up."

Lensom meekly silenced himself at her urging. He had served in EshCal's fleet when she launched her pivotal counter-mutiny. Ever since, his respect for her turned to fear whenever he found he had drawn her ire.

"Thank you," Spril nodded, "Back to the point, most of Ouristihra still sees us as a potential threat. Why am I, the leader of our military, also the authority on our economy, on education, on infrastructure? I may have proven myself as a soldier and as a military leader. But what of that qualifies me to rule on other issues?

"In a certain respect, CreSam's had a noble vision for ArcNos, but it was bastardized by his megalomania and the Avatars of Fate. He sought to advance ArcNos in such a way that our fellow Ouristihrans could only advance with us. But as long as the Brigadier General Elite commands the height of political authority, we remain susceptible to infiltration. And as long as we are susceptible, we will always be looked upon with suspicion. Does anybody have any comments or questions?"

"That's all well and good, sir," an elderly Representative agreed, "However, you must recall that Parliament was disbanded before the Avatars invaded. So long as we and the Committee Chiefs remain to keep you in check, we have nothing to fear from the Avatars."

"That's only what the public saw," SenRas sighed, "Before their presence became widely evident, the Avatars of Fate launched a series of scandals to have Parliament discharged one Representative at a time."

"Remember that, Representative TolRou," Phylus urged, thoughts of his own victimhood vivid in his memories, "All of your predecessors lost their job and their livelihood when only a handful of people had heard about these mysterious foreign agents."

"I stand corrected," TolRou humbly accepted, "Let me say, however, that if this is a matter of feeling overwhelmed, I certainly understand."

"I'm not afraid to admit it," Spril said as he scratched a few greys around the edges of his goatee, "I have been rather swamped these past five years. But my top priority is the good of ArcNos. I swear it.

"Now, when we last met, I provided you with recommendations for the leaders of each Ministry. If anyone has any alternatives in mind, your suggestions will be met with serious consideration."

"Actually, I have one," TolRou insisted, "You may not like to hear this, but I think Brigadier Elite EshCal should head up the Ministry of Defense. She is considerably more experienced, and she was on the inside during the ArcNosian Civil War."

"I served as a traitor for most of that time," EshCal sorrowfully countered, "Spril assembled a resistance to restore order. Therefore, I formally reject any nomination for his post."

"Actually, I have every intention of promoting you, in a manner of speaking," Spril said, "As expected, the Ministry of Defense will be largely comprised of high-ranking officers. These officers will be known both as Ministers and by their military rank, with the exception of the Prime Minister of Defense."

"What are you saying?" LenSom cut in, "You're promoting yourself above Brigadier General Elite?"

"Only in regards to military authority," Spril specified, "Why? Is there a problem?"

"No. No problem here, sir," LenSom dismissed, slumping in his seat.

"Very good. Now. Since I'll be shedding my current title to take on the seat of Prime Minister of Defense, that leaves the rank of Brigadier General Elite open. I motion for Brigadier Elite EshCal to be promoted to such rank along with the title High Minister of Defense."

"You have my vote then, sir," LenSom announced, his voice still a tad shaky.

"You had me convinced when Colonel SenRas and Chief Negotiator Phylus reminded us what became of the last Parliament," TolRou conceded.

"That's Prime Minister of Foreign Affairs Phylus," Spril corrected with a smirk, "Now, as I recall, you two were the last ones undecided. Has anyone else changed their mind, or has the motion passed?"

Everyone scanned the room, looking for hints of distrust or uncertainty. As nobody raised any objections, Spril nodded authoritatively and clapped once to return their attention to the dais.

"Very well then, the motion passes. If we come to need a single authority figure to oversee the Ministries, we will convene to discuss such an issue. Beginning after the upcoming assembly, representation in the Ouristihran Union will default to the Prime Minister of Foreign Affairs. I will attend the next meeting, as our fellow Ouristihran leaders anticipate. No changes are to be made to Parliament at this time. This meeting is adjourned," Spril concluded.

The populous of the room stood to applaud their landmark transformation of the federal paradigm. Spril shuffled down the steps and hurried to meet his friends along the wall. SenRas and Biroe greeted him with congratulatory handshakes, Phylus with the same as well as a pat on the shoulder. As they cleared away, EshCal congratulated him with a firm handshake but showed her personal gratitude with a spontaneous one-armed hug.

"Thank you, sir," EshCal beamed, struggling to rein in her stoicism.

"For what?" Spril shrugged as he pulled back, "You deserved a promotion. I recommended you."

"Exactly! You didn't pass me over like most men would, given my position," she elucidated, "You've enabled even more upward mobility for the women in our military."

"Hah! Here, I thought I was just giving due credit," Spril laughed as they walked to the elevator, "Look at us, making history without even knowing it."

"Speaking of history, there's someone I'd like to invite into the Ministry of Foreign Affairs. Someone from the Subtransit Resistance," Phylus said.

"Yes? And? Why so secretive?"

Phylus raised his finger to pause the conversation while they waited for the next car. He anxiously drummed his fingers together as they boarded and waited for the doors to close. Only when it began its ascent did he resume the conversation.

"Legally, he doesn't exist. The Ouristihran Citizens Registry has no records on him."

"We can use a tracking pigeon to deliver the invitation," Biroe suggested.

"Yes, but without valid identification, I can't hire him."

"Leave that to me, young man," SenRas smirked.

"You?" Phylus asked incredulously, "I'm open to suggestions, but what puts you in a position to make this happen?"

"His new title," Spril interjected from the front of the car, "Prime Minister of Covert Affairs."

Eytea leaned on the wooden doorframe, her wings splayed to catch the Harvest wind. The cabin behind her stood in a state of disarray, but she focused on the forest beyond the lawn. She watched a rustling in the shadows as the sun plunged behind the horizon. Sinkua emerged from the trees, Sestak and Seschnel coming behind him.

"Okay. You were right," Sinkua conceded as they crossed the lawn, "They do still know their way home."

"See?" Eytea teased, "Just because they're getting old, doesn't mean they're losing their minds."

"Of course not. But I'd still rather they were healthy enough to bring in money."

"It was your decision to move out," Eytea reminded, "Not that it matters, I guess. We'd be just as bad off there as anywhere else."

"I didn't realize it'd be this hard to find steady work," Sinkua sighed, slumping in the doorway.

Aside from sporadic odd jobs, he had largely failed to find work since the end of the ArcNosian Civil War. He had two identities, and both were unemployable. MeiLom was dead, and Sinkua didn't exist. Eytea had similar luck, her wings effecting discomfort in most. Worse still, the west coast docks had the greatest abundance of jobs, but they were unwilling to hire a young woman of her physique to do manual labor, regardless of whether they could admit it.

"Maybe you should try the Tournament of Duelers again," Eytea cautiously suggested.

"If you'll do it, I guess I can, too," Sinkua bargained.

"I don't wanna compare scars, but I think I've had it worse than you."

The year after the ArcNosian Civil War, Eytea and Sinkua had returned to Quarun to compete in the Tournament of Duelers. Neither of them considered the reputations they had developed and were thus unaware that most of the competitors saw them as prime targets. Bound from flight and electromancy, Eytea lost in her preliminary bout. Sinkua reached the first round but fell to a cheap gut shot and questionable judgment.

The following year, they both reached the first round. Sinkua suffered too many injuries in the preliminary though, and his opponent made short work of him. Eytea won her match in that she knocked out her competitor, but she repeated her mistake from her first appearance. Just as back then, the Commissioner disqualified both of them.

Neither of them had lost their edge. Rather, with Ouristihra being more in peacetime, they had little need to sharpen it. Regardless, it became apparent that their reputations had turned too many competitors against them, more to prove themselves than out of hatred.

"Well, the boat ride and registration are free. The worst that could happen is we lose again," Sinkua pondered, "We are running out of stuff to sell."

"We could go back and stay with my mother," Eytea suggested, "Sell the cabin and the plot."

"If that's what you want to do, I can't stop you," he accepted, "But we know there's not enough room there for all of us."

"Well, that's not gonna happen," she protested, nuzzling his shoulder, "I don't care if you say you were okay on that island. I'm not gonna leave you out here by yourself."

Sinkua ran his fingers through her still vibrant hair, tracing her ponytail with his thumb and forefinger. Quite abruptly for that time of evening, a tracking pigeon landed on the lawn. It hopped about, searching for its target in the growing darkness. Eytea tapped her foot, and the bird hopped to them to offer the letter. She took the letter and unrolled it, handing it to Sinkua as the pigeon flew away.

"I can guess who this is from," he said, "I hope he's at least doing better than us."

"It's not who you think," Eytea smiled, having glimpsed the bottom of the letter.

"Who do you think I think it is?" Sinkua challenged.

"Galo. Inviting you to celebrate the fifth anniversary with him."

Sinkua read the letterhead. It came from the office of Prime Minister of Foreign Affairs Phylus. She was right on both counts.

"Damn," he remarked, partly at having guessed wrong but more at Phylus's new title, "Looks like our old sharpshooting friend got promoted to Prime Minister of Foreign Affairs."

"I didn't know ArcNos had such a Prime Minister of Foreign Affairs. So, what does he want?"

The more he read, the farther his mouth gaped in disbelief. Ever the cynic, he reread it several times, trying to find some error or evidence of a hoax. Still in disbelief despite finding neither, he shoved it into Eytea's hand. She read it aloud.

"Sinkua:

As of the posting date on this letter, the former Brigadier General Elite Spril – known henceforth as Prime Minister of Defense Spril – and the Parliament of ArcNos have enacted a collective of federal Ministries. Included among these is the Ministry of Foreign Affairs, of which I have been appointed Prime Minister. Given your diplomatic contributions to Parliamentary ArcNos, beginning prior to your enlistment in the Subtransit Resistance, I hereby formally offer you a position of employment within this Ministry.

Affixed to the back, you will find two tickets for a ferry from Ferya to ArcNos. You may use these tickets at your convenience, but I implore you to come quickly and take advantage of this opportunity.

Respectfully,

Phylus
Prime Minister of Foreign Affairs"

"Hot damn!" Sinkua exclaimed, pumping his enflamed fist, "Looks like we're not entering that stupid tournament after all."

"Sounds great, but what about your identity?"

"He knows Sinkua is an alias and that MeiLom is legally dead."

"Right. So how can he offer you a government job if you don't legally exist?"

"Eytea. This is Phylus we're talking about," he assured, rubbing her shoulder, "He wouldn't go to the trouble if he didn't already have a solid plan. Trust me when I say we can trust him. Okay?"

"You mean like how he had a solid plan when he led everyone underground to start their own country?" she muttered.

"Hey now, Uulan told us that snag that Olsa put out wasn't on the level. That law was overturned," Sinkua snapped, "Phylus was gonna go back and deal with it the following Swelter, but we ended the war before then."

"I know. I'm sorry," Eytea sighed, "I shouldn't have brought it up. I knew it was wrong."

"Besides, we know Phylus has gotten a lot more careful since then. They all have."

"You're right," she smiled, "So, when do we leave?"

"First thing in the morning," Sinkua nodded, giving her a quick kiss.

KalChi knocked on the double doors, a stack of papers tucked under her arm. A voice from within beckoned her.

"Biroe?" she called back.

"That's Prime Minister…"

"Oh come on! You've had the title for a week now," KalChi sighed exasperatedly.

"And it still hasn't gotten old!"

"Fine. Prime Minister of Treasury Biroe? I have those budget figures you requested, sir."

"Excellent!" Biroe exclaimed, flipping a switch under his desk to unlock the door, "Please. Come in. Have a seat."

"That's the last time I do that in private," she insisted teasingly.

"Whatever you say, KalChi," Biroe flirted, "So you've determined what we can spare from our infrastructure budget like you promised?"

KalChi chose to let the numbers speak for her, laying before him several pages of projected budgets for each district, derived from five years of records. At the end of each section, she had calculated how much they could withhold without eliminating any projects. On the last page, she outlined how much she could designate altogether, based on the sum of the reports and additional predicted infrastructure spending over the next year. The total boded well both for ArcNos's economy and for their relationship with Berinin.

"This sounds fantastic. Thank you so much for your help," Biroe beamed.

"Have you finished analyzing the other reports?" KalChi asked, "I can help with them if you'd like."

"I did, but none of them had anywhere near this much of a surplus."

"Well, just so you know, I'm available if you need me."

"I suppose they could use a second look. Are you available now?"

"You know I am," KalChi smiled, "Phylus and Vielle are going to Berinin in two days, right?"

With his deployment date closing in, Phylus grew increasingly anxious. Despite the lack of correspondence from Sinkua, he remained certain that his old friend would accept his offer. He knew enough of his circumstances to know the letter would, at the very least, draw Sinkua back to ArcNos. Even if he doubted the veracity of the offer, which he had plenty of reasons to do, he would sooner use the tickets to come see him in person than write back and forth for weeks on end. Still, Phylus could only bide his time for so long before he would need to reopen the position, perhaps to someone easier to hire.

EshCal's shortcomings on her promise further compounded his troubles. Granted, she didn't hold fault alone, but the soldiers she deemed most suitable all had prior engagements on those days. Still, if she failed to find an additional guard, he would soon find himself at sea with a pilot, his daughter, and an inordinately large sum of money. Judging from Biroe's boastings, their final contribution could rival the sum of the last four donations.

"You know," Eytea pondered as she and Sinkua boarded the lobby elevator, "The last time I came here was with Colonel SenRas, making sure Kabehl was really dead."

"Did you ride the elevator that time?" Sinkua asked, recalling the first time they rode an elevator together.

"Heh, of course not. But I wonder if SenRas still works here."

Five years after his diagnosis, Ophalin had yet to see any signs of remission in Sinkua's condition. Worse still, he had made no progress toward a functional cure. Every idea hinged on knowing the exact chemical formulae of each component, and that had become inextricable from Sinkua's genetic material. However, the longer Sinkua went without an episode, the stronger his long-term memory became.

The elevator dinged as it stopped on the forty-eighth floor. The doors hummed open, and Sinkua and Eytea stood across from the double-door entrance to the Platinum Hall.

"Right through there is where he showed me the body," she reminisced, "This place looks a lot nicer now."

"I'll bet, what with those assholes not being around."

As they each opened a door, an office door up the hall opened almost in unison. A sparsely decorated elderly soldier emerged, familiar to both but with far more history with one. All three paused.

"Sinkua? What are you doing here?" SenRas puzzled.

"SenRas!" Sinkua barked.

SenRas fixed his eyes on Sinkua as he approached in long forceful strides. Eytea followed casually, keeping her distance and trying to hide a creeping smile. Sinkua stopped before him and looked him over, taking stock of his decorations. He had collected a few more since their last meeting. Sinkua abruptly grabbed SenRas by the shoulders and pulled him into a familial hug.

"It's good to see you again, Grandpa."

"I, um… Grandpa?" SenRas stammered, "I've never been called that. Well, except maybe as a half-assed insult, but…"

"I figured it out on my way to Ferya," Sinkua explained.

"He's been waiting five years to do that!" Eytea laughed as she caught up.

"But I'm only your grandfather in blood. I never even knew your mother."

"I know. But considering what you did for me and CreSam, I'd say you've redeemed yourself."

"I had begun to worry I could never atone for what I had done," SenRas sighed, his shoulders relaxing as though his burden had manifested as tangible weight, "Thank you, MeiLom."

"Oh cool! Does this mean I can call you MeiLom now, too?" Eytea joked.

"Don't get any ideas," Sinkua snickered, "He's the only one who can call me that."

"What about XalRut?" SenRas asked, "Your grandmother?"

"Maybe," Sinkua shrugged, "So, did Phylus not tell you about the job offer?"

"He did actually, but I didn't know you were coming today. Come into my office."

SenRas reached behind Eytea and locked the door as they followed him into his office. He directed them into a pair of chairs as he poured himself a mug from his new coffee brewer. Spril had given it to him, along with a connoisseurly collection of grounds and filters, as a gift for his new position. Eytea and Sinkua scanned the plaques adorning the walls, pointing out and mumbling conversations about particularly interesting ones.

"Now then," SenRas began, sighing contentedly as he sipped his dark roast, "I have something in my desk that you're going to need."

"The deed to the old house?" Sinkua asked.

"Eh? No, that's in an undisclosed location," SenRas dismissed, sifting through his top desk drawer, "You'll need these before that would be of any use to you anyhow."

SenRas's offering took them both by surprise, despite their knowing it to be necessary for Sinkua's employment. SenRas presented a stack of identification papers, complete with birth certificate, medical records, school transcripts, employment history, and Ouristihran Citizens Registry certification. According to these papers, Sinkua legally existed.

"Are these real?" Sinkua gaped, worried that his condition could have distorted his memories of his name's origin.

"As real as they need to be," SenRas snickered, "These copies are for you. Digital copies were uploaded to the Ouristihran Citizens Registry's database, and an associate planted physical copies in their document library in Poravit. All of them have been validated and notarized."

"That's wonderful," Eytea beamed, keeping her voice cautiously low, "But how did you pull this off?"

"That's what I'd like to know," Sinkua agreed, "I didn't know a Colonel had this kind of pull. Did you get a promotion?"

"In a manner of speaking, yes, but in another manner, no. I'm still Colonel SenRas, but these days, that's more a formality for people not in the know."

"In the know?" Sinkua pried.

"Officers of the Platinum Hall and my Ministry. The only paper we exist on is restricted to internal circulation those groups and is digitized, encrypted, and destroyed once it serves its purpose," SenRas explained, "I am the Prime Minister of Covert Affairs."

"You just broke your own rule," Eytea snickered.

"Perhaps, but now if there's a leak, I'll know it was you," SenRas taunted, "Besides, you kids are family. One of you literally."

"Well, I hate to ask for more favors after everything you've done..."

"What I did was my job."

"... Okay then," Sinkua continued, "Does this mean we can get the deed to the old house?"

"I'll work on drawing it out. In the meantime, go see Phylus. He and Vielle are leaving for Berinin soon, and he wants to see you sign on with his Ministry before he leaves."

"Oh, does Vielle work here, too?" Eytea beamed.

"Yeah, got herself a degree in sociology and a public sector job as a Junior Consultant. Anyway, I'll see you kids around."

Eytea stuffed the papers in her coat pocket, hers being considerably larger, as Sinkua gave SenRas a firm handshake and a one-armed hug across the desk. Sinkua held the door for Eytea, and she smiled back at SenRas and thanked him yet again. Phylus had presented the job offer, but without SenRas, none of it would have mattered.

She followed Sinkua to Phylus's office, where they eschewed manners and barged in to take their old friend by surprise. Phylus jumped in his seat, having come to accept that Sinkua wouldn't report before he left for Masnethege. As his pulse settled, he looked up to find he had written his fate prematurely.

"Sinkua!" Phylus exclaimed as he rose, "Why didn't you write?"

"Never crossed my mind," Sinkua shrugged, "but I'm here now. When and where do I start?"

"Actually, I've got a lot of paperwork you need to fill out and no time to go through it with you before I leave," Phylus confessed.

"Yeah, SenRas told us you were about to go to Berinin with Vielle," Eytea interjected, "Delivering your annual donation, right?"

"The paperwork can wait until you get back," Sinkua compromised, "SenRas is gonna get the deed to my childhood home. We can go get settled in while we wait."

"Or you can do it on the way to Berinin," Phylus offered, "Long story short, I need a guard on the ship. Someone other than Vielle and me. EshCal said she'd assign someone, but everyone she thought qualified is already busy, what with it being on such short notice. Plus, she's been busy assembling the Ministry of Defense with Spril."

"You want us to come with you?" Eytea asked.

"If you don't mind. I mean, I know you're not officially soldiers, but after what you two did in the war, you're closer than either of us. Myself especially."

"If we don't mind? You're asking if we don't mind going to Berinin with you?" Sinkua asked, "I don't care if it's a business trip. I'm pretty much always willing to go to Berinin. Especially if we're going to Masnethege."

"Hah! I figured as much. Just know there's a good chance we'll run into trouble on the way. Only a few people know we're taking this money by hand, but you know how rumors tend to reach the wrong kind of people. And this is a bounty worth jacking."

"How much are we bringing them, if I can know?" Eytea asked.

"You'll need to if you're going to guard it. Which reminds me, I'll need to have you sign on as an independent contractor for this trip," Phylus derailed, "Anyway, we're taking..."

"Five hundred twenty-nine million, two hundred twenty-seven thousand, and ninety-three iolas," Biroe interjected from the door, holding it open with his wheelchair, "Vielle asked me to tell you she's gone home to pack and to call her if you need anything."

"Okay, thanks. Was she too busy to tell me herself?"

"No, she just saw these two getting on the elevator and thought you might need to talk business for a while," Biroe explained, "By the way, welcome back, you two. Really fantastic seeing you again."

"Likewise," Sinkua nodded, "Especially in far better circumstances."

"Hope to see you around, then. Stop by the Treasury sometime."

"I'll stop in for coffee as soon as I get a chance."

SenRas nearly tripped over Biroe's wheelchair as he backed out of the doorway. He staggered and sidled, bracing himself on the back handles.

"Heading out for a break, Mister SenRas?" Eytea politely asked.

"Eh? Not exactly. Just going downstairs to drum up those housing documents for you kids. Standard boilerplate stuff," SenRas sidestepped as he righted himself.

"I've got a couple of hours until we leave for Berinin. You want me to come with you and knock it out before we shove off?" Sinkua offered.

"No, no," SenRas insisted, "Focus on your trip. Besides, this could take more than a couple of hours."

Sinkua raised an eyebrow, puzzled by the notion that signing a deed with two different names could take so long. Being that he only had experience buying a small plot from the Feryan government, he supposed this could involve considerably more paperwork. Dismissing his cynical urge to distrust his once estranged grandfather, he shrugged and returned to his conversation with Phylus.

SenRas slipped out of the Platinum Hall, breathing deeply to steady his pulse. His acumen in covert operations ran deeper than he wished any of them to realize, so the thought of deceiving what little family he had retained unnerved him.

For Sinkua's sake, he endeavored to keep his paternal origins from spreading beyond their most trusted friends and associates. CreSam's reputation had improved to that of a puppet tyrant, but it was still that of a tyrant.

On the surface, SenRas only needed to keep this transaction a secret. CreSam had relocated sometime after MeiLom's disappearance, but the home that MeiLom fled had remained deeded to his family. However, the disappearance of that deed complicated the issue.

SenRas had locked it in a safe in his office on the night of the imperial surrender, and he had never bothered to look upon it since. Now, he had come to find someone had stolen it, and he had scarcely a notion as to when or by whom it could have been taken.

Chapter 2

Vielle watched salty waves roll by as she leaned on the starboard rail, the setting sun illuminating the faint shore of her birthplace along the horizon. Eytea and Sinkua conversed behind her, talking of his trip to his island of refuge. From what she could hear, his memories of the voyage had endured the decade since, but his time on the isle had blurred.

Similarly, she could remember dim fragments of her childhood in Ivaria, but she recalled even less of the mother who had abandoned them. To wit, Phylus was the only parent to appear in even her earliest photos. Spril figured prominently as well, enough to imply his being her brother. Yet, her mother never showed up. Granted, Vielle had no desire for a reunion, but the totality of her absence was awfully curious, all but begging for examination. It was as though she birthed a daughter and vanished.

"Got a minute, kiddo?" Phylus asked, startling her from her introspection.

"What? No, I'm totally swamped here," Vielle snickered, hiding her internal discomfort.

"We never got to talk about this trip. What you did to make it happen," Phylus continued, "Thank you for making sure my work would get done while I was away. I should've given you more credit."

"Yes, you should have," Vielle agreed.

"I'm not done," Phylus cut back in, "That was a bad time for surprises. Signing me up for this without telling me was one thing, but you should have told me I'd be covered while I was gone. Okay? Next time you want to surprise me like this, let me know my job will be left to someone trustworthy."

"Yeah, I know," she sighed contritely, her mind drifting back to her absent mother, "I didn't really think it through. Sorry."

Sinkua and Phylus had spent the day filling out paperwork for his position in the Ministry of Foreign Affairs. His primary function would be to monitor opportunities for international collaboration, particularly with Haprian and Ivaria. Phylus had umbilical roots in Ivaria, but their leaders knew about Sinkua's role in restoring their rights to the aquatic steam engine.

Eytea and Vielle had caught up on their time apart. When they last saw each other, Vielle had decided to study sociology after high school, and she had since earned a two-year degree. Eytea and Sinkua had purchased an eight of an acre and built a cabin on it. She talked of her mother giving them the two horses and the wearing of age on their bodies. They lived well outside of her hometown barter community, and Sestak and Seschnel's diminished capacity for work provided little more than spare change.

Eventually, their conversation turned to their honing of their Hybrid abilities. With no recent combat applications, they had mostly become an afterthought. They had continued developing their skills though, if nothing else, to keep them under control. Feeling spry and competitive, they took potshots at jellyfish schooling along the side of the ship.

The seas had roughened throughout the evening, but their pilot's capabilities reduced the disruption to an afterthought. Her navigating the tossing waters let them concentrate on protecting the haul. Given their cargo of over half a billion iolas, they anticipated an invasion of pirates. Though he kept silent, Sinkua considered an Avatar of Fate, perhaps a replacement for The Criminal. Yet, for all their anxiety and preparation, little more than ferries and mail boats passed within shouting distance.

"You know, Dad," Vielle mused, brushing her hair behind her ears, "I haven't seen Galo since we tore down the fence."

"I know," Phylus nodded, staring off toward the distant shore, "Been quite busy in Berinin."

"Right, taking over as Chieftain Sage. Think it's changed him much?"

"Of course it has," Sinkua interjected, taking a seat beside her on the rail, "but I wouldn't worry about it."

"I'm gonna head to the bunks," Phylus abruptly announced.

"Suppose I should get some rest, too. Ought to be fresh in case we get marauded tonight."

"Thanks, I needed the worry," Vielle snarked with a crooked grin.

While Sinkua's condition stayed ubiquitously ingrained in his daily life, his insomnia had largely subsided. He no longer needed to collapse after an episode to get a decent rest. The nature of his parents' deaths still troubled him, but he had come to cope with it somewhat. Finding a bit of family in SenRas, as well as a home with Eytea and Elemeno, offered much needed solace. Learning CreSam had manipulated the Avatars also helped, but the more he tried to understand it, the longer he mentally scribbled on the ceiling at night.

A ball of light whizzed past Vielle, nearly dropping her from the rail it so startled her. She glanced back to see Eytea approaching and pointing to the orb. Vielle returned her attention to it as it exploded into sky lightning. For a couple of seconds, the sky shone like midday. Vielle gasped with a wide smile.

"You miss it dearly, don't you?" Eytea asked, "Ivaria, I mean."

"To be honest, I barely remember it. I know Spril joined the military in ArcNos when he was fifteen, so I guess I was about six when we left," Vielle reminisced, "But that's what worries me. I barely remember leaving, and all I remember from before is what I've seen in pictures."

"Remember how Sinkua was having trouble with his memories? I mean, he still does, but you remember, right?"

"Yes and his panic attacks that came with it."

"What if this is some side effect of being a Hybrid, but it manifests in different ways?"

"That's troubling to think about," Vielle sighed, "Have you had problems with your memory, too?"

"Not that I can remember," Eytea stated, her stoic expression holding back a snicker.

"Oh, you two are just full of it tonight!" Vielle exclaimed, Eytea's laughter spilling forth.

"Come on, Vielle. You're just worrying too much. You'll be fine," Eytea assured between laughs, "Do you know what your problem is? Why you can't remember life in Ivaria? You've done most of your living in ArcNos. The most important moments in your life, aside from the basics like literacy and not shitting your pants, happened in ArcNos. And there have been a lot of them."

"You really think that's all it is?"

"Of course! Why? Is there something else?"

"Yeah, kinda related, I think," Vielle sighed, "All the pictures of me as a kid, my dad is in a lot of them. Spril's in quite a few, too. But my mother's not in any of them."

"She left when you were pretty young, right?" Eytea asked, taking a more somber tone.

"Dad says it was when I was a baby. But there's a picture of him holding me when we got home from the hospital, and she's not even there."

"Maybe he got rid of the pictures of her holding you," Eytea suggested, "They might have troubled him, or maybe he wanted to keep you from looking for her."

"I know she abandoned us, but what could be so terrible about her that I shouldn't know who she was? Unless Dad found out she was an Avatar of Fate, it's not his place to say I can't know anymore."

"Not at all," Eytea agreed, "But we can only guess what happened to her and the pictures. Anyway, I'm off to bed. Goodnight, Vielle."

"Goodnight," Vielle sighed.

The southern tip of the Ivarian coast reached the northern edge of the horizon, faintly visible under clear night sky. Lighthouses dotted the coast atop rocky outcrops, their beacons shining like flashlights through pinholes. Vielle rested her head on her forearms atop the rail, pondering Eytea's insights.

Her idea about muffled childhood memories made sense, despite being a touch dismissive. Eytea's thoughts on her mother's photographic absence, however, stirred troubling thoughts. Her father could rationalize hiding the pictures from himself and from her as a child, but continuing the charade into her adulthood seemed so unlike him. This brought her to defend her father against herself, which circled her back to her mother possibly being an Avatar of Fate, the most worrisome thought of all.

Vielle staggered back, flailing her arms and grabbing at the rail. She steadied herself and took stock of her surroundings. Righting herself, she rubbed the back of her neck and shuffled off to the bunks. For all her troubling over her childhood, she had dozed off slumped on the starboard rail.

With Ierodhesan classical music filling his home, SenRas thumbed through his phone book, sipping from a mug of tea in his other hand. Though the phone in his office could not be tapped without his knowledge, his calls could still be overheard in the Platinum Hall. Normally, he could tolerate that, as those in hearing distance would already know of his pursuits.

This matter, however, beckoned greater secrecy for more than his personal failure of security. Sinkua's parentage had not become common knowledge beyond a core group, and a premature leak could evoke a scandal. Finding her number, he dialed and waited.

"Hello?" a distantly familiar voice called back.

"Is this Farim?" SenRas asked, walking to the stereo to turn it down.

"Yes. Who's this?" Farim confirmed, sounding puzzled.

"Colonel SenRas from ArcNos. We met a few years ago."

"You're that old guy that kept jacking with the Avatars, right?"

"Ah good, you do remember me."

"Not your face, but I remember your name and the sabotage I heard about."

"Yes, I certainly caused my share of trouble. I should say you made quite a name for yourself as well, young lady."

"Well, you know, I do what I can," Farim laughed, "So, what brings you to call? Still working in ArcNos, I take it?"

"Yes, Spril took my story to heart and kept me on his staff. What about you, dear?"

"I went back to Poravit a few days after we tore down the fence. Been working in criminal forensics and private investigations ever since."

"Sounds exciting," SenRas remarked, "Also sounds like you might be able to help me."

"I can't promise I can help much over the phone or that I can visit any time soon," Farim warned, "But I'll do what I can and refer you to someone local if you want."

"Well, something important disappeared from my office," SenRas began, "It's a deed to a house. I locked it in a safe shortly after CreSam killed The Scout. I went to check it this morning, and it was missing."

"The safe or the deed?"

"Just the deed."

"So, the last time you saw the deed was five years ago. Where was it before that?"

"CreSam's office."

"Why was it in there?"

"It's the deed to his old house. I took it into safekeeping in case his son turned up alive, and I had found a promising lead."

"I see," Farim pondered, drumming her fingers on her desk, "Those offices were heavily monitored back then. Even if you were alone, somebody could have seen you hide it."

"As I feared," SenRas confirmed, "Do you also think an Avatar of Fate is behind this?"

"That's my hunch at the moment."

"I figured as much, but what about…"

"Who, when, why, and how?" Farim cut off, "That much, I don't know. I'll have to examine the area personally."

"I thought you couldn't promise a visit in the near future."

"But I never said I couldn't come at all. I don't know how soon it will be, but I'll call before I leave for the docks."

"Sounds wonderful. I'll see what else I can learn in the meantime."

As he hung up, his eyes fixated on XalRut's phone number.

Nautical bells echoed in the distance, scattering gulls across the salty morning sky. Barefoot children ran down to the beach, waving excitedly and curling their toes in in the warm Southland sand. A lone figure stood on the bowsprit with a rope coiled around his shoulder, his ragged hair draped in red. Roused by the commotion on the beach, someone stirred in a house toward the north end of town.

"I think they're a little young to remember you," Eytea teased, poking Sinkua's hip.

"What? I'm just up here to throw the rope," Sinkua joked, tightening his jaw.

As the ship reached the shore, Sinkua tossed the rope overboard. Children scattered to let it land, and a cluster of them gathered to tie it to a nearby palm tree.

"An ArcNosian ship approaches," a familiar voice called, "and the children feel safe enough to run to it. Times certainly have changed, my friends."

"Galo!" Vielle called as she dropped from the ship on a milystic vine.

"Nice robe, brother," Sinkua said as he landed, having leapt from the bowsprit.

"Well, I figured I ought to look the part," Galo boasted, extending his arms to flaunt the garment, "if I mean to strut about calling myself the Chieftain Sage and such."

"Masnethege looks like it's thriving," Eytea encouraged, folding back her wings as she lit upon the sand, "You can hardly tell someone tried to burn it down a few years ago."

"Inappropriate compliments," Galo laughed, "You and Sinkua must still be together."

"We just moved back to ArcNos," Eytea smiled, "Sinkua got a job with the Ministry of Foreign Affairs."

"They're lucky to have you, brother. I presume that has some bearing on everyone's business here, then."

"My dad will explain when he gets down here," Vielle assured.

Phylus exchanged greetings with Galo as he reached the gathering of Hybrids. Before he could explain their unannounced arrival, Galo invited them to his home. Of course, he suspected the purpose of their trip, but he preferred to discuss it in private.

Survivors of the imperial assault waved to Sinkua as he passed. Though he could not recall their names, nor if he ever knew them, he recognized their faces with notable clarity. He waved back to all and pumped his fist encouragingly to the more energetic ones.

"Sit wherever you'd like," Galo invited as they filed into his home, "I'll pour us some mango juice."

"That reminds me, are the pomegranates in season yet?" Sinkua asked.

"Pomegranates? Those don't grow in the Southlands," Galo answered, puzzled by the obviously foolish question.

"Of course they do. I had one my first day on the island."

"I know not what you ate, but I assure it was no a pomegranate. The climate is much too warm in this region."

Sinkua sat in a wicker chair, mulling over his memories from a decade past. Eytea sat on the arm of the chair, rubbing his shoulders. In the Northlands, grocers kept pomegranates in stock most of the year, so he grew up believing they grew year-round. His every attempt to grow his own while in exile had failed, but he had blamed it on inexperience and misfortune. Now his cynicism brought him to contemplate other reasons. As Galo returned with a tray of drinks though, Sinkua swallowed his brewing paranoia.

"I can guess what's brought you all down here," Galo began as he circled the room, "Come to deliver the final donation, correct?"

"Of course," Phylus nodded, "Seemed appropriate to come in person."

"We're not interrupting anything, are we?" Eytea asked from behind her glass.

"Nothing that can't wait through a visit with friends," Galo smiled.

"We'll try not to keep you from your work for long," Phylus assured, "I imagine you're under a lot of pressure, following behind Chieftain Sage Gijin and all."

"You would think so, would you not? As it turns out, outside of Masnethege, most people don't expect much of me because of my age. I work just as hard all the same, but they're actually quite easy to impress."

"I thought they would expect more of you because of your age," Vielle observed, "like you need to prove yourself to them."

"I thought they would, too, but the last Chieftain Sage as young as I was my great-great-grandfather, Vahi. He abandoned our famed medical research and cultivation, advocating for crude fossil oils instead," Galo explained, "That caused the failing economy that Grandpa inherited. So really, as long as I don't break anything, nobody complains."

"Well, our last donation will certainly help," Phylus bragged, slipping him the memo, "and from the looks of Masnethege, it looks like you can invest it well beyond the reconstruction effort."

"Truth be told, the first donation covered that with money to spare. An advantage of our lifestyle, I suppose. Any unfinished work is an issue of labor power, not funds."

Ancient memories flickered to life as Sinkua approached the copper statue. The Triad Titan had virtually annihilated the capital, but the fountain and its semicircular shrine had survived unscathed, save for a few wisps of blood. Sinkua let the water run over his hand, searching for buried memories of his first visit.

Gijin's death left him alone in knowing Galo's origins, but he hadn't inherited any knowledge of when or how to explain such an anomaly. Even twenty-two years later, he could hardly explain it to himself, and had begun to doubt his memories of it.

"Are you sure ArcNos can stand to part with this money?" Galo asked, "Surely, CreSam and the Avatars left a deep scar in your economy."

"Biroe says we can, and I take him at his word," Phylus reassured, "He'd stake his name on it."

"So, what sort of plans do you have for the money?" Eytea pried.

"I was going to invest it and let it grow for a few years, but that was when I thought it amount similarly to prior donations," Galo explained, "With half a billion iolas, I can skip ahead to the next phase of my plan, once I acquire the approval of the Ouristihran Union at next month's meeting."

"I'll let Spril know you'll be looking for his support," Vielle offered.

"Thank you. By the way, could you ask him to bring Sinkua? If he can take the time off, I mean."

"I'll see if I can spare him for a few days, but I'll need to know why you need him there," Phylus insisted.

"The island he lived on is rich in exotic flora. I want to claim it for Berinin, and Sinkua can help me make a case for it."

Sinkua cocked an ear as mention of the island breached his introspection. His thoughts returned to his first day there, internally arguing over whether the fruit or the memory lied to him. Paying a visit could settle the debate, but he hadn't the time for it. Were he to help the Berininites claim it though, they might ask him to assist with their expansion as well.

"I'll help however I can," Sinkua offered, returning to the group, "At the very least, I can argue that you would make good use of it."

"Thank you. Always comforting to have such dependable friends, is it not?" Galo smiled, "I'm confident we can make a case for Berinin being best suited to colonize it."

"Wouldn't proximity make that the case?"

"It helps, but if it would be of better use to another country, they should have it."

"Of course, the plant life would be a boon to your medical industry," Phylus noted, "By the way, Yrlis still hasn't figured out how to duplicate your results."

"Well, she certainly won't grow them in a laboratory," Galo scoffed, "But yes, that's exactly why we need that island."

"We'll tell Spril what you have planned, so he can build a case in your favor," Phylus offered, "Well, I hate to cut this short, but we should be going soon."

"Actually," Sinkua interrupted, clearing his throat, "I need to speak with Galo. Alone. Do you mind?"

Galo and Sinkua watched each other pensively as the others filed out of the hut. They mumbled amongst themselves, wondering what Sinkua could need to discuss in private. Anxiety over his lifelong secret had stirred in his gut too soon after he swallowed this new worry over his first day on the island. No amount of fortitude could keep him from regurgitating either.

"Is something wrong in ArcNos?" Galo asked.

"It's nothing like that. It's just…"

"The Avatars haven't made a move, have they? No word from Tanelen?"

"No, they're still hiding. Now please," Sinkua urged, "just listen. How did Grandpa Gijin tell you your parents died?"

"They both fell ill and died before my first birthday. You already know this. Why ask now?"

"Has your Aunt Nalygen said anything about it?" Sinkua pried, somewhat unsure of his memory of Nalygen as his aunt.

"We never discuss it. What are you getting at? Brother, do you know something about my parents?" Galo eagerly asked.

"Not so much about them. More about you," Sinkua began, "Come sit back down."

"Grandpa Gijin told me you witnessed my birth," Galo recalled as he returned to his seat, "I suppose that means you know more about me than anyone else now."

"Right, well," Sinkua continued, scratching the back of his head, "I wouldn't exactly say you were born. At least not in the traditional sense. But I was there for it. In fact…"

"Oh, I was cut out surgically? That must have been stressful for my father to watch."

"No, there was no surgery. I'm sure he would've been worried if there had been, except that he wasn't there for it."

"He wasn't?" Galo recoiled, "That's awfully rude of him, but it's hardly a secret worth keeping for so long, much less that can't be spoken before mutual friends. It's a tad depressing, but it happens often, sometimes with good reason."

"I'd say being dead was a pretty good reason," Sinkua said, "Gabdur died when Zheal was pregnant. That's why I could never tell you anything about him. Not because I was too young to remember. But because I never met him in the first place."

Galo stared into his cup, swirling the mango juice and trying to see to the bottom. For nearly twenty-two years, he had been indoctrinated into believing his father passed away during his infancy. Instead, he had been born to a widow.

"My mother was widowed while pregnant?" he gasped, shaking his head, "No wonder she fell ill so soon after I was born. The stress must have been unbearable."

"Galo. My brother," Sinkua consoled, "Your mother died before you were born. I'm not entirely sure that she ever even was pregnant."

"That's awfully macabre. I owe my life to Grandpa in more ways than I ever imagined. But of course, she was pregnant. She must have been," Galo argued, "Premature babies grow into healthy children all the time, but he had to have a baby to work with when she died. I'm proof enough of that aren't I?"

"Well, the common belief around here is that she was pregnant when she died," Sinkua said, beginning to regret that he had started this conversation without preparing an explanation, "And that might be true. I don't know. I never met her. But if she was, it wasn't with you, and Grandpa Gijin couldn't save that child."

"Sinkua," Galo sternly beckoned, "Who am I?"

"Galo, of the Berininite Chieftain Bloodline."

"No. Who am I really?"

"I wouldn't lie to you, brother."

"You have lied to me my entire life!" Galo bellowed, standing so hastily, he toppled his chair, "Bad enough I should be made to endure the burden of being a Hybrid. But now I learn the burden of Chieftain Sage was thrust upon me illegitimately?"

"No! Listen to me!"

Sinkua stood and grabbed Galo's shoulder, hoping to calm and seat him. A meaty fist plowed into his cheek and across his face, the Serpent Bracer scraping his features. In a split second of heightened awareness before falling back, Sinkua discovered his answer.

"I'm sure people learn all the time that they were adopted, having spent their whole lives believing a comfortable lie," Galo snarled, "But who could lie so heinously to a child in my position, knowing they were forcing upon me a burden that I was never meant to inherit?"

"Galo, it isn't like that," Sinkua insisted, still sitting on the dirt, "You're part of the Chieftain Bloodline. I swear it."

"And who are you to keep perpetuating these lies!?"

Sapphire milystis coursed through the Serpent Bracer as Galo pointed at his Hybrid brethren with rage. Anxious heavings bounced his chest in fractured rhythms. Crystals gathered around his fist, coalescing into a frozen spear. Sinkua grunted and raised his hand, a plume of flame bursting upon Galo's abdomen and sending him stumbling. Galo lost control of the crystalline weapon, launching it through the thatch roof.

"That. Right there," Sinkua snapped, returning to his feet, "If Chieftain Sage isn't your birthright, why does the Serpent Bracer answer you like it did Gijin?"

"The mind can play cruel tricks if it believes a lie strongly enough."

The flap tore back, and Eytea, Vielle, and Phylus barged into the hut. The dispute had grown so loud, it had reached them near the southern coast.

"What are you kids shouting about?" Phylus demanded, "Galo, the last thing your people need is to have you threatening your friends and blasting holes in your roof because you're too stubborn to shut up and listen."

"You can't just…" Galo protested.

"Shut up and listen!" Phylus barked, "That has always been your problem. I don't know or care what the deal is here, if you were adopted or what. But Sinkua's trying to explain it to you, and you end up threatening him. What should you have done?"

"Shut…"

"Shut up and listen!"

"Thank you, Phylus. Now…" Sinkua began.

"As for you!" Phylus cut off, "You work for the Ministry of Foreign Affairs. Do you remember that? Do you know what that means? It means you're a diplomat. Act like one! Learn some tact, and stop setting our allies on fire!"

"Dad," Vielle urged, "You're just going to make them angrier."

"I know what I'm doing. Stay out of this, young lady."

"Galo. Look," Vielle beckoned, holding his shoulders and staring up into his eyes, "I can't pretend I know what you're going through. I haven't lived your life. But I know what it's like to have responsibilities you didn't ask for. So does Sinkua. So does Eytea.

"I also know what it's like to have to live a lie. I spent years hiding the fact that I was a Hybrid to protect Dad and Uncle Spril. Maybe you were raised on a lie. Maybe you weren't. But I promise it won't do you any good to push away the people who have always been there for you."

Galo held her shoulders, staring into her deep brown eyes. He brushed her chin-length hair behind her ears, withdrawing the shadow from her face. With a remorseful sigh, he closed his eyes and leaned his forehead against hers.

"I'm sorry," he groaned, "I know not what to make of this, but I need all of you to leave."

"For what it's worth, I'm still figuring out how to explain it, but let me try," Sinkua pleaded.

"Not today," Vielle insisted, "Think it over. Write a letter when you know what to say."

"That sounds like a better idea."

"I'll look forward to it," Galo promised.

"Just keep on with your plans for that island. And Sinkua?" Vielle urged, "Stop setting our allies on fire."

"Let's just head home and let everyone calm down," Eytea suggested, "Sinkua and I still need to sign the deed to that house."

Sinkua squeezed Eytea's hand and, after bowing his head to Galo, left with her at his side. Phylus followed shortly behind them, but Vielle lingered a moment longer, waiting until the flap had shut behind her father.

"By the way," she added, "you're not the only one here wondering about their parents. If I learn anything you should know about yours, I'll tell you. But you have to promise to do the same for me with my mother."

"You have my word."

XalRut reclined in her ageworn easy chair, losing herself in another chapter of a classic Lenguardian novel. Vermillion streaks of setting sunlight slipped between the vertical blinds and stretched across the kitchen floor. All else was dark, save for a lamp behind her shoulder.

The phone rang, breaking the calm. With an exasperated sigh, XalRut erected herself and snatched the phone.

"Hello?" she grumbled.

"XalRut? It's SenRas. I need to ask you something."

"Sure, honey," XalRut sighed, "What's going on?"

"Do you know what became of AinZun?" SenRas asked nervously, fearing the ground he dared to tread.

"Why in the world would you bring her up?" XalRut snapped with disgust, "It was bad enough that I lost custody. It was worse when I heard whom her son had fallen in with. And it was worst of all when I learned how he died."

"Okay. I'm sorry I brought it up. It's just that..."

"No. I haven't heard from her. Not in over forty years. If you manage to find her, tell her to call her mother. Her real mother."

SenRas sat in silence as the phone hummed in his ear. He knew the call would end as it had, but the lead beckoned investigation. XalRut had spent forty years despising him. He could endure a few more days, especially knowing he once again deserved her anger.

Chapter 3

SenRas rubbed his fingernails against his thumbnails, excavating black residue from their beds. Little good it would do, as the stench lingered long after scrubbing. XalRut had begrudgingly come to accept the smell so long as the substance didn't end up on her face.

He crept through the partially open door, wary of the creaky hinges, and paused. She snored lightly, the sheets rising and falling in rhythm with her nasally breath. He undressed to his undergarments and slipped under the sheets behind her. Sighing both contently and contritely, he rubbed her smooth dome belly.

"Mmm… Got a letter from the court today," she mumbled.

"Any good news?"

"No. Not at all," she sighed, "Said I can't see AinZun anymore."

"That's terrible, honey," SenRas commiserated, "Restraining order?"

"Might as well be. Her father got full custody, and I lost all visiting rights."

XalRut ran her fingertips pensively along serpentine ridges on her arm. Scabbed spots dotted the lines, and she shuddered as her fingers grazed them. Bitterness consumed her memories of the man she had once loved, the father of her firstborn.

"I'm sorry. I feel like this is my fault."

"SenRas, honey, you know that's not true. You gave me a way out before I even realized I needed one," XalRut insisted, "If it's anyone's fault but mine, it's his for putting me in that place at all."

"I wonder how he got custody then."

"I guess that's not for us to know, but I'm worried about her being raised by him alone."

"She just turned four, right?" SenRas asked, "Did it ever occur to them that she might forget her real mother?"

"They don't care. But we can still keep this one," XalRut sighed, rubbing her belly.

"I'll do everything I can to help. Have you come up with a name?"

"Well, um… What do you think of BeiLou?"

"It's a perfect name," SenRas smiled, "I'll do everything I can to help us keep BeiLou. Get a real job with regular pay. Quit creeping around at night from one job site to the next."

"Get a job that doesn't take you from the factory to the testing site for quality control?"

"Of course."

They lay spooning for several minutes, breathing in unison. As their eyelids drifted together, their pulses harmonized into synchronicity. The light of a single full moon peered through the window, casting a stretched pane of pale light across the carpet.

The fitted sheet hummed beneath SenRas's hip. He groaned and rolled away.

A lone woman traversed the long corridor, her shadows scissoring as she passed each pair of sconces. Darkness consumed all beyond the luminous solace of the lamps, the hall stretching for distances she could only imagine. All these years with them, and she had never ventured beyond the light alone. A muscular arm reached forth from the dark.

"Were you followed?" a gruff voice asked.

"They've suspected nothing. As I promised."

"Take my hand. Follow."

As she complied, she pondered what manner of device enabled him to walk through this darkness with such confidence. His did not live in it, thus ruling out natural adaptation. Rather, he only ventured into it when duty called for such.

Lost in her thoughts, she nearly walked into him when he stopped. He turned and grunted, indicated only by the breath on her neck. A blue outline shimmered around his hand as he placed it against the wall at the end of the hall. Swirling lines traced outward in chaotic patterns. A cerulean rectangle outlined the perimeter, and the panel split and parted.

He led her into a circular room with illuminated chairs posted at precise intervals. Various luminous arcs traced the floor. Rays bloomed from the center of the dome ceiling, reaching behind each chair. A significantly larger chair stood at the head, floating waist-high above the floor. All seats but this one were empty, leaving their shimmering insignia exposed. She squinted to see a slight glare covering his shadowed face.

"Why have you called for me, sir?" she opened.

"You are slipping," he accused, his breath strong with the smell of mutton.

"How do you suppose, sir?"

"The Document has fallen from our hands. You were to keep them from it."

"You have my apologies, sir."

"Apology means naught with a wake of inaction."

"Of course. I'll see to it that it gets back to us."

"It is as nothing without him," he reminded, "Know that his grandfather seeks it for him, as well. He must not learn of your responsibility for its absence."

"If I find it first, should I let it fall into his hands?" she asked, "His grandfather, I mean."

"Yes. He has earned a home. He will protect our interests there until he may come to know of them."

"Understood, sir. Will that be all?"

"What word of The Diagram?"

"They have not translated it."

"Guide their hands."

"I shall, my lord."

"One of your achievements beckons both congratulations and gratitude," he added, "Your sabotage of The Politician has succeeded. Our reports indicate she suspects not your betrayal."

"It's as I intended it, sir. If that's all, may I ask what's become of my daughter?"

"She has yet to outlive her usefulness to them. I know not her location, only that she lives, but I can put you on her path," he offered, "The depth of a kinship will soon be realized. Seek out her brethren. When the time comes, they will help you find her."

"Thank you, sir."

"You are dismissed. Send word of your progress."

The same stout figure returned to her side to escort her to the sconces. As they neared the lighted expanse of the hall, he released her hand. He continued to walk alongside her to the edge of darkness, out of duty and camaraderie.

"Have a safe trip to ArcNos," he bade, "Give them my regards."

In the neon chamber, a figure approached from another entrance. His robe dragged the floor, scattering the dust motes floating above the glowing tracks. A short holster clung to his hip with a disproportionately large hilt, and he walked with a ceremonial staff topped with concentric rings of precious alloys.

"What brings you before me, Pahres?"

"Something appeared in my possession this morning, my lord," Pahres explained as best he could reason, "Quite literally, as it was upon my nightstand this morn but not as I fell asleep last night."

"Show it to me," his superior beckoned, suppressing his bewildered curiosity.

Pahres opened his outstretched hand. Resting atop half an insignia tattoo was a small orchid either encased in platinum or wholly formed of it. His superior plucked the flower from his hand and examined the relic.

"Might it portend what I suspect?" Pahres asked.

"I can conceive of no better theory. It explains your apostatizing and dichotomous conscience. However, nor can I of how it came to exist."

"Then we are of the same mind, my lord."

"Yes. It would appear that by some ripple in truth, your mother has returned. You are free to investigate further."

Sinkua shuffled up the dock, his hands in his pockets and his eyes on his boots. He had scarcely spoken for the duration of the ride home, only giving brief answers to direct questions. Vielle and Phylus left him to his thoughts, knowing wiser than to pry deeper than he invited. Eytea silently kept by his side all the while.

Yet he never spoke on the matter. None of them had ever suspected any sort of oddity in Galo's family history. They only knew it to have been tragic and accepted it as such, just as he had. Still ignorant of its details, they had been surprised to learn Sinkua had known some dark secret for Galo's entire life.

Stranger still, he kept it silent even throughout the ArcNosian Civil War. As they and strangers entrusted their lives to him, he withheld truths from those who never knew they had been lied to. Before he left ArcNos, he had allowed the truth of his parentage to become known among the core of the Subtransit Resistance, but no mention of Galo's crossed his lips.

Although if he could protect Chieftain Sage Gijin's secret so fervently, it stood to reason that he could be trusted with their lives. As such, Vielle saw beyond accusations of mistrust and clandestinity to find a unique opportunity.

Sinkua stopped at the edge of the shore and reached back. Eytea smiled and jogged to catch up, tucking her wings to reduce wind resistance. She clutched his hand and walked inland alongside him. Vielle and Phylus respectfully kept their distance.

"Have you figured out what you need to say?" Eytea asked.

"Not yet. You'd think I would after all this time, huh?"

"I'd say the right words will come to you when the time is right, but that's crap."

"Or maybe that wasn't the right time," Sinkua admitted, "So now I have to force it."

"Gotta make your own opportunities, sometimes. You know that."

"Exactly. But there's no point in brooding over it. Brooding never got me anywhere."

"That's my man," she encouraged, patting his abdominals.

"Do you think Grandpa has that deed ready by now?" Sinkua wondered aloud.

"You really like saying that, don't you?" Eytea teased, "I don't know. I mean, I hope so, but he didn't really sound all that confident when we left."

"Not really, but I guess he's swamped with all the recent changes," he reasoned, "I think I saw a signing bonus in my contract though. We can use that to get an apartment outside of the city. Rent is cheaper, and it'll still be close to work."

"That sounds good," she beamed, "And I'll look for work once we're settled in. Can't have you winning all the bread, now can I?"

Phylus and Vielle reached the joint of dock and pavement, walking alongside each other. Vielle smiled as Eytea patted Sinkua's stomach.

"Looks like his shell finally cracked," she noted.

"Yeah, lucky he's got her with him," Phylus agreed, "Otherwise, that could've gone much worse."

"He just mentioned a signing bonus," Vielle said, dragging her fingertips along the rough bark of a conifer, "Is he right?"

"Yes, but keep quiet about it," he smiled, "It's not standard. I slipped it in as a favor."

"Oh, that was sweet of you! How much did you get them?"

"Three thousand iolas. One month's pay," he said, "By the way, how long have you been wondering about your mother?"

"Pretty much always, but it's been getting stronger lately," Vielle admitted, "I'm forgetting what life was like in Ivaria, so I've been looking at some old photo albums. I haven't seen her anywhere."

"She was barely around. She spent her pregnancy planning her disappearance," Phylus explained, "So, she insisted we couldn't take any pictures of her with you at the hospital. It was nothing against you, but she said where she was going, she couldn't have anyone knowing about her family."

"Where was she going?"

"Never explained that one. Probably for the same reason."

"Witness protection?" Vielle asked, to which Phylus shrugged.

As they drove back to the capital, Eytea asked Phylus to drop her off outside of the city. She planned to browse apartments while Sinkua worked. Phylus recommended the south side of town, mostly for their budget but in part for his convenience.

Vielle split off into the maze of cubicles. She felt guilty showing up more than halfway through her shift, even though had been approved for the time off. Sinkua and Phylus, meanwhile, continued to the Platinum Hall to finalize their paperwork in Phylus's previous office.

"Do me a favor and keep quiet about the signing bonus," Phylus urged as they entered the hall, "It isn't exactly protocol."

"Well, you're doing us a favor, so I guess I owe you one," Sinkua said, "And thanks."

"Now that that's out of the way, let's get you that check and put you to work."

SenRas barged into the office, clutching a mug of coffee. He explained in sketchy detail that they could not yet transfer the deed. MeiLom's being CreSam's only next-of-kin somehow did not guarantee his inheritance of that house. The fact that MeiLom had died some three months before CreSam further compounded their troubles. Hence, that house had become government property, and a preservation order barred private ownership.

SenRas grew increasingly anxious as he rambled on, partly for the lie he perpetuated but more for having broken his promise. He worried that he had helped his grandson come home only to have him live on the sidewalk.

As soon as he paused for breath though, Sinkua assuaged his guilt by explaining the signing bonus Phylus had authorized. Sinkua broke his promise in doing so, but telling the Prime Minister of Covert Affairs hardly seemed like a cause for concern. Phylus shrugged it off.

SenRas returned to his office and to his work of monitoring the Avatars of Fate. Though only a secondary motive at best, they hoped the reform might rouse the sleeping beast. That beast, however, hadn't so much as snorted.

He scoured his office, searching for derelict surveillance devices. Even evidence of bugs could have sufficed, as it would have at least told him what to search for within the walls. He inspected every surface of his chairs and desk, meticulously combed the carpet, and traced the grooves in the hardwood wall panels. He went so far as to disassemble the coffee maker, though he couldn't imagine what manner of tap he might find in there.

As he put it back together, a faint glimmer caught his eye. For all his digging and scraping, he had thrown up a fair amount of dust and residue from areas not often polished. Though his office had received its usual spot cleaning last night, a few surfaces looked to have been hastily passed over at best, particularly the area around the safe. With a spark of epiphany, he took a pinch of coffee grounds from an open bag.

He blew the dust away and sprinkled the grounds. Without a proper brush, he crouched and blew softly, dancing the grounds into a corner. As he hoped, they pooled and clumped in a few spots, creating rough fingerprint patterns. The first he recognized as his own. The others he had no hope of identifying, as they were completely bare.

This verified his and Farim's theory about an Avatar of Fate having stolen it, but realistically, it brought him no closer to an answer. He had never entertained any other possibility than an Avatar taking it. He sneered as he swiped the grounds away, begrudgingly accepting that he needed to wait for Farim.

Vielle sat on yet another call, slowly whittling away at her queue of callbacks that had accumulated in the last hours of her absence. Either her boss had forgotten she was to be away for most of the day, or she had grown impatient and cancelled Vielle's call-forwarding. Still, the calls she returned were nothing unusual. She talked through them quite routinely.

She had personalized her cubicle with various pictures, framed ones upon her half desk and snapshots pinned to the modular walls. She plucked one from the wall and stared at it. As an infant, she slept on Spril's arm. Her exposed ears told her their shape had not been as much of a secret as she believed.

This became an afterthought behind her next realization. Despite her father's explanation, her mother might have left because of her deformity. Perhaps they embarrassed her, or maybe she knew what those ears entailed and needed to get away. Even though she knew she might have just been paranoid, her stomach churned at the idea of her mother being an Avatar of Fate. She had made the comment in passing, but she never thought it could be true.

Still, it evoked one more epiphany. She spent the rest of her current call thumbing through her black book and put off her next callback to make a personal call.

"Hello?" a voice crackled in her headset.

"Farim? Is that you?" Vielle asked, keeping her voice down.

"That's me. Who's this?"

"Vielle. From ArcNos."

"Vielle! How ya been, girl?" Farim exuberantly greeted, "What's up with the hush-hush? You keeping secrets, too?"

"Too?" Vielle asked, unwittingly raising her voice.

"Forget I said anything," Farim dismissed, "What's up, kiddo?"

"I'm at work, so I've gotta be quick. I need you to help me find my mother."

"Is she missing? I know your dad is single, but we never talked about what her deal was."

"Missing is putting it lightly. I don't even know who she is."

"What about your birth certificate?"

"Come on. You know me well enough to know I already checked that. That part's blank."

"You know I love hearing from you folks back in ArcNos, but there are people over there who can handle this stuff. I'm not the only forensics analyst or private investigator in Ouristihra, and if I am, I'm demanding a raise."

"I know you're not, but you have more experience investigating the Avatars of Fate than any I've heard of. So, I really need you on this case."

"Say what now?" Farim blurted.

"You have more…"

"No no, I got that. What's that have to do with this? You don't really think…?"

"Yes. Spril and my dad knew about my ears when I was a baby, but they didn't know I was a Hybrid until just before the war," Vielle explained, "My mom could have left because she knew, and only way she could've known back then is if she was an Avatar."

"That's, um, actually a pretty solid hypothesis," Farim admitted after a long silent pondering, "Listen, I've got some business with one of your colleagues this weekend. Can't say who or what, but it also relates to the Avatars. I'll tend to both of you then."

"Okay. Thanks so much, Farim! I've gotta get back to my callbacks now. B'bye!"

Sinkua sat on a bench in the mailroom, thumbing through a stack of envelopes. Cigarette butts in stale water stained his boots. As usual, junk mail dominated the haul, credit card offers and such.

He didn't know why he still bothered to check the mail, seeing as he had accepted by the second day that he would throw it all away. Like an inexplicable compulsion, he kept at it nonetheless, never knowing what he could have been searching for. When the insignia of the Radial Axiom Arena on a handwritten envelope caught his attention, he chalked that up as his answer.

His eyebrows arched as he read the proposal, sent directly from the Commissioner himself. Without acknowledging the rest of the stack, he pitched the other letters in the rubbish bin and hurried back to his apartment.

When Sinkua returned, having just arrived home from work, he found Eytea lounging in her sweats. She had cleaned the place to their liking, and the hour had grown too late for calls about job openings. He plopped down beside her and handed her the letter.

"What do you make of this?" he asked.

"Well, it's um," she began as she read, "Are you thinking about going?"

"Not to compete. But for this, I might," Sinkua said, "This sounds like it might be fun."

"Yeah, it does, but don't you think it's suspicious?"

"Not really. I mean, it's short notice, but they probably couldn't reach me until Grandpa set me up with a proper identity."

"I know that. I mean that he invited the runner-up instead of the champion."

"That was a fluke, and we all know it," Sinkua scoffed with a chortle, "Seriously though, I think it's because Spril used an alias, didn't he?"

"He did. He wore a disguise and called himself Namias."

"Right, so the Commissioner probably just couldn't find him," he reasoned, "Either that, or it's because I was credited with assassinating CreSam."

"I guess that makes sense. It could go either way," she accepted, "Still, you need to be careful. Something about Mortvill seemed odd."

"Was it the mask?" Sinkua asked, remembering that faint glimpse ever so vividly.

"Yeah, that was part of it. I'm surprised you could see that from down there. But he had this air about him. Polite enough, but something about him didn't sit right with me."

"Well, the tournament is in a week. I'll tell you if I notice anything strange about him."

Flurrying fists pummeled the salty air, followed by a pattern of barefoot kicks with wisping arcs of mist. Galo drew back into a defensive stance, breathing heavily and focusing on the Serpent Bracer. Rather than as a conduit for his hydromancy, he focused on it as merely an object. He reared back and punched the air.

Just as always, the bracer radiated its usual cool glow, and a spire of ice launched forth. Frustrated, he jerked it from his forearm and shouted into the serpent's face.

"Why are you still answering me?" he bellowed, "I'm not one of them! Whatever you are, whatever they did for you, you don't owe me anything! Stop it! Just stop it!"

With a swelling in his throat, he slammed the Serpent Bracer onto the ground and stormed back to the front of his home. Inside, he sat with his face in his hands and his elbows on his worktable.

He looked up at the fountain in the back of the room, contemplating his troubles as though confessing them telepathically. It reminded him of Gijin, but speaking aloud to a statue, even in private, still felt rather foolish. Narrowing his eyes, he rose to approach the fountain.

"Wait a moment," he said, breaking his silence, "Sinkua was looking at you just before he spoke of Gabdur and Zheal. You know something, don't you? What secrets are you hiding?"

He carefully hoisted the bowl from the upper left arm. He discovered how the water flowed into the bowls. It came up through holes in the finger tips, which branched out into dozens of holes just below the rim. Admirable as the artisanship was though, it said nothing of Sinkua's story.

He skipped to the bowl held in offering, suspecting he would find no more answers in the right hand bowl. In the offering bowl, he discovered a pair of sealed glass vials lying in the bottom.

"Grandfather, what were you hiding?" he asked as he took the vials, finding them full of water, "A way to find my parents perhaps, in case you might not live to tell me of them?"

Galo stared into the water, contemplating if it could have been milystic. The Serpent Bracer had reacted to his grandfather, and the four sleeves of the Chieftain Sage Robe meant the statue could have represented a real person. More pressingly though, he noticed stray crimson specks floating in the water. A vague yet nearly complete red line traced the bottom of one.

Realizing what they might have been, he rushed back to his worktable to pen a letter. Though Berinin had plenty of people who could help, he thought better than to spread this news among the locals. Stirring up controversy with doubts of his lineage would only cause trouble, especially with special interest groups protesting a Hybrid holding federal office. Fortunately, he found a mostly untouched vial of Farim's tracking essence in his collection.

When he went outside to find a pigeon, he returned to the back of the house and retrieved the Serpent Bracer. He wouldn't accept his lineage without proof, but he would acknowledge it as a possibility in the meantime. Finding the first step to an answer had opened his mind.

Malia grunted as she pulled the iron-laden door to the cavernous chamber, architecturally similar to the last she had visited though far less luminescent. The chairs stood in a nearly identical pattern, down to the floating throne at the head of the room. Her superior of the moment sat in the hovering chair, impatiently drumming his fingers on the arm rests. Her colleagues had already arrived as well.

"Get to it, Investigator," he huffed, "I've neither the time nor the patience for your fussing about."

"My apologies, my lord," she excused, bowing as she shuffled to her seat.

"Geneticist, what progress have you on the girl and her cellmates?" he asked, ignoring Malia's contrition.

"They protect her fervently," answered the Berininite Avatar, "and she them in rare instances. They give our guards a great deal of trouble, but we have brought them into submission. They remain in our possession and continue to move with us as we command."

"I speak of the genetic testing, not of your social concerns."

"Most of the subjects do not react with any utility to the agents we've developed. Her bodyguard was an exception," The Geneticist explained, "We assumed the formulae would only need be matched to particular genotypes; however the necessary specificity has proven more minute."

"What are you trying to say?" scoffed a middle-aged Northlander, "Your blood grafts are only compatible with one host? How do you explain all of us?"

"They are not as versatile as I had hoped, but neither are they so restrictive. And I would explain us with the law of averages, Engineer," he scolded, "We are a handful of successes among thousands of failures. As it were, the proper nomenclature is gene grafts, you philistinic nincompoop."

"Shut it!" their superior boomed.

"Yes, Lord Harvester," they shakily complied.

"You have The Diagram to work from, do you not?" The Harvester asked indignantly.

"Recall that The Diagram fell from our hands before ArcNos fell to civil warfare," The Engineer said, her steely eyes fixating on Malia, "The Investigator has failed to recover it."

"You claimed to have restored it to its rightful place, Investigator," The Harvester insisted, "What of this talk that it still eludes our hands?"

"I said no such thing," Malia protested.

The Harvester raised his upturned fist, slowly uncurling his fingers toward her. Deep purple fog swirled from his wrist and hand, smoky tendrils stretching from his fingertips. Malia clutched her chest and coughed chokingly, gasping for air as the pigment drained from her face.

"I might remind you that she wields our most direct influence in Eprilen," a colleague interrupted, "Since The Politician has fallen out of favor there, The Investigator's tenure as Judge gives her the greatest leverage among us in controlling history, as it were."

The Harvester lowered his hand, the smoke dissipating, and Malia inhaled deeply as she regained her olive complexion. She looked to the one who had spoken on her behalf and nodded her gratitude.

"We have already set out to take The Politician in new directions," The Harvester announced, "Your errors have been grave, Investigator, but The Prophet presents a valid argument. Eprilen remains a priority. See to it that history continues in favor of our destiny, and you may retain your name among the Avatars of Fate."

Soon thereafter, he dismissed the assembly, and all went their separate ways. Malia watched her feet as she walked, mulling over what manner of history The Harvester could have referred to. They had not run a political scandal since ArcNos. She worried that she might have overlooked something or perhaps was no longer as privy to their exploits as she believed.

The Harvester showed no suspicion of her ongoing betrayal. In fact, he seemed wholly ignorant of his brother's clandestine hindrance of his operations. So, he could not have suspected any of his agents as turncoat, but that failed to silence her worry of losing her cover.

Outside of the abandoned house, she leaned against the siding and sparked a cigarette. They were his brand, smelled like him. He hadn't turned her on to smoking, but he had introduced her to this flavor. Even after just over two decades without seeing him, except for an all too brief encounter in an Eprilenese hotel, she could shake neither the habit nor the memories the smoke elicited.

A jangling of metallic rings startled her. She turned to see The Prophet standing beside her and brushed stray ash from his robe with a quiet apology.

"Thank you," she professed, "For saving me in there, I mean."

"Twas nothing. You'd have done the same for me," he insisted softly.

"True enough. I suppose you followed me out here?"

"I did indeed. Worry not. They did not see me."

"Good," Malia nodded, hurrying down the porch steps, "Any idea what he meant by history continuing in our favor?"

"His words are always up for interpretation, my lady. I cannot tell you how to receive them," The Prophet reminded, "I would implore you to start small however. Small for us at least. See to it that one of us attains a position of greater influence, perhaps restore Olsa to her once glory."

"Hmph, so the only way to save my ass is to save one of theirs? I don't care for the sound of that."

"You did set back The Politician and The Geneticist considerably."

"As was my duty."

"Yes, but in your position, subtlety is often the better part of success."

"I understand, but I'm not exactly fond of having to undo my handiwork. We both know I'll just turn around do it again. Probably do even more damage the second time. So, maybe it's time I was armed better."

"If it is protection you seek," he said, setting his hand upon her shoulder, "I would be pleased to oblige."

She turned to study him, assessing his body language. His demeanor appeared unobtrusive, but his quickened pulse and sweaty palms dissolved his façade of chivalry.

"You know what happened the last time I got involved with a colleague in that manner," she refused, "Thank you, but I'll find my noble guardian elsewhere."

Pahres sighed and bade her farewell, and the two parted ways.

Chapter 4

Two spoons clanked together as they scraped the last remnants of pork stew from the bottom of a can. XalRut grinned sheepishly as SenRas split the last chunk of meat and scooped out one half for himself. She furrowed her brow at the sight of his hand, having only just now bothered to look up from the meal.

"How did you get blood there?" she asked, rubbing dried bits of it from the side of his hand.

SenRas swallowed anxiously as he scratched the side of his head. He pulled his hair aside to show a wound, small but deep and scabbed over. XalRut leaned in and cooed apologetically.

"Looks like it stung. What happened?"

"Got bumped on my way back to the line after having a smoke. Dragged my head on the pegboard and snagged it on a broken thumbtack," he explained, scratching his leg from inside his pocket, "Stung a bit, yeah, but it's hardly a bother."

"I'll clean it for you," XalRut insisted, "I think we're out of rubbing alcohol, but I can use a spot of whiskey."

"I was gonna drink that," SenRas protested.

"It's just liquor. What's more important, getting drunk or not getting an infection?"

"Just...? Listen to you. It's something to drink! Something that doesn't smell like a fucking Kirtsian took a bath in it! Don't waste it on a little cut."

"Watch your language. BeiLou can hear you," she hoarsely whispered.

"We both know that's just a myth."

"Oh my goodness," XalRut gasped, shaking her head, "Those kids were talking about me. But how could they know?"

"What kids?" SenRas asked, forgetting the argument, "Right about what?"

"Some of our neighbors send their kids to the same private school as AinZun. She's been getting picked on because of her family," she explained, nearly sobbing, "SenRas, they're talking about us."

"What have they been saying?"

"That her mother is a baby-making junky whore who ran off with a stupid alcoholic!"

"Okay, maybe one of those labels is true, but it ain't yours," he protested, "What kind of parents teach their kids that language anyhow?"

"It doesn't matter if it's true or not," she argued, shaking her head in frustration, "If these kids keep running their mouths, they'll ruin any chance we have at a normal life here."

"The parents are the problem. Not the children."

He searched his pocket with his index finger, maneuvering it back into his ring. He worked it down just past his first knuckle, finding the tip still warm.

"Find out who's been saying what," he continued, "I'll have a word with their parents."

"Just don't get hurt, okay? I at least want one of my daughters to grow up with both of her parents."

"Don't worry," SenRas comforted, kissing the top of her belly, "I don't bruise easily."

Farim sprinkled white powder over the safe dial while she shook her brush to loosen the soft bristles. As she wiped the residue on the side of her pants, she teased the dust from the surface, careful only to move what would go willingly.

"What do you make of it, miss?" SenRas politely asked in a low voice.

"Blank fingerprints. Just like you said," she hesitantly confirmed, uncompliant with his quietude, "I thought maybe it was your technique."

"Well, if there had been any marks, I doubt I could have drawn a proper print from it," he conceded.

"In any case, you were right about their being blank, and my research connects that to the Avatars of Fate."

"That means we're looking at Kabehl, Amirione, or Malia, respective code names, The Scout, The Hunter, and The Investigator."

"As far as you know, those are the only three suspects."

"I don't want to think any others have been here, but I suppose I must. The Investigator is the only of those three who could be alive, but she's been unaccounted for since CreSam banished her."

"I'll need to run a second test to confirm that this was an Avatar though."

"I thought the fingerprints were the second test."

"No, that's the first data point," Farim explained, "The fact that CreSam's property disappeared from here doesn't prove anything by itself. But with foreign prints on your safe, we can prove the deed was stolen. Their being blanks is a strong argument for the Avatars being behind it."

"So, we've got proof that it was stolen and reasonable suspicion that one of them was dicking around with my safe?" SenRas reiterated, "Sounds to me like we have enough to peg it on them."

"Only that they probably stole it. But the more I know, the better I can confirm it and the further I might be able to narrow it down," Farim reminded as she dug through her kit, "Plus, the more proof we have, the better our chances at getting a conviction. You know they have a way of swaying the courts."

SenRas grumbled as he recalled their manipulation of the Ouristihran Union Parliament. He watched Farim more closely now, studying her meticulous pursuit of whoever had lifted the deed. She dabbed the prints with a series of tiny cotton swabs long sticks and slid each one into a long narrow tube.

"What do you plan to do with those?" he asked, hoping to see it through.

"I'm looking for traces of DNA. I don't know how much I'll find after this long or coming from them," she cautioned, "As far as I know, their genetic leavings could, um, break down after a while."

"How could that even be possible?" SenRas guffawed, forgetting his clandestinity.

"I don't know, but that doesn't really matter unless it happens," Farim shrugged, "Anyway, I'll see what I can pull from this and check the official databases."

"Will that tell us who it is?"

"Maybe. If I get a hit, we'll know who it is, but it won't be an Avatar of Fate. If I don't, it was one of them, but we won't know which one."

"So, one gets us a dreadfully puzzling answer, and the other only proves what I already know. I hope you have more of a plan than this."

"You don't know me that well, so I'll let that one slide," Farim sneered, "If it's not one of them, the bare prints suggest either an impersonator or a saboteur. We can use that to our advantage. If it is one of them, I can run it through a specialized database my old mentor started."

"Of course, see if it's someone you've sampled before. That's quite clever," SenRas complimented with an appreciative nod.

"If I don't have a name, I'll check where else the suspect has turned up, and that should tell us who stole the deed," she continued, "By the way, what do you know about CreSam's missing son? It might help with the search."

"I have nothing to tell, I'm afraid," SenRas humbly refused.

"Well, if you learn anything about MeiLom, let me know," Farim implored.

"Of course," he nodded, "Now then, if you're done here, I'll let you get on with your weekend."

"I've got some business downstairs, and then I'm heading back home," she casually shared on her way to the door, "I'll call you when I have an answer."

At that, she left his office. He remained where he stood, listening to her footsteps until he heard her leave the Platinum Hall. Once that door shut behind her, he reached for his phone.

"Hello?" called a voice, drifting in from down the hall as well.

"You left your door open."

"What did you find out?" Phylus asked.

"She's mostly certain it was an Avatar. So, she's checking for DNA, which ..."

"Not about that," Phylus interrupted, "We'll get to that later."

"Her other business is a case downstairs. It's probably Vielle," SenRas reasoned, "There are, however, thousands of people working in this building, and many of them know or know of Farim."

"The pieces fit," Phylus sighed, "Not that it matters. She's gotten too far for me to stop her."

"I might say she's too old as well, young man. Like it or not, your little girl is a grown lady now, young and naïve as she may be."

"Even so, I don't like the idea of her finding out who her mother is. Not since I found out myself."

"What do you know of this woman?"

Farim squinted through the frosted glass as she knocked on the door. Only what sunlight pierced the blinds lit the path behind her. The handle jostled, and the door creaked opened. Vielle looked out nervously and beckoned her inside.

"Thanks for coming," Vielle hoarsely whispered.

"No trouble, kiddo," Farim shrugged, "You worried the Avatars might be running surveillance here?"

Vielle's eyes widened, and she gave a more thorough look outside the room. She slammed the door and locked it with trembling fingers.

"Well, now I am!" she exclaimed, "I was just worried my dad or one of his friends might hear us."

"Don't worry about that. Nobody's here but the cleaning crew," Farim lied, "Go have a seat by the vending machines, and we'll get started."

Vielle complied, rolling up her sleeve as she sat. Farim dug in her bag and, holding the fingerprinting kit aside, withdrew out a syringe with exchangeable vials.

"So, how is this going to work, anyway?" Vielle asked, "Won't you need a sample from my dad, too?"

"No, I can get his from the database," Farim said as she wrapped a tourniquet, "Clench your fist."

"What about me, then?"

"You're in there, too," she assured, pausing to compose her explanation while she pricked Vielle's arm, "I can use Phylus's data to figure out which half of your DNA came from him."

"Can you really know that for sure?" Vielle wondered aloud.

"It's hard to say. The computer does most or all of the work. I just load samples and push buttons," Farim laughed, "Without a mother candidate, it might not get a single definite sequence. But it can pull the most likely sequences into a probability distribution."

"I guess that's why you're taking so many samples," Vielle noted, visually counting the vials.

"You got it. Then, it'll isolate those genes, leaving the half of your DNA that most likely came from your mother. I'll run those sequences through the databases to look for matches."

"Couldn't you just do the same thing with our database records, though? I mean, that way you could run all the combinations you want."

"I can isolate sequences, but I can't cross-check without samples."

Vielle rolled down her sleeve, struggling to wrap her mind around this almost alien technology. Before this meeting, she hadn't seen much peculiarity in Farim's request for blood samples. Now, the methodology grew stranger the more she learned about it.

"Wait, does that mean if you collect DNA from a crime scene, you're screwed if you lose the sample?"

"No, once the sample is uploaded, we can do whatever we need to from the digitized sequence. But only if we upload a full sequence," Farim explained.

"Hmm, you'd think it'd let you use whatever portion you need," Vielle puzzled.

"You'd think, but it turns out this sort of thing doesn't come up very often," Farim teased, "Paternity cases always have a known mother, a known child, and a pool of candidate fathers."

"Oh, of course. I guess if you have no idea who my mother is, that'd complicate things, wouldn't it?"

"Exactly. This is daughter minus father against every woman of age on file. We don't know where this woman lives, where she was born, where she went to school. Nothing. And I'd imagine any of your dad's friends who know are sworn to secrecy."

"Of course!" Vielle snapped in frustration, "I think Spril knows, but I can't even get a hint out of him."

"Hah! So, that's where he draws the line, huh?" Farim jabbed, "Anyway, yeah, I've never had this come up before. Even the loosest women I've run paternity tests for have at least had a list for me. I meant, their pool of candidates could actually fill a swimming pool, but you work with what you can get."

"Oh, that's just dirty," Vielle laughed, stealing a glimpse of Farim's cleavage as she leaned down to grab her bag, "How do you work with that stuff? I'd be so worried about catching something."

"There's always some risk," Farim smiled, nodding pensively as she packed her equipment, "We wear really durable gloves."

"Yeah, but I bet it dries out your skin, huh?" Vielle asked, diverting her eyes with less subtlety than she intended.

"Nothing a little moisturizer can't handle," Farim shrugged, "Anyway, I'll call you when I've made progress. Just know that it could take several weeks to get your answer."

"Of course. No hurry. I'm sure you've already got plenty to do."

Vielle offered her sweaty palm for a handshake. Farim accepted, locking eye contact with her. While she kept Vielle's attention on her face thought, she distracted herself as Vielle pulled her into her arms. This hug wasn't friendly, familial, or even a formal salutation, as was done in some regions of Lenguardia and Ierodhes. Farim kept her arms pinned to her sides, wriggling to urge Vielle to stop.

"Right. I'll just be on my way now," Farim dismissed, patting her on the shoulders, "Don't be a stranger, but um… don't be too familiar either."

Vielle watched in silence as Farim left her alone in the break room. Leaving the door unlocked, she collapsed into her seat with a regretful sigh. She set her hand above her left breast and found her pulse racing, as she had anticipated.

"That confirms that," she sighed, "Too bad I still have no idea what I'm doing."

Gray clouds advanced from the horizon, swallowing the blue as they raided the sky. Thunder rumbled as rain began to trickle. With each breath of wind, the storm drew nearer to the brick and concrete rooftop. Eytea hovered a few meters above, looking toward the approaching storm.

"We can wait until the rain passes if you want," Eytea taunted as she descended.

"Oh, what's wrong?" Sinkua goaded as he unraveled his morningstar, "Afraid your wings might run?"

As Eytea's feet hit concrete, raindrops struck asphalt only a few blocks away. They drummed ever nearer as she yanked her halberd from its holster and charged at her boyfriend. Sinkua ducked under the blade and hook kicked behind it, pulling the weapon down and her arms with it. Eytea jerked her halberd out from under his foot, sending him staggering back.

Sinkua caught himself on his hand and swung his morningstar, tangling the chain around her halberd. Eytea stumbled as he tried to erect himself against her. She pulled back to keep aright and retain control of her weapon. Sinkua disarmed her with a forceful yank. He returned to his feet, boots striking stone as raindrops first battered the ledge.

As he turned to fetch her halberd, she lunged with an elbow leveled at his jaw. She met her mark with diminished impact, as Sinkua looked her way only in time to disrupt her with a hasty palm heel to the sternum. Her leg sprang up, and her foot smacked against his chin. His head snapped back, raindrops shattering against his upturned face.

Eytea bounced on the balls of her feet, goading him to test his mettle against a moving target. Sinkua dropped his morningstar, still entangled with her halberd, and lunged with a backhand punch. She ducked and punched at his kidney. He snatched her wrist and twisted her arm into a hammerlock, kneeing the base of her spine. She stomped on his foot, and he released her, shoving her away with the bottom of his boot.

As she turned around, he untangled her halberd and tossed it back to her. Lightning cracked and thunder poured forth from the horizon as raindrops shattered against their bodies. Eytea charged and jammed her spearhead into a crack, launching herself at him. Her feet plowed into his clenched abdominals, but he wrapped his arms around her legs and dropped her on her back. He followed through with an elbow drop to the chest, knocking the breath from her lungs.

Gasping for air with rain beating down on her face, she kicked upward and sprang to her feet. Before the scattered droplets settled around her feet, Sinkua launched a flurry of fists into her stomach. She doubled over in pain but watched his breathing as closely as she could manage. Within a gasp of respite, she struck back with a sharp jab to his clavicle, grinding her knuckles against the pressure point.

As he winced and reared back, Eytea grabbed his ruby pendant, pivoted behind him, and yanked it back. He struggled to wriggle his fingers between the chain and his neck. She perforated his spine with an alternating series of palm heel strikes and punches with her middle finger's knuckle protruded. Gasping for breath, he choked on the rain as it rolled down his face. He stomped at her feet, but she dodged every strike.

Finally, the chain could endure no more tension, and the clasp snapped against his throat. Steam spewed from the concrete as the ruby smashed the surface of a puddle. Heaving, he whipped around and bashed the side of her face with the back of his fist. He swiftly followed with a swing of his recovered morningstar, wrapping the chain around her neck. The ball settled over her sternum, just short of puncturing her skin only by his control.

She tapped her foot thrice, and he stepped in to unwrap the chain, still catching his breath.

She stood as still as she could while he freed her. She watched his eyes and smiled. No matter the punishment she doled out, he still saw it as a friendly sparring match. He returned her look only to avert his eyes with a contrite muttering.

"Sorry about, um, you know, hitting you in the face like that."

"We were sparring. Shit happens," Eytea shrugged.

"Well yeah, but I mean," Sinkua fumbled, "Your mom and Kabehl."

"Oh, that? Don't worry. You didn't remind me of him. As long we're sparring, it's fine," she assured, "Besides, you throw a punch a lot better than he ever could."

"Is that right? I guess I shouldn't be surprised that I hit a lot harder than him."

"Harder, yes, but your form is better, too. Frankly, it would be an insult to say you remind me of him when you hit me in the face while we're sparring."

"You have a strange way of trivializing him, you know that?" he noted as he stuffed his broken necklace in his pocket, "Come on, let's go inside and get cleaned up."

She took his hand, and they returned to the stairwell. Back in their apartment, with raindrops pattering against the window, Sinkua kicked his boots into the corner while Eytea replaced his chain with one of comparable length from her modest jewelry collection. He thanked her and followed her to the shower.

Evening had begun, and late the next morning, they were to make for the coast. This had been their last opportunity to train before the Tournament of Duelers. Though she never spoke of it, Eytea had contemplated enrolling if the opportunity arose during the trip.

Farim held her coat shut as she fished her keys from her pocket. Back at the other end of the nearby docks, the last of her fellow passengers dragged cumbersome luggage down the ramp. She had taken the tourist route, allowing her a longer reprieve before she picked up after half a decade off from openly meddling in the exploits of the Avatars.

Researching them didn't particularly trouble her, not after so long doing it. Mostly, she found herself anxious over how abruptly her old friends became involved with them again. Divining from experience, she knew the stirring about them, no matter how subtly handled, would find its way to them. When it did, they would once again show themselves.

Granted, Sinkua had told her CreSam had similar intentions, but political instability abounded in Ouristihra. Eprilen entered a state of flux after Olsa's impeachment, and ArcNos struggled to rewire its political power grid.

As she opened her car door, a tracker pigeon fluttered above, unaware that the message it brought would further complicate her uneasiness. It released the rolled paper and continued.

Farim furrowed her brow, a lump in her gut screaming in her ear in pessimistic anticipation. She wasn't expecting any correspondence, certainly nothing from ArcNos so soon. Sitting in the driver's seat with her feet on the frosted pavement, she contemplated how this letter could pertain to the Avatars. Finally, accepting the futility of ignoring it, she shut herself in her car and opened the letter.

She let out a coo of pleasant surprise upon seeing the letterhead of Chieftain Sage Galo. They had passingly exchanged brief letters, but months had passed since either of them last wrote. That pleasant surprise turned to stern worry, however, when she noticed the length of the letter. To her relief, his message beared no evident relation to the Avatars of Fate, but rather to her chagrin, it smelled of instability in Berinin.

Galo presented a strained explanation of how he learned he might have been adopted. Though even for her experiences with the absurd, Farim found it all but impossible to swallow. Perhaps it could have been more a matter of his trouble explaining the matter, having only recently come into his knowledge. From what ramblings she could understand, it seemed Gijin's only son and his wife had died well before Galo's birth, but Sinkua insisted he belonged to the Chieftain Bloodline nonetheless.

Her fingers explored the back of the sheet as she read about the vials he had found in a bowl of water. The issue grew stranger with every sentence, but she kept reading, oblivious to the dusting of premature snow gathering on her windshield. Fastened behind the page, as promised, she found three plastic pouches. Two held flakes of dried blood from the aforementioned vials, and the third held Galo's blood, squeezed from his fingertip. She placed the letter and samples in the glove compartment and started her car.

She found some solace in his request though. At the very least, he had samples from all three people in question. Logically though, Sinkua must have lied to him, either about his lineage or about the timing of his parents' deaths. Supposing he had somehow been honest, her mind turned somersaults trying to piece together the logistics of the situation. She turned up the radio and sang along to distract herself.

EshCal dug in her desk, donning street clothes in lieu of her usual formal attire. She had taken vacation time, but she needed a few effects from her office. So far, she had managed to slip through the bustle unnoticed, so she presumed her departure would be just as unhindered. Instead, an abrupt voice so startled her, she nearly banged her head on the underside of a drawer.

"EshCal?" it spoke from her intercom, "Er, High Minister of Defense EshCal?"

"You know I prefer the other title," she sighed with a crooked smile, "How'd you know I was in here?"

"I heard you unlock your door. You're not as quiet as you think, young lady."

"Should've figured. Just means you're better at your job than I'd be."

"Of course. Could you come see me before you leave?"

"What do you need?"

"Just for you to deliver a parcel in Quarun."

"This isn't anything…?"

"Unsavory? I should think not. This is strictly a personal matter."

"Good. I'll be over in a few minutes."

"I'll leave the door cracked for you."

SenRas polished the box once more while he waited, more to busy his hands than for appearances. Upon finishing, he opened it and cleaned the velvet lining, plucking away specks of dust and cobweb strands. After several minutes of meticulous inspection, his door opened.

EshCal presented herself as something of a sight, as SenRas realized he could not recall having ever seen her out of uniform. She dressed in an entirely unassuming manner, showing regard for sexuality. Her nonchalance reminded him of how he imagined XalRut had looked at her age.

"Well, don't you look lovely," SenRas complimented as he rose from his seat.

"Eh? If you say so," EshCal shrugged, "I don't dress to show off."

"As you shouldn't," SenRas insisted, beckoning her to sit across from him, "Should you ever look to settle down, be wary of men who expect you to dress to stir their loins on a daily basis."

She laughed nervously at his phrasing, the awkwardness of having this conversation with a colleague being made even more so by his age.

"I get what you're saying," she nodded, "So, is the parcel in that box?"

"Actually, the parcel is the box," he corrected, sliding it to her.

Curious, she opened it and found it empty. The velvet lining looked to have long been undisturbed, short of a recent cleaning. Scattered bits protruded upward as though they had just been pinched.

"I suppose this is for Sinkua."

"You suppose right. He left it in the Subtransit when he left for Ferya."

"What is it?" she asked, examining the outside, "Aside from a box, I mean."

"It's the box he kept his medallion in as a child. He can't use his pyromancy in the Tournament, so I thought he might like to keep it in there during his match."

"I'm sure he'll appreciate that," EshCal nodded, "I wonder if he even remembers where he left it."

"Perhaps so, perhaps not, but from what I understand, he never could come back for it until recently," SenRas shrugged, rubbing a cramp in his leg, "In any case, best of luck in the Tournament."

He extended his arm for a handshake, and she reciprocated with a firm grip. With the box tucked under her arm, she left his office and closed the door behind herself. Once she had shut the door, he inspected the side of his hand.

She had only left partial fingerprints in the powder, but the vague whorls eliminated her as a suspect. He reached under his desk and grabbed a bottle of rubbing alcohol and a rag, both drawn from his first aid kit before the meeting. His phone rang while he scrubbed.

"You could've just asked," EshCal snarked before he could offer a greeting.

"Supposing you were, would you have told me?"

"Probably not, but your way was just as discreet."

"So it would seem," SenRas mused, "but if you were one of them, I wouldn't say what I'm about to tell you."

"Which is?"

"Wash with rubbing alcohol."

"Why? What is this stuff?"

"Fingerprint dust."

"What else?" she sighed.

"A topical necrotizing toxin activated and accelerated by skin oils."

"Shit. You don't mess around, do you?"

"I most certainly do not," he asserted, "Now, go wash with rubbing alcohol. That batch will start sloughing off your skin in about twenty minutes otherwise."

"Thanks for the warning. I got a bit of it on the box, so I'll get that, too."

"As you should. If you pass that toxin to my grandson, even by accident, my disposing of you would be far less modest."

Chapter 5

SenRas slowly turned his key to lock the deadbolt, fearing the smallest noise could wake XalRut. He loosened his tie and wiped the sweat from his neck, half from anxiety and half from seasonal heat. Once he had locked the door, he patted his pockets. At so late an hour though, he thought more of how to do without than of replacing anything he had forgotten.

Tonight's job only took him six blocks away. Close enough to walk. Starting his car would have drawn unwanted attention. He checked the address once more and started on his way.

He stopped at the first corner to light a cigarette. Watching the street and the opposite sidewalk in the corner of his eye, he fed the corner of his assignment paper to the cherry. He walked casually while it burned, the fire creeping toward his hand. As the flames licked the hair on his knuckles, he let the last of the paper fall. The ashen material crumbled against the sidewalk, the fibrous embers smoldering to dust.

He repeated the address in his mind as he walked. He had memorized it, but his lack of recognition troubled him, given the proximity. The street was familiar, but he could not think of any businesses operating along that stretch.

He stopped and stared at the mailbox. Tonight's assignment took him to a residence. The contractors hadn't lured the perpetrator back to the scene. Instead, he was to strike in their home.

"Must be a slippery one," he mumbled, "We'll see."

As he circled to a side window, he locked the safety on his sidearm. Had he known he would be working in someone's home, he would have left it at home.

The first window led into a bathroom, but he found it locked. He pressed the tip of his knuckle ring against the glass, slowly melting through it, and carved a hole big enough to reach through to unlock the window.

SenRas took stock of the bathroom. The mark had a child, a young daughter judging by the pink cartoon character toothbrush. By tradition, she would receive a portion of the bounty as an insurance benefit. Nonetheless, his stomach turned at the thought of taking a man from his child. He would need to work quickly, before guilt turned to hesitance.

The target slept alone. SenRas stepped lightly, almost gliding across the floor. He pushed the tip of his still-warm ring against the man's trachea. The man gurgled and stirred as the searing tip bore through his flesh. He hacked violently as blood welled up. In a frenzied panic, he sank his fingernails into SenRas's wrist, struggling to push him away.

SenRas pulled a length of chain from his coat pocket and cracked it across the mark's face, knocking out a tooth and loosening another. The man cried out in bewildered pain. Someone stirred down the hall. SenRas jammed the chain into his mark's mouth, wedging it behind his back teeth. He brought the two ends together and pulled it taut as he continued driving the hot spike deeper into his trachea.

"Go back to sleep," he hissed.

Blood pooled around the wound. The mark's eyes screamed when his mouth no longer could. His pupils dilated and retracted erratically. His eyelids fluttered. His complexion slowly faded. His body became limp. SenRas withdrew the small blade, the heat cauterizing the wound, and pocketed his manriki.

As he stepped out, his footsteps drowned out another set from up the hall. His were not particularly loud, quite the opposite in fact. Rather, these other footsteps were simply small.

They were to cross paths in the hall, she going to check on her father, and he coming from disposing of him. This defied protocol. Children were never to discover the body. SenRas trembled, his face cloaked in darkness.

"Go back to bed, honey," he murmured incoherently, "Strange dreams."

Either her fatigue clouded her judgment, or he mumbled vaguely enough to pass for her father's drowsy voice. She rubbed her eyes and returned to her room, answering him meekly.

"Goodnight, Daddy."

A lump grew in his throat. His hands trembled. That had to have been her voice.

No longer concerned with stealth or protocol, he barged out the front door. He jerked the knot out of his tie, straining to breathe as he staggered away from the house.

Many times, he tried to run, but for all his distress, he could only take a few steps before tripping over himself. His breathing grew increasingly ragged, sweat matting his hair.

Inebriated with contempt, he threw his body against a phone booth door. Trying again, he jerked the door open and thrust himself inside. He locked it with his manriki, wanting nothing of whatever intoxicated creature might happen along, and dialed with trembling fingers.

"Who the fuck did you send me after?" he snarled.

"Did you forget the address, young man?"

"No. I already made the hit. Listen!"

"Then, we have no problem."

"It's my stepdaughter!"

"That is impossible. Your target was male."

"You made me orphan my stepdaughter. You assholes sent me to kill my wife's ex-husband!" SenRas roared, tears beginning to overflow behind his eyelids.

"The client said nothing of a name. Gave only an address."

"What about the crime? What was his crime?"

"What significance is that to you?"

"Humor me, you sack of shit! What did he do?"

"Temper. Temper. I doubt I could simplify it for you, but it was investment fraud. He was hired to manage their retirement funds, but he stole the money instead. So, they cut the contract short and, well, you know the rest."

"Bullshit," SenRas spat, his voice tremoring, "I need out."

"I'm as sorry as I can be that you were connected to the target, but we cannot let you walk away every time you become emotional."

"No! Listen to me! We were set up. That man was not an investment banker. He worked on an assembly line."

"What proof do you offer?"

"Search my wife's court records, and you'll find him."

"We will investigate the matter and alert you of any relevant findings. Your bounty is to be found in the usual place, less the allotment for your stepdaughter."

"Send my cut," SenRas ordered, "Tell her I was in an accident."

Without waiting for confirmation, he banged the phone onto the receiver, pocketed his manriki, and stepped out into the night. SenRas took a long gaze to the northeast, toward the home he shared with XalRut and their unborn daughter. He had destroyed a family, but to protect his own, the only option he saw was to leave it behind. No matter which way he walked, he would endanger them, but he supposed whoever had set him up was only after him.

He dropped his tie and headed west.

Sinkua leaned into the corner of the couch, his arm around Eytea, who lay against his body. The television in their quarters picked up movie channels they couldn't afford at home, thus making up for what it lacked in size. They watched a film from the months leading up to the ArcNosian Civil War, one of but a handful of blockbusters that didn't propagandize the political climate.

Eytea's halberd and Sinkua's morningstar hung from a rack in the corner. Without the pressure of poverty, Eytea had decided to enroll in the Tournament through a scout on their boat. In helping Sinkua resharpen his edge, so too had she repolished her own. She thought it such a waste to tag along only to watch his exhibition fight. Sinkua, however, could not enter without forgoing his match with Mortvill.

Neither could see the other's face, but both assumed the other to be awake and so forced themselves to stay awake as well. To the contrary and despite their efforts, both carried heavy bags of fatigue in their eyelids. Their eyes reluctantly began to shut, but a knock at the door startled them alert.

Eytea rolled off the couch, rubbing her eyes with her wing as she shuffled to the door and fumbled with the lock. EshCal smiled at her as Eytea opened the door. If she noticed she had awoken them, she didn't appear the least bit contrite. She had a familiar box under her arm.

"May I come in?" EshCal asked, presenting the box.

A spark of recognition glistened in Sinkua's fatigued eyes. He nodded and yawned, waving her inside as he sat upright on the sofa. Eytea closed and locked the door behind EshCal. Sinkua noted the empty holster on her hip.

"Didn't know you were in the Tournament," he observed.

"Yeah, I've actually never been in one. Thought it might be fun," EshCal shrugged, sitting on the ottoman, "I suppose my reasons are political as well."

"What do you mean?" Eytea asked.

"With the ongoing power shift in ArcNos, there are people who think we're weak and vulnerable right now."

"Not to mention having our first female Brigadier General Elite," Sinkua added, drawing an ireful glare from Eytea but an affirmative nod from EshCal.

"That too," EshCal added, "But if I make a strong showing here, that will reinforce our public image."

"I can't believe you said that," Eytea disdained, shaking her head at him.

"I never said I didn't think a woman should hold the position," Sinkua corrected, "But I won't pretend people don't think that way."

"Remember Eytea, he trusted me to lead hundreds of troops on an ambush and to go after The Hunter," EshCal added, "You know most people are sexist when it comes to my line of work. Even the women."

Eytea shrugged and nodded acceptingly. She knew Sinkua never thought less of either of them in any militant metric, and if he did, their gender did not factor into it. She blamed her lashing out on her fatigue.

"Anyway," EshCal continued, "SenRas asked me to bring this to you. He also said he'd kill me in a most unpleasant and garish manner if I accidentally kill you. So do me a favor, and don't die before we get home."

Sinkua chuckled as he accepted the gift. It looked cleaner than he remembered it being, the finish shimmering as though it had been prepared for display in a market. He opened it and found the vials missing. He had no particular use for them now, but he wondered what might have become of them all the same.

"That does sound like something Grandpa would say," Sinkua grinned, "Where did he find this?"

"He said you left it in the Subtransit, so there, I suppose. He held on to it this whole time, waiting for an opportunity to give it to you."

"But why would he have it delivered to you here?" Eytea asked.

"To put my necklace in," Sinkua gleaned, "Gijin gave me this box to keep it in, and Grandpa knows I'm barred from using my pyromancy in my match."

"But does he know what happens to you when you don't wear it?"

EshCal crookedly pursed her lips and arched an eyebrow.

"Nothing happens, really. My body feels colder, but I can get along just fine."

"Oh please! You get sluggish and stupid, and we both know it."

"Well, it's not like we can try it out now. I'm already half-asleep."

EshCal stood up and backed toward the door.

"I'll let you two get to bed," she said, "Good luck, Eytea. Give them a good show, Sinkua."

Eytea and Sinkua both bid her good fortune and goodnight as she let herself out. Sinkua locked the door behind her and followed Eytea to the bedroom. He wore his necklace to bed and kept the box beside him on the nightstand.

They awoke early the next morning. Sinkua's insomnia had waned considerably, but long sleeps still came rarely.

Up on the ground level, the floor shimmered with a faint red hue as the rising sun cast a long shadow through the wrought iron gate. Sinkua and Eytea slipped over to the bar and diner to have some breakfast before the commencement ceremony.

When they reached the diner, they found it already crowded. Assorted strangers sat inside, most keeping to themselves as they gorged themselves on pig meats and eggs. Others went straight to the sauce, but from the looks of them, most may have been left over from last night. Eytea's wings brushed the doorframe as they entered, prompting the more lucid patrons to turn toward the odd noise.

"Eytea?" a gruff voice called.

"MalVek?" Eytea answered, spotting his waving hand.

"Finally decided to come back, huh?" he asked, standing as she and Sinkua met him near his table.

"Yep. Sinkua got a decent job, so I'm not under as much pressure to hit the money. So I thought it would be fun to give it another go," Eytea beamed, "Oh, and he's going up against Mortvill in an exhibition match."

"I heard about that. But how did you know the Commissioner's name?" MalVek puzzled, "Not many people know that. It's part of why he wears that mask."

"He told me it was because of his leprosy," Eytea said.

"I suppose that's as good a reason to give as any."

"Wait, how did you know about my exhibition match?" Sinkua interjected, "That wasn't made public."

"EshCal here told me about it," MalVek answered, nodding backward over his shoulder.

For all their surprise and conversation, they had failed to notice who shared his breakfast table. Neither of them knew the two to be any closer than by the most tenuous of connections, though. EshCal and MalVek had only started working together near the end of the ArcNosian Civil War, and EshCal had never mentioned being in contact since.

"Hey guys. Sleep well?" EshCal asked, to which both nodded as they took seats perpendicular to them.

"This lady was asking me if I knew any weaknesses she could exploit," MalVek taunted, shoving his thumb at EshCal.

EshCal laughed nervously and shook her head. Sinkua eyed her shrewdly, though not to glean what she might have learned. Rather, he pondered what they had actually discussed. The laugh sounded inorganic, and he didn't know EshCal as the type to steal an advantage going onto a level field.

"Well then, we'll let you get back to that," Sinkua wryly insisted, "I've got a few pointers to cover with Eytea, if that's how we're gonna play this."

"Right, we've seen you in action. I want to freshen up on my memories," Eytea agreed.

Her eyes darted between EshCal and MalVek, as well as Sinkua's eyes. She hadn't noticed any cause for suspicion, but she knew when Sinkua's mind had set out on a hunt. Hence, she followed his lead, knowing it to clearly be of concern to her.

On their way to another table, she explored her memories of EshCal and MalVek in combat, but chaos muddled those recollections. Sinkua hurriedly ordered their breakfasts, knowing what Eytea would want on such a morning.

"Okay, what do you remember about them?" she asked in a low voice, "I can hardly keep track of the details from our battles, especially the ambush by the train tracks. There was so much going on."

"There was, but that's not what I'm worried about," Sinkua brushed off, his attention obliquely toward EshCal and MalVek.

"I thought you might have suspected something. You had that certain glimmer in your eyes. Well then, what is it?"

"I'm not sure. That's why we came over here," Sinkua insisted, "I know EshCal wouldn't ask MalVek how to get one over on you."

He leaned on his elbow with his hand cupped behind his ear, slightly amplifying the noise in the dining room. As long as he could tune out everything else, he could eavesdrop on their conversation more clearly.

"Any idea what they're hiding?"

Sinkua raised his finger. He let his eyelids droop, focusing on diminishing the ambient sounds of the diner. Fragments of EshCal's voice penetrated the dull roar of conversation and the clanking of dishes and cutlery, but MalVek's voice, being an octave deeper, drowned in the din. What little he caught of their conversation, however, was unassuming and thus of no consequence to his hunch. He dropped his arm, shaking his head as his hand landed on the table.

"Never mind. I can't hear them from here."

"Well, what do you think they could be plotting over there?" Eytea grinned, finding it all delightfully intriguing.

"Hard to say. MalVek and his brother were always pretty reclusive, NalSet especially," Sinkua recalled, "If they're hiding something, EshCal must be privy to it."

"Now that you mention it, I've always thought those two were a tad odd," Eytea agreed, "I'm not too keen on technology, but their level of genius seems almost inhuman."

"I've thought that, too, but neither of us has any scale to measure by," Sinkua added, "For all we know, they could be average among their colleagues."

"They figured out those barrier towers rather easily. I thought the Avatars of Fate were supposed to be decades ahead of our time."

"Right," Sinkua nodded as their breakfast arrived, "but they had a broken prototype to work from. Maybe just about anyone in their field could have put it back together. Reverse engineering, I think they call it."

"That's possible," Eytea nodded, furrowing her brow.

MalVek leaned on his elbow and turned away from Sinkua and Eytea, watching their distorted reflections in his glass. As Sinkua put his hand behind his ear, MalVek curled his finger, dragging the fingernail over the tabletop. EshCal darted her eyes and stole a glance. They grinned at the effort, more out of respect for his untrained technique than derision at his relative transparency.

They exchanged small talk in dull mumbles until Sinkua gave up his eavesdropping efforts. MalVek straightened his finger when he saw Sinkua drop his hand. He and EshCal returned their voices to normal levels.

"What do they know about your involvement?" MalVek asked.

"Only that I sought to work with the Avatars of Fate until near the end of the war," EshCal said, "and that I was biding my time for a chance to kill The Hunter."

"Keep it that way if you want in."

"What about you?"

"They only know as much about me as I allow."

"How can you be sure they won't figure out more?"

"I'm more practiced in the art of secrecy than you think."

"True, but he figured out where they operate from."

"Partly because of deliberately scattered bread crumbs, but I see your point. He's more astute than we gave him credit for, but her mind is sharper than his," MalVek explained, "Were he as clever as her, I'd be in trouble."

"And if they learn to brainstorm more fluidly?" EshCal asked.

MalVek downed the last of his iced tea and slapped a few bills on the table.

"In a few hours, it won't matter."

With his travel bag slung over his shoulder, Galo paced his home, dousing candles and drawing the curtains. The horizon looked of rain by tomorrow afternoon. He paused before the statue fountain, gazing reverently into its face. He lowered his head and sighed, his decision firmly made.

As he stepped out, someone snatched his arm. He spun defensively and grasped at whoever had grabbed him. He clutched his assailant's forearm, but they both paused when he met her eyes. She looked back at him sternly, almost maternally.

"Aunt Nalygen?" he asked, knowing the title would startle her.

"Aunt?" Nalygen gasped, releasing his arm, "Who gave you that idea?"

"Judge Nenbard told me the night I left for ArcNos. I had been keeping it to myself until you were comfortable enough to tell me," Galo recounted, "But I suppose it just slipped. My apologies"

"Well, that just means I don't need to have my talk with you," she smiled.

"What talk?"

"If you believe Nenbard that I'm your aunt, then you must believe Sinkua that Gabdur and Zheal really were your parents. So, we'll have no more talk of you resigning."

"I don't know. I want to believe him, but it doesn't make sense if they both died before I was born."

"It would if you could understand how wonderfully skilled Chieftain Sage Gijin was, both with natural and manufactured medicines. He extracted you from your dead mother's womb and nursed you to health," Nalygen recalled, "He marked your birthday as the day you would have reached full term, the same day you came off life support."

"That's not what Sinkua told me," Galo recoiled, "He said he didn't know if Zheal was pregnant when she died, but if she was, it couldn't have been with me."

"That's absurd! She certainly was pregnant. The Chieftain Sage went into reclusion over his grief and focused on nothing else but keeping you alive. Judge Halciem took over on governing affairs."

"So either Sinkua lied to me, or Grandpa lied to everybody, including me."

"If I were you, I'd be more concerned with what they're hiding," Nalygen cautioned.

"What do you mean?" Galo countered, adjusting his shoulder strap.

"The only reason either of them has ever had to lie to you is to protect you. Not to deceive you. Not to betray you. But to protect you until it is safe for you to know the truth, whatever that may be."

"I know the point you're working toward, and you don't need to worry," Galo said, "I'm not going to Eprilen to post a resignation. If I ever do, it will be for political or medical reasons. I've decided that whether I'm adopted is hardly reason enough to resign. Besides, I'm sure the question of my parentage is being figured out as we speak. If I am of the Chieftain Bloodline, I'll just have to invite Sinkua down here and slap the truth out of him."

"Very well, then," Nalygen smiled, "In that case, have a safe trip, and good luck with whatever you have planned for the conference."

"That much is a surprise," Galo grinned, "By the way, I understand you first heard of my doubts because I had been shouting with the curtains open, but do me a favor and refrain from speaking so freely of it in the open."

EshCal wove and pivoted through the testosteronean battle royale of the Alpha Preliminary. She exploited each sighted opening with epee lunges to pressure points, often going unnoticed until after she struck. Despite losing much of its combative utility in dulled oaken form, she still opted for her standard melee arm. Much like when Spril first faced CreSam, their presumption of its weakness worked to her advantage.

She also spent much of her time strategically turning her more formidable opponents against one another. Many times, she used her epee only to open their defenses and dropped them with bareknuckle aggression. MalVek watched from the outer ring, nodding approvingly at her technique, which landed her in the final four with scarcely a bruise beyond welts on her knuckles.

Eytea's showing in the Gamma Preliminary proved her assertion that she could fare better without the stress of overwhelming poverty. Unfettered by monetary woes, she ducked and dashed through the crowd, slashing weapons from hands and checking guts with her oaken spearhead. Even with her wings tied down, she still bounded lightly and agilely, her motions fluid even in the most hectic of parries.

Her offensive style stood in stark contrast to the acrobatics of her defenses and evasions. She struck with vicious intent, having assimilated Sinkua's propensity for brute force into her own brand of angered grace. Her backswing sent men near MalVek's size collapsing and tumbling as it clapped their skulls. She swept the legs from under aggressors and slammed their bodies into the sand with the butt of her polearm to their abdomens.

Sinkua watched her intently, a satisfied smile spreading over his face. Her skills had not waned in peacetime after all. In fact, she had improved, both in learning from him and building on prior knowledge. MalVek watched him, nodding in approval as he found Sinkua's eyes moving in unison with Eytea's motions.

As the announcer delivered the winners and statistics of the Gamma Preliminary, Sinkua circled the gate to meet Eytea. She returned to the outer ring, panting with sweat running down her neck. He took her by the hand and congratulated her heartily. Between accolades, he glanced pensively behind his shoulder.

"You were incredible out there!" he remarked, adding under his breath, "Follow me."

"Do you really think so?" she excitedly answered, cooperating with his cover though uncertain of its purpose, "What's going on?"

Sinkua darted a glance toward MalVek. Eytea took Sinkua's hand and followed him to the diner. They stopped at the door, and Sinkua looked back. They could no longer see EshCal. The dull rumble of the crowd swelled into a cacophonous uproar as the members of the Delta Preliminary took the field.

"Too obvious," Sinkua insisted, "Keep walking."

Nearly on the opposite end of the outer ring, they found new seats among strangers. Here, they could speak more openly. Delta had already begun, with MalVek showing no hesitation in thinning the crowd.

"What did you figure out?" Eytea asked.

"MalVek is sizing us up again," Sinkua muddled, scrutinizing MalVek's technique.

"You mean like he and Spril did the first time we came here?"

"No. Different this time. He wasn't watching you fight so much as watching me watch you."

"What, so he wanted to see what you thought of my performance?" Eytea pondered, "Or do you think there's more to it?"

"I'm not sure. I only caught a few glimpses, but he was watching my face whenever I did."

"It sounds like he was seeing how well you could follow me," she suggested after a moment's consideration.

"I was tracking your movements with my eyes," he confirmed, "But why would he be interested in that?"

"Oh, were you? Have any trouble keeping up?"

"Not really. My eyes moved right along with you. Damn near synchronized even."

"Interesting," Eytea smiled, "I bet that has something to do with it."

"Do you think he wants to see how well I know you?"

"We're the only Hybrid couple in Ouristihra. People are going to, you know, study us."

"Sure, but why is he suddenly so interested in us?" Sinkua pried, "Why be so secretive about it? Why here? Why now?"

"I'd say he's keeping it to himself to be polite, but I know that answer wouldn't sit well with you," Eytea suggested, "Now that I've heard myself say it, I don't like it either. That's just not his way. But I'm sure he'll let us know what he's up to when he's ready."

"You're probably right. But now I have a bad feeling about my exhibition match."

"Oh, you think you're nervous? I'll either have to fight EshCal or someone who bested her if I reach the semifinals."

"Could be worse."

Sinkua nodded toward the battlefield. MalVek mercilessly bludgeoned ribcages with a wooden sledgehammer, knocking the breath from his contenders and slamming their bodies onto the sand.

In the back of his mind, Sinkua pondered if a match between EshCal and Eytea would be the first time two women faced off in the semifinals. At the fore of his thoughts, he worried what sporting punishment Eytea might endure from MalVek were she to eke out a victory against the more seasoned EshCal. Admittedly, he mostly contemplated these matters to distract himself from his worry over his exhibition match, which had been scheduled between the last semifinal and the championship.

He reflected on their first foray in the Tournament. That glint of light from the announcer's box had grabbed his attention, and through the glare, he had noticed that metallic mask. At the time, he had thought it some eccentric mark of aristocracy, a mad quirk of someone wealthy enough to own such a grand arena.

Eytea had found Mortvill friendly enough but insisted he had a strange and enigmatic air about him. Moreover, Sinkua had grown suspicious of their having all been placed in separate preliminary groups. His and Galo's joint exploits had become a recurring theme in the rumor mills of the time. The Commissioner may have sought to fund the rebellion, but with Imperial ArcNos as a shareholder, he could only do so covertly.

Sinkua recalled MalVek's surprise at their knowing the Commissioner's name. He revisited the reaction, obsessing over it until he finally gleaned the truth behind it.

"I think I figured it out," Sinkua spat, ending a long pensive silence.

"What did you come up with?" Eytea hastily urged as MalVek strong-armed the Delta Preliminary to a close.

"MalVek knows the Commissioner personally."

"Wait. Are you sure?" she gasped.

"Sure as I can be."

"But how?"

"I don't know. I haven't completely made sense of it, but it all fits."

"Care to explain how you came up with this?" Eytea asked, her thoughts scrambling to piece together the implications of such a notion.

"I'll explain later."

Sinkua nodded out to the field, noting MalVek heading for the exit. He got up out of his seat, Eytea following, and they made their way back the way they had come.

Just before EshCal came into sight, they began carrying on as they had been when they walked away. They put on an image that they had gone off for a celebratory drink and now returned to join EshCal and MalVek with mirth spilling over. They reached their seats around the moment when MalVek returned to his, sweaty and catching his breath.

"It's occurred to me that we haven't really heard from you since the war," Eytea opened, "What have you been up to all this time?"

"Eh?" MalVek shot back, puzzled by the sudden prying, "I've been in ArcNos. Rebuilding, you know."

"What about your brother?" Sinkua added.

"They've both been incredibly busy," EshCal interjected, "Dismantling the streetlamp surveillance system. Rebuilding our communication lines. They even helped reopen the blockaded Subtransit routes."

"The Avatars also left a few presents in the inner capital," MalVek added.

"Hey, could you help me with something?" Eytea diverted, turning to Sinkua.

"Sure, what do you need?"

"This harness is cramping up my shoulder blades. Can we go to our room? Maybe you could give me a back rub?"

"They've got a drug store on site," MalVek offered.

"Thanks, but I need something more than just a pill."

"Not what I was going to say," he sneered, still just as irritated by presumptive interruptions, "Get some magnesium sulfate. Put it in your bath water and soak until it's almost time for your next match."

"Oh, thank you. I'll give that a try," Eytea smiled.

EshCal watched through the corner of her eye as Eytea and Sinkua walked away. They passed the gate to the quarters, but they both slowed and looked back a few steps later. EshCal turned away and smiled before they saw her.

"They went downstairs. Well played," EshCal complimented.

"I knew they would. And they think we think they went to the drug store."

"Do you think they'll figure us out while they're alone?"

"There is no us. Not yet anyway. But it doesn't matter. I'll tell them soon enough."

"Does that mean I'm in if the plan works?"

"If your part of the plan works, yes."

"Why did you send them away, then?"

"Privacy."

A buzzing reverberated from his pocket, and he reached for his phone.

"Excuse me, I need to take this," he insisted before answering, "Hello?"

"The door is unlocked," a woman responded.

"Has he come in?"

"He's hanging his coat."

"Good. And the other guests?"

"They've already arrived."

"I cleaned out the closet."

"Is everything okay?" EshCal asked as he stuffed his phone in his pocket.

"Time to start the party," MalVek signaled, "You're up, miss."

While EshCal took to the field, Sinkua and Eytea talked in their quarters. Eytea had overstated her aches as a scapegoat, but Sinkua made good on the back rub all the same.

"So, how do you figure MalVek knows Mortvill?"

"He thought it was weird that we knew the Commissioner's name, like it's privileged information," Sinkua explained, "He wasn't surprised like he just learned it for us. He was surprised that we also knew it."

"Why would he be on a first name basis with him?" Eytea asked, casually baring the front of her naked torso as she rolled onto her side.

"I'm more concerned with what they're doing together than with how they met."

"Why, what do you think they're doing?"

"They're studying us," Sinkua asserted, "You know how MalVek was watching me watch you?"

"Yeah, we went over that."

"Right, well I think the Commissioner separated us our first time here so he could study us individually."

"What interest could the Commissioner have had in us?"

"Well, we can assume MalVek wants us for further defense against the Avatars. He might suspect they're about to make a move."

"That's possible," Eytea nodded, "Maybe the Commissioner separated us to maximize our winnings. If he and MalVek are both working against the Avatars, the Commissioner would have been interested in the Subtransit Resistance."

"Right. But he would have to fund them covertly, what with Imperial ArcNos being one of his top shareholders," Sinkua added, "I've considered that, but I'm not entirely convinced. He hasn't shown any interest in the Avatars since then."

"What do you suppose, then?"

"I don't know. Maybe he's just curious. Maybe he hoped to see two Hybrids in the championship," Sinkua spitballed, "Maybe he told you his name because he thought you deserved to know it just because you're one of only four Hybrids in the world."

"Five if you count the one in captivity. Assuming she's still alive, that is."

"Hm, right. I forgot about her," Sinkua admitted, visibly perturbed by the memories, "Whatever their reasons, I find it off-putting that they've been using the Tournament to study us. That can't be a coincidence."

An electronically amplified voice resonated through the ceiling. Sinkua and Eytea paused and looked up. Concrete and rebar muffled and distorted the words, but Eytea smiled knowingly.

"EshCal won her match."

"And this excites you?"

"Of course!"

"You do remember that she'll be your opponent in the semifinals, right?" Sinkua reminded, "I mean, if you both make it that far."

"I know," Eytea beamed, "That's why I'm excited."

"I thought you said you were nervous."

"I can be both."

Malia leaned over the announcer's console in stunned curiosity. EshCal had just felled her first opponent with the graceful ferocity that had made her an infamous legend on the battlefield. Monitors lined the booth, but in her surprise, her kneejerk reaction had been to lean in for a better look. Realizing her gaffe, she quietly laughed at herself as she drew back and looked over her shoulder.

"Mr. Commissioner?" she beckoned.

"Yes?" the Commissioner sternly answered.

"Which way to the restroom?"

"Bottom of the stairwell. On your left."

Malia shuffled past him, thanking him as she left the booth. The Commissioner stepped forth and stared down at the field with his arms folded. He scanned the sand field, sneering behind his mask.

Malia locked herself in a bathroom stall. She squatted atop a closed bowl and pulled out her phone.

"How are you doing in there?" she whispered.

"I am rather perturbed that I cannot see my Tournament, but I've been worse," a man mumbled, his voice slightly echoing.

"Do you need anything?"

"Only to know that you are certain of this plan."

"Absolutely, sir. This is the best way I can think to expose them," Malia reassured.

"If you truly believe so, then I suppose our best option is to trust you."

"Thank you for cooperating. I promise this will be worth your trouble."

"Just make sure I get my match with Sinkua. I would prefer it to be a public event, but a private bout might suffice if need be."

"I'll see what I can do for you."

"Oh, and do try to bring me some lamb jerky and a lager without drawing undo attention. I find I've grown a mite peckish."

Chapter 6

Farim thumbed through a stack of papers with one hand, while her other fed a steady chain of unsalted potato chips into her absently chewing mouth. At the opposite side of the room, a centrifuge quietly hummed as it separated three blood samples. Scattered before her were clippings from Berininite newspapers, wherein she searched for news of Galo's alleged parents.

Nearly every newspaper reported that Gabdur and Zheal had died a few months after he was born. This meant had Sinkua lied about their dying before Galo's conception, but she couldn't think why Sinkua would perpetuate such a lie. Two newspapers, however, corroborated his story.

They were both small-town papers, the kind unknown to most people beyond their barely triple-digit population. On one hand, they could have been working from misinformation or poor research. On the other, Gijin could have set out to rewrite the details of their deaths and overlooked those two newspapers. Granted, that broad of a cover was unlikely, but with what she knew of Gijin, the possibility was worth considering.

The centrifuge stopped spinning and beeped loudly. Farim wiped chip crumbs on her jeans and rolled her chair across the room, spinning to face the machine. She stopped herself against the table, popped out the vials, and plugged them into another machine. This one would check Galo's sample against the other two and bear out any commonalities.

Down at the other end of the table, which ran the length of the wall, another computer beeped several times in rapid succession. Farim glided to it, hooking her foot around a table leg to stop herself, and clicked the mouse to stop the alarm. The screen displayed a list of Phylus's possible genetic contributions to Vielle, sorted by calculated likelihood.

Before running that test, she had already loaded six vials of Vielle's blood into that computer's centrifuge. She pulled the top six paternal contributions into another program and fired up the centrifuge. As a precaution, she set aside the next half dozen for later.

While she waited, she returned to the first computer. Before she started working on Galo's parental concerns, she had loaded the sample from SenRas's office. As expected, she failed to make a hit in the Ouristihran Citizen's Registry. This all but confirmed the thief as an Avatar of Fate, but beyond that, she only knew the perpetrator to have been a woman.

When Eytea returned to the surface for her first match, Sinkua followed and took a seat with EshCal and MalVek. He figured that, while he may not be able to read any more into MalVek's designs, his presence would deter him from further plotting.

Having done all that he needed however, MalVek found no discomfort in Sinkua's presence. Similarly, EshCal took solace in knowing Sinkua and Eytea wouldn't discuss their suspicions in front of them.

Eytea won her first bout with little trouble. She and EshCal eked out victories in each of their second bouts as well. This brought to fruition what Eytea, as well as EshCal in secret, had craved since Eytea passed her preliminary battle. As the last representatives of the Gamma and Alpha Preliminaries, they would face each other in the semifinals.

With a show of unrestrained brute force, MalVek had muscled his way into equal standing. Eytea and EshCal silently shared the expectation that the winner of their match would have the displeasure of battling him in the finals.

"Alright, you're more agile than her, and you have a longer reach, depending on how low you hold your halberd," Sinkua reassessed as he adjusted Eytea's harness, "But she's faster and stronger."

"I know," Eytea assured, "The lower I hold my halberd, the more of a reach advantage I have, but the more of a speed advantage she has."

"Right," he nodded, "If you hold it higher, you can swing faster, but you sacrifice your reach advantage."

"I'll find a good middle ground."

EshCal carved a series of lines in the dusty air, ending her display by pointing the oaken epee at Eytea. Eytea looked up and pushed the dull blade back with her fingertip. EshCal shoved the fencing sword in her holster and offered her hand as Sinkua finished with the restraints.

"You ready to do this?"

"Hey, I came here ready!" Eytea boasted as EshCal helped her to her feet.

"That's what I like to hear!" EshCal exclaimed, "Let's give 'em a show for the ages."

"I'd have it no other way," Eytea insisted, "By the way, is it true what they say? Is this the first time two women have fought each other in the semifinals?"

"Sure is. Pretty historic, huh?" EshCal confirmed, "In fact, it's the first time there's been two women in the semifinals at all."

"Has there ever been a female champion?" Sinkua asked.

"Not yet," MalVek answered, "A few have passed the semifinals, but they all lost the championship match."

EshCal and Eytea entered the field alongside each other, their gaits almost synchronized. Each stole glimpses of the other from the corner of her eye, analyzing one another for potential weaknesses. At the center of the sand field, they each assumed the stance of their choosing.

For all their stillness, they stood in the eye of the raging storm that had become of the Radial Axiom Arena. Spectators whooped and shouted, their collective voices coalescing into a thunderous roar. The stands resonated under stomping feet, flakes of stucco raining from the ceiling in the outer ring.

The blaring of the horn drilled a hole through the roar of the crowd. Eytea opened with a sudden thrust, gripping her halberd at the center and the butt. Taken by surprise, EshCal leaned back and let the blade stop just short of her chin. Eytea withdrew and swung her polearm around to sweep EshCal's legs.

EshCal erected herself synchronously with Eytea's withdrawal. EshCal sidestepped Eytea's next swipe, kicking off the side of the axe blade on the ball of her foot. At Eytea's open side, EshCal lunged her epee at her unguarded kidney. Eytea twisted to parry and responded with a kick to EshCal's bared underarm.

EshCal reared back and squeezed her arm for a split second. Eytea circled her halberd over her head and brought it down on EshCal within her blink of distraction. Jolting to lucidity, EshCal stepped into the attack and punctured the Harvest wind with an upward thrust of her epee. The tip of her fencing sword impaled Eytea's halberd, their coupled momentum driving the epee through to its hilt. They froze and stared at one another in mutual disbelief.

Eytea offered her knee, and EshCal braced her foot on it and pulled back, freeing the sword. Even as they stumbled away from each other, they resumed their brutal yet artful volleying of attacks, parries, and ripostes. EshCal dodged under Eytea's widely arcing swings, while Eytea weaved around and pivoted away from EshCal's piercing strikes.

Aside from the odd kick or jab, strikes scarcely found their mark. Most that landed did so through such hindrance as to be rendered largely ineffective. As Sinkua had predicted, EshCal dashed around Eytea's long-reaching attacks, seemingly taunting the halberd itself. If the rippling of EshCal's shoulder muscles gave any indication, any one of her ripostes would have reduced Eytea to an agonized fetal position.

EshCal leaned back as Eytea's wooden axe blade screamed at her face, the wind from its edge tossing her hair. Her spine began to tighten as she bent further. Eytea grimaced as though she knew what she forced upon her elder opponent.

EshCal answered with a devastating riposte thrust, but she failed to account for the split seconds Eytea had afforded herself. Eytea dropped her halberd to her hip, holding it behind the head, and watched the tip of EshCal's epee screech toward her face.

A wake of dust swept up as Eytea glided into the attack. With one hand, she grabbed EshCal's epee, passing it over her shoulder, and with the other, she thrust her halberd.

Despite EshCal's superior strength and speed, she failed to react before impact. The spearhead jammed into her stomach, distorting the relaxed flesh before she could tighten her abdominals. Eytea drove the weapon in until the top of the axe grinded against EshCal's sternum.

EshCal's eyes widened, her face gnarling with anguish as she doubled over and wheezed for air. Eytea ripped the epee out of her hand and pitched it backward, simultaneously discarding her halberd. With her arms extended back, she exploited EshCal's pained stupor with a sharp kick to the chin.

EshCal's body snapped erect, sending her staggering. Eytea followed with a palm heel strike to the base of EshCal's sternum, driving with enough momentum to push her back to her arm's full extension.

EshCal coughed violently, gasping and spitting blood. Eytea held her at arm's length, watching the composure drain from her body. EshCal grew disoriented, the edge of her vision jaggedly flickering with the hastening rhythm with her pulse. Eytea pulled back her arm as EshCal began to grasp at it. EshCal collapsed onto her knees, and Eytea watched in statuesque silence as she fell to her hands and slapped the sand thrice.

The exuberant announcement of Eytea's victory boomed from the speakers, resonating throughout the stands. An uproarious clamor swelled from the audience, seemingly more for the match itself than the outcome. Eytea crouched beside EshCal, wrapped her arm around her, and helped her to her feet. EshCal braced herself on her final opponent as they ambled off the sand field in tandem.

Sinkua looked up to the announcer's booth, his attention taken by moving shadows. Truthfully, his eyes had been diverting up there quite frequently, given that only the next bout stood before his fight with Mortvill. He narrowed his gaze and flared his eyes to overcome the dusty Quarunite air.

In the middle of the announcer's speech, the Commissioner turned and walked away from the console. Malia stepped aside, nodding respectfully. As their shoulders brushed, the Commissioner reached under the mask and pulled at something.

"This had better work," he muttered, his voice sounding distant and vaguely feminine.

Malia gasped with widening eyes, freezing with fear as the doppelganger stepped out of the booth. She squeezed her earpiece but received no response. Frantically, she pulled her cell phone from her pocket, but it had no signal either.

"Could I borrow your phone, please?" she nervously asked.

"Sure, just be quick about it," the announcer complied, taking pause as he opened his phone, "On second thought, no. Sorry, but I don't have a signal."

"Is that normal in here?"

"Not usually. Let me check something," he answered, pulling his walkie-talkie from his hip, "Ah no, this isn't normal at all."

"Shit!"

Malia threw the door open and scrambled out of the booth. Her heart jackhammered her ribcage as she spiraled down the stairwell. An undeniable truth behind her paranoia sank into the most inextricable recesses of her rationale.

She anchored herself on the door handle as she ran past the storage closet. She pounded on the door, panting heavily and calling between breaths. A masked figure with a bag of jerky opened the door with urgency in his posture.

"What has occurred?" he asked.

"It isn't him," Malia gasped, "Commissioner. You must leave."

"What do you speak of? Who did they send in his stead?" Mortvill barked.

"It's The Engineer, sir. I don't know what she plans to do," Malia confessed.

"I suspect she intends to send a message," Mortvill suggested, "That being that your most recent attempt at sabotage has been exposed, and you with it."

"I know it has. But why her? Why not The Geneticist? Or The Politician? Someone I've actually sabotaged."

"Preemptive retaliation, my dear."

"What does this mean for my daughter?" Malia panicked.

"Well, I should presume to say it does not bode well," Mortvill prophesied, "According to my contacts, you have approximately one week."

"One week? One week until what?"

"Until a kinship is realized. It will occur a dozen kilometers eastward across the sea from Masnethege. Seek your guide in ArcNos."

"Should I warn the others first?"

"By what means, and to what ends? You only know he sent an associate in place of himself. Hardly a thing to do about it, given such meager observations. Go save your daughter."

Heads swiveled as a cloaked figure swept down the stands. Those in the midst of phone calls found their conversations silenced, their devices abruptly blacking out as the Commissioner passed. Down on the sand field, MalVek and his semifinal opponent stared up at the approaching figure.

"Sinkua!" MalVek shouted, "Looks like you're up!"

"What's going on?" EshCal called back before Sinkua could answer.

"I thought my match was between the semifinals and the championship," Sinkua added as MalVek neared.

"He's coming down now, and he's armed," MalVek insisted as he reentered the outer ring, "Get out there and greet him."

An ominous settled fell over the audience. Sinkua strode onto the sand field, a wooden morningstar slung over his shoulder. His luminous eyes fixated on the distantly familiar figure descending the stairs, his searing gaze trying to burn through that mask and meet the face living beneath.

The Commissioner walked silently across the field, his cloak obscuring his footprints. He kept his face oriented on Sinkua, who returned the fixed stare. He reached over his shoulder and gripped a handle nearly the girth of his forearm. He pulled from his back a beastly sword with a blade nearly a meter and a half in length. Sinkua arched an eyebrow and took a step back. Worse than its size and the ease with which the Commissioner carried it, it looked and sounded metallic.

"You've brought the wrong weapon, sir," Sinkua insisted.

The Commissioner pointed his blade at Sinkua. A pensive sneer consuming his expression, Sinkua defiantly stepped toward the Commissioner.

"What do you mean by this?" Sinkua demanded.

Sinkua snarled and jerked the chain of the borrowed morningstar, testing its durability with great dissatisfaction. His eyes flared brightly. The Commissioner grimaced behind the mask.

"MalVek, you obviously know Mortvill," Eytea revealed, somewhat to MalVek's surprise, "What is he trying to do?"

"He doesn't seem like himself today," MalVek said, "Go get Sinkua's morningstar."

Eytea nodded and fled, brushing past fellow competitors as she made for the gated staircase. MalVek opened his phone, but quite to his chagrin, found it had no signal. At his urging, EshCal checked hers as well, but it yielded the same failure. He had the same luck with his earpiece.

"He's on to us," he muttered.

"What do we do?" EshCal blanked.

"Our lines have been cut. If we make a move, we'll draw attention and out ourselves," he said, "Stand by to intervene should your part of the plan fail. Expect to improvise."

The Commissioner bellowed ferociously as he slashed at Sinkua's head. Sinkua ducked and pivoted to the Commissioner's side, exploiting the brief opening with a sharp jab to the ribcage. The blade wholly eliminated any reach advantage Sinkua could have had. He inevitably withdrew to dodge the Commissioner's next swing.

By now, most of the audience had dismissed their inoperative phones for more urgent matters. Those with pacemakers clutched their chest, doubling over and choking on their own breath. Nearby spectators scrambled to find medics and ripped through bags in search of medication.

Sinkua bobbed and weaved around the furiously slashing blade, sticking quick punches wherever he could. Despite the gradual volley of jabs though, the Commissioner showed no signs of pain or weariness. Sinkua's breathing destabilized. Uncomfortably salty sweat coated his skin and matted his hair. He had long ago given up on reasoning with this cloaked psychopath, as every plea brought only silence and mounting aggression.

His patience thoroughly depleted, Sinkua tried to snatch the Commissioner's blade with the oaken morningstar. The ball knocked against the blade and deflected sharply. Although Sinkua's counter proved largely ineffective, the Commissioner's upper body flinched as he turned to follow with a downward slash. Sinkua's eyes fixated on this twitch as he kicked up the studded ball and grabbed the chain, pulling it taut.

"Prepare to deploy the unit," MalVek ordered.

"You're sure this will work?" EshCal asked.

"If you're going to work with us, you need to trust the work we've done," MalVek barked, "That device is the result of over five hundred thousand labor hours of research and development, and that was with the target's brother at the top of our organization."

Eytea threw open the quarters door and slammed it behind herself. She snatched Sinkua's morningstar from the coat rack and strapped her halberd on her back. As an added precaution, she grabbed the wooden box from the nightstand. She ran out the door, kicking it shut behind her, and rushed to the stairs to the outer ring.

The blade pressed against the wooden chain, held back by little more than Sinkua's futile resilience. The Commissioner jerked and flinched. Sinkua coughed hoarsely, sweat pooling in every crevice as the blade wedged into the chain. Finally, the oaken fibers snapped and splintered, the Commissioner abruptly stabilizing as his sword plummeted upon his curmudgeonly opponent. Sinkua pitched the split failure of a weapon off from his sides as he sprang back to evade the falling blade.

A fan of coarse dust spewed upward as the sword sliced the sand field. Instinctively, Sinkua tried to hurl a ball of flame through the shroud of dust, but his hand turned up only smoke. At that moment, he noticed what he had been too occupied to acknowledge, the relative chill that consumed him. Overexerting himself with that single failed effort, he wheezed and hunched over.

"Sinkua!" Eytea shouted from the open gate to the outer ring.

Sinkua looked back as his morningstar left Eytea's hands, its head pounding the dense air as it spiraled forth. Gathering the remains of his composure, he ran to it, grabbing at the air until his hands found the handle. The Commissioner charged from behind, snarling viciously with his broadsword drawn back.

"Oh! Let me see your halberd!" EshCal beckoned, "You just gave me an idea!"

"You'll have to retrieve the device if you miss," MalVek warned.

"Just trust me."

Eytea handed over her halberd, puzzled but too worried about Sinkua to question any of it just yet. EshCal whipped out her belt and strapped the unit to the side of the spearhead.

The massive blade carved yet another wake of screaming wind. Sinkua snapped loose the bindings on his morningstar, spinning and swinging it with a bellow of raw ferocity before the chain fully dropped at his side. Their weapons collided again, only this time, the broadsword snapped backward.

Tiny sparks popped from the blade as the spikes roughened it. The Commissioner staggered back with the ricocheted momentum. Sinkua crouched in answer to an urging shouted from behind.

MalVek and Eytea stepped aside. EshCal rushed to the open gate, modified halberd mounted on her shoulder. As the Commissioner stumbled, she called to Sinkua and sent the polearm screaming across the sand field. MalVek clenched his teeth. Eytea gasped and held it in as though that breath might be her last.

Eytea's halberd, fortified with MalVek's mysterious device, careened over Sinkua's head. Once it passed, Sinkua rose to his feet again, standing in arrogant contempt. The spearhead plunged into the Commissioner's chest, stopping at the strapped device. Rather than blood pouring from the wound though, sparks arced and spat erratically. Sinkua sneered in bewilderment.

A pulse of energy blasted from the device, spreading throughout the Commissioner's body. He jolted as he collapsed onto his knees. Sinkua stepped back. The Commissioner spasmed and convulsed violently on the sand.

"So," EshCal smiled victoriously, "Am I in?"

"No. Something's wrong," MalVek refused.

"What? What's wrong?" Eytea panicked, "Is he not supposed to look like that?"

"No, it's just supposed to knock him out."

The Commissioner dropped his broadsword, and it lost its opacity, leaving a wireframe outline. That dissolved into nothingness as well. MalVek ground his fingernails against the stone wall.

"Why does he have a weapon generator?" Eytea demanded.

"He's a decoy," MalVek snarled.

"Wasn't that the plan?" EshCal asked.

"Plan?! What plan!?" Eytea shouted.

The decoy sparked and jolted, its frame contorting and expanding chaotically. He grew considerably taller, his shoulders widening and limbs lengthening in proportion. His clothing and mask somehow stretched as well, as though they were extensions of this shifting phantom. His cheeks and jawline contorted as his obstructed visage restructured itself.

"No time to explain," MalVek insisted.

The new form erected itself, standing just over six meters. It unceremoniously flung Eytea's halberd away, its baritone breath loud enough to resound over the terrified screams of the crowd. A dense wooden rod grew from his hands, shaping into a colossal warhammer.

"Eytea, get…"

Before MalVek could finish, Eytea rushed out of the gate. She fought with her harness as she sprinted across the sand field, jerking the buckles undone and tossing it aside. In her haste, however, she had left Sinkua's box on her seat.

"MalVek!" EshCal urged, her voice shaky with anger as much as fear, "Who is that?"

MalVek swallowed and gasped, "Someone who shouldn't exist!"

Biroe buried his knuckles in his hair as he clawed through a disheveled heap of paperwork. His lips curled into a bewildered sneer as he examined the numbers yet again. He shifted in his seat, trying to peel the sweat-matted khaki fabric from his leg. Quite to his startling, another chair scooted up alongside his wheelchair, and an arm reached across his backrest.

"Having trouble, sir?" KalChi asked.

"What are you doing here?" Biroe puzzled, "Oh… Wait, that's right."

"Yes, you paged me ten minutes ago," she affirmed, "Sorry, I was a bit tied up. What's going on?"

"You used to work for these people, right?" Biroe asked, showing her the letterhead on one of the pages.

"Yes, but I left seven years ago. Why?"

"There's an anomaly in their equity accounts. What can you tell me about the owners?"

"I only met them a few times, but they were decent enough. For corporate executives."

"Were any of them part of the Subtransit Resistance?"

"No, when the company shut down, they took a core crew and relocated to Lenguardia," KalChi recalled, "They moved back shortly after the war, but I had already been offered a better salary and benefits package here."

"Well, I'm glad we won you over," Biroe smiled, "Anyway, you've never suspected them of fraud?"

"No, I could never see them cheating anyone. Why? Do you think they might be embezzling?"

"Their equity payouts dropped eighteen percent this year."

"What about sales and buybacks of shares?"

"Consistent with their history since they came back to ArcNos."

"So, there's no spike in investors selling back their shares," KalChi reiterated, "but payouts have dropped. How is their stock value holding up?"

"Solid!" Biroe remarked, throwing up his arms, "That's just it! Based on net changes in active shares and their stock value, money is literally missing. It's not in any accounts traceable to the owners. It's just gone."

"Sounds like foul play, then."

"But you just said the owners were of solid merit."

"Not on their part," KalChi corrected, "The money went missing, so they deducted it from their net profits. What I mean is that some of their investors might have been cut off."

"I have found a few other companies exhibiting similar anomalies."

"Really? Why are you just now consulting your staff about this?"

"This is the first one that anyone in the Ministry of Treasury has worked for," Biroe justified, "I was going to send the files to our investigative unit, but I became preoccupied with researching it myself."

"Don't bother. They'll just sit on it," KalChi insisted, rising from her seat.

"Not the people I have in mind, but if you have another suggestion, I'm open to it."

"I'll call the company and get a list of their top shareholders."

"Will they give you that?"

"Maybe, maybe not," KalChi shrugged, "Depending who I get on the line, I might be able to coax it out of them. At a minimum, I can learn if any shareholders active during my last month there have since withdrawn their investment."

"And we'll dig up the same information on the other ones," Biroe epiphanized, "Cross-reference and find the common investors."

"Exactly. Then we'll isolate and investigate those shareholders," KalChi confirmed, "Anyway, I need to be going. I have an appointment, and I'll be late if I don't get on the next Subtransit train there."

"Alright. Thanks so much for your help. I'll see you in the morning."

The new monstrosity rushed across the sand field, sending Sinkua backpedaling. With a resonating bellow, the titan crashed the hammer down upon his prey. Sinkua leapt back, a cloud of sand whipping over his face, and dropped into a crouch as he landed on the tremoring ground. The giant followed with a swing from the side, the chills of dependency leaving Sinkua disoriented.

A foot lit upon Sinkua's back, planting him face down and out of the Warhammer's path. Eytea, her discarded halberd in hand, sprang from Sinkua's back with a beat of her unencumbered wings. The hammer passed between them, thrumming the air with its momentum. She aimed her weapon at the beast's outstretched arm as the other hand barreled at her from beyond the edge of her vision.

"What about the others? Can we call for backup?" EshCal urged.

"Circumstances called for skeletal presence. The plan was to knock out The Harvester and send him off," MalVek reiterated, "Even if we could expel this one, there's no safe place to send him."

"Right, but..."

"Can't do it without exposing ourselves anyhow, and it's too soon for that one to know about The Omnimath," he added, pointing across the field with three fingers curled around Sinkua's box and his sledgehammer drawn back in his other hand.

"Then, what are you doing?"

"Protecting our interests."

From the edge of the field, MalVek let his sledgehammer fly. Eytea came screeching down upon the titan's arm. MalVek's hammer pummeled the incoming hand, knocking it from its deadly trajectory. Eytea plunged both heads of her halberd into the beast's forearm and swung to the underside, carving his flesh with the full weight of her body. Electric sparks arced with in the wound.

The giant whipped his gashed arm out to the side, flinging Eytea from it. He plucked the sledgehammer from the ground, his fist nearly consuming it. MalVek charged across the sand field, only for the giant to hurl his sledgehammer back at him. His reflexes failing to match the incredible momentum, MalVek took the crushing blow to the ribcage. He collapsed back through the open gate, gasping and clutching his chest.

The beast threw up a wake of sand as its foot plowed into Sinkua, sending his weary body skipping across the field. MalVek weakly pitched the box, landing it far short of Sinkua.

Recovering her balance, Eytea circled to the front of the giant, drawing its attention away from Sinkua and MalVek. Between her halberd hanging from the titan's arm and fear of collateral deaths from a milystic strike, her offensive options were cripplingly depleted. Instead, she wove around his attacks, making her way toward Sinkua's box.

Sinkua dragged himself to his feet, hocking bloody phlegm and sand out of his throat. His torso slumped, feeling too heavy to support itself. Hearing something land behind him, he turned his head as much as the constant strain in his joints would allow. He turned and ambled toward the box, drooling a trail of blood and dragging his morningstar. From the corner of his eye, he saw Eytea dodging the giant's tormenting advances.

Sinkua hacked violently, doubling over in pain. He choked on his own breath as sanguinary mucus flooded his airways. Holding his chest and desperately trying to stabilize his breathing, he dragged his feet along an expedition of a few meters.

A single scream thrust him over the threshold.

Eytea circled an incoming fist, diving in close to reclaim her halberd as it dropped from the colossus's forearm. The titan swung ferociously as she came within reach. Giving up on her weapon, she launched herself back with a surge of lightning. Relative to the titan's size, it only grazed her, but relative to Eytea's, the warhammer crashed against her side. She screamed in agony as her wing fractured and her shoulder cartilage shredded between the impacted bones.

Eytea cried out as she landed on her injury and rolled along the sand. Sinkua gasped in horror as she settled before him, the clearest breath he had taken in several minutes. He coughed hoarsely, his heart erratically bludgeoning his ribs. Eytea lifted her head and looked to him with widening eyes.

Recalling Sinkua's experience upon returning to ArcNos shortly before the war, Eytea exhaled a rapid stream-of-consciousness monologue. It didn't matter what she said, just that he could hear her voice as the episode set in. Another voice called out to him.

"Sinkua!" MalVek shouted, "Catch!"

Sinkua held out his arm, placing his trust in MalVek's aim. He closed his fist around the chain as it draped over his hand. That familiar nurturing heat flowed down his arm. He grimaced as he dropped it around his neck. The ruby medallion bounced against his sternum, radiating its warmth throughout his body.

Sinkua turned and walked toward the giant, his eyes glowing fiercely. The colossus drew back his hammer. Sinkua discarded his morningstar. Whorls of flame burst around his hands. The beastly maul rushed down upon him. He grinned wickedly as he lowered his head and raised his arms. He clutched the handle of the warhammer, stopping it even against the giant's strength.

The two struggled against each other, the titan to retract his weapon and Sinkua to pull it from his clutches. The fibers grew brittle and ashen under Sinkua's fiery grip. He twisted his hands, raining ember fragments in a cascade of sparks. The giant snarled ferociously.

The reinforcement rod cracked through, the rupture vomiting sparks. From the depths of his throat, Sinkua expelled an animalistic roar and hurled the decapitated hammerhead back at the giant. It bludgeoned his abdomen, sending him doubling over.

Sinkua launched into a sprint, leaving a trail of fire in his wake. He sprang off the hammerhead as it landed, grabbed the beast by the collarbone, and pulled himself onto its shoulders. Repeatedly, he pounded his enflamed fist against the mask, denting it and caving it in on that hidden face. The fire spread across his torso, incinerating Sinkua's shirt. The beast writhed as Sinkua bored his fingers into his deltoids.

The titan pulled him from his face, a trail of melted flesh and seared tissue connecting Sinkua's fingertips to his shoulders. Sinkua wriggled for freedom but found no avail as it threw him to the ground. He slid on his back, sand violating his wounds, but kept his eyes fixed on the wretched monstrosity.

Sinkua slowly sat up. The colossus staggered toward him, its steps shortening, and eventually stopped. He stayed seated, watching in bewilderment as his episode subsided along with the threat of the titan.

The loss of opacity began with the severed hammerhead and rippled throughout the colossus's body. Green lines shimmered through translucent surfaces. The surface faded away, leaving a luminescent wireframe. That dissipated as well, leaving only a black disc. The disc skidded along and fled the sand field. Sinkua collapsed on his back, his eyelids drooping.

"MalVek?" EshCal beckoned as she sat beside him on the ground.

"Yeah?" he answered, his head still shaky from the blow to the chest.

"I'm not sure I can handle working with you," she confessed.

"No. You did great," he assured, bracing himself on her shoulder, "Your part of the plan went fine, given what we had planned for."

"Thanks, but I mean… This? What just happened here?"

"Would you believe me if I said it makes more sense than what I thought had happened?"

"I'm listening."

"Then wait until they are, too."

Chapter 7

A loud humming resonated in Sinkua's ears, waking him. He opened his eyes to find himself face down on polished wood. Puzzled, he turned to survey his surroundings. He lay in a train car similar to the last one he recalled riding in Quarun.

Eytea sat beside him, smiling sweetly. She had watched him sleep with his face planted on the wooden windowsill. EshCal and MalVek sat across from them. He tried to sit up only to tremble as he beared down on his arms.

"Your upper body won't be able to handle much stress for a while," MalVek warned all too late.

"What happened?" Sinkua grunted as Eytea helped him up with her good arm.

"You threw a hammerhead that weighed more than Eytea as though it was a bag of apples," EshCal answered, "The adrenaline numbed the pain, but you destroyed a lot of muscle tissue in your arms and torso."

"Most people don't consider that tradeoff," MalVek nodded.

"What? No. No, I know about that," Sinkua dismissed, "Of course I know about that. I mean what happened to my match, and how did I get here?"

"You collapsed after the fight," Eytea said, "But you didn't black out like you usually do after an episode. It was more like you were letting yourself rest."

"Well, people typically faint after having that burst of superhuman strength," MalVek added, "Once the adrenaline wears off, they pass out and sleep through the pain."

"Right. Well, I think I woke up too soon," Sinkua sneered, "How's your shoulder, Eytea?"

"Hurts a ton."

"We'll get you both fixed up once we get where we're going," MalVek promised.

"Sounds nice," Sinkua smirked, "Got any pain killers in the meantime?"

"EshCal, could you please?" MalVek beckoned.

"Now, what happened out there?" Sinkua pried.

"I can't go into much detail here, but what you fought was a highly concentrated organic hologram," MalVek began.

"The way it faded into a grid," Eytea recalled, "it looked like the weapon Kabehl used."

"Same principle but much more advanced."

"So, it's the Avatars' technology?"

"They wish it was their technology," a familiar voice scoffed as it approached.

"Hello, NalSet," Sinkua greeted.

"Hello to yourself, young man. Been staying out of trouble?"

"Not so much, no."

"Good answer," NalSet commended, "Now like I said, they wish they had come up with that technology. They stole it from us. Same with the barricades."

"You mean you had all these advantages during the ArcNosian Civil War, and you didn't use them?" Eytea scolded.

"It's not as simple as that," NalSet insisted, "We couldn't risk being accused of fraternizing with the Avatars. Much like how Sinkua felt the need to keep his relation to CreSam a secret."

"I suppose that's reasonable," Sinkua nodded.

"We also needed to cultivate the lot of you, given that most of the Avatars of Fate were still at large. Helping you become strong enough to contend with them meant helping you level the battlefield on your strengths, not simply handing you advantages. Plus, we didn't want to start an arms race. At least not another one," MalVek added, "I'll go into that more when we arrive."

"There's quite a lot we need to discuss, really, but we can't here," NalSet added.

"Why not?" Sinkua asked, "We're in a private cabin."

"That doesn't mean we can't be overheard."

"Okay, but who was that first projection if it wasn't Mortvill?"

"His brother. Leader of the Avatars of Fate," NalSet answered.

"His Avatar alias is The Harvester. Nobody but Mortvill knows his real name anymore," MalVek added.

"And the giant?"

"That's one of the things we can't discuss here."

EshCal set an open bottle of painkillers and a glass of water on the table. Sinkua thanked her and popped a couple of pills. Eytea did likewise.

They had been right to think MalVek and NalSet had been hiding something, but neither imagined anything as heavy as this. Their injuries hurt enough on their own, but learning a rival group guided their dealings with the Avatars induced migraines. Stranger still, while Spril had scouted them for the war in ArcNos, MalVek and perhaps Mortvill had been scouting them for greater ambitions. Internally, they both debated whether these people had called on them because the Avatars had marked them or the Avatars had marked them because these people had called on them.

Perhaps that was what MalVek had meant by not wanting to start another arms race.

A woman near the end of her third decade jammed a metal probe into the soil beside a flowering plant. She pushed a button and, while holding it, watched the screen on a handheld device linked to the probe. She sneered with distaste at the results as she wiped the sweat from her neck. She winced as she brushed her artificial sunburn.

"Crap in a coffee cake!" Spril exclaimed, "Think you keep it hot enough in here?"

"Geez! I didn't hear you come in!" Yrlis gasped, catching her breath, "And yes. I do. This is how hot it is in Berinin."

"During Harvest?"

"These are Swelter blooms," Yrlis sighed impatiently.

"Well, this makes sense, then," Spril conceded, "You need this drink more than I thought."

"Oh, thank you," Yrlis professed, accepting the icy beverage, "What is it?"

"Mango lemonade."

"Mango?" she bit with a crooked sneer, "Now, you're just teasing me."

"What? Why do you think that?"

"Galo's favorite drink was mango juice!"

"I'd forgotten about that," he shrugged, "Sounds like you've had him on your mind."

"Oh sorry, are you jealous?"

"Not in the slightest. I just know your work out here is about figuring out his secret."

"Now, that just makes it sound sinister," Yrlis chided.

"You know I don't mean it that way," Spril insisted, "But what do you plan on doing when you figure out how this stuff works?"

"You mean if it works."

"He got you with the ipthkys root."

Yrlis cringed at her memories of the days following that wager, days spent entirely too much on the toilet.

"Fine, but that doesn't mean all of it works," Yrlis partially conceded, "Anyway, if I can figure out his secret, I'm going to talk to him about advancing the technology."

"You're not expecting to exploit their work, are you?" Spril worried.

"What? No! I just want to help synthesize them for mass production and wider availability."

"And if he won't?"

"I'll ask Phylus to help."

"Vielle might work better."

They laughed together over that remark. Even though Vielle had no romantic interest in him, the way Galo had eyed her stayed memorable even five years later.

"Anyway," Spril continued as Yrlis downed the last of her now-diluted mango lemonade, "You've yet to reproduce the results they apparently get all the time after five years in a greenhouse. Are you sure they even can be synthesized."

"I mean the chemical composition," Yrlis specified, "Not the plants themselves."

With that comment, she returned to her work. Her results had all been negative, but she dutifully continued to test every plant. This species was said to fight influenza, but so far, none of the variants in this crop reacted to the virus.

"What if you prove him wrong?"

"Honestly, I haven't thought about it. I've been giving him the benefit of the doubt this whole time."

"That's big of you, but doesn't that go against burden of proof?" Spril cautioned.

"I know. Onus goes to whoever makes the claim, not the naysayer," Yrlis confirmed, "Maybe I should confront him about it."

"Why not? You've simulated every environmental condition, haven't you?"

"Yeah. I even went down to that exotic pet store on the south end of town. You know the one I'm talking about?"

"Yeah, I've passed it a few times. Smells too weird to forget,"

"Smells even stronger on the inside," she laughed, "Anyhow, I got some stool samples from a few…"

She trailed off there, losing herself in thought. Spril watched her curiously as her eyes deepened. Behind her gaping stare, her mind sifted through years of data and research.

"Stool samples from some animals indigenous to Berinin?" he asked.

"Right. That."

"Are you okay? I didn't know if you were having a breakthrough or blacking out."

"First one. Definitely the first one," Yrlis lit up, "When can we go to Masnethege?"

"I'm leaving for Eprilen in the morning," Spril reminded, "You can ride along and continue southward."

"Right! Your Ouristihran Union meeting," she recalled, "Since Galo will be there, I can just talk to him then."

"Sounds great!" he remarked, "I'll pack your suitcase while you finish up out here. So, do you really think you've figured it out?"

"Definitely!" Yrlis boasted, "I just can't simulate the conditions. It's impossible. They've all naturally come together, waiting to be found but not to be copied."

As much as his injuries would allow, Sinkua cocked his head as he stepped off the train. The aerodynamic body and single-track mounting were curiously new to him. NalSet sidled up next to him.

"First time seeing a mag-lev train?" he probed.

"Mag-lev?" Sinkua asked, "Looks expensive. What's so special about it?"

"It's short for magnetic levitation. Makes railways a lot more efficient and sustainable. Been running these lovelies in Quarun for three years."

"Huh. I think the last time I was on a train was after my first Tournament."

"Last time I was on one was in ArcNos," Eytea remarked, "I got to ride in the driver's compartment and everything."

For most of the ride, sarcasm and snide humor had been her coping mechanisms. The crack in her wing radiated throughout her shoulder blade into a deep throbbing cramp, and that arm had become largely immobile. Those aches made it exceedingly difficult to contemplate what MalVek and NalSet had dropped on them, much less to anticipate what secrets they still held. Snark and sarcasm distracted her and Sinkua from pondering answers to questions they couldn't yet ask.

As had been discussed on the train, their destination would be Country Living Bed & Breakfast. Upon departure, they melded with the crowd, exchanging pleasantries among strangers. As the masses dispersed, they did as well.

MalVek and NalSet traveled together by taxi. Sinkua and Eytea took a bus, and EshCal rode in a separate taxi on an alternate route. The arrangement was meant to divert the spying eyes of the Avatars of Fate.

Sinkua and Eytea arrived last, finding the other three waiting on the porch. NalSet stood in front of the door with his arms crossed behind his back.

"Good, we're all here," he welcomed, "My brother and I will head in first to sort out a few things."

"Making sure Mortvill made it home?" Eytea pried.

"Have we become that transparent? Yes, we need to see if he's ready to receive company."

NalSet reached across his torso as though to scratch himself and peeled a narrow mechanism from the doorframe. Knowing he had drawn attention, he mimed passing the device to MalVek. They walked into the darkened interior and shut the door. A Berininite a few years their junior welcomed them.

"Splendid scenery in the Northlands this season," he professed, "How was the operation, sirs?"

"Two of them are on the inside track, and we have a new recruit," MalVek boasted, "But the sabotage didn't go as planned."

"Do you suppose they're on to us?"

"I see no other possibility."

"Well, The Omnimath arrived nearly an hour ago. He's waiting for you in the chamber."

"Thank you. How are matters progressing on your end?"

"Quite well, thank you. I've kept him from settling into a base of operations for any extended period."

MalVek watched his colleague leave as they exchanged salutations. The Berininite laid a strip of material on the frame and opened the door to warm salty breezes. As he peeled the strip away, the scenery warped and skewed, shifting to a frosted urban landscape. NalSet and MalVek continued to the chamber.

"What became of the mission?" their superior scolded as they crossed the blue track lighting winding along the floor.

"We're still trying to…" MalVek began.

"An affront to our research!" NalSet boldly remarked, "To think they would use our technology to resurrect so abominant a creature!"

"That is not what I speak of," The Omnimath insisted, "I have known since we came here that he was capable of such measures, were he to acquire our work. What happened to the plan? How did they figure us out?"

"You'll have to ask Malia about that," MalVek deferred.

"The two of you have no theories on the matter?"

"Given her unsubtle overachieving with The Coalition, they most likely began to suspect her of treachery," NalSet offered.

"They deduced that her plan to have them sabotage the Tournament was actually a trap for them. So they changed the operation to catch her in the act," MalVek complemented.

"I knew she would eventually slip. Natives always do," The Omnimath sighed, "but I trusted her nonetheless. At least she made good on her promise of lamb jerky."

"Plus," MalVek cut in, "we've brought those two into the fold."

"Sinkua and Eytea, correct?"

"Yes, sir. This may not be the best news after what happened with Malia, but we've also brought in another recruit. An ArcNosian Native named EshCal, the first female Brigadier General Elite in the nation's history."

"I'm familiar. I'll not be receiving company at this time however," The Omnimath excused, "I need to further review the logistics of today's mission. I will speak with Malia in due time. You two are dismissed."

Sinkua paced nervously, trying to distract himself from his unanswerable confusion. Worse, the painkillers had started to wear off. EshCal leaned against a tree, soaking in what shade its sparse branches still offered. Eytea sat on the porch steps, her eyes panning the landscape. She held out her fingers to frame the scenery.

She abruptly rose to her feet, drawing Sinkua's and EshCal's attention with slight alarm. Eytea dashed across the field, bum wing bouncing with each footfall. She crouched briefly and returned with her hands cupped over each other.

"What have you got there?" Sinkua asked as they approached one another.

"Check it out!" Eytea remarked, opening her hands, "I didn't know these grew here."

In her hand sat a rose blossom with a length of stem between her fingers. It spanned the width of her palm and, quite curiously, exhibited a rich sapphire hue.

"Strange. I've never seen blue roses."

"They're not natural, and technically, they're not roses. A botanist in Ferya crossbred roses with some other flowers and eventually came up with these."

"Fascinating," Sinkua remarked, taking the flower for a closer look, "How long have they been growing in the open?"

"I can't remember when they weren't, but I've only ever known them to grow in Ferya," Eytea recollected, "We had a trading partner that grew them. We never met him, but after we buried Kabehl, he started putting one in most of the barter parcels he sent to us. He stopped a few weeks before you and Galo showed up."

She slid the stem between locks of her hair, perching it over her ear. Against the darker strands, the brilliant tones of the flower almost appeared to glow.

"What do you think?" she asked.

"Never saw you as the flowers-in-your-hair type," Sinkua shrugged, "but you look beautiful."

Heads turned as the door opened. NalSet peeled the mechanical strip from the frame and stuffed it in his pocket before anyone saw him or the inside of the cottage. He and MalVek beckoned the others to the porch.

"Mortvill hasn't arrived yet," MalVek half lied, "But I called him, and he said he won't be receiving guests today."

"I had a feeling he wouldn't after what happened today," Sinkua agreed.

"Of course, well, he needs to discuss what went wrong with the rest of our staff."

"Where do I stand on my recruitment?" EshCal asked.

"He didn't reject you."

"If he asks for your input, you're in," NalSet assured, "You played your role without issue. Even adapted when conditions changed."

"Okay, now what about our injuries?" Eytea piped up, "I don't mean to whine, but the painkillers have worn off."

"Of course, come in," MalVek invited, "We've rented a room upstairs with two beds. Our chief biomedical technologist is on his way."

The interior of the cottage resembled a countryside home, excepting the reception counter, ATM, and outdated vending machines. The décor centered on light browns and pastels accented with oil paintings of Spring and Swelter landscapes. It smelled faintly of fresh lightwood with a tinge of nicotine.

They found their room near the top of the stairs. Sinkua and Eytea sat on each of the two beds, settling in as best as they could manage. MalVek and NalSet pulled EshCal aside to the window. NalSet opened the window, letting the cool rural breezes flow through the room, and nodded to MalVek.

Sinkua watched and smirked. Even after all he and Eytea had figured out, all they had confessed, they still kept them at a distance, whispering behind their backs in front of their faces. It reminded him of Gijin's conditioning, always being told that the rest would come in time. Eytea watched with him as MalVek stepped aside to make a phone call.

"That was our doctor," he announced as he hung up, "He'll be here shortly."

"I didn't hear your phone ring," Eytea said.

"I called him," MalVek clarified, "I was worried he might get lost since he hasn't been here in a long time."

The front door opened. The conversation between the receptionist and the new arrival faintly permeated the floor in a dull grumbling. When MalVek turned from Eytea, Sinkua mouthed an urging not to instigate. She nodded in compliance.

An expected knock came at their door. MalVek opened it to a middle-aged Berininite gentleman. He wore a grey suit with a matching fedora over tightly cropped hair. A dusting of greying stubble framed his jawline, connecting his sideburns.

"Long time since I last made a house call. You must be the one with the broken wing, right?" he chuckled, pointing at Eytea.

"Wow, no wonder you're their chief doctor," Eytea snarked with a mischievous grin.

"Biomedical technologist," he corrected, "Now, you are Eytea, and you, sir, are Sinkua. Is that correct?"

"That's right," Sinkua greeted, "And your name? Or are we not allowed to know that?"

"Are you familiar with The Geneticist?"

"No, we're not. Is that one of the Avatars?"

"Yes, he is," he answered, furrowing his brow, "Let's just say I'm his antithesis and leave it at that for now."

"Good enough for me," Sinkua shrugged, "Not like I expected to get any more answers today anyway."

"That's the spirit!" the Berininite encouraged, perhaps sarcastically, "Now, I'm going to give each of you two shots. Then, I want you to try to sleep for a few hours."

The sun had already begun to sink behind the horizon, the dim triad of moons suspended high in the sky. EshCal bade Sinkua and Eytea farewell, wishing them luck with their recoveries, and excused herself with MalVek and NalSet. They had nearly reached the lobby by the time the quirky Berininite first punctured flesh.

He delivered Eytea's first shot to her shoulder. She cringed as the needle penetrated the tattered remains of her cartilage. The second went into the crack in her wing, causing her to arch her back as the shooting pain radiated to her shoulder blade. As the Berininite withdrew the needle, she lay face down and closed her eyes.

They shot open again as Sinkua yowled. He took his first shot to the base of his spine. The second went just under the base of his skull and his brainstem.

"So, how do these work?" Eytea asked, aiming to distract Sinkua.

"Truthfully, it just speeds up the recovery time," the Berininite answered as he administered the last injection, "It works at a cellular level to repair the damaged tissue. That's all you need to know, right?"

Galo shifted in his seat, nervously scratching the cushion as he scanned the room. Perhaps he only imagined it, but his peers seemed to judge him, sizing him up as though they doubted his worthiness. He found solace in having Spril beside him. They smiled and nodded to one another as the Grand Sultan of Ferya delivered his opening statements as predesignated officiator of the assembly.

It then came time for each of the leaders to present orders and concerns to the committee, beginning with Spril.

"As always, it's an honor to be here, ranked among the great men and women of our time," Prime Minister of Defense Spril opened, "But I intend for this to be my last appearance."

"Do you intend to resign?" the President Elite of Ierodhes asked.

"He has taken a rather long time to correct the damage done by Lord CreSam," the High Magistrate of Haprian suggested.

"By what measure is that relevant?" Chieftain Sage Galo stepped in, "The improvements are real and measurable."

"Ah-ah, thank you, but you're arguing over a statement I did not make," Spril interrupted, "I'm retaining my authority over our military. However, we have delegated further governmental authority into a collective of Ministries. I have been named as Prime Minister of Defense with former Brigadier General EshCal serving as Brigadier General Elite and High Minister of Defense."

"In other words," the High Magistrate cut back in, "you've given yourself more authority."

"An elected committee has given me more authority over the ArcNosian military and diminished my power in all other aspects of governing," Spril corrected, "That being said, my seat here is being relinquished to someone far more educated in the science of diplomacy, Prime Minister of Foreign Affairs Phylus."

"Congratulations on your civil revolution," the Grand Sultan professed, "We'll miss seeing you but look forward to meeting your replacement."

"Many here are already familiar with Phylus," Spril said, trading knowing glances with Galo, "He helped assemble the Subtransit Resistance, many of whom have since laid the foundation for ArcNos's newly reformed federal government."

"Yes, I remember him well enough," the Grand Sultan agreed, "Did you have a proposal to be voted upon?"

"Unless we have to vote for me to step down as ArcNos's representative, I do not."

"That's your business. Moving on. Chieftain Sage Galo of Berinin?"

"Right then," Galo opened, clearing his throat, "There's a stretch of land twelve kilometers due east of Masnethege across the Southland Sea. After the strike on our homeland, the survivors took shelter there. During their stay, they discovered an abundance of rare and exotic plants, many of which are suspected to possess revolutionary medicinal qualities."

"So then, you've found yourself something of an iolite mine," the Prime Duke of Eprilen congratulated, "That is, assuming you intend to continue on the path set by your grandfather."

"That reminds me, Chieftain Sage Galo, I've brought a guest who wishes to meet with you after the assembly," Spril cut in.

"Thank you, Prime Minister of Defense Spril," Galo said, "And yes, Prime Duke Norum, we have indeed. For that reason, we wish to designate that island as an annex of Berinin. Its resources are of greatest value to us, and we are best suited to use them to the benefit of all Ouristihra."

"Do you intend to build research facilities on this island?" the Grand Sultan asked.

"Research and development, yes, as I believe it would be best to study these plants in their natural habitat."

"And should the yield be non-medicinal?"

"We can find some medical quality in virtually any plant grown in its indigenous habitat," Galo boasted, "But should it be nothing of particular use, we'll use the rich soil and additional land to offset the burden of producing food and raising livestock for our citizens. We also invite Lenguardia to research the land and perhaps help us all gain a better understanding of how it came to be so rich in exotic flora."

At this time, the matter came to a preliminary vote. A second would follow the next morning, giving everyone time to consider the issue further. The practice let the presenting party know who they needed to convince, though it often led to coercion and browbeating instead.

In this instance, nearly everyone sided with Galo, except for the High Magistrate of Haprian, the Noble Doyen of Tanelen, and the Magnate Supreme of Poravit. The remaining seventy percent would be enough to pass the motion. However, Galo thought better than to coast through the ordeal, knowing those three would spend the evening coercing their colleagues into changing their vote.

Between the High Magistrate's behavior and his residual suspicion about Tanelen, he knew convincing them would be an uphill, perhaps futile, pursuit. The Magnate Supreme's vote might have been worth seeking, even if just to keep her from talking anyone else out of their position. Then again, it may have been more effective, as well as easier, to prepare a statement to hold those already voting in his favor.

Yrlis sat on the front steps of the Ouristihran Union's meeting hall, bundled in a trench coat against the biting wind. She shivered in fits, crumpling the papers tucked in her coat. Presentation was of little consequence, but she still worried that it would detract from her merits.

Galo stepped out into the cold to find a woman sitting alone. She glanced back at him, enough to see his face but not enough to show hers, and rose to her feet. Galo cocked his head slightly. He had assumed that he would meet with Spril's guest elsewhere, not that she would wait outside in the blustery weather. Before he saw her face, a voice from behind grabbed his attention.

"Yrlis! What happened?" Spril called as he came out onto the steps.

"I got lost," Yrlis confessed, "I couldn't find this Half-Shell Pearl anywhere. So, I came here to wait."

"Half-Shell Pearl?" Galo perked up, "I could guide you there if you'd like."

"Oh, you've been there?" Yrlis asked, playing coy, "How is it?"

"Best I've had that I didn't see come out of the ocean," Galo boasted, "But don't pretend you didn't know I'd been there."

"What? Well, I didn't really, um..."

"What's your proposal? Buttering me up with an oyster platter won't affect my answer."

"I should've known you'd see through us," Spril laughed, shaking his head, "Phylus told us you guys went there when you came to postpone your inauguration."

"I figured as much. Now, the proposal?"

"I think I figured out your secret," Yrlis bragged, "but I need to work with you for a while to confirm it. If I'm right, then I have a proposal."

"Scarcely a matter to be discussed in the open," Galo insisted, "Follow me. We'll discuss it over an oyster platter."

Chapter 8

Spril and Yrlis stayed aside while Galo negotiated with the host in the restaurant lobby. Until now, seeing him speak without hearing him, she hadn't noticed the animation of his hands in conversations. As he slipped the host a tip, she chuckled to herself, imagining him dressed as he had during the war. He still wore the Chieftain Robe, but now it framed a meticulously tailored black suit. He turned to them and nodded back toward the dining room.

They wove through a sea of nattily attired patrons. Classical music played at a low volume, the tone changing minimally from one table to the next. Black curtains covered the back wall.

The host pulled one aside, uncovering a door with a deadbolt lock. He peered at them as he surreptitiously unlocked it, softly signaling for them to stay quiet. The illusion of only a curtain isolating celebrities and executive affairs enhanced the cultured ambience.

Heads turned on rubbery necks as ArcNos's Prime Minister of Defense and Berinin's Chieftain Sage entered one of the private dining rooms. The unknown woman in tow added a certain scandalous intrigue to the curiosity. Rumors spread swiftly in hushed tones, patrons who knew of their joint involvement in the Subtransit Resistance easily distinguishable from the rest. Scattered throughout were a few naysayers, those who thought the Triad Titan should have permanently severed ties between ArcNos and Berinin.

"Okay. I've spent the past five…" Yrlis began once the host shut the door.

"Let me stop you there," Galo interrupted, "Let's wait until we have our food before we start talking business, okay?"

"Afraid the waiter might cash in on what he overhears?"

"A tad, but it's more that I hate to be interrupted during negotiations."

"He's probably just hungry," Spril joked.

Galo shrugged and flashed a crooked grin, his first show of vulnerability since he outed their gambit. Yrlis squeezed Spril's leg and smiled at him.

At Galo's recommendation, they ordered two of the sampler platters he had shared with Phylus. Some twenty minutes later, the waiter arrived with the platters, an umami symphony melding under the ceiling fan. Galo's stomach grumbled audibly, and he swallowed the first oyster before the waiter locked the door. Yrlis started in with her proposal while Spril casually snacked.

"As I was saying, I've been running experiments over the past five years, simulating more and more of the conditions in Berinin," she began.

"Concentrating on the fauna, correct?" Galo asked with a cheek full of oyster.

"Yes, I tried introducing some indigenous animals, ones whose dietary staples included the plants I was testing. I thought perhaps the plants were only medicinal as a fecal extract."

"Wait," Galo interrupted, "You didn't… You know?"

"What? Oh! No no no!" Yrlis refuted, "This was all done with petri dishes. I was only able to commission the animals for a few weeks, but it didn't work anyway."

"I know it didn't."

"Of course," she continued, snatching another oyster and dipping it in hollandaise sauce, "Later, I thought maybe the key was indigenous fertilizer. So I returned to the exotic pet store to request stool samples."

"Sounds like an awkward conversation," Galo mused, hiding his anxiety.

"Surprisingly, not so much," Yrlis shrugged, "Anyway, that got the occasional positive result, but they weren't consistent. That brought me here to you."

"Why? Are you giving up?" he monotonously taunted.

"No. I'm confronting you. I know the secret, but I need you to confirm it."

"Oh? Well, go on then. I'm listening."

"Indigenous fertilizer."

"You just said yourself that it didn't work," Galo argued flatly, leaning in as he swiped another oyster without breaking eye contact.

"No, I said my experiment didn't work, but a few samples tested positive. I'd have to recreate the entire ecosystem to replicate the results that occur naturally in Berinin," Yrlis countered, "Wouldn't I?"

Galo leaned back and stared at her, more time passing between his bites than had since the platters landed. Yrlis returned the stare, continuing to eat at her usual pace. Spril's eyes darted between them, occasionally pinching oysters like a child sneaking bites before supper. A smile slowly spread across Galo's face.

"You're right. Medicinal properties can change with the seasons. They all come together under the indigenous species' natural behaviors," Galo confirmed, "Do you concede that they work now?"

"Almost. First, I want to test some of the plants you claim to be medicinal, in their natural habitat."

"Then, will you be satisfied?"

"Probably."

"You have more in mind, don't you?"

"Nothing to pervert your legacy or reveal your secret," Yrlis assured.

"Hey, so what happens if a foreign species is introduced into the ecosystem?" Spril interjected.

"We'd have to rework everything coming out of that area," Galo flatly answered, "but the list of regulations on that sort of thing is longer than my arm."

Yrlis chuckled to herself at the volatility of Berinin's system. Her proposition would prove immeasurably valuable to them. Now, all she needed to do was convince Galo of this.

Biroe rolled across his linoleum floor, reaching for the microwave as it beeped. He threw open the door and took the plate within the duration of the signal. Tonight, he had Feryan takeout.

The phone rang as he grabbed his plate. He nearly dropped it on the counter, the phone so startled him. Pausing to gather his composure, he shoved off to the other end of the kitchen and answered the phone as it rang for the fourth time.

"Y'hello?"

"Biroe? I'm not interrupting anything, am I?" KalChi answered.

"No, KalChi, I was just about to sit down to dinner. Not that I sit down somewhere else to do that, but um…" Biroe fumbled, "Anyway, what's going on?"

"Oh, this can wait. Go ahead and have dinner," she insisted.

"No, go ahead. It's okay. It's just leftovers."

"Really?"

"What? Is it weird that I eat leftovers?" he wondered aloud.

"Haha, no. Not that," she excused, "Is it really okay if I go ahead?"

"Oh. Yeah. Sure," he encouraged, blowing on his food, "What's up?"

"I got the list of current shareholders from that company we discussed, and I figured out who's terminated their investment since I left."

"Anything interesting?" he asked, his attention drawn away from dinner.

"Well, yes and no," she floundered, "I compared what they would have been paid to the anomalous amounts."

"And? Did you find a match?"

"I wish it was that easy, but no matter what combination I tried, I couldn't even get within five percent. So, I looked at their current shareholders, and I found an exact match."

"Interesting," Biroe nodded, chipmunking a bite, "That means the payments are being deducted, but the transactions aren't processing correctly. Now, we just have to figure out why and, after that, why the companies aren't documenting the returned funds."

"They've designated that money to specific shareholders, regardless of whether they could reach them by their usual means," KalChi spitballed, "Or maybe they suspected foul play and thought this would trigger a third-party audit."

"Sounds like a stretch, but I suppose it's plausible. After the weekend, I'll examine the current shareholders at the other organizations on the list."

"Actually, sir, I already started on that, and I think I'm on to something. One is a subsidiary of my last employer, and another is a sister organization. It took some sweet-talking and a lot of phone tag, but I got part of their shareholder lists."

"Based on what parameters?"

"Everyone whose equity payments were no greater than our anomalous amount. Come to think of it, their tone always changed when I mentioned that number," she trailed off, "Anyhow, I was able to find exact matches in both of those sets as well."

"Three for three," Biroe reaffirmed between bites, "I think it's safe to call this a trend. I'll have one of my contacts dig up some history on the investors. See if they can find any other common ties."

"Well, I can't say I've conducted background checks, but I did cross-reference the lists against each other. There are only two people who show up on all three," KalChi said, "JalRov and IlcBei."

"IlcBei? I knew her. She owns the Subtransit. Real nice woman."

"Apparently, someone doesn't agree."

"Apparently not. Same with JalRov," he added, "By the way, are you at the office?"

"Yeah, why? Did you need something?"

Biroe swallowed anxiously, swigging from his can of punch. He smacked his lips as his palate became dry and pasty. His nerves frayed as he worried over the split seconds crawling by since she last spoke.

"As a matter of fact, yes, I do," he insisted, feigning a tone of authority, "Get out of the office and enjoy the rest of the weekend."

"Of course, sir," she smiled.

"And come have some leftovers with me."

His heart plummeted at the sound of his words. Somehow, they sounded worthwhile in his mind, but hearing them aloud, they sounded ridiculous. Steadying his breath, he waited for his one shot at recovery.

"Oh, um, I'm not really hungry," KalChi rejected, flattered at the sentiment but puzzled by the offer.

"It's Feryan takeout," Biroe blurted, clenching his teeth in distraught anticipation.

"Oh! I love Feryan food!"

"So, now are you hungry?" he teased.

"I suppose I could eat a bit," she flirted, "Where do you live?"

A mischievous smile took over Biroe's face as he gave her his address. He had remembered her once professing her love of Feryan cuisine. Ever since, he had taken to developing a taste for it until he had the courage to ask her on a dinner date. After they hung up, he dialed the restaurant. Fresh takeout would go over much better than twice-reheated leftovers.

Farim stared into her monitor with bloodshot eyes and a pallid complexion. She could have packed groceries in the bags under her eyes, she had worked so far into the morning. She took a long swig from her fifth cup of coffee, gasping as it rushed down her throat.

The sample from SenRas's office had yet to yield any wholly positive results, but it had turned up a few near matches, suggesting possible blood relatives. She traced their genealogy, but none of them turned up an answer.

Her search for Vielle's mother had yielded a few possibilities, but the best results didn't exceed eighty percent. She set those aside to compare against Phylus's full sequence.

Down at the other end of the table, another computer beeped loudly. The sudden outburst in an otherwise quiet room so startled her, she nearly dropped her coffee mug. Heaving as her heart calmed itself, she clicked a few lines of text and scooted to the machine.

"What do we have here?" she asked, speaking aloud to keep from going stir-crazy, "Galo is..."

She paused to think how to explain the results to herself, as though she would doubt them the moment she heard them aloud. It inarguably defied logic.

"He's... the true Chieftain Sage," she accepted, bewildered by the outcome, "He was born nearly two years after Gabdur and Zheal died, but he's their son."

Farim rolled her chair back to the first console, repeatedly reviewing the results of Galo's test. She knew she must have run the test incorrectly. It seemed like the only logical explanation. Perhaps, she had run the wrong samples, or maybe she had used the wrong parameters. Whatever the case, a quick glance at the screen ripped her attention away.

"What? No, no, no! Abort! Abort!" she shouted, furiously clicking, "Ah, son of a bitch!"

Infuriated with her fatigued carelessness, she banged her forehead on the table and lay there, arms hanging limply and muttering profanities. Entirely by accident, she had changed the parameters on her search for Vielle's mother. Not only did it restart the search, it purged the ongoing list of results from the Ouristihran Citizens Registry. Three straight days of scanning records, analyzing sequences, and compiling matches had been wiped out. That is, until that telltale beep lifted her head from the table.

"One hundred percent match?" she guffawed, "To who?"

In her haste to check the other console, she had unwittingly added the sample from SenRas's office into the search list for Vielle's mother. The computer checked the new sequence first, and in a remarkable turn of serendipity, it yielded a perfect match.

"Damn. Vielle was right."

Unfortunately, Farim couldn't report success to Vielle just yet. Not only would Vielle not be awake yet, Farim had only learned that Vielle's mother was the same Avatar of Fate who had infiltrated SenRas's office. She and her mentor didn't have this one in their database.

She considered calling SenRas instead. If he knew the thief from gender and age, she would know Vielle's mother. At the very least, he could provide her with a short list of suspects to research. She looked up SenRas's number and slowly punched the keys in her fatigued excitement.

"Ministry of Human Resources. SenRas speaking," he answered.

"SenRas?" she asked, "I didn't know you worked in human resources."

"Yes, it seems I have a bit of a way with people," SenRas dryly boasted, "Now, to whom am I speaking?"

"This is Farim."

"Ah, of course. Good morning, Farim. What news do you bring?"

"Actually, I have a question for you, sir."

"Go right ahead. Anything to help the investigation along."

"What women frequented your hall during the Avatars' occupation? My mentor and I don't have the culprit on file, but I did determine that it was a woman."

"Well, there was Malia, EshCal, and the mail lady. A few others passed through on appointments, but those three were the most regular."

"Do you know the mail lady's name?"

"No, but I can get it if you'd like. I can also tell you EshCal is in the clear," SenRas added, "That is, unless fingerprint removal is reversible."

"I don't see how it could be," Farim said, "So you got a look at her fingerprints?"

"Yes, and they're not blank. If you'd like to be more thorough, I can get a blood sample," he offered, "She knows I checked her fingerprints, so if she has nothing to hide, I'm sure she'd submit to one more test. She did pose as an Avatar candidate of her own volition, after all."

"I might ask you for that if I don't get a match from the others, but for now, it's down to Malia and the mail lady," Farim pondered, "No luck on the Ouristihran Citizens Registry so far, but I'm still scanning the database."

"My money is on Malia, given the history we had."

"Why didn't you tell me this earlier?"

"I needed hard evidence, not conjecture."

"Fair enough. Anyway, I'll be there in a few days to follow up. Oh, and let Vielle know I'm coming, please."

"I'll do just that. Catching up with an old friend?"

"Not entirely," Farim dodged, unnerved by memories of their last meeting, "I've been researching some stuff for her, and I have some news to share."

"Very well then. I look forward to meeting with you."

The call ended there, and SenRas dialed Phylus.

"So, you knocked up an Avatar?" he accused as soon as Phylus picked up.

"What?!" Phylus shot back, shaken by the remark.

"Farim found Vielle's mother. She matched the sample left by whoever emptied the safe in my office," SenRas explained, "No fingerprints points to her being an Avatar of Fate. So, you and Malia used to be an item, then?"

"Yes, but she doesn't know about Vielle," Phylus confessed, "I've been wracking my brain trying to figure out how to approach this, and now Vielle's gone behind my back."

"Your ex-girlfriend doesn't know she's the mother of your child. Well, this just gets more curious every day, doesn't it?"

Sinkua jogged up the stairs from the Subtransit station, shielding his eyes from the sunlight as he emerged from under the sidewalk. The hum of the train echoed behind him as it started toward its next destination. He looked around at the top of the stairs, taking stock of his surroundings.

Ever since he awoke that morning, he had felt disoriented, out of place even. Perhaps, it was a side effect of the drugs. Maybe he had a bout of nausea left over from his injuries. Most likely though, he felt that way because he woke up at home with no recollection of how he had gotten there from the bed and breakfast. Getting up with the alarm, he had left Eytea to sleep and headed off to work.

Looking up to the clock tower, he discovered something even more disconcerting. He had missed the last two days of work. In fact, he had completely lost the past three days. Sneering pensively, he felt for the puncture marks at the bottom of his spine and the base of his skull.

"Okay," he assured himself, "That part was real."

The receptionist called to him as he entered the building.

"Sir, the Prime Minister of Foreign Affairs has requested to speak with you as soon as you've arrived," she reported.

"Well, I'm here as far as I can tell," Sinkua sighed, "Where can I find him?"

"In his office. Shall I page him to let him know you're coming?"

"Yes. Thank you."

While the receptionist paged Phylus, Sinkua shuffled to the elevator. His mind rolled over itself, trying to come up with a rational explanation for his extended absence. He and Phylus may have had history, but he couldn't expect special treatment. Such an offense, especially so early, should have cost him his position.

Phylus's office stood at the center of the Foreign Affairs department, the other rooms arranged in a wheel-and-spoke pattern. Sinkua found Phylus's door partially open. He sat behind his desk, studying a large detailed map of Ouristihra. Pins of different colors denoted various landmarks and events, lengths of yarn connecting some.

"Prime Minister of Foreign Affairs Phylus," Sinkua greeted, "You wished to see me?"

"Dispense with the formalities, Sinkua," Phylus smiled, rising from his chair, "We've saved each other's lives. No need for titles here."

"Okay, well," he nervously continued, "did the receptionist downstairs tell you I was coming?"

"She did. That's why I had my door open. So, how was your trip?"

"Uh, more than a tad odd, I'd say. Not sure if news of it has gotten here yet," Sinkua dodged, "Sorry about the extended absence."

"No need to apologize, buddy," Phylus assured, patting Sinkua's shoulder, "Frankly, I'm impressed that you're taking such initiative, given what EshCal said happened to you."

"Well, I mean, you helped me something serious with this job. Would be a shame to squander it just doing the minimum," Sinkua shrugged, realizing an alibi had been established without his knowledge, "But I do feel a bit guilty for not asking if you had another assignment lined up for me first."

"Spril mentioned there might be something on the horizon for you, depending how his conference in Eprilen pans out. Haven't heard anything further just yet, but if you need help with anything, just let me know."

"Alright. Thank you," Sinkua nodded, "Why did you call me in here, then?"

"Making sure you were still in one piece, what with the beating you took. Holding up okay?"

Sinkua nodded again and headed out to his cubicle. He concentrated on his feet, mindlessly dodging coworkers and office equipment. He obsessively mulled over what he could remember between confronting Mortvill's impostor and waking up at home. Most of it felt like a blur, worse so after he had collapsed in the arena.

This brought him to question the very authenticity of the memories after his collapse. Perhaps, he was still blacked out on the sand field or asleep at the bed and breakfast. Maybe he had lost consciousness earlier than he remembered, and his mind had filled in the gaps. After all, he had three days of lost time to account for.

His condition had been dormant for most of the past five years. Triggering it after so long, especially as violently as it had, might have intensified the symptoms. CreSam's deterioration suddenly began to make a lot more sense.

Sinkua dropped into his chair and took stock of his surroundings. Everything felt familiar and real enough. If he was in a lucid dream, he had gone too deep to realize it. He shuddered at the thought of being so trapped in his subconscience.

An unmarked disc sat in a case beside his monitor. Having no recollection of it, he felt compelled yet hesitant to check its contents. He internally argued with himself to the humming rhythms of his computer starting. Hoping the disc might settle his uncertainty, he shoved it in the drive before nagging doubts could cripple his hand.

The one file on the disc appeared to relate to ArcNos's sponsorship of the Radial Axiom Arena. Perhaps, Sinkua had written this document, but by all sensibilities, it seemed impossible.

Apparently, after he awoke and recovered from his episode, they found The Commissioner locked in a storage closet. They suspected the whole ordeal to have been the work of the Avatars of Fate, and regional authorities came to investigate. Naturally, they encouraged ArcNos's participation. Working from this proposal, the rest of the document focused on preserving ArcNos's relations with the Radial Axiom Arena as well as Quarun at large.

Destroying his hopes for closure, this report detailed events of which he had no memories. Nor did he recall writing it, even though, perhaps all the more odd, he followed the thought processes exactly as though they were his own. As he read, he pondered how to preemptively discredit slanderous rumors, where most would elect for the easier and less confrontational cover-up. The section on public relations panned out exactly as such. The whole thing read as though he had written it.

In fact, the real author of this report mimicked his writing style and thought processes so well that his even his closest friends would have mistaken it for his. That thought inspired an idea to confirm his memories, once he finished the report. He continued reading in persistent hopes of a rational explanation and, much to his relief, found it at the end of the document.

The reported events were all real, with the exception of his participation in them. The real author, left unnamed, belonged to the same organization as MalVek and NalSet. The brothers had relayed details of the investigation to their colleague, and EshCal supplied copies of Sinkua's reports for analysis and mimicry. Thus an uncanny likeness had been born.

Absurd as that may have been, their courtesy in easing his uncertainty comforted him. As such, he took their means as more of their science that he didn't understand but accepted as working. Still, he had a phone call to make, though now more for the comfort of a familiar voice. He dialed briskly and drummed his fingers as he waited.

"Hello?" Eytea muttered, still half-asleep.

"Hey, babe. Did I wake you up?" Sinkua innocently asked.

"Um, no. I was just getting out of bed," she half-lied, "What's up?"

"I was just wondering what color vase you think would go best with a blue rose."

"A blue what?" Eytea puzzled, forgetting about the flower until her scratching fingers found the stem, "Oh yeah, the blue rose. Eh, how about lavender?"

"Lavender, huh?" Sinkua contested, "I was thinking about something darker."

"Something between fuchsia and violet, maybe?"

"Sounds like a nice fit. I'll pick one up after work."

He scribbled a note to himself and started reading the report for a second time. Best that he knew it as well as if he wrote it himself. Also, he needed to cut off the addendum before he submitted it.

A couple of hours into his shift, his phone rang.

"Ministry of Foreign Affairs," he answered.

"Sinkua? It's Phylus. I have someone on the line who needs to talk to you."

"Alright, patch 'em through."

"Actually, he needs to talk to both of us. Hold on."

After a click and a beep, a third person came on the line, shouting, "Hello? Are you both there?"

Phylus and Sinkua shrank back, Phylus shaking his head in frustration.

"Galo, I told you, you don't have to yell. The distance isn't a factor," Phylus reiterated.

"Sorry," Galo dialed back, though still somewhat shouting, "Sinkua, are you there, too?"

"Yes, I'm here. What's going on?" Sinkua asked.

"Your island has been declared as a Masnethegean territory. It's officially Berininite land," Galo boasted, his voice finally waning to a tolerable volume, "We've begun researching the local flora, and I'd like to meet with the two of you."

"We're Foreign Affairs," Sinkua reminded, "You should talk to the Ministry of Research and Development."

"Oh, it's not that. I've already acquired the aide of a mutual colleague," Galo assured, "I'm meeting with diplomats to discuss their country's most common and most urgent medical needs."

"I'll send Sinkua down there next week," Phylus offered, "but I don't think I'll be able to join him. Sinkua, can you let him know if I'm going with you before you leave?"

"Sure. So, I'm leaving after the weekend?" Sinkua confirmed.

"That should work," Phylus agreed.

"I'll look forward to your arrival. Thank you," Galo closed.

Galo hung up the phone and handed it back to Yrlis. She had spent his call biting her lip to hold back her laughter. With the absence of telephones in Masnethege, he assumed that the sound faded as it traveled. A loud sharp laugh breached Yrlis's restraint.

"Did you get everything taken care of?" she asked as she pocketed her phone.

"Yes, thank you. Sinkua is coming next week."

"What about Phylus?"

"He won't be joining us," Galo sighed, "His position keeps him rather busy, I should assume. Imperial sympathizers and loyalists are still all too common, after all."

"I certainly don't envy him," Yrlis agreed, "By the way, thank you again for inviting me here. This place is even more breathtaking than I had imagined."

Dense green foliage swallowed their legs nearly to their waists. A stretch of beach lay to the west, and to the east, a thick forest rich in lush flora. A wide strip of plants between the beach and the forest grew considerably lower than the rest, as though recently cut or possibly trampled. The trickling sound of waterfalls came from the depths of the woods.

"It really is something," Galo beamed, "Just think of all the potential."

"I'm glad I can recognize it, now," Yrlis smiled, "Perhaps in return, I could offer you a different way of seeing it?"

"If you're thinking to grow factory gardens, I won't go for it," Galo cautioned, "It wouldn't work, anyway."

"I know that much. My experiments showed that plants grown in simulated habitats don't yield consistent results."

"I figured as much. So, what's your proposal, then?"

"I want to study the chemical compositions of your medicinal plants," Yrlis explained, "The list of reported side effects is damn near immaterial next to the ones from other pharmaceutical companies."

"You're pushing for mass production."

"Yes, I am. Just the medicinal components. We could revolutionize the industry and practically eliminate side effects."

"Not to sound greedy, but what about Berinin's dominant market share? Our economy depends on that."

"They'd be sold as plant extracts and branded as products of Berinin."

"I wouldn't go that far," Galo refused, "It wouldn't be fair for you to make this possible only for Berinin to claim all the credit. We'll brand them as joint products of Berinin and ArcNos."

"Does that mean you're up for it?"

"It means I'm considering it, but keep in mind that Berinin has an image to uphold."

"What do you mean?" Yrlis curiously pried.

"We're known for promoting general wellness, not just curing diseases," Galo explained, "For instance, we produce a line of teas cultivated to prevent illnesses and protect against seasonal allergies."

"Well, right off hand, we could treat common tea leaves with the medicinal compounds and add natural flavors to simulate what's currently on the market," Yrlis suggested, "Perhaps we could use a factory garden, as you called it, and dose the seeds with the compounds."

"Either approach may show promise," Galo pondered, "By the way, I should warn you that our research could take us elbow-deep in excrement. In some cases, the medicinal quality comes more from the fertilizer than from the plant."

"I've had my fingers inside people's brains, but thanks for the warning," Yrlis laughed, "But if it's in the droppings, why do you market the plants as medicine? People drink energy drinks with guano extract. Besides, isn't it less concentrated?"

"Yes, but we boil down the plant extract to nearly the same concentration as the droppings," Galo assured, "As for your first question, people are more willing to drink strange and exotic teas than to sprinkle dried scat on their salad."

Galo leaned down and plucked a dark violet flower from a tangle of vines. He inhaled deeply of its aroma and exhaled a long sigh. Gently pinching the base, he plucked a petal and held it up to the sunlight.

"One more thing," he continued, rolling the petal between his thumb and forefinger, "You're thinking of guarana extract."

Chapter 9

Malia stepped back on the sidewalk, staring up the monolithic tower. Her mind rushed over memories of her last days there, losing CreSam to his degeneration and her overly devoted reverse infiltration. Of course, even SenRas had fallen for her façade to the point of threatening amputation. Still, the sight of that building unhinged her usually steady conviction.

An elderly woman set her hand on her shoulder, jolting her a bit. Malia turned and glanced down, checking the uniform.

"Good morning, ah, Representative TolRou," Malia smiled warmly, trying to hide her discomfort.

"I'm sorry, have we met?" TolRou asked, looking down to see her name and title embroidered on her breast pocket, "Oh, of course. Can I help you with something, miss?"

"I'm looking for someone. Someone to help me find someone," Malia stumbled, "I've been here before, but that was years ago. I'm not sure who I need to talk to."

"Have you tried the Ouristihran Missing Persons Committee?" TolRou suggested.

"They can't help," Malia refused, fidgeting at the name, "My best lead brought me here, said someone would be able to help me find the person I'm looking for."

"This person. Are they supposed to be in ArcNos? The one you're ultimately out to find, I mean."

"No, if I understand correctly, she's in Berinin. Either that or my guide is there."

"Your lead sounds pretty vague," TolRou scoffed, scrunching her nose.

"Quite so! He believes it's more helpful to give people just a bit of direction and let them figure out the rest," Malia explained, "Anyway, I need to find someone in Berinin, but I'm supposed to start here."

"In that case, I would suggest the Ministry of Foreign Affairs. Perhaps, they can help you bridge the gap between what you need here and who you need in Berinin."

"Okay, thank you so much."

TolRou nodded with a smile and headed into the building. Malia took a deep breath and entered behind her, grabbing the door before it closed. She made a note to seek SenRas's help should her visit to Foreign Affairs yield fruitless, even if it meant ironing over old conflicts. Ironically, she knew him only for his role in cutting off the Avatars of Fate from ArcNos, entirely unaware of his new position as Prime Minister of Covert Affairs.

At the reception desk, Malia asked to speak with a member of Foreign Affairs, as well as directions to the department. The receptionist paged Phylus after sending Malia's visitor badge and facility map to the printer. Her mind wandering around the lobby, Malia failed to notice when the receptionist mentioned his name. Oblivious, Malia accepted her map and badge and shuffled off to the elevators.

Malia navigated the offices and other facilities in the wheel-and-spoke of Foreign Affairs, zeroing in on the center. On her first attempt, she found the center but no door. Two more tries, and she found the entrance, blaming her frayed nerves for her incompetence with the map.

Their eyes locked when she opened the door, eyebrows scaling foreheads.

"Phylus?" Malia gasped.

"Malia? What are you doing here?" Phylus asked, circling to the front of his desk,

"Is it true? Are the Avatars are coming out of hiding?"

"My evidence suggests it, but I don't know if these are isolated incidents or setting the groundwork for a full-blown resurgence."

"How can't you know? I thought you were one of them."

"And yet," Malia countered, sitting on the corner of his desk, "you're comfortable talking to me about this. Why do you suppose that is?"

"Well, it's not because…" Phylus blushed.

"Certainly not seduction. No, last time I tried that, I couldn't get any intel out of you. Well, unless you count that bug I planted on you," she teased, cracking into laughter, "I asked you to tap me so I could tap you."

"Yes, I remember," he sneered, unamused by her joke, "But I thought it over while we were tearing down the fence, and I realized something. You knew exactly where to station guards to stop our incursion. Instead, they were positioned near manhole covers and abandoned Subtransit entrances. You falsified your report. Why do you suppose that is?"

"Damn, you're good," Malia conceded, "I'd have to step up my game to get one over on you. But then again, you always have been a good judge of character."

She rolled up her sleeve, showing her Avatars of Fate insignia. She rubbed it vigorously, and when she drew back her hand, the tattoo had vanished. No ink stained her hand.

"Tsora-kinetic transdermal ink," Malia explained, "It reacts to my energy to move through my epidermis."

"That is just… bizarre," Phylus marveled, "So, what brings you back here anyway?"

"I need help finding someone, and I was told somebody in ArcNos could help me find someone to find that someone."

"That sounds like a shitty scavenger hunt."

"I agree it's something of a mess. But since I apparently need someone in ArcNos to help me find someone in Berinin, TolRou suggested I try the Ministry of Foreign Affairs."

"Sounds reasonable. Who are you looking for? Ultimately, I mean."

"This is awkward to ask of you, given our history," Malia stumbled, "But I need your help to find my daughter."

"Your daughter?" Phylus puzzled, though absent the look of suspicion Malia had anticipated, "How do you know about Vielle?"

"Vielle?!"

Vielle and Farim rode the elevator together, separated by more than an arm's length. Farim had come promising news about Vielle's investigation, but she refused to explain their trip to the forty-eighth floor. Farim fidgeted anxiously.

To distract herself, Farim thought back on a conversation she had overheard in the lobby, trying to fill gaps of unheard dialog. They spoke of some urgent matter in Foreign Affairs. Nothing pertinent to her, she supposed, but enough to distract her on the long shared solitude.

"Listen, um," Vielle said, puncturing the silence, "Sorry about last time."

"It's okay," Farim uneasily smiled, "I just never knew you were, well, you know."

"Yeah. Guess I am."

"You know I'm not, right?"

"I never thought you were a lesbian. I just needed to be sure that I was," Vielle shrugged, "So again, sorry about that."

The elevator car squealed to a stop, and the door opened.

"I'd say you could've just told me what was on your mind, but I don't think that would have been any less awkward."

"Heh. Probably not."

"Well then, do you have someone in mind?"

"I don't know. Maybe. But I thought I should be sure before I go looking for a date I shouldn't even be on," Vielle explained, "Does that make sense? It makes sense when I think about it, but it sounds weird when I hear myself say it."

"Eh... No, that's actually pretty reasonable. Weird, yes, but still reasonable," Farim agreed, "Just to be sure then, you weren't trying to hook up with me?"

"Haha, no. No, you're pretty, but I don't think you're my type. Plus, you're what, twelve years older than me?"

"Hey! I'm only thirty-two!"

"And I'm twenty-one. Fine! Eleven years. Excuse me!" Vielle teased.

Farim laughed and shook her head. Phylus had often said his daughter had a way with people, and clearly, she had honed that gift into adulthood. Here, Vielle had taken an awkward situation with Farim and deflected the embarrassment. Farim's thoughts returned to her task as SenRas invited them into his office in the Platinum Hall via intercom.

"Good morning, you two," SenRas greeted as they entered his office, "Coffee?"

"This could get strange," Farim mused, trailing off as she panned his office, "Stranger than it's already been. So yeah, coffee sounds great. Thanks."

"I'll take a cup, too, please," Vielle accepted.

"So, I suppose," SenRas pondered as he poured their drinks, "that you brought us together because the people we asked you to find turned out to be the same person."

"Yes, they are," Farim nodded as she sipped her drink, "Or well, she is."

"In that case, I've met your mother, Vielle," SenRas said, shattering her illusion of secrecy, "She comes off rather as a bitch at first, but there's a certain underlying warmth if you can navigate the upper layers."

"Whoa. Wait. What?" Vielle gasped, "Who told you I was looking for my mother?"

"It wasn't me," Farim covered.

"No, it wasn't. Not exactly," SenRas confirmed, "I don't wish to share my methods, but I assure you nobody was spied upon. Suffice it to say, I glean much from subtext. Something of a gift I've developed with time."

"I'll say," Farim agreed, "I guess that means you already know what's coming, then. But Vielle, you really ought to sit down."

Vielle took a seat in front of SenRas's desk. She turned it to face them and nodded.

"Okay, go on," Vielle urged.

"Your mother worked here in the Platinum Hall," Farim opened, "during the ArcNosian Civil War. Her name is Malia."

"Judge Malia of Eprilen?" Vielle asked.

"Former Judge," SenRas corrected, "And she's from Ivaria originally. She never lost the accent."

"Right. Former Judge. But yes, that's who I mean," Farim agreed, "This may be hard to hear, but I know you've been searching too long for me to withhold information. Your biological mother has no fingerprints."

"No fingerprints? What does that mean? I mean, what does that imply?" Vielle fidgeted, refusing to accept what she feared, "Was she in a witness protection program? Is that why she left us?"

"No, they only do that in the movies," SenRas interjected, "Removing the fingerprints, that is."

"Given that, as well as her work during the war, I believe she's a member of the Avatars of Fate," Farim confessed.

"Was she in your database?" Vielle asked, swallowing a lump in her throat.

"No, but you know that list isn't exhaustive," Farim insisted, slowly sitting beside her.

"Then, maybe she wasn't one," Vielle gasped, choking on her words, "Maybe it's just a coincidence. Maybe, well…"

"No, I'm sorry, but I really don't think it can be."

"Oh geez," Vielle choked up, tears welling in her eyes, "When I got that bad hunch, I thought maybe I'd be ready for it by now. But I'm not. I'm not ready for her to be an Avatar of Fate. I liked it better when I didn't know her."

"If you need help," Farim offered, rubbing her arm, "you could always talk to Eytea."

"It's not the same with her, but I guess I could try."

"Actually," SenRas cut in, "You may be right, Vielle. It isn't all a bizarre coincidence, but you might not have to accept that your mother is an Avatar."

"What do you mean?" Vielle asked, smearing tears across her sleeve, "Did she not have that tattoo?"

"She did, but your father and I have discussed her behavior, and we have evidence indicating that she was a mole," SenRas explained, "That is, a mole within the Avatars who they sent here as a mole to keep tabs on CreSam. It's all very hush-hush, double agent, secret spy. Makes sense if you've been watching from here."

Vielle slouched in the chair as the bombardment of news settled into her thoughts. Eytea might be a good confidante, but she had learned about Kabehl's secret life much earlier in her life, before she knew of the Avatars by so malevolent a reputation. Vielle had never met her mother and now learned she could be affiliated with the Avatars, knowing the chaos they had inflicted on ArcNos and tried to spread throughout Ouristihra.

On the other hand, she took puzzled solace in SenRas's words. As bizarre as it sounded, she trusted that it made sense from his perspective. Without context though, his justification meant nothing. She knew she would need to meet Malia to sort matters out.

"SenRas?" a voice called from the speaker on his desk.

SenRas pushed the intercom button and answered, "Yes, Phylus? I'm a meeting. Can you be brief?"

"I know. Is Vielle with you like you expected?"

"She is. Farim was just giving us our news."

"So much for surprises, then. Send her to my office when you're done, please."

"Her being me?" Vielle asked.

"Yes, dear, come see me when you three finish talking, okay?"

"I think we're done here," Vielle dismissed, "I'll be right over, Dad."

Vielle profusely thanked Farim for her work and SenRas for the coffee and bewildering but comforting insights. They watched her leave, and Farim locked the door behind her, turning back to SenRas with a curious glimmer in her eyes. He nodded and waved her over.

"So, what tipped you off about Malia?" she asked as she took a seat across from his desk, "Was there something wrong with her insignia tattoo?"

"Ah-ah, nothing so droll, I'm afraid," SenRas rejected, "It was an accumulation of factors, such that might take some time to discuss."

"I have twenty minutes until the next Subtransit train to the docks comes."

"Well, for instance, she sabotaged a surveillance operation, thus giving the Subtransit Resistance the upper hand on an infiltration," he summarized.

"Are you sure she didn't just slip?"

"Phylus said they weren't encrypting their conversations because they didn't suspect espionage. She heard what he meant. But that's all I can say on that matter."

"I suppose I'd have to talk to Phylus about the rest then."

"I'm afraid so. But for now, go catch your train. I've work to do," SenRas dismissed.

"By the way, can you break a five for fare?"

"Of course. But when did they start charging?"

"They didn't used to? I thought it was only free during the war."

"No, it's been free as long as it's been under its current ownership. The Ministry of Treasury may know what happened. I would presume it's a budgetary issue."

Vielle knocked on Phylus's partially ajar office door. She peered in curiously as she slowly opened the door, trying to glean his reason for summoning her. He had a visitor, an olive-toned woman of middle age, fidgeting impatiently. As this woman turned to see her, their eyes fixed on each other's faces, mouths agape. She looked so much like her.

"Dad, is this woman…?" Vielle asked.

"Phylus, this girl is…?" Malia asked, almost simultaneously.

"Vielle, meet Malia. Your biological mother," Phylus nervously introduced, "Malia, this is your daughter, Vielle."

"But… how?" Malia gasped, "You never got me pregnant. I've only given birth once."

"Yeah, to me!" Vielle protested, "But you couldn't be with us, so you ran out of the hospital as soon as they let you."

"No, not to you. The girl I'm looking for is fifteen," Malia rejected, "Your father and I used to be a couple, but that ended twenty-two years ago."

"And I'm twenty-one," Vielle countered, "Plus the tests matched!"

"What tests?" Phylus and Malia accusingly asked in unison.

"Dad, I had Farim track down my mother by comparing our gene sequences," Vielle explained as best she could, "It was completely serendipitous, but the person who tampered with SenRas's safe was a perfect match for my test. That was you, wasn't it, Malia?"

"It was, but I don't understand how I could possibly be your mother," Malia refused.

"Artificial incubation," Phylus shakily interjected, "Do you remember how we had stored our, um, personal products?"

"Yes, I do," Malia recollected, "We agreed that it was in case something unseemly happened before we were ready to have kids."

"Exactly."

"That was supposed to be for an emergency, like if one of us became impotent or infertile. Or incapacitated. Or dead!"

"I was busting my ass trying to build a life for us, and you bailed! I needed purpose."

"So you jacked my eggs and made a test-tube baby?"

"Hey! I am standing right here!" Vielle erupted, approaching Malia, "And I wouldn't be if it wasn't for what he did. You left your eggs in his possession. Nothing he did was illegal."

"It's the principle of the matter, young lady," Malia derided.

"Young lady? Don't try to go all Mom on me now. You had no knowledge of and no obligation to me for twenty years," Vielle spat, "The way you're talking, you would've bailed even if you knew about me. Probably would've run faster."

"They wouldn't have taken me away if I was pregnant," Malia insisted, "But this? I feel so violated!"

"Just to assure you, I never even intended to put any pressure on you or ask anything of you, regarding Vielle," Phylus said, "I only wanted to know the child you and I could make together."

"Who wouldn't have taken you away?" Vielle asked, ignoring her father's platitude, "The Avatars of Fate?"

"Not them. They came later, but I'm no longer affiliated with them, anyway."

"Then prove it."

"Her tattoo is fake," Phylus offered, "She's with a counter-ops group called The Coalition."

"She'll have to do better than that," Vielle argued, "Malia, return whatever you stole from SenRas. I know he was always trying to sabotage those jerks."

"I'd love to," Malia agreed, "but it was stolen from me."

"Nice excuse, but you're not fooling me."

"I'm not trying to fool you."

"And why should I trust you? Because you're just such a compassionate person who's been inconvenienced by an offspring who never asked you for anything? Bullshit."

"Fine, you want proof that I'm not in league with the Avatars?" Malia protested, "I'll explain why I came here."

"Go right ahead."

"My other daughter, your half-sister, is a hostage of the Avatars of Fate. I was told to come here and then go to Berinin to get help rescuing her," Malia asserted, "If I were one of them, why would they take her prisoner? If I were one of them, why would I look for help from a key member of the Subtransit Resistance?"

"It could be a trap," Vielle suggested, grasping for an excuse.

"My boss told me a connection would be made. A kinship would be realized. This might be what he meant," Malia said, "I've seen what your friends can do on the battlefield. If this were a trap, clearly, I'd sooner expect it to backfire than trip."

"This daughter," Phylus stepped in, "Is she a Hybrid?"

"She is. That's why they have her," Malia explained, 'They've been using her for genetic experiments since she was a baby."

"Vielle, I always thought you were one because of an accident at the geneticist's office," Phylus said, "but it sounds like Malia, you might be the influencing factor."

"I would've thought the same thing," Vielle agreed, "but maybe you're right. I think we should help her."

"Hold on. You're a Hybrid?" Malia gasped, "There's only supposed to be three others."

"There are four of us," Vielle said and specified, "Sinkua, Eytea, Galo, and myself."

"This is so unexpected. My boss will be thrilled to hear about this."

"So, a bit off topic, but is the father of your other daughter still around?" Phylus asked.

"No, but he never had any part beyond impregnation anyway. It was part of our arrangement," Malia explained, "But he died almost exactly five years ago."

"Wait," Phylus epiphanously remarked, "Last time we were together, you said I was better than CreSam. Did you mean to say that…?"

"Whoa! You and CreSam?" Vielle recoiled, "Damn, even I know you traded down."

"We did. Yes," Malia confessed, "The Imperial Brigadier General Elite was the father of your half-sister."

"If your boss doesn't know about Vielle, he was referring to a different connection," Phylus deduced, "And I think I know who."

"CreSam's son, right?"

"Yes. Sinkua is in Berinin this week."

"On a small island twelve kilometers east of Masnethege?"

"Yes. How did you know?"

"My boss told me it would happen there."

"But how did he know?" Vielle interjected.

"I could postulate, but I don't think anybody will like the answer."

"I don't like the sound of that," Vielle worried, "But when you talk to Sinkua, have him send for me before he sets off to help you."

"Vielle, are you sure about that?" Phylus asked.

"Absolutely," Vielle solemnly nodded, "Nobody should lose their childhood to those assholes. Besides, no matter how I feel about Malia, that girl is my half-sister and a fellow Hybrid. We have to stick together."

"Thank you," Malia professed, "I won't forget all you've done for me. Both of you."

"Don't think I'm doing this for you, Malia," Vielle scolded, snidely emphasizing her name, "That girl means more to me than you ever could."

Malia nodded and added, "Gijin named her Nikasu."

A knock came at the door almost in unison with the phone ringing. Biroe wheeled his way to the door, fishing his wallet from his back pocket, and called back over his shoulder for KalChi to answer the phone.

The delivery boy on Biroe's doorstep wore a dime-store knockoff of what television dramas passed for old-time traditional Feryan garb, minus the musk from sleeping on tanned animal hides and the transparent imperfections of hand-stitching. Biroe suppressed a pitying laugh at the ridiculous as he paid for the meal.

"Hello?" KalChi answered, "Oh sure, he's right here. Hold on, okay?"

They met in the kitchen, Biroe with dinner and KalChi with the phone.

"Do you always have girls calling when you order out for Feryan?"

"Only from this place," Biroe joked as he took the phone, "Hello? Biroe speaking."

"Oh, good! I finally reached you. Maybe you can help."

"Well, that would depend on what you need help with," he shrugged, "Who is this?"

"Oh, pardon me. I'm so sorry. I suppose it has been quite some time," the woman blushed, "This is IlcBei. Remember? From the Subtransit Resistance?"

"Ah, of course," Biroe smiled, slathering on his most cordial demeanor, "I remember you fondly. How have you been?"

"Lately, not so well. Do you have a few minutes?" IlcBei pleaded.

"Trouble with your stock investments?" Biroe predicted.

"Why, yes! How did you know?"

"Prime Minister of Treasury. Your blocked equity contributed to multiple discrepancies large enough to trigger high-order audits," Biroe explained, "The statements were so off-kilter that they went straight to the top of the Ministry of Treasury for investigation."

"What have you been able to discover?"

"Equity payments to key investors are being intercepted and rerouted by a third party. The money is being written off the company ledgers but isn't reported as being returned. The trail goes cold after a pending return payment transaction, meaning whoever is doing this doesn't want the shareholders or the companies to have the money. In fact, that may be more important to them than taking the money for themselves. It's like the money simply vanished."

"A conflict between her bank's security measures and the hijacking protocols may be expunging the funds," KalChi suggested from across the kitchen.

"Oh goodness! I forgot you had company. I can call back later, if you'd like," IlcBei offered, hesitant to delve further into this mess of a scandal.

"KalChi is only here on business," Biroe insisted, winking to KalChi and lip-syncing otherwise, "She thinks the money might be vanishing because it's trapped between your bank's security features and whatever this third party put in place to stop it."

"I see. I'll ask my bank if that's possible," IlcBei offered, "Could the companies themselves be doing this as a form of tax evasion?"

"It's possible but highly doubtful," Biroe insisted as he poured two glasses of white wine, "Too many unlikely coincidences. Most of the companies have nothing in common except a few key independent shareholders, primarily you and JalRov. So, assuming the culprit has it out for you two, we've been analyzing what we can access of your personal records."

"I'll disclose anything you need to know. Whatever it takes to fix this problem."

"Don't worry," Biroe encouraged between bites, "We'll get you back to the life of affluence you're used to."

"Now, don't get the wrong idea. I'm sure you've heard all this before, but I live a pretty normal middle class life," IlcBei countered, "I use those investments to keep the Subtransit free and my apartment community sixty percent below average rent of the rest of the local market. I keep enough to live more than comfortably, of course, but most of my equity payouts go into running these businesses without having to ask much of my clientele."

"That is, well, fascinating. You're a paragon of altruism," Biroe beamed, "Why would anybody have a problem with that?"

"I don't know, but if this keeps up, both systems are going to collapse," IlcBei foretold, "I'm behind on maintenance and getting down to skeleton crews. I've lost thirty percent of my Subtransit customers since I imposed a fare, but the more passengers I lose, the more I have to charge to catch up. Most of my tenants can't afford much more in rent, but the place is falling into such disrepair that I can't attract new tenants who can. At best, I can only cover four more months of expenses without my equity payments."

"IlcBei, I promise you I'll do everything in my power to set this right. Nobody should have their lifeline severed like that," Biroe promised, "Speaking on your clientele and tenants, not just you personally. I know now where your concerns lie."

"Thank you, Biroe. I knew you could help."

"Of course. Anything for an old friend and more for the good of our people. Now, I'm about to sit down to a business dinner with my High Dinner. We'll discuss how to proceed with the investigation," he vowed, "Every dog with half a nose will be following every trail we kick up."

"Thank you again! Enjoy your dinner date," IlcBei smiled.

"What did you find out?" KalChi asked as Biroe hung up the phone.

"Subtransit and those cheap apartments on the northeast side of town are falling apart because of this scandal," Biroe explained, his attention returning to their meal, "Turns out, IlcBei uses her investment income to pay for nearly all of it."

"Sounds pretty heroic of her," she beamed, "What do you think will happen if she's unable to fund it much longer?"

"We could be looking at any of a number of possible outcomes, and none of them are good. Government assistance programs are already stretched thin."

"That much I know."

"If the government expenses these projects, we'll run up a deficit, but…"

"B we'll net a positive return at some point in the future."

"Exactly. And if we don't do it, we'll throw the lower labor class out to rot. The economic suicide of it notwithstanding, the inhumanity of it would be inexcusable."

"But if we support them, their labor will sustain reconstruction and growth efforts, which will eventually offset the deficit."

"Eventually being the key word there. It's hard to say how long we can endure it before we fall into another recession. Especially this soon after the war."

"It sounds like this scandal could destabilize our economy if we can't stop it quickly enough," KalChi foretold, "Or at all, for that matter."

"I'm afraid so," Biroe agreed, "Either our government or our labor class goes bankrupt."

Chapter 10

Galo grabbed near the base of a small flowering vine and gave a few firm tugs, pulling it from the ground by the roots. Clods of soil falling from the gangly roots, he passed the sample to Yrlis. She bagged it, sealed and labeled the bag, and dropped it in her specimen kit. By the time she finished, Galo had found yet another unfamiliar species and busied himself uprooting a specimen.

All over the island, Berininite laborers and researchers harvested the local flora for examination. Others came through behind them, spreading seeds to fill the voids. Earlier, they had picked clean a series of paths, dusting them with a layer of infertile soil, to serve as temporary roads.

Galo and Yrlis looked to the northwestern horizon as nautical bells resonated through the bustle of commerce and research. Yrlis gave a puzzled look, while Galo simply smiled and jogged away.

Sinkua stood at the end of the ramp, gazing into the island from its last beach he had stood on. Memories of that night flooded back, so distant they felt like visions of someone else's life. The foliage had thickened since then but smelled just as it always had.

Galo ran faster as Sinkua came into view. Sinkua cracked a smile and waved to him. Galo appeared far less bitter than he had been when they last spoke.

"My brother!" Galo called, "I believe I owe you an apology."

"I'm sure I owe you several, but I thought we didn't get hung up on that sort of thing," Sinkua shrugged, "What's your point?"

"My parents, Sinkua!" Galo clarified, pulling him into a one-armed hug, "They are exactly as you said."

"Aside from that whole thing where they're dead, that's great news. So, you're keeping your position?"

"As long as it's here to be had."

"Remember what happened last time you put someone else in charge?"

"Hah! That I do, brother," Galo laughed, "I've since set Nalygen and Borret straight. They honestly believed their words reflected my wishes."

"How did you figure it out, anyway?" Sinkua asked, following him into the thicket.

"I found vials with bits of congealed blood in the fountain shrine. I sent them to Farim, and she wrote back saying they belonged to Gabdur and Zheal, who she confirmed as my parents."

"And you thought I might be lying," Sinkua scoffed tauntingly.

"Surely, you can't blame me," Galo protested, pulling aside a thick tangle of vines, "I do still have my doubts, but it's more that I can't understand how it was possible. Farim suspects they died nearly two years before I was born."

"I know they weren't there when you were born. But how does she figure that?"

"All but two small town newspapers ran their obituaries less than a year after I was born. Those two reported it nearly three years before the others, identical listings on the same date," Galo recalled, "It's possible they were working from bad information, but it's also possible that Grandpa Gijin was running a cover-up and let two of them slip."

"Two papers slipping in that big of a scandal sounds plausible," Sinkua agreed, "But if I knew nothing about this, I would say the idea of that big of a cover-up is ridiculous."

"But you do know about it," Galo solemnly asked, "Don't you?"

"Yeah. But look at it this way. How likely is it that two random newspapers that probably have no contact with each other got the same two obituaries wrong in the exact same way?"

"More likely than thousands of others doing it. But those two are more likely to be overlooked in a fixed story, so I see your point."

"Right, when Gijin covered your parents' deaths, he went after the high-profile papers and worked his way down."

"That makes sense," Galo agreed, opening a path into the woods, "So, if my parents weren't present for my birth, how did it happen?"

"You know those vials of blood?" Sinkua reminded, digging for the right words as he paused, "Gijin poured those into one of those bowls of water, mumbled a few things, and it made a bubble with a baby in it. That baby was you."

Galo jerked around, mouth agape. He didn't look offended by the story, as Sinkua worried he would be. Of all the emotions fighting a territory war on Galo's face, bewilderment and fascination held the dominant ground. Such sorcery must have been, by any sensibility, medically impossible.

"How would that even work? A human fetus takes forty weeks to fully develop, and our bodies must be more complex," Galo insisted, "Do you mean to tell me I developed in, what, forty seconds?"

"Roughly," Sinkua shrugged, "Like I told you, I don't know how to explain it, and I've spent more than twenty years trying to comprehend it. That is one memory that has been indelibly burned into my mind."

"If you're lying, I'm going to knock you for a loop," Galo promised, "But if you're telling the truth, we have a medical marvel waiting to be discovered."

"In that case, call in the journalists for the press conference," Sinkua joked, "So, is that why you called me down here? To clear up the record on your parents?"

"No, I truly do wish to discuss the needs of ArcNos's medical industry. Were you able to gather any statistics?"

"Cancer research is always a hot-button issue, and our pneumonia outbreaks are always pretty harsh. If you want specifics, I'll need more time to get in touch with the right people."

"I'm sure there's something on this island that can help with pneumonia. But there's something else here that I wanted to show you. Do you recognize this place?"

"Hard to tell with all this overgrowth, but I think we're near where I built my camp."

"Precisely. Which means you surely ate from these plants until your first crops were ready to harvest," Galo said, reaching up to his shoulder into a massive tangle of vines.

"Yeah, as far as I remember," Sinkua confirmed, "Why? Are you thinking of selling produce?"

"Not so much selling, but we are allocating a sector for farmland," Galo answered, cocking his head away from the foliage, "That's beside the point however."

Galo grabbed the bulbous fruit, wrenching and pulling. It snapped free, and with the abrupt loss of resistance, he stumbled back as his hand whipped out of the foliage. He handed the fruit up to Sinkua and smiled as Sinkua pulled him to his feet.

"A pomegranate?" Sinkua asked.

"Yes. A pomegranate. They actually grow here! But what's especially strange..."

"I told you I had pomegranates when I lived here."

"Yes, but I told you they don't grow this far south."

"What, so it's easier to think I lied or remembered wrong than it is to think you were wrong about something agricultural?"

"Not at all. What's strange is that I pulled this from a vine."

"I know. That's where I got them when I lived here."

"Do you honestly not see where I'm going with this?" Galo asked, arching an eyebrow, "Pomegranates grow on trees."

"Really? Are you sure?"

"Yes, of course. I thought you knew that."

"No, I always used to get them at the grocery store. Never saw them growing before I came here, so I assumed they were supposed to grow on vines. What do you think this means?"

"It may be a new species of fruit, possibly not a true pomegranate," Galo suggested, "Given all the strange and exotics species we've been discovering here, it would seem as though something occurred to, in a manner of speaking, disrupt evolution."

The idea sounded absurd, suggesting something had redefined the natural forces on this spit of land in the middle of the Southland Sea. Sinkua brushed it off as Galo's imagination running amok. Isolation, he figured, must have caused the island to develop differently. Such a phenomenon wasn't unheard of, and it definitely sounded more sensible than this nonsense about disrupting evolution.

A bit further inland, they came to a rectangular plot with significantly lower growth than the surrounding area. Lengths of dead vines hung from squeezed and swollen cross-sections of the corner trees. Sinkua stood in the middle and closed his eyes, breathing deeply.

The smell was still familiar, near enough to tempt old memories. His thoughts flashed through that most landmark night of his nearly five years there, the night he discovered his pyromancy. The ruby shimmered and warmed against his chest as he reminisced, fists clenching incrementally tighter.

He opened his eyes and released a long exhale.

"Are you well?" Galo asked, carefully grabbing his shoulder, "For a moment, I thought you were going to set fire to the woods."

"No, I'm good. Just reinforcing memories," Sinkua sighed, "Eytea still has that hyena coat, you know."

"I don't know a lot about women," Galo admitted as they continued their trek, "but if she'll hold on to something like that, she's probably a keeper."

"She certainly is," Sinkua smiled, "But she can't wear it anymore. It's gotten too tight around her chest and shoulders."

A worker came running from the edge of the woods, his shouting only vaguely audible from that distance. He flailed his arms broadly, and Sinkua and Galo hastened with longer strides. In clear shouting distance, he called for them by name. Sinkua didn't recognize him but assumed this man knew him either by reputation or a mutual acquaintance.

"Galo. Sinkua. Sirs," the worker panted as they came together, "We've discovered something."

"Well, that is what we're here to do," Galo snarked, "Once the surveyors find a suitable spot, we'll build a formal research facility. Until then, bag it up to examine on the mainland."

"I don't mean a plant," the man protested, "Come with me. It's just beyond the forest."

As they followed the hurried worker back to his post, both considered what he might have unearthed. Galo thought it may have been a prank. It couldn't have been anything so grand as to be so rushed, probably some fungus or a tree frog they didn't recognize. Sinkua's thoughts, however, were far more hectic. After what he learned with the pomegranate, he expected something to the effect of a hyena skeleton that didn't belong to a true hyena. Perhaps, they would tell him it was technically a furry reptile.

It turned out to be nothing like either of them anticipated. Researchers and their assistants had eschewed their duties to scrape sediment from their discovery. Running well over five meters so far, a stretch of weatherworn masonry lay embedded in the soil.

"Was this a wall?" Galo asked.

"Yes, sir, that's what it looks like," the worker who had fetched them answered, "As you can see, we're still trying to find where it ends."

"Could we have unearthed an ancient civilization?" another optimistically suggested.

"If you did," Galo qualified, crouching to pick up a stone, "these remains were remarkably preserved. These don't look particularly old."

"They really don't," Sinkua worried, also taking a stone to examine, "Also, the edges are too perfectly angled."

"Many old cultures used molds to make building blocks," Galo explained.

"I've heard about that, but feel the faces," Sinkua countered, "They're too rough to have come out of a mold, even on the bottom."

"Huh. You're right," Galo agreed, comparing the stones.

Working outward from Galo and Sinkua, researchers and their assistants examined the enigmatic building blocks. Sure enough, the faces weren't uniform enough to have come from a poured mold.

"These were ground down mechanically," one assistant noted, "The tool markings run in tight spirals."

"Do you mean to say these were produced by modern machines?" Galo asked, to which the worker nodded, "This isn't an ancient culture at all. Someone else was here recently, but this was all they left behind."

Sinkua's heart plummeted into his stomach as a harsh epiphany grabbed him by the throat. Everything made sense now. His disease. His disjointed memories. His visions in the Feryan lab. The Criminal's omen. They all became clear.

"I," he gasped weakly, "can only think of one group."

"One group...?" Galo fearfully encouraged.

"One group," Sinkua nodded, "who could clear their tracks this thoroughly."

"Everyone back to the boats!" Galo shouted, his eyes widening as his voice rolled over the crowd, "Bring back anything you can dig with!"

Eytea smiled longingly as she trickled water into the narrow reddish purple vase. The blue rose thrived, even appeared to have grown. Moonlight shining through the window, she reflected on the day she found it.

That moment stood as a beacon over the pain and fear of the rest of the day. Even besting EshCal in the semifinals paled as a means of solace. Truthfully, her injury had been a relatively minor nuisance, especially having been healed by the time she awoke at home. She had briefly awoken in transit and so didn't come into to the same unsettling confusion as Sinkua.

Rather, it was the lack of answers unnerved her. MalVek and NalSet would only offer so much, and she knew EshCal didn't know enough to leak anything of use. Besides, every answer she got from them only seemed to give her more questions.

She lay in bed and blankets hiked up to her neck, staring at the ceiling. NalSet had said the weapon generator was their technology, stolen by the Avatars of Fate. Now, the Avatars could generate fully mobile people with it, their greatest disadvantage being artificial intelligence or remote control. She shuddered at the thought of facing Kabehl again, even a holographic recreation, or worse, what they could have developed from his nanochip had his corpse not been exsanguinated and the blood destroyed. Too tired to obsess any longer, Eytea yawned and closed her eyes, settling in for another night alone.

The moonlight flickered to pitch blackness, followed by a blinding flash of light. Eytea sat on the edge of the bed, squinting as the light waned. All went black again for a split second, her torso wobbling in disorientation. She grabbed the side of the bed, finding metal bars beneath the mattress.

This bed was wrong.

Looking over the side, she found she sat on a gurney. Strangers in white coats walked along the other end of the room, two of them dragging a near-lifeless body. Blackness flashed again as she scooted off the edge. Legs dangling and arms flailing, she grabbed the bars only to pull the gurney down on herself with a cacophonous bang.

Sitting perfectly still, she rolled her eyes up to surreptitiously look toward the coated strangers. They didn't notice her. She slowly scooted out from underneath the gurney, only to realize she no longer felt its weight upon her. Looking back over her shoulder, she found the gurney upright and unruffled. She looked to the pair dragging a body.

Darkness consumed her vision in fleeting and nauseating flashes as the body's head slumped and bobbed. Light returned as its eyes opened, flickering with disorienting intensity. Grabbing split seconds, she focused on the body, and in a blink, she shifted across the room and walked alongside them.

They stopped in the corner. The subject began to raise its head, and one of the coated strangers lifted a weighted leather pouch across his shoulder. Eytea called out in protest, her voice reverberating between her lips and rebounding into her throat. She reached out to intercept the weight, but it passed through her hand incorporeally and struck the subject's head. Everything went black.

Within this existence, she had no metric for how much time passed. In dim fleeting glimpses of light, she only knew they had moved. Either that or the room had changed. Elaborate machines surrounding an array of occupied gurneys emitted ghastly orange and yellow glows. A horrible symphony of groans and screams accompanied the flickering lights.

The dragged person looked toward the end of the hall. A diminutive figure sat huddled in the corner of a holding cell. The subject blinked slowly, and in an opportune moment of unfettered lucidity, Eytea walked down the corridor. She braced herself against the wall, thrusting herself forth through the disorientating flash floods of darkness. The distance stretched on as she closed it, but she faintly recognized the figure in the cell as the one she had followed here years ago.

"Doesn't he know he's one of them?" one of the coated strangers asked.

"Of course he does. That's sort of the point here," the other answered.

"What should we do with this thing?"

"Take it off him. Make sure he gets it back before he leaves."

Eytea turned and saw them pull a necklace from the subject's neck. The room ceased to exist.

Sinkua sat up with his sleeping bag and vomited beside it. Perhaps it was only an artifact of such a vivid night terror, but his mouth tasted more of blood than digestive acids. Using his hand as a torch, he checked the puddle of vomit. It had a slight crimson tint, though that could have come from the pomegranate he had eaten, perhaps unwisely.

Sleep now impossibly distant, he shuffled out of his sleeping bag and kicked it into a heap. The night air clawed through his coat, letting damp wind cling to his body. Flurries dotted the sky like stars on an overcast night. Twice now, a nightmare on this island had awakened him to rare snowfall.

This new nightmare, though unfamiliar upon waking, felt more like a memory within itself. Yet at the same time, he felt entirely detached, as though he had stolen the memory. He saw it through his own eyes, but the young man in the nightmare was a stranger.

He trudged across the plain, stepping around sleeping researchers and laborers. The tumbling sound of breakers rolled through the high-pitched howl of the early Frigid wind. An array of vernal aromas mingled with ambient ice particles, creating an olfactory symphony conducted by the salty winds of the Southland Sea. Nautical bells marked an intermission, startling him from the approaching calmness he longed for.

"A boat?" he muttered.

A few others stirred, but nobody awoke more than briefly. Sinkua stood alone in his insomnia and curiosity. He jogged toward the shore from which the ringing had come.

A newly arrive ArcNosian boat sat by the beach. A uniformed sailor anchored the bow to a tree with the help of a Midlander woman in civilian clothing. They exchanged a few words, shook hands, and parted ways. The sailor returned to the ship while the woman headed up the beach.

"Rather late for an unannounced visit, wouldn't you say?" Sinkua called.

"It's an urgent matter," the woman answered, "Sorry if the bell woke you up."

"Hardly," Sinkua dismissed, now within speaking distance, "Is your crew in distress?"

"I am. Personally. You're the one they call Sinkua, correct?"

"I'm Sinkua, yes. Do we know each other?"

"To wit, we haven't met, but I know of you by your reputation. My name is Malia," she introduced, offering a handshake.

"Why do I recognize that name?"

"I used to be the Judge of Eprilen, under Prime Duchess Olsa. Or Phylus might have mentioned me. Apparently, I'm Vielle's mother."

"In that case, it's nice to meet you, I suppose," Sinkua absently professed, trailing off as he stared at the coarse dirt in his nailbeds, "I guess you're either looking for me or Galo, then."

"Just you," Malia verified, obsessively picking at her fingernails, "I need you to help me find somebody."

"That isn't exactly what I'm known for. Who recommended me?"

Malia bit her fingernail, rolling it on her tongue against the backs of her cuspids. In transit to the island, she had devised a theory about The Omnimath's prediction. Not only was she correct, Sinkua had discovered the secret as well.

"My boss," Malia sternly answered, "Most people know him as The Commissioner."

"Ah, you're one of Mortvill's associates."

"MalVek let you in on us. This will be easier than I thought."

She rolled up her sleeve, wincing against the icy wind, to show the tattoo on her bicep. Sinkua recoiled and sneered at the sight of their insignia. Malia rubbed her hand over it, and it faded as though melting through her skin.

"I was a mole in the Avatars of Fate," she explained, "They took my daughter hostage for genetic experiments. I swore loyalty in exchange for keeping her alive and ambulatory, but I siphoned intel back to Mortvill and my affiliates. But my cover has been blown, and now she's in danger."

"I think I've heard of her, actually," Sinkua noted, "Is she a Hybrid?"

"She is. But that's not the only bond you've gleaned, is it?" Malia ventured, "How much have you learned on your dig?"

"My dig?" Sinkua dodged.

"Your palms are dusted with mortar and cinder block particulate," Malia pointed out, "Judging by how you keep looking at your hands, you must have found something personally unsettling. I'm familiar with your condition."

His stomach turned in on itself, threatening to expel whatever remained of last night's fish. Just speaking of it was nigh unbearable. They fractured his present and ruined his future, but to cover their tracks, they had blacked out his past.

Two days of digging had only unearthed greater depths of hollow subterranean chamber, possibly a tunnel to a deeper facility. The smell of the walls triggered sporadic flashbacks, strengthening as they ventured deeper. He experienced them as his own and yet so distant, as though he had been imprinted with the intimately unfamiliar memories of a stranger. Perhaps, Eytea had spent her adolescence grappling with such a paradox. Memories from beyond a void screamed over the abyss, only reaching him as distorted mumbles.

"Then it's true," he sneered, "They took me in, too. Didn't they?"

"I think so. I think that's one of the reasons Mortvill sent me here," Malia deduced.

"How can't you know?" Sinkua scolded, "I thought you worked for them!"

"The Geneticist never let me near his work, probably to keep me away from Nikasu. All I was allowed to know was what lab they kept her in."

"Or maybe they suspected your sabotage for longer than you thought," he suggested.

"I don't think so. They never appeared suspicious of me until shortly after the war," she recalled, "Olsa, The Politician, assigned me to shadow Lord CreSam and act as a medium between Imperial ArcNos and The Harvester, leader of the Avatars of Fate. To my utter chagrin, he didn't recognize me."

"He spent most of that war losing his mind," he solemnly reminisced, "How did you two know each other?"

"He was Nikasu's father."

Punched in the gut by the sound of this news, Sinkua lowered himself on shaky legs, crouching on the beach. His eyes flared and jaw tightened. His fingers curled and knuckles paled, death-gripping clods of sand in his fiery palms. Bad enough they had taken him. Worse still that they had done the same to a fellow Hybrid. But this affront, another strike at his family, was inexcusable. Unforgivable.

They turned his father against his mother and himself and weaponized him and his cousin against each other. His sister, they had used to make such living weapons. Desperate and hubristic people turned monsters. Counterfeit Hybrids. They had picked apart her gift, turned it into a curse, and used it to bring ruin upon his family and his people.

"In blood only, but ours was a union of necessity," Malia continued, tempting Sinkua's fury, "I took her to Chieftain Sage Gijin to have her adopted into a safe home, but somehow she ended up with the Avatars."

"Where is she?" Sinkua snarled, shards of malformed glass falling from his hands as he thrust himself to his feet.

"I'm afraid I don't..."

"Take me to every lab you know of. I will hollow out every one of them and burn down all the ones where she isn't being kept," Sinkua promised, "And when I find where they have her, I will slaughter every motherfucker who dares to get in my way."

Profanity aside, Malia had aimed for just such an answer. She felt a bit guilty, indeed a sign her indoctrination had failed, about prodding the scars of a mending man so freshly rebroken. Incapable of undoing their damage to him though, she could only help him direct and focus his rage.

"Thank you. If you'd like, I can arrange a meeting with someone who may be able to help with your condition," Malia offered.

"My doctor said I need a marrow transplant from a living blood relative. My only ones who haven't been infected in some way are too old to undergo the extraction," Sinkua refused, "Besides, I need this if I'm going to save Nikasu."

"Suit yourself, but in that case, I can't justify sending you alone."

"Eytea and Galo would both be willing to come, though she's better suited for an infiltration and rescue."

"Vielle has also offered to join you," Malia relayed.

"I thought she would once she knew the hostage was her sister," Sinkua nodded, "I'm curious to see what side of her this situation will bring out."

"Just make sure all of you come back alive," she urged, "I hear Nikasu made friends on the inside, so you should be at more of an advantage once you've made contact. And what about Galo?"

"Come to think of it, his first duty needs to be to his country," he decided, "Besides, we need someone on the outside in case something goes wrong."

"A sound strategy," she professed, "Do you want to come aboard and sleep for the rest of the night?"

"I don't know how much sleep I'll get, but lying on a bed sounds nice," he accepted, "Just give me a few minutes to leave a note for Galo."

"Then, when you get back, I'll tell you everything I know. Where the labs are. Where she's been. When they move her. Anything I can think of that will help you save her."

Malia faded toward the horizon as Sinkua walked inland, a furious chorus of voices consuming his thoughts. He had long ago concluded CreSam hadn't been of sound mind when he killed BeiLou, but it sounded like he had impregnated Malia deliberately. Either his psychosis came later, or he had an affair. Scattered thoughts glanced off the idea of CreSam killing his wife to get her out of the way of the other woman.

Sinkua found a notebook sticking out of the top of a researcher's kit, a pen nestled in the binding rings. He pulled it out and flipped to the back page where he wrote a note to Galo. He didn't delve into any particulars, only that he confirmed his suspicion that they had experimented on him. Galo would take pursuing answers and vengeance to be enough reason for Sinkua to leave without a personal farewell.

Malia returned to her quarters on the ship. Atop a large table, she unrolled a map of Ouristihra with color-coded landmarks but no key. She pulled a roll of clear plastic from a second cubby and unraveled it over the map. Rotating and shifting the overlay, she aligned its constellation of markings to the landmarks. She taped the corners of the overlay to the table and squeezed one of her stud earrings.

"He's in. Where is our target?"

"Facility 3891. Lenguardia. Test if he can track her location before you move out."

"Understood, sir. By the way, were you aware I had a Hybrid daughter before you mated me with CreSam?"

"Such a dehumanizing manner of phrasing. But no, I alas was not. Our search was otherwise complete, and we had not found that young man to be a Carrier."

"Would you still have asked me to do it if you knew about Vielle?"

"I'm afraid I cannot make such a promise. There are only supposed to be four, but..."

"So how can there be five?"

"You must let me finish. There are to be four, but Vielle is not one of them. By all conceivable logic, she should not exist. At least not as a Hybrid. Nikasu completed the Revival as it was intended."

"Then who or what is Vielle? A spare? An anomaly?"

"We have yet to determine that. I will speak further on the matter with the brothers."

"And if she really is a fifth Hybrid?"

"Where you are concerned, that means rescuing Nikasu is your sole agenda. If my brother knows a fifth was born, he will perceive a threat and either execute Nikasu or launch a preemptive offensive. You are excused from all other duties until she is safe. EshCal will assume your mantel in your absence."

"Thank you, sir. He's coming."

A knock came at the door. Malia squeezed her ear stud, silencing the static.

"Malia?" Sinkua called, "Are you in there?"

"Just a moment. I just need to get this thing taped down."

"Thing?"

"I have a map of their labs," Malia explained as she opened the door and waved him inside, "I've lost track of Nikasu, so I'm looking for a pattern."

"Are you sure there is one?" Sinkua asked, looking over her shoulder, "Even if there was, they'd probably change it to shake you off the trail."

"No, The Geneticist is a man of inescapable habit. Every subject is moved on their own pattern. The trick is pulling an individual pattern from what looks like chaos."

"I have a knack for spotting patterns. Show me what you have so far."

Malia spent several minutes detailing Nikasu's forced movements, peppering her account with stories from The Geneticist's reports. They stunted her body and mind with squalid conditions, the food and drink sounding little better than what Sinkua had found under the house in Ferya. They provided barely more than enough to keep her alive and producing Hybrid blood. Several times weekly, they sampled her plasmatic delicacy, lacing it with other substances in pursuit of weaponizing humans.

"Enough with the stories!" Sinkua barked, his eyelid twitching, "You've already talked me into this, so just show me on the bloody map!"

Malia sheepishly apologized. Abandoning the emotional angle, her account became strictly technical. She traced Nikasu's path on the overlay, marking the date of each arrival and departure. The movement looked erratic, even irrational. Her stays ranged from a few days to just over a year. Sinkua's lips curled with agitated bewilderment.

"I don't see anything," he grumbled, "She's been moved over twenty times, and she hasn't been to the same lab twice. The order of countries hasn't even repeated."

"If I showed you how some of the other subjects are being moved, would that help?"

"Do you think maybe where they move one decides where they move another?"

"I've considered it," she qualified, "Where or when. Possibly both."

"Let's figure out where first and get her next few destinations. Then we'll deal with when," Sinkua insisted, "You might be on to something, but I want to look at this some more before we make it too complicated."

"We're dealing with a man who reads genomes like magazines," Malia warned, only somewhat facetiously.

"What are these numbers?"

"Code designations. He uses them in place of names."

"Do the numbers themselves mean anything?" he asked, "Order of construction? Coordinates? Postal code? Phone code?"

"They're completely arbitrary, as far as I know. Why?"

"That's where the pattern is, then."

"Of course! I assumed that was a red herring, but you could be on to something. Do you think you can use them to track her?"

"No, I'm no good with numbers. But I do have a friend in ArcNos who can help us," Sinkua offered, "But just by looking at these lines, I'd say her next stop is in one of these regions in Quarun, Lenguardia, or Poravit."

"We have to go back to ArcNos to get Vielle," Malia reminded, "We'll visit your friend while we're there."

MalVek and NalSet walked down the blackened corridor, their nervousness making its length seeming all the greater. Their summoning had been both abrupt and urgent, and he had sounded especially perturbed. NalSet did a better job of hiding it, but both housed a torrent of unrest as they silently mulled over the possibilities.

The doors opened against MalVek's palm. Their superior sat in his levitating throne, serpentine patterns of cerulean track lighting flowering along the floor from beneath it. He leaned forth and peered down at them.

"The two of you have much to explain," The Omnimath began, "What do you know of Vielle?"

"She's Phylus's daughter," NalSet explained, MalVek too choked to speak, "Phylus was Spril's caretaker after his parents passed."

"I know who Phylus is!" The Omnimath barked, "Of course I know who he is. I know Vielle is his daughter. What I didn't know was that she was a Hybrid. Why have you kept this from me?"

"To give her a chance at a normal life," MalVek insisted, "We knew what she might have been, what she could become. We didn't want to let you take her down that path. She had been through too much already. They all have."

"Theirs are neither lives of comfort nor convenience. But unlike the billions of petty lives to slip in and out of this world, they are among the few born with purpose beyond their mortal span. Thus, if that purpose demands sacrifice, then so shall it be."

"How many of them must we sacrifice? How much can we expect them to give?" NalSet snarled.

"As much as is necessary, even if necessity dictates her life be forfeit. Pahres has dispatched to find her."

"We can't treat people like this. Otherwise, we're no better than him," MalVek warned.

"The shadows of their lives are consumed by our cause," The Omnimath proclaimed, "Yggdrasil will take root once more."

Chapter 11

Galo looked down at the rumpled sleeping bag, rubbing his chin apprehensively. He reached inside and rooted around, finding nothing. He picked it up and shook it. Still nothing.

"Sinkua!" he called out, his voice echoing, "Sinkua!"

"He left last night," a field researcher called back, jogging into conversational distance, "Another boat came in last night. Woke me up briefly, but Sinkua was already tending to the visitor."

"Did you see who it was?"

"Sorry but no, sir. Whoever it was, they didn't come far enough inland for me to see."

Galo curled his lips disapprovingly, not at the researcher's shortage of information, but at the overall situation. He shuffled his feet through the foliage around Sinkua's sleeping bag and turning up nothing. A second rummaging through the sleeping bag proved just as fruitless.

"Did anybody see who Sinkua left with?" he called out.

"Didn't he leave a note?" a woman called back.

"If he did, he didn't leave it with his sleeping bag," Galo argued.

"Well, I'm sure he wrote one," she said, "The last page of my notebook was torn out."

"Why would he write a note and forget to leave it?" Galo pondered aloud, his voice drifting as he walked away.

She stared at the strip of paper between her thumb and forefinger, grinding it in her trembling digits. No details were given, only where he had gone. Five years had passed since they last spoke, and now she had the audacity to ask a favor of him at such a time. She sighed disdainfully and reached for the telephone.

The phone rang. A timeworn hand crept over the remote. With tremoring fingers, his bones grown frail, he paused the film and reached for the telephone. He shifted the bed upright, sheets bunching under his buttocks as he squirmed into a more tolerable posture.

"Hello?" he coughed.

"Uulan? Have I reached you at a bad time?"

"Yes, but at this point, perish any thought of waiting for better. Who is this?" Uulan answered, "I think you sound familiar."

"It's Farim. Remember?" Farim gently coaxed, "From the Subtransit Resistance?"

"Ah yes, I remember you. Rather the ambitious young lady, you were. What brings you to call on this old man?"

"I think the Avatars of Fate are making a comeback," Farim explained, "I've gotten multiple cases that traced back to them. Plus there was that fiasco at Radial Axiom."

"I heard about that one. Are our old friends well?"

"Yeah, they all made full recoveries."

"That's certainly nice to know," Uulan hoarsely whispered, "But where exactly does this concern me? Not to be rude, but I have better things to do than stick my nose in such affairs."

"At the risk of sounding insensitive," Farim countered, "what's taking up so much of your time that you can't even share your wisdom to help the rest of us deal with them?"

"First of all, I thought I was done with those people the first time I dealt with them," Uulan grumbled, "Secondly, stage four bone cancer is taking up what's left of my time."

"I'll make this short then," Farim meekly accepted, "Is there any historical precedence I should consider? Something that might help me understand their agenda or what to expect?"

"Yes, quite a bit, actually. Start at the beginning and work backward," he muddled.

"What does that even mean?"

"Look into their past. You'll find what drives each of them," Uulan clarified, "And you must consider the connection between the Avatars and the Hybrids. Seek the Hybrids' families as well, and you'll learn more about them as enemies of the Avatars of Fate."

"I already know Vielle's parents, but Sinkua's and Galo's parents are all deceased. That just leaves Eytea's mother."

"We only knew Vielle's father. If you can find her mother, I'm sure you'll learn plenty."

"Well, we did just find out who she was."

"Sinkua's parents having passed needn't be an obstacle. There are those who knew them well and a lifestyle to be found in what they left behind."

"What about Galo's parents? Everything about them is pretty hush-hush, what with the cover-up on their deaths."

"Actually, that isn't entirely true."

"What do you mean? Do you know someone who can teach me about them?" Farim hungrily beckoned.

"My tenure and reputation have privileged me a glimpse into particular circles," Uulan boasted, "Circles that say you might speak with one of his parents, should you know where to look."

"What?! Are they still…!?"

The line cut to static. Farim stared at the pile of newspaper clippings on the corner of her desk, her face a mask of bewilderment. Her lips stretched into a sneer of aggravated confusion. What had once been implausible had now become incomprehensible.

"This friend," Malia opened as they crossed the parking lot, "Is he somebody I know?"

"I don't know," Sinkua half-shrugged, "You might know him. He defected and helped me escape the capital after I delivered the war papers."

"That sounds familiar. I remember hearing about an accountant abetting you."

"Yeah. Partially deaf, one leg, rides a wheelchair," he added, "Probably a stunt driver in a past life, if you believe in that sort of thing."

"Well, I don't know about all that," she laughed, more at his description than the belief in reincarnation, "But he's the guy that can help us track Nikasu?"

"Yeah, his name's Biroe. Heads up the Ministry of Treasury now."

"Will he have time for us?" Malia worried as they entered the elevator.

"For you, probably not," Sinkua asserted, "For me, yes. Whatever he's doing, he can put it off or find someone else."

Their conversation in the lobby had elicited strange looks, mostly glares of derision and disbelief, from those bothered enough to react. The facility was largely staffed with people who had lived in ArcNos during the war and thus knew about the declaration of war and the daring escape to the outer lands. Speaking freely of the event only alarmed then-outsiders and the perhaps paranoid.

Engrossed in an endless matrix of hypothetical figures, Biroe all but sprang from his seat when a knock at the door jerked him from his trance. KalChi held his shoulder and let out a small laugh as he calmed himself. He spat an expletive and rubbed the bridge of his nose.

"Who's there?" Biroe called.

"Sinkua. Do you have a few minutes?"

"Come on in here."

Sinkua pushed both doors and walked through with an urgent stride. Malia came in tow, carrying a sheet of paper and a rolled-up map.

"What can I help you with?" Biroe asked, shrewdly eyeing Malia.

"We need you to find a pattern," Sinkua ordered, "Malia has a list of numbers, and we need to know what comes next."

"You interrupted us for that!? Do you have any idea what we're doing here?" Biroe challenged, "We are on the verge of economic collapse, and…"

With a swipe of his arm, Sinkua jettisoned Biroe's paperwork and desk supplies onto the floor. He grabbed the map from under Malia's arm and unrolled it atop the bare desk, the transparent overlay still aligned and affixed.

"Each of these marks is a lab where the Avatars of Fate have been conducting experiments on people. The kind of experiments that made The Hunter bulletproof, gave The Scout his regenerative powers, and made me as fucking volatile as you know I can get," Sinkua asserted, "They have Malia's daughter, and we need your help to find her before she's executed. Or worse."

"Or worse?" Biroe asked incredulously, "I'm sorry to hear about your daughter, Miss Malia, but this is neither my priority nor my field."

"What if I told you my daughter is their source for creating human weapons?" Malia challenged.

"She's a Hybrid," Sinkua added, "And she's my and Vielle's half-sister. So, you can understand why this is important. They know Malia betrayed them, so they're either going to kill Nikasu or amp up the operation."

"Either way, we're all pretty much screwed," Malia said, "They kill her, that means they saw her as a threat, but we missed out on an advantage. They start weaponizing people more quickly, they'll build an army we can't possibly be ready for."

"This does sound pretty urgent," KalChi noted, "Should I come back later?"

"No, stay here and straighten up, please," Biroe requested, staring up at Sinkua and Malia, "Gather a committee and run scenarios. I'll take these two upstairs."

Biroe rolled out from behind his desk and brushed between his invasive guests. Sinkua and Malia sneered as he passed without acknowledgement and continued to the door.

"Where are you going?" Sinkua barked.

"The Platinum Hall," Biroe flatly answered, "If you want me to help you find your sister, follow me."

Sinkua nodded to Malia and waved her out the door behind Biroe. She took long strides to catch up with Biroe, ultimately failing and resigning herself to find the Platinum Hall by memory. Sinkua rolled up the map, careful to keep the overlay fastened in position, and nodded to KalChi. KalChi stood in dumbfounded silence as the man who had wrecked her boss and boyfriend's desk left with him unapologetically.

"Why do they still use the Platinum Hall if they have Ministry offices?" Malia asked as Sinkua came to her side.

"I don't know," Sinkua admitted, "I think it's a private meeting area for the Prime Ministers."

"I would assume it's where they keep confidential and sensitive materials."

"I wouldn't know anything about that. I can ask Grandpa about it, if you're curious."

"I'd rather not deal with SenRas right now," Malia slipped.

"Wait," Sinkua said as, in a single swift motion, he took a long stride ahead, turned, and halted her with his fingertips pressed against her clavicle, "I never told you SenRas was my grandfather. Not even CreSam knew that. What did you learn about me before you came looking for me, and who did you learn it from?"

"I already knew who your parents were before I came looking for you. Mortvill has been watching your family for several years, since before your mother was born," Malia revealed, "There are no legal records of SenRas being anyone's father, much less grandfather, but he had traced him to you."

Sinkua found him such a bizarre voyeur, this Mortvill. Sure, his interest in the Hybrids fit with his position against the Avatars of Fate, but he had watched his family for at least three generations. That level of stalking straddled the territories of absurdity and perversion.

"How could he have known that long ago?"

"That's not for me to know," Malia dismissed, "But I did wrong by him. SenRas, I mean. I need to set it right before he knows about it."

A traitorous Avatar of Fate had surreptitiously wronged his grandfather. His eyes flared up with epiphany as the elevator opened to invite them inside.

"You stole the deed!" he accused "The hell would you do that for?"

"The Avatars wanted it. I don't know why, but they did. The Coalition thought it would be safer with us than with SenRas," she explained as the car climbed the shaft.

"And yet," he countered, stepping off at the forty-eighth floor, "you lost it anyway?"

"Yeah," she meekly admitted, "But if I hadn't stolen it, one of them would have killed SenRas to get it, and you would never have known he had it."

"I guess that's true. Wouldn't be fair to ask you to get it back in return for saving your daughter though, what with her being my sister and all."

"It would put me on better terms with Mortvill and the rest of The Coalition. But tracking that deed is more my forte. I'll let you know if I need your help."

"I'm sure Grandpa could help. He did figure out how to kill The Scout. Behind everyone's backs, at that."

Malia sighed in exasperation, the undeniably sound advice weighing heavily on her conscience. Her actions had saved SenRas's life, but he would surely manage to refute this hypothetical scenario. After the trouble she had caused him, he had no reason to give her an audience, much less cooperate with her.

He would be an indispensable asset to her investigation though. After all, he had seen through the first layer of her cover rather quickly. Had CreSam not dismissed her, SenRas may have proven astute enough to see through to her true designs.

Malia let out a small breathless laugh as Sinkua knocked once to announce their arrival. Biroe had her old office in the Platinum Hall. Better a member of the Subtransit Resistance than some Imperial loyalist, she thought.

"Now then," Biroe greeted, "what's this pattern you think you've found?"

"Technically, we haven't. We were hoping you could help," Malia explained.

She set the sheet before him, a list of four-digit codes for the labs where Nikasu had been kept. To avoid perhaps unnecessary complications, she excluded any indication of location or timing or duration of stay. Biroe mulled over it, leaning on his elbow. His brow furrowed incrementally tighter every time his eyes reached the bottom of the page.

Sinkua and Malia watched pensively as Biroe scrawled the numbers in varying formats, spacings, and kernings. He tried building a matrix, thinking to decode some ongoing hidden message, but that yielded only gibberish. The same happened when he assigned letters based on their alphabetic position, even when he displaced them using various metrics.

"Do you think he needs…" Malia piped up.

"Shh!" Sinkua cut off, "Let him work."

Biroe drew a graph and plotted the codes as pairs of two-digit coordinates. He gritted his teeth as no pattern emerged. Plotting them as radians proved equally fruitless, as did all attempts at plotting on a three dimensional graph.

"What about four coordinates, one for each digit?" Sinkua suggested.

"And how do you suggest I draw a four-dimensional graph?" Biroe snarled, "I can only draw three dimensions on paper, and…"

"Can you model it on your computer?" Malia asked.

"Four spatial dimensions? I don't have that kind of software. Believe it or not, accountants don't usually need that sort of thing," he snapped, "Besides, the fourth coordinate is time. How am I… Hold on!"

Biroe swept his failed attempts onto the floor with epiphanic haste. He laid out ten fresh sheets, on each of which he wrote a single digit and drew a three dimensional graph. Realizing his mess, he nodded to Sinkua, who crouched to gather the discarded papers with a simper and a shake of his head.

Biroe diagramed ten scatter plots using the first three numbers as coordinates and the fourth as the header digit. When he finished, he transferred the plots onto the zero graph. A pattern began to emerge, but it needed something more.

He tried connecting the points with common header digits. What had been nearing a pattern now left him staring at a mess. He muttered under his breath about changes over time.

On an eleventh sheet, he drew the merged scattered plots again. His eyes and pencil darting between the list and the graph, he connected multiple sequences running from zero through nine. He tapped his way down the list, mumbling to himself and checking off entries with a quick swipe of his pencil. Finally, a pattern emerged.

"What does this look like to you?" he asked Malia.

"Whoa, look at that," Malia remarked, her lips curling into a fascinated smile, "It's Elchimerian's Whorl."

"Elchi what now?" Sinkua asked.

"Elchimerian's Whorl," Biroe reiterated, "Elchimerian was a Kirtsian mathematician who lived three hundred years ago. He created an algorithm to diagram the movements of multiple phenomena in relation to each other, primarily in meteorology and cosmology."

"Okay, so you have an algorithm to work from. That means you can figure out where she is now, right?"

"Elchimerian's Whorl isn't quite that simple, especially after this many iterations. I can give you a few possible paths she was taken on, but it's up to you to know how many times she's been moved. That and which path to follow"

"I'm sure they've only moved her once," Malia insisted, "Moving her twice this quickly would disrupt protocol."

"As much as I hate to say it, if their protocol needs to do without her, they'll just off her," Sinkua macabrely predicted, "Sooner they eliminate an asset themselves then lose her to an expatriate."

"Okay, I… guess that's… good to know… I think," Biroe trailed off, "Anyway, her next stop will be 3241, 3891, or 1341."

"Hey!" Malia urged, elbowing Sinkua, "Where did you think he took her?"

"You already had an idea?" Biroe interrupted.

"Yeah, but it was a dead end. Only a guess, really," Sinkua excused, "We needed solid math on this. Anyway, it was, eh, Lenguardia, Poravit, and ah, Quarun."

At Malia's behest, Sinkua unrolled the map and overlay on the floor. Peering from scarcely a nose's length away, Malia found and highlighted the Laboratories 3241, 3891, and 1341.

"3241 is in Eprilen, and 1341 is here in ArcNos," she began.

"Probably a derelict lab left over from the war. We should see about having someone check into it though," Sinkua suggested, helping Malia to her feet, "Biroe, let Spril know about 1341 while I'm gone, okay?"

Biroe nodded as Malia continued, "3891 is in Lenguardia, right in the middle of one of the regions you predicted. I think I can trust you guys on this one."

"Damn right, you can," Biroe boasted, "This guy plotted our course to take down the Imperial motor cavalry and cornered them into ending the war."

"And this guy singlehandedly fixed our budget to accommodate the incoming citizen resistance," Sinkua added, "Wherever our patterns cross, that's where we need to go. Now, let's go get Vielle, pick up Eytea, and get back on the water."

"I need to speak with Phylus first. Go ahead and talk to Vielle without me."

"Okay, we'll meet you at Phylus's office and go from there."

Malia nodded in compliance, restraining a victorious smile. Her directive to have him track Nikasu had gone swimmingly. Perhaps, she thought, the latency of his condition had given his intellectual faculties time to rebuild themselves. This could have meant that the weaponizing factor had diminished as well, but better that than his mental capacity.

"Biroe, do you mind if I use your phone?" Sinkua requested as Malia left.

"Go right on," Biroe agreed with a smirk of mutual pride, "Need to call your lady?"

Sinkua nodded as he accepted the phone and dialed home. Eytea answered before the end of the first ring.

"Hello?"

"Eytea? It's me," Sinkua answered, "I'm back from Berinin."

"Oh wonderful! I was starting to go stir-crazy," Eytea sighed, "This apartment is too damn quiet when you're gone.

"I'd imagine so," he snickered, "Anything promising on your job search?"

"Pretty much all been a bust. My most promising lead is an as-needed delivery position with a Feryan takeout spot," Eytea explained, "So, how was your trip? Are you and Galo back on good terms?"

"We are, yeah. He figured out I had been telling the truth about his parents, so he's in a better mood now. But..."

"That's good. What about his research?" she continued, dancing around the issue that gnawed at her thoughts.

"Got a lot to work with. Too soon for promises," Sinkua hastily dismissed, "Eytea. Listen. We've got an emergency. Get dressed. Get our weapons ready. I'll be there in thirty minutes with Vielle and Malia."

"Why? What's going on?" Eytea beckoned, anxiety swelling her throat.

"Remember the little girl on the lab?"

"I do. I had that dream the other night, but this time, well..."

"It was me. I know. I had the same dream. We think they experimented on me while I was living on that island, but somehow I don't remember."

"Does this mean we're going to an active lab to procure an antidote?"

"No. It means we're going after that little girl. They're either about to execute her or use her to launch a mass offensive. Malia, Biroe, and I tracked her to a lab in Lenguardia."

"Shit. We'd better hurry, then," Eytea agreed, "By the way, who's Malia?"

"She was a mole within the Avatars of Fate, but she had to cut and run when they figured her out. This girl, Nikasu, is her daughter," he explained, "So is Vielle."

"Ah wow, so they're half-sisters. That's pretty cool for Vielle. Finds out her mom wasn't an Avatar after all, and now she has a sister," she beamed.

"Yeah, it is. All around," Sinkua nodded, "Nikasu's also my half-sister."

"Wait! Wait, what?" Eytea stammered, nearly dropping the phone.

"CreSam was her father. Malia calls it a union of necessity."

"Let me make sure I have everything straight," Eytea recapped, "There's a teenage Hybrid hostage, who they're using to make living weapons. Either she's about to be executed, or they're about to kick production into overdrive. And she's your and Vielle's half-sister."

"That's about the sum of it."

"Fuck the restaurant. We're going to Lenguardia. I'll leave the rent check on the mail table," she asserted, "Who's coming?"

"Just you, Vielle, Malia, and me. But I think Malia's just gonna help us find the lab and maybe get us inside."

"No Galo?"

"We need him outside in case something goes wrong. Plus he has his expansion work to coordinate."

"True. We should try to bring Spril, too, in case we have to split up inside the lab."

"I'll have Vielle talk to him."

Malia stopped before the double doors and looked down at her shoes, taking stock of herself as her attention panned upward. She breathed in deeply, releasing it slowly and savoring her moment of composure. More than twenty years since she left him, save for one night in Eprilen, and he could still get under her skin in a way she thought long dead. She smirked with partially feigned confidence, brushed off her shirt, and hiked up her bra.

"Prime Minister Phylus?" she called, knocking on his door, "Can I speak with you?"

"Come in. State your business," Phylus answered, either feigning ignorance or too engrossed in his work to recognize her voice.

"I'm back from Berinin," Malia reported, closing the door behind herself, "Do you have a moment?"

"Not particularly, no," he refused, eyes fixed on hers, "But I suppose you shouldn't be made to wait."

"Thank you, this is quite urgent. I need to take Sinkua for a while," she said, taking a seat across from him, "I don't know how long he'll be gone."

"After your last visit, I assumed you would. I've already cleared him for an open-ended business trip. It's a bit in the grey area, but your being a former Judge mitigates the boilerplate stuff a mite."

"You didn't say anything about my work with the Avatars or The Coalition, right?" Malia worried.

"I wouldn't think of it."

"Good. We also need Vielle."

"I know. She's getting vacation time."

"Well, I just want to make sure you're okay with it. She's more your daughter than she could ever be mine, and I'm risking her life to save her half-sister on my side."

"As far as I'm concerned, Nikasu is as much family to me as she is to Vielle. If I weren't so damn busy, I'd go with you as well. Is anyone else going?"

"We're picking up Eytea shortly."

"If she knows Nikasu is related to Sinkua, she's already at the docks by now," Phylus snickered, "What about Galo?"

"Sinkua thinks it would be best to have a Hybrid outside and out of the loop."

"Sounds reasonable," Phylus nodded, "Too risky to put all of them on an infiltration mission, even if they're out to rescue another of their own. Less the one left out knows, the less they can accidentally give up."

"He didn't go that far, but that sounds like the size of it."

"Classic Sinkua. Won't divulge his plans until each factor becomes pertinent," Phylus recalled, "Good to see the boy's still got it. Anyway, try to get Spril or EshCal to go in with you. Any top-tier soldier ought to do, but they'd be best for the job."

"I'll talk to Spril about it," Malia agreed, glossing over her intelligence on EshCal, "I saw EshCal earlier, but she looked too swamped to ask."

Vielle yanked her headset down to her neck, wiping sweat from her crescent ears. Tension spreading throughout her back, she scratched the back of her head and squirmed in her seat. The news had left her restless, minutes crawling past like hours as she awaited her long-absent mother's return with her friend.

Regardless of having never met her, Nikasu was both family and a fellow Hybrid, another of only five in the world. Their bond was undeniable, an unfathomable magnetism pulling her toward her kin. Yet, she could only sit and wait, talking people through issues each pettier than the last. She massaged her forehead, pinching the bridge of her nose between her thumb and forefinger.

Sinkua perched on the bottom shelf of an abandoned delivery cart, looking out over an array of cubicles. Spotting Vielle's skullcap, he stepped down and set off in long strides.

He found Vielle with her head in her hands, her headset hanging from her neck. Hurrying to her side, he noticed redness in her cheeks and unevenness in her breath, disrupted by an urging chime from her headset. She had a caller waiting, but that concerned neither of them.

"Vielle," he whispered, crouching beside her and holding her shoulder.

"Sinkua!" she sighed, wiping moisture from her eyelids, "You're back. Yay."

"Our sister is in Lenguardia," Sinkua reported, locking eyes with her, "I have immediate clearance to go find her. Can you leave today?"

"Yeah, of course," she assured, sniffling as she tugged the still-chiming headset from her neck, "I just have to go home and get my cat-o'-nine-tails."

"Did they let you have time off again already?"

"No. I put in the request three days ago, and they refused. So you know, screw them. This is our sister and a hostage of the Avatars. If they don't think that's a priority, this job can suck it."

"Good enough," he snickered, "By the way, I need you to talk Spril into coming with us, in case we need to split up once we're inside."

"Isn't Galo coming?"

"No, we need him outside in case something goes awry while we're in there."

"Makes sense. I'm sure he'll be eager to meet Nikasu though."

Sinkua grinned and nodded, offering his hand. Rising to her feet, Vielle grabbed her skullcap and pulled it down over her disheveled hair. She wiped the last traces of tears from her face, reclaiming her composure.

"But um, if I lose my job over this," she dialed back as they started walking, "Can I stay with you and Eytea until I find something else?"

"Yeah, we can set you up on the couch," he offered, patting her upper back, "Anyway, go to the Ministry of Defense and talk to Spril. I'm heading back to Foreign Affairs to meet with Malia. She went to talk to your father."

Vielle cupped both of her hands around one of his. The redness had faded from her cheeks, but the brief onset of tears left a trail of salty skin, faintly tinted by her eyeliner. She looked up at him and smiled, feeling secure within his shadow. As much as she hated waiting around for a hero, knowing Sinkua would join her in rescuing Nikasu bolstered her confidence.

"Thank you," she exhaled.

She squeezed his hand once more, Sinkua reciprocating the gesture, and split off to seek out Spril. They had been out of touch recently, Spril being rather preoccupied with the transition. EshCal's workload had overflowed into his office during her extended absence following the Tournament, word being that she was on a reconnaissance mission. Still, she felt confident that Spril would be willing to join them.

Of course, that left the matter of whether he could go. His desires notwithstanding, his duties couldn't be quite as easily eschewed as hers. On top of the restrictions of his authority, transitioning into this new system had been, from Vielle's perspective, administrative chaos.

The Ministry of Defense bustled with soldiers and personnel shoving past each other, each with business more pressing than the last. Vielle ducked and wove through the empty spaces under elbows, turning her diminutive stature into an advantage.

A long queue grew out of Spril's office doors. Even from the end and with his door shut, she could hear him in heated debate with his current visitor. She forced her way to the front of the line, stoking a commotion of angry objection.

"Uncle Spril!" she called, throwing the door open, "I need to talk with you. Right now."

"Hold your tits. Me and your uncle are having a man-to-man here. Got it?" the visiting soldier objected.

"Step out, clamhead. I'm trying to prevent a war."

"Who do you think...?"

Before Spril could intervene, Vielle grabbed the man's shoulder, fingernails digging through his uniform shirt. Vines sprouted from the back of her hand, wrapping around his neck and opposite shoulder. Having apparently never witnessed a Hybrid's powers, his eyes grew with shock and fear. He ripped one off his neck, but it branched off and wrapped around his hand instead.

"First rule, don't ever address me like that," Vielle hissed, "Second rule, disrupting the Avatars of Fate takes priority over whatever you came in here to bitch about. Now, step out before the thorns come out."

"Vielle. Stand down," Spril ordered.

The soldier smirked arrogantly as Vielle gave a defeated sneer and complied. He reached for her shoulder, looking down in contempt at her petite frame. For someone so petite to confront him as she had was surely a joke at best, an insult at worst.

"Hands off the personnel, soldier," Spril barked.

"What?! You're gonna stand up for her after what she just did?"

"That wasn't an order. That was a warning," Spril corrected, "I won't stop her if you agitate her a second time."

"Do you seriously think...?"

"Stand down and step out, soldier!" Spril bellowed, "That was an order."

The soldier's eyes darted between Vielle and Spril. Vielle inclined her head, serpentine vines growing from her shoulders like vestigial wings. Grumbling bitterly, he dropped his hand and walked to the door.

"Remind everyone out there that EshCal came back yesterday," Spril added, "They'd know that if they listened to morning announcements."

The soldier's hands trembled as he fiddled with the door handle. Clearly not sniper material like her father, Vielle thought.

"Haven't seen you in a while," Spril mused, his tone becoming more cordial once the soldier had shut the door, "How have you been?"

"Oh, it's been crazy. I guess you heard I found my mother, huh?"

"It does seem like SenRas or your dad said something about that. Eprilen's former Judge Malia? Used to work undercover in the Avatars of Fate?"

Of course, he had known about Malia since the beginning, but Phylus had sworn him to secrecy. Without discovering some part of it herself, they feared Vielle might never understand, much less accept, the reality of her origins.

"Yeah, apparently she stole something from SenRas for them, but then she lost it. But that's not why I'm here," she explained, pausing to compile her thoughts before she broke the news, "Malia has another daughter."

Spril looked her over, reflecting on the tone of her words. For a long awkward moment, he dissected her demeanor. With such discomfort in her voice, this was more than learning her egg-donor mother had birthed a child herself.

"Also a Hybrid?"

"Of course. She probably wouldn't be in this kind of trouble if she wasn't."

"I sensed the tone. What kind of trouble?"

"The Avatars have been using her to make living weapons, but they found out Malia's been sabotaging them. They're probably kinda pissed about losing CreSam, too, what with his being the girl's father," Vielle explained, "Sinkua thinks they're either going to execute Nikasu or use her to kick off a huge assault."

"There's some gray area in there, but those sound like their most likely reactions. What do you need from me?" Spril asked, still processing the idea of Sinkua and Vielle sharing a sibling.

"Sinkua and Biroe tracked her to a lab in Lenguardia. Malia is taking the two of us and Eytea over there on a rescue mission. Sinkua says we need a fourth in case we need to split up."

"Galo's staying out for tactical purposes, I suppose?"

"That's what Sinkua says."

"Go wait for me in the main lobby. Give me a few minutes to clear up my schedule, and I'll be right down," he promised, "EshCal owes me one anyway."

"I'll call Sinkua and let him know you're joining us."

Chapter 12

Sinkua and Malia stepped off the bus, moving with a swarm of fellow commuters. An arm reached up from behind the sidewalk crowd, followed by a sharp whistle. Eytea tucked back her wings and spear-armed through the shoving masses.

"Hey, where are Spril and Vielle?" she asked.

"Coming on his motorcycle," Sinkua reported, pecking her cheek, "I thought we were picking you up at home."

"Faster this way," Eytea reasoned, pulling a strap off her shoulder, "I brought our weapons."

She handed him his morningstar in its back harness. She had cleaned it and capped the spikes. Even after all the blood and sinew it had hosted, the ball and spikes fairly glimmered in the waning sunlight. Sinkua professed his gratitude as he adjusted the straps on her halberd's harness, noting the handmade leather sheaths over the blades.

"By the way," Malia cut in as they shuffled out of the crowd, "I'm Malia. It's nice to finally meet you."

"Oh, have you heard a lot about me?" Eytea asked, presumptively flattered.

"Sinkua talked about you some on our way here from Berinin," Malia laughed, clearly understating the matter, "But in all seriousness, I learned quite a bit about all of you while I was planted within the Avatars of Fate."

Granted, she only spoke a partial truth, since she had only recently learned about Vielle. Previously, she had suspected The Harvester or The Geneticist might have known about their relation. Keeping that a secret to shorten her leash would have suited their agenda. However, the truth she had learned from The Omnimath was that much more unsettling.

This was hardly the time to mention that their kindred friend wasn't supposed to exist, no matter the manner of speaking. If Vielle believed her existence and Hybrid status to be fraudulent, she might not be so willing to risk her life for another. Worse still, she might rationalize that Nikasu's death would legitimize herself as one, being that it would reduce the headcount to the requisite four.

"We'll have to get up to speed with each other on that later."

"I'm not sure I ever mentioned this to you," Sinkua cut in, "but she's the reason SenRas has had so much trouble with the deed to my parents' old house."

"Seriously?" Eytea asked, taken aback, "I'm assuming you did it for the Avatars and not your other people, but what have you even done to set things right?"

"Sure, rub it in. I screwed up," Malia grumbled, "I did steal it for the Avatars, but I was protecting it for The Coalition instead. But now it's gone missing. I was trying to track it, but I blew my cover."

"If she hadn't done it, someone else might have killed Grandpa for it. And we might have never known we had a claim on that house," Sinkua defended, "Then, she might not have come to us about Nikasu by now. But Malia, if you'd like, you can go back to searching for it once we've found the lab. Given your recent treachery, you ought to stay outside anyway."

"Mortvill said saving Nikasu is my only priority right now. EshCal is surrogating for me on all other matters in the meantime."

108

An electric motorcycle slowed to a crawl as it pulled onto the sidewalk. Pedestrians parted, many with looks of spite and disdain, as the driver walked it along. The soft hum of the motor resonated off the walls of the human corridor. Vielle removed her helmet and waved to her friends and egg-donor mother.

"Vielle thought we'd find you three here," Spril explained as he parked the bike.

"Good thinking, because the sooner we find Nikasu, the better off we'll all be," Eytea insisted.

"I took a cat-o'-nine-tails from the armory instead of getting mine from home," Vielle noted, "Now, where exactly are we going?"

"Laboratory 3891 is in north central Lenguardia, which is at the far eastern end of the Midland Sea," Malia explained, "Most of their facilities operate largely underground, short buildings with several subbasements. Laboratory 3891, however, is one of several exceptions."

"Any military grade vessel can get us to northern Lenguardia by this time tomorrow, sundown at the latest," Spril informed.

"Should we take one with an armored vehicle on board, so we can drive to the facility?" Malia suggested.

"Bad idea," Sinkua rejected before Spril could answer similarly, "That'll draw too much attention. We don't know how wide of a surveillance perimeter they've laid out."

"By that logic, they could be watching the coast, too."

"Even if they are, we can move more freely and are harder to track on foot," Eytea added, "Unless someone wants to deal with us up close, but that's yet to end well for them."

"Alright. Vielle and I will go on ahead to the docks," Spril reported, "Two of you take a cab out there and the other a bus."

Spril flipped his visor down, and Vielle put on her helmet as he started the motor again. Sinkua pumped his fist, while Eytea nodded affirmatively and Malia nervously waved. Spril swerved the bike back onto the asphalt and sped eastward.

"Thank you for meeting with me, Mrs. Elemeno," Farim professed from behind her mug of tea.

"Oh, I haven't been Mrs. Anyone for almost ten years, dear," Elemeno insisted, "But I must say, it's nice to finally meet more of Eytea's friends. How has she been? She doesn't write or call nearly often enough, you know."

"She and Sinkua are renting an apartment on the south side of town, right outside of the capital. Close to where we all lived during the war," Farim said, "Except now they're living above ground."

"Well, it's nice to know they're getting along alright. I've been worried about her, you know. She always felt so burdened growing up, like it was her fault Kabehl became the way he was."

"You mean that he was an Avatar of Fate?"

"Yes, she thought her wings drove him to join them."

"Have you considered she might be right?" Farim callously suggested.

"I refuse to enable that sort of thinking. She has enough problems already, and even if her life was easy, I would never blame her for his decisions."

"I mean by virtue of being a Hybrid. No conscious fault."

Elemeno stared into her nearly empty mug, reflecting on the last day she dealt with Kabehl. They gave him to the soil with such cold dismissal, but his words still resonated so many years later. She never wanted to admit to herself what she had gleaned, but time and age had left her with little other choice but to accept it.

"I don't know exactly when he joined. For all I know, he joined before I had my Eytea. That man even made intimacy impersonal," Elemeno trailed off, "I didn't see the tattoo until Eytea was eight years old, but he despised her markings since her birth."

"Her markings?"

"She had two purple spots on her back. Looked like bruises. Kabehl hated those spots. Hated her for having them. I thought maybe birth defects upset him. Maybe his anger was just misguided," Elemeno continued, "Later, he said his employer taught him what her wings meant. He was … particularly eager to try to kill her."

"So, he knew before you did? Did he know before Eytea?"

"More or less. Chieftain Sage Gijin delivered her halberd to me when she was a toddler, but he only described her as a destined heroine. We didn't learn the name Hybrids until Sinkua and Galo visited us."

"It sounds like the Avatars of Fate know more about Hybrids than anyone else, ever since they assassinated Gijin."

"But what do the Avatars know that makes them want to kill the Hybrids?" Elemeno worried, "And just who are they anyhow?"

"That's what I'm trying to figure out, Miss Elemeno," Farim assured, "The two clearly have some kind of bad blood between them, but only the Avatars know what it is anymore. But I can tell you, I don't think Kabehl joined because of Eytea."

"How do you suppose that to be?" Elemeno pried.

"Their entire operation seems to be predicated on a shared hatred of the Hybrids. Their most notorious exploits all connect to them."

"Yes, and Kabehl hated Eytea. If he were looking for likeminded folks, they would be the obvious choice."

"Well yes," Farim conceded, "but you said they taught him what she was and what her wings meant. He hated her, but he didn't try to kill her for them until she was a teenager."

"Why else do you suppose he joined?"

"I think he was recruited because of his discontent over her markings," Farim insisted, "Another Avatar learned about Eytea's anomaly and Kabehl's resentment. They used that to draw him in and indoctrinate him against the Hybrids in general. Not to make him sound like a victim. He's still just as much an asshole as he always was."

"I would never think you were spinning his life that way, dear," Elemeno assured, "I suppose there's no telling what the progression of his hatred was anymore."

"Exactly. But what we do now is that these people have intimate knowledge of Hybrid births. Every Hybrid has had a parent figure baited, indoctrinated, or in some way victimized by the Avatars of Fate."

"Do you have any idea how they know who's having Hybrid children?"

"No, but it sounds like Chieftain Sage Gijin knew before everyone else, too. I'm making my way to Masnethege to see what I can learn about him."

"Have you ever studied their insignia?" Elemeno suggested, "I'm no symbologist by any stretch, but I doubt it's arbitrary."

"Symbology is hardly a real science, by any stretch," Farim sarcastically dismissed, "Everything has different historical significance depending on the culture and the era, and we don't know when or where they originated. If you have some solid intel about it though, I'd be glad to hear it. Somewhere else you saw it, maybe?"

"Not unless you count process of elimination as solid intel. Kabehl said it had to do with an excavation project. I went to Lenguardia and asked around. I was directed to a facility in the north, but the people there dismissed it as a hoax. Rather hastily at that."

"I suppose that's a start."

"That building had a peculiar engraving over the door, though," Elemeno continued, "It looked like the letters y, n, o, a, all lower case. The o had a line across the middle, the right half of the n was too long, and the a and y were curly. That sign has always stuck with me. So odd."

"YNOA? Ynoa?" Farim puzzled, "Any thoughts on what it could mean or stand for?"

"I've drawn naught but nonsense and blanks."

"Maybe ynoa meant something in one of the dead languages. I'll look into it and tell you if I find anything relevant," Farim promised, rising to her feet.

"Oh, must you be going so soon?"

"Yes, I really shouldn't linger. I need to continue on my way to Berinin," Farim apologized, "The tea was delicious, thank you."

"If you'd like, I can find directions to that facility," Elemeno offered, "I kept detailed records, so I could cross-reference if I found something else. If you can wait a bit, I'm sure I can dig them out."

"In that case," Farim reconsidered, "I suppose I should stay."

Malia grabbed a low branch and braced her foot against the steep hill, pulling herself onto the street from the valley forest. The branch bowed and cracked against her weight. She crouched on the road side and held out her hand, taking the sheathed business end of Eytea's halberd and helping her up. Eytea assisted Sinkua in similar manner. Sinkua hoisted Spril by his quarterstaff, who brought Vielle onto the pavement by the same means.

A vast park lay just beyond the other side of the street. Unleashed dogs chased squirrels, who searched the newfallen snow for their food caches. Parents picnicked, watching their children play. Others biked or jogged in spite of the weather, while elders busied themselves with Remchuk and chess. Tall buildings loomed over a strip of forest along the back of the park.

"Laboratory 3891 is directly south of here, a short ways beyond the park," Malia explained, "I'll know it by the engraving over the door."

"We found an abandoned one in Ferya a few years ago," Eytea recalled, "It had been sealed off and converted into a house. If they hide their labs in plain sight..."

"... we're definitely dealing with one of their taller labs," Sinkua finished.

"Spread out and head south," Spril ordered, "Stay within shouting distance, and make sure you can see Malia. Malia, when you find the building, your signal will be to light a cigarette."

"If anyone is being followed, intervene discreetly," Sinkua added, "The more attention we draw, the harder it will be to rescue Nikasu."

The five of them fanned out, losing each other in a long line of parallel-parked cars along the opposite side of the street. Each headed down the hill and into the park, meandering through with the nonchalance of a scenic early evening stroll.

Malia took care to keep Vielle in her sight. It felt rather odd having maternal bonds manifest despite having never known her beyond rumors about the Subtransit Resistance. She had given one daughter to the Avatars, but she found a small measure of redemption and solace in gaining a daughter she never knew.

Finding this impossible child ignited hope that they could save Nikasu against odds just as improbable. It also reinforced her dwindling maternal pull toward Nikasu, atrophying for a near void of interaction. Obsessing over her mistakes, she contemplated if Nikasu remembered her anymore.

Vielle caught Malia staring, but she pretended not to notice. It felt awkward at first, but it became easier to tolerate the longer it went on. Rather than fade to background noise, it became something of a means of comfort. If this supposedly phony Avatar now showed her true self, she had been taking measures to protect the Hybrids for years. Now, she showed a keen interest in Vielle's wellbeing, even so soon after she fretted over their relation.

Vielle often felt she spent too much of her adolescence looking out for her father. Between losing his job, their house, and Spril, he had fallen into damaging tendencies. She had managed to keep his depression and subsequent chain-smoking in check, and that burdened her enough without the stress of finding food and employment. Now, she had someone watching her back the way she watched his.

Spril's eyes continuously swept the expanse of his visual field, seeing all as a potential battlefield. He paused for a split second on each of his comrades. Tracking Malia's movements, he plotted possible trajectories into a mental shortlist of destinations. He then sized up the potentials for structural weaknesses or unconventional entry points.

Eytea tucked her wings back, hiding them behind her shoulders. The nightmares replayed in her mind, Nikasu's face becoming clearer with each repetition. From what Eytea could see of her, Nikasu bore a considerable resemblance to Sinkua. Such perspective may have come from knowing their kinship or, more likely, having seen Sinkua in her place.

With that thought, Eytea went back to obsessing over Sinkua's condition, contemplating the thought of Nikasu being the source of his infection. Whether Sinkua blamed Nikasu would hinge on his mental state when they found her, and Eytea forecasted that as unfavorable.

Sinkua kept Vielle in the corner of his eye, not noticing when Spril or Eytea looked his way. Having grown more adept in the art of subtlety, he watched Vielle without her realizing, though her attention on Malia surely helped.

Losing family was familiar ground for him. Not that he had grown comfortable with it or even accustomed to it, but he had experience enough to brace himself against the likelihood of losing Nikasu. The only personal loss Vielle had ever known proved temporary when Spril returned. Her losses had been largely impersonal, watching her community fall apart while keeping what family she had. Between that and her charismatic façade hiding her pain, Sinkua worried how Vielle might react if they lost Nikasu.

The south side of the park proved far livelier than the north, active with commerce from street vendors to towering markets. Buildings both modern and vintage lined the sidewalks, overlooking parallel parked cars.

Malia paused before the concrete stoop of an archaic building resembling a repurposed courthouse. Deep chills washed over her as she gazed up at the engraving, breathing deeply in vain hopes of steadying herself. She leaned against the wall, and by both order and urge, she sparked a cigarette, the taste eliciting memories to assuage her anxiety.

One by one, they closed in around her, Sinkua arriving last as the cherry neared the filter. They found her staring up at the engraving, a nervous shudder occasionally washing over her. Pedestrians swerved around her, paying little mind to whatever hypnotized her.

"What does ynoa mean?" Eytea asked.

"It says 3891," Malia revealed, "It's written in an ancient script."

"Are you fluent in it?" Sinkua asked, "We found a genome map shortly before the war. I think it was in this language."

"Sorry, no," Malia sighed, relieved to learn that particular exploit had panned out, "I only know of three people who are fluent."

"How much can you read?" Spril encouraged.

"Just numerals and identifying the letters. Everyone knows their names, but most people don't know them as linguistic characters. These ones are gamma, eta, theta, and alpha."

"Those are names of Subtransit boarding docks," Vielle noted, "Does that mean they were built in ancient times."

"No, those were built long after the ancient scripts fell out of use."

"So, how does everyone know the names without knowing they're letters?"

"The story goes that there are historical figures with the same names," Malia explained, "I don't know how much of it is true, but they've been credited with some of the most revolutionary acts in the history of Ouristihra."

"We can ask Uulan what he knows about them," Eytea suggested, "But for now, do we just walk in the front door?"

"You four go inside. This is as far as I can take you," Malia insisted, "I don't know what you'll find in there, but I'll endanger everyone if I go in with you."

"Fair enough," Spril dismissed, "Wait for us at the boat."

Galo sat under a palm tree at the head of the beach, carving into a mango with a paring knife. Breakers reached up the sand, washing within centimeters of his outstretched feet. From the east, a long shadow on the water caught his eyes, its wake sloshing the tide up to his ankles. He turned to see an ArcNosian ship approaching.

"Coming in a rather wide," Galo mumbled as he rose to his feet, "Even Sinkua navigates better than that."

The ship closed in on the coast over the next several minutes. Fellow Masnethegeans congregated on the beach, curious about the visitor. Unannounced ArcNosians approaching from this side had often been welcome visitors. It was the ones pushing through from the northern shores who worried them. This vessel was no bigger than a sloop, suggesting a minimal crew, perhaps a lone traveler.

An unfamiliar figure stepped out to the starboard railing as the boat neared the shore. He donned a black suit stained by the nautical air, much to his chagrin, judging by the way he swiped at the salt and sand embedded in the fabric. Retaining his composure, he raised his hand to the silent crowd, seeming to have expected a more clamorous response.

Galo narrowed his eyes, shrewdly sizing up this overdressed visitor. Odd enough that this outsider would arrive on the beach of Masnethege without forwarding word of his approach. Stranger still that he would come so inaptly dressed.

A crewmember tossed the anchor, while another lowered the gate and ramp. The gentleman walked down with one hand in his pocket and the other holding a portfolio. He nodded to the Masnethegeans, who returned befuddled glares.

"Welcome, friend," Galo tactfully greeted, "What brings you to our beach?"

"You are Chieftain Sage Galo, correct?" he asked, "Or are you some child playing in your father's clothes? I thought you'd be older."

"It's the melanin. Does wonders for the complexion," Galo sneered, "I'm the man you're looking for. If you expected someone older, you're as out of the loop as you are out of touch."

"In that case, it's a pleasure to meet you. I am Chairman LenSom of the ArcNosian Parliament," LenSom introduced with a plastic smile, "I have orders to place you under arrest."

"What!?" Galo exclaimed, "On what grounds?"

"War crimes, sir," LenSom stoically reported, snatching Galo's wrist and snapping one end of a set of handcuffs around it.

"I've committed no war crimes! Who issued this order?"

LenSom sighed impatiently as he withdrew the warrant and held it out for Galo to see.

"The order was written and signed by Foreign Affairs Minister Sinkua," LenSom reported, "and subsequently approved by Prime Minister of Foreign Affairs Phylus. Pending your trial, you are to be placed under arrest in ArcNosian custody."

LenSom tried to remove the Serpent Bracer, but Galo's searing stare taught him better. He maneuvered the other cuff under the head of the copper serpent instead. Galo snarled as LenSom locked his hands behind his back, his fury genuine but his incompliance feigned.

The image of that warrant had burned itself into Galo's memory. He could scarcely recall seeing Sinkua's penmanship, but the signature seemed reasonably genuine. Such matters called for investigation, and the only way he knew how to get his answers was to cooperate and await his trial.

The door groaned as Sinkua opened it by its ornate handle. Vielle and Spril stood at his flanks with Eytea two steps behind him, all poised for an assault upon entry. The plastic odor of office equipment and furniture polish swept over them instead.

Behind a lone desk in the back corner of the lobby sat an indifferent receptionist, more aware of something between her teeth than of her visitors. Seemingly by the total vacancy otherwise, they had arrived after office hours. Vielle scanned the layout the room.

"This doesn't look like the lobby to a laboratory," she loudly whispered, "Eytea, do you recognize any of this?"

"No, but you're right," Eytea confirmed, "It looks more like a marketing agency."

"I was thinking public relations research."

"Either way, this is obviously a cover."

"Then, we don't have to worry about her triggering an alarm," Sinkua cut in, nodding toward the receptionist, "If this is a cover, she won't know it."

Vielle split off from the crowd and approached the desk. She smiled and waved as the older woman fixed eyes with her, scrutinizing this unannounced visitor. Vielle had strapped her whip to her back, hiding it from the front, but the top of her right ear peeked between strands of her neck-length hair.

Spril watched pensively as they conversed. The receptionist's demeanor steadily shifted from puzzled discontent to pleasant agreeability. Vielle was quick to adopt her Lenguardian inclination for supplementing conversation with hand gestures. They spoke too softly to hear, but both nodded affirmatively at the close.

"This is a shared facility," Vielle reported as she returned, "This section is a market research agency. Second basement houses a research lab with a military contract."

"Which military?" Sinkua asked, seeking evidence for the Tanelen theory.

"She doesn't know."

"This is our place."

"Elevator is at the end of that hall."

As they passed the receptionist, Spril caught the faintest motion in the corner of his eye. He slowed as he passed beyond her peripheral vision, listening through the ambient hum of central heating. Noticing Spril's lagging, Sinkua patted Eytea and Vielle on their shoulders and looked back. Spril cocked his head toward the lobby, then nodded them onward.

The receptionist's chair rolled forward half a wheel turn, the seat creaking as she leaned forward with all the surreptitiousness she could muster. Faint tones of her deception resonated like bass notes in Spril's ears. In a single fluid motion, he whipped his quarterstaff out of its harness and snapped it between her hand and her desk. She froze with her finger and the button separated by little more than the width of the weapon.

"Lower your hand," Spril sternly demanded, "Trip that alarm, and you're gonna have a whole mess of trouble on your head."

She slowly retracted, returning her hand to its armrest. Spril glanced at her purse, noting the abundant key ring clipped to the strap. On a key fob the size of his thumb, he spotted what looked to be the edge of their insignia. He turned her chair to face him and pressed his staff against her clavicle.

Sliding his hand down the weapon as he closed the distance, he crouched and grabbed her purse. She watched in nervous silence as he hung it from his quarterstaff and found the suspected key fob. It bore their mark.

Spril whistled to the others and pitched the keys down the hall. Sinkua caught them and rifled through them, finding the Avatars of Fate key fob. Vielle took it and inclined her head toward the elevator. The three looked back to the lobby.

Spril held each end of a phone cord, stretching the knots and twists out of it. The receptionist trembled, still too alarmed to speak. Spril and Sinkua nodded to each other as Sinkua backed into the elevator, urging Vielle and Eytea to join him.

Inside the car, a small scanner under the keypad emitted a flickering red glow. Vielle swiped the key fob across it, granting them access to the second basement. A split second after that beep echoed up the hollow corridor, an empty hand reached out. Sinkua took back the keys and whipped them back to Spril.

The doors closed, and the car slid down the shaft nearly in silence. All three pairs of eyes moved between each other and the digital display above the door. After a moment, they all shared an almost arrogant laugh.

"Your uncle's a real piece of work," Eytea joked, "I can't believe no one else heard that."

"Yeah, he's really something," Vielle agreed.

"Well, I'm glad you got him to come along," Sinkua added.

"Once he heard who Nikasu is, he dumped his schedule on EshCal," Vielle said, "There's no way he wouldn't come with us."

The elevator opened to a scene familiar to Eytea's and Sinkua's subconsciences, minus the nauseatingly erratic split-second blackouts. Medical and mechanical equipment lined the walls and crowded the floors. Subjects lay borderline comatose on stretchers and gurneys. Intravenous needles anchored them to the machines, while studded leather straps bound them to the beds.

"Let's wait for Spril," Sinkua suggested.

They stepped off and backed into a storage outlet a few meters aside.

The key ring hooked the middle finger of Spril's outstretched hand. Holding the wrapped phone cord with his free hand, he snapped the key fob off with his teeth and dumped the rest of the keys onto the receptionist's purse. He pulled the knot tight, disconnected each component of her computer, and used those cords to bind her wrists to the armrests.

Using a jar of rubber cement from a desk drawer, he stuck her shoes to the floor. He then tightened the laces to keep her from wriggling out of them. As he ripped a sleeve from her blouse, he took pause upon noticing two unopened meal shakes on her desk.

"When is your shift over?" he asked.

"Morning," she meekly answered.

With a roll of tape from a nearby supply cabinet, he secured the two cans to her body, one against each collarbone. Leaving without explanation, he headed to a break room he had noticed in the hall and returned shortly with a pair of straws. Taking something resembling mercy on this blindly compliant crony, he opened the two cans, stuck a straw in each, and leaned the straws against the corners of her mouth.

"There," he concluded, "We can't risk you setting off the alarm, but that's no excuse to make you go hungry."

Careful not to dislodge or block the straws, he gagged her with her torn-off sleeve. After inspecting her bindings to his satisfaction, he locked the front door and headed for the elevator.

"If you behave yourself," he said, flaunting the key fob, "you might get this back when I'm done with it."

The receptionist tried to scream through the fabric. Spril snarled and whipped around.

"What?" he barked, to which she nodded toward her crotch and sank her head in lieu of shrugging, "Your bladder. Your problem."

Ignoring all further muffled pleas, Spril walked to the elevator, quarterstaff held at his side, and rode to the second basement.

"How is she?" Vielle asked, peering around the corner as Spril stepped off the elevator.

"Silenced," Spril concisely answered, "Where do we go from here?"

"If it's like the others," Eytea recalled, "there's a hidden elevator in a corner. From a certain angle, the staircases and catwalks and such form their insignia. The elevator shaft is the center stroke."

"And these people?" he continued, panning the cold room.

"I don't know how involved they are in what goes on below. This looks like it's mostly a holding area."

"We thought the receptionist wasn't involved either," Sinkua reminded, his eye twitching, "Besides, Nikasu and I were both knocked out before they took us downstairs."

Sinkua broke away and wove through the maze of gurneys and machinery, sneering at the memories he stirred up. Spril looked to him with deep concern at his parting comment, having only just learned that he had once been a subject.

"Will you be alright in here?" Spril asked as he caught up, Vielle and Eytea close behind.

"Once we find Nikasu," Sinkua asserted, ripping cords from equipment without breaking his stride, "I'm burning this whole damn place down. Make sure the building doesn't fall on me, and I'll be fine."

"You brought your pills, right?"

"No. They wanted a monster. I'll give them their fucking monster."

A peripheral monitor beeped furiously at each piece of equipment he unplugged. This drew the ireful attention of several technicians, their lines of sight converging on the advancing cause of the ruckus. Subjects groggily awoke in the wake of disruption, propping themselves onto their elbows.

Bringing up the rear, Vielle guided them toward the elevator and implored them to leave the receptionist as they would find her. Spril stayed within arm's reach of Sinkua, while Eytea studied the corners of the room. She kept Sinkua in the corner of her eye, anticipating a volatile reaction to the first act of aggression.

Sinkua locked stares with the foremost technician. As the technician reached for something at his hip, Sinkua reared back and launched a screaming ball of fire. The flames swallowed the man's head and shoulders, wisps of fire trailing down his shirt and coat as he flailed madly. Sinkua barreled forth, forearm braced before him and morningstar drawn back.

Tasting the bitter calcium of human bone for the first time in five years, his morningstar cracked through the searing skull. He whipped it sideways and dispatched an interloper, strands of flesh and sinew rippling from the spikes in the wind of its momentum. With his other hand, he swept forth a spreading wave of fire at approaching assailants.

They closed in faster now. Spril wove through the tumult, snapping away sidearms as they drew them. He cracked windpipes and rammed sterna as he and Sinkua advanced across the room.

Vielle continued unplugging test subjects, confirming that the machines kept them subdued. She tried to believe Sinkua suspected or knew the same, but in his state of mind, she knew he might have only wanted to cause trouble. Nonetheless, they gradually sat up and steadied themselves with moderate success.

Eytea took aggression only as needed, leaving the brunt of the forward fighting to Spril and Sinkua. Her attention split three ways, she continued to check the corners while she watched those two and dispatched whatever assailants came her way. From across the room, a particular alignment caught her full attention. She shot a branching fan of electricity into a cluster of aggressing technicians, buying a moment's focus. They writhed as the searing charge arced and surged through their bodies.

"Hey!" Eytea called over the morbid madness, "I found it!"

Sinkua and Spril dismissively swaggered away from their tussles, their opponents thoroughly disarmed and incapacitated. Vielle pulled herself away from a subject's bedside, pensively watching the crowd as they rose from their beds as though waking from death. They would need to fend for themselves. Her concern waited just beyond the next elevator.

Chapter 13

Galo stood before the ArcNosian Parliament with Chairman LenSom sitting at the center of the oblong table. The garish stench of tanned leather and polished mahogany invaded his nostrils. Such arbitrary displays of power baffled Galo, and he grumbled at the thought of having helped liberate ArcNos into the hands of these elitists by another name.

"Chieftain Sage Galo," LenSom began, "In accordance with the decree of Foreign Affairs Minister Sinkua . . ."

"Where is he?" Galo interrupted.

"Parliament asks that the defendant not speak out of turn," LenSom diverted.

"I'm sure you would," Galo snarked, "Where is Sinkua? I will not speak on these charges until I have spoken with him."

"In accordance with the decree of Foreign Affairs Minister Sinkua, as approved by Prime Minister of Foreign Affairs Phylus," LenSom restarted, "you are hereby placed under the custody of the ArcNosian federal government."

"I know. On what charges?"

"In the weeks leading to the ArcNosian Civil War, you, as Chieftain Sage of Berinin, engaged in multiple acts of aggression against Imperial ArcNos."

"They attacked Berinin!"

"And were subsequently punished accordingly. Your participation in battle implicates Berinin as a militant ally of Parliamentary ArcNos, but you neglected to issue an official declaration of war or militant allegiance," LenSom explained, "Furthermore, your interference in Haprian demonstrated lethal force in the impedance of an international negotiation. Whether Imperial ArcNos was entrapping Haprian or not, you drew first blood as representative of an otherwise uninvolved third party. Thus, all further bloodshed can logically be traced back to you."

"Technically, Sinkua drew first blood," Galo corrected, "Why don't you throw him in the gallows, while you're at it?"

"Sinkua was a citizen of ArcNos at that time. Being a civilian, he could only have been excommunicated pending a trial to be held had Imperial ArcNos proven victorious in the war."

"Where is he?" Galo reiterated, "Once again, I am withholding all further discussions of this matter until I have spoken with Sinkua."

"In that case, you concede to the crimes," LenSom ordered, "You are to be assigned to a holding cell, pending the determination of the length of your sentence, which is to be carried out in a maximum security facility. Foreign Affairs Minister Sinkua will be notified of your arrest and may visit as he sees fit."

Galo lowered his head in shame and disgust. He supposed, the charges sounded legitimate, though he knew less about ArcNosian international law than he would have liked. The splintering state of the union at that time surely compounded matters. He found himself more troubled by who had issued the order than by any possible legislative abuses.

Sinkua had disappeared from the island without notice on the same night they discovered a decommissioned underground Avatar lab. Early analysis had placed its construction within his time there. It all pointed to his notion that they had experimented on him and blotted out the memories. His unannounced departure made sense, but his betrayal

118

was inexplicable.

    Something foul hung within the whole affair.

    Groans of agony and protest resonated inside the elevator as it reached the nethermost bowels of the underground laboratory. Vielle winced, clutching her abdomen. Spril calmly set his hand on her shoulder. Eytea closed her eyes, conjuring memories of the dreams to ready herself for what lay beyond. Sinkua trembled as he struggled to even his breathing, the very sound of the lower reaches agitating unknown memories.

    A blinding flare sparked against Eytea's mind's eye, illuminating silhouettes. She braced herself against the wall, easing down to a crouch as the elevator car came to a stop. It flashed again, holding a split second longer. A swelling of perfectly white light blurred the edges of solid black shadows. Another person occupied the vision, a scraggly man with long unkempt hair. A curious mass of indeterminate form loomed behind him, his shadow moving in and out of it. Perhaps only a product of flickering light, the mass vaguely expanded and contracted, as though breathing.

    "She's communicating with me," Eytea gasped as the elevator opened.

    "What?" Spril asked in disbelief, holding the doors while they stayed in the car.

    Sinkua gazed into the torturous chamber, hypnotized beyond acknowledgment of Eytea's situation. The stench flowed into the elevator car, reminiscent of the lab in Ferya but much stronger her. Macabre images forced their way through his mind's eye. He saw himself break a handle off a gurney and plunge it through an technician's sternum. A muffled and warped voice passively likened it to an event in Ferya.

    "It's like my shared dreams," Eytea specified, closing her eyes again, "Except, I think we're both awake."

    "She knows there are others like her, then," Spril deduced, "She knows you've been in her dreams, and she figured out how to link to you."

    "I don't think she's doing it on purpose," Eytea corrected, straining to hold the connection, "There's someone else with her. A cell mate."

    Spril unwittingly removed his hand from the elevator door as he hunkered down to watch over Eytea. Sinkua clutched his head and collapsed to his knees, a sickly torrent churning in his gut with each flash of forcibly recovered memory. All else drowned into silence as the reality before him warped into a devastating hallucination.

    Subjects transformed into eldritch, tearing apart the fragile bodies of their once-technician slavers. The altered beasts turned on each other and upon themselves as well, experimenting with humanly intolerable torture on their new bodies. That smell had was responsible, that stink of chemicals, blood, tissue, and whatever else these people had used to disrupt evolution. No matter how thoroughly they buried the memories, that overwhelming stench could always draw them to the surface.

    The doors banged against his shoulders. His body jarred with each strike, his hallucination jostling violently. With each stretch and twist, imaginings of perpetual violence bled through the illusions. His pulse grew arrhythmic, and his breathing destabilized, growing hoarse as blood pooled in his throat.

    "Guys," Vielle urged, grabbing Eytea and Spril each by a shoulder, "Sinkua's having problems."

    Eytea opened her eyes, pausing to reacquaint herself with her immediate surroundings. Spril looked beyond Sinkua and out to the laboratory, assessing what he faced that so troubled him. Eytea looked down to see her boyfriend entranced and beaten by a pair of stubborn elevator doors. She spat an expletive and grabbed the doors.

    Sinkua rose to his feet, his torso slumping under the burden of arrhythmic pulse and uneven breath. He staggered out of the elevator, surveying the grounds as he tried to separate hallucination from actuality. Their mutual exclusion hinged on his capacity to believe in the possibility, but they overlapped so deeply that illusion devoured reality.

He charged into the facility with his morningstar ferociously flailing, immersing himself in his hallucination and thus giving it credence. Confusing subjects for creatures and technicians for slavers, he spared the beasts and slaughtered their keepers. His knuckles became raw, his blood mingling with his that of his victims.

Avatar operatives collapsed into heaps of themselves, eruptions of flame scorching their freshly sundered flesh. Within Sinkua's illusion, their bodies contorted into something wickedly inhuman in their final moments, as though the fires melted away a façade to reveal their true selves. In reality, their subjects recoiled in horror, fearing the blazing madman who they briefly thought came to free them.

"Vielle, stay with him," Spril ordered, "Eytea, let's find Nikasu."

"What am I supposed to do?" Vielle panicked, "I can't talk him down! We don't have his medicine! Make Eytea stay here. He's dating her, not me."

"Eytea's the only one who can lead us to your half-sister," Spril countered, "Just pick off the stragglers, and make sure he doesn't get killed."

Eytea clenched her eyes, squinting in her mind's eye in an effort to sharpen the visions. Nikasu faced the exit, an imposing door with no handle and a high window. A marking in the window caught Eytea's attention.

"What was the second symbol out front?" Eytea asked.

"Eta. Why?" Spril answered.

"It's on the window in the door to her room," Eytea relayed.

Eytea and Spril worked their way around the perimeter of the room. Several hallways sprouted from the testing area along the semicircular wall opposite them. The smoke of Sinkua's fires grew intolerably dense as they reached the first corridor.

The walls stretched on as nothing particular. A lone door stood at the end with a ship's wheel lock jutting from its center.

"Which one is that?" Spril asked.

"Fourth symbol from the door. Alpha."

The screams tapered off, replaced by the shrieking and hissing of various melting substances. Within the blinding mask of smoke, the testing area fell into stillness. The deceased no longer collapsed. Those with their shoes and feet melted to the floor slumped across equipment, swathed in flame and fused to their deathbeds. Others became encased in ash and airborne metal and plastic particulate, images of their final agony to be preserved as their bodies decayed within.

Reality collapsed entirely into illusion, becoming nothing as the choking landscape consumed his awareness. Infuriated but without an outlet, Sinkua dropped to his hands and knees. The throbbing in his skull and chest raged on, growing with each pulsation. He coughed violently, blood spraying from this throat.

It had never been this bad, not that he could recall in his last moment of lucidity. This state of mind, these consuming hallucinations, and this prolonged suffering in the aftermath had never felt so pronounced. Coming to this place, it seemed, awoke whatever they intended to create. Fooling him into believing he had tamed it, his disease had only grown stronger in its half-decade of supposed dormancy.

Vielle covered her nose and mouth with the bottom of her shirt, affording herself some protection against the wall of smoke. She navigated the sputtering inferno by the sound of his coughs, forcing herself to ignore to the ruined bodies along the way. In the periphery, she glimpsed a few survivors, test subjects judging by the tubes hanging out of

120

their arms, scrambling out of the bedlam.

She found him face down in a puddle of blood and vomit, his torso still. The fires had begun to shrivel as their source fell unconscious. Arms shaking with fear, both of him and for him, she rolled him onto his back. Sickly crimson fluid spilled from his open mouth as he came up on his side.

Encasing her fists in bark, Vielle pounded Sinkua's sternum. His mouth gaped, ejecting traces of whatever morbid cocktail had rendered in his throat. Getting no further response, she pounded again. His neck pulsed vaguely, rhythmically at that. She pried his mouth open, inhaled to the capacity of her lungs, and pressed her mouth to his, releasing her breath into him. With one more desperate pound on his chest, he gasped for air.

She sat and watched him, idly rambling about what sort of person she thought their half-sister might be. His eyes stayed closed, but as the seconds crawled by, his rib cage swelled and retracted with growing prominence and frequency. Finally, he breathed regularly but continued to sleep on the floor. Vielle huddled over and laid her head on his smoke-stained shoulder

The second door had an unfamiliar symbol, and the third gamma. Spril noted that the search progress more efficiently if Malia had taught them that ancient alphabet. Judging by the names used in the Tournament of Dueler preliminary bouts, Eytea rightly predicted the fourth to be delta. With two dozen halls, however, they feared they could search every hall before they found eta. Sinkua had all but cleared out the testing area, but that didn't necessarily mean they had that kind of time.

Eytea and Spril found another unfamiliar mark in the fifth hall. Looking to the floor, Eytea noticed their once long shadows receding markedly. The warm orange glow of the otherwise drab hall faded. Eyes wide with fear, she whipped about and dashed up the hall. Spril came close behind.

Returning to the testing area, they found Vielle huddled over Sinkua and surrounded by smoldering debris. From their poor vantage point, he didn't appear to be moving.

"Sinkua!" Eytea called out.

"He's okay," Vielle called back, "At least, he will be. Soon. Keep searching."

Eytea froze between the fifth and sixth corridors, staring worriedly into the smoky mausoleum. Sinkua lay among the dead, looking painfully similar to those he had slain. Vielle kept his head propped up to keep any more bloody mucus from running down his throat.

There lay the man to whom Eytea devoted her adult life, and she realized then the depth of the impact of his condition on her psyche. Perhaps, it had been worse than she recalled from the war, back before they were a couple, but only became so apparent as they grew closer. More likely, though, she had grown complacent about it during its repose. In times of peace, he could tame it, but it never died. It only waited, latent and patient.

"Eytea," Spril beckoned, holding her shoulder, "Come on."

At the feeling of Spril's hand, Eytea jolted out of her anxious introspection. She smiled warmly at Vielle as she watched over Sinkua, wishing she could take Vielle's place but knowing she would never let her. Whether Vielle realized it or not, Eytea saw how she often looked to him like a big brother, trusting him in her times of distress and watching over him in his. How suitable that they would share a sibling, and Eytea alone could lead them to each other.

She pried herself away and followed Spril into the sixth hall. Halfway down, they found yet another unfamiliar glyph. Eytea huffed impatiently and turned about sharply.

Finally, in the seventh passageway, they found the eta symbol in the window. Eytea let out a sighing laugh at having found the door so soon, but Spril's doubts suspended her moment of relief.

"Can we really be sure that's the only door with that letter in here?"

"Do you really think there's enough halls down here for the old alphabet to repeat?" Eytea countered, "If there's another Eta door down here, that means the old alphabet had no more than seventeen letters, and I don't think that could work."

"And what's your frame of reference for that? The one alphabet you've ever known?" Spril challenged, "Besides, we don't know if there are deeper subbasements. Try to connect to her and check if you see my quarterstaff through the window."

Her mind and eyes wandering back to the testing area throughout his counterpoint, Eytea nodded in agreement. She hesitantly pulled her attention back to the window. Spril held up his quarterstaff and waved it side to side. Eytea closed her eyes and saw the silhouettes of Nikasu's cell almost immediately.

Eytea saw a waving black bar through Nikasu's eyes as she faced the window. Her mental vision blackened as Nikasu approached the door and stood under the window. The hall abruptly returned to view as Nikasu, as far as Eytea could tell, hoisted herself up by the lock base.

"Eytea! She's..." Spril urged.

Eytea caught a split-second glimpse of a winged silhouette through Nikasu's eyes. She looked back at herself looking back at herself, like some bizarre telepathic mirror. Her vision stretched and telescoped, ending in a blinding flash and a pop. Eytea doubled over and collapsed.

"Son of a bitch," Spril muttered, "Two Hybrids down, and they're supposed to be this great nemesis the Avatars of Fate?"

He called back to Vielle, summoning her to accompany them to Nikasu's cell. Vielle shot back in frustration that Sinkua still lay passed out and had become deadweight. Spril hunkered down in front of Eytea and shook her by the shoulders. Her eyelids fluttered and head wobbled as she tried to focus on half a dozen Srils.

"Ow. Damn. What just happened?" she mumbled.

"She looked out here and saw you while you were still linked," Spril explained, "Your head snapped back, and you collapsed. Are you okay?"

"Um... I think so. I just need to sit down for a minute."

"Alright. I'll go help Vielle bring Sinkua back here so he isn't lying out in the open."

Eytea nodded absently, staring at a stain on the concrete. She pressed a sore spot on the side of her head, tangling her fingers in her hair as she dug to her scalp. To her relief, she hadn't made the stain, but it held her attention almost hypnotically nonetheless.

Spril found Vielle wiping blood from Sinkua's facial hair with her shirt. She smiled down at him, still passed out, both pityingly and admiringly. Spril gave a knowing glance as he hoisted Sinkua and dragged him to the Eta hall. Vielle followed, vigilantly watching Sinkua for any change in his vital signs.

Spril laid Sinkua down by the wall opposite Eytea. Vielle tapped her shoulder. Eytea jolted and snapped her head upright. She took stock of the changes in her surroundings, first noticing Vielle beside her, then Sinkua lying across from her. Seeing the end of a staff in the corner of her eye, she followed it to find Spril had returned as well.

"Oh good," she exhaled, "You're all here."

"Can you stand?" Spril asked.

"Kinda. Maybe. I think."

Palms pressed firmly and fingertips curled against the stucco, Eytea clawed the wall as she pulled herself upright. Her legs still uneasy, she staggered as though inebriated. As long as she kept her hands planted on the wall though, she managed to keep her balance.

At Spril's behest, Vielle stayed by Eytea's side. He lifted Sinkua again, hoisting him onto his back this time. His knees buckled, but once he braced and recomposed himself, he kept stride with Vielle and Eytea.

His head forced downward by the burden, Spril noticed several stains like the one that had entranced Eytea. Blood not being so queer in such a place, Spril only found it curious that these came in such varying shades of red. The drip trails appeared to run in both directions. He initially presumed most of the stains came from Nikasu, but knowing two other products of her lineage, he realized they just as likely came from technicians who tempted her anger.

Spril lifted his head to find himself standing before a ship's wheel lock. With a loud grunt, he rolled Sinkua off his shoulders and sat him on the floor. Sinkua stirred and grumbled. Spril bent backward, popping his back. Eytea managed to stand upright without the wall.

A tap at the window caught all but Sinkua's attention. They looked up to see a hand with long thin fingers drumming on the glass. The index finger traced a series of arcs and circles, alternating clockwise and counter. After a few movements, it paused briefly and repeated the pattern.

"It's the lock combination!" Spril deduced.

Nikasu flashed a thumbs-up and demonstrated the pattern again. Spril copied it precisely as he saw it, assuming she had learned it flipped and thus showed it to him correctly oriented. A deep clank reverberated through the wheel as the locking mechanism retracted the bolt. The great iron door moaned on its hinges as Spril pulled it open.

Sinkua's eyes slowly opened to see Eytea by his side. He looked around, examining his new surroundings. Not particularly pleasant by any definition, but he did notice the renewed quiet of his once forgotten rage.

The moment he stepped off the elevator was the last in his lucid recollection, the rest blurred by the attack, perhaps mercifully so. Now, he woke up in a poorly lit corridor, distinguished only by its bloodstains, before an imposing iron door. From beyond it came the dank stench of mildew and quasi-edible rations. With Eytea's help, Sinkua got to his feet, and they followed Spril and Vielle into the cell.

A muffled scream resounded from deeper within the building as another wave of the traumatized staggered out the door. The cry fell silent as the door fell shut, resuming when more people came stumbling out. Whoever caused such a ruckus, the crowd appeared wholly indifferent, perhaps unaware, of this individual's plight.

Farim was more concerned with them anyway. They appeared to be escaped hostages, freed from bondage with little more than the remains of their wits. Zeroing in on their gaits and ticks, as well as exposed flesh, she conducted flash examinations as they passed. They moved as though unsure of each step, untrusting of every shadow, and unaware of themselves. Track lines adorned most forearms.

"Who did this to you?" she demanded of a passer-by.

They wouldn't answer, perhaps couldn't. None would look her way for more than a split second, barely being comfortable with each other's eyes, much less a stranger's. Anyone could be the enemy, could be one of them. Whoever they were. Her behavior so starkly different, Farim knew the screamer couldn't have been another paranoid wanderer, but that assuaged her worry only slightly.

In a long pause between outpourings, her eyes trailed upward to the stone carving. It looked just as Elemeno had described it, that strange word written in an even stranger text. Her knowledge of dead languages and lost alphabets began and ended at their existence. Farim considered this obscure carving may have been derived from one such ancient script, rather than a stylization of the modern alphabet as Elemeno had theorized.

She looked to the surrounding buildings, grasping for anything from which she might derive an answer. They all had their building number carved in the same place and in the same size. Following the sequence, she realized the carving fit into the pattern without breaking it.

"Ynoa means 3981?" she asked herself aloud.

Farim stepped aside as another group abruptly poured out the door. Hands tremoring violently, the last locked it behind himself. Farim moved down the steps with them, careful to match their pace to keep from upsetting or disrupting them.

She stared up the stone tower from the sidewalk. Judging by the wounded psyches of those leaving, Kabehl's story had obviously been a cover. Elemeno needed to know the depths of his deception, but stuck outside, Farim could only draw from conjecture.

A frail figure cowered behind the iron door, her emaciated arm trembling with her fingers curled around the metallic slab. Spril took hold of the door as the others filed in after him. She looked up at Eytea, her eyes masked by matted bangs, only to hastily lower her head again.

"Sorry," she hoarsely whispered.

"For what?" Eytea asked, kneeling to look up at her hanging face.

"Hurting you. Sorry."

"You're Nikasu, right?" Sinkua asked, his composure restored by the necessity of the moment, "Your mother sent us here to rescue you."

Her head turned in sharp, sudden twitches, studying their lower halves. Vielle tried to peer through the mess of hair to see her face, careful not to touch so psychologically frail a person without invitation.

"Our mother," Vielle reiterated, "She's waiting outside for us."

Nikasu lifted her head to look directly at Vielle, trembling as they made obstructed eye contact through her tangled locks. Vielle grazed the tips of Nikasu's bangs with her fingertip, awaiting permission. Hesitantly, as though the movement physically pained her, Nikasu nodded. Vielle gently brushed aside the shroud of hair and softly gasped at the sight of her face.

"Sinkua," she quietly beckoned, "She has your eyes."

Nikasu twitched her neck to look at Spril's abdomen. Sinkua waved his hand across her line of sight, and she turned to see his instead. She trailed up his torso, pausing on the hedge around his mouth, and stopped on his eyes. The rest of her body still trembling with deep-seated discomfort, the corners of her mouth twitched as though trying to form a smile.

"You," Nikasu weakly greeted, "You look like me. Our eyes."

Nikasu kept eye contact with Sinkua longer than anyone had thought possible moments earlier. Just as Vielle said, they had the same shape and manner of eyes. Nikasu's pupils were a dark rich shade of violet, fading along a steady gradient through her the irises and into pastel lilac hues along the outer edges of her sclerae.

"It's nice to meet you, Nikasu," Sinkua smiled, crouching to eye level, "I'm Sinkua. Your big brother."

Her mouth twitched again, as though fear imprisoned her smile. She darted her eyes between Vielle and Sinkua.

"You two are," she began, pausing to rein in her errant thoughts, "brother and sister?"

"Not quite," Sinkua said, "She has the same mother as you. I have the same father."

Nikasu turned to Eytea, her attention captivated by those wings. She trailed her eyes up her figure, tracing the outline of her wings, and stopped at her face. Unable to bring herself to look at her eyes, she fixated on her hair instead.

"I like your flower," Nikasu said, "A nice man gave me one. He had skin like Father's. But I have not seen him since then. I think Father tried to hurt him."

"CreSam didn't know about this place," Sinkua insisted, "Can you tell us more

124

about this man? The one who brought you a flower?"

"CreSam? I do not know who he is," Nikasu refuted, "Father is The Geneticist. Mother was a liar."

"CreSam was their protégé during the war in ArcNos," a voice from the corner offered, "As was EshCal."

A tall scant figure emerged from the shadows, stout forearms coated in coarse hair over an array of puncture scars and track lines. Facial hair consumed the lower half of his face. His filthy unkempt hair dangled to his shoulders, lashing out in tangled mats. Close behind him came a creature most bizarre.

Its tail scouted forth, manifesting from the shadows as a python looming above this haggard stranger. Its tongue flicked out, tasting the air beyond the darkness. Fluorescent light seeped from the back wall as the creature emerged in its entirety, its body responsible for much of the shadow. With a growl came the head of a lion, and with a grunt, that of a goat. The goat head spoke as the lion head grumbled contentedly.

"Both thought to extort and defy the Avatars of Fate," it said in a smoky feminine voice, "Only EshCal made it out alive."

"What..." Sinkua gasped, pensively approaching the creature, "What are you?"

"I could ask the same of you, young Hybrid," the creature scoffed, "I am a chimera, and my name is Ozzera. And you? Which one are you?"

"Sinkua. This is Vielle. That's Eytea," he introduced, "And that's Spril."

Ozzera stalked past the others and stood over Spril, lowering her lion and goat heads to his eye level. She sniffed both of his cheeks, her snake tail lurching forth to taste his forehead. Spril held still, though he struggled to retain his composure and stoicism.

"You smell odd," Ozzera observed.

"Pardon her," the odd man offered, "She's forgotten the notion of personal space, having been caged for so long."

"It's nothing really," Spril dismissed, absently rubbing Ozzera's scruffy goat cheek as she withdrew from such discomforting proximity.

"Unhand me. I am not some lap pet," her lion head protested as the goat head closed its eyes and snarled blissfully.

"We've yet to be introduced to you, though," Spril continued, "Being in here with her, should we assume you're also a Hybrid?"

"That I am. My name is Yahsek."

"You two are the silhouettes I saw," Eytea observed, "When Nikasu was showing me this room."

"You are the dream walker, correct?" Yahsek asked, "Nikasu told me she often saw a girl with purple wings in her dreams."

"But how could she connect to me when we're both awake? I don't understand," Eytea puzzled, "Nikasu, how did you do that?"

"I... I don't know. I started seeing you in my mind. Then I heard you talking about what I saw," Nikasu explained, "I'm sorry I hurt you."

"You already apologized, but I told you there's no need for it," Eytea reassured, "You helped bring us here. As far as I'm concerned, that makes you a hero. You just helped us save the world."

Nikasu's eyes widened, neck twitching violently. This anxious tick spread throughout her torso and grew into a crippling tremor. She settled on the floor, curling into a ball and rocking on her buttocks.

"What's wrong? What did I say?" Eytea panicked as Sinkua and Vielle dropped to Nikasu's sides.

"Saving the world," Yahsek said, "Just the thought of something so grandiose overwhelms her. She doesn't take well to pressure, so we strive to minimize it while she's in her cell. After all, she suffers quite enough out there."

"Oh, dear. No. No, no," Eytea doubled back, devising an alibi as she knelt before Nikasu, "I didn't say 'save the world.' I said 'save the girl.' Your mother told us you were in danger and asked us to save the girl."

"Right," Sinkua played along, "I'm sure you've done things you didn't understand, not knowing how you did them. Now that you've helped us rescue you, maybe we can help you understand yourself better."

Nikasu gradually stopped trembling, though she continued to rock on the floor. She looked up at Sinkua, almost making eye contact again. That anxious twitch of fearful contentment returned to her pale lips.

"You can help me?" she asked, "But Father will hurt you if you take me away."

"The Geneticist is not your father," Sinkua protested, "No father would do this to his child. CreSam was emotionally abusive, but he was a pup compared to The Geneticist."

"It's more dangerous for all of us if we leave you here," Vielle reasoned, "Besides, we couldn't bear to leave you behind. You're family."

"And not just because you're related to them," Eytea added, "There's only one more of us in the world. We need to stick together."

Ozzera cocked her ears and closed her eyes.

"They are coming," she warned.

"Who?" Spril asked.

"Those above us. They have discovered your infiltration. They are most displeased."

"How well do you know this place?" Spril urged.

"If we beat them to the elevator, we can slip out from under them on the ground floor," Yahsek suggested, "Ozzera will take the stairs."

"I will not fit in the elevator," Ozzera added.

"I still don't understand what you are," Sinkua interjected, helping Nikasu to her feet, "What is a chimera?"

"What is a Hybrid?" Ozzera countered, "I suppose it would not do to describe what you see, would it?"

"No, it wouldn't," Sinkua insisted, puzzling over her question behind stern eyes, "Did The Geneticist breed you?"

"Find the man who brought Nikasu a flower like Eytea's," Ozzera insisted, "He can tell you what you wish to know."

"First, we need to leave this place," Yahsek urged.

His tattered pants rustled as his leg muscles bulged, the mass of his calves shifting into his thighs. Ghastly pale flesh darkened while long matted hair retracted and thickened. His bare callused feet hardened and atrophied, blackening as they shaped into hooves.

Yahsek snatched Nikasu by the wrist, his sudden contact going unresisted. She clutched his shoulder as he pulled her to his side, and she climbed onto his back. With the others still trying to comprehend what he had done, Yahsek burst into a bipedal gallop. Hunched nearly to running on all fours, he rushed up the hall and through the testing area.

Spril presented the stolen key fob, tilting his head up the Eta hall. Ozzera lowered her mammalian heads, inviting him onto her back. She gripped his quarterstaff behind her teeth like reins, and he held onto its exposed ends. With Spril securely mounted, Ozzera roared out of the cell, cracking the doorframe and knocking it loose from the foundation.

Yahsek's legs returned to their human form as they arrived at the elevator. Nikasu slid off his back and hit the button. A mechanical hum assured them of the car's approach. Their chances of a bloodless escape looked favorable.

Sinkua, Eytea, and Vielle followed from a safe distance as Ozzera barreled up the hall, ramming the walls out of both fury and spatial necessity. They trailed her through the testing area, Sinkua smirking with vicious satisfaction as she left a wake of demolition.

Spril pulled his quarterstaff from Ozzera's mouth and drew up into a crouch. Ozzera veered toward a corner awash in shadows. Spril leapt from her back, propelled by her shifting momentum, and landed in front of the open elevator. The thunder of combat boots on reinforced concrete reverberated in the car as he dropped into a kneeling crouch.

Navigating the fresh wreckage, the others reached his side as Spril erected himself. He called his gratitude to Ozzera as she searched the darkness for the stairwell. The five of them safely inside the car, he swiped the key fob and pounded the lobby button.

"So, you can change parts of your body to mimic other animals?" Sinkua confirmed as the doors closed, "Is that your power or your anomaly?"

"Both," Yahsek answered, "What about you? I know you caused those fires, but what's special about your eyes?"

"I can clearly see through smoke and fog. That sort of thing."

"Sounds useful."

"What about you, Nikasu?" Vielle encouraged, "What do your eyes do that's special?"

"Yeah, and what's your Hybrid power?" Eytea egged on, "It's safe to talk about it now. You're in good company."

"Hey, I hate to ruin a good reunion or whatever this is," Spril interrupted, furrowing his brow at the screen above the doors, "but we just passed the second floor."

"Are you certain?" Yahsek asked, fear tinging his voice.

"Why would I lie about that?" Spril snarked, pounding the emergency stop button, "How is this happening?"

"Emergency protocol. Elevator function override," Nikasu muddled, more parroting than explaining, "Access the operational command database. Delete destination. Override local commands via remote access henceforth."

"What did you just say?" Sinkua asked, "Why are you talking like that?"

"Someone hijacked the elevator," Yahsek clarified, "They know you are here. They wish to speak with you."

Chapter 14

EshCal shuffled a pile of paperwork, much of it frayed around the edges from mistreatment, into a more manageable stack. She shook her head in disdain, more at the situation she created than at the mess she inherited. The task of acclimating to Spril's workspace alone had proven nigh overwhelming. This came on top of the pile of work he left for her, much of it passed from her desk during her earlier absence with The Coalition.

A scrap note fell from a stack of documents. She dropped the stack on her lap, reverting it to disarray, and bent down to grab the note off the floor. It beared a simple message scrawled in black marker. EshCal puzzled over the message for what could have been several seconds or several minutes, finally pinching the communication implant embedded in her earlobe.

"Agent?" a voice buzzed in.

"Sir. Does the term Lab 1341 mean anything to you?"

A long awkward pause ensued. EshCal shifted uneasily.

"Sir?"

"It does."

"Anything I should be aware of?"

"It is one of theirs. Northwest of your position. Highrise district."

"Directive?"

"Pending. How did you learn of this?"

"It was on Spril's desk. I'm covering for him while he's away."

"I see. Perhaps, they considered they might find their parcel there. Where did they go?"

"Lenguardia. What parcel?"

"Agents have been dispatched for backup."

"Wonderful. What parcel?"

The line went silent. Frustrated, EshCal pinched her earlobe and ended the call. Either she had not yet earned access to this knowledge, or its sensitivity barred it from remote discussion. Striving to put the unanswerable from her mind, she returned to her work, all the while consumed by what that note might portend.

Sinkua furiously jabbed the lobby button as the elevator ascended into double digits. Yahsek sighed and shook his head at this display of futility. His patience depleted, he grabbed Sinkua's wrist.

"That will do nothing," Yahsek insisted.

"You don't know that," Sinkua argued, "Maybe we'll go back down when we stop."

"Remote override procedures in effect," Nikasu parroted, "All internal directives ignored. Commands from current remote access station granted autonomy."

"It'll only listen to the computer they used to hijack us," Yahsek simplified, "No matter how much you punch that button, it won't do anything while they're overriding it."

"What about physically stopping it?" Eytea suggested, trying to see past the lighting panel in the ceiling.

"Our combined strength is insufficient," Nikasu insisted, "Sinkua must generate a

128

temperature of one thousand one hundred thirty degrees centigrade to melt the mounting assembly. Such a feat is highly improbable and would cause us to plummet. My assistance would be insufficient."

"Why does she keep talking like that?" Sinkua asked Yahsek, failing in his efforts to refrain from shouting.

"It's the sort of dialect she's been exposed to her entire life," Yahsek reasoned, "She cut her conversational teeth on a mix of hatred and jargon."

Eytea stepped on Spril's interlocked hands, and he hoisted her to the ceiling. She pushed the light panel aside and smashed the bulb with her halberd, finding a locked access panel in the ceiling of the light housing.

The elevator crept toward the topmost floor as Eytea hung from the ceiling, stabbing through the access panel. Sinkua held her legs, granting her more leverage. Four floors shy of the top, she punctured the roof, the spearhead jutting into the elevator shaft.

"The drive mechanism is in the ceiling, right?" Eytea asked.

"They are in ArcNos," Spril confirmed.

"Good enough."

Eytea's body jerked downward, taking Sinkua with her, as a brilliant arc of lightning exploded from the head of her weapon. The blast reverberated throughout the last meters of the shaft, rattling the car against the tracks. With the control gears fried, the drive mechanism howled and clunked to a reluctant yet inevitable halt. It whirred in futility, straining to carry out its override directives.

"Did that actually work?" Yahsek asked pensively.

"Feels like it," Sinkua confirmed, "One floor short of the top."

"Are you kids always this reckless?"

"Only when we have to be," Vielle joked, laughing nervously.

"Okay... Well, if Sinkua and I can pry the doors open, we can ..."

The car jostled abruptly, dropping the conversation into an anxious silence. It shook again, Nikasu collapsing into a trembling ball as the car groaned against the frame.

"Sinkua! Yahsek!" Spril bellowed, "On the door!"

Yahsek's arms elongated, hair thickening and becoming reddish orange. His hands blackened, taking on a leathery texture. He jammed his fingertips into the slot between the doors. Sinkua followed suit, save for the brachial transformation.

"Nikasu," Spril continued, kneeling beside her, "You said your help by itself wouldn't be enough, right?"

Chin quivering, Nikasu nodded vigorously.

"It's okay. No need to cry. Anything you can do to help, we need you to do it," he implored, "We're gonna work together. We just need you to try."

"That's right, sis," Vielle added, "We're in this together. Whatever you can't do on your own, someone will help."

"That's how we survive. How we take ground against them," Sinkua added through gritted teeth while Eytea jammed her halberd between the doors, "Anything you can do will help."

The groaning steadily amplified, crescendoing into a thunderous crack that echoed throughout the car. Sinkua, Yahsek, and Eytea pulled at the door, their efforts thus far producing little more than a sliver of light. The car howled and, with a cacophonous snap, propelled into its surely fatal plummet. Nikasu shrieked at the sound, clapping her hands over her ears.

"This is it, Nikasu!" Sinkua snarled, straining on the door, "Show us what you've got!"

Nikasu panted erratically, her heart slamming against her rib cage as though trying to escape from her chest cavity.

"Everyone here believes in you," Vielle added, "Help us save each other."

The doors parted by a few centimeters, enough to pick out flashes of detail as rooms screamed upward. Sinkua, Yahsek, and Eytea groaned as they struggled to break through the locking mechanisms.

"Come on, Nikasu," Sinkua growled to his shaky half-sister, "Everybody out there wants you to fail. They expect you and all of us to die here!"

"Sinkua, what are you…?" Yahsek cut in.

"They've convinced you that you're incompetent. The only thing holding you back is the bullshit they fed you," Sinkua asserted.

"Listen to your brother," Vielle softened, "They lied to you. You're stronger than you believe."

"Now show these human-trafficking motherfuckers how you piss in the face of death!" Sinkua roared, "Show them what they feared!"

Nikasu's tremors stopped. She lifted her head and looked to the display above the door. They had dropped halfway to the bottom. Her violet eyes shimmered brilliantly, and she planted her hands against the floor. The pitch of the squealing deepened, dropping a full octave over the next five floors.

"What in the…" Eytea gasped, "Is she stopping the elevator?"

"Slowing it down," Yahsek specified as they forced the doors further apart, "Isolated gravity manipulation. She's going to soften our landing."

"It will be insufficient," Nikasu insisted, "Serious injuries still probable. I am sorry to all of you."

"Don't apologize! Just prove them wrong!" Sinkua commanded, "Eytea, aim your halberd at the back wall."

As Eytea complied Sinkua nodded to Spril to grab Yahsek's arm, and for Vielle take hold of Eytea's arm. Eytea braced her halberd along the same arm and hooked her other around Sinkua's elbow. With their other hands, Spril and Vielle held Nikasu under her arms. Everyone's bodies lightened upon contact.

Nikasu's body quaked with her continuous swelling of psychologically suppressed milystis. With resonating bellows from deep within the throats of Sinkua and Yahsek, the locking mechanisms snapped, and the doors spread wide. The car plummeted past the fourth floor.

"Eytea, blast it!" Sinkua shouted.

Knuckles paled as Eytea fired a concentrated surge of milystic lightning against the back of the car. The condensed impact of the lightning ball recoiled and launched her backward. Sinkua and Vielle slid back with her, dragging Nikasu along, who completed the chain to Spril and Yahsek. Between the strength of Eytea's blast and Nikasu's depletion of gravity, all six of them barreled through the open doors on the ground floor. Its acceleration restored, the car jerked downward and crashed violently into the bottom of the elevator shaft.

Their bodies pounded the tiles, joints cracking and popping. They tumbled freely as the chain broke, each halting by their own means. Nikasu landed sprawled across Eytea, who winced in pain, unable to move her arms without excruciating pain. Nikasu muscled her way up to her hands and knees and, body wobbling from the strain, puked violently.

"I like your flower," she chirped before collapsing face down in a puddle of blood-laced vomit.

Sinkua dragged himself across the floor, scrambling to roll her over.

"How is everyone?" Spril asked.

"I think I dislocated my shoulders," Eytea winced.

"Just a few cracked ribs here," Yahsek added, eyes clenched.

"Pretty sure I threw out my back," Sinkua groaned, lying by Nikasu's side.

"My head is loud," Nikasu muddled, "And I vomited blood. I need water."

"I think I broke my nose," Vielle whimpered, her bloody hand cupped over her nose.

"Well, at least all of you yet live," a familiar voice announced.

Yahsek opened his eyes to see Ozzera rounding the corner into the elevator hub. Her lion head snarled in greeting as she approached.

"I heard the elevator come loose," Ozzera said, "but I did not arrive down here soon enough to stop it."

"Down here?" Spril asked.

"Yes. When I heard the elevator pass this level, I realized they had initiated override procedures," Ozzera explained, Spril's eyes steely with skepticism, "I tried to get ahead of you and stop it."

"But we stopped it first," Nikasu added.

"Indeed," Ozzera agreed, her goat head nodding, "I know not how you managed, but when I heard it drop, I hurried back down here to stop the elevator before it crashed."

"Thank you for coming for us," Yahsek professed as he sat up, "Are they pursuing us?"

"You and I are obligated to one other, dear Yahsek," Ozzera reminded, "They are scrambling, but if we hurry, we can slip out before they find us."

Ozzera galloped up the hall toward the lobby, her snake tail beckoning them to follow. Spril rolled Eytea upright and hoisted her onto her feet. Clutching the side of his chest, YahSek offered Vielle his free hand. She accepted it with her less bloody one, keeping the other cupped over her nose. Still stricken by a touch of delirium, Nikasu laid her hand on Sinkua's chest. His body steadily lightened, feeling almost as though he might not fall if he jumped with enough momentum. In spite of his thrown back, he sat up somewhat easily. Nikasu's lips twitched pensively.

"Thanks for yelling all those nice things at me," she smiled.

"Thanks for…," Sinkua returned, "…well, whatever you did in there. You're a big part of why we're all alive."

"Come on. Let's catch up."

Nikasu and Sinkua got to their feet with their arms around each other's shoulders. As long as they stayed in contact, he could ignore his injured back. Better still, he could pull her along on longer strides than he otherwise could. Nikasu scrambled to keep up, knowing how abruptly he would normalize if they lost contact. Vielle smiled as they approached, masking traces of jealousy.

All but Ozzera emerged into the lobby as they reunited. Spril stopped by the receptionist, who pleaded with her eyes, and ordered the others to wait.

"I'm done with this," he announced, showing the key fob, "First, I need you to answer one question. Did you tip them off?"

She shook her head in denial, and he firmly backhanded her.

"I already caught you trying to screw us once. Now. I'm going to ask again. Did you tip them off?"

"They probably saw all those…" Sinkua offered, surveying erratic trails of bloody footprints from down the hall.

A shower of glass and wood cut him off, spewing inward from the front door. Sinkua turned with a start, alarmed by the explosion but more perturbed at the interruption.

"Ah good. You kids are safe," NalSet greeted as he reached through the gaping hole and unlocked the door, "These spider mines are a real bastard to assemble, you know. Gotta make 'em by hand, one at a time."

"NalSet? How did you know we were here?" Vielle puzzled.

"Malia reported that she had escorted you folks here to rescue this young lady.

Mortvill dispatched me to serve as backup," he explained, "By the by, she's waiting at your boat."

"I happened to be in the area for other reasons," Farim announced as she entered behind him, shaking out her hair and wringing melting snow out of her wool hat, "I got a lead on this place from Elemeno. She was right to be suspicious."

"What do you mean?" Eytea asked.

"She came here several years ago to check out Kabehl's line about the excavation project, what he said the tattoo on his arm meant. She told me about the engraving over the door," Farim said, "I don't suppose any of you figured out what ynoa means, did you?"

"That's the building number and the facility's code designation," NalSet answered, "It's 3891 written in one of the ancient scripts."

"Is it the same script that the genome map was written in?" Farim gasped.

"Yeah, but don't get your hopes up. I can't read it. Just know the numbers and the names of the letters."

"Then, you're not one of the three Malia told us about," Vielle deduced, "She said she knows three people who can read that language."

"Mortvill and the Harvester are both fluent. So's The Prophet, I think," NalSet recalled, "Mortvill will send help with translating the map soon enough."

"Actually, make that four people who can read the forgotten languages," Ozzera boasted, lowering her heads as she trotted into the lobby, "As much as you might wish to call me people."

"What the shit is that?" Farim recoiled, the others nonchalant.

"My name is Ozzera, and I'm a chimera," Ozzera huffed, "I much prefer to be called a who than a what."

"Sorry, I... just, um... You caught me off guard," Farim retracted, "And with how things have been going lately, that's really saying something."

"Look, can we just get out of here so I can torch the place, and we can all go home?" Sinkua cut in, "We're gonna lose enough time just getting Ozzera to the coast without causing a panic."

"I shall find my own way," Ozzera insisted.

"Hold off on the pyromania," NalSet urged, "I need to bring in some agents to scout and loot the place first."

"Come back to ArcNos with us, and you can loot Lab 1341."

"What do you know about 1341?"

"Biroe figured Nikasu might be there, after he cracked The Geneticist's algorithm," Sinkua said, NalSet's eyebrows flying up his forehead at that last remark, "Spril's gonna have some troops look into it when we get home."

"We're still awaiting Mortvill's directives on 1341, but I guess you can go ahead and torch this one then."

In a show of something vaguely resembling mercy, Spril untied the receptionist's shoes and loosened her bindings. She scrambled to free herself as the others filed out, but she froze in her seat with white knuckles, wide eyes, and a deep swallow as Ozzera destroyed the doorframe around her hulking mass. In all her time there, she never imagined such a beast had been held captive in the basement, much less that it could exist at all.

"Are you coming or not?" Spril asked, "Hurry up before I change my mind about you."

She snapped out of her trance and launched from her seat, a half-empty can spilling down her shirt, and she rushed out the door. Spril offered her key fob as she came to his side.

"My friend was about to make a case for your innocence, but he's busy now."

Sinkua closed his eyes and inhaled deeply. His ruby emitted a pulsating glow, growing stronger as he pushed the limits of his lung capacity. The glowing swelled to encompass his shoulders, and he raised his hands into the swirling mass of crimson milystis.

"I think he was going to say they saw everyone leaving out here," Eytea suggested, her eyes following intoxicated trails of bloody footprints up the sidewalk, "That must have tipped them off."

Sinkua's body quaked as he lowered his hands, drawing from the milystic orb and splitting it in two. His hands trembled as though their very molecules might resonate into decoherence. Yahsek held Nikasu back.

"Sounds reasonable enough," Spril agreed, "But how would they know we used her key fob?"

The chaotic surges slowly took on coherence, shaping into nearly spherical whorls. Flames flickered on their surfaces as Sinkua struggled to maintain their raw form. Everyone took a few steps back.

"I've never been scheduled to go down there myself," the receptionist defended, "And nobody was coming in with an appointment, either. Walk-ins have to be cleared with management."

"Fair enough," Spril nodded, offering her key fob.

"You know what? Keep it. Maybe it'll help you at their other place," the receptionist insisted, "I am so done with these weirdos. No way I'm sticking around after this."

Sinkua whipped the torrential masses of nigh pure pyromantic milystis into the towering laboratory. They left trails of flames hanging in the air as they roared into the face of the building, scattering streetlamp shadows under the midnight sky. Sinkua raised his arms as the roaring whorls exploded in spectacular blasts, guiding the destruction upward.

Milystis shredded through the ceiling, converting to flames as it ascended the tower. Windows exploded under the intense heat. Floors buckled, cracked, and collapsed into the levels beneath. Desperate and capitulant operatives threw themselves through emptied window frames. Sinkua watched stoically as the first broke against the concrete, his seared flesh splintered by his shattered bones.

"Come on," Sinkua said, "We're done here."

KalChi sat before a heap of paperwork, which lay piled up beside a monitor displaying several open documents and spreadsheets. They all pertained to IlcBei and JalRov. Some explored IlcBei's ownership of the Subtransit as well as a low-income apartment community. Others spoke of how JalRov used his investment income for comparably altruistic means.

This indicated a trend, and to KalChi, that meant someone had targeted the investors rather than the companies. She buzzed Biroe on her intercom.

"Yes, KalChi?" he calmly answered.

"Prime Minister of Treasury Biroe?" she politely teased.

"You know you don't need to be formal. What did you find?"

"Wow, that confident in me, huh? I found a link between JalRov and IlcBei."

"Really? Whatcha got?" Biroe beckoned.

"JalRov owns a staffing company," KalChi said, "but what's interesting is that he reports no personal income from it."

"How do their agency fees look?"

"Market norm. Companies get charged a pretty middle-of-the-road premium on top of wages, but until recently, JalRov didn't take any commission for himself. Instead, he used it to provide ninety-percent coverage health insurance for every one of his employees from their first completed pay cycle. Fully company funded."

"Damn!" Biroe blurted, "There's enough for him to do that?"

"There was. In light of recent events though, he had to cut back to fifty-percent coverage," KalChi continued, "He used his equity payouts for personal income and in some scant months to cover what the agency fees couldn't."

"Both he and IlcBei have amassed great wealth and used it to help the disenfranchised. Someone doesn't appreciate the lower class getting assistance from the upper class."

"What do you think? Are we looking for someone who thinks the poor are getting undeserved entitlements?"

"That's one of several possibilities. We could also be looking for other successful investors who want to keep their wealth without being made to look miserly," Biroe theorized, "A certain caste of our wealthier citizens believe minimizing philanthropy validates their wealth to the less fortunate."

"But you have something else in mind," KalChi gleaned from his dismissive tone.

"Cross-reference every transaction with banks operating out of Tanelen."

"Sir, do you really think...?"

"I do. This reeks of their work."

Yahsek awoke on the main deck, breathing deeply as he basked in the salty sunrise. Being cramped in prison cells for so long had rendered him a mite claustrophobic. Not even the cold spitting mist discouraged him out of the open. The planks beneath his lounge chair creaked with heavy footsteps.

"Come to see the sunrise?" he asked, gazing off toward the orange horizon.

"I have missed it so," Ozzera professed, "I wish to have a word with you."

"We both know what our release portends."

"How did you escape the elevator?"

"Sinkua and I pried open the doors. Nikasu slowed it down. We all linked arms, and Eytea launched us out," Yahsek recounted, scrutinizing the events as he heard them aloud.

"She truly slowed its fall? She did not simply lessen its acceleration?"

Yahsek turned from the sunrise to lock eyes with Ozzera's goat head. It hadn't occurred to him at the time, but Nikasu had exceeded what they knew to be the limits of her powers. Impossible.

"She did. I'm sure of it," Yahsek asserted, "Even though..."

"We believed she was capable only of fractional reduction," Ozzera said, "What she did requires a full reversal. Negative gravity."

"That might account for the vomiting."

"I would imagine so, yes."

"Hopefully that was only excess in the face of desperation," Yahsek sighed, "She has a destiny to fulfill. We can't risk her overexerting herself in the meantime."

"Indeed."

Malia sat at the foot of Nikasu's bed, watching her sleep through the sunrise. She had awoken in the wee hours of morning, hardly able to sleep more than a handful of hours. The rush overwhelmed her, first discovering a daughter she never knew and now a reunion with the daughter she had lost.

She set her hand on Nikasu's leg. The frail teenager slept so peacefully, that military surplus cot clearly the most comfortable place she had slept in years, perhaps in her entire life. Malia snickered at the memory of how Nikasu sank into the mattress, her tension diffusing, and fell asleep within seconds. On some level, she could scarcely believe she ever let her go, shame bubbling up for having let it happen. On another, she knew they would never have been safe together.

Now she had an entourage of Hybrids, activists, and revolutionaries.

"Mother?" Nikasu asked, stirring as sunlight bathed her face, "How did you get in my cell?"

"Wake up first, dear," Malia smiled, "Then talk. You're on a boat to ArcNos. You're with friends."

Nikasu sat up, shrewdly examining the cabin. It did seem strange that her cell felt like it was moving. They no longer tested those sort of drugs on her, and they would never allow her to wake in transit. Memories of the previous night shifted into a coherent arrangement. The corners of her lips twitched.

"I remember. My brother and sister came for me," she smiled, managing brief eye contact, "Father said you were a liar, but they said you brought them to save me."

"Sweetie, we lost your father in the ArcNosian Civil War."

"Father is The Geneticist!" Nikasu blurted, her temples glistening with new sweat, "Father is alive, and he's going to come for us!"

"No. No, no. Please, calm down," Malia said, "Nobody is going to come for you. That man wasn't your father. Didn't Sinkua tell you?"

"I… I don't know what to believe," Nikasu fretted, clutching her tangled hair, "What if they're all lying to me? What if they're using me, too?"

"That won't happen," Malia promised, tipping Nikasu's chin up to hold eye contact, "These are good people. They take care of each other. They need you just as much as you need them, and they know that. Understand?"

Nikasu timidly nodded. She couldn't imagine being part of such symbiosis, the very concept being entirely foreign to her. The lab techs disregarded her as an expendable commodity, despite her being integral to their operations. Instead, they indoctrinated her to believe she needed them to live, that the outside world was inhospitable.

"What happened to you?" Nikasu boldly asked, "After they took me, what happened?"

"I worked for them until earlier this year," Malia said, contrition heavy in her voice.

"You worked for my captors?"

"Yeah," Vielle chimed in, leaning against the doorframe with her arms folded, "What's the reasoning there?"

"I do owe both of you an explanation," Malia sighed, "But I also owe one to Phylus. Would be easiest for all of us if I address the three of you at once."

"Fair enough," Vielle muttered.

"At least tell me why you worked for them," Nikasu beckoned, "Please?"

"It was so I could keep you safe. At least, that's what I told myself. Really, I was just letting them keep me on a leash. I turned you over because otherwise they would have hunted both of us. I thought temporary captivity would be better than running for the rest of our probably-short lives," Malia explained, "I spent my time with them sabotaging them, usually subtly, but when I got too ambitious, they figured me out and cut me off. I knew you would be in danger, so I went looking for Sinkua."

"My brother. CreSam's son."

Malia nodded, her mind rushing backward through the years leading to the war.

"And she found me. Your sister," Vielle added, "Come on, let's go see who else is awake."

"Malia?" a gruff voice called from behind Vielle.

"NalSet," Malia nodded, "Good morning."

"I need to speak with you alone."

Eytea sat up in bed with the blanket draped over her legs and her back against the wall. She looked down at Sinkua, still asleep and clearly spent from last night's episode, and smiled warmly at him. For several minutes, she sat in silence, enjoying their solitude on the calmly rolling sea.

Her mind drifted to Galo, wondering how his work on their new province had been progressing. Unearthing those ruins must have warranted an interruption, perhaps a complete overhaul of their operations. Such thoughts had hardly crossed her mind before. Sinkua's act of retribution freed her mind to contemplate other impacts of their experiments.

A small wind from the partially ajar window fluttered her rose. She pulled it from her hair, smiling at how accustomed to it she had become. Just like the ones he used to send, it thrived long beyond its harvest. Having kept it in a vase helped, but an ordinary flower would have wilted long ago, especially on this trip. She pondered how it could have survived, noting to ask Galo about it.

She found it curious that Nikasu had received one as well, especially that someone had delivered it to her while she was in captivity. It sounded like someone had given them to girls in distress, perhaps female Hybrids and their families, except that Vielle never received one, as far as Eytea knew. It served no measurable function, but she and her mother had always welcomed that occasional splotch of brightness. With that thought, an epiphany shot across her mind.

"Sinkua," she beckoned, shaking him by the shoulder, "Wake up."

"Hrmph. What?" Sinkua stirred.

"I remember his name!"

"I remember lots of names. What's your point?"

"The guy who used to send us those flowers."

"Yeah? Anyone we know?"

"No, but it's been bugging me, and now I remember," Eytea remarked, "It was Aleepo."

"Aleepo? Strange name. Where's he from?" Sinkua muttered.

"Ferya, I guess. I never met him, so I don't know if he was a native or what."

A knock on the door stirred the old man under disinfected linens. He cringed as he opened his eyes and shut them again. Reaching through his disorientation, an outside voice endeavored to clarify.

"Professor Uulan?" a young man beckoned, "I have the information you requested."

"Office visiting hours ended an hour ago," Uulan grumbled, "Come back tomorrow."

The door creaked as the man crept in, careful not to startle the elderly patient. His answer may have been the product of fatigue or an interrupted REM cycle, but the young man couldn't rule out dementia.

"Uulan?" he asked, "You're not at the university. You're at Hillside Oncology."

Uulan opened his eyes, scowling at the brightness of the room, particularly the emphasized whiteness of his bed sheets. He scanned the room, reacclimating himself. Looking to the nurse, he grumbled incoherently.

"Remember sir? Your cancer treatment?"

"Of course I remember!" Uulan growled, "You kids pumped me full of isotopes and stuck me in here to waste away. I had students your age, and they had the common decency not to irradiate their elders."

"I'm sure you were a wonderful teacher," the nurse tactfully excused, "I found that information you asked me for this morning."

"Well? What took you so long?" Uulan snapped, trying to recall what he had asked for.

"Terribly sorry, sir. I've had people trying to die on me all day," he spat, dropping the paper on Uulan's lap, "Quite rude of them, actually."

Uulan snatched the paper as the nurse left, shiftily watching the young man until he shut the door. Returning his attention to the paper, he quickly remembered what he had requested. As much as he would have loved to be done with those people, he still had one final responsibility.

He reached for the phone and lingered over the keypad for several minutes. They hadn't spoken in years, decades perhaps. Even when her daughter passed, he failed to reach out to her. He couldn't imagine how she might take to someone who had become a stranger evoking such painful memories.

With shaky fingers, he brought himself to dial. An elderly woman answered shortly, her voice vaguely familiar in its tenuous resemblance of the one he remembered.

"Am I speaking to Mrs. XalRut?" Uulan asked.

"This is she. Who's calling?"

"This is Uulan. You and I were on the faculty at Quarunite University Southwest."

"Oh yes, the name is familiar. History department, correct?"

"That's right. You were in neurology, I believe?"

"Neuropsychiatry, but I suppose that's close enough after all this time. Tell me, how have you been?"

"I've seen better times, but I'm afraid I didn't call to reminisce," Uulan apologized, "Your daughter was one of my students."

"I remember," XalRut sighed, "You were BeiLou's favorite professor."

"And she my favorite student. She had such potential," he reminisced, despite his insistence otherwise, "Did she tell you about the graduation present I gave her?"

"No, I'm afraid not. I suppose you're aware of her passing. Otherwise, you would have asked how to reach her."

"I am, and I apologize for not contacting you when it happened."

"You have your own life, Uulan. No need to fret yourself with such guilt."

"Thank you, XalRut," he humbly accepted, "Now then, I entrusted BeiLou with a collection of tomes from Ouristihran antiquity. The spines were cracked, and the pages were melded together. Several museums were in a bidding war over them, but they would just put them on display as they were. That wasn't what I wanted. I wanted them opened. I wanted to share that forgotten era with the world. Showing off some timeworn covers would never do."

"There are companies that specialize in restoring historical artifacts."

"Yes, but I didn't want them subjected to corporate interests. Whatever record of antiquity is in those books, it needs to be shown exactly as it is. Not through the eyes of the highest bidder," Uulan insisted, "Besides, when BeiLou graduated, I hadn't made tenure, so I didn't have a lot of money to invest. But I knew her curiosity and competence would serve my purposes. I knew if any of my students had the acumen to pull it off, it was BeiLou."

"I'm honored you would say that," XalRut sighed, choking back tears, "Did she... Did she pull it off? Did she open them?"

"Not as far as I know. I heard from her on occasion, but her last letter was when her son was very young. She hadn't succeeded, but time to work on it had become scarcer each day since her pregnancy."

"I'm sure you understand how hectic that time can be," XalRut insisted, "You have children, don't you?"

"Had, actually," Uulan corrected, his voice thick with remorse, "But let's not discuss that, please. I just want to know what became of those books."

"She never wrote a will. All of her possessions were left to her next of kin. As I understand it, that would mean Sinkua inherited them, seeing as he and MeiLom are one in the same."

"This is the first I've heard about that. I worked with Sinkua as a member of the Subtransit Resistance. But he left with hardly more than a suitcase. He couldn't have taken the books."

"In that case, I suppose they're still in the old house. I hear it's under federal protection," she suggested, "May I ask why you've waited until now to ask after them?"

"I assumed you had inherited them after CreSam died, what with MeiLom having been declared dead," he reasoned, "That was all well and good for the time, but only recently have they come to be of interest to me again."

"I see. And what brought them back to your attention?"

"I believe they've come to be of interest to someone else," Uulan reported, "I need to keep them out of the wrong hands."

Chapter 15

Phylus took a long drag off his cigarette as he reread his summons. The charges were unfamiliar, undoubtedly falsified. He knew he would have no trouble disproving them, but their origins baffled him. Furthermore, he couldn't perceive of Sinkua committing such an atrocity.

Still, the charges had been laid out, and regardless of who had issued the order, his leadership and sense of diplomacy had thus come under scrutiny. The veracity of the accusations aside, he and a fellow Subtransit Resistance operative had come under attack. Considering other events that had recently come to his attention, this appeared to be another of their gambits.

He drained the last bit of life from his cigarette, hoping to level his thoughts before he braved the courtroom. Grunting disdainfully, he stuffed the summons in his coat pocket and flicked the dying cigarette butt on the concrete. He crushed it under his boot as he turned and headed into the courthouse.

"Chief Negotiator Phylus," LenSom welcomed, "So glad you could make it to your hearing. Most people wouldn't have that kind of resolve."

"LenSom. Parliament," Phylus nodded, making note of the incorrect title, "You know perfectly well my philosophy on running away."

"Of course," LenSom wryly smirked, "Are you familiar with the charges being leveled against you?"

"Yes, I'm familiar with the concept of diplomatic endangerment," Phylus answered, scanning the spread of Representatives, "You're accusing me and one of my employees of damaging relations with an ally and acting with disregard to diplomatic immunity. However..."

"That would be the sum of it. What is your defense of these allegations?"

"As I was saying..." Phylus continued, pausing to let his words linger emphatically, "However, I am not familiar with the charges leveled against Chieftain Sage Galo. I have no record of these allegations nor of Foreign Affairs Minister Sinkua issuing a warrant for his arrest."

"According to our transcript of your intra-departmental communications, you were made aware of the charges and approved them," LenSom insisted, "Your signature is on the warrant."

"I have no recollection of this. Do you have carbon copies?" Phylus asked.

"Of course, we do. Should your mental acuity be brought under scrutiny as well, if you would forget authorizing the incarceration of our top foreign ally from the ArcNosian Civil War?" LenSom goaded, "Or perhaps, you crave the relevance you gain from conflict?"

"I refuse to stand here and be insulted," Phylus spat, "You want to throw accusations? What about your efforts to absolve once Brigadier General Elite CreSam and the Avatars of Fate of any responsibility for the floundering state of our economy?"

"What are you implying, Phylus?" LenSom asked, sourly emphasizing his name.

"I'm implying that you have shown more motive than anyone in my Ministry to arrest Chieftain Sage Galo, Sinkua and myself especially," Phylus pointed, "Perhaps your fealty to our nation should be brought under scrutiny."

"You have nothing to go on," LenSom snickered, "Only the accusations of a traitor.

But as much as I might wish otherwise, I must concede that I cannot legally force you to resign."

"In that case, what are my charges?" Phylus sneered, burning through LenSom with his glare, "And what will become of Sinkua?"

"What happens to Sinkua is between Sinkua and Parliament," LenSom insisted, "As for you, we hereby dock your pay by twenty-five percent and implore you to resign voluntarily."

Sinkua jostled the door handle, flattening his brow as he confirmed it locked. Odd that they would send for him only to lock him out, he thought, but legislators had always seemed like a needlessly cryptic bunch.

The handle abruptly turned in his hand, and the door flew open, yanking his arm. Phylus shouldered his way past him, dodging eye contact. Phylus paused, preoccupied with frustration, as he realized whom he had passed. He turned and jerked Sinkua's hand from the door handle.

"What are you here for?" Phylus asked in a low tone.

"I don't know. A courier brought me a summons to stand trial," Sinkua shrugged, "I thought I might have caused some collateral damage in Lenguardia."

"Why? What happened in Lenguardia?" Phylus asked, briefly sidelining the situation, "I understand you found Nikasu and a couple of others."

"We did, and I burned down the lab."

"Well, that might be what this is about, but I doubt it," Phylus denied, "Do you know anything about Galo getting arrested?"

"What? No! What did he do?"

"You honestly haven't heard about this?"

"Dead honest. I assume it happened when I was out of the country."

"Yeah. Otherwise, you'd undoubtedly have been the first to know."

"Do you think this summons is for me to testify in his defense?" Sinkua asked, reaching for the door.

"No. Don't go in there," Phylus insisted, grabbing his arm, "In fact, don't speak a word of this with anyone except me, unless I say otherwise."

"Where is he?" Sinkua urged as Phylus dragged him down the courthouse steps.

Phylus shook his head, his focus fixed straight ahead. He had kept Sinkua out of the courthouse, but his stomach turned somersaults hoping Parliament, especially the recently promoted Chairman LenSom, hadn't seen him.

Sinkua pulled his arm from Phylus's grip and took a couple of long strides to catch up. He looked Phylus over as they walked, scrutinizing his demeanor and gait. He tried to think what crime Galo could have committed, but nothing believable came to mind. Stranger, he could conceive of no other reason why they would summon him except to speak in Galo's defense.

Phylus, meanwhile, moved with a sense of bitter urgency not seen since the war.

For a moment, Sinkua considered that Galo's arrest might have been tied to the war. That sounded preposterous though. Galo had served an integral role in their victory. Anybody accusing him of war crimes must have been in bed with the Avatars of Fate.

"Wait," Sinkua urged, "Was he arr…"

"Have you talked to Malia since you got back from Lenguardia?" Phylus interrupted, "Vielle said she wanted to speak with me."

"What? I, um," Sinkua fumbled, "She came for dinner the day after, but I haven't talked to her since then. I assumed she went to see you at your house."

"No, as I understand, she wanted to talk to me, Vielle, and Nikasu together. But otherwise, you really haven't seen her since then?"

"I really haven't."

"How is Nikasu, by the way?"

"Having trouble adjusting. She won't leave the apartment. Doesn't talk much. But she's starting to come around. How's Vielle?"

"Relieved that she kept her job, but she's still nervous."

"I mean her busted nose."

"That's why she's on edge. The drugs make her a tad woozy, but she can't get time off because of how she walked out."

Sinkua eased his stride as he tried to accept Phylus's silence on Galo's arrest. He feared his forced nonchalance to be a poorly presented façade, though.

Phylus led Sinkua into his office and locked the door. He paced the room restlessly, checking for holes and glints of reflected light. Sinkua joined him in his search for eavesdropping apparati. Phylus opened the control panel on his personal elevator and flipped a switch, shutting it off.

Even having scoured his office twice, Phylus still couldn't convince himself that it hadn't been bugged. He motioned for Sinkua to stand before him, to which Sinkua swiftly obliged. Phylus pulled Sinkua's lower eyelids down, inspecting his pupils. He roughed up his hair and pulled his ears forward. He patted his shoulders, down his arms, and along his torso. Finding him clean, Phylus nodded approvingly and signaled for Sinkua to reciprocate.

Still unconvinced, even after he came up clean himself, Phylus grabbed a blank sheet of printer paper and handed a pen to Sinkua. He sat at his desk, leaning over the sheet. Sinkua sat down across from him.

"War crimes," Phylus scribbled, then flipped the sheet facedown and slid it to Sinkua.

"How do they figure?" Sinkua wrote back.

"Act of war. Berinin's involvement not official. Interfered in Haprian."

"Ridiculous. Who put out the warrant?"

"They say you did and that I approved it."

"Impossible. I've been out of the country."

"Warrant was dated two days before you left."

"Damn. Where is he?"

"Holding cell."

"I'm going to see him."

Sinkua shoved the paper at Phylus and nearly toppled his chair as he lunged out of it. He threw the door open, only to be interrupted by Phylus tapping on his desk. His patience already threadbare against such ludicrous accusations, Sinkua whipped around and glared at him. Phylus shook his head, silently calling Sinkua back to his seat. As Sinkua hesitantly complied, Phylus scrawled out his counterpoint.

"You'll expose yourself if you go now."

"And draw them out of hiding."

"Or create a scandal. Go at night."

"Fine. Can I bring Nikasu as a guide, or should we leave her out, too?"

"Bring her," Phylus wrote. He paused partway through the handoff, then retracted the paper and added, "No details."

Malia tapped the reinforced glass panel, startling the idle guard inside the booth. He pulled the window open and looked at her flatly.

"Business?" he grumbled.

"Visitation."

"ID?"

"Right here," she complied, handing over her card.

"Serial number?" the guard asked as he scanned the card.

"159-72-584."

"Go through."

The guard handed her a guest pass and closed the window. Malia clipped the pass to her shirt collar and pushed the door as the lock disengaged. What extended beyond contrasted deeply against the welcoming cleanliness of the lobby and the guard station.

Paint flaked from the cinder block walls, which had been done in a moldy shade of milky urine. Putrid drips splattered arrhythmically on the cracked concrete floor. Prisoners called out perversely and pleadingly.

Malia hesitated, breathing deeply to calm herself as she surveyed the grounds. A large hand landed on her shoulder, startling her. Slowly, she turned to cast wide eyes on another guard, one of impressive stature.

"159-72-584?" he asked, to which she sheepishly nodded, "Come this way."

He released her shoulder and headed deeper into the prison. Her eyes darted nervously as she followed him, convicts shouting lewdly at her. Malia slouched and hunched her shoulders, trying but failing to hide the very existence of her breasts. That did nothing to deter them.

Near the end of the hall, the guard stopped and unclipped his key ring from his belt loop. Malia tapped her foot anxiously as he thumbed through the collection. A hoarse voice came from within the cell.

"This isn't your wing."

"It is now," the guard dismissed.

"What happened to TenWan?"

"Transferred."

"Pheh. Scared. He sent you in his place," the prisoner goaded, "Trust me, if I wanted to get out when you open the gate, you couldn't stop me."

"I'm sure you think so," the guard nodded with more than a tinge of sarcasm, "Whatever helps you sleep at night, big guy."

"I've found my own reason to stay," he insisted, his sneer evident in his voice, "Doesn't matter how big a guard they assign to my cell."

The guard unlocked the cell and stepped inside. The prisoner presented his upturned hands, and the guard cuffed his wrists to the bed frame. Taking special precautions, the cuffed the prisoner's ankles as well. The convict smirked viciously, taking a small victory from the extra measures.

"He's all yours," the guard offered, his iron conviction faltering in his voice.

Malia slipped past him and into the cell. The prisoner looked her over as she sat at the head of the bed. For more than a minute, they sat in silence, studying one another.

"You are Chieftain Sage Galo," Malia uneasily opened, "correct?"

"I am," Galo verified, clearing his throat, "And you are?"

"I don't think we've met. My name is Malia," she introduced, "I need to ask you something."

"These charges are unsubstantiated. They can't hold me on them."

"I'm sorry, but I don't have the means to help you with that."

"How can you expect me to help you if you won't help me?"

"Vielle may be in danger."

"How do you know Vielle?" Galo urged.

"I'm her mother. I was a spy within the Avatars of Fate, but I lost my cover," Malia revealed, "She and I have since been united, but I've had to distance myself again for the time."

"Is that why she may be in danger?" he asked, struggling to hide how this news overwhelmed him, "Because you blew your cover?"

"Possibly, but it might come from my people."

"Your people? Other spies within the Avatars?"

"Not entirely. The primary function of The Coalition is to undermine the Avatars of Fate. Planting moles is just one of our methods," Malia explained, "Most of our work is preventative, but when that fails, there are those who work to empower the victims and enemies of the Avatars. You worked with two of them actually. Brothers, in fact."

"MalVek and NalSet."

"That's them."

"They always were rather abstruse," Galo mused, the extent of their intellects and resources made clear, "I can nary say I'm surprised."

"Does that mean you'll help me?" Malia pleaded, "My people have already helped you more than you could possibly know. Our work hasn't been perfect, but things would be far worse if we didn't intervene."

"I was ready to help when you said Vielle was in trouble," Galo confessed, "I was merely distracted by curiosity. I'm sure you can understand."

"In that case," Malia began, "I need to know who's visited you. Anybody suspicious? Anybody you didn't know?"

"All of my visitors have been strangers. Quite sad, in fact," Galo worried, "None of my Subtransit Resistance comrades have come to see me. It makes me wonder if they were involved in this at all or if they simply lack the scrotal fortitude to face me."

"Who has visited you, then?" Malia pressed, holding back a snicker at his phrasing.

"Mostly the media. Reporters, editorialists, and the like. Who are you looking for?"

"Have you seen this man?" she asked, pulling a photograph from her breast pocket.

Galo studied the picture, searching his memories for any hint of familiarity. Capitulating to ignorance, he confessed, "I can't say I have. Avatar or Coalition? Or some other person of interest?"

"He could be working for either one. If he comes, ask his name."

"If he comes on behalf of the Avatars of Fate, would he not report any information he gets from me to The Coalition, as well?" Galo pondered.

"If he can remember it, he will. But I've already nearly lost one daughter, letting them use her as bait. I refuse to take that risk again."

"And if he comes on behalf of The Coalition? What will become of Vielle?"

Malia's eyes wandered, fixing on a blend of stains from across the ages. Timeworn blood, urine, and vomit had given an uneasy color to an otherwise drab floor, the pigment so unfathomably nauseating as to render the gray inviting. She contemplated what NalSet had divulged of Pahres's intentions. She knew much of it had been conjecture, but she still struggled to wrap her mind around and accept it.

Whether out of incomprehension or nonacceptance, she couldn't answer his question. Instead, she stuffed the photograph in her pocket and got to her feet. Brushing residue and sediment from her buttocks, she turned to address him.

"I'll come back in a few days to see if he visited," she reported, "and who he came as."

Disappointed again, XalRut hung up the phone and checked her list of numbers. She crossed out the one she just called and, holding the paper at arm's length, confirmed what she feared. She had run out of numbers and still hadn't found what she was looking for.

"Nobody can get me clearance?" she wondered aloud.

Between the circumstances surrounding CreSam's actual death and MeiLom's legal death, access to their old house had fallen through a tangled mess of red tape. Technically, it no longer belonged to anybody, but until a deed holder or an executor of their estate was found, it couldn't be repossessed by the state. It had come under federal protection without actually being owned by the government.

Insufficient evidence confirming MeiLom's passing further compounded matters. Typically, the statement by the OMPC would have sufficed, but these circumstances, particularly the last known owner's status, demanded conclusive proof. This being a rather unique situation, none of the offices she called had the slightest notion of how to handle her request.

This barricading of all legal avenues left her with one choice. She would have to work around the roadblocks, and she knew one person especially adept at driving on the sidewalk without leaving tracks. He did still owe her for mortalizing The Scout, and it would be as much for his own good. Despite this, she hesitated with her hand hovering over her phone.

Powering through her reluctance, she snatched up the phone and dialed before her resolve gave out again.

"ArcNosian Ministry of Human Resources," he answered.

"Is this SenRas?" XalRut asked.

"It is. Who am I speaking with?" SenRas asked between sips of light roast.

"Honey, it's XalRut."

"Oh! Oh, I'm sorry. You sound different on this phone. I'm in the office."

"Yes, I gathered as much. Did you transfer?"

"Eh? No, I've always worked in this Ministry. Ever since we established them," SenRas insisted.

"Oh, of course," XalRut comprehended, "Listen, we have a situation. It's about BeiLou."

"Oh, no. What happened now?"

"It's not so much what happened now as what happened after college. She received several antique books. Her professor intended for her to restore them."

"Ah, quite fascinating. What did she find? Anything we should be worried about?"

"As far as Professor Uulan knows, she never opened any of them. But now he's worried the wrong kind of people are looking for them."

"I would venture to say they're still in their old house," SenRas suggested, sensing the direction of the conversation.

"I've come to the same conclusion," XalRut agreed, "Look, I'm sure you have a lot on your plate already. But is there any way you can recover those books without getting hurt or arrested?"

"You want me to break into our daughter's old house?"

A car parked in front of the house across the street. XalRut peeked through the blinds curiously, but she didn't recognize the car or the man and woman who stepped out of it. She returned her attention to SenRas.

"I'd rather not ask that of you. If you're caught, even after the fact, the books could be confiscated."

"Yes, that would be problematic. I'm not certain where they would end up, but they'd be even further out of reach than they are now."

"Is there anything else you can do?"

"Quite possibly. I've been working to get the deed signed over to…"

The knob and lock ripped out of the door and bounced across the room, a metallic alloy boot thrusting profanely through the hole in the wood. XalRut shrieked and dropped the phone. SenRas jumped at her scream and winced as her phone hit the floor.

"XalRut! What happened? Are you alright?"

XalRut watched fearfully as the ruined door swung open, banging against the wall. The man and woman from across the street walked into her living room. The woman swaggered through, sizing up the room with a derisive sneer, as the man followed in silence. She stomped on the discarded doorknob, crushing it under her alloy boot. As XalRut saw her profile, a spark of distant familiarity flared from the depths of her memories.

"Ain.... AinZun?" XalRut gasped.

"AinZun!?" SenRas shouted, "Is AinZun there? Is she alright? What's happening?"

"How do you know my name?" AinZun demanded.

"I... I'm your..." XalRut sputtered.

"Oh. Right. Dad's old fling. Guess I'm doing you a favor, then."

AinZun produced a pistol from her hip, a blue light blinking on the barrel. She wiped her right eye, a contact lens sliding down from behind her eyelid. A second blue light blinked over her iris, matching rhythm with the one on her gun.

"AinZun! What are you doing?" XalRut pleaded.

"What's going on?" SenRas demanded.

"Is that him on the phone?" AinZun snarled, "Is that the man you left Dad for?"

XalRut nodded timidly. AinZun leveled the pistol and pulled the trigger. SenRas called out in desperate opposition at the thunder of gunfire. The bullet roared from the barrel with a burst of smoke and a rippling orange trail in its wake.

The bullet ripped into XalRut's forehead, scattering her thoughts as it bored deeper. She writhed in agony as it drilled through her brain, her grip on reality floundering erratically in that infinite instant. The bleeding wound radiated a swelling red glow, and the bullet exploded against the back of her skull.

AinZun stepped over XalRut's body and picked up the phone.

"The next one is for you, old man."

She dropped the phone and signaled her comrade.

"Anything unusual, Prophet?"

"Not a thing, no."

"Good. Then let's go. Our next target is at Hillside Oncology."

"Actually, my lady, if it's all the same to you, I would prefer to move on to ArcNos," The Prophet requested, "Ready the stronghold for occupation, as it were."

"Phase One is just getting underway. It's too early to be making active arrangements toward Phase Three."

"The first piece has been moved into position. I need time to prepare for their riposte."

"If you think it's necessary, I won't question your judgment further. Just don't get ahead of schedule," AinZun complied, studying his posture, "I can take you as far as the bus station."

"That will suffice. Thank you, Engineer."

SenRas hung up his phone and lifted it to dial again, his hands trembling with fury. His chest bounced with each ragged breath, becoming ever more erratic with each pulse of the keypad. He bashed the receiver against his ear as it rang, as though to expel the trauma from his thoughts. Tears welled in his eyes, and his throat swelled as she answered.

"Ministry of Defense."

"I ... I ..."

"Can I help you with something?"

"This is ... I need to ..."

"Who is this?"

"I want in."

"SenRas?"

"Yes."

"I'll be right over."

"Thank you."

Sinkua unlocked his apartment to find Eytea, Nikasu, and Yahsek scattered about the living room, eating Feryan takeout. An unopened container sat on the coffee table, still steaming through the latch hole. Yahsek nodded to him, and Nikasu flashed a smile.

"Hey babe, I brought home dinner," Eytea boasted, "I got my first paycheck today, so my employee discount kicked in."

"It's really quite good," Yahsek complimented, "And I'm not just saying that because of what I was living on."

"Yeah, it smells great. Thanks," Sinkua absently agreed, "Nikasu, how do you feel today?"

"Too heavy," Nikasu muddled, "Milystic manipulation is operating below desired levels. Progression of recovery is below projected parameters."

Sinkua sighed and shook his head as he took his spot on the couch. Trying to distance himself from his anxiety for even a moment, he looked to Nikasu and smiled as he grabbed the unopened carton. Nearly two weeks had passed since they returned, and such jargon still peppered her speech.

"You really need to stop talking like that," Sinkua insisted, "You sound like a robot, and not the whimsical humanoid ones in the movies. Not everything has to be so technical."

"If we take her out on the town, she ought to pick up some more, well, normal dialect from the locals," Yahsek suggested, "What do you think, Nikasu? Are you comfortable enough to leave the apartment?"

"I, um, I don't know," Nikasu hesitated, "Will all of you come with me?"

"Of course we will," Eytea insisted, "And if we ask nicely, I'm sure Ozzera will stay nearby just in case there's any real trouble. Right, Yahsek?"

"She'll help if I ask her," Yahsek agreed, "but her proximity will depend on where we go."

"We should go at night when there aren't quite as many people out," Sinkua suggested, "It'll do you good to see the town before you deal with crowds. Do you think you'd like that?"

"Oh yes, certainly," Nikasu delighted, "That sounds like it could be fun."

"Of course it would be fun," Sinkua snickered, "We can be each other's guide. I'll point out landmarks, and you'll point the way in the dark."

"I would like that very much," Nikasu nodded, "Thank you."

"In that case," Sinkua continued between bites, "why don't we go after dinner?"

"All of us?" Nikasu eagerly asked.

"I was thinking just the two of us. Brother and sister out for an evening stroll."

Nikasu's expression flattened. She looked to Yahsek for guidance. Eytea shot Sinkua an accusing and doubtful glare from across the couch. Yahsek nodded to Nikasu reassuringly.

"Go ahead," Yahsek insisted, "It'll be good for you."

"See? It's perfectly safe, and I'm sure it'll be more tolerable than whatever else you've had to use your Hybrid vision for."

"Well, I guess you do have a lot of sibling bonding to catch up on," Eytea reluctantly agreed, "I don't like this idea, but maybe I'm worrying too much."

"Don't worry," Nikasu oddly comforted, hugging Eytea around her shoulders, "I can always make time for my sister-in-law."

Eytea's expression quickly shifted from worry to confusion. Sinkua dropped his fork and whipped his head to the side. Yahsek raised his head, one eyebrow slowly scaling his forehead. All three stared at her now, each more puzzled and shocked than the last. All tried to speak at once, only to trip over each other's words.

"Do you..." Eytea began.

"Who told…" Sinkua started.

"They're not…" Yahsek cut in.

"Sorry," Nikasu shrugged, shrinking away from Eytea, "I thought since you two are a couple, that meant you're my sister-in-law. Then, I'd be related to all of you."

"Oh, is that all?" Eytea nervously laughed, "No, we'll only be sisters-in-law if Sinkua and I get married, and I don't think he could settle down even if he wanted to."

"What's that supposed to…?" Sinkua recoiled.

"So, nobody finds it weird that she just said that she's related to me?" YahSek interrupted.

"No, not particularly. I'm assuming it's because you both used to refer to The Geneticist as Father," Sinkua dismissed, "So Nikasu, what did you mean by…"

"I've never called that little bastard Father. No, I'm Nikasu's cousin once removed. When I heard my cousin had her child abducted by the Avatars of Fate, I went in to rescue her," Yahsek recalled, "Obviously, the bad news is that I was captured. But it turned out I was also a Hybrid, so they had reason to keep me alive. We managed to negotiate a few terms to our captivity."

"So is that how you ended up in the same cell?" Eytea asked, playing along with the distraction.

"You know she still won't be related to all of us when we get married, right?" Sinkua asked, "Or are we just going to overlook Galo?"

"I apologize for misspeaking," Nikasu excused, "I suppose my subconscience is still adhering to the concept of The Geneticist being my patriarch."

"She still forgets the little bastard wasn't really her father," Yahsek explained, "And as I'm sure you know, the young Chieftain Sage is his nephew."

Sinkua, having returned to his meal after giving up on defending his position as husband material, spat a mouthful of food back into his carton and turned his head sharply. Eytea put her carton on the coffee table and turned to give Yahsek her attention. The news itself didn't come entirely as a surprise. All the other Hybrids had ties to the Avatars of Fate, but Galo had thus far been the only exception. How casually Yahsek blurted it out caught them off guard though.

"What?" Yahsek shrugged, "You mean I've been in captivity and know more about your friend than you do?"

"He didn't even know he had any aunts or uncles until a few weeks before the war," Sinkua remarked, "But never that any of them were with the Avatars."

"Ozzera overheard The Geneticist talking about Galo and Gijin once or twice. Does this mean you know his real name?"

"Galo should. I can't remember it right now."

"In that case, one of us should visit him as soon as possible."

"That's exactly what I was thinking."

All returned to what remained of their dinner, forgoing conversation to avoid any more awkward interruptions. Nikasu's slip was excusable, given her circumstances. Yahsek, on the other hand, had clearly lost all sense of tact and inhibition.

Sinkua could only remember fragments of their conversation with Nenbard, Sanus, and Ocronn about Galo's family. He didn't have enough to piece it together without Galo's help though. He dug up trace memories of talk of a woman bringing a baby to Gijin, and Galo's mother's brother taking the child when he moved away.

Whoever that man was, everyone must have believed that he adopted the baby, never suspecting that he abducted it for the Avatars of Fate. Surely, Grandpa Gijin couldn't have known. For him to endorse such an atrocity would have been absurd.

Sinkua pitched his empty carton in the garbage and threw his jacket around his back. He tossed Nikasu's jacket to her and gave Eytea a peck on the cheek.

"Will you bring your morningstar?" Nikasu pleaded, "If something bad happens, I want you to be able to protect us."

"Sure. We'll work on getting you a weapon sometime, too," Sinkua agreed with a wink.

"I'll contact Ozzera and ask her to keep a lookout," Yahsek offered.

Sinkua thanked him while he held the door for Nikasu. She squeezed her brother's hand as she brushed past him. Shivers resonated down her spine, a coupling of her nerves and the harsh freezing wind.

"We're gonna be fine," Sinkua assured as he locked the door behind them, "Just stay close and tell me what you see when it gets too dark for me, okay?"

"Okay. I can do that," she said, nodding vigorously as they descended the stairs, "There's a lot of cigarette butts on these stairs. That looks like a beer stain. Or maybe urine. And…"

"I don't need that much detail," he laughed, "It's light enough out here. I mean where there aren't any street lights."

"Okay, good. My brain will get tired if I do that all night."

Eytea cleaned the last bit of mess from dinner. As she wiped a stain from her shirt, she realized she had never changed out of her uniform. She laughed quietly at herself as she unbuttoned her top. A forced cough stopped her.

"You want me to step out?" Yahsek asked.

"What? Oh sorry, I'm still used to it just being me and Sinkua here," Eytea apologized.

"It's fine. We're trying not to be in the way."

Red in the face, Eytea slipped into her bedroom and closed the door. Yahsek continued their conversation through the wall to keep from ending on an awkward note.

"Are you really okay with Sinkua taking her out like that?"

"No, not really. But I can't exactly forbid it, now can I?" she called back.

"I suppose not. But who are you more worried about?"

"Nikasu, of course. Sinkua can handle himself."

"Are you certain of that? He's escorting a high-priority fugitive. He hasn't faced the worst of what they can and will send after them."

"I'm sure he's already considered that. Knowing him, he was hoping for it when he agreed to break her out of there," Eytea suggested, "General consensus was that the Avatars would either execute her or go on the offensive after Malia defected."

"You suppose he saved her in order to force their hand?" Yahsek clarified.

"Probably, among the more obvious reasons," Eytea qualified as she stepped out of her bedroom in a sweatshirt and sweatpants, "That's how he thinks."

"It's a sound tactic on its face, if we can assume the assaults will be isolated to areas where Nikasu has been sighted."

"And if we can't?"

"Too soon to know."

"So, now that you've drilled me about my relationship, why don't I ask you about yours?"

"Anything you need to know."

"What's the story behind you and Ozzera? She said you were obligated to each other."

"That story is a long and messy one, I'm afraid."

"Well, is she your pet? Or maybe an old friend who the Avatars experimented on?"

"More the second, minus the experiment," he nodded, "Certainly not a pet. If anything, we're more the pets. Those who remain don't seem to see us that way though."

"Those who remain?" Eytea pried, sitting on the couch and leaning on her knees.

"I'm afraid I've said too much," Yahsek apologized, looking away, "If you haven't learned yet, I'm not in a position to tell you."

"Tell me what?"

"The outside world isn't ready to know. I've suspected as much since we escaped. They're controlling history by suppressing information."

"In that case," Eytea pondered aloud, "I know who I need to talk to."

Sinkua and Nikasu walked in nearly matching strides, his eyes fixed straight ahead while her attention zipped about childishly. As she grew more comfortable, finding a sense of security in his proximity, a look of wonder spread over her face. Without people, save for the occasional straggler, she found this metropolis truly fascinating.

Sinkua shared his knowledge of shops and other businesses. He pointed out discolored patches in the asphalt and described how the Subtransit Resistance had blasted holes through the street to attack the capital. Still matching his gait, Nikasu stared up at him in amazement as he recounted nearly losing his arm to an explosive bullet and Phylus taking one across his ear.

"I still have a scar from the bullet," Sinkua boasted.

He rolled up his sleeves to show the hairless scar tissue on his bicep. Nikasu looked at it curiously, smirking as she poked it.

"That feels so weird," Nikasu laughed, "My scars are too small to feel like that."

"Be grateful for that. I don't know much about what you went through, but sometimes it feels like the bullet is still in there," Sinkua said, "It's not, of course. I watched the surgeon take it out. Have it as a souvenir somewhere, I think. Unless I lost it when we moved back here from Ferya."

"You've lived in Ferya, too?"

"Yeah, I've lived in ArcNos, Ferya, and a little island off the coast of Berinin. It's actually a part of Masnethege now, but it wasn't back then," he recalled, "I've also visited Ivaria, Eprilen, Haprian, and um, Quarun. Oh, and Lenguardia, obviously. My first time in Ferya, we found one of the labs where they used to keep you. It had been decommissioned and abandoned, so we were actually glad you weren't still in there."

"I think I've been to every country in Ouristihra, but this is my first time seeing any of them," she regretted, "Do you think maybe you could show me around some other places sometime?"

"Let's not rush into it, but yeah. Next time Phylus sends me out on a business trip, I'll see if you can tag along, okay?"

"Phylus is the guy that lost his ear when he was saving you, right? After you got shot in the arm?"

"Yeah, that's him. Bit high strung sometimes, but he's a real solid bloke," Sinkua complimented, "Damn eagle-eye with any gun he's ever gotten his hands on. Better than The Hunter, I'd say, and I'm sure that pissed him right off."

"And now he's your boss?"

"Yep. He was a Negotiator before ArcNos split, and now he runs our Ministry of Foreign Affairs. Galo and I had helped bring people together and build support on our way here from Berinin, so he offered me a job."

"Well, that was nice of him. And didn't Vielle say he's her father?"

"I don't know if she said that to you, but yes, Phylus is Vielle's dad."

"So, that makes him my...?"

"Stepfather. But I bet you can get away with calling him Dad," Sinkua smirked, patting her shoulder.

The streetlights ended a block ahead of them. Vague silhouettes of masonic monoliths stood shrouded in foreboding darkness. Nikasu's eyes flared brightly, then faded to a shimmer. Her luminescent pupils plucked ambient photons from the darkness and cycled them through her optic nerves to create natural night vision.

"What do you see up ahead?" Sinkua asked.

"I think that's a bank over there. Maybe a real estate office," Nikasu pointed out, "They still look the same to me."

"What about over there?"

"I don't know what that is. It has a big fence around the front with barbed wire on top."

"That's where we need to go," he asserted.

"What? Why?" she gasped, "That place looks scary. There can't be anything we need to do there."

"Of course there can. None of us have gone to see Galo, so now that I've shown you around, that's what we're going to do."

"Why is he in there?"

"He was arrested for war crimes, and they told him I issued his warrant."

"You didn't, did you?"

"Of course not. But aside from Phylus, everyone who knows about it believes that I arrested him," Sinkua worried, "So, we're going to visit Galo and straighten things out, make sure he hasn't fallen prey to the scandal."

"Does Eytea know?"

"I only found out today, so no, she doesn't yet."

"Okay, so what do you need me to do? Will we have to fight our way in?"

"Of course not. It's a government facility, and I'm a government employee, strange as that still is for me to say. Just be my eyes through the dark."

"Alright," she agreed, nodding rapidly, "I can do that. I'll tell you if you're about to fall or if someone is sneaking up on us."

"Attagirl."

Under the shroud of darkness, the stenches of the street grew all the stranger as they mingled with those from the prison. Residual exhaust from increasingly popular combustion engines hung thick, lacing with oil stains and old tar. The homeless and societally discarded sat in their own alcoholic sickness. Nikasu quietly pointed them out to direct Sinkua around them.

Sinkua showed his card to the gatekeeper at the perimeter fence. The gatekeeper hesitated to grant Nikasu entry without identification, but he complied when Sinkua insisted upon her relevance to Galo's case.

"His serial number is 159-72-584," the gatekeeper read from his roster, "Guard in the lobby will expect you to know it."

Sinkua and Nikasu thanked him and continued to the lobby. The guard in his booth gave only a dismissive glance before returning most of his attention to whatever they had interrupted.

"What do you want?" he grumbled as he opened the glass panel.

"Here to see a prisoner," Sinkua flatly reported.

"Visiting hours are over. Go home."

"Prisoner 159-72-584," Sinkua firmly resisted, shoving his card in the booth, "Apparently, I'm his arresting officer."

"I'm relevant to the case," Nikasu parroted, her confidence bolstered by Sinkua's assertiveness.

"Inside. Next guard will take you to his cell."

The guard returned Sinkua's card and gave him a pair of visitor passes. Through the next door, they found the stench from outside intensified to nauseating levels. The squalor that the prisoners lived in edged on inexcusably inhumane, evidence of the prison's floundering and perhaps overstressed budget. Nikasu barely flinched at it, having endured worse.

A tall burly guard walked them down the hall, idly recounting how he had taken a woman to see the same prisoner a few days ago. He recalled her resemblance to Nikasu, except that the other woman was quite a bit older. Nikasu listened intently, trying to tune out the lewd callings and wolf whistles. As the guard paused though, their perversions burned through her defenses and, with them, her patience.

"Fuck off! I'm only fifteen!" Nikasu shouted.

In the instant those words left her mouth, Nikasu shrank back behind Sinkua. He laughed, quite audibly at that, as the misogynistic heckling fell into stunned silence. The guard, trying to maintain his professionalism, stifled a chuckle. Sinkua gave her his hand, and they continued walking.

Toward the end of the hall, a trail of blood droplets glared with deep contrast against the milky gray floor. The guard quickened his stride, trying to hide his worry lest the prisoners found his conviction shaken. He pulled his walkie-talkie from its holster. Nikasu squeezed Sinkua's hand, trying to comfort him as much as herself. The guard stopped, standing dumbfounded before the cell, and dropped his walkie-talkie.

"What is it?" Sinkua called as they neared the burly guard.

Speechless, the guard simply pointed. Sinkua and Nikasu joined him in bewildered silence as they stared at the evacuated cell. The cross beams had been snapped in two, and a pair of bars had been bent wide enough for an adult body to easily fit through. Partially congealed blood smeared the bars, concentrated at the widest part of the gap.

"Did you mention that he could do anything like this on his warrant?" the guard asked.

"No," Sinkua refuted. He sampled the blood with his fingertip and smeared it on the inside of his jacket. "Because he can't."

Chapter 16

"Are you the one she told me about?"

"I know nothing of being announced."

"I should think not. What's your business?"

"I'm here to help you."

"How so?"

"I can get you out."

"I'm listening."

"I can help you find the ones who did this to you."

"I already know them."

"In that case, I have something that belongs to you. An heirloom from the confiscatory."

"What's your name?"

"Of what consequence is that?"

"What is your name?"

"You may call me The Prophet."

"Very well, then. Let's be on our way."

"What do you mean the prisoner escaped!?" Chairman LenSom shouted, his voice through the speaker echoing in the vast office.

"I mean the bars were ripped apart, and he's not there anymore," Phylus called back from the middle of the room.

"How?! How do you explain this?"

"I don't!"

"How could he have done that? Is there something we don't know about him?"

"Ministry of Healthcare is checking the blood sample. We suspect that he had an accomplice."

"Is Sinkua in there with you?" LenSom pried, "Does he know how the prisoner could have done this?"

"Now, why do you assume I would know that?" Sinkua spat.

"You tell me. You're one of those people," LenSom derided, "Maybe, you're the accomplice. Rather convenient that you two just fell ass-first into this hunch."

"Why would I arrest him just to break him out? And if I did, do you honestly think I would let someone like you find out about it?" Sinkua snarled, "For that matter, why would I arrest him in the first place?"

"I'm well aware of your history with each other," LenSom accused.

"Exactly!" Sinkua snapped, "History that an ivory tower bitchboy like you could never understand!"

"Minister, I order you to…"

"I order you to shut your whore mouth!" Sinkua fumed, "You lost your right to speak. Now, sit down and shut up."

"Sinkua, you're going to…" Phylus cut in.

"Cut it, Phylus. This is between me and bitchboy up there," Sinkua interrupted, "Did you really think you could get away with forging a warrant in my name?"

"I've done no such thing," LenSom indignantly defended.

"Bullshit! For that matter, where the hell do you get off using me to turn one of our most valued allies against us?"

"I could ask you the same."

"And what makes you think you should turn us against each other? Do you have any idea who we are?"

"Sinkua!" Phylus urged.

"I know perfectly well who you are!" LenSom rumbled, "Inhuman, inhumane, and exceedingly privileged!"

"We're the reason your silver spoon ass gets to sit in that circle, jacking off on other people's work," Sinkua challenged, "You wanna come after us? Piss on an eel!"

"Consider your employment terminated!" LenSom ordered, "Evacuate the premises within the hour."

"He'll be gone shortly," Phylus answered.

Phylus cut the transmission, sneering to hold back a snicker. He turned to Sinkua with a victorious grin and nodded approvingly.

"It worked," he conceded, "Head home and wait for my call."

"You're sure you can hold up your end of the deal?" Sinkua asked.

"Absolutely. Civilian advisors get paid from the petty cash fund," Phylus explained, "Nobody in Parliament has access to the records, not even the Chairman."

"Alright. I need to fetch a few things out of my desk, and then I'll be on my way."

Sinkua put on a disdainful sneer, a mask for his elation, and shuffled out of Phylus's office. Word of his termination would spread quickly, and if he looked at all content, fabricated hearsay would spread even faster. Back at his cubicle, he realized he only had one piece of personalization on his otherwise standard-issue desk.

He looked at the picture, mulling over whether to steal the frame or just take the photograph he had put in it. Noticing a once-coworker staring at him blankly, he flashed an overstated smile as he pulled the picture out of the frame. For punctuation, he gingerly returned the frame to the corner of the desk and, his expression darkening, backhanded it into the modular wall. Grunting disdainfully, he shouldered past the gawking employee and headed to the elevator.

Employees chattered amongst each other as he walked just beyond what they assumed to be earshot. He couldn't pick out specific words, but the timing and attempted secrecy said enough. They could think what they wanted, anyway.

While he waited for the elevator, he felt a buzzing in his pocket. He pulled out his phone, first noticing the Ministry of Foreign Affairs insignia engraved on the back. He reminded himself to return it to Phylus, then answered bitterly.

"What do you want?"

"Sinkua? Is something wrong?" SenRas asked.

"Hey, Grandpa. I'll tell you later. What's going on?"

"The deed to your old house has resurfaced."

"Really? Where was it?"

"I haven't a clue. It wouldn't be fair to say I found it. More that it was returned."

"Did you meet the person who found it, or did they just drop it off?"

"It was a gentleman from Berinin. Looked to be a few years older than Phylus. He simply walked in and said he had something that I'd been looking for," SenRas recounted, "He didn't give his name, but he said to give you and Eytea his regards. Does this sound like someone you know?"

"I could guess," Sinkua nodded, leaning against the wall beside the elevator, "Probably one of Malia's associates. Coalition, that is, not an Avatar."

"Alright well, hurry up here and fetch this thing before it vanishes again."

"I'll be right up. Thanks."

"Perhaps while you're here, you might tell me what has you so riled up as to be answering the phone like that."

"If you really have to know, I got fired," Sinkua spat, "Apparently, LenSom can't handle being called out on his bullshit. He can mouth off all day, but if anyone pushes back, they get canned."

"Screw that guy. I'll get you your job back."

"Thanks, but don't worry about it. Phylus is gonna put in some calls and help me find something in the private sector. I need out of the government business anyhow."

Vielle drummed her fingers on her desk, playing a card game on her computer while she waited for her next call. She mindlessly flicked the metal covering her nose, the sound echoing inside her kinked nostrils. Her thoughts wandered back to that night in Lenguardia.

Sinkua had insisted on having Nikasu and Yahsek stay with him, partly to keep Vielle on track toward moving out of her father's house. Grateful as she was, she wished she had more time for her long-estranged half-sister. Her stomach twisted into unnamable knots, having barely spoken to her since they came home.

NalSet's nonchalant insider knowledge of the Avatars of Fate had been particularly curious, running deeper than he or MalVek had ever let on. He did corroborate Malia's story about sabotaging the Avatars however, which meant they both belonged to an organization focused on such work. That meant, of course, that she had worked with them without knowing it. Both sides, it seemed, had their own designs on the Hybrids.

Necks craned at the sound of footsteps in the maze of cubicles. None of the managers had been scheduled to come through, and the mail wouldn't arrive for another hour. Curiosity overcoming her contemplation, Vielle turned to see who had come just as the visitor reached her row.

He cocked his head curiously as their eyes met. Flashing a charismatic smile, he smoothed a stray lock of hair hanging from his fedora. Entranced by his demeanor, Vielle stared at the nattily dressed visitor as her headset beeped urgingly. A cerulean boutonniere adorned his breast pocket in bright contrast to the stone gray fabric.

The strange gentleman stopped beside her, nodding as though they had long been friends. Vielle became exceedingly self-conscious of the bandaging on her nose. She cupped her hand over the metal bracing and managed an embarrassed smile for the mahogany gentleman as he hung his fedora beside her skullcap. Women in nearby cubicles, most of them older, stared in bitterly envious silence, their mouths slightly agape.

"I could help you with that, if you'd like," he offered, his breath smelling of sage.

"Oh, this? No thank you, it's healing nicely," Vielle dismissed, "Can I help you with something?"

"I believe you might. Would you perhaps be the Lady Vielle?"

"Well, I don't know about the Lady part," she specified, laughing at her unintentional lewd pun, "But I am Vielle. And you? Have we met before?"

"In that case, I have something for you."

He plucked the boutonniere from his pocket and offered it to her.

"For me? Really?"

"Truly."

"You came here just to give me this blue rose?" Vielle asked, "What's your deal, man?"

"I do apologize for having taken so long."

"What are you talking about?"

"Those you don't know you're looking for are always the hardest to find," he muddled.

"Yeah, I still don't follow. Thanks for the flower though. It's beautiful," she professed, her expression flattening with the onset of cautious cynicism "It isn't going to collect my sweat for a doomsday device or anything weird like that, is it?"

"Hah! Of course not. I've never been one to fraternize with their kind," he assured.

"Nice to know. Being who I am attracts strange company. Some, the kind I shouldn't be taking gifts from," Vielle insisted, "By the way, you haven't told me your name."

"My name is Aleepo. Another like you has known my face but not my name, and another the opposite," Aleepo introduced, "You are the first of your people to know both."

"Wait!" Vielle urged as Aleepo palmed his fedora onto his head, "You mean you've..."

"I'm afraid I can't stay and chat. I've other business to tend to on the premises. By the way, if you happen to see Galo before I do," Aleepo urged, "Please tell him that I am sorry."

Sinkua knocked on the office door as he opened it. SenRas sat at his desk with a mug of coffee. Sinkua cocked an eyebrow at the sight of EshCal sitting across from him. He hadn't realized SenRas had any guests when he called, and to his knowledge, all work between Defense and Covert Affairs, or Human Resources rather, went through Spril.

"Good morning, Sinkua," EshCal greeted.

"Not really," Sinkua refuted, "What are you doing here?"

"Auditing your grandfather. Lock the door, please."

"What do you mean?" he asked, complying with her request.

"You know of the counter-operatives out to sabotage the Avatars of Fate, correct?" SenRas asked.

"Right, The Coalition. Malia's one of them. She led us to Nikasu, Yahsek, and Ozzera."

"Any others you know about?" EshCal prodded.

"We learned about them from MalVek and NalSet," Sinkua recalled, "They recruited you at the tournament, right?"

"They did. I was starting to worry that you either didn't remember or didn't catch on," EshCal nodded, "SenRas has asked to join The Coalition. The man who recovered the deed to your house is one of ours."

"Was it the doctor who put me and Eytea in a coma?"

"He prefers the term 'curative hibernation,' but yes, it was him. His name is Aleepo."

"The guy that gave blue roses to Eytea and Nikasu?"

"I don't know anything about that, but I remember Eytea putting one in her hair."

"Yeah, she said someone named Aleepo used to put one in the trade packages he sent to her and her mother, but they never met him," Sinkua recalled, "She said he bred them himself and has been spreading them across the Northlands."

"Huh. Well, I'm still new to the group, so I haven't pinned down everyone's idiosyncrasies," EshCal shrugged with a smile, "Sounds like a pleasant enough hobby."

"Yeah, it does. So, what made you want in, Grandpa?" Sinkua asked, "Finally get tired of running solo against them?"

"The bastards killed my ex-wife," SenRas spat.

"Wait, what?" Sinkua gasped, "They got Grandma?"

"Shot her while we were on the phone. Said the next one was for me."

"I can't believe it. What business do they have preying on a defenseless old woman?"

"Hardly defenseless, young man," SenRas argued, indignant at such a reduction, "She gave me the means to eliminate The Scout. She was searching for some antique books that belonged to your mother. Said she had to keep them away from the wrong kind of people."

"I remember those books. She kept them in their bedroom. I never thought they were worth killing over," Sinkua reflected, "Then again, it never occurred to me that the Avatars would be interested in them."

"I didn't even know about the books until XalRut called. She said BeiLou got them from one of her college professors. Fellow by the name of Uulan."

"I've met him. He was part of the Subtransit Resistance. But he never said anything about my mother."

"I suppose he didn't know who you were. Anyway, there must be something important to them in those books," SenRas considered, "Or maybe I'm not ready to accept that this was revenge."

"Revenge for what? Kabehl?" Sinkua guessed.

"No, her father."

"Whose father?"

"The Engineer's. AinZun's," SenRas clarified, "XalRut was killed by her estranged daughter from her first marriage."

"Did she know?" Sinkua asked, "I mean, did AinZun know she'd been ordered to kill her mother?"

"Yes, she did."

"What happened to her father?"

"Killed by a professional assassin when she was five years old, after her parents had divorced" SenRas recounted, painful memories rushing to the forefront of his thoughts.

"Then why kill her own mother? That doesn't make sense."

"Because I was the assassin."

"Shit. Seriously?"

"Yes, an unfortunate relic from a past I'd rather not remember," SenRas sighed, "But for the record, I didn't know who he was when I made the hit. It wasn't until I heard her in the hall that I realized what I had done."

"Do you know who ordered the hit?"

"Not conclusively, but I have a theory. They marked him on false accusations. Charged him with corporate embezzlement, but he worked on an assembly line."

"SenRas and I were discussing it when Aleepo showed up with the deed," EshCal interjected, "He suspects an earlier generation of the Avatars of Fate put out the hit."

"Why?" Sinkua puzzled, "What do they gain by killing a blue collar divorcé only to take it out on his widow, what, forty years later?"

"Forty-six," SenRas clarified, leaning on his elbow as he stared into his coffee mug.

"We have reason to believe they weren't specifically concerned with him. Evidence points to his being more a means to an end," EshCal explained.

"That end being AinZun?" Sinkua deduced.

"That's what we think, at least for one," SenRas confirmed, "They used me to destroy both of XalRut's families and create a future recruit in her first daughter and possibly one in her expected second."

"My mother," Sinkua supplied, "But they took CreSam instead."

"And they got Masfaru as well. AinZun's son."

"What about her husband? Masfaru's father?"

"Status unknown," EshCal answered.

"Let me make sure I have this right. They create future recruits by destroying families and building psychological profiles that suit their needs?" Sinkua reiterated, to

156

which both nodded, "And in the cases we know about, they have blood ties to the Hybrids."

"Spot on," EshCal nodded.

"So, if they cause tragedies to create each new generation of Avatars, then that would mean…" Sinkua trailed off, his emerald eyes widening with horrified epiphany.

"What? What does it mean?" SenRas pried.

"Galo's parents. They weren't just sick. They were infected."

"If we can get the bodies, Aleepo can tell us for certain," EshCal suggested.

"You two look into that without me," Sinkua insisted, "I'm going to a meeting to figure out what happened to Galo."

"He isn't in his cell?" EshCal asked, her brows knitted tight with concern.

"No, when I went to visit him, he was gone. That's part of why LenSom fired me."

"What's the other part?" SenRas snickered.

"I may or may not have called him an ivory tower bitchboy," Sinkua shrugged.

"When did you try to visit Galo?" EshCal asked through SenRas's explosion of laughter.

"Last night. I took Nikasu with me to meet him."

"Go ahead to your meeting. We'll do what we can from here," EshCal said, she and SenRas exchanging a knowing glance, "SenRas, how far back do the audio records on your phone go?"

"One week. Why?"

"That will work," EshCal affirmed.

Sinkua shut the door behind himself, hearing nothing more of their conversation.

A pair of alloy boots clanked against the tile floor, reverberating in the cold white hall. AinZun walked with a small figure draped in a blanket leaning on her shoulder. She patted it in rhythm with her footsteps, smiling somehow both warmly and dismissingly at all who addressed her.

Alongside her walked a Berininite in Northlander street clothes. He watched the bundle on her shoulder with a proud smile, nodding confidently to men smirking knowingly. As a room number caught his attention, he gently took hold of her shoulder.

"What is it, hon?" AinZun asked.

"I think this is it," he suggested, pushing a button on the side of his watch, "Yes, this is the room."

"Then let's get to work."

Weakened by the battle between pain and morphine, Uulan struggled to turn his head as a pair of strangers entered his room. They appeared to be new parents, perhaps out to share the joy of newborn life with those nearing death. Such an odd custom, pleasant as the babies may have been to see. Uulan eked out a smile and gasped a greeting.

The husband locked the door as the wife unwrapped the bundle, revealing an intravenous bag instead of a baby. Uulan's eye twitched, fearing what manner of treatment might be in the pouch if they had to smuggle it into the room.

"What is that?" Uulan gasped.

The Berininite sneered as he hung the bag.

"Who are you?"

"You helped her," he asserted, disconnecting Uulan's current bag.

"Her? I don't know her," Uulan refuted.

"Not me, you idiot!" AinZun snapped.

"You know perfectly well who I mean. So, we're going to take care of you," the man continued, "in much the same way as she helped that old ArcNosian take care of ours."

"That nanochip was my pride. Our pride!" AinZun hissed, crouching beside the bed, "It took us years to perfect, but because of her, we can't mass produce it. Now that you've helped her..."

"... We're going to ruin you just the same," the man said as he connected the illicit bag.

The sallow substance trickled toward Uulan's vein. He watched the two strangers pensively, his hand impatiently braced to pull the needle out of his arm. They watched with folded arms and stoic faces. As much as he feared that fetid drug, he somehow harbored a greater fear of what they might do if he tried to escape it.

The first drop reached his blood. As he writhed in pain, his arm searing from the inside out, they turned and left the room. No longer paralyzed by fear, Uulan yanked the line out of his arm, blood and putrid fluid dripping on the floor. He clutched his arm to stanch the bleeding, wincing as he pressed too hard against a fresh bruise.

He pulled his hand away to find, to his ever-growing horror, a bruise rapidly spreading up his arm. It crept along his shoulder and behind his neck. He screamed out in shock and anguish, his throat feeling shredded by the exertion, as the bruising reached his chest. It spread throughout his torso and crept down his other arm, his skin becoming a sickening blend of purple, black, and yellow.

He furiously jabbed the call button as pain consumed his other arm, the one that had taken the drug now hopelessly immobilized. Someone outside jostled the handle, calling to him that his door had been locked. Gasping for breath and his pulse weakening, Uulan pounded his chest in a ditch effort to keep his heart beating.

In an act of pure desperation, he reached behind his head as the bruises spread down his legs. He pulled the defibrillator paddles down by the cords, gasping hoarsely as they bounced off his ribcage. He laid the paddles on his chest. The door handle clicked and turned. Gritting his teeth, he squeezed the triggers.

The cords dangled freely. Impotent paddles atop his chest, Uulan looked to the nurse with fearful desperation. She could only stare back in slack-jawed mortified silence as her patient, every bit of visible skin covered in abusive bruised, choked on his final breath.

Sinkua leaned against a lamppost, its beam diffusing the glare of his eyes. He kept his head low to keep from standing out, figuring sunglasses at night would draw the wrong kind of attention. He looked up periodically, rubbernecking to look down the street, and mumbled under his breath as he checked his watch.

Eytea paced under the light, her wings crammed into an overcoat. She fiddled with the flower in her hair as the minutes crawled by. At every approaching set of headlights, she took hopeful but ultimately disappointing pause.

"This is the right place, right?" Eytea worried.

"Phylus said the old boarding dock," Sinkua confirmed, "I assume he meant Epsilon."

Eytea eventually gave up her anxious pacing. Shortly, they both retired to sitting under opposite sides of the lamppost, passing the time with idle conversation.

Well over an hour past schedule, a sedan and a pair of motorcycles parked alongside them. The foremost rider dismounted and took off his helmet.

"Good, you haven't left," Spril greeted, "Sorry we're late."

"We're just glad you showed up," Eytea excused, "What happened?"

"Standard protocol for dodging party-crashers," Spril explained, "Anyone on a stakeout would've given up by now."

"Well, you could've done with letting us know," Sinkua insisted.

"Probably," Phylus agreed as he stepped out from the passenger's side of the sedan, "but we couldn't risk the possibility of your lines being tapped."

"Besides, we know you two can take care of yourselves if anyone brings trouble," Biroe added as he lowered his wheelchair out of his car.

"Hey, Biroe. Good to know someone still trusts me," Sinkua greeted.

"Right. Let's head inside," Phylus invited.

KalChi exited from the back of the car, as did EshCal from the opposite side. SenRas shuffled out from the middle of the bench seat. The second rider dismounted, SenRas and EshCal flanking her and shrouding her in street-lamp shadows as she removed her helmet.

They engaged in idle chatter for a few minutes, exchanging pleasantries and introductions where necessary. One by one, the crowd dispersed. As the conversation dwindled to two, Phylus and Sinkua, the rest turned back at irregular intervals and headed down the Subtransit entrance across the street. Sinkua and Phylus followed shortly behind the last of them.

Beyond the view of any street level cameras, EshCal and SenRas drifted away from the second rider's flanks. Vielle stretched her arms in her renewed personal space and smiled at her father as he fell into step alongside her on the stairs.

"Good cover. Nice to see you're being thorough," Phylus complimented.

"Cover?" Eytea asked, "What's going on?"

"MalVek contacted me earlier, after Sinkua left my office," Phylus recounted, "He said Vielle needed to lay low. Some people have their eyes out for her."

"Did he say why?"

"No, but he generally gives good advice," Vielle noted.

"I wonder if Galo is connected to this," Sinkua mused, mostly thinking aloud, "Maybe whoever is after you is using Galo to get to you."

They wove through the bustling crowds of the Epsilon Boarding Dock, fluidly separating and reuniting. They exchanged no acknowledgements with each other beyond the bottom of the stairs. Eventually, they converged on a little hamburger joint with a familiar door.

Sinkua brushed the carved letters with his fingertips, memories of the last days of the war flooding back. Despite his weakened retention of long-term memories, those marked with bloodshed held on more tenaciously. The scar on his arm served as a pestering reminder, throbbing seemingly whenever he started to put it out of his mind.

A lone patron looked up from his meal as the entourage of nine entered the diner. The clamor of footsteps drew the attention of the cashier, who elbowed the fry cook.

"Take the corner booth," Phylus said, "I'll put in our order."

"Hey, um, welcome to Epsilon Burger," the cashier nervously fumbled as Phylus approached the counter, "Can I, uh, help you with something?"

"Yes sir, you can help me with some burgers for my friends and me," Phylus said as he slid a sheet of paper across the counter, "I went ahead and wrote everything down."

"Oh ah, thanks," the teenage associate accepted, mumbling the list as he poked at the register, "So, is something going down? You know, like some kind of, uh, inside job or something?"

"I can see where you might say that," Phylus smiled as the cook dumped a sack of fries into the oil vat, "Though I'm not at liberty to say one way or another, mind you."

"Oh, yes sir. Understood, sir," the cashier agreed as he accepted Phylus's money, "It's just, I recognize some of you from, you know, back then. I was just a kid when it all happened."

Something about the boy's tone compelled Phylus to give him a more scrutinous look. Perhaps he expected to recognize him as well. It was then that he noticed the vague but undeniable stripe of scar tissue running from the corner of his lips and tapering off just before his jaw joint.

"Right. Our Parliament for the Subtransit Resistance," Phylus said, his tone sobered, "This was our meeting room. Nice to see the old door is still here."

"Yeah, my boss says it's some kind of landmark. Like a piece of history or something. He wanted to keep it 'cause he thought it'd bring in customers."

"Actually, I was hoping I might be able to take it. Of course, I'd provide a replacement and install it."

"I'll have to check with my manager, but I don't think he'll have a problem with it," the cashier said, "That door's not scoring us any business. You guys are more customers than we've had all day."

"Do you think it's turning people away?"

"Nah, we just got a lot of competition around here, and this place is still pretty new to the game."

"Well, good luck with that, then. I'll stop by tomorrow to talk with the manager."

"Sounds good, sir," the cashier nodded as he slid the high-piled tray across the counter, "You folks enjoy and stop by Epsilon Burger any time."

Phylus joined the others in the corner booth with a tray of precariously heaped burgers and cartons of fries. He filed in next to Vielle, Biroe shifting his wheelchair aside to let him through. They waited pensively, exchanging shrewd glances and silently deciding who should speak first. The cashier brought a tray of drinks and set in the midst of nine pairs of hungry and eager eyes. As the cashier shuffled away, Phylus cleared his throat.

"For those who don't already know, a dear friend of ours was recently arrested for war crimes," Phylus opened, "Chieftain Sage Galo, a key member of the Subtransit Resistance, was detained by Chairman LenSom of Parliament."

"The official story is that I was the arresting officer," Sinkua added.

"Galo is the one with the snake around his arm, right?" KalChi asked.

"Yes, the Serpent Bracer," Sinkua confirmed, "I went to visit him last night, but he had broken, or been broken, out of his cell."

"Literally, in fact," Phylus qualified, "The bars were bent and broken. We suspect he didn't work alone. Sinkua took a sample of blood that had been left on the bars. The Ministry of Healthcare is analyzing it. The results are scheduled to be ready tomorrow."

"In the meantime, I got myself fired from the Ministry of Foreign Affairs. LenSom brought Galo in and blamed me for damaging foreign relations, and now he's accusing me of abetting a prison break," Sinkua explained, "Since I'm no longer working for the government, he'll have a harder time tracking me. Assuming he tries. Could be that he thinks he won, since I'm out of the picture."

"Possibly," Phylus added, "Civilian surveillance goes through more channels and red tape, so we'll have more time to stop a tail if he tries to pin one on you."

"It may be that he was out to ruin Galo, but he settled for you instead," Spril suggested, "It's obvious that he was trying to turn you two against each other. Firing you was just, pardon the pun, stoking the flames."

"On a tenuously related note, my ex-wife XalRut was recently assassinated by an Avatar of Fate," SenRas transitioned.

"Assassinated? Was she also a diplomat?" KalChi asked, still catching up on past events.

"She's behind our taking down Kabehl, also known as The Scout. He was one of the more resilient Avatars of Fate," SenRas boasted, "At least at evading death, that is. Not so much at taking a punch. In any case, the killer said that I'm next on her list. So we know they're coming to ArcNos."

"That being said," EshCal followed, "we have a lead on who broke Galo out of jail."

"Someone involved in XalRut's murder?" Sinkua asked.

"He was present but, from what we can tell of the recording, not actively involved. His name is Pahres," EshCal reported, "He also goes by The Prophet sometimes. He's a rogue Avatar now working for The Coalition."

"He told AinZun, The Engineer, that he wanted to move ahead to ArcNos. She apparently assumed the line was no longer connected at that point," SenRas explained, "Thus a Hybrid is falsely arrested, then broken out of prison shortly after a rogue Avatar plans to come here. It's conjecture, but it's a lead worth exploring."

"If you're right, then Sinkua is probably right about this having to do with whoever is after Vielle," Eytea suggested, "But why would he be after her specifically?"

"That much, I don't know," EshCal confessed, "That depends on whether he came here as Pahres or The Prophet."

"Where do his allegiances ultimately lie?" Spril asked.

"I think I might know," Vielle interrupted, "Not about his allegiances, but why someone's after me. Malia said there's only supposed to be three other Hybrids besides Nikasu. She didn't know I'm a Hybrid. Or about me at all, for that matter. But she knew Sinkua is Nikasu's half-brother, and Mortvill even knew where Malia could find him a week before he was there."

"What are you getting at? Do you think you might not be a real Hybrid?" Eytea asked.

"I don't know," Vielle said, "but as far as Mortvill's concerned, it sounds like I'm not supposed to exist."

"The Commissioner has been watching my family for at least three generations," Sinkua noted, "How could he have overlooked you?"

"And what about Yahsek and Ozzera?" Eytea added.

"The man and the chimera from 3891?" EshCal asked, to which Eytea nodded, "I don't know. We're getting into conjecture here, but maybe the Hybrid gene sequence is propagating beyond what he thought its limits were. It's possible that he can no longer keep track of when and where it will appear."

"That could be why The Prophet asked to come here and ready the stronghold, as he put it," SenRas suggested, "The Engineer called him that after she made the hit."

"So, he came here as an Avatar of Fate," Sinkua noted, "Or at least he made the decision as one."

"The stronghold most likely refers to Laboratory 1341," Spril suggested, "We found a building in a highrise community to the northwest. A carving over the front door looks like it says ayda in stylized text. We know from Malia that these are numerals from an ancient language, reading one, three, something, one."

"One in eight chance that's our place, then," KalChi noted, "Did you find anything else?"

"One of our recon soldiers turned something up. I sent him in under the cover of requesting a job interview, working from the fact that the receptionist at 3891 was unaware of its real operations," Spril said, "He reported that the interior of the facility appeared to be incomplete, but a scanner in the elevator read the key fob given to me by that receptionist. Clearance had been revoked. That soldier is now under protective surveillance. We suspect he may have tripped a security alert."

"I suppose this is a good time for me to butt in, what with this stronghold being incomplete," Biroe interjected, "KalChi and I have been researching a pair of economic anomalies, possibly a full-blown scandals. The owners of the Subtransit, a low-rent apartment community, and a philanthropic job placement agency have had their personal equity income blockaded. These two investors, IlcBei and JalRov, have long funded their operations through quarterly equity payments from ownership of stock in several companies throughout ArcNos."

"To put it in non-accounting words, something Biroe struggles with when he gets going like this," KalChi offered, squeezing his thigh, "They put money into a bunch of companies, and they get a cut of the profits every thirteen weeks. IlcBei uses hers to fund the

Subtransit and that apartment complex. JalRov heads up a job agency. He spends his salary on health benefits for his workers, uses the money from his investments to cover other business costs, and lives off whatever's left."

"Right. They're connected by their philanthropy and altruism, helping the lower class at minimal expense to our government. From a short-term fiscal standpoint, we can't afford to take up the mantel if the estates of IlcBei and JalRov lose their financially stability," Biroe cautioned, "But long-term, as well as from a moral standpoint, we can't afford not to."

"So, they're trying to screw the economy while we're rebuilding it?" Vielle simplified, "What a bunch of clamheads."

"I couldn't put it better," KalChi smiled, "Biroe and I have yet to find the source of the interference, but all intel indicates that the money is being rerouted to a series of trust accounts at multiple banks in Tanelen."

"And Tanelen is the unwitting host to the Avatars of Fate," Spril added, downing the last bite of his cheeseburger, "Five years of silence, and now they're emerging with a multi-pronged attack. Cripple our economy, turn Sinkua and Galo against each another, capture Vielle, and establish a base of operations in the northwestern highrise district."

"Their endgame?" KalChi asked.

"Short-term, my first impression is that they're trying to take ArcNos again. If they're based in Tanelen, ArcNos is the next logical step in expanding their dominion, given our proximity."

"Spril, are you overlooking the fact that they enlisted the highest authority of Eprilen and, at the time, the Ouristihran Union," Phylus reminded, "Former Prime Duchess Olsa is an Avatar of Fate."

"From a martial perspective, they need to establish a dominant presence in ArcNos in order to spread beyond their outlying northwest corner of Ouristihra," Spril explained, "From ArcNos, they'll have access to Quarun and Ivaria with minimal room for third party interference. Planting Olsa as Prime Duchess of Eprilen was a seed, the fruit being the means to pincer several nations, including ArcNos, and stage more subtle and gradual takeovers. Taking a nation by force is more like uprooting and relocating an entire forest. Incredibly burdensome, but the effects are more profound and immediate."

"I bet that's what they were trying to do when they set CreSam up as Brigadier General Elite," Vielle suggested, "But can this really all be a matter of martial dominance?"

"I suspect there's more to it," SenRas cut in, "Just before she was murdered, XalRut asked me to recover some antique books from the house where Sinkua grew up. His mother received them from one of her college professors, a man named Uulan. Professor Uulan, who I recently learned to have been a member of the Subtransit Resistance, told XalRut he was worried the wrong kind of people are after them."

"I can't remember exactly how the writing on the outside looked, but it wasn't Modern Ouristihran," Sinkua recalled, "There's other circumstances, but her knowledge of the books was probably one of the reasons they killed her."

"Oh no," Eytea fretted, "That means Uulan is in trouble."

"I'll dispatch a protective unit to his location," Spril assured, "As for those books, you and Sinkua will move into that house as soon as the necessary paperwork has been filed."

"Nikasu and Yahsek will need to come with us," Sinkua insisted.

"Having them there will make it easier to guard the books," Spril agreed, "but it could also draw unwanted attention from the Avatars of Fate."

"At this point, shouldn't we want to get their attention?" Vielle challenged, "We've been so occupied with staying off their radar that we let them fall off of ours. We need to encourage more activity out of them, so we can draw them out of hiding and fight back."

"Point noted," Spril conceded, "Sinkua, Eytea, Nikasu, and Yahsek will take up residence in Sinkua's childhood home. At least one of you must be on the property at all times. For the time being, safeguarding those books and protecting each other are your top two priorities."

"Biroe and KalChi, see if you can get that money back to IlcBei and JalRov," EshCal ordered, "Also, keep digging for names on those trust accounts. Vielle, continue keeping a low profile. I'll give you a picture of Pahres. If he approaches you, insist upon introductions. Avoid him if he calls himself The Prophet, but do nothing to evoke conflict. Spril and I will continue investigations of Laboratory 1341."

"We'll finalize the paperwork for the housing deed in the morning. I'll have a courier deliver it to your apartment and bring it back to me once you've filled it out and signed it," SenRas told Sinkua and Eytea, "I'll take care of it from there."

"Does that cover everything?" Phylus asked, to which all nodded after a moment's reflection, "Good. Then, this meeting is adjourned. Everybody go home and get some sleep. Starting tomorrow, we're moving into position to prevent another war from starting."

Chapter 17

Galo approached the dark wood altar, which was draped in velvet speckled with sapphires. Flickering sconces danced shadows across his face, deep within the hood of his new four-sleeved robe. Cerulean serpentine embroidery adorned the fabric, mapping a chaotic path along his body.

The Prophet lit incense on the altar as Galo knelt before it. Producing a scroll from behind his dais, The Prophet approached his new disciple. He thumped the ground with the base of his scepter, the jangling of the concentric rings summoning Galo to his feet. The Prophet unfurled and presented the scroll.

"These symbols," he beckoned, "Tell me what they mean to you."

"They look like scribbles," Galo dismissed.

"They are runes, you heathen!" The Prophet hissed, circling him.

"Is that supposed to mean something to me?" Galo challenged, turning his head to keep him in his sights.

"The true heir can read these runes."

Galo searched his childhood memories. Days spent with Sinkua highlighted his clearest recollections, despite his efforts to recall his time alone with his grandfather. Had Gijin ever spoken of any runes, Galo's mind prioritized them behind Sinkua.

"Suppose the true heir had never been taught about the runes," Galo dodged.

"Inconsequential," The Prophet muttered, "The knowledge is in your blood."

"I'm afraid you don't know how knowledge works," Galo scoffed, "It isn't hereditary."

The Prophet scowled at his insolence. This boy had such nerve, speaking to him so derisively. He could still serve his purpose though, regardless of his attitude. Hiding his frustration, The Prophet tightened his hold on his ringed scepter and countered Galo's assertion.

"In a manner of speaking, you are evidence to the contrary."

"What do you mean by that?" Galo challenged.

"Precisely as I say. If you are the true heir, you are capable of reading these runes."

"What does it mean if this is the only criterion I don't fit? The rest is psychosomatic?"

"Nothing so absurd. The mind can play spectacular tricks but not to such extent."

"Then, what of the test?"

"This is a piece of architecture. Not some test," The Prophet scolded, his cloak billowing vaguely as his body jerked at the indignation, "Your hindrance is external."

"Someone has kept me from knowing the runes?" Galo asked, laying bait to feed his suspicion.

"Yes. Your brother, as you oft call him, has diminished you."

Galo's subconscience refused to access childhood memories that did not Sinkua. Even in adulthood, even in losing his grandfather, he had prioritized Sinkua's endeavors before his own. While he kept secrets for him, Sinkua kept them from him. While his own people scraped and struggled, Galo helped Sinkua save the people he had denounced, people who already had a stable and growing community. That parasitic pyromancer had leeched from him, and Galo had enabled those feedings at the expense of his people and his livelihood.

"He is my impedance," Galo agreed.

"Transcend above him," The Prophet urged, setting a hand upon Galo's shoulder, "and find the knowledge within."

"When I read the runes, will the architecture be complete?"

"Yes. Your true potential will be realized," The Prophet promised, "And from the greatest depths, shall Leviathan once again rise."

Galo rolled up his sleeve and gazed into the Serpent Bracer, eyes narrowing as he studied its scales. The crevices granting a measure of protection against humidity, their outlines had retained some of their original copper hue. Contrasting the otherwise greened bracer, Galo's eyes traced the lines as though reading a strange map absent of legend.

"I'm going to meditate."

Heads turned as Yrlis walked northward and inland. She could hear their mumblings but not their exact words, feeling self-conscious nonetheless. She paused before Galo's hut and looked around before shaking the flap.

Nobody answered. In the corner of her eye, she noticed Masnethegeans pensively approaching. She shook again, but her attention waned from the door. An old man patted her shoulder.

"Have you not," he shakily began, "heard the news, young miss?"

"No, what's going on?" she shrugged, shaking her head.

"I'm afraid our Chieftain Sage is away."

"Away on business?"

"You'll find the Interim Chieftain Sage next door," the old man directed.

"Interim Chieftain Sage?" Yrlis worried.

The old man had already turned his back, paying no regard to her question. Moments ago, she avoided eye contact as they closed in, and now she yearned for it as they walked away. She knew of nothing that should have kept Galo away long enough to warrant a surrogate authority.

Yrlis shook the flap on the house next door and received an answer almost immediately.

"Please, come in," a smooth voice invited.

"Thank you, sir," Yrlis accepted, pulling the flap aside, "Maybe you can clear some things up for me. The locals don't seem too keen on answering my questions."

"Yes, I heard you talking outside. By the way, I'm Nenbard," Nenbard introduced, "Judge Nenbard, typically, but it's Interim Chieftain Sage Nenbard for now."

"Yes, I recognize you. I've seen you on the news a few times," Yrlis said, "So, why are you here? What happened to Galo?"

"You honestly haven't heard?" Nenbard puzzled.

"Nope."

"Strange. There was news coverage on it. I get the impression that you're well-informed and generally intelligent."

"Yes, well, at this point, I'd really like to know what it is."

"There's no comfortable way to say this. Our Chieftain Sage has been arrested," Nenbard unveiled, "He's imprisoned in ArcNos on war crime charges."

"War crimes?" Yrlis sneered incredulously, "If anyone should be jailed for war crimes, it's the Avatars of Fate."

"Apparently, someone in ArcNos thinks otherwise."

"Who was it?"

"Beg your pardon?"

"Who arrested him?"

"The locals are saying Sinkua issued the warrant, and that Phylus signed off on it."

"Well, that's bullshit. They have no reason to do that."

"Well, the press release said otherwise. Chairman LenSom took all the responsibility. Or credit as he apparently saw it. He was the one to come and arrest him."

Yrlis shook her head and sighed. She had been out of touch for a few weeks while she worked on her research grant application. They had their work on the newly annexed island, and she had endeavors unbefitting of so tropical a climate. Without Galo's consultation though, she ran relatively blind in this field. A partnership had formed across conflicting schools of thought, but now her partner had fallen into some absurd scandal.

"What sort of press release was it?" Yrlis pried, "What media channels did it go through?"

"There was a newspaper article, a radio address, and a television spot. Not the kind of technology the locals are accustomed to, so filming was rather comical at times," Nenbard inappropriately chuckled, "Not that this is a laughing matter. No. No, not in the slightest."

"Then, why haven't I heard about this?"

"I could guess, but you won't like the answer," Nenbard warned, "Or maybe you will, because you've had the same thought and are already devising counter-measures."

"Do you think the press release was a sham?" Yrlis deduced, "Part of the façade to make his arrest appear legitimate to the locals?"

"When actually, LenSom never intended to broadcast it at all," Nenbard added.

"Because he isn't officially named as an arresting officer. But no Masnethegean would believe that anyone who's met them would think Sinkua had ordered Galo's arrest. So, he assuages them with a phony press release," Yrlis agreed, "By the way, how did they find out? About Phylus and Sinkua being implicated, I mean."

"Surprisingly, LenSom told them. Galo asked him who ordered his arrest, and he spilled it," Nenbard relayed, having only heard the story himself, "Seems he lost his foresight for a moment."

"Either that or he wanted the Masnethegeans angry at Sinkua and Phylus."

"Or maybe just Galo."

"Maybe. And he thought they were too ignorant and poorly resourced to get the word out."

"Well," Nenbard mused, leaning back in his armchair, "It would seem LenSom has something of a compulsion for underestimating them."

"Clearly. But I know just the young woman to help me spread the news," Yrlis smiled.

"By the way, if you don't mind my asking," Nenbard redirected, "what was your original business in coming here? Perhaps, I can help."

"Oh, I had some news for Galo. Somewhat business, somewhat personal," Yrlis explained, "More personal to Galo, that is."

"Well, let's have the somewhat business part, then."

"It pertains to our developing endeavors on Berinin's new satellite island," Yrlis began, "I've acquired a grant to conduct research in the coniferous forests of Tanelen."

"What?" Nenbard perked up, leaning forward, "Do you mean to say...?"

"Yes. Yes, I do," Yrlis grinned, "We're going to research the Sisyphus Fir."

"Just put that in the middle of the room, facing south," Sinkua guided.

A pair of movers shuffled past him, carrying a sofa. They hauled it into the sunken living room and set it in position. Eytea watched beside him, sitting on the stairs while he stood in the foyer.

"So, are you really comfortable with this?" she pried, "I mean, you have to admit, talking about it is nothing like actually being here."

"Yeah, I know. But I'm fine with it."

"Look, you don't have to act so strong all the time. I won't think any less of you if you want to back out," Eytea promised, "We can just take the books and sell the house."

"I'm not pretending, and I'm certainly not doing this to impress you," Sinkua argued, inclining his head toward Nikasu in the kitchen, "I'm doing it for her. This is where I grew up. She should have grown up here, too."

"Sinkua, we can still give her a proper home without a bunch of hypotheticals tied to it."

"My mind is made up, Eytea. We already subletted the apartment, and selling this house could take months, plus a few weeks more to find a new place."

"But do you really want her to covet the house where your family fell apart?" Eytea challenged.

"She never even had a family," Sinkua countered, his voice raising enough to draw glances from Yahsek and Nikasu, "Plus, as far as we know, that family might have stayed together if she had been here. At worst, maybe my parents would have gotten a divorce and been done with it."

"You can argue hypotheticals all day, honey," Eytea begrudgingly accepted, "but it won't change the fact that this could be really bad for you. Just being here could stir up memories you're better off forgetting."

"That won't happen."

"How can you possibly know that?"

"Remember how picky I was when we were shopping for furniture?"

"Yeah. You spent three hours just looking at coffee tables."

"I got stuff that looked nothing like the furniture I grew up with," Sinkua reassured, "and I'm making sure none of it's arranged the same way."

"Perhaps, we should consider remodeling the kitchen, then," Yahsek piped in, "Sorry, I didn't mean to eavesdrop, but you two had become too loud not to hear."

"I was thinking about that, actually," Sinkua agreed, "We can look into it after we settle this scandal with Galo."

"Ozzera and I would be glad to help. Nikasu as well, I'm certain."

Finding Sinkua preoccupied, one of the movers approached Eytea to tell her they had finished. She surveyed the living room and dining room and nodded approvingly, thanking them for their work.

"I'll need you to sign off on the truck," the mover reminded, "That and payment."

"I can write you a check," Eytea offered, following him to the truck.

"So, how does it look to you?" he asked, standing behind the empty trailer.

"Quite empty."

"Good. Sign here, then," he ordered, holding out a contract on a clipboard.

"Confirming you unloaded everything?" she asked.

"Yep, and that we didn't just toss it on the lawn," he said, "Unless that's what you asked for. Get some weirdos every now and again."

Back in the house to write a check, Eytea found Nikasu sitting on the kitchen counter, her legs dangling freely. Sinkua regaled her with childhood memories of watching his mother cook breakfast from that very spot. From his expression, Eytea suspected those were among his only remaining pleasant memories of this house. Engrossed in the idea of remodeling the kitchen, she absently waved to the mover as he returned to the truck.

"So, we have a house now," Eytea awkwardly announced.

"Yeah, it's really something, huh?" Sinkua beamed, "Never imagined I'd be here again."

"I'm gonna take a look around," Nikasu exclaimed, dashing to the stairs, "I love this place already."

"I'd give you a tour, but well, you know," Sinkua excused.

"I know," Nikasu accepted, leaning down the stairs, "You had the furniture arranged differently from how it was when you were growing up here."

"Exactly," Sinkua grinned as Nikasu ran up the stairs, returning his attention to Eytea and Yahsek, "She's gotten pretty good about how she talks. It's not just me, is it?"

"It's because she's excited," Yahsek laughed, watching the stairs and listening to Nikasu's remarks from the upper level, "But yes, she's loosened up quite a bit. By the way, where did your mother keep those books?"

"They were in a hole in the wall under her bureau," Sinkua said, moseying up the stairs, "I asked the movers to leave it when they were taking out all the old stuff in the first truck. I'll move it after I figure out where to move the books to."

By the time they reached BeiLou and CreSam's old bedroom, Nikasu already sat on the bed with a timeworn book on her lap. She grazed her fingernail over the mold encrusting its pages, curiously studying its antiquated cover. Sinkua rushed in and snatched her hand.

"Please, don't touch those too much," he urged.

"Don't worry. I'll be careful with them," Nikasu insisted, "These don't look like they're in the modern language."

"Of course they aren't. They wouldn't look that old if they were."

"Well then, how are we supposed to read them if we get them open?"

"For now, I'm just worried about keeping them away from the Avatars," Sinkua said, "They must be who Uulan was talking about."

"Yes, but she brings up a valid point, even if by accident," Eytea countered, "If whatever is in those books is valuable to them, it's probably valuable to us, too."

"Or it might just be something we don't want them to know."

"Or something they don't want us to know."

"Or both," Yahsek mediated, "If it was simply something the Avatars shouldn't know, Uulan would have destroyed the books."

"He's a tenured historian, so not necessarily," Eytea asserted, "Besides, if he knew enough about what's in them to make that decision, he would just tell us what's inside."

"In any case," Yahsek dismissed, "Once we get these open, I can have Ozzera translate them."

"Speaking of Ozzera," Sinkua interjected, "Do you think she'd want to live in the basement here?"

"She'll be fine as long as it's in better shape than our last cell. But that beckons the question," Yahsek said, "There's a basement here?"

"No, but we can have one put in so she doesn't have to hide out in the wilderness."

"Oh! Is Ozzera going to live with us, too?" Nikasu asked, "That sounds great!"

"Sounds like that decision's already been made," Eytea laughed.

An unexpected knock came at the door. Anxious over the possibilities, Sinkua descended the steps slowly. He craned his neck to see through the narrow smoky windows running along either side of the door. Fist clenched, he threw the door open, hoping to surprise the potential assailant.

"Hey, buddy," Phylus greeted, also holding a door.

"Ah. Hey, Phylus. What's with the door?" Sinkua asked, his tension calming, "This isn't some corny door-to-door salesman gag, is it?"

"Haha, no, it's a housewarming gift."

Phylus turned the door around. That familiar carving rekindled memories Sinkua had tapped into a few days ago. He ran his fingers over the letters, reminiscing about the reassurance he had given Eytea before their invasion of the imperial capital. The scar on his bicep flared up.

"I bought it from Epsilon Burger," Phylus explained, "I figured you and Eytea should have it."

"So, you know the story behind it, then?" Sinkua pried.

"Yeah, but I'm not sure how much I believe it. I've never seen you as the kind of guy to wax philosophical, even in private."

"I have my moments," Sinkua smirked, his tone turning sober, "But apparently, there's a lot about me that even I don't know."

"Speaking of which, did you ever find out exactly what happened to you in that lab?"

"Not yet, but the way Galo was talking, it sounded like the local plants were, um…" Sinkua stumbled, "Well, they were wrong."

"Wrong how?" Phylus asked, "Oranges were green, and apples grew underground?"

"Probably. Pomegranates grew on vines instead of trees, and they found too many new and deviant species not to be suspicious. He said it was like evolution took a different course."

"Either that, or the Avatars conducted some overly ambitious experiments and mutated the ecosystem," Phylus suggested, "Is anyone investigating the facility?"

"Last I heard, Yrlis was working with Galo on the island. So, I assume she's waist-deep in it while he's here."

"I'll find out if she told Spril anything," Phylus promised, "Well, I need to be going. Enjoy your new home."

Farim grimaced at the odometer as she pulled into one of the last open spaces in the lot. As she put the car in park, she took the letter from her pocket and reread it.

"Farim:

A patient in our care has passed on in a nature most macabre and unanticipated. It is my professional assessment that the cause of his death is beyond the ken of modern medicine. Our internal investigative unit has proven grossly ineffective in this matter.

I've elected this archaic means of correspondence due to current suspicions. I've chosen you for this job because of your involvement in a recent military operation. Please, come to SQHO as soon as possible. None of us feel safe as long as this matter is unsettled."

Farim stuffed the letter back in her pocket along with the rental car keys. The subtext of the letter had been obvious enough. They wanted her to investigate the murder of a patient, allegedly carried out by an Avatar. Sending it by tracker pigeon evaded any conceivable means of interception, but she found the attempted subtlety both unnecessarily paranoid and largely transparent. A brief search for the acronym had brought her to Southwest Quarunite Hillside Oncology.

Snow and ice crunching under her boots, Farim held her longcoat closed around her body. Harsh wind blew snowflakes through her hair as she hustled to the canopied sidewalk and onward to the entrance.

The automatic doors opened as she wiped icy mud from her boots, an inviting warmth pouring from the vestibule. Standing in that minute cusp, she couldn't feel her fingers but neither could she see her breath. She paused to admire the curiosity.

"Are you the detective?" a nurse asked.

"What?" Farim jumped, "Oh. Yes, I'm Farim."

"Jevana," she introduced, leading Farim into the lobby, "I thought with how you were standing there, either you're the detective, or you're at the wrong hospital. What were you doing, anyway?"

"It was the air currents. You'd think I'm crazy if I explained myself."

"Most of us already think you're crazy because of the people you've investigated. But that's also why we called you."

"The Avatars of Fate," Farim blurted, "It's okay to say it. They're not going to magically appear just because you say their name. Avatars of Fate. Avatars of Fate. Avatars of Fate. See? Nothing."

"After the security breach, we have all grown a mite superstitious," Jevana confessed, "We knew of the patient's involvement in the Subtransit Resistance, but between his terminal illness and their reported dormancy, we thought additional security was a frivolous expense."

"A lot of us haven't been hunted down," Farim excused, masking her anger at their carelessness, "I presume the patient was Uulan, then."

"It was. You two were familiar?"

"We served together in the Subtransit Resistance," Farim recalled, a previously deferred lump swelling in her throat, "I called him a few weeks ago to ask for his help with some research. It was the first and last time we'd spoken since we left ArcNos."

"I'm awfully sorry to hear that," Jevana consoled, "His killers left minimal vital information behind. Their fingerprints were blank, but I assume you already knew that."

"Killers?"

"Yes, two people went into his room shortly before he was pronounced dead. A Northlander woman and a Southlander man, both middle-aged. The woman had something bundled in a blanket, leaning on her shoulder."

"They posed as new parents to get inside his room and murder him," Farim deduced, recoiling, "That is beyond contemptible."

"We thought so, too," Jevana agreed, "But we hoped if you could find out who did it and perhaps help us understand how, we might restore a semblance of security."

"I'm more concerned with why than who," Farim clarified, "If I know why they killed him, I can determine if you're still at risk. You're better off avoiding these people altogether."

"We have no record of their time inside his room. Audio and video security feeds were wiped clean, as though they shut off when they walked in and came back on when they left. Any idea what can cause that to happen?"

"Electromagnetic interference. One of them carried a transmitter. Could I get the feeds anyway?"

"I don't see how they'd be of use to you, but of course," Jevana complied.

"A few frames might have slipped through," Farim explained, "Did anybody outside of the room hear anything?"

"Nothing of substance. Just something about a ship."

"That doesn't help by itself, but if I can get those surveillance feeds, I'll take them back to my lab in Poravit and see what else I can extract."

"Do you think maybe you could do your research on site?" Jevana pleaded.

"Sorry, I need my lab for this," Farim dismissed, "If your investigators couldn't pull anything, I assume you don't have the equipment I'll need."

"Our equipment is police grade, the same as what you use, I should assume."

"Not quite the same. My work has given me access to some more advanced technology," Farim boasted, "But if it will make everyone here feel better, I'll start my investigation here."

"Thank you. We've assigned you a research station with full autonomy," Jevana offered, "Anything you need, just ask."

"In that case, I'm also going to need Uulan's autopsy records."

Jevana's mouth flattened pensively. She stared at Farim for a few dragging seconds, blinked lingeringly, and said, "Let me just take you downstairs, then."

Her shoulders deflating with preemptive relief, Jevana led Farim through the halls and into depths privileged only to employees of particular standing. Coworkers watched with reserved optimism as they passed, Jevana's wide-eyed nod confirming their hunches. Perhaps the one person who could bring closure to this bizarre murder had finally heeded their call.

Farim watched straight ahead, catching glimpses of their stares in her periphery. Her mind scrambled with possibilities, most of them ultimately faulting herself. In fact, from her thus far limited perspective, it seemed like the most reasonable explanation. She had called him to ask about the history of the Avatars and the Hybrids, and he wound up murdered. The more reason she found to believe she had unwittingly marked him, the more self-consciously she dodged eye contact.

Through an unmarked door and down a long corridor, Jevana took Farim to a service elevator only accessible by a six-digit security code. Its scent betrayed its usual purpose to Farim. A blend of hard candy and formaldehyde had stained the metal walls with its sweetly pungent aroma.

At the bottom, they entered a morgue with cold storage lockers covering the back wall almost entirely. A medical examiner paused awkwardly in midstride as two people stepped out of the elevator without a gurney between them. He smiled nervously and shuffled back to his current subject.

"Farim, this is Seirakh, one of our investigative medical examiners," Jevana introduced, "Seirakh, this is Farim, the detective we sent for. Can you pull Professor Uulan and his records, please?"

"It really isn't necessary for me to see the body," Farim insisted, "I just need his records and the surveillance feeds."

"Well, that's just the problem, madam," Seirakh fumbled, "We're not sure what killed him."

"How can you not be sure? It's been more than a week since I got your letter, and you haven't even determined cause of death?"

"Oh, we've determined the cause of death. That was easy enough," Seirakh scolded, "What we can't understand is what did it to him."

"Just look at him first," Jevana pleaded, "I don't know. Maybe it will help you."

"Well, I did use a gun to track them to Tanelen," Farim mumbled, boasting under her breath, "Alright, pull him out."

Seirakh scanned the wall for Uulan's patient record code. Those being in large bold print, he remembered the alphanumeric sequences the way most people remembered names. He took a bound folder from the front of the drawer and pitched it to Farim.

Farim opened it, reading the statement of death as she approached the body locker. Uulan's cause of death sounded pedestrian enough, but the details of his internal bleeding sounded like the Avatars' work. His muscle tissue exhibited a thus far unidentifiable foreign contaminant.

"I'm sure you have a lot of questions, but first look at this," Seirakh insisted, "Tell me what you make of it."

Seirakh opened the drawer slowly, Farim's mask of calm professionalism collapsing into disgust as Uulan came into the light. Sickly purple and orange bruises covered his swollen flesh. He looked as though he'd been bludgeoned over every square centimeter of his body. Farim spread his fingers and toes, finding bruises even in the crevices.

"So, when you said internal bleeding, what you meant was internal exsanguination," Farim observed, choking back the urge to vomit, "How did this happen?"

"We don't know what…"

"I don't mean the unknown contaminant. I'll get to that. I mean what happened inside his body?"

"The lining of his circulatory tract was destroyed," Seirakh explained, finding his own words impossible, "It's like his white blood cells mistook his arterial walls for infectious tissue."

"His circulatory system destroyed itself from the inside out," Jevana simplified.

"Yeah, I got that. Do you have any samples of the contaminant?"

"Plenty," Jevana assured, "They left an IV bag hanging by his bed. It was dripping on the floor when the nurse found him. He must have pulled the needle as soon as the stuff got into his arm."

"Why would they use an entire bag if they only needed a shot?" Farim pondered aloud.

"We can assume they didn't expect him to put up a fight," Seirakh eliminated, "He was three decades their senior, I'd say, and the advanced osteosarcoma had rendered him decrepit, and he was bordering on dementia."

"Perhaps, they didn't know how much it would take," Jevana spitballed.

"That's not it. Even if they didn't know the exact amount, they wouldn't be that far off," Farim insisted, "In any case, Doctor Seirakh, you said you haven't been able to understand this stuff?"

"I've run samples through everything. Spectrometer. Chromatograph. Even the spectral comparator," Seirakh reported.

"That last one isn't exactly standard protocol," Farim interrupted.

"I know, but I'd gotten desperate," Seirakh defended, "They all came up as unidentifiable. This compound does not and, to wit, cannot occur in nature."

"Thankfully!" Jevana blurted.

"Quite so. But there are also no records of it having ever been synthesized."

"Meaning this is a private development," Farim explained, "It wouldn't the first."

"It gets worse," Seirakh said, "Some of the elements have never been successfully synthesized either. They've even stabilized isotopes either never attempted or with half-lives best measured in microseconds."

"Well, I'd appreciate any information you have about this compound," Farim requested, "It might help me track them down and predict their next move. Can you do that for me, Doctor Seirakh?"

"I'm not sure how much you'll be able to comprehend, but it can't hurt to humor you."

"Great. Now, Jevana, can I get those surveillance feeds?"

"Right this way," Jevana nodded.

Behind a door looking from a distance like a column of cadaver lockers, Jevana showed Farim to an expansive forensics laboratory. A vast collection of investigative equipment occupied the majority of the floor. A pair of investigators worked feverishly. The elder of the two welcomed Jevana by name, while the younger kept his nose in his work.

"Is this your Poravitian detective?" the elder derided.

"Yes, she is. Listen, I know how you feel about bringing in an outsider. This is your lab. I get that," Jevana defended, "But she's dealt with these people. It's what she does."

"I didn't even know I had a reputation," Farim interjected, "Except with the others from the Subtransit Resistance, I mean."

"Word travels in our circles," the elder and as yet unacquainted investigator said, "Your station is back in that corner. Professor Uulan's records are already loaded."

"What about the surveillance data?"

"It's in there, but it's nothing but static."

"Well, even if all you have is police grade software, I can get something out of it," Farim boasted.

Letting the arrogance of her claim sink into his already tense form, Farim slipped past the elder investigator and headed to her station. With a taunting smile, she watched him in the corner of her eye, finding him giving her the side-eye with a frustrated sneer. Stepping out of her social victory and into her work, she dropped into the seat and closed everything but the security files.

She isolated and looped the disrupted video feed. Every few repetitions, she reduced the playback speed. Minutes crawled by, soon marched, and eventually jogged into hours, her attention consumed by the flickering static. With fatigued eyes and depleted hope, she closed the file.

"I've broken each frame into six layers but found no sign of a break in the static," she reported, grasping for human contact.

"Deepest that software goes is four layers," the elder investigator argued.

"Maybe for you, but I know a trick to break down certain formats into six," Farim smirked, "But anyway, if it's all static even at that depth, your restoration software won't get anything."

"Told you there was nothing there," he derided, "Thought you said you could get something even if all we had was police grade software."

"I still have the audio feed to work on," she defended. She suppressed the urge to blow raspberries at her host and instead muttered, "Not my fault your equipment's outdated."

Donning a set of headphones, Farim moved on to the audio feed. Just as with the video, static dominated the playback. As she slowed it though, she heard warped syllables behind the incessant buzzing, traces of recorded sound bleeding through the interference.

Slowing it further did little more than verify the sounds as voices. For all the static and warping, however, she couldn't make sense of them. Not yet anyway.

With each playback, she reduced the white noise until the distorted voices became the dominant layer. The surviving words had been stretched, compressed, pitch shifted, and even reversed. She feverishly scribbled every distinguishable word on a notepad.

"Did you find something, Poravitian?" the elder investigator asked.

"Yeah, I pulled a few words," Farim nodded, fatigue softening her boastful edge, "Helped, ArcNosian, chip, produce, and ruin."

"He helped someone in ArcNos ruin them?" the younger investigator suggested, speaking for the first time since Farim arrived.

"He helped a lot of people in ArcNos, but," she argued, pausing to sort her thoughts, "Wait. One of the Avatars involved in the war had a nanochip in his blood. It made him sort of indestructible. Did Uulan talk to a man named SenRas?"

"Possibly. The name sounds familiar. Gimme a sec to check his phone records," the younger investigator urged, "Still have them open from earlier, but…. Ah. Yes. Here we are. He called a woman named XalRut. Retired neuropsychiatrist. Tenured professor at Quarunite University Southwest. Next of kin, BeiLou and MeiLom, both deceased. Marital status: divorced. Most recent spouse: SenRas. That's where I knew his name from."

"You got all that from Uulan's phone records?" Farim asked, briefly sidetracked.

"We have automatic cross-referencing on caller identification records. Does this mean anything? The fact that he called XalRut?"

"I think so. SenRas managed to disable the nanochip that I mentioned. If his ex-wife was a neuropsychiatrist, she probably had something to do with it," Farim deduced, "So, XalRut helped the ArcNosian, being SenRas, destroy The Scout's nanochip. Which means we're dealing with whoever designed it."

"Why kill Uulan over a phone call, then?"

"They exchanged information. Either, she told him something important or vice versa. Possibly both. That would mean XalRut is…"

"She was murdered. Explosive tracer round to the head," he interrupted, "Sorry."

"Son of a bitch! If they already cut both ends, there's no telling where they might…" Farim ranted, trailing off into a dawning horrible epiphany.

"…Where they might what?"

"I can't believe this didn't occur to me before!" Farim spat, hastily closing Uulan's surveillance files.

"What didn't occur to you?" the younger investigator pried, 'What's going on? Are we safe here?"

"I know who they're after. You're safe as long as you keep your mouth shut," Farim insisted, "Destroy every record that I was ever here."

Chapter 18

Surrounded by blue sconces casting translucent shadows of themselves, Galo meditated atop the dais in his chamber. His body trembled with each breath, milystis coursing like blood. That very energy traced the scales of the Serpent Bracer, many arrangements of such resembling the runes from The Prophet's scroll.

Since noticing this, Galo had endeavored to etch the runes upon his bracer in milystis. Progress had been significant, as he sharpened his finesse to hold multiple glyphs. Placing them in order, or even in total, was still well beyond his ken.

A faint breeze swept down the side of his body, and Galo opened his eyes. His face twitched as, in his heightened awareness, he felt he could count the microorganisms in the wall. A metallic clink drew his attention to the floor, and he pensively rose to approach the object.

It was an orchid, either composed of platinum or coated in it. He studied it from several angles, rolling it throughout the light as his lips curled into puzzled curiosity. Interrupted by a faint smell of sage, his attention turned to the nearest wall.

As he approached, he found a hole barely a few centimeters wide. He shifted his head, trying to find a well-lit vantage point. He had no such luck, but the smell grew stronger near the hole, waxing and waning in respiratory rhythm.

"Who's there?" Galo called.

"A friend," someone answered from behind the wall, "Though I fear you would disagree at this time."

"Is that why you hide? Cowardice?"

"I prefer tactical clandestinity, but if you would call it cowardice, I cannot stop you."

"What do you want?"

"To help you. The Prophet is not who you think he is."

"I must awaken Leviathan. No voice from the wall is going to stop me."

"Indeed. But not for the man he is now. Certainly not for the man you have become."

"What is this orchid?"

"We have named it the Platinum Orchid. It is, in point of fact, a seedling for something much greater."

"A relic for an arbormancer? Or are you familiar with my studies?"

"I know of them better than you might suppose, but it is ultimately for an arbormancer."

"You have found the wrong one, then. Vielle is the one you seek."

"I know. I learned of such through MalVek."

"You know MalVek?"

"As well as NalSet. Again, better than you might suppose."

"You claim to know much, but you have still brought this to the wrong one."

"Quite to the contrary, young Chieftain Sage. It is neither my duty nor my position to deliver the Platinum Orchid to Vielle at this time."

"Do you presume it to be mine?"

"I do not. However, it is to save lives in this place, should our theory pan out."

"I will entertain your musings, as long as you answer one question. Why will you not show your face to me?"

"You and I know each other, although we have never met. I do not want our first encounter to be on terms such as your current state engenders."

With the rising sun shining through the window, Sinkua sat at the foot of their bed, rubbing the fatigue from his eyes. He looked back to find the bed otherwise empty. Eytea had awoken strangely early, probably roused by his sister. His sleep had ended prematurely, as it often did, but further slumber still eluded him.

Still not entirely awake, he tangled his body in his clothes as he dressed himself. All the while, he scanned the room for his bandana.

"Must be in the living room," he muttered.

He heard a muffled giggle as he staggered down the stairs. The smell of bacon permeated the air, coaxing him into a more lucid state. He hastened down the remaining steps and turned the corner, expecting to find Eytea cooking breakfast.

"You're up early," he noted, shrewdly eyeing Yahsek.

"Is it morning?" Yahsek asked as he flipped the bacon, "Sorry, my internal clock is still a bit out of sync."

"Well, we have external clocks in this house. But if you're going to wake people up, at least you're doing it humanely," Sinkua said, "Have you seen Eytea? She wasn't in our bed."

"Sorry, I haven't, but…"

The laugh repeated, drawing Sinkua away from their conversation. A red mound peeked over from behind the recliner. With a crooked grin, he stalked across the dining room. He grabbed the back of the chair with a sudden outburst, trying to startle his stalker.

Her hair bunched into his red bandana, Nikasu launched herself over the armchair and tackled Sinkua. She watched with triumphant amusement as her planning and waiting coalesced into his smirk exploding into a fit of surprised laughter. Lying across his stomach, she joined in the laughter, his spasming abdominals shaking her and cracking her up all the harder. She failed to notice he had taken back his bandana until he wriggled out from underneath her.

"I thought you might need a laugh this morning," Nikasu smiled, catching her breath.

"I'll take one any morning I can get it," Sinkua agreed, his tone sobering as he adjusted his bandana, "But I get the feeling you have bad news."

"Possibly. Eytea is gone, but we do not know when or why she left," Nikasu reported, her voice abruptly turning somber, "She left a presumably handwritten letter, so she cannot have been abducted."

"That's what I was about to tell you," Yahsek interjected as he plated the bacon alongside a pile of scrambled eggs, "She might have had personal matters to tend to. Errands or called to work maybe."

"Were that the case, I believe she would have awakened him or perhaps left an unsealed note," Nikasu contended, "Her sealing the envelope indicates that the matter is more private and thus is likely more dire."

"Nikasu. Please. Quit with the robot talk," Sinkua urged, rubbing the back of his head, "Where's the note?"

Nikasu hung her head solemnly and nodded to the coffee table. Sinkua approached it slowly, as though the truth would only manifest once he read the letter. Breaking through his inhibitions, he swiped the envelope and ripped it open.

Fear became relief as he read the opening line. Further down the page, it turned to a different sort of fear, for her life rather than their relationship. Setting the letter aside, he turned to Nikasu and wrapped his arms around her.

"She's on her way to Ferya."

Eytea's eyes fluttered open, one buried her pillowcase, the other drinking what droplets of moonlight trickled through the windowpane. She listened to the creaks of the old house among the chirping crickets and hooting owls, wondering how she had awoken so abruptly. A loud knocking came from the front door.

She rolled out of bed halfheartedly and hobbled down the stairs. The knocking continued, steadily growing louder. Not anyone else to be awoken by the knocking, Eytea stomped on the stairs. The nocturnal visitor apparently understood, as they knocked only once more, this time softly.

Eytea opened the door to find Farim on the stoop, clutching her longcoat around her body. Her expression spoke of overwhelming urgency, the kind driven by mortal fear. Eytea's spine straightened, her consciousness rushing back by the urgency of necessity.

"Farim," Eytea greeted, trying to calm her with her voice, "Get in here. Get out of the cold."

"Thank you," Farim accepted, shutting the door behind herself, "But I'm afraid I can't stay long. Neither can you."

"I'll go wake the others," Eytea excused, turning her back.

"No!" Farim protested in a sharp whisper, grabbing Eytea's arm, "Just you. The others need to stay here."

"What's going on?"

"It's your mother. You need to sit down."

"What about her?" Eytea asked fearfully.

Farim nodded assertively to a dining room chair. Eytea scrutinized Farim's expression as she paced backward to the chair.

"If something happened to my mother, Sinkua will want to come."

"Eytea, listen to me," Farim urged, sitting across from her, "Nothing happened to your mother. Not yet, anyway. But if both of you go, I can assure you that something will."

"What do you mean 'not yet'?" Eytea remarked, "And what will happen to her if we both go? If she's in trouble, she needs our protection."

"Too much protection will bring them on in force. I have reason to believe she's on their hit list. They'll get suspicious if both of you go right now," Farim explained, "There's a lot of speculation about Sinkua in the media, between his arresting Galo and breaking him out. If he gets on a boat with you, they'll know you're onto them."

"Whoa, hold on. Sinkua was set up," Eytea hissed, "But for now, what's going on with my mother?"

"Do you remember Uulan?"

"Yes, the historian from the Subtransit Resistance. What does he...?"

"He was killed a couple of weeks ago. Two Avatars of Fate poisoned him, for lack of better terms."

"Oh my goodness! Who could do that to such a kind old man?"

"Obviously, the same kind of people who could assassinate HarEin and Gijin," Farim spat, "They also killed XalRut, and I think I found a connection."

"The books in this house. Uulan told XalRut about them," Eytea relayed, "XalRut was telling SenRas about them over the phone when she was shot."

"First I've heard about that, but it sounds like all the more reason for Sinkua to stay here."

"I'll concede that," Eytea agreed, leaning forth into a panel of moonlight on the table.

"But there's more to it," Farim continued, "I could only pull distorted audio fragments from the surveillance feed, but they said something about helping an ArcNosian, a chip, and ruining. Uulan helped XalRut by telling her about those books…"

"And XalRut helped SenRas destroy Kabehl," Eytea added.

"Exactly. It's tenuous and ass-backwards revenge, but they have strange ways of operating," Farim confirmed, "Extrapolating from the audio I pulled, I suspect they told him they were killing him for helping someone who helped someone else kill one of their own. I'd say we're dealing with the Avatars who created The Scout's nanochip."

"One of them was probably The Geneticist," Eytea insisted, "I would think the other was The Engineer, but she told SenRas he was next."

"When did this happen?"

"After she killed XalRut. The Prophet was with her. He asked to go ahead to ArcNos without her. SenRas heard them over the phone."

"So, The Prophet is in ArcNos, and The Engineer is hunting SenRas," Farim recapped, "Well, the good news is that you only have to protect your mother from The Geneticist."

"I would think he's after Nikasu and Yahsek, maybe Ozzera, but you could be right about my mom," Eytea agreed, "Either of them might go after her before they come here."

"You'll be going, then?" Farim baited.

"Yes, and I know Sinkua needs to stay here. There's too much at stake," Eytea accepted, "Just let me leave a note for him."

"Of course."

Eytea took a notepad and pen from a kitchen drawer and scrawled feverishly. Her mind raced as she scribbled note after note, ripping each poorly worded failure. Eventually, she managed something coherent.

"Sinkua,

I'm going to visit my mother. Don't worry. Our relationship is wonderful. I love you as much today as I did yesterday. But she needs me right now.

The Engineer and The Geneticist killed Uulan, and they told him something about a chip. Farim and I think they were talking about Kabehl's nanochip, so we're worried they might go after my mom.

I know you'll want to follow me, but please don't. You have too much to protect here. If you go, they'll notice and might make their move while you're at sea. Leave this to me. I'll come back as soon as I know my mother is safe.

I love you. Hug your little sister for me.

Eytea"

She folded it, sealed it in an envelope on which she wrote Sinkua's name, and left with Farim.

Nattily dressed pedestrians shouldered by the underdressed pair standing in the middle of the sidewalk. Their hands in their pockets, the pair stared up at a tower across the street. Despite its impressive height by any other standard, here it passed as average.

"Doesn't look like anything special," EshCal remarked, "But I suppose that's the idea."

"What have they told you?"

"Directives are still pending."

"You know we can't withhold our investigation," Spril reminded.

"They know we've peeked," EshCal nodded, "If we stop, the Avatars will know we've been in contact with The Coalition."

"Have they suspected you?"

"They haven't pursued me."

"Perhaps news of your treachery died with Amirione, then."

178

"We could hope to be so lucky," EshCal mused, stepping into a clearing in the traffic, "Or we could be realistic. I joined for their protection, both for myself and for ArcNos."

"Have you considered you might have endangered both of us?" Spril prodded, walking alongside her, "If the Avatars learn you're working with The Coalition, they'll know critical technology and intelligence are in the hands of ArcNos's top brass."

"I have," she insisted, "I needed to trigger a relapse, so we could treat the underlying problem more effectively. That's why I brought a gift from them."

They stopped before the tower, gazing up its foreboding height. It stood a few stories higher than the capitol building, but to stand within such a monolith's shadow was to truly know its intimidating demeanor.

"That one that looks like a curled lowercase d, that's their number 4," EshCal said, indicating the third figure carved above the door.

"Noted."

They walked into a lobby that could have swallowed the entire ground floor of Laboratory 3891. Symmetrical staircases curved near the walls, which stretched six stories into vaulted ceilings, from which hung crystal chandeliers, shimmering prismatically. At the center stood a colossal marble fountain, encircled by a trough of exotic foliage.

Spril and EshCal parted to opposite ends of the fountain. Spril watched the receptionist go about his afternoon routine. As the receptionist turned his back, Spril tapped the fountain with the sole of his shoe, and he and EshCal dashed for the stairs.

They each ducked behind a potted plant at the base of the twin staircases as the receptionist turned toward the door. Once his attention returned to his work, they rushed deeper into the lobby, EshCal a bit behind, being hindered by her backpack. They converged at the back of the room, before an unmarked door. They found it unlocked, as reported by their reconnaissance soldier.

At the end of a long corridor stood an elevator door nearly the width of the hall. EshCal swallowed anxiously at the sound of distant humming as she pushed the button. Undoubtedly, they monitored this elevator, and each second that rattled past was another chance for the Avatars to stymy their efforts.

"Looks like we're in luck," Spril said as the doors opened, noticing EshCal's angst.

"I prefer not to count on luck," EshCal said, leading him into the elevator, "I don't exactly believe in it."

"I have no choice," he insisted, tapping the back of his head.

"Sure, if you want to call it that."

As the doors closed, and before Spril could question her remark, EshCal dropped to one knee and opened her backpack. From it, she pulled a console with a mounted piston and a tuning fork attached by a long wire. She powered up the console and nodded to Spril.

Spril bounded onto the handrail, leaning against the wall with his arms spread for balance. EshCal hung the console from the opposite rail, unraveled the cable, and gripped the tuning fork in her teeth. With agility unlike he knew she possessed, she leapt and twisted her body, pressing one hand to one wall and both feet to the opposite.

Shimmying down until she balanced on the handrails, EshCal struck the floor with the tuning fork. She watched the screen as the prongs reverberated and, once the reading stopped, placed the console in the center of the floor. With the pull of a trigger, a bolt in each corner secured the console where it lay. She pushed a couple of buttons and set the piston into motion.

The floor wobbled gelatinously, ripples resonating from the console. The rings gradually tightened, ripples stretching higher and deeper. EshCal tapped Spril's leg and pointed to his quarterstaff.

Mouth agape in disbelief, Spril drew his quarterstaff from its back holster. He crouched and, holding the rail with his free hand, pushed the staff into the floor. It passed through as though the floor had shifted into a mesophase.

He swirled the staff, widening the hole. The surrounding floor drooped and stretched into the elevator shaft. Cracks formed at the edge of the slope, the joint effect of resonant disruption and structural warping. Spril withdrew his quarterstaff and returned it to its holster.

EshCal turned off the console, and the floor gradually reverted to its solid state. Cracked bits rained into the elevator shaft. She lowered herself onto an undamaged area, Spril following shortly.

"I have seen some weird shit, and I still don't understand what you just did," he admitted, "Did you just liquefy the floor?"

"I don't fully understand it either, but it's something to that effect," she said, lying on her stomach, "I think it cracked because it got brittle where you compressed it."

"That explains the break in Galo's prison bars."

"Yeah. Looks like a two story drop."

"Just like at 3891."

"Hold my ankles."

Spril rolled up EshCal's pants and grabbed her bare calves, just above her ankles. EshCal wriggled forward, arms reaching down into the shaft. Spril shuffled forward with her, lowering her into the hole.

EshCal looked up to find Spril's torso fully submerged, his shoulders just below the deepest stalactites. Dangling upside down, she drew her pistol, checked the clip, and took aim. Her first shot hit wide to the left, the rubber bullet striking reinforced concrete with a dull thump.

Her next shot found its mark on the back of a pressure sensor, activating the elevator with a loud hum. Spril scrambled to hoist EshCal out of the shaft as the locks disengaged. EshCal thumbed her belt loops and curled her torso upward. As the elevator began to descend, she held his arms and let her legs drop. He curled back, and she climbed up his arms and out of the hole.

"Very impressive," Spril grinned as they both got to their feet, "Especially for someone your age."

"I'll ignore that last part. This time," EshCal sneered, "So, thank you."

Sunken fragments crumbled against the bottom of the elevator shaft. The doors opened to a vast chamber, just as in Laboratory 3891. Only, this room was empty. No machinery lined its walls. No gurneys dotted its floor. In fact, nothing suggested anyone had been there since its construction, aside from its unnatural cleanliness.

"Not what I was expecting," Spril remarked, "Do you think this is why your boss said directives were pending?"

"Because he's still determining what they'll use this place for? Possibly," EshCal pondered, "But with his foresight and intellect, he ought to have a working theory by now."

"Isn't The Harvester the same way though?"

"True. His brother may be the only factor he can't account for," she agreed, "And I mean that both ways."

Spril paced the perimeter, his eyes tracing the moulding along the base of the wall. After a long stretch of uninterrupted white banding, he snapped his gaze away at the corner. He squinted and squeezed the bridge of his nose.

"Did you find something?" EshCal called, her attention halfway up the wall at the opposite end of the room.

"Yes. No. Everything. Nothing," Spril muddled, "Damn, that's maddening."

"What are you going on about?"

"There should be another level further down. I was looking for evidence along the floor. Something subtle like a wire or an air valve."

"I thought the same but up above. It doesn't make sense to have a second basement without a first."

"This entire wall is immaculate though. No flaws, not even the slightest off-shade," Spril worried, "Even the moulding and the walls are the same shade of white."

"Simple but powerful psychological device. Subjects feel trapped without feeling closed in. Without abnormalities, they can't form perimeters, much less patterns."

Spril nodded somewhat absently, his attention drifting away as he cocked his ear. A scratching like metal on concrete resonated from afar, dissipating throughout the chamber as a faint tremor in the stale air. He closed his eyes and held his breath, seeing in his mind's eye a rippling outline of the room, brightest at the source of the sound.

"Something's scratching over there," he asserted, "Meter and a half from the corner."

"I don't hear anything," she dismissed, "but it's probably only a rodent."

"I'm not sure I do either, but if it's a rodent, it sounds like it found a way down."

Spril walked to the corner, flashing a grin as he heard a second set of footsteps behind him. The scratching grew louder, breaking into the edges of assured audibility. Spril ground the heels of his palms against his ears, wincing and gritting his teeth.

The sound echoed and accumulated upon itself, shaking his brain with rusty fingernails. His vision melted into an ivory void as his upper body twitched and spasmed. A hand on his shoulder snapped his mind back to stability.

"Are you alright?" EshCal worried, "If you need to go back, we can."

"I'm fine. I was concentrating so hard on hearing that noise, that it sounded too loud when it became easy," Spril explained, as much to himself as to her, "Everything's back to normal now."

EshCal stayed by his side, keeping watch over him out of both curiosity and concern. Strange enough that he heard things so long before she could, but stranger still that it should throw him into spasms. For what little sense she could make of the situation, it seemed something about this room overloaded his senses.

"Stay back here," she whispered, grabbing his shoulder to stop him, "I'll set up the resonant disrupter."

"It's okay," he assured at a conversational volume, "I told you everything's back to normal."

They both turned and watched in fearful and curious anticipation as a section of wall began to tremble. Whatever or whoever came from beyond that wall surely brought a wealth of answers and dread, knowledge drenched in mayhem. Spril grabbed the end of his quarterstaff, preparing to defend against whatever manner of beast approached from the greater depths.

The rectangular segment sank into the wall with a harsh scraping sound. With a smoky hiss, it split in two and spread open. A Berininite in a grey suit and a fedora stood before them.

"Aleepo!" EshCal exclaimed, "What are you doing down here?"

"I could ask the same of you," Aleepo countered, stepping out of the secret elevator, "You're breaking protocol."

"The Engineer and The Geneticist have assassinated two people in Quarun," she reported, eliciting an anxious tic from Aleepo, "XalRut and Uulan. After XalRut, The Prophet asked to come here to ready the stronghold. We suspect he was referring to this facility."

"You are not to be accompanied by outsiders on leads exclusive to The Coalition, especially not by high-ranking government brass," Aleepo challenged, "Where did you get your information?"

"SenRas, before he enlisted with your group," Spril defended, "He was on the phone with XalRut when she was shot."

"Ah yes, he told us about that," Aleepo nodded, "In that case, I do apologize. Clearly, you have come by your own intel. By the way, it's nice to see you're doing well, sir."

"Have we met before?" Spril puzzled.

"No, but I have heard tales of your exploits," Aleepo clarified, "You look rather healthy for a man who's been dead for seven years."

"I've heard some people get to avenge their own death," Spril said, "Maybe I'm not done yet."

"Well, now that we've established why we're down here," EshCal rerouted, "Why are you down here? I wasn't notified that you were in the area."

"Emergency action. Two persons of interest are in a compromised state further down, below the prison cells."

"Is one of them Galo?" Spril asked.

"Yes, and the other is The Prophet."

"What are they doing down there?"

"They were ruining our plan," Aleepo said, "Should our theory pan out however, they'll be back on course shortly."

"What was the plan?" EshCal challenged, "And why didn't I know about any of this?"

"Your ignorance on the matter was part of it," Aleepo explained, "When Galo was arrested, Mortvill dispatched Pahres to release and educate him under the guise of kidnapping him for the Avatars of Fate. To complete the illusion, we needed you to behave as though Galo had truly gone missing."

"Well, what happened to Pahres? Why did he take Galo down here?"

"He shifted to The Prophet. His mind has been trapped in that state for weeks now," Aleepo worried.

"What is The Prophet doing with Galo?" Spril pressed.

"Physically, Galo is unharmed," Aleepo assured, "but he seems to have been indoctrinated on false runes. I came here to save both of them as well as to learn The Prophet's intentions."

"What do you mean by 'false runes'?" EshCal asked.

Aleepo smiled at her, searching for the words to explain his statement. His trouble came not from their nonexistence or elusiveness, but rather from the inevitable spiral of questions which would surely follow. He pulled her epee from its holster and, her face contorting into defensive confusion, pressed the tip into his palm. Blood trailing down the blade, he returned it to its holster.

"Take that to your detective friend," he advised, "Farim, I believe. She will find your answer."

"Okay," EshCal nodded, watching him shrewdly, "In the meantime, what are we to do about Galo and The Prophet?"

"Tell Sinkua. It will do Galo well to see him."

Chapter 19

"What's troubling you, old pal?" the waitress asked over a sea of noisy patrons and kitchen mayhem.

"Hrm?" Sinkua grunted, glancing up, "I came for the muffins, not a conversation."

"They're complimentary for my old favorites," she smiled, "Or do you not recognize me? You certainly remember my muffins."

"You're... NieRie?" he guessed, looking up only long enough to make eye contact.

"None other. You and Spril got those pomegranate muffins on my menu, and they've made me a nice few iolas. So, the way I see it, you're right decent people," NieRie recollected, "Now, what's got you so glum? I didn't think you could look sad holding one of them."

"Just worried," he muttered, cracking an ephemeral smile at her remark.

"Sweetie, I pride myself on two things. The first is baking things what people like to eat. The other's helping people I like with what's eating them. Now, I like you well enough, but you have to give me more to work with here."

"Eytea went back to Ferya. Her mother might be in danger. She didn't wake me up to say goodbye because she thought I'd try to go with her."

"Well, would you have?"

"Yes."

"You afraid the love might be dying?"

"No, it's not that. She knows I would've gone with her to help her protect her mother," Sinkua insisted, "But she also knows I need to stay here."

"Because of your job?" NieRie guessed.

"No, I got fired for shooting off at the mouth to the wrong asshole. At least, that was the only legitimate reason," Sinkua grumbled, "Galo got arrested and then broken out of jail. Somehow, I got framed for both. Last I heard, he was only convinced of the first."

"So, talk to him and set things right," NieRie insisted, setting her hand atop his, "What a bunch of strangers believe can't measure up to what you and yours know."

"I'm going to, but we have to find him first."

"Well, if you're working on setting things right with Galo and know things are okay with Eytea, what are you worried over?"

"I've got plenty more going on in my life, but I'm not going to bother you with it," Sinkua insisted from across his cup of dark roast, "But suffice it to say, you obviously don't know what happened the last time I was isolated from the people closest to me. Or what runs in my family at times like this."

Sinkua glared at NieRie as she rose from his table, dropping her benevolent demeanor. Never blinking, never wavering, he watched her walk away. When she finally stopped looking over her shoulder, he took another bite of his muffin.

Muffin and pomegranate mush stuffed in his cheek, he pitched the rest of the pastry on the plate and dropped his head in his hand. He plowed his fingers into his hair, scratching slowly and deeply. He closed his eyes and sighed, spitting an expletive under his breath.

His isolation had largely been his own doing, he knew. He shunned anyone who tried to connect with him. His barricade even attenuated his relationship with Nikasu,

Hybrid bonds and kinship dissolved by years of separation and ignorance.

The door chime interrupted his unfortunate realization. He had no delusions that this new patron came to see him, but a new face offered a brief distraction. Quite to his surprise, a familiar face entered the diner, though he hesitated to see it as any sort of solace.

"There you are," Spril remarked, weaving around tables to join Sinkua, "EshCal went to check your house. I'll call her in a moment."

"Why were both of you looking for me?" Sinkua asked, "What happened?"

"Some good news, hopefully. We found Galo. Or rather, we found someone who found him. He's in Laboratory 1341."

"What the hell is he doing there?" Sinkua exclaimed, nearly choking on his coffee, "So, it was an Avatar who broke him out? The one that was coming to ready the stronghold?"

"Yes but no. It's hard to explain," Spril muddled, "I don't think I even understand what's going on. It's the one that Vielle is supposed to look out for."

"Pahres?"

"Well, right now, he's The Prophet. Apparently he has Galo pretty well indoctrinated on some false runes or some such."

"How is any of this even possibly good news?" Sinkua snarled, "And for that matter, how can Pahres be The Prophet just right now? Kabehl was Kabehl, The Scout, and an asshole all at once, all the time."

"That's the part I don't understand. But another member of The Coalition, a Berininite named Aleepo, said he set things into motion to bring him back around. He also said Galo needs to see you," Spril explained, "I'll take you there this evening when you're ready."

"I've met Aleepo. He put me in a coma in Quarun, and I woke up three days later in my own bed," Sinkua recalled, "Can I bring Nikasu?"

"Her gravity manipulation may prove useful, but we need to travel light," Spril pondered, "Nikasu can come, but leave Yahsek and especially Ozzera out of this."

Elemeno ran her fingers through Sestak's mane as she brushed a dusting of snow off his coat. Coarse bristles through ice crystals left shimmering streaks in his hair. Flurries drifted lazily from the sky, melting upon the shoulders of her jacket.

A doorknob rattled from the other end of the lawn. After a thorough shaking, the unannounced visitor knocked furiously. Curious but cautious, she sent Sestak to join Seschnel in their stable and stalked around toward the front of the house. Unsure if she should expect trouble or someone in it, she instead found her daughter and thus no immediate clarification.

"Eytea!" Elemeno called, "What brings you back this way? Is Sinkua with you?"

"Sinkua stayed home, Mom," Eytea answered, "Let's go inside. I need to talk with you."

Elemeno motioned for Eytea to wait and entered through the side door. Eytea waited with her arms folded and foot tapping anxiously on the icy stoop. Unable to focus a steady warming current throughout her body, as she had long since learned to do, she shivered and bounced in her duster. She grabbed the doorknob once she heard her mother stop fumbling with the lock.

"When did you change the locks?" Eytea asked, slipping inside.

"After Farim visited. I helped with her investigation on the Avatars of Fate," Elemeno said, shutting and locking the door.

"What did you tell her?"

"I told her about Kabehl's explanation for his tattoo. How he said it pertained to an excavation project," Elemeno recounted, "I also gave her some notes about a building that I found in Lenguardia when I was researching his claim."

"Did it look like it said ynoa over the front door?"

"Yes! It was an excavation research facility, but they didn't recognize the symbol. But how do you know about it?"

"It's an Avatar laboratory. They've changed the cover to a market research agency," Eytea said, "We rescued Sinkua's little sister and a couple of her friends from there."

"Oh goodness!" Elemeno gasped, "Is his sister also a Hybrid?"

"Yeah, she manipulates gravity. Her friend and former cellmate can transform parts of his body into animal parts. He also has a chimera who's unshakably loyal to him."

"What in the world is...?"

"It's a creature with a lion head, a goat head, and a snake for a tail. Both of the mammal heads can talk, and it has incredibly keen senses."

"How could that even exist? Was it created in the laboratory?"

"She," Eytea specified, "And she said she wasn't. She told us Aleepo, the guy who used to send us blue roses, would be able to explain it."

"I can't imagine what he has to do with it, but I was waiting to ask you how he's been. I couldn't help but notice the rose over your ear. It's quite lovely."

"Oh this? I found it in Quarun. He must have started growing them outside of Ferya," Eytea explained, "But enough pleasantries for now. You're in danger, and we both need to understand what's at stake."

"Is it because I helped Farim?" Elemeno guessed, "Did she help you save those two new Hybrids and the chimera?"

"No, but if they know you've worked with someone who's investigating them, they won't look too kindly on that either," Eytea said, "They killed XalRut, a neuropsychiatrist who figured out how to disable Kabehl's regeneration chip. They also killed Uulan, a historian and a member of the Subtransit Resistance. They told him it was because he helped the person who helped destroy the chip."

"Seems rather a strained reason to kill a fellow," Elemeno remarked, "Guilt by association gone too far."

"Sounds like just their kind of logic. There's more to it, but Sinkua is covering that end," Eytea reasoned, "Anyway, if they're that worked up over the chip..."

"They'll probably come after me for breaking his neck and putting him in a shallow grave."

"Exactly. EshCal said he died dozens of times before they dug him out of his grave. So I guess we did help test the chip."

"But I'm sure it bungled up their research plenty. Plus there's the whole principle of trying to kill one of their little agents or whatever they call each other," Elemeno patronized, "Well now, how long will you be staying?"

"Until we know the heat is off. I may have to take you back to ArcNos or sneak another guard out here though."

"We'll just deal with that as it comes. But for now, your bedroom is open to you. Nobody has rented it in weeks."

"Rented?"

"Yes, the horses are getting on in years, so I've had to find other ways to bring in the necessities. I've been renting out your old bedroom to travelers."

"I should go say hello to them."

Nikasu stared across the corner of the table, focusing on her opponent's hole card. With a drawn-out blink, she took a breath to sort her thoughts and turned to the deck of cards. Her eyes shimmered faintly as she opened them, consumed light reflecting and multiplying within. Relaxing her posture with a long exhale, she tapped her cards.

"Hit me," Nikasu said.

"What?" EshCal asked, "I thought you had the hang of this game."

"Hit me... please?"

"You have eighteen, and the dealer is showing an eight. The odds are..."

"Just give me a card, okay!" Nikasu demanded.

"Alright, it's your call," EshCal agreed, turning the next card, "Two. Lucky for you, I suppose."

"I'll stay."

"I would hope so," EshCal snarked, flipping her hole card, "Ace makes nineteen. Dealer loses."

Yahsek chortled from the living room, stifling his laugh at the sound of a chair legs dragging along the floor. Looking back over his shoulder, he took to explaining himself preemptively.

"You're never going to beat her now that she knows how the game works," Yahsek insisted, "Not with a normal deck anyway."

"What do you mean?" EshCal asked, more curious than insulted, "Nikasu, can you count cards?"

"Hah! Don't you wish that's all it was?" Yahsek scoffed, "She can see through at least the next four cards. Her eyes can amplify light."

"What? You little cheat!" EshCal exclaimed, her voice laced with laughter, "You are definitely Sinkua and Vielle's sister. As long as I've dealt with either of them, they've never hesitated to fight dirty."

"She also counts cards," Yahsek nonchalantly added.

"Okay, now I see more of Sinkua in you."

"I think I should take that as a compliment," Nikasu meekly accepted, the very notion of praise still awkward to her, "After everything he did to help save me, it has to be one. Right?"

EshCal smiled and nodded.

An idling and fading hum outside caught EshCal's attention. She leaned her chair back and parted the blinds. Without a word, she gathered the cards and stuffed them back in the box.

The door opened, taking Nikasu rather by surprise. She sprang from her seat defensively, not immediately recognizing Spril from their first and only meeting. Sinkua entered behind him, a borrowed helmet hanging from his fist.

"Sit down, Nikasu," Sinkua said, rolling his eyes, "Spril's our friend."

"Hey, look who I found," Spril boasted to EshCal.

"You've brought him up to date, then?" EshCal asked.

"Yes, we came back here to discuss our entry plan," Spril said, "Which beckons the question, why are you still here?"

"Yahsek told me where Sinkua went. So I thought I'd teach Nikasu how to play blackjack while we waited for you guys."

"She said I remind her of you," Nikasu said, smiling at Sinkua.

"What? I know she's our ally, but you shouldn't just sit there and take that," Sinkua argued, "EshCal, what did you say about my..."

"It was after she learned your sister counts cards and can see through the top of the deck," Yahsek interrupted, not bothering to turn away from the television.

"Oh..." Sinkua paused, "Never mind, then."

"It's okay," EshCal excused, "I know you're on edge with Eytea out of the country."

"Right, sure," Sinkua brushed off, not wanting to linger on the subject, "So, Nikasu, does your mind feel good and sharp?"

"It's had a nice warmup. Why?"

"Feeling confident?"

"Well enough. Again, why?"

"I'm taking you on a rescue mission. They found Galo. He's in a facility like the one we found you in, except larger and less occupied, and he's deeper down."

"I would advise against that," Yahsek challenged, rising from his seat, "Returning to an Avatar laboratory would prove detrimental to her recovery. Not to mention, she is entirely unfit for combat. Ozzera and I will enter first and clear the way for you."

"You will do no such thing," Spril barked, "Marching that eyesore of a beast in there is begging for a preemptive strike."

"Understood. In that case, I will accompany Sinkua in Nikasu's stead. Should he have one his episodes, I would be better suited to defend his unconscious body," Yahsek boasted.

"We don't anticipate any combat," EshCal countered, "The basement was completely empty, aside from one of my colleagues tending to a related situation."

"But what of the lower levels where Galo is being kept?"

"He's with one person, a person of interest to my colleagues, at that."

"Even if Sinkua has an episode..." Spril added.

"If I start to lose my shit, my sister has a better chance of stabilizing me," Sinkua spat from the frayed end of his patience, "Her voice is more familiar and comforting. With the attitude you're pulling, all yours'll do is piss me off."

"Hey!" Yahsek protested, "I have spent years looking out for her! And I am not about to let you just..."

Nikasu slumped uncomfortably, clutching her head and trying to block out their argument. Such bickering over her, and all spoken of her in the third person. She sank deeper into herself, feeling less like a person the longer they quarreled.

"Here's a thought," Nikasu muttered, "How about we listen to what Nikasu has to say!"

Yahsek halted his diatribe. In awkward silence, all four of them turned to the usually timid girl who had just demanded the floor. Yahsek cleared his throat.

"Okay, Nikasu. What do you think you want..."

" I know I want to go with him," Nikasu insisted, "I was with Sinkua when we found out Galo had been broken out of jail. That's when I was supposed to meet him."

"That doesn't put you under any obligation to him," Yahsek grasped.

"No, but I was there for the event that led to Sinkua losing his job, so I want to be there to help straighten things out," Nikasu argued, "Besides, I know how much they mean to each other. This is my way of thanking my brother for coming for me. And I know if Galo could've done anything to help save me, he would have."

"Then why didn't he?"

"We needed a Hybrid on the outside in case of trouble on the inside," Sinkua muscled in, "One who couldn't lead anyone to us. Galo is responsible for an entire nation, so he had the greatest need to stay out. Now, as long as you live in my house, you are never to challenge the loyalty of my friends. Do you understand?"

"Yes. Whatever you say," Yahsek sneered, returning to his seat.

"Speaking of trouble," EshCal diverted, "We can't expect to always keep her clear of it. Nikasu, do you have any combat experience?"

"Nothing formal. Yahsek and I used to spar in our cell for fun," Nikasu recalled, "And a few times, I wrestled the doctors when they came to draw samples or take me out to the testing area. Sometimes, I'd stab them with the needles they were trying to inject me with."

"That's my girl," Sinkua smirked, patting her shoulder.

EshCal looked her over, studying her physique. She assessed Nikasu's structure, accounting for the extent and style of her fighting experience. EshCal flipped through a mental database of melee weapons. With each note on Nikasu's build, experience, and mentality, she eliminated anything from individual entries to entire categories.

"I think a handheld scythe would suit you," EshCal suggested.

"Two could work better," Spril added.

"Possibly. Nikasu, are you ambidextrous?"

"Is that where you're good with both hands?" Nikasu asked, to which EshCal nodded, "No, I'm not."

"The off hand would be used for defense," Spril said.

"Good point. I'll get you a pair from the armory," EshCal offered, "I can train you on them whenever you'd like. Just ask, and I'll make time for you."

"Actually, um," Nikasu said, pausing to clear her throat, "Can we get them now? Maybe you could train me a little before we go get Galo? We have time, don't we?"

"Yeah, we're not going until it's dark out," Sinkua confirmed.

"Okay, good. I know you said you don't expect any fighting, EshCal, but I wanna be as ready for this as I can," Nikasu asserted.

"Alright, but first I need to go over the entry plan with…" EshCal began.

"Don't worry about that," Spril cut off, "I'll take care of it. You two go train. We'll get Nikasu up to speed when you bring her back."

Malia pinched her earlobe as a beckoning hum vibrated within.

"What's the news?" she asked.

"Aleepo has acquired the Platinum Orchid."

"Where is he now?"

"We lost him in the highrise district of northwest ArcNos, but we caught his trail again in the same region. We suspect he handed off the relic."

"Where exactly was he when you found him again?"

"Leaving Laboratory 1341. We presume The Prophet has taken Galo then."

"You presume?"

"Pahres was supposed to break Galo out of prison, but The Prophet took him instead. Laboratory 1341 is the most logical place to take him given that… Well, you know."

"Actually, I don't," Malia steamed, "If he's The Prophet, why would Aleepo take the Platinum Orchid to him?"

"Our prevailing theory is that the Platinum Orchid is the key to stabilizing Pahres."

"I don't know. I don't trust the guy," Malia grumbled, "I'd just as soon let him die if it'll save Vielle."

"Bold words from a double agent, but recall that even after he defected to The Coalition, he stayed with the Avatars to protect you. He leaked intel to us for years, working as an independent informant, up until his Avatar alias became a discrete personality. Of course, we can't know for certain what has come of any of it without infiltrating the facility."

"Get clearance from the Omnimath. Tell him we suspect foul play if you have to."

"We have no reason to suspect Aleepo of foul play. Besides, EshCal already infiltrated."

"The new recruit got clearance over me?"

"No, she entered as the ArcNosian High Minister of Defense and Brigadier General Elite, not as one of our operatives," her colleague assured, "Spril and Sinkua are entering tonight to rescue Galo and check on The Prophet or Pahres."

"Very well, then. Keep me posted."

"EshCal is also taking Nikasu to the armory for a combat briefing," he slipped.

"What? No! He is not taking her back into one of those places!"

"Malia. Relax. She'll have two of the best warriors from the Subtransit Resistance

188

with her. Three if EshCal goes in, too."

"I don't care. It's too soon."

"Others will be scouting the area, as well."

"You can dodge this all you want, but I've made up my mind."

"If too many of us converge on that facility, they'll suspect…"

"MalVek!" Malia snapped, "Meet me at Laboratory 1341."

"We'll wait outside. I'll bring a tap for EshCal."

Nikasu fidgeted as EshCal paced the perimeter of the room. All manner of melee weapons lined the walls, most largely foreign to her but a few intimately familiar. Many of the test subjects and her fellow prisoners, scarce and short-lived as they were, had been tortured with implements such as these. Others, spectacular failures in the eyes of their captors, they gruesomely dispatched. Even knowing she should trust EshCal, Nikasu trembled as EshCal brushed her fingertips across these familiar devices.

EshCal decidedly started beside the handheld scythes and circled back to them. Rather than simply trusting her and Spril's decision, she examined each type of weapon, sizing it up as a potential match with Nikasu. Having completed the perimeter, she pulled a pair of handheld scythes from the rack.

"You know," EshCal opened as she turned around, "Spril was your age his first time here. Fifteen is our minimum enlistment age, and he, ever ambitious, signed up on his birthday."

"Oh, um, I don't… think I want to…" Nikasu nervously rejected.

"No, no, don't get the wrong idea," EshCal retracted, offering the scythes, "I don't mean for you to enlist. You're a fugitive. They'd find you too easily. No, I'm just making small talk."

"Okay then," Nikasu meekly smiled, accepting the weapons, "Which one did he pick?"

"Quarterstaff. Spril always goes with the quarterstaff. Just a stick of wood, but it's amazing what he can do with it," EshCal remarked as Nikasu held the blades up to the light, studying them, "In fact, his first time here, his commanding officer faced him with a broadsword, and Spril still took him down. Rumor is that he broke the staff over his head. Of course, Spril started that rumor himself, but I've seen enough not to doubt him."

"Oh goodness!" Nikasu gasped, stifling a laugh, "What did his commander do?"

"That's, um…" EshCal fumbled, "Well, that's a long story. That's about when things started going wrong, and well…"

"I get it. You don't have to say anything else."

"Of course. Thank you. Shall we get on with this now?"

Nikasu nodded assertively and shifted into her image of a functional combative stance. EshCal looked her over, nodding in approval at some details but wrinkling her brow at more. She lightly but firmly kicked Nikasu's ankles to reposition her feet, her knees to bend and straighten them. She took her by the wrists and elbows to pose her arms. Lastly, EshCal patted Nikasu's back to correct her posture.

"Good form, good form," EshCal complimented, "Now, try exhaling. Let off some tension. Let this stance feel natural."

"Okay, but it's just that you're really finicky about this, and I don't want to disappoint you."

"Trust me. You'll be more comfortable if you relax. Your stance must allow for fluidity of motion, both in striking and in defending. You must be able to fall back and advance with ease. And you must," EshCal asserted, drawing her epee with an evanescent glimmer, "be quick about it."

EshCal lunged with a sharp jab at Nikasu's chest. In a kneejerk reaction, Nikasu thrust a scythe upward, ungracefully knocking the epee off course and instead toward her face. EshCal stopped well short and withdrew with a smirk.

She stepped in and struck again, this time aiming for Nikasu's face. Nikasu yelped and swept the other scythe, hooking the epee. She pulled it aside and craned her head in the opposite direction.

EshCal rolled her sword out of its snag and circled it back to her side. With Nikasu's chest unguarded, EshCal thrust again. Nikasu lunged and swung her offensive scythe overhead. EshCal lowered her blade and grabbed Nikasu's wrist, stopping her short of a stabbing strike.

"See what I mean?" EshCal grinned.

"Yes, that works very well," Nikasu nodded.

"Do you want to try it the way you…?"

"No, no. I believe you. Let's keep going."

"Okay. First, let's go over some combat basics. I'm going to teach you a few general techniques as well as some situational tactics."

"What should I do if my brother starts having one of his attacks?"

"Just talk to him. I don't think it matters what you say, but hearing a friendly voice helps him keep his head together. But if he gets so far gone that even that doesn't help, keep your distance. Protect him as best you can, but stay out of his reach."

"Whoa, is it really that bad?" Nikasu gasped.

"Nobody knows where his mind goes when his attacks go that far. He might not recognize you. Hell, he might not even recognize himself."

"What is it that's, um… well…" Nikasu fumbled, "What's wrong with him anyway?"

"He was taken hostage and poisoned so to speak by the Avatars of Fate. We don't know exactly what they doped him with, but it escalates his pain and anger into a blinding rage and blacks out his memories. The infection is systemic now, too deeply ingrained to simply be treated with an antidote. Two of my colleagues are working to develop a cure."

Her brother's story weighed heavily on Nikasu's conscience. Given the origins of his illness, she suspected they had crossed paths to neither of their knowledge. Worse, she feared they had developed his poison from her blood samples. If such detriments were typical of the surviving infected, her ignorance could never suffice as atonement. Now, she saw a chance for redemption, no matter her hatred for the needle.

"If they need to use my blood," Nikasu began, unable to hold eye contact, "to make a cure for him or anyone else who got infected, they can have it."

"Nikasu," EshCal said, "Why do you think you need to…?"

"Because they probably used me to poison him," Nikasu asserted, "I need to make it up to him, and if his sickness came from me, maybe the treatment can, too."

"Nikasu, nobody expects…"

"I know you said you can't just give him an antidote, but maybe your two colleagues can figure something out from my blood samples."

EshCal looked steadily into Nikasu's eyes, studying her demeanor without betraying her own emotions on the matter. Nikasu appeared steadfast, immovably certain that she should go back under the needle for Sinkua's benefit.

Silently, EshCal returned to the rack and grabbed a second pair of handheld scythes. She then rejoined Nikasu, fluidly demonstrating the stance she had put her in.

"Alright," EshCal began "Watch me and copy what I do."

Spril scribbled a rough sketch of the area around Laboratory 1341, caring more for relative positions than any semblance of scale.

"The area might be staked out when we show up, so walking right in won't be the best idea this time," Spril warned, rotating the sketch for Sinkua.

"We'll need to create a diversion, then," Sinkua added.

"Right, but first we'll need to reroute when we get into the area. Otherwise, we'll look like we're casing the building. There's an all-hours department store nearby with a men's wear section in front," Spril said, "If the building is staked out when we get to the highrise district, we can rework our entry plan from there."

"Sounds good," Sinkua agreed, "What should we expect once we're inside?"

Spril ripped the first drawing from the spiral bindings and, the lobby being rather simple in its layout, swiftly sketched an overhead diagram of the room.

"Each of these are tall enough to hide behind if we crouch," he said, indicating the stone planters, "But the receptionist can see us anywhere if we're standing on ground level."

"Is the desk round, or were you just drawing too fast?" Sinkua pointed out.

"It's a ring. The receptionist sits inside it. We'll need to wait for him to turn his back before we move past the fountain."

"Or make him turn his back."

"Right. While his back is turned, we'll need to get past this point before he turns around. From there, we move to this door at the back of the room. It should be unlocked, but we'll need to create or wait for a diversion to mask the sound of the door."

"I assume that leads to our elevator."

"Yes, but the key fob from 3891 won't work."

"Then how did you and EshCal get down there?"

"She used a machine that more or less melted the floor," Spril said, "I lowered her into the elevator shaft, and she shot the back of the call sensor with a rubber bullet."

"Sounds ridiculous," Sinkua snickered, "I like it."

"I thought you might," Spril laughed, "Anyhow, the room below is similar to the second basement in 3891, except it's much larger and, well, empty."

"Empty? No test subjects?"

"No test subjects. No beds. No tables. No machines. No furniture. No fixtures. Nothing. The next elevator was in the same spot, but we never went down it."

"Safe to assume the same wheel and spoke layout as in 3891," Sinkua suggested.

"Probably. Aleepo said Galo was further down than that with his associate Pahres, currently The Prophet. Aleepo's going to meet us there."

"Okay, now that we're clear on the entry plan," Sinkua said, "can you explain the situation with Pahres and The Prophet?"

"Like I told you at NieRie's, I really can't."

"You did? I don't remember asking you."

"I did, and you did. Have you been taking your medication?"

"Yeah," Sinkua shrugged, "I remember taking it this morning."

"Well anyway," Spril said, rising from his seat, "Best I can figure is that he suffers from an extreme case of split personality disorder, one being Pahres and the other The Prophet. I have no idea what causes it, if he knows when he's about to change, or how much of what happens in one state he remembers in the other. He can probably fake it, but if he could ever truly change on command, he can't anymore."

While explaining Pahres and The Prophet, Spril had dismissed himself to a bathroom. He searched the medicine cabinet for a bottle of Sinkua's prescription from Doctor Ophalin. Finding it, he checked the refill date and intake directions.

"What makes you say that?" Sinkua called back, "That he can't change on command anymore, I mean."

"Aleepo said he's been stuck as The Prophet for weeks," Spril answered, furrowing his brow at the prescription details, "Either he can't change back or he doesn't want to."

"Let's hope for the first," Sinkua insisted, "I don't put any stock in talking an

Avatar into changing their mind. I'd sooner expect to fall ass-first into whatever causes him to change."

Spril stormed down the stairs and slammed the bottle on the table.

"How do you explain this?" he demanded.

"That's my prescription," Sinkua defended, "You were just asking about it."

"This was filled on the twenty-eighth of Librus. Three month supply. What day is it?"

"I don't know the exact date. Middle of Saggitus? What of it?"

"It's the fourteenth of Capricus! You should have run out two weeks ago, but you've still got two weeks of pills left in here."

"Yeah? What's your point?" Sinkua barked, snatching the bottle and popping a pill, "I only take them when I need them."

"You can't just pop one whenever you feel like you're about to have an episode," Spril insisted, "I let it slide when you didn't bring your pills to Lenguardia, but clearly, I was wrong. You need to follow Doctor Ophalin's orders, or else you're going to keep getting worse."

"Hey, I don't know if you've noticed, but this sickness is making me strong enough to take on the Avatars!"

"How do you plan to face them if you're…"

"Remember how The Hunter was bulletproof? When I took the war papers to CreSam, I clocked the shit out of him. You think I could've done that if I hadn't been exploiting my sickness?"

"You know what? I don't know. But what I do know is that…"

"Bite me, Spril. You stood in front of a bullet to keep them out of ArcNos. And I've heard about how you rushed through physical therapy. So don't lecture me about taking risks," Sinkua scolded, "What I'm doing is nowhere near as dangerous, and the payout keeps proving itself."

Spril scowled at the accusations, knowing the truth they carried. Of course, his faults didn't absolve Sinkua of his own, nor did they make Spril wrong to point them out. Spril studied Sinkua's body language, gauging how strongly he held to his convictions.

Spril couldn't deny the comparability of their risks, much less that his own had been retrospectively foolish. They had eventually worked out, but at a cost both unknowable and immeasurable. Challenging Sinkua to compare the dangers they each incurred seemed unwise.

Sinkua thought his dangers being less severe rendered Spril's accusations moot. He wouldn't listen to any counterpoints Spril might have had, because his anger dictated his thoughts.

The door opened, and in walked EshCal and Nikasu. Nikasu expressed a new level of confidence in her gait, a pair of handheld scythes strapped to her hips. Spril and Sinkua set aside their argument to greet them.

"How'd the training go?" Sinkua asked, stuffing the pill bottle in his pocket.

"Your sister's a natural," EshCal bragged, "Guess that runs in the family, too."

"Both families," Spril smirked, "Between Sinkua's and Vielle's bloodlines, we should've known you'd be a scrapper, Nikasu."

"Well, I don't know about that," Nikasu shrugged, trying to sound humble, "I did get one over on EshCal a couple of times. She'll say she was going easy on me, but she's lying."

"What?" EshCal gasped, feigning offense, "That's some serious lip. Maybe we'll just have a go at each other in next year's tournament. See if you can walk as strong as you talk."

"You're just bitter because Eytea took you down," Sinkua teased, making for the stairs.

"You can't stop getting a kick out of that, can you?"

"That my girlfriend bested someone who thought she could be CreSam's personal guard?" Sinkua answered from the top of the stairs, "No. No, I can't."

"Don't forget, she got a lot of her weapon training from me," Spril added.

"Go ahead and gloat with me, then," Sinkua snickered, returning to the dining room with his morningstar and dagger, "Come on, let's get going."

Nikasu and EshCal headed back to the driveway, Nikasu still laughing at the exchange. She had long suspected that a better life could be found beyond those horrid cells. Never had she imagined, however, being surrounded by such lively and interesting people. They all had so many stories of such fascinating exploits.

Sinkua followed, checking the binding on his morningstar, and Spril stepped out with him. Spril grabbed his shirt as he locked the front door and pulled him back, leaning over his shoulder.

"We're not done," Spril insisted, "For now, get in the car, and let's go save Galo."

Chapter 20

They walked along an unbreaking rhythm of street lamps, their destination still a few blocks away. Crystalline dust clung to their clothes ephemerally, a steady headwind blowing them into wisps of water. Highrises stretched moonlight shadows over the streets.

Spril paused on the corner, EshCal, Nikasu, and Sinkua following suit. He nodded toward a certain car, one of several parked along the curb, and squinted to see through the distortion of darkness and distance.

"I think there's someone in that car," Spril announced.

"You can see that from here?" EshCal asked.

"Which one?" Sinkua asked, "You think someone's staking out?"

"The green one," Nikasu clarified, her violet eyes shimmering, "Beside the lamp post."

"They're out of the receptionist's line of sight," Spril noted.

"Well-hidden from both of those buildings, as well," Sinkua added, nodding to a couple of neighboring establishments, "Whoever they are, they've also taken measures to hide from a counter-stakeout."

"Sounds complicated," Nikasu said, "But yes, they're definitely watching something. There's a man and a woman. He's probably in his fifties. She looks forty-something."

"What else can you tell about them?" Sinkua encouraged.

"He's local. Or at least regional. She's from further south."

"A Northlander and a Midlander," EshCal noted, "A few possibilities come to mind."

They all took pause from their deliberation as Nikasu pointed out a third figure approaching the car. They took turns at passing glances toward the trio, eventually compiling an image of a middle-aged Southlander in a grey suit and fedora.

"Wait,"Nikasu gasped, ancient memories wakened by the mention of the fedora, "That's him! That's the guy who brought me my blue rose."

"Aleepo?" EshCal asked.

"Oh, you know him? What's he like?"

"I wouldn't so much say I know him. He's a fellow member of The Coalition."

"The first time we met, he put me in a coma," Sinkua recalled, "But I think he's the one who found the deed to my house, so he's alright by me."

"So why is he…?" Nikasu began to ask.

"He said he was going to meet us out here," Spril reminded, "Either those two are also Coalition, or he's clearing out accidental witnesses."

"For their own safety. Keep them off the Avatars' watch list," EshCal preemptively answered.

"Well," Sinkua said, breaking off from the group, "there's only one way to find out."

At the first sign that Aleepo noticed him, Sinkua nodded in mutual acknowledgement. He stared through the windshield, wishing his ability to see through translucencies afforded him the same night vision as Nikasu. He processed what few details he could discern, subconsciously filing through disjointed memories to cobble together identities.

Aleepo tipped his hat and righted himself. He turned to approach the oncoming entourage, again tipping his hat and holding up a small round curiosity between his other thumb and forefinger. Sinkua waited for the others to catch up, making Aleepo to come to them.

"Very good, you've all made it. Wonderful," Aleepo smiled, "By the way, EshCal, I've been asked to give you something. Would you mind wearing this inside?"

"What's this?" EshCal challenged, "A tap?"

"It is. So, would you mind?"

"That's Malia in the car, " Spril deduced, "Who is she with?"

"Our own MalVek. He asked me to give you his regards, by the way."

"I'll wear it. I'm sure she's just worried about her daughter," EshCal sympathized, "I can only imagine."

"Yes, both of them," Aleepo specified, affixing the tap in EshCal's ear, "Obviously, she fears for Nikasu coming to such a place so soon."

"This is my decision," Nikasu objected.

"And noble though it is, Malia contends that it is both dangerous and foolish," Aleepo explained, "But while I am inclined to agree with her, I do understand the necessity."

"What danger is Vielle in?" Spril asked.

"To hear Malia tell it, the worst kind imaginable," Aleepo said, "She believes my means of saving Pahres will endanger Vielle, perhaps that they will ultimately mandate her sacrifice."

"You'd do no such thing, would you?" Spril challenged, holding the end of his quarterstaff.

"Perish the very thought, good sir! I merely delivered an artifact believed to be linked to his conditional identity," Aleepo defended, "The Platinum Orchid. It quite literally manifested shortly after he defected wholeheartedly to The Coalition. The Omnimath theorizes it to bear a connection to his cognitive transformations. He has, however, been without it for a disconcerting length of time."

"What's a platinum orchid?" Sinkua asked, "And if it's supposed to fix him, why does he still have Galo locked away down there?"

"The matter of fixing him, as you so myopically put it, is more complicated than merely having it in his possession. As deeply entrenched as he is in his darker persona, he would likely attempt to destroy it. I delivered it to Galo with instructions to pass it on to Vielle. His indoctrination is strong, but I sensed doubt in his voice. He's considering fulfilling my request, and the more resolute his decision to do so, the weaker The Prophet's hold on Pahres."

"I'm sorry, but your methods don't make sense," Sinkua confessed, shaking his head, "If Vielle needs it, why don't you just give it to her? And you still haven't told us what it is."

"He wanted to save both of them," Spril answered, "He knows what Vielle means to Galo, so he gave him a responsibility to her."

"Precisely, my friend," Aleepo smiled, "Now, as for your first question, Sinkua, it is a seedling to a great eldritch tree. One capable of spanning the very concept of reality."

Sinkua raised his eyebrows at the thought of such a tree. Considering the Serpent Bracer as well, he looked down at his ruby, contemplating how the three might be connected. In the corner of his eye, he saw Aleepo turn and walk away. As the others followed him, so too did he quite mechanically.

If the relic Vielle was to receive possessed such power, it stood to reason that his and Galo's held comparable potential. His had proven to either be the source of or a converter for his milystis. Galo's seemed to serve more as a conduit than a mere power cell, however, one apparently accessible to all members of the Berininite Chieftain Bloodline.

"Hey, you said it was empty down there, right?" he asked, interrupting a conversation that sounded to him like mumbling.

"The staging area in the second basement is," Spril verified.

"The testing area at the bottom of the hidden elevator is as well," Aleepo added, "Galo and The Prophet are further below."

"What did it look like down there?" Sinkua asked.

"What little of it I could see resembled a sort of shrine or temple," Aleepo recalled, "Though it had an oddly mechanical feel to it."

"Fits my hunch," Sinkua asserted.

"Care to share with the rest of us?" Spril pried.

"Yeah! What have you figured out?" Nikasu eagerly encouraged.

"If they meant to replace you with him, Nikasu, they'd have medical equipment set up at least in the testing area. They wouldn't lock him in an underground temple. Makes you wonder what they're doing down there, doesn't it?"

"When Galo was arrested, The Omnimath dispatched Pahres with instructions to release and awaken him," Aleepo interjected, "The Prophet kept to those basic instructions, except with different and thus far unknown designs on the matter."

"Wait. Awaken him?" Sinkua worriedly diverted.

"More precisely, he endeavors to have Galo awaken Leviathan," Aleepo explained, "The great serpent of the seas, capable of either embracing or strangling the world."

"That, um, certainly fits my idea," Sinkua stammered, "Since they haven't taken him for human enhancement experiments, it could be that they intend to use him to power a machine."

"What? You mean they're harnessing milystis as an energy source?" Spril challenged, "Is that even possible?"

"The device we used against the decoy at the tournament was based on organic energy frequencies," EshCal said, "It stands to reason that they could be used to power machines as well."

"Both are quite possible to harness, but milystis is vastly more potent than tsora," Aleepo explained, "Thus, it's equally more troublesome to control..."

"But that much greater a power source once properly harnessed," Nikasu interrupted, "Like connecting a car battery to a reading lamp. The real trouble lies in safely containing the energy in an incompatible device insufficient of such capacity."

"Basically, it's hard and dangerous to move milystis out of a Hybrid and into a machine, because only a Hybrid is suitable to wield it," EshCal clarified, noticing Sinkua's confusion.

"Of course," Sinkua agreed, "But what if they had a willing Hybrid with a conduit? Say, the Serpent Bracer?"

"Yes, of course!" Aleepo remarked with inappropriate exuberance, cutting into Sinkua's last syllable, "In that case, we must bring MalVek inside with us. Should your theory of a subterranean apparatus prove out, he may be able to determine their function."

"What? No," Sinkua denied, "We need to get the Serpent Bracer away from Galo until we can talk him out of there."

"Oh, yes. Of course, that as well," Aleepo agreed, hastily nodding, "I will go and speak with MalVek once more. The rest of you continue on and discuss how you might get that, ah, Serpent Bracer away from our Hybrid friend."

Sinkua watched Aleepo hurry away, dissecting his sudden change in behavior. It couldn't have been so extreme as the psyche shifts Pahres suffered from, apparently because of this Platinum Orchid. Aleepo certainly had an adverse reaction, though, seemingly to the mention of the Serpent Bracer. Following the others, Sinkua obsessed over Aleepo's awkward pause before repeating that name.

Having mentioned Leviathan so passively, his discomfort at the mention of another serpent, especially one so small and inanimate, seemed irrational. Sinkua considered that the Serpent Bracer may have been Galo's key to awakening Leviathan. If it could serve as a conduit to power some machine, it being Galo's link to the great serpent made sense.

"I hear there's a machine you want me to look at," MalVek opened as Aleepo returned with him.

"Not my idea," Sinkua corrected, "but it's good to have you along."

"Good to see you, too. You look like you've seen better days. Guess that's to be expected though," MalVek noted, "NalSet told me you'd recovered the captive. Looks like her rehabilitation's coming along just fine. Damn good work there, my boy. Don't believe she and I have been introduced though."

"We'll make acquaintances along the way," Sinkua insisted, "I'm sure we all have a lot of catching up to do, but first we need to reach Galo before he does whatever they want him to do with the Serpent Bracer."

"Y-Yes, of course," Aleepo stammered, his cool demeanor once again shaken, "Whatever they've built down there, we must stop them from using Galo to activate it."

"A machine powered by a Hybrid. Crazy thought, isn't it?" MalVek remarked, "Can't promise I can decipher what exactly it does, least not while we're in there. But if I bring him some pictures, NalSet and I can pick it apart and work it out."

"Very well, then," Spril said, "Let's get on with this."

Having expanded the infiltration team, they needed to rework their entry strategy. Aleepo and MalVek debated alternatives, feigning body language indicating a more casual exchange. After much deliberation, they reached an agreeable arrangement.

Being most comfortable with each another, Sinkua and Nikasu were to enter together. After their training session, Nikasu could have perhaps gotten by with EshCal, but Sinkua needed Nikasu in case he had an episode. Spril paired with Aleepo, being that he had the least personal connection and would thus be the least of a distraction to Spril in times of peril. This left MalVek and EshCal together largely by default, though MalVek justified it with his having initiated her into The Coalition.

EshCal and MalVek entered first, ducking onto the bench behind the fountain. Spril nodded as the receptionist turned his back, and they diverged to the staircases. Spril, watching out of the corner of his eye, cocked his head to the side as the receptionist began to turn back around. EshCal and MalVek rushed for the back of the room, keeping low and close to the wall. The receptionist lifted his head and looked about as EshCal grazed and jostled the doorknob at the back of the lobby.

The receptionist's moment of alarm waning, Sinkua and Nikasu entered next. Nikasu fidgeted nervously on the bench, her breathing growing heavy as she stared down at her feet. Sinkua set his hand on her shoulder, but she refused to look up.

"What's wrong?" he whispered, "I thought you were sure about this."

"I am. I'm just…"

"Do you want to stay up here?"

"No, I…"

"We can ask Spril to wait with you."

"No!" she sharply whispered, "If we split up, one of us can get caught no matter which way that man turns."

"Only if we're too slow or not low enough," Sinkua assured.

"I don't want them to take me back," Nikasu trembled, "And I couldn't handle them taking you. But if we get caught together, we can fight them off."

"Alright," Sinkua conceded, "I'll signal Spril."

Sinkua waved to Spril. He tipped his head back, indicating the receptionist and, with a quizzical expression, drew a circle with his index finger. Then he cocked his head, first to the left, then to the right. Returning the expression, Spril pointed into the lobby, then out. Sinkua nodded. Spril drew a circle, pointed into the building, then back, and nodded to his right. Sinkua mouthed his gratitude.

"Okay, we'll go together," Sinkua agreed, "When the receptionist turns back around, he's going to go to his right."

"So he'll be facing that way?" Nikasu confirmed, pointing to the left.

"Yes. When Spril gives us the signal," Sinkua said, squeezing her hand, "we'll break to our right."

Spril nodded to them, and Sinkua shot off the bench, pulling Nikasu with him. She stumbled as she hustled to match his stride, their grip on each other keeping her on her feet. Crouching by the stairs, Sinkua stroked her back as she caught her breath. When Spril signaled them again, he patted her shoulder, and they ran to the back door.

EshCal and MalVek caught Nikasu and Sinkua respectively before either of them crashed into the door. As they caught their breath, MalVek patted Nikasu's shoulder, intending a show of respect. Nikasu winced and shrank back, driven anxious by the unfamiliar touch. EshCal shook her head and nudged MalVek's hand away. Sinkua nodded apologetically.

Spril and Aleepo joined them shortly. For several minutes, they waited for a diversion, crouching around the door. Nobody else came into the building. Nobody came down the stairs. Nobody called.

"It occurs to me," Aleepo whispered, "that we haven't come across anyone else here but this fellow, The Prophet, and Galo."

"Do you think this place might be otherwise vacant?" EshCal asked.

"Yes. This whole room, including this man, may be a decoy," Aleepo suggested, taking his phone from his breast pocket.

"Meaning if we kill him, we're in the clear," MalVek concluded, beginning to rise while Aleepo dialed.

"No. Sit down," Aleepo ordered, yanking MalVek's arm, "They left the building phone number painted on the front door. If we're lucky..."

The reception desk phone rang. With the jangling as their cover, Aleepo opened the door, and they filed into the hallway. On the next ring, Aleepo shut the door and disconnected the call.

"Do we need a key fob for the elevator?" Sinkua asked.

"No, that won't be an issue," Spril said, sneering with his back to Sinkua, "We made it without one earlier today. This time will be faster."

"Yes, I saw your handiwork on my way out," Aleepo said, "Nearly fell into it, in fact."

"Work of the resonant disrupter, no doubt," MalVek boasted, "How did you go about getting into the basement?"

"Spril lowered me through the hole, and I shot the call sensor with a rubber bullet," EshCal said, "Aleepo, since you're the tallest, I'd like you to do it this time."

Nikasu held Sinkua's hand as they stepped into the elevator. Everyone filed in and pressed against the walls. MalVek snickered at the hole, the product of his and NalSet's ingenuity.

"Come here, Aleepo," EshCal beckoned, lying on her stomach, "Hold my ankles, and I'll slide down."

Nervous about the responsibility, Aleepo clutched EshCal's ankles with uncomfortable tenacity. She grabbed the broken edges and lunged, lowering her body up to her waist. She flipped over, Aleepo crossing his arms to keep his grip, and squirmed up to her knees.

"That's low enough," Spril insisted, discomforted by another handling his High Minister in so haphazardous a manner, "EshCal, take the shot."

Aleepo tightened his hold on her ankles as EshCal wrestled her pistol out of its holster. The elevator shafted swayed around her, drifting in a nauseating and hypnotic rhythm. Blood rushing to her head, the target melted in and out of itself and retreated into the wall.

EshCal squeezed her eyes shut and took as a deep a breath as she could hold. Slowly exhaling as she opened her eyes, the shaft came into focus, moving in perfect harmony with the swaying of Aleepo's uncertainty. She aimed her pistol and took the shot, hitting slightly to the left.

The echoing gunfire jostled her senses back out of alignment, the pistol rolling around her finger by the trigger housing. Fighting for control, her other hand shot out in a kneejerk reaction.

EshCal's legs jostled in Aleepo's cross-armed grip as she lunged downward. The sound of his chin clapping against the edge of hole echoed in the elevator shaft. He tightened his grip on her ankles and she on her composure. Her next shot found its mark.

The elevator humming to life, Aleepo hastily shuffled back to withdraw EshCal from the shaft. Just as she had with Spril, EshCal hoisted herself by her belt loops and climbed Aleepo's outstretched arms. Spril snickered at Aleepo's dumbstruck expression.

"Don't get to be Brigadier General Elite without being pretty damn fit," Spril boasted, smirking at EshCal.

Nikasu shuddered as the elevator descended into the basement. The first one always felt the same. Being among friends changed nothing. Something in the air, perhaps something intangible or imperceptible, conjured inescapable traumatic memories. Swallowing a lump in her throat, she looked to Sinkua and squeezed his fingers as the doors opened.

Sinkua returned the glance and smiled vaguely, hiding his discomfort for the sake of easing hers. Though his history with such places surely paled beside hers, these catacombs had a proven habit of spiraling him into acute episodes. Regardless of its reported vacancy, he couldn't shake the worry that his catalyst remained, especially with Galo's life and mind at stake deeper within.

The staging area cohered with Spril's report, vast and empty. Sinkua's pupils dilated and contracted as he searched the walls for abnormalities. He jerked his attention away, wincing at the endless expanse of white. Spril nudged him as he passed.

"Sorry, forgot to tell you not to look directly at the walls," Spril warned all too late, "They got to me earlier, too."

Nikasu's eyes darted between Spril and Sinkua, worried more for her brother than her friend by degrees. Curious, she looked to the wall to see what Spril had meant. Her eyes consuming light with unintentionally heightened efficiency, the ivory sea nearly blinded her. She cringed and turned away as she felt its first hypnotic tugging.

"Keep your heads down," Aleepo ordered, heading for a distant corner.

Nikasu grabbed Sinkua's wrist and blindly followed his lead, her eyes cast down toward her feet. Sinkua watched the back of Aleepo's head, his mind wandering to an unknown familiarity about this odd Berininite, something in his posture or gait perhaps.

"Nikasu," he whispered, "Did you ever see The Geneticist's face?"

"Hm? Not that I can remember. How come?"

"I am not he," Aleepo corrected without turning around, "Though we were once acquainted. But that you deduced him to be a Berininite is naught to scoff at."

"I actually didn't, I don't think," Sinkua confessed, straining to clarify what restricted knowledge had brought him to such an assertion, "Nikasu has been worried that he would come after her, and you're the only one here that we don't know."

"Think on it a bit more," Aleepo encouraged, "I suspect you'll find a greater foundation to your deduction."

Silent as his assertion sank in, Aleepo pulled something from his pocket as he stopped by the corner. Feeling warm breath on his neck, he looked back to find Spril watching him. Aleepo opened his hand, showing a severed and cauterized Northlander thumb.

"When it comes down to it," Aleepo boasted, "their security can be rather laughable at times."

He opened a panel on the wall and pressed the thumb against it. A series of angular lines blossomed from under the digit, and the console hummed to life. The wall split open, revealing the next elevator. The doors spread ajar to invite them into its maw, a throat into the abysall catacombs.

Sinkua focused on his breathing as the secret elevator hummed down the shaft. He squeezed Nikasu's hand, as much for his wellbeing as hers. He held his breath and closed his eyes as the doors opened to the greater depths.

Braving depths she had frequented but never consciously seen, Nikasu led Sinkua into the vast nothing of the testing area. It lacked that maddening stench and sickening groans of minds and bodies shredded asunder and turned monstrous. She patted the back of his hand and wriggled out of his grip.

"It's okay. It's not like the other ones," she assured, "You can breathe now."

"Thank you," he exhaled, gasping for air, "You're right. Same walls as the staging area, but this place looks mostly harmless otherwise."

"Yes, for now," Aleepo sneered, "He's yet to install his apparati in this one. Miserable bastard."

"You and The Geneticist have some history?" Sinkua pried, "Besides having opposing philosophies on medical sciences, I mean?"

"Do you recall my calling myself his antithesis?"

"No, I remember meeting you in Quarun, but I don't remember that. Sounds like something you'd say, though."

"Well, the bastard owes me his life," Aleepo grumbled as he counted the corridors, "And I don't mean that to say he owes me favor in return for my having saved his life."

"What does he mean?" Nikasu asked Sinkua.

"He means The Geneticist took someone he loved, and now he's out to kill him."

"A few someones, actually," Aleepo corrected, "But I'll make right where possible soon enough. Come on. The passage is in the Eta cell. Seventh hallway."

"Same one where we found you, Nikasu," Sinkua recalled.

Nikasu folded into herself as they walked that discomforting offshoot of the testing area. When she last traversed it, she told herself it would be her last time. Even so, a sliver of her subconscience had remained skeptical. Much as she tried to suppress it, that doubt asserted that she would need to return not in captivity but in retribution.

Without the iron door, the cell failed to radiate that familiar air of intimidation. In spite of its incompletion though, the walls pulsated with sickly potential.

"There's a false panel in that corner," Aleepo said, "It opens to a hidden passage inside the wall of Galo's chamber."

He lifted a section of the floor, revealing a dark hole. The catacombs ran deeper than any of them had previously known, his telling of still further depths now becoming real. Aleepo swung his legs into the hole.

"Don't worry, it isn't too deep. Perhaps four meters tops," he assured, "Just give me a moment to get out of the way."

Aleepo dropped into the hole, his landing echoing in the chamber shortly. After a pause, Sinkua followed. Nikasu came after, shoulders faintly trembling as she floated to the ash-strewn bottom of the pit. In moment's intervals, Spril, EshCal, and MalVek joined them as well.

"He's meditating," Aleepo whispered, peeking through a slit between wall panels, "Spril, draw your quarterstaff and…"

"Stand aside," MalVek asserted.

MalVek pressed his knuckles against the sliver of light. He reared back and plowed his fist into the wall, debris scraping his knuckles as they barreled through.

Fragments of wall exploded forth, scattering across Galo's lap and jolting him out of his trance. He turned to spit his indignation, disgust consuming his expression at the sight of his once brethren.

"What is the meaning of this?" Galo demanded, "What business do you have coming here, brother?"

Though his voice oozed with sarcastic contempt at the kinly calling, Sinkua approached Galo nonetheless.

"I'm here to set things right," Sinkua insisted, "and to free you. There's been a misunderstanding."

"You're damn right there's been a misunderstanding," Galo snarled, rising to his feet atop the dais, "I put aside everything for you. My birthright. My home. My people. All of it! All to chase your impish demons. And for what?"

"We both know you chased the ArcNosians to protect Berinin," Sinkua deflected, "Don't act like I coerced you."

"Every aspect of my life revolved around you. I always put you first."

"I'm sorry you feel that way, but that's never what I intended," Sinkua said, "But remember that I risked my life to save your people. Do you really think that was all about getting to CreSam?"

"And just as I start to make good on my promise to revitalize Masnethege," Galo continued, descending from the dais, "you have the gall to arrest me for war crimes."

"I had no part in that. Those papers were forged. I was coming to set things right, but The Prophet reached you first."

"How do you sleep at night?" Galo challenged, the Serpent Bracer radiating cerulean, "For that matter, how do you let Eytea sleep with so worthless traitor as you?"

"Is that what this is about?" Sinkua diverted, "Look, I know I didn't visit as much as I used to after the war, but that wasn't her coming between us."

"This has nothing to do with her!"

Galo closed the distance between them and smashed his fist into Sinkua's sternum. The pent-up milystis channeling through the Serpent Bracer exploded violently, sending Sinkua staggering back.

"Galo!" Sinkua barked, steadying himself, "You have to listen to me!"

"Shut up and defend yourself!"

A flurry of radiant fists closed in. His eyes and reflexes incapable of matching their ferocious rhythm, Sinkua raised his forearms to protect himself. Each impact resonated through his bones and muscles. Sinkua clenched his teeth, fighting back an episode despite the assault coming from his lifelong friend.

"Galo, don't do this," he snarled, "You know what can happen. It's worse than you remember."

"That's exactly why I'm doing this. To transcend above you!"

"Vielle still needs you!"

"I'll tend to that next," Galo dismissed, his assault slightly waning.

"Galo. Listen. Assuming you trigger one of my attacks," Sinkua snarled, "what makes you so sure you'll survive?"

"I am the avatar of the great Leviathan," Galo boasted, "Your fury and strength are nothing against such power."

"Fine!" Sinkua snapped, clocking Galo across his jaw through his flurry of punches, "If you awaken Leviathan in this shitty cult hole, what makes you so sure you'll survive? What makes you think any of us will survive?"

"Leviathan is my…"

"Leviathan is your fucking death knell if you summon it here. That's what The Prophet wants. You mean nothing to him," Sinkua scolded, "Once they have Leviathan, you're expendable."

"Stop it!" Galo bellowed, his conviction faltering, "You are my past. They are my future. My duty is now to them and theirs to me."

"Your duty is to Vielle. If you release Leviathan here, all of us will die. Would you really do that to her? Not only leave your duty unfulfilled, but also murder Spril?" Sinkua challenged, "And what do you think she'll do when she learns you killed yourself in service to the Avatars of Fate?"

"I'll not have you speaking so ill of them!"

Galo drew back his fist, milystis surging through the Serpent Bracer and manifesting as a spire of ice. Sinkua stood his ground, staring into his demise upon the crystalline spike. Closing his eyes and steadying himself, a frigid gust swept over him as his brethren's icy fist devoured the space between them.

The rush of cold abruptly stopped. Sinkua opened his eyes and found the frozen spire trembling just short of collision.

Nikasu squeezed Galo's oblique muscle, her fingertips grinding against his kidney. Trembling in pain, he withdrew his fist, encasing ice crumbling. His knees buckled under his own amplified body weight. His vision grew blurry and his head light. He collapsed onto his knees. He coughed up a mouthful of vomit, choking on a trail of stomach acid tracing his esophagus.

"I can't allow you to do this to my family," Nikasu warned, "I don't want to hurt you, but if you fight back, I will push harder."

"Wh-what are you?" Galo gasped.

"A Hybrid. I would say like you, but I would never sink this low."

"How are you doing this to me?"

"Nikasu manipulates gravity," Sinkua explained, "We came to rescue her, but she ended up saving our asses instead."

"I would never choose to serve the Avatars of Fate," Nikasu flatly accused, "I've spent my entire life trying to escape them. And you have the gall to put them before us? Your own kind?"

"Remember the girl who Eytea saw in her dreams? The one we looked for in Ferya?" Sinkua asked, crouching beside Galo.

"Y-Yes. That's when The Criminal came after us for the second time," Galo recollected, "You faced him alone to protect Eytea."

"To protect both of you. This is that girl. She spent her whole life until recently being abused and tortured. They used her blood to try to turn people into monsters."

"I… I never imagined."

"Look. You obviously care about Vielle," Nikasu said, "Whatever happened between you and Sinkua, you don't want to do wrong by her, do you?"

"I suppose not," Galo acknowledged.

"Good. Now listen to me," Nikasu continued, releasing him.

"But The Prophet has gifted me with…"

"Don't interrupt me!" Nikasu snapped, slapping Galo across his face, "Go ahead and wake up your stupid serpent in here. I don't give a flying shit. Kill yourself for all I care. But wait until I leave first."

"You're just as selfish as he is," Galo sneered.

"It doesn't particularly bother me to die down here as opposed to anywhere else," Nikasu proclaimed, "But I can't let you take me from Vielle."

"What do you...?"

"I'm her half-sister."

"You're her what?" Galo gasped, "Phylus had a second child?"

"Not Phylus," Sinkua corrected, "Malia. Used to be the Eprilenese Judge. Served under the Avatars of Fate as a mole for an opposing organization."

"You're familiar with my father as well," Nikasu continued, "The late Lord CreSam."

"Y-You mean you two are..." Galo stammered, "You're half-sister to Vielle and Sinkua?"

The door flew open, and all heads turned to find The Prophet filling the frame.

"What are you doing here?" he demanded.

"Pahres!" Aleepo remarked, "We need to borrow your disciple."

"How do you know my name?" The Prophet shouted, his voice trailing off, "Why are we down here?"

"Prophet, are you well?" Galo asked, approaching him.

"Get back up there and meditate, you miserable pawn!" The Prophet snarled, "Did you really think your friends could just..."

"Galo, you need to go see Vielle," Aleepo interrupted.

"He's right. I'm afraid I have unfinished business with Vielle," Galo confirmed, turning his back to The Prophet.

"What has happened? Why are we down here? Why are you dressed like that?" Pahres pleaded, clutching his head.

"Don't worry about your old mentor, Galo," Aleepo consoled, "He'll figure it out."

"How dare you speak ill of me in so sacred..." The Prophet countered.

"Sorry, but mind is made up," Galo asserted, shouldering past The Prophet, "You can have me when I'm done, but first I have something I must deliver to Vielle."

"Stop," Pahres urged, grabbing Galo's robe, "What is the meaning of these runes?"

"I do not yet know, though I've meditated on them for weeks."

"But why do you wear them?"

"I assumed they were to summon Leviathan, as you commanded me to do."

"Why would I want you to do that here? We're eighty meters underground in the middle of a city," Pahres puzzled, "Besides, these runes..."

"They have nothing to do with summoning Leviathan," Aleepo cut in, "At least not that I've ever seen."

"What's going on here?" Galo asked, "What happened to The Prophet? And how do you know the Leviathan Runes?"

"He is no longer The Prophet. He has returned to his true persona of Pahres since you asserted to deliver the Platinum Orchid to Vielle," Aleepo explained, "But as many questions as that answer calls for, that to your second question would beckon all the more so."

"You can clear it up later, after you explain to Vielle why Pahres's psyche hinges on whether she has this relic," Galo insisted, "Now again, how do you know the Leviathan Runes?"

"I've studied them for most of my adult life, often at the guidance of Pahres and the man you know as Mortvill. I've worked to correct my transgressions of abandonment, ones of which I am ashamed to speak here."

"I've known some rather unpleasant stories of such," Galo countered, cocking his head toward Sinkua, "Speak your piece and make peace with it."

"Very well then," Aleepo sighed, "All but one of you knows me as Aleepo, but that is a pseudonym derived by a form of alphabetic shift cipher from my given name."

"I don't follow," Galo admitted, "What bearing does this have on your transgressions?"

"The encryption combines the modern alphabet with one of many ancient ones, letters such as you likely noticed on your way down here. My real name," Aleepo explained, pausing to steel himself for his confession, "is Gabdur."

"Wait! Y-You mean... you're my..." Galo stammered, to which Gabdur solemnly nodded, "But... b-but how? H-How could you even...?"

"It was for your own safety that I could not stay," Gabdur apologized, "But know that I intend to make right for what I have put you through."

"How can you be alive?" Galo corrected, "Grandpa, Sinkua, Nalygen, Nenbard, Ocronn, Sanus, everybody! Everybody swore you died long before I was born!"

"Even if it only comes at the confirmation of your grandfather as you knew him, it's nice to see you trusting your Hybrid brother again," Gabdur smiled, "The tale of my survival is best told later, perhaps after we've escaped this horrid temple."

"I concur, old friend," Pahres said, bowing his head, "MalVek, EshCal, thank you for escorting these friends here to set affairs to rights."

"A little persona distortion won't sever the bonds," MalVek assured.

"Sinkua, thank you for coming to speak to Galo, even such as I had made him."

"I've heard that wasn't really you. From what I understand, you and The Prophet are two different people," Sinkua dismissed, "I can kinda sympathize with that."

"Nikasu, I apologize for having orchestrated your return to such a place so soon after Malia had you freed. But I also thank you for having braved it," Pahres continued, "Not only did you save Galo and myself, you have prevented me from committing a great atrocity against Malia and my bloodline."

"What do you mean by your bloodline?" Nikasu asked.

"And Spril," Pahres concluded, disregarding Nikasu, "It's nice to see you're doing well, sir."

"What's that supposed to mean?" Spril challenged, "Why do people keep telling me that?"

Pahres simply smiled at him, MalVek and Gabdur grinning knowingly.

"Come on, let's get back upstairs," MalVek urged, "Pahres, you lead the way. Good chance there's a machine down here I need to check out."

Pahres waved for the crowd to follow as he exited the chamber, and they filed out into the hall. Alternating sconces cast crossing shadows along the floor and up the walls, the corridor shimmering with their interrupted glows as the line of eight passed through their light.

"Um... Father?" Galo fumbled, moving in alongside Gabdur.

"Call me Gabdur until you're comfortable calling me something more paternal," Gabdur said, "I understand that may never come."

"Okay, Gabdur," Galo continued, "When you mentioned Grandpa, you said 'as you know him.' What did you mean? Was he different when you were growing up?"

"Entirely so. His personality was vaguely similar, but well..." Gabdur struggled to explain, "That story ties into the one of my abandonment."

"So then, you'll tell me when we get to the surface?"

"Yes. I'll tell you everything outside," Gabdur promised, "About your grandfather. About your mother. About her siblings. What became of them. What became of me. Everything. It's time to come clean."

"... Thank you."

Chapter 21

Sinkua walked behind Galo and Gabdur, listening to them exchange strained pleasantries and exaggerated promises. Perhaps, Sinkua had maintained the charade longer than necessary, but he had done so at Grandpa Gijin's behest. This man, were he truly Gabdur, had spent more than his son's entire life hiding from his responsibilities. The network of lies had only needed to be implemented because of him.

Worse still, he had long been active with The Coalition. Gabdur or Aleepo had infiltrated at least one Avatar facility prior to 1341 and had made frequent trades with Elemeno and Eytea. While Galo faced political ruin, Gabdur went off chasing teenage girls with blue flowers. Judge Nenbard took up the charge of Interim Chieftain Sage so Galo could go to war, while Gabdur hid from the burden of his lineage.

Sinkua considered that Galo may have become so desperate for a patriarch that he could believe any comfortable lie. After the beating Sinkua took though, seeing Galo warm up so quickly to Aleepo somewhat offended him. Frankly, he found it absurd that Galo would accept Aleepo's claim of paternity so easily.

No sensible person would shoulder the blame for such abandonment and negligence. Anyone who knew the atrocities wrought by shirking those responsibilities wouldn't dare claim to be that man.

"Galo," Sinkua urged, shouldering between them, "Hey, I know you trust this guy when he says he's your father, and after what you've gone through, I can't really blame you for wanting to. But don't you think you're being a bit too trusting?"

"Brother, he saved all of our lives," Galo protested, "If I've learned anything from this, it's that I should be more willing to trust those who have come to my aid."

"I understand that. I really do. But isn't that exactly the sort of thinking that got you in here?"

"No, that was this sort of thinking coupled with believing my best friend had overshadowed and betrayed me. But don't worry. I'm over it now."

"Galo, please," Aleepo beckoned, shifting between them, "What he says makes sense. The answer to distrusting your friends is not to trust all who speak what you wish to hear. Both extremes inevitably result in hardship."

"Bold words from the man under scrutiny," Sinkua snipped.

"You're protecting for your friend from me, even though I've saved both of your lives. I respect that."

"He's saved me countless times. And I him."

"Hence why it's sensible for you to protect him so fervently. Regardless of what I've done for any of you recently, it's perfectly logical for you to suspect that I'm lying."

"Now, don't get me wrong. I don't necessarily think you're lying," Sinkua corrected, "I think you don't know what Gabdur's death did to everyone around him. If you did, you wouldn't claim to be him. Sure, you've been helpful lately, but you're treading ground better left untouched. Because if you change your story after learning the blame you're accepting, you're just a liar. But if your story holds up, you might be the biggest asshole any of us ever had for a father."

"Sinkua!" Galo gasped, "Don't you think that's a mite harsh?"

"No, he has a valid point. No right-minded stranger would claim to do the things your father has done," Aleepo agreed, "Either I'm an ignorant liar, or I'm an honest asshole."

"Fine then. Galo, give him the Serpent Bracer."

"I, ah… I'm really not comfortable with that," Aleepo protested as Galo slid it off his forearm.

"Why not?" Galo prodded, "Was Sinkua right about you."

"No, I… Um… It's just that… Well," Aleepo stammered, "I have some unpleasant history with that relic. That's all."

"Get over it!" Sinkua barked, shoving the Serpent Bracer onto Aleepo's forearm.

Aleepo's arm trembled under the burden now girding it. He clenched his fist, reflecting on memories of his betrayal. Zeroing in on that shame, he turned it into the pain from which he drew his strength. From deep within the nigh inaccessible recesses of his subconscience, he felt an eldritch voice call out to him. He opened his eyes, and the Serpent Bracer emitted a blue glow. Galo and Sinkua recognized it as the same as Gijin had conjured before he destroyed the Triad Titan's defense system.

"Well," Sinkua said as Galo reclaimed the Serpent Bracer, "Guess this means you're just a patent asshole."

"I suppose it does," Gabdur meekly smiled, his composure deeply wounded.

KalChi examined yet another spreadsheet through bloodshot eyes, cross-referencing it against others she had previously inspected. Every time they moved the pilfered funds, they threw out five false deposits, doing likewise with each subsequent transfer of those phony transactions. Thus, the wrong path never reached a dead end with any simplicity.

KalChi had discovered a few lines of data indicating the fraudulence of the red herring transactions. Unfortunately, this required extensive backtracking, which sometimes took longer than tracking them to their nigh inevitable dead end. She had also learned, quite dreadfully, that she lost her momentum if she put aside her work for more than an hour.

"Hey hon," Biroe called with a rap at the door.

"What the…?" KalChi ricocheted, yanked out of her mental solitude, "Oh! Hey babe. What are you still doing here so late?"

"Bringing you a hazelnut mocha. What are you still doing here?" Biroe countered, moving to her side.

"Getting my favorite coffee from my favorite boyfriend ever," KalChi smiled, blinking the dryness from her eyes, "But seriously, is this why you're still here?"

"Partly. I'm hanging around in case you need me. How's it coming?"

"I've determined that the interception does originate in Tanelen. I remember hearing the Avatars worked out of there during the war, so I've been digging for more evidence. I haven't found anything incriminating yet, but I did find something curious."

"Curious can be good."

"The Commissioner of the Radial Axiom Arena banks there. You'd think he would bank in Quarun, right?"

"I'm sure he has accounts in every country. The Commissioner is a man of the world."

"Yeah, but you have to admit it's strange that he'd have an account at the same bank as our thieves."

"Maybe," Biroe half-heartedly conceded, rubbing his stubbly chin as he mulled over the happenstance, "Let me see your computer for a minute."

"Just for a minute?"

"Fine, more than a minute, but you'll have it back before you lose your mojo."

"You have forty minutes."

KalChi sipped her coffee and watched over Biroe's shoulder as he examined databases of Tanelenese banks and the Commissioner's accounts.

Biroe's eyes zipped and glided along the screen, absorbing and filtering information. His certainty in his hypothesis grew with almost every bit of relevant data. He quickened as he moved down the list, blinking less frequently with every line of data he analyzed. At last, he rolled back and threw his hands behind his head, squeezing his eyes shut as he realized how irritated they had become.

"Right there. What does that tell you?" Biroe asked, rubbing his watery eyes.

"The Commissioner has multiple bank accounts in Tanelen?" KalChi asked, "Isn't that normal?"

"Had. Look how many he has now."

"Ah, just the one. What do you suppose it means?"

"He should at least have separate personal and business accounts in each country that he banks in. It's common sense for business owners. Instead, he closed all his other accounts in Tanelen and moved his money and all scheduled account activity into this one."

"Maybe we're dealing with the world's ballsiest identity thief."

"I don't think anyone hijacked his accounts, but if someone could pull it off, they'd definitely be that," Biroe laughed, "No, I think the Commissioner is sending us a message. You know how EshCal and SenRas have been working with that anti-Avatar group, The Coalition?"

"Right! And they're led by…"

"… the Commissioner of the…."

"… Radial Axiom Arena! Oh shit!"

"My point exactly!" Biroe agreed, "He figured out where the thieves were redirecting the stolen equity payments to, so he used his finances to create a bread crumb trail."

"Then we know it was the Avatars of Fate," KalChi asserted, reclaiming her computer with hazelnut breath, "And I'll bet I know what they're doing with it."

Rather than check every transaction on every layer, she traced each path the money took down the branches. Four movements of the stolen money ended with one valid transaction and nearly thirteen hundred fraudulent ones.

"What exactly are you…?"

"Shh! I'll tell you when I find it."

KalChi traced money trails for another hour, working well into the hundreds as she honed a method for efficiency. Her heel feverishly drumming the floor with caffeinated anticipation, she eventually found her answer. Ascertaining her assertion, she traced the money back its initial interception. Every transaction checked out.

"Boom. Look where the money ended up."

"Doesn't sound suspicious," Biroe shrugged, "Or is that why it's suspicious?"

"Oh, now I get to upstage you, huh?" KalChi teased, "Come on! 1341 West Heniokhos Boulevard? Doesn't that sound familiar?"

"The others were investigating a place called Laboratory 1341."

"West Heniokhos Boulevard is in the highrise district to the northwest."

"Say no more," Biroe insisted, nudging KalChi's chair away from her desk, "Go eat, nap, whatever you need to do."

"What are you going to do?"

"They still have money coming down the pipeline. Which means that place isn't fully funded yet. Which means Laboratory 1341 isn't fully operational," Biroe theorized, "I'm going to cut the bastards off."

"But if you do that, won't they figure out that we did it?" KalChi protested, "We being ArcNos, seeing as you and I aren't Coalition?"

"Probably. So what?"

"So what!? They'll attack!"

"Yep. But they won't have whatever they're building there, and right now, we've got advantages to spare. Especially if Phylus and Sinkua fix the scandal with Galo."

"Alright, do what you need to do. I'm coming back in three hours to relieve you," KalChi promised, "If we're going to challenge the Avatars of Fate, we're doing it together."

Pahres stopped, motioning for the others to do likewise, as a perpendicular corridor captured his attention. At the end of a long stretch stood a set of foreboding double doors, rich mahogany panels adorned with goldleaf overlaying intricate engravings and ivory handles mounted to plates of gold. Pahres approached the doors with distantly knowing curiosity.

"Did you find something?" EshCal asked.

"This seems familiar," Pahres puzzled, "This room was important to him."

"These carvings look like the runes you had me studying," Galo added, "Sorry, I mean that The Prophet had me studying."

"No need to apologize," Pahres excused, "But I believe you may indeed be right. That would establish a connection among the runes, this room, and the Serpent Bracer."

"The runes are exactly the same," Gabdur confirmed, rubbing the back of his neck, "It's a lost Berininite script of the ancient language used upstairs."

"Can you read it?" Galo asked.

"I... I'm afraid not," Gabdur refused, the light shimmering yellowish off beads of sweat between his fingers, "The lost scripts used to be passed through our family, but we abandoned that custom many generations ago."

"Seeing as we've established a connection here," MalVek asserted, shouldering to the fore, "this room'll be where we find the machine. If there is one."

Before anyone could protest his methods, MalVek yanked an ivory handle. Much to his chagrin, they scarcely budged. He pulled again, but they moved so little it seemed like someone had bolted door handles to the wall as a practical joke.

Galo reached past him and grabbed a handle. The ivory glowed with the same shade of blue as the milystic light radiating from the Serpent Bracer. His arm trembled as the glow snaked through the gold leaf overlay, outlining the runic inscription with a river of cerulean light. Swallowing nervously, he opened the door.

"It only opens for the Chieftain Bloodline," Galo concluded.

"Yes, it would appear so," Gabdur anxiously sighed, wiping glistening sweat from the back of his neck, "Are you sure you want to go in there?"

"I must," Galo insisted, "I need to see where my anger was taking me. It's the only way to keep from becoming so lost again."

MalVek and Galo entered the chamber and closed the door. A towering circular ziggurat stood before them, the circumference of the bottom tier occupying most of the floor space. A multitude of pipelines sprouted from each layer, running down the sides and snaking along the floors and up the walls.

MalVek traced the path of one of the pipelines with his eyes, craning his neck to find the walls stretched into darkness. As far as he could tell, the line neither penetrated the wall nor left the room otherwise. He then followed each line from the base of the ziggurat to the bottom of the wall, noting changes in spacing.

Galo took off the Serpent Bracer and placed it on the floor. He scaled the ziggurat, secure in believing only his copper heirloom would satiate the appetite of this bizarre contraption. He gazed into a hole atop the device, an helictic carving lining the inner surface. The hole expanded beyond the helix, yawning into impenetrable darkness. He rubbed his elbow, suffering sympathy pains for the man he nearly became.

"Have you figured anything out?" he called.

"I can't see where these pipes end up from here," MalVek admitted, taking snapshots with his pocket camera, "But I'm drawing a pattern from how their spacing changes from the bottom layer to the walls. It's incredibly inefficient, which means there must be a purpose to it."

"Can the pattern tell you what this does?"

"Not by itself, but with a floor plan and utility layout, I'm sure NalSet and I can come up with a few theories. There a hole for the Serpent Bracer up there?"

"There is," Galo cringed, "The inside of the hole is carved out for it. It has to be screwed in."

"Ensures a secure connection," MalVek noted, scowling as he observed pipeline spacing shifts up one of the walls, "Makes sense that they'd design it that way. Strange though, seeing as that's about the only thing that makes sense about this whole fuck-forsaken room."

"Right, but a member of the Chieftain Bloodline has to be wearing it," Galo reminded, "Do any of these daises look to you like they could rotate?"

"Well no. Whole shell of this contraption looks to be solid," MalVek mulled, "Ah damn! This thing'll twist your arm right off! It's an auxiliary port and a torture device."

"Uh-huh. You guys were right. The Prophet was going to sacrifice me to activate the Mechanical Crypt."

Yrlis unlocked the front door and peeked inside. Finding the lights out, she furrowed her brow a moment, but her lips curled into a mischievous grin as she slipped inside the house. With carnal pursuits in mind, she quietly locked the door and crept to the hall.

She snuck into their darkened bedroom. Fixating on the outline in the blankets, she disrobed with a smile growing slyer with each discarded article. He didn't stir. She slipped under the covers and ran her hand down his side.

Only, nobody was there. Yrlis turned on the lamp and found herself alone in their bed, stroking heaps in the comforter. Disappointed, she dressed herself and wandered out of the bedroom.

Pacing the hall, Yrlis looked over every portrait and every fixture as though new and unfamiliar. Days spent working had flown by as her research into the Sisyphus Fir thus far came up fruitless. Nights spent alone lagged on. All this added up to weeks of growing unfamiliar with her life at home.

While she waited for Spril or an explanation for his absence, Yrlis poured herself a drink. Leaning on the countertop, she sipped the minutes away. Sips became glasses as minutes became hours, the first birdcalls of the nearing dawn gently chiming in the otherwise quiet kitchen.

She grabbed her phone to call him, but she stopped halfway through dialing. Surprising him with a phone call could have been a bad idea for any number of reasons. She shuddered at the thought of a ringing phone blowing his cover in the heart of an Avatar stronghold, all because of her impatience and perhaps his forgetfulness.

She understood that their careers left them little time at home together, even if she didn't like to accept it. Assuring herself that he would come home safely and soon, she dialed Vielle instead. Postponing intimacy, she had other plans to carry out.

"Hey girl, what's shaking?" Yrlis remarked.

"Oh my gosh, Yrlis! Is that you?" Vielle elated.

"Yeah, it's me. We hit a wall in our research, and I've got other stuff to take care of here. How have things been?"

"Things have gotten, well, complicated. That's really the best way I can put it," Vielle muddled, "I guess you know what happened with Galo, then?"

"Uh-huh. Arrested for war crimes. Sinkua's and Phylus's names on the warrant. Real shady shit from Chairman LenSom. I've got an idea who put him up to it."

"More specific than just the Avatars?"

"Assuming your dad was right about her, I'd theorize he works for Olsa. Seeing as she got impeached in the middle of her tenure as head of the Union Parliament, she might be using him as a proxy or protégé."

"Of course, he was right. She has the tattoo, and she's never given anyone a reason to think she was a mole like Malia," Vielle confirmed, "But not to put you on the spot or anything, but if you knew what happened, why'd you wait so long to come home?"

"Too many chefs will spoil the stew," Yrlis countered, "I knew a lot of people here would be investigating, but what I was working on, only I could do. At least until Galo was out of captivity."

"What were you working on?"

"I obtained a research grant to study the Sisyphus Fir. I'm going to try to succeed where the guy who bred the Glaucus Fir failed. Bring the fruit to full ripeness and study its medicinal properties."

"Ooh, sounds fascinating," Vielle elated, "I wouldn't think you'd want to do that without Galo though."

"That was the plan. I couldn't accomplish as much as I would've liked without him, but it was more than I could do to help him with his incarceration. All I can do there is teach you what I learned about it in Berinin so you can spread the news," Yrlis explained, "But if we start while Galo's still in prison, there's no telling how LenSom will retaliate. He might even go so far as to have him executed."

"I don't want to think about that!" Vielle protested, "Okay, okay, I see your point. As soon as they get him out, I'll start spreading the news and get everyone's names cleared. Do you want to come over and iron out the details?"

"Actually, I've been up all night, so I thought I might try to…"

"I'm cooking breakfast before Dad goes to work. I'm off work today."

"In that case, I'll be right over."

Pocketing her phone, Yrlis grabbed a bottle of iced coffee from the refrigerator. She popped the lid off and threw it back, pouring the drink down her open throat. The caffeine and sugar flooded her body, the rush jolting her senses to an almost heightened state after long travels and a restless night.

Once on the road, Yrlis watched inbound traffic accumulate while those leaving town remained comfortably sparse. A curious thing, all those people with their individual lives, yet so many operated on the same basic itinerary. So many went deeper into town for work, yet so few came out for it.

Insomnia had a strange way of stringing her thoughts along into curiosities otherwise taken for granted. Her efforts to concentrate ended with her mind awash with anxiety. She worried, bordering on panic, over what could have had Spril so intensively occupied and what might have become of Galo. Despite reacting as though it rang hollow, Vielle's accusation struck deep.

She knew she would endanger Galo's if she circulated what she had learned from Nenbard about Galo's arrest. She also knew herself unfit to break Galo out, and her information didn't exonerate him. It only relieved Sinkua and Phylus of the blame for arresting him. So, she had helped where she could instead, researching the Sisyphus Fir.

Yet despite all her reassurance and affirmation, she couldn't shake the guilt of abandonment.

Yrlis stopped before the driveway, letting Phylus back out. He stopped and rolled down his window as she waved to him.

"Hey, sorry I can't stay and chat," he excused, "Good to see you though."

"You too. Any idea where Spril is?"

"At work, maybe?"

"He was gone all night."

"In that case, I have some ideas," Phylus suggested, pausing thoughtfully, "But I need to get going. Ask Vielle to catch you up."

"Okay, enjoy your day."

She let his words settle as she watched her feet amble to the front door. Phylus had some ideas about where Spril could be. Nothing solid. Just some ideas. Clearly, much had developed in her absence, enough to warrant multiple possible explanations for why Spril hadn't come home last night. Yet, Yrlis was unaware of all of them.

She worried over what it could portend for their relationship, but at the same time, she fretted over what manner of corruption Spril had been contending with. Struggling to quiet these two warring fragments of anxiety, she rang the doorbell.

"Hey, Yrlis, You just missed my dad," Vielle welcomed, "Come on in."

"Yeah, we talked for a bit in the driveway," Yrlis said, accepting the invitation.

"Eggs, bacon, and waffles are on top of the stove. I already ate, so have as much as you want. Dad had to eat and run, so there's a lot of leftovers."

"Thanks. I'm fiending for carbs after staying up all..."

"And there's half a pot of coffee. I made a second pot, and Dad took half to work."

"You always anticipate just what your friends need," Yrlis smiled as she made for the coffee brewer, "That's what I like about you."

"Oh, please. You like lots of things about me," Vielle teased, "So, what news have you got?"

"Well, Nenbard taught me some pretty interesting tidbits about Galo's arrest," Yrlis began, coughing on the first hasty swig, "Has it been on the news up here?"

"Now that you mention it, no," Vielle pondered, "I mean, I get all my news about stuff like that from Spril and Dad and them. So, it never occurred to me before, but no one else has been talking about it."

"Well, LenSom staged a press release in Masnethege. He recorded a radio address and a television spot and dictated a newspaper article," Yrlis recounted, "But apparently, it hasn't been distributed. Nenbard and I think the whole thing was a sham, something to make the techno-illiterate Masnethegeans believe everything was on the level."

"Given his story, he'd have to. Nobody there would believe Sinkua ordered Galo's arrest," Vielle said, "But if he acts like he has nothing to hide, then they might accept it."

"They're acting like they have, but it's only a cover. Nenbard figured LenSom out when what he told Galo didn't match what he said in the press release. He asked them to play along until they could prove his contradiction."

"What was the contradiction?"

"LenSom said in the press release that he ordered Galo's arrest, not Sinkua and Phylus. If we can generate suspicion of a scandal or a cover-up ..."

"... we can have his recording equipment submitted to the court. We can clear up Dad's and Sinkua's names and run LenSom through the mud. If we play it right, we may be able to pull Olsa out of hiding and dig up some more intel on the Avatars."

"But unfortunately, it won't exonerate Galo. Trumped-up charges or not, it only proves Sinkua and Phylus were framed."

"Well, that's not exactly our problem at this point. Turns out, somebody broke him out of jail a few weeks ago."

"Really? Who?"

"Actually, they think it was an Avatar. There was blood on the bars," Vielle recounted, "Ministry of Healthcare found it came from two people. One was Galo of course, but the other one wasn't in the international database."

"Weird. Why would an Avatar want Galo out of prison?" Yrlis pondered.

"Beats me. Either they needed him for something or they wanted to do something worse to him," Vielle suggested.

"Maybe both."

"Well, Spril was running with the theory that it had something to do with Laboratory 1341. You know, the Avatar lab we learned about when we were trying to figure out where Nikasu was being kept."

"Nikasu? That's the new Hybrid girl, right?"

"Yeah, she's living with Sinkua in the house where he grew up, along with Eytea and Yahsek. That's her friend who was in captivity with her."

"Sounds like a lot happened while I was gone."

"Enough to make me dizzy. But anyway, what have you learned about the Sisyphus Fir? Think it might be true what they say? You know, about how it can cure any disease?"

"Panacea is a sci-fi myth," Yrlis explained, "Maybe there's some universal derivative, some common denominator in every medicine. And if there is, maybe it can come from the Sisyphus Fir."

"You're pursuing it on a hunch and some legends? That's not like you."

"I read several papers by scientists who have studied the chemical properties of the Sisyphus Fir. Turns out, it's a bonanza of organic bonding agents, antibacterial enzymes, and potential for antiviral manipulation. Someone even had this idea that it evolved to protect animals that spread its seeds against certain viruses."

"Oh, that's beyond cool," Vielle remarked, "Now, when you say organic bonding agents, you mean...?"

"It can adhere to organic compounds such as, say, vitamins or other nutrients in a person's blood," Yrlis hinted, "It could potentially use those nutrients to reproduce and protect against relapse. If this pans out, it could completely overhaul how we treat cancer."

"It could also be the answer to Sinkua's condition."

"That also occurred to me. Even if the cure itself isn't derived from the Sisyphus Fir, it may serve as a distribution agent."

"Well that's great news. I'll keep my mouth shut about it so you can tell him yourself."

"Well, let's not get his hopes up prematurely," Yrlis continued, "Now then, what were you saying about Spril and Laboratory 1341?"

"Well, it's an Avatar facility, obviously, in the northwest highrise district."

"I know that much. He told me about it before he went to Lenguardia."

"Ah, right. Of course. Anyway, Spril suspected that whoever took Galo might have taken him to Laboratory 1341."

"Thinking they're using him to replace Nikasu and Yahsek?"

"Something like that."

"You suppose Spril was casing the lab last night?"

"It's the most likely place. You wanna head that way and look for his car?"

"Yeah, my nerves won't settle until I at least know where he is."

"Alright, just give me a few minutes to get dressed. I was about to head out in that direction anyway," Vielle said, "Do you mind if we pick someone up on the way?"

"Not at all."

Galo sank into himself, dawdling behind while Pahres struggled to navigate the labyrinthine crypt. He watched them try to decipher its silent machinations, pitying them yet at the same time feeling unworthy. They had become so engrossed in this maze, it seemed they had already forgotten his transgressions, perhaps even forgiven them. He could only hope.

The Serpent Bracer believed Aleepo to be Gabdur, and that sufficed to convince him for the time. However, he couldn't comprehend how this man could hide for so long, through so much suffering, only to come to his rescue so soon before he was to be sacrificed. Surely, he could have saved him sooner, rather than let matters worsen as much as they dad.

Sinkua seemed unwilling to discuss why he had excluded him from Nikasu's rescue. Galo hadn't asked, but he wondered if it portended a permanent scar on their friendship. Years ago, they would never have left each other out of such an excursion. Yet, even as he mourned the decaying bonds with his fellow Hybrids and the rest of the Subtransit Resistance, they had gone to great lengths to save him.

Though perhaps, their greatest priority was to prevent the awakening of the Mechanical Crypt. Maybe, he thought, Gabdur had only come out of hiding to keep that horrible contraption dormant. That ziggurat had seared an image of itself into his memories, disrupting his composure with every thought of giving himself to it.

Yet to think that iconoclastic bastard only cared to come to his aid when that machine became an issue almost made Galo want to abandon Gabdur in the labyrinth. Countless lives had suffered and ended because of deception, and only now did he bother to help.

As much as Galo tried to distance himself from the fact though, Gabdur was still his father by blood and thus a fellow Chieftain. Regardless of his priorities and motives, he had saved his life and returned him to his friends. He had saved him not only from The Prophet, but from his own blinding hubris. Galo decided he'd watched him struggle long enough.

"We're never going to get out this way," Galo asserted.

"What do you mean, son?" Gabdur asked as everyone stopped and turned.

"Do not call me that. You have not earned the privilege," Galo firmly objected, "In any case, we're not moving any closer to the perimeter."

"You mean we're walking in circles?" MalVek asked.

"Not exactly. More that we're being moved in circles."

"I've kept track," EshCal insisted, "We've moved forty meters from your chamber, approximately forty-five degrees westward from true north."

"Yes, your sense of direction is very astute," Galo snarked.

"There's no need to…" EshCal scolded.

"But your listening skills need work," Galo cut off, "I said we're being moved in circles."

"You mean the halls are moving?," MalVek puzzled, "Rearranging themselves?"

"Yes. I figured it out when The Prophet first brought me down here."

"And I hitherto had come here only as him," Pahres said, "Thus, I haven't a conscious memory of it."

"Yes, well, he led me in circles, but we never ended up back where we started. Before the indoctrination took hold, I used to listen to the walls," Galo recounted, "It's faint, and I've never felt them move, but I heard mechanical sounds from inside the walls. I never heard them from my chamber though."

"Maybe the nearest moving halls were too far away for you to hear," Sinkua suggested.

"That's why they run so quietly," Nikasu asserted, turning her gaze toward Galo, "Keep the sacrifice on a leash he never knows he wears. And should his cavalry come for him, they too will find themselves ensnared, never suspecting they've been bound to this place. You should feel honored. They only used blunt force sedatives to keep me from learning the exit route."

"Is she always this macabre?" Galo mumbled to Sinkua.

"It comes and goes."

"Or maybe it isn't running quietly. Maybe it's running far away," MalVek suggested, "There are probably motion or thermal sensors in the walls, programmed to prohibit movement within a certain radius."

"Why do you sound like you're guessing?" Sinkua challenged, "Your idea makes sense, but you don't sound sure about it. One of you guys said the Avatars stole tech from you, but you seriously don't know how this maze works?"

"You're right that they stole tech from us, including the barricade towers and the resonant disrupter," MalVek conceded, "But they also have their own technology. We've designed rearranging walls, but we've never built them on this large a scale. And I can think of a dozen ways to keep their inner workings virtually undetected. If you honestly think I'd be holding out..."

Galo encased his fist in a thick layer of ice and pounded the wall, disrupting MalVek's heated protest. He pounded a few more times, gouging a gaping hole wide enough to fit his arm through.

"Reach around in there," Galo directed, "See if you can find your sensors."

"And if I'm right?" MalVek asked, groping about in the hole, "Do you have a plan, or did you just want to figure it out?"

"I have an idea, but it depends on whether you're right."

"Well, I'm finding a series of nodes and daisy-chain wiring in here. Definitely a motion detection system. Complex one at that," MalVek reported.

"If we destroy them, this section will be able to move with us in it, right?"

"Theoretically, yeah. Or something close by, at least."

"If Eytea were here, she could just stick her hand in the wall and overload the sensors," Sinkua yearned, "How do we go about this without her?"

"Well, you could overheat them, but we don't want to risk burning this place down with us in it," MalVek began, "But it shouldn't..."

"Circuitry for subterranean application is designed for optimal functionality at below standard temperatures and oxygen levels," Nikasu interrupted, her robotic cadence drawing a bewildered stare from Galo, "Therefore, it also overheats at considerably lower temperatures than pedestrian circuitry."

"Yes. That's more or less what I was going to say. Works colder, overheats at a lower temperature," MalVek agreed, "Now Galo, you coat the inside of the walls with ice, and Sinkua, you set them on fire. The melting ice will put out the fire, and the steam will wreck the sensors."

Galo set his hand inside the wall. Ice crystals manifested from his palm, spreading down his fingertips and along the inner surface. Meanwhile, Spril gouged a hole in the opposite wall.

As Galo continued to the second wall, Sinkua reached inside the first. Flames surged from his hand, spreading virally over the crystalline coating. His arm trembled under the exertion, struggling to balance the intensity between vaporizing the ice and setting the wall ablaze. Sweat smeared his temples and the nape of his neck.

Steam pouring from the bludgeoned wound, Sinkua yanked his hand out of the wall. With Nikasu at his side as he caught his breath, he turned to find Galo had finished with the other wall. Swallowing anxiously, Sinkua approached the second wall.

His mind fixated on Eytea while he burned the ice. Having her around would have simplified matters, this task being relatively easy for her. It seemed no matter the extent to which she used her electromancy, the exertion never shook her. She had saved him and others numerous times, the effort never seeming to fatigue her.

His face and neck painted with anxious sweat, he pulled out of the second wall.

"And now we wait," MalVek said, sitting on the floor.

The others joined him, quietly listening for movement. Minutes crawled past, gradually collecting into hours. After what could just as well have been two hours as five, the walls began to rumble.

With Sinkua offering his hand as a torch, MalVek looked inside the wall.

"We've got movement!" he victoriously announced, "Galo, what's next on your plan?"

"I remember what the hall to the elevator looks like," Galo said, "We'll head back to it, destroy the sensors, and wait for it to carry us to the exit."

"Great, but how do we get back to it?" Sinkua challenged.

"We passed it a short ways back. If we get in range of some working sensors quickly enough, we should be close enough to hold it in place."

"Your plan hinges on a lot of what-ifs and maybes," MalVek criticized.

"Yes, but it's a brilliantly laid one, given our limitations," Gabdur boasted, "We should be so lucky that he could offer such insight. We'll head back the way we came until Galo finds the elevator hall."

"Even if it moves, I'm certain I can find it," Galo assured, following Gabdur on his enthusiastic backtracking, "As loud as those gears are, we'll hear them should they begin to turn."

Sinkua grinned at his friend and Hybrid brethren's confidence and ingenuity as he turned to follow. The others came just behind him.

Yrlis parked on a cross street to Heniokhos Boulevard. They walked up the boulevard, odd-numbered buildings ticking upward, until they reached series of tinted floor-to-ceiling windows. All but the phone number had been scraped off of the glass double doors. Vielle stepped off the sidewalk.

"This is the place," she confirmed, noting the obscure characters in place of common numerals, "Now what? Do you want to wait out here?"

"I suppose," Yrlis sighed, "I mean, we can't go in looking for him, can we?"

"I'd like to, but we don't know where to look," Vielle reasoned, "If this is where they took Galo, it'll be heavily guarded. It took most of us to break Nikasu out, and they probably took Galo because of that. So…"

"Never mind!" Yrlis exclaimed, her face alight, "Spril just came through the back door of the lobby."

"Anyone else?" Vielle asked, rushing in to look with her, "There's Galo, Nikasu, and Sinkua! But where's Eytea?"

"MalVek and EshCal are with them, too. Plus a couple of guys I don't recognize," Yrlis added, "Hmm, Galo looks upset."

The door swung open, and the exhausted entourage poured out. Spril took pause, puzzled by the unexpected greeting. He smiled and yanked Yrlis into a tight embrace.

"When did you get back?" he asked, that being the first question he could fully process.

"Last night. I had plans for you when I thought you were in bed, you know," Yrlis snickered, "But I guess that can wait a little longer."

"Sorry, we took EshCal's car out here. They had taken Galo hostage, but this gentleman helped us free him."

"Vielle and I have met," Gabdur clarified, emerging from the group, "But, as with most of you, under somewhat false pretenses. By the way, did you ever find a chance to apologize to Galo on my behalf?"

"I'm afraid not, Aleepo," Vielle shrugged, "But I still have the flower you gave me. I'm keeping it somewhere special."

"I see that," Gabdur said, nodding toward the blue rose, "Who's your friend?"

"Oh! Sorry. There's so much going on, I forgot to introduce you guys. This is

MarLys," Vielle said, "She's my girlfriend."

"Hey-hey!" MarLys greeted, "Vielle told me she runs with an odd crew, but you folks are a hell of a spread."

"Well, this certainly explains a lot," Galo remarked.

"Oh, come on," Vielle protested, "You can't still be upset about that, can you?"

"I might be wrong here," Sinkua said, rubbing his jawline contemplatively, "but I'm pretty sure I called that one"

"Haha, yes you did," Vielle laughed, "Now Galo, you're not still upset about what happened back then, are you? Or does my being a lesbian offend you?"

"Never mind him for now," Gabdur excused, "My son just made some unsettling discoveries, so he's rather perturbed at the moment."

"Say what now?"

"Yeah, I thought you said your friend from Berinin lost his parents," MarLys added, "Makes me wonder what kind of secrets the rest of you might be carrying around."

"Sinkua and I have a common half-sister who we didn't know about until a couple of months ago," Vielle recalled, cocking her head toward Nikasu, "But I told you about her."

"That would be me," Nikasu introduced, flashing a wave and keeping her other hand stuffed in her pocket, "Nikasu."

"Yeah, you said that after your mom ran off, she hooked up with his dad shortly after his mom died," MarLys confirmed, indicating Sinkua and flashing a smile to Nikasu.

"There's more to that story, and you know it," Sinkua protested, "How much aren't you telling her?"

"I know it's not my place to give this sort of advice" MalVek opened, "but if you want a healthy relationship with this girl, there are things you can't hide from her."

"Speaking of relationships," Galo cut in, digging in his pocket, "I was asked to give this to you. Apparently, much that I don't fully comprehend depends your having this, including Pahres's existence."

"Hm, well that answers that question. I wasn't sure if you'd apprehended The Prophet or he'd come as Pahres," Vielle said, eyeing Pahres as she blindly accepted the offering.

She rolled it in her palm, admiring its texture. It somehow felt both metallic and organic, like flora screaming through a mineral coating, yet registering only as a muffled growl. Opening her hand, her smile of quiet awe turned to a gasp of bewilderment. The Platinum Orchid radiated a pulsating green glow, tiny vines involuntarily sprouting from her palm.

"Whoa, what's happening to you?" MarLys asked, holding Vielle's shoulders.

"Nothing to worry about. I just," Vielle assured, squeezing her eyes shut, "need to concentrate."

"Gabdur!" Galo barked, "What the hell did you have me give her?"

"She is unharmed, I assure you," Gabdur promised, "That was merely an acclimatory reaction, as was to be expected."

"What is this thing?" Vielle asked, "Which one of you is responsible for it?"

"It appeared to me a few months ago," Pahres said, "Our employer learned that it belongs with you. As it turns out, you…"

"I'm an anomaly. I'm not supposed to exist. I know," Vielle spat, "What does that have to do with this flower?"

"You're not supposed to exist?" MarLys puzzled.

"No, child. It's not that you are not meant to exist. It's that one of your caliber was not a conceivable likelihood," Pahres explained, "But I assure you that your existence, while unforeseeable, is in no way invalidated."

"Thanks, but that doesn't answer my question. What is this thing?" Vielle

216

reiterated.

"The Platinum Orchid is a seedling of Yggdrasil," Pahres said, "the great tree capable of spanning the very concept of reality."

"Does that have something to do with how she exists even though you didn't think she could?" MarLys asked, "Oh, and you have so much to explain to me now, babe."

"I believe it may. That being the case, you ought to thank whoever preserved it for her."

"Damn right, I oughtta," MarLys smiled, "But I'm pretty partial what she gave me."

"Blue does look better on you than platinum," Sinkua pointed, "Eytea wears hers in the same place."

"Your girlfriend, right? From Ferya?"

"Yes, and just to prepare you, she has wings."

"You know, after what I've seen today, I don't think much would surprise me anymore."

"Don't be so sure," EshCal said, "But yes, as I recently learned, Gabdur bred those blue roses and gave them to all of the Hybrid girls."

"They all grew up under such unfortunate circumstances," Gabdur commiserated, "I wanted them to know they were special. That someone cared."

"That's great that you can wax poetic," Galo sneered, "But what about the male Hybrids? What about Sinkua and Yahsek? What about the son you abandoned?"

"I'm not familiar with this Yahsek, but you and Sinkua were looked after by Gijin. In a manner of speaking, that is," Gabdur excused, "But I did promise you I'd explain myself when we got out here."

Chapter 22

"It's right through here," Gabdur pointed, opening his umbrella as they neared the forest's edge, "Masnethege is just ahead."

"Thank you again for inviting me, sir," Nenbard beamed, "It's an honor just to be invited to your home."

"Authority has no place here, my friend, so let's do away with the formalities," Gabdur insisted, "You're my most apt pupil to date, and I need your counsel. Today, we're equals."

"I understand," Nenbard nodded, donning his umbrella as well, "How is her condition?"

"Worsening, but the progression appears to have slowed."

"Without better treatment, how long do you suppose she has?"

"Nenbard!" Gabdur snapped, whipping about so quickly he flung the rain on his umbrella onto himself, "We never speak in timetables."

"I'm sorry. I didn't mean to be so insensitive."

"Insensitive indeed, but such talk is inexcusably reductive."

Gabdur led Nenbard to the front of his hut, where he gently pulled back the flap and peeked inside. Nenbard leaned in to peer over his shoulder.

"How is she, Father?" Gabdur asked in a projected whisper.

An elder of diminishing stature rose from his knees at the wilting woman's bedside. He brushed back his long grey hair, matting from sweat and stress, as he looked up to face Gabdur. His four-sleeved robe dragged along the sandy floor, obscuring his footprints.

"I wish I had better news for you, my son," Gijin sighed, "but I have made no headway against Zheal's condition in your absence."

Nenbard waited in the foyer as Gabdur approached the cot, his eyes fixed sorrowfully upon his wife. Zheal slept almost constantly, though rarely in quietude. Her body writhed as she moaned in agony. Gabdur winced at the sound, choking against a swelling in his throat.

"Zheal," he exhaled, "I brought a friend and colleague. Nenbard is going to help us."

"O...Okay," Zheal choked.

"Don't speak. Save your strength."

"Na... Naly.... gen."

"You want to see your sister?" he consoled, "Okay. I'll bring her in the morning."

"Nalygen.... Sou.... Soup."

"Of course. I'll ask her bring..."

"Nalygen came today," Gijin interrupted, filling the cracks in the fragmented statement, "She brought a pot of her addax soup. There's plenty of leftovers, if either of you want some."

"Ah, well that sounds nice. I'll have to thank her for that."

"Don't get your hopes up. She put too much caliptrium in the broth and killed the flavor," Gijin complained, "That woman thinks far too reductively of our research."

"Never mind her," Gabdur excused, "My sister-in-law means well enough."

"Eb… Ebralgi," Zheal gasped.

"So does he," Gabdur insisted, "Save your strength."

Gabdur stayed at Zheal's bedside while Gijin and Nenbard discussed the progression of her illness. He only heard fragments of their conversation, mentally ensconcing himself and his wife. Running his fingers through her hair, he comforted her as he checked for open sores. He strained a pitying smile as he stroked her cheek, checking for a fever.

His fingertips painted her cheek with darkened blood. He smelled the blood on his fingers while he cleaned her cheek with his shirt. It stank of pungent metals. He smeared it on his pants, shaking his head in bewilderment.

"Yesterday nothing, and today this?" he puzzled, "Whatever this is, I fear it's advancing to its next stage."

"Wh… What…. is it?"

"I don't know. Up through yesterday, you tested anemic. Enough so that I could smell the deficiency," Gabdur explained, "But today, your blood smells too metallic, like you have too much iron and copper."

"Li… Like…. men…. menst…"

"Menstrual blood? Yes, I suppose it does smell like that."

"What is it?" Nenbard asked, "Is she having complications with her menses?"

"No more than anything else," Gabdur corrected, "It's the blood from the sores on her scalp. It smells like menstrual blood."

"That's bizarre. Could I have a look?"

Nenbard's nose wrinkled as he smelled the darkened blood on Gabdur's freshly wetted fingertip. Gabdur examined its texture while Nenbard considered the odor.

"We need to test it," Nenbard insisted, "but I believe this actually is menstrual blood."

"I'll take care of that," Gijin insisted, leaning over Zheal to swab one of her welts, "Stay by her side, son. She needs you."

"But how?" Gabdur choked, Gijin silently leaving the room with the sample, "How is that even possible?"

"Her bloodstream must be absorbing her menstruation somehow," Nenbard said, "But medically speaking, I don't know what could cause that. I've never heard of anything like it."

"The how will have to wait until we've treated the what, then," Gabdur accepted, stroking Zheal's cheek, "First, we need to address her blood toxicity."

"Once the rain clears, we can take her to the hospital for hemodialysis."

Gabdur stared down at the Serpent Bracer encircling his forearm. Legend spoke of its ability to influence the flow of water. He recalled with wonder and perhaps hyperbolization how his father could stand in the breakers and remain dry. Despite his best efforts though, Gabdur had failed to impose his will upon it.

"Yeah," he sighed, "Once the rain clears."

"Gabdur. Nenbard," Gijin called as he returned, "I found traces of deceased ova in the sample."

"How are her toxicity levels?" Gabdur asked.

"Not yet lethal, but she'll need hemodialysis within the next two hours."

"Her immune system is too weak for her to survive this storm," Gabdur argued, "Can you bend the rain?"

"That falls to you, son. I've grown too frail for such an exertion."

"We'll build a canopy," Nenbard mediated, "We passed a hospital about forty-five minutes before we got here. Adjusting for the extra weight gives us about thirty, maybe forty minutes to build it, I'd say."

"You and I will work on that, boy," Gijin insisted, "Gabdur, go speak with your brother-in-law. He visited after Nalygen left. Perhaps, he noticed something relevant."

Entrusting his pupil and his father with the task of constructing a canopy, Gabdur stepped out into the now raging storm. Having left his umbrella behind for them, the rain soaked through his clothes within seconds. The cool evening air chilled him through, his body trembling as he trekked southward through the capital village.

Shivering horribly, he vigorously shook the flap to his brother-in-law's hut. Dragging moments later, a man a few years his elder answered. He appeared disheveled and disoriented, grunting an unwelcoming greeting to the man who had wed his little sister.

"How is she?" Ebralgi muttered.

"Can we talk inside?" Gabdur pleaded.

"You'll get my floor wet."

"Your floor is sand, you twat!" Gabdur shouted, "I'm sorry, but I don't have time for your pedantry."

"That's always the problem with you," Ebralgi sneered, "You don't have time."

"Listen. Your sister is in serious trouble. The sores on her head are leaking menstrual blood," Gabdur reported, "Did you notice anything strange when you came to see her?"

"Yes, her blood iron was dangerously low. I took measures to correct it," Ebralgi said, "If it smelled too high to you, it's only because her body hasn't flushed the excess. Either that, or you've grown too accustomed to the smell of her low-iron blood."

"You're responsible for this? Why did the Chieftain Sage find dead ova in her blood?"

"I know nothing of that," Ebralgi assured, "You'd best be going. She mustn't have long to live without hemodialysis. And here you are without safe transport for the poor dear."

Ebralgi nodded to the Serpent Bracer, mocking Gabdur for his failure to fulfill the reputation of the Chieftain Bloodline. Gabdur turned away bitterly, leaving the relative shelter of the front of Ebralgi's house. He ran back to his family's hut, his bare callused feet sloshing the drenched sand.

"Son!" Gijin exclaimed, "You've returned just in time. We need a third set of hands."

"You two got a lot done while I was gone. Wish I could say the same," Gabdur grumbled, admiring the nearly completed canopy, "How can I help?"

"Fetch your Chieftain Heir Robe from your quarters," Gijin ordered, "We need it to cover these thatch holes."

Gabdur retrieved the robe as requested, gazing longingly at it as he walked. He rarely wore it out of the house during these unseasonably stormy days. People outside of Masnethege often didn't recognize him as the Chieftain Heir without it. With each storm he endured without it, he felt further detached from his inheritance. Now, he would sacrifice this increasingly foreign garment to help save his wife.

After Nenbard and Gijin covered the holes, Gabdur checked the durability of the canopy, and they carried the bed out into the storm. Much to Gabdur's begrudging, Gijin still insisted on stayed behind, being too frail to endure such violent weather.

With Nenbard at the fore, Gabdur stayed by the head of the bed, keeping watch over Zheal. Perhaps just as importantly, he kept himself within her reach and sight. Roused by the thunderstorm and the jostling of her bed, her eyes flickered open.

"Whe... Where?"

"We're going to a hospital, honey. Your blood toxicity is rising. You need hemodialysis."

"Menst...."

"Yes, it was menstrual blood," Gabdur confirmed, "We don't know how much is in your system, but toxic shock is a serious concern."

"H…. How?"

"We don't know. We're going to look into it once you're being treated. Try to rest until we get there."

"Eb… Ebra… Ebralgi came," Zheal meekly smiled.

"I know. Dad told me he visited you after Nalygen left," he nodded, "I spoke with him."

"Shot," she exhaled, curling her wrist to point at her bicep.

"He told me your blood iron was low, so he corrected it," he reported, "Your brother can be quite the malcontent, but we should thank him for taking care of the details while I was out."

"N…. No," Zheal choked, "Not iron. Wr… Wro… Wro… Wrong… c … co…"

Zheal hacked and seized violently, odiferous blood spewing from her throat. With tears flooding her desperate eyes, she clutched Gabdur's shirt and pulled him nearer. Panicked and heaving, he dropped his end of the bed and wrapped his arms around her shoulders, leaning his forehead against hers. Nenbard lowered the foot of the bed, mouth agape and chin quivering as he watched the poignant spectacle unravel.

Gabdur pivoted to Zheal's side, tears falling from his eyes and into hers. She blinked them away along with her own, her corneas bloodshot. Blood trickled from every orifice on her head as well as the sores on her scalp. Clinging to Gabdur as he held her close, Zheal gurgled through the toxic blood filling her throat.

Gasping to speak once more, Zheal choked on her last breath.

Clinging to her a moment longer, Gabdur sobbed over Zheal's lifeless body in bitter denial. Nenbard rushed to his side as Gabdur desperately pounded her chest. Wholly unaffected the stink of dead blood, Gabdur breathed into her open mouth. He inhaled through his mouth, drawing back only slightly.

"Gabdur," Nenbard urged, choking up as his conviction crumbled, "Gabdur! Stop it!"

"Don't you tell me to stop, you cock!" Gabdur roared, persisting in his hopeless efforts, "When it's Sanus on the bed, you can decide when it's alright to stop!"

"You don't know what you're exposing yourself to."

"Who cares?! I don't menstruate! Help me sit her up!"

"Gabdur!" Nenbard shouted, pulling him away, "I'm sorry! She's gone! There's nothing anybody can do about it!"

"How can you possibly be so calm about this?"

"Because if I can't calm him, my tutor is going to kill himself trying to save a dead woman," Nenbard asserted, his eyes fixed unwaveringly on Gabdur's.

"Pick up the bed," Gabdur ordered, lifting the head of the bed, "Go! Keep walking!"

"What do you…"

"We're taking her to the hospital," Gabdur asserted, "We need to understand what took her, and we can't do that here. I'll deal with Ebralgi when I get back."

Eyes holding on his disfigured spouse, Gabdur ambled along behind Nenbard. His feet dragged through rocks and brambles, indifferent to their lashings. Ebralgi's last words to him repeated in his mind, echoing and consuming his thoughts.

Gabdur's wife, Ebralgi's sister, had suffered on the edge of death, and Ebralgi had dismissed her out of petty selfishness. Zheal's departing revelation had fallen short, but it told him enough.

Bitter and remorseful, Gabdur stretched his sleeve to cover the head of the Serpent Bracer, the nose creeping into his peripheral vision nonetheless. As much as Ebralgi had betrayed Zheal, Gabdur had failed her. He panted unevenly, shaking the bed with trembling arms. He squeezed his eyes shut, fighting back tears.

"I failed you with the Chieftain Heir Robe," he muttered through grinding teeth, the rain drowning his words, "I failed you with the Serpent Bracer. I failed you with my education. I failed you..."

"Gabdur," Nenbard beckoned, "We're here."

A fatigued orderly met them in the lobby, his eyes locking on Gabdur's bitter face. He jolted alert at the macabre spectacle, an emaciated bloody-faced woman lying motionless on the bed they carried. Gabdur watched in growing aggravation as the orderly's eyes darted about, assessing the situation in befuddled silence. Gabdur rolled up his sleeve to show the Serpent Brace, but the orderly remained where he stood in mortified confusion.

"Unless you have casters in your pocket, I suggest you go fetch us a hospital bed," Gabdur ordered, "Or are you so dumbstruck that you'd have me carry her on my back?"

"N-No, sir," the orderly stammered, "I'll get a wheelchair and take her to intensive care straight away, sir. Paging a doctor for you now, Chieftain Heir, sir."

"Are you bloody daft?" Gabdur snarled, "She doesn't need intensive care. She needs an autopsy."

"She'll need hemodialysis first," a pale man in the waiting room butted, "I'd advise you not to stand too close either. It may have become airborne, and the antidote is in short supply."

"A blood borne infection that's also airborne? Not possible," Gabdur challenged, "Go back to your tabloids. Leave the real medicine to the experts."

"Fine. You're right. I'm not a medical expert," the stout man conceded, lowering his newspaper and standing to approach them, "I'm not even an expert on her disease. In fact, I'm little more than a messenger."

"What are you rambling about?"

"Gabdur. Be careful. Con artists prey on the mourning," Nenbard warned.

"Sure, my timing could have been better. Would have been if it hadn't been for certain complications," the man excused, "One of my colleagues has been keeping close tabs on your brother-in-law's research. To put it..."

"Do you mean to say," Gabdur interrupted, "that Ebralgi was, in fact, responsible for this?"

"Yes. But obviously, you already knew that."

"I knew he was behind her last symptoms."

"Menses in her wounds?"

"Yes. Who are you?"

"A messenger, just like I told you," he reiterated, "My name is NalSet."

"Well, NalSet, what else can you tell me?" Gabdur encouraged, "And how do you know so much?"

"To get your second question out of the way, I have connections," NalSet reminded, "My colleagues, the one tracking Ebralgi plus another, have worked to develop an antidote. They almost had a viable sample during her early stages, but they were slow to consider that he would complicate the disease."

"Working under the cover of correcting her nutrient levels," Gabdur nodded, "Clever bastard. Do you know why he was doing it?"

"I could guess, but it'd just make you ask more questions. We're better off talking about it in private," NalSet said, "By the way, that your blood on your lips?"

"It's hers," Gabdur sighed, watching as Nenbard and the orderly wheeled Zheal's lifeless body into a service elevator, "I suppose that doesn't bode well if you're right about it being airborne. Seeing as you have been about everything else, which I'm finding hard to swallow."

"I wish I could explain myself further, but I can't risk blowing their cover. It'd jeopardize all of us. You understand, right?"

"No, but I suppose I'll have to accept it. Will I need hemodialysis as well, then?"

"No, just inject this into your aorta," NalSet said, pulling a vial from his pocket and sounding entirely too nonchalant, "Careful with it. We only have three doses."

"Do you mean to say that if I'd only been faster, you could have saved Zheal with a single injection?" Gabdur gaped, shaking his head in self-loathing and disbelief.

"No. The shot is enough for you, because you were only just exposed. She would have needed her blood cleaned first."

"I suppose nothing I could have done would have saved her then."

"You're better off not obsessing over what you could've done, especially when you can't change the outcome," NalSet advised, "Now, get a pair of syringes from the nurses' station."

"Why a pair?"

"One for the antidote. One for a blood sample."

"Ah, of course. We'll need to check my blood to monitor the efficacy of the treatment," Gabdur comprehended, "I'm sorry. I'm still rather disoriented by all of this."

"It's fine. By the way, have you had a son yet?"

"I'm afraid not."

This realization added a horror that Gabdur hadn't yet considered, now weighing heavily as he shuffled to the nurse's station. Men in the Chieftain Bloodline always sired one child, always a son. Soon after the child's first birthday, the father became irreversibly infertile. Only those whose sons didn't survive their first year had ever been an exception. Postulations and legends were never in short supply, but a proven explanation had never surfaced.

Because Gabdur never impregnated Zheal, custom dictated he remarry and sire a child with his second wife, but he had no idea how long his natural fertility might hold out. Otherwise, the line of succession would end, hurling Berinin into political tumult.

After a condensed lifetime in introspective isolation, Gabdur returned to NalSet with a pair of syringes, a cotton ball, and a flask of isopropyl alcohol. NalSet filled the first syringe with the antidote. Gabdur stretched his own shirt collar down and swabbed alcohol on his chest.

"This is gonna sting," NalSet warned, "Only at first though. You'll feel a cooling sensation once it starts circulating."

"Fire away," Gabdur said, closing his eyes.

"Hold on," NalSet paused, lowering the syringe, "We just met, and you're gonna let me inject something into your heart?"

"Into my aorta," Gabdur corrected, "But you're obviously on the level. You were right about Zheal's symptoms and about Ebralgi's involvement."

"Yeah, but that could be 'cause I work for him."

"Normally, I would agree with you," Gabdur said, "But if you were working for that miserable bastard, you wouldn't expose yourself in front of everyone like this. Now, fire away before the infection has a chance to proliferate."

"You're a good judge of character," NalSet complimented, "Astute, too. You'll need it if you're gonna work with us."

NalSet plunged the needle between Gabdur's ribs. Gabdur winced seethingly, but the chill spreading from his heart swiftly overpowered the burn. He panted heavily, clinging to his pants to keep from clobbering NalSet in his aggravated stupor.

The cold grew more tolerable as it dispersed throughout his bloodstream, permitting his body to return to a healthy temperature. Gabdur clutched his chest as NalSet withdrew the needle, pressing his finger against the puncture wound.

"Cold on the blood. Just like you said."

"Good. Let's wait a few more minutes, then we'll get your sample."

"Will we be able to test it here?"

"No, we don't have access to the necessary equipment here."

"I'm sure I could throw my weight around and gain access to it," Gabdur boasted, "You should know who I am."

"You're Chieftain Heir Gabdur. Everyone knows that," NalSet shrugged, "I mean they don't have it here."

"In that case, I'm going to go check on Zheal."

"Shouldn't do that. She's on a cold slab by now, cut open and hooked up to machines. Not what you need to see right now," NalSet warned, "We need your mind at peace, much as it can be. All you can do for her is wait."

"Hmph. I suppose you have a point. What do you suggest in the meantime?"

"Normally, I'd say whiskey, but seeing as who you are and where we are, coffee'll have to do."

Gabdur rubbed his puncture wound as they made for the cafeteria. With each passing moment, he noticed white noise discomforts leaving his body. Oddly, they didn't so much diminish as become entities independent of and then expelled from his body.

Perhaps it was a beneficial side effect of the medicine, but more likely, those discomforts had been symptoms. Ebralgi had been painfully devious on the matter, hinting at his involvement only shortly before Zheal died. It didn't seem irrational that Ebralgi would have Gabdur's illness advance more slowly, taking hold under the guise of distress. With enemies like that, NalSet's resources would clearly serve Gabdur well.

"I believe you said something about working with you?" Gabdur announced as he poured a cup from the waiting room coffee pot.

"That's right. You're gonna come work with us," NalSet asserted.

"And exactly who are you?"

"NalSet. There's also my brother MalVek, our colleague Chekov, and our boss Mortvill."

"Small crew," Gabdur smirked, "Big talk for a four-person operation."

"Saved your ass. We just choose to travel light," NalSet countered, "Get what we need when we get where we're going."

"And what is it you need from me?"

"Plenty of things. For starters, we need your blood."

"My blood? So, you mean to fight a war?"

"If it comes to it, yeah. But for now, I mean a sample. We also need a clean one from Zheal."

"What about my father's blood?"

"Gijin's? No, the samples are for him, so to speak. We also…"

"What do you mean 'so to speak'?" Gabdur interrupted.

"Forget I said that," NalSet insisted, continuing before Gabdur could object further, "We also need your medical expertise."

"My medical expertise? You just cured me of the disease that killed my wife, and I didn't even know I was infected."

"We lost contact with the person who developed the base for it. If this becomes an epidemic, they'll be working blind once these samples're gone. But if anyone can help them recreate it, it's you. Except maybe Gijin, but you've got time and potential in your corner."

"I'd rather not think about losing him any time soon," Gabdur sighed, following NalSet back to the lobby, "But do you really think I'll surpass him?"

"It's what every parent wants when their child shares their vocation."

"Fair point. Even while Zheal was ill, I obsessed over ensuring our son could make better use of his time as Chieftain Heir than I have."

"In that case, you won't like what I have to ask of you next."

"What? That I relinquish my title?" Gabdur laughed.

"Yes," NalSet solemnly insisted, "We need you to leave with us."

"What? You can't be serious. I just lost my wife. My father is probably sick as well. And you expect me to pack up and leave?"

"I'm completely serious, and your father is definitely sick. Ebralgi thinks you are, too. So, what do you think'll happen when you return home alive and healthy?"

"I'll have Ebralgi deported."

"On what evidence? You're the only witness. I could back you up, but they've got no reason to trust me. It'll be your word vers' his, and you're emotionally compromised," NalSet prodded, "Besides, that little shit got to you and you didn't even figure it out 'til today. You need our protection."

"And I suppose you can't offer it if I stay in Masnethege?"

"No. We need to keep moving to stay off their sensors."

"Whose sensors?"

"You familiar with the Avatars of Fate?"

"Secret underground organization rumored to control the world's governments?" Gabdur asked with an arched eyebrow, "They're just a myth, a convenient conspiracy theory for people who don't agree with every decision their government makes."

"Not exactly. People do blame them for things they've got no part in or that aren't even happening. They don't control the world's governments either. But they do exist, and they're getting stronger," NalSet warned, "Our job is to keep them from getting too powerful."

"How do you go about that?"

"Wrenches in the gears. Enable their victims. That sort of thing."

"So you're fighting an underground group from even further underground?" Gabdur deduced, "Coin the tracks and watch the chain reaction?"

"You catch on quick. One variable can change everything. Think where you'd end up if you hadn't come here today or I'd kept my mouth shut when I saw you. You'd be dying your ass off with no one to save you."

"Hmm. I suppose you have a point. I never thought about life like that, but I could attribute that to mine having been laid out for me since birth."

"In that case, you're in for a thrill with us. Not gonna say we can tell the future, but Mortvill's kind of a statistical oracle."

"Sounds like an interesting fellow. I might like to meet him."

"That'll happen soon enough," NalSet promised, "First we need to get that sample from Zheal. Then we'll go to Masnethege."

"You know what?" Gabdur piped up as NalSet walked away, "You go get the sample by yourself. I'll meet you in the lobby."

"You sure?".

"Yes, I'm sure. I don't want the last time I see her to be like that."

"Smart man."

"Oh, if you see Nenbard, tell him I went to get some rest. And that I said he should do the same."

Gabdur sat in the lobby, pondering the events of the evening. No other day better proved the potential for momentous changes born from seemingly irrelevant decisions. NalSet had introduced him to a new line of thought, unconceived in his preordained lifestyle. Without Nenbard, he wouldn't have reached the hospital in time for NalSet's antidote to stave off his infection. His father may have died as well with Zheal's disease perhaps becoming airborne. Had he not sought Ebralgi's counsel, he would have continued trusting him, leaving Masnethege none the wiser to the true assassin of the Chieftain Bloodline.

Gabdur followed the chain of decisions and outcomes even further back, so far that foreseeing this day from that time should have been impossible. Had he not taken Nenbard as a pupil, he may have never learned the source of Zheal's blood toxicity. If he hadn't married her, Zheal might have still been alive or at least perished in less pain. At that moment, Gabdur realized the greatest reason why he needed to leave Masnethege.

Tradition destroyed his family. If not for the arbitrary custom of eschewing technology, he would have had immediate access to a dialysis machine or any other medical device he may have needed. Instead, they were forced to hike to the next town for what should have been a routine procedure. The Chieftain Bloodline and this custom had become codependent. Tradition bound him to uphold the practice, and the practice proved his family's authority. Were he to relinquish his title, a new order could free his people from that antiquated custom.

Gabdur stood to meet NalSet as he returned to the lobby.

"Ready to go?" Gabdur asked.

"Just as soon as I get your sample," NalSet reminded, showing the first vial of blood.

Gabdur rolled up his sleeve while NalSet readied a needle. They made quick work of it, and NalSet pocketed the second vial as they walked out the door.

"I already cleaned Zheal's with a shot of the antidote," NalSet assured.

"Good to know," Gabdur said, "By the way, I've done some thinking about what you said. About changing one variable. And well, I've accepted that I truly cannot stay in Masnethege."

"Yeah? You realized you'd be doing your people a favor if you walk away?"

"Yes, but there's more to it. If Masnethege wasn't so bent on eschewing technology, we would have had the equipment we needed to save Zheal. We may not have been able to cure her, but we would have kept her alive for longer. Long enough for you to find us there."

"You're probably right."

"I know I am. But even as Chieftain Sage, I wouldn't have the authority to change that. Those two traditions are so tangled up in each other, nobody knows which thread to pull. I'm bound by custom."

"You think if you step down, whoever takes your place'll have Masnethege catch up to everyone else?"

"Yes, I do. I don't know if it'll happen right away, but if they're forced to develop a new system of authority, they'll be forced to confront other arbitrary customs."

"You're a quick study, y'know that?" NalSet smirked, "Mortvill's gonna like working with you. But that's not exactly in line with our plans."

"What?" Gabdur snapped, the rain barely muffling his shouting, "My father cannot sire a second child. I am leaving Masnethege at your behest, and should I father a child during my absence, they will not accept him as the rightful Chieftain Heir. How can my self-exile even possibly not break the chain? And more to the point, how can you continue to support such a ludicrous tradition after you've shown me how absurd it is?"

"We don't support the tradition. Neither do the Avatars of Fate. But it's up to Masnethege to change. So we take the diplomatic approach. In this case, offering you a job and our protection."

"Do you mean to say that," Gabdur realized, "Ebralgi was working for them?" NalSet simply nodded.

"But if you wish for the Masnethegeans to break that tradition, how else but ending the Chieftain Bloodline could you accomplish that by removing me as an influencing factor?"

"Y'know, damn near everything you say is a fucking mouthful," NalSet spat, "Yes, we want Masnethege to change on its own. Yes, taking you away plays into that. But have you ever tried waiting to see what'll happen?"

"I'm a doctor. I have to do that all the time."

"Fine. What about looking in two directions at once. Ever try that?"

"I, ah, well... I suppose I um..."

"The farther they split, the harder it is to focus on both," NalSet said, "But if you bring them together, sometimes you find what you're looking for somewhere in the middle. Not always. But sometimes."

"I've yet to take you for the type to wax philosophical," Gabdur mused.

"The hell said anything about philosophy?" NalSet challenged as they neared the edge of the forest, "Figurative maybe. Take the two most likely outcomes, and what'll happen is either somewhere between or way the hell off base."

"What do we do when it's off base?"

"Improvise."

The sky had grown dark and swollen by the time they returned to the Sacred City. Three patches of moonlight diffused through storm clouds provided the only natural light between the village and the horizon. Rain ripped through leaves and slashed thatch roofs, the violence of it all having subsided only marginally since Gabdur and Nenbard's departure.

Gabdur faintly heard a cough through the shredding rain, rushing home as he realized how harsh it must have been to travel so far. NalSet stayed close behind, seeming to be in considerably less of a hurry. Gabdur ripped the flap open, scattering reeds and mud.

Gijin lay in the middle of the room, huddled beside a puddle of mucosal blood. Crimson caked his grey beard, his mouth agape and drooling red. He lifted his head, struggling to hold it up as his pupils dilated and contracted erratically. Gabdur rushed to his side, laying him back on the ground.

"NalSet! Bring the antidote!" Gabdur shouted.

"We need to move him first. He's too exposed here," NalSet insisted as he came to Gijin's side.

"There's a shrine in the back."

"Perfect."

Within the shrine stood a copper statue said to have been of the first Chieftain Sage. What moonlight reached it through the roof refracted through the water pouring from its bowls, waterfalls shimmering prismatically. Gabdur and NalSet laid Gijin, limp and wheezing, before the fountain, the ancient leader watching over his ailing progeny.

NalSet readied the antidote while Gabdur tore open his father's shirt. Gijin's pulse fluctuated erratically. He coughed and hacked violently, clutching his chest.

"Gabdur! Get his hand out of the..."

An audible swelling from above interrupted NalSet, the bizarre sound deferring their moment of panic. The statue radiated a cool blue glow, the same shade as Gabdur had seen his father evoke from the Serpent Bracer. A paradoxical wind, cool to the skin yet warm to the bones, flowed like breath from the shining statue.

Gabdur stared dumbfounded. NalSet placed the syringe in Gijin's open hand and shuffled back. With a pulsating glow, an eldritch voice poured forth from the statue, riding the wind and flowing inaudibly into their minds.

"The bloodline must not end."

"What...?"

"Shh!"

NalSet grabbed Gabdur by the back of his shirt and yanked him to his side, pressing his finger to his own lips. Though bewildered, Gabdur nodded in compliance. Gijin's back arched, thrusting his chest upward as though to meet this strange wind. His throat raw, he drank of the eldritch breath and exhaled the words of the voice on the wind as they repeated.

"The bloodline must not end."

NalSet handed Gabdur the vials of blood and nodded to the statue, signaling for him to drop the sealed containers into one of the higher bowls.

Balancing on the rim of the basin, Gabdur noticed the flow of wind had separated from the sculpture. It persisted even detached from its source, circulating faster as the cycle tightened. He gazed at the statue as he dropped the vials into an upper bowl. Its blue glow waned as the eldritch wind grew more distant from its copper body.

Gijin's body settled, briefly motionless, and the rhythm of breath slowly returned. Gabdur began to kneel beside him, but NalSet grabbed his shoulder. Gabdur looked back to see his new associate shaking his head.

"We have to go," NalSet mouthed.

Gabdur looked to his father, an abundance of questions rattling through his mind. Nothing in his studies or their history, not even legends and campfire tales, ever spoke of that statue performing such feats. Somehow, it either healed his father or, perhaps more rationally, gave him departing peace. Knowing that didn't explain what exactly had happened though, the glowing, the paradoxical wind, or the voice.

The answers would have to wait. This much he knew. Whatever might become of his father, he had to leave. To protect his people from the Avatars of Fate, he needed to abandon his budding feud with Ebralgi and become a stranger. Removing the tradition that stunted their growth required he deny his heritage.

Gabdur walked away with an unfathomable weight in his heart. He set the Serpent Bracer on a table in the front room and, standing in the open doorway, looked back one last time. The statue returned to its usual greened copper shade, the blue glow wholly subsiding. As he let the flap fall shut behind him, he heard a voice from inside, foreign yet with a cadence of familiarity.

"So shall it begin once more."

Chapter 23

Galo stared down at his knees as he absorbed the story of his family's collapse. The Serpent Bracer hummed pulsatingly in response to his anxious rumination. He felt their eyes on him, Sinkua and Gabdur awaiting his reaction. A comforting hand lay on his shoulder, and he set his atop it.

"I know it's a lot to take in," Gabdur consoled, "But I hope you now understand why I had to leave."

"I… I don't know. You could have faced Ebralgi. You could have had him arrested," Galo flimsily protested.

"Like I told you, it would have been my word against his. I had no way to prove…"

"You could have done it. You could have stayed in Masnethege. We would have fought the Avatars of Fate together."

"Actually," MalVek interjected from the front of the car, "if he stayed, you wouldn't exist. Hence the vials of blood and 'The bloodline must not end.'"

"Then, I came from those vials, just like Sinkua said?"

"As I understand it, yes," Gabdur confirmed, "Under the right circumstances, the water in the fountain can be used to create a child of the Chieftain Bloodline."

"What about the forced impotence?" Sinkua interjected.

"Aha! Now there's a pertinent question," Gabdur remarked.

"That's how we planned to end the low-tech tradition," MalVek interrupted, "Disrupting the Chieftain Bloodline."

"Precisely. After your first birthday, Galo, siring a child was still possible for me."

"Have you?" Galo asked, arching an eyebrow.

"I should think not. Far be it for me to claim celibacy, but I always use protection," Gabdur said, "Once you and Nenbard have Berinin well on the path to restabilization, I'll find someone to settle down with and have her bear me a son."

"I know I'm new to your customs," Nikasu chimed in, peeking up from behind the back seat, "but doesn't this mean you're the Chieftain Sage, Gabdur?"

"No, I'm legally dead. But if I have another son, Berinin will have an unprecedented two living Chieftains within the same generation."

"Which will result in an upheaval of Masnethegean tradition," Galo nodded, "Before today, I might have opposed such a plan."

"That was why you were kept unaware…."

"Please! Let me finish," Galo snapped, "Knowing my mother died because of that tradition, I think it's time to change our ways."

"Galo, do you understand that you owe your existence to her death?" Malia asked, watching him in her rearview mirror, "If she had lived, the son she had for Gabdur wouldn't have been you."

"I wouldn't have known the difference," Galo argued, "I only agree with his decision to leave because it was necessary to influence a revolution in Masnethege. We've trailed behind the rest of Ouristihra for too long. If not for that, I would still blame him for leaving me to shoulder the burden alone."

"I don't mean to instigate," Nikasu interjected, "but Ebralgi held me captive and experimented with me. He's also the reason Sinkua has his condition."

"He also helped make The Hunter bulletproof," Sinkua added, "And he helped give The Scout the ability to regenerate from fatal injuries."

"His work in genetic grafting were foreseen likelihoods, but Mortvill calculated them to be a manageable risk," MalVek assured, "Countermeasures were implemented."

"Nikasu, instead of taking you and Sinkua home," Malia abruptly offered, "would you like to go to Phylus and Vielle's house? I need to explain why I left and what happened after. It may help you to understand why you ended up with The Geneticist."

"You're the Midlander who Nenbard spoke of," Galo deduced, "On the night Grandpa died, Nenbard told us about a Midlander who brought an infant to Grandpa. He said Ebralgi left with the child. That would have been fifteen years ago."

"Yes, that was me," Malia confessed, "But there's more to it. Nikasu, are you ready to hear your story?"

Nikasu gazed out the back of the hatchback, watching the scenery rush away from the rear windshield. She had spent much of her time in captivity wondering how she had ended up in such a detrimental lifestyle. She had accepted The Geneticist as her father, but she had never known her mother as anyone but a liar and a deserter. Having learned the truth of her family, however, these concerns returned with greater intensity.

Despite her indoctrination to the contrary, she had not been born in one of their facilities. The Geneticist had taken her hostage, and from the sound of it, others had allowed it. Rescue efforts waited fifteen years to be set into motion, either to serve some convoluted ends or purely out of apathy. Nikasu shook her head in contempt. At an absolute minimum, that woman owed her an explanation.

"Nikasu," Sinkua said, setting his hand on her shoulder, "If you want me there, I'll stick around."

"You should," Malia agreed, pulling into Phylus and Vielle's neighborhood, "Her story pertains to your father, as well."

"Actually, we need to go to our house first," Sinkua suddenly recalled, "Gabdur, didn't you say you don't know who Yahsek is?"

"I did."

"He's another Hybrid. He was in captivity with me," Nikasu explained.

"That can't be right," Gabdur argued, "There are only supposed to be four Hybrids, and we have a working theory to account for Vielle."

"He told us he was Nikasu's cousin once removed," Sinkua added, "Malia, do you have a cousin named Yahsek?"

"No," Malia said, turning the car around in an empty driveway, "I have one male cousin, and his name isn't Yahsek."

"Besides, even if there are other Hybrids out there somehow," MalVek added, "you're the oldest, Sinkua. Everything begins with you."

"What do you mean?"

"The onset of Zheal's illness coincides within a week of your birth. The Harvester learned of a Hybrid birth and set out to prevent others," MalVek explained, "That's also when he began Kabehl's indoctrination, in order to prevent or destroy Eytea."

"How can you possibly know all of this?" Galo challenged.

"Behavioral analysis, mostly," MalVek said, "Mortvill has an incredible proficiency for tracking probabilities. I admit a lot of it is over even my head, but it pans out most of the time."

"So, what's your take on Yahsek?" Malia asked, "He used my name and my daughter to get close to the other Hybrids. Did you think he figured into The Omnimath's analysis?"

"Unfortunately, I don't think he was a foreseen likelihood," MalVek confessed, "If he was, he was too remote to constitute countermeasures."

"Whoever he is," Sinkua interjected, "he just spent the night alone in my house with a collection of books that the Avatars assassinated Uulan and my grandmother over."

"Your grandmother was also killed because of Kabehl," MalVek added, "But yes, you left a Faux-Hybrid alone with those books."

"We need to hurry," Malia said, merging onto the highway, "The Harvester is almost as good as The Omnimath at behavioral analysis and circumstantial foresight. He could have planned this. I'm sorry, Nikasu, but we'll have to have our talk with Phylus and Vielle after we deal with Yahsek."

Snow settling on her shoulders, Elemeno dug her workworn boots into the icy mud. She leaned into a large sheet of plywood, holding it against the open end of the stable. The Frigid had been unusually cold and wet even for Ferya, and at their age, Sestak and Seschnel could hardly be expected to endure it.

Eytea hovered by an upper corner, the rachides of several feathers pierced with nails, securing the new wall. Snowflakes rolled down the nails in her wings, encapsulating the tips in ice. Self-conscious over Sestak's snorting, she tried to hammer more softly. Realizing that to be too impractical, she tried ignoring his protests instead. Sestak butted his head against the wall on her next strike.

"Mom, Sestak's not gonna let me finish," Eytea called down, "I can't hammer hard enough to drive the nails without him head-butting the wall."

"I hear him. Maybe we should try another way," Elemeno suggested.

"Suppose we gave them some blankets for the night," Eytea offered, "It'll be warmer in the daylight tomorrow. They can roam the yard while we work."

"Don't let them run too far, now," came a voice from the frozen darkness, "I'll advise you from experience, it's unwise to allow your pets much slack in their leashes."

"Who's there?" Eytea called, "Show yourself!"

"But you know all about that," the shrouded voice continued, "Don't you, Eytea?"

A dark-skinned figure stepped into the security lighting around the perimeter of the estate. His ebony hair hung to the middle of his back over a suede hide trench coat. He favored his left leg, a shadow behind his coat suggesting an encumbrance along his right.

"Who are you?" Elemeno challenged, "What are you doing here?"

"Honestly, I only expected to see you," he answered, striding deeper into the yard, "But with your daughter here, it looks like I've been spared the additional travel."

"Roll up your sleeves," Eytea demanded, sidling toward the house.

"Well, I see you have a theory about me. I'll just tell you, then," he said, "What you seek is there. I am The Geneticist of the Avatars of Fate."

"Your name is Ebralgi," Eytea revealed, "Galo's uncle. Brother to his deceased mother. Kidnapper of Nikasu and Yahsek."

"Ooh, somebody's been doing her homework. I can appreciate that," Ebralgi taunted, "Too bad you didn't tie off all the loose ends after you cut Nikasu free."

"If that's why you were looking for me, why have you come after my mother?" Eytea challenged, "How does she factor into this?"

"Aside from cultivating this indignant attitude toward your betters?" Ebralgi sneered, "She took The Scout out of commission for months. Do you have any idea how much of a setback that was for us?"

"Oh, spare me the drama, crybaby. We all know those deaths were temporary, and only the first one was on purpose," Eytea derided as they began circling each other, "But if it hurt your business, we'll gladly take credit for it."

"Such a deficient mind as yours will never understand our work! The regeneration nanochip took years to develop!" Ebralgi nearly shouted, "His body could not endure its full potential immediately upon implantation. Nobody could. Not even Lord Harvester. It needed to grow with him."

"Aww, did we stunt his growth? Poor wittle man."

"Enough talking!" Ebralgi snapped, whipping an oversized tonfa from his leg holster, "The Engineer will be pleased to know I eliminated both of you when we rendezvous in ArcNos. Once she's finished with SenRas, our masterpiece will be properly avenged."

"Speaking of poor little man," Eytea snickered, drawing her halberd from her back holster, "Compensating much there?"

The Geneticist rushed forth with and infuriated snarl, his tonfa drawn across his chest. Eytea leaned back as he swung, the wind from his weapon tussling her hair. With a twist of his wrist, he knocked the offshoot across her face. Eytea winced and dropped back onto her hand.

She sliced through falling snow, hooking his tonfa between the blades of her halberd, and used his momentum to pull his weapon to the ground. Pinning his weapon to the ground, she traced a swift arc along the snow with the tip of her boot. As her foot closed in on his abdomen, his midsection rolled back with unnatural fluidity.

Eytea sneered at the bizarre spectacle and kicked at his side. The Geneticist avoided her attack just as he had the first, chuckling at her futile persistence. His lower back appeared to stretch and pull his abdomen away from her attack. It moved independently of the rest of his body, as though absent of the impedance of bones.

Frustrated, Eytea unpinned his tonfa and slashed at his arms. The Geneticist jerked back, losing his hold on his weapon. He charged forth as the blade rushed past, ducking under the predicted thrust strike. He snatched his tonfa out of the air, bracing it along his forearm, and slammed it against her neck.

Eytea dropped her halberd and clutched the tonfa, stepping back with the impact. The Geneticist's enraged breath burned against her chilled face as he strained to drive his weapon into her throat. Turning the handle toward her face, he slid his hands further apart, squeezed, and twisted.

Eytea dropped backward upon hearing a click from within the oversized tonfa. The ends parted open and out jutted three hand-length blades. As her wings struck frozen grass and soil, she pulled him onto her upstretched foot and hurled him behind her head.

His weapon ripped from his clutches, The Geneticist rolled through the frigid mud. Dead grass clung to his coat as an insult to his pride. Eytea charged with her halberd in one hand and his tonfa in the other.

"Here's your surrogate dick back, you fucking prick!" she shouted.

She launched herself with a thrust of her wings and an explosive surge of lightning. Unleashing a menacing hiss, she pitched her halberd between his legs and skewered his coat to the ground. With a second jolt of lightning, she screamed down at his entrapped body.

She stabbed with the long end of his weapon, the blade aimed at his spine. It punctured his coat with little resistance, but his flesh parted to grant the blade and handle harmless passage through his body. Her eye twitched with bewilderment as he chuckled tauntingly.

Eytea withdrew the tonfa and hurled it against the broad side of the stable. Sestak and Seschnel grunted. She yanked the halberd from his coat and leveled the tip at his back. Before he could right himself, she unleashed a massive surge of lightning from the blades, strong enough that the recoil sent her stumbling back.

The potentially fatal current dissipated harmlessly throughout The Geneticist's coat. As Eytea stood infuriated and dumbfounded, he rose to his feet, swiping at the mud and dead grass on his shirt. With a bitter sneer, he ripped away her halberd and hurled it in the direction of his tonfa. The horses grunted again, butting against the partially fastened wall.

"You irreverent little bitch!" The Geneticist snarled as he muscled forth, "Do you have any idea who I am? What I'm capable of?"

"Yes. Overcompensating," Eytea defied, "Obviously."

"Quiet!" Ebralgi shouted, smacking her across her face, "You want to talk about surrogate dicks? About overcompensating? I should…"

A ring of cold steel pressed against the back of his head, silencing his threat.

"You shut your filthy mouth," Elemeno commanded, pushing the pistol barrel harder against the base of his skull, "You speak to my Eytea like that again, and they'll be your last words."

"Heh. Well, I see the old cow just can't wait to put her life on trial," The Geneticist snickered, "Your blood should do nicely for experimentation."

"I don't think you fully appreciate the circumstances," Elemeno challenged, "Which do you think is faster? Your artificial reflexes or the next bullet in the chamber?"

"And suppose you're wrong? Your precious little freak isn't much shorter than I," The Geneticist taunted, "Are you willing to risk…"

Crystalline mud spattered off his trench coat as the bottom of her boot crashed into the small of his back, his enhanced evasive maneuvers useless against the surprise attack. He collapsed onto Eytea, who staggered back in an effort to let him drop without her. Elemeno turned and unloaded the clip at the broad side of the stable. Six bullets ricocheted off the steel paneling.

Three zipped off into the distance. One buried itself in the side of the house. The fifth shattered a window, and the sixth glanced off Elemeno's shoulder, grinding into her collarbone. The partially installed wall collapsed as a twisting trail of blood rippled along the wake of the sixth bullet.

Undeterred by the decaying of age, Sestak and Seschnel grunted and kicked at the fallen panel. Eytea shoved The Geneticist off herself, and Elemeno grabbed him by the back of the coat. She spun with him and sent him staggering into the open. The sibling horses rushed from the stable with piercing whinnies.

Sestak butted his forehead against The Geneticist's chest, the confusion overwhelming his defenses. He gasped in pain and humiliation, the very breath knocked from his lungs. Seschnel circled to his side and butted his arm, and he screamed in anguish as his shoulder buckled and cracked in the socket. Sestak pivoted to his opposite side.

Dizzied by the pain, The Geneticist stumbled toward the stable. His equine foes closed in, the sleeker Seschnel gaining more quickly than her bulkier brother. Seschnel reared onto her hind legs, and The Geneticist dropped to his hands and knees. Seschnel came down upon his back with a furious neigh, her front hooves kicking wildly.

The Geneticist recovered his discarded tonfa. Throbbing pain radiating from his ruined shoulder, he rolled onto his back and kicked up into a crouch, thrusting his weapon upward as the enraged equine came down. The blade punctured her sternum, the combined momentum driving the entire long end of the tonfa into the wound.

Seschnel collapsed to her knees as her hooves hit mud. The Geneticist ripped the tonfa from the wound, a gush of blood trailing behind it. Seschnel whinnied and grunted before him. Sestak hesitated. The Geneticist examined his bloodied weapon with a grimace. He wiped the handle on his coat and retracted the blade still wet with crimson.

"Thank you for this sample," he taunted, "I'll ensure his sacrifice won't have been in vain."

"Mom, are you alright?" Eytea called, rushing to Elemeno's side, "What happened to you?"

"Never mind me," Elemeno dismissed, "Check on Seschnel! Hurry!"

"What the…." Eytea puzzled, looking across the lawn to find Ebralgi standing over Seschnel, apparently wiping her blood on his coat, "You son of a cunt! What did you do to her?"

Sestak put himself between the murderous intruder and the humans he called family. Eytea launched a jolt of lightning at Ebralgi's tonfa. He dropped it as his hands surged, and Sestak headbutted him again, following with a kick to his ruined shoulder.

Crying out in agony, Ebralgi turned and fled. He hurdled the fence and rushed off into the darkness. Sestak pursued him furiously, crashing through the wooden fence. Footsteps and hoof clops circled the estate, accompanied by Sestak's angry grunts and Ebralgi's fearful panting.

"That's right!" Elemeno shouted, choking back tears, "You stay off our property!"

"Mom, sit down," Eytea urged, "You're losing a lot of blood."

"Bah. I'll be fine, dear. It's only a scratch," she insisted, complying nonetheless.

"Only a scratch? I can see the bone, and I think there's a piece of it missing."

Ebralgi's distant footsteps stopped, followed shortly by a car door slamming. The engine started with a loud hum, and he tore off into the night. Sestak gave chase briefly, but the sound of his steps soon retracted homeward.

"Huh. How about that?" Elemeno guffawed, "Very well then. Let's give Seschnel a proper burial, then you can call one of our neighbors to take me to the hospital."

"I'll call you an ambulance now."

"You will do no such thing, young lady. Not until that poor girl gets the funeral she deserves. Now, fetch us a pair of shovels while I gather flowers."

"Of course," Eytea solemnly conceded, "But once you've been bandaged, we're leaving for ArcNos."

"We're not safe here anymore, are we?"

"If he comes back, he'll either bring back-up or a bigger stick. If he doesn't come back, that means he found a better reason to go after Sinkua and the others," Eytea explained, "Either way, we're not helping anyone by staying here, not even ourselves."

"Alright. You know more about these things than I do. I should trust you," Elemeno reluctantly agreed, "But what will we do with Sestak?"

"Loan him out to a neighbor," Eytea suggested, "Collect a cut from any services he provides when you get back."

"So, you're at least optimistic that I'll come home?"

"Of course," Eytea smiled, "The smoke has to clear eventually."

Vielle sped out of the neighborhood on her motorcycle, MarLys's thighs clutching her hips from behind. MarLys turned her head at a passing van, what little hair hung past her chin rustling in the wind. She lifted the visor on her helmet and leaned over Vielle's shoulder.

"Hey, wasn't that the van some of your friends left Heniokhos Boulevard in?" she shouted over the wind.

"Yeah. They were probably coming to visit," Vielle said, "Turned around when they saw us leaving."

"Why would they be coming to visit? We just saw them."

"We'll talk about it when we get where we're going," Vielle insisted, "Put your mask down. We're getting on the highway."

MarLys swiftly complied, her nerves not being nearly as resilient to riding on the highway. She squeezed Vielle's hips and wrapped her arms around her waist. The wind pulled hard against her auburn hair as they zipped down the ramp.

Vielle's contagious sense of calm flowed into MarLys, easing her tension. MarLys peered over Vielle's shoulder, watching her composed body language against the contrasting backdrop of rushing asphalt. Even in so hostile an environment, she appeared unflappable.

MarLys recalled that being the first thing she had noticed about Vielle's personality. No matter the trouble, if she could conceive of a way through, she kept a cool demeanor. She thought back to the first time she noticed her, couriering a package to her call center during peak volume. While others panicked, Vielle calmly pressed onward.

Vielle shot a glance to MarLys, grinning at her girlfriend thinking she watched her surreptitiously. It had always been that way since they first crossed paths, her deflecting MarLys's attempts at discreetly eyeing her. She remembered looking up from her desk, feeling those eyes linger upon her, and how entranced she then became by this svelte young woman.

She burned the image into her memory, willing herself to seek out the auburn-haired courier. After the weekend, she received a visitor during lunch. The object of her admiration introduced herself as MarLys, admiration becoming elation as she invited her on a date.

Time and distance rushed past as they rode in shared introspection, their thoughts laced through one another's. MarLys looked up from the dash display as she noticed their surroundings quieting. She looked around as they cruised along the tranquil avenue, taking stock of the area.

"What are we doing way out here?" she asked.

"Making sure we're alone."

Vielle scanned the spread of coffee shops and diners, finding most either too busy or too vacant. Once she found one with a moderate crowd, she parked the bike, and they headed inside.

"I thought you wanted to be alone," MarLys pried.

"Not 'alone' alone. I just don't want to run into anybody we know, and an empty café would be too obvious" Vielle explained, "But I don't wanna go someplace crowded either. Y'know, just on principle."

MarLys headed to the front counter while Vielle claimed a table. Vielle shook her head and laughed to herself as she overheard the barista flirting with her, blissfully unaware that she had as much interest in him as he would in the waiter. She turned away, mulling over the conversation they had on Heniokhos Boulevard.

As much as she wanted to be angry at Galo for holding her rejection over her head, she still found herself to blame. She didn't particularly worry that she should have humored his advances, but she had been so consumed with questioning her sexuality that she had failed to be honest with him.

Following that accusation, Sinkua's question rang deeper than it may otherwise have. Despite his cognitive shortcomings, that man always had deeper insights than he probably realized. His cadence and expression prominent in her memories, it felt like he saw through to the dark secret in her relationship.

Just as the doctors had written off her crescent moon ears, Vielle explained them to MarLys as a cosmetic birth deformity. MarLys had presumably heard of Hybrids, given their prevalence in the ArcNosian Civil War, but Vielle had denied nearly all of her involvement. Yet again, she had come to live two lives, hiding each from the other.

She sneered at the irony, a girl who shouldn't exist leading a double life with both defined by lies. Pahres's words on the matter gave her no solace. Consolation from someone whose inner beast had hunted her didn't sit particularly well. After hearing so much about the impossibility of her existence, validation from her once-predator meant nothing.

"Hey hon, I got you an orange scone," MarLys offered, "They were out of cherry."

"That's fine," Vielle sighed with a faint smile, accepting the plate, "Orange scones are Spril's favorite, you know."

"He's the bald guy, right?"

"Mm-hmm. He helped raise me. Moved here with us from Ivaria," Vielle said,

"Now he runs the Ministry of Defense. Crazy how life goes, huh?"

"Maybe for you!" MarLys remarked, "So, between him running the Ministry of Defense and your dad being the Prime Minister of Foreign Affairs, I bet you saw some pretty interesting stuff during the war, huh?"

"Well, actually I …"

"I know, I know, you weren't involved. Your dad helped start the community and establish the base laws. You always say that," MarLys interrupted, "But I can't help but feel like…"

"I've been holding back on you," Vielle confessed, "I've kept more than my share of secrets, and now it's my turn to come clean. Besides, if they say my life itself is some kind of lie, I shouldn't live one. Not if I can help it, right?"

"It certainly doesn't sound healthy. So what is it?" MarLys asked, biting into her bagel as she watched Vielle intently, "Are you a high-bred?"

"We're called Hybrids," Vielle smiled, holding back scone crumbs as she stifled a giggle, "During the war, we thought the four of us were all there are. Or at least, I did."

"Did the others know about someone else?"

"Yeah. Nikasu," Vielle nodded, "Sinkua, Galo, and Eytea had clues that she was in captivity but no way to track her. Her mother, our mother, came to us a while ago and asked us to rescue her. That was pretty awkward, meeting my mother for the first time."

"Wait. How can you be meeting your own mother for the first time?" MarLys puzzled, "Didn't she have to, you know…"

"Yeah, that's what I thought, too. Turns out, I was conceived and incubated in a genetics clinic. I'm a test-tube lesbian Hybrid paradox. Ain't that some shit?"

"Guess I'm lucky to have you," MarLys mused, nudging Vielle's cheek with her knuckle.

"Bet your pretty little ass you are," Vielle teased, "Anyway, the four of us were on the front lines of the war along with Spril and Dad. So was MalVek as well as EshCal, once she defected from the empire. Farim fought when she was needed. You haven't met her yet. She's a forensic scientist. Really brilliant. You'll like her."

"Oh wow. I wish I knew you while I was in school. You could have helped me so much with my political history classes," MarLys remarked, "Now, what exactly are Hybrids anyway? I mean, are you guys humans, beasts, what?"

"All our parents are human, so I guess we're a special variant of humans. I don't know, maybe evolution got the hiccups and coughed us up," Vielle pondered, "We could be an old subspecies that went extinct but still somehow blips back every now and then. But whatever we are, the Avatars of Fate hate and envy us. They've been hunting us both to kill us and to use us for human enhancement experiments. That's what happened to Nikasu."

"That is just awful!" MarLys exclaimed, bagel crumbs falling from her parted lips, "How is she doing now?"

"Adjusting to civilian life. Just like the rest of us but from more dire circumstances," Vielle answered, "I don't know how much control she has over her powers though."

"Do you mean like the vines that came out of your hand?" MarLys asked, "So, you all have some kind of superpower? Is that why these Avatar people hate you?"

"Probably. It's why they want our blood. To weaponize people using our genes," Vielle explained, "But yeah, we've all got different powers. Sinkua works with fire. Galo's is water. Eytea can create lightning. I'm sure you'll meet her soon. I can manifest flora. And Nikasu manipulates gravity."

"So what you're saying is that your little sister could make a fortune as a weight loss guru," MarLys joked.

"Haha! Oh, that would be terrible. I could almost see her doing that if she spends too much time with Sinkua," Vielle laughed, "Not that Sinkua's a bad person. Far from it at the end of the day. It's just, as long as I've known him, he's never been afraid to get his hands dirty to get what he's after."

"Yeah? Like what?"

"Well, he climbed the fence around the imperial capital, walked right into the city, and marched up to CreSam's office to declare war in person. So, they're sitting up there thinking it's an empty threat, like they could just roll right over us. You know, since they were so much bigger than us," Vielle recalled, "But really, his plan was to bring in foreign aid and build our forces literally underground where the imperialists couldn't reach us. Since we were officially at war, our reinforcements were guaranteed safe passage if they came as civilians.

"He fights dirty, too. It's actually pretty macabre sometimes. Uncle Spril is the only person I've ever seen take him down, and he only did it by fighting even dirtier."

"Yikes! A fire wizard with a mean streak. I'd better stay on his good side."

"As long as you don't break my heart, he'll be okay with you," Vielle winked, "He's kinda had a big brother complex with me ever since I saved his life with my powers when nobody else knew I had them."

"That's just... I don't know. Wow," MarLys gaped, "You've got so many stories I want to hear about that I have no idea where to even start."

"Everyone has their stories."

"But I guess keeping secrets has been a habit of yours for a while, huh?"

"I had a good reasons for those," Vielle defended, wincing at the scathing of MarLys's words, "But yeah, I realized what I've been doing this morning."

"Was it because of all that stuff about anomalies and how you technically shouldn't exist or whatever?"

"Living lies because my life itself is a lie? I don't know. It's an interesting parallel. Poetic even. But I don't think that's why I did it. Can't have been a conscious decision, seeing as I just recently found out about this anomaly business."

"Why do you think you did it, then?" MarLys pried, "Pahres said they didn't think a Hybrid like you could exist, but he insisted that doesn't make you any less of a person."

"I honestly don't know, but I'm guessing it has something to do with that Yggdrasil seedling he gave me," Vielle pondered, "But whatever the reason, I've had enough of running and hiding. Maybe I'll disappear when Yggdrasil grows. Maybe I'll disappear if it doesn't grow soon enough. I don't know, but..."

"You know I'll stay by your side no matter what happens to you or where you need to go," MarLys comforted.

"Thank you. In the meantime, if my existence is a lie, I need to stop living them myself."

Yrlis gazed out the window, counting the passing broken lines along the highway. Much had changed in her absence, all of it seeming to collide and collapse into a single moment.

Her thoughts raged with the nature of Vielle's existence, the influence of the possession of precious metal flora, Hybrid experimentation and indoctrination, and bonds to eldritch beings from the likes of folklore. All her knowledge felt useless here, whether inadequate or inapplicable. Even if she tapped into the medical potential of the Sisyphus Fir, formulating it for Hybrid application could prove to be a monolithic task all its own.

The biochemistry of the Hybrids had always mystified her, even frustrated her to the point of lashing out. This flood of new information overwhelmed her with the possibility of having to accept defeat. No matter what she learned from isolated observations, she might never understand the Hybrids. With little more than a fool's knowledge of their biology, she had no hope of deciphering and curing Sinkua's disease, not even with the Sisyphus Fir.

"Thank you again," Pahres piped up from the back seat, jarring her introspection, "For letting me stay with you, I mean. It will only be for tonight. I shall be on my way in the morn."

"It's no trouble really," Yrlis excused, clearing her clammy throat, "Just don't expect any company. Spril and I are going to bed when we get home."

"To be clear, I only agreed because we were the only ones with room in our car," Spril interjected, "Besides EshCal, but she's going to work so I can take the day off."

"Sir, are you implying that you…"

"That I don't trust you? No. I'm not implying it. I'm saying it. You kidnapped a falsely accused prisoner. You nearly sacrificed a Hybrid and the Chieftain Sage of Berinin. And in doing so, you triggered a chain reaction of conspiracy theories and paranoia," Spril spat, "So no. I don't trust you. And I won't trust you until I'm sure this Prophet business is purged from your mind. Until then, you are not to approach any of the Hybrids."

"Hmm. Here I presumed you were being hospitable," Pahres sighed, "I do suppose I understand your position on the matter. I did arrive here as The Prophet, but that cannot absolve me of his transgressions. Just understand that this incarnation of me, my true self, knew nothing of his actions or intents. Those memories now are less than a blur."

"And don't even get me started on all this 'It's nice to see you're doing well, sir,'" Spril continued, ignoring Pahres's tenuous apology.

"It is nothing, really. Those of The Coalition are well aware of what you have suffered in your pursuit of the Avatars of Fate and the protection of the Hybrids," Pahres explained, "The wellbeing of anyone so devoted to our causes is to be preserved and respected."

"Don't go thinking flattery is the way to my good side."

"You'll have to excuse him," Yrlis insisted, "He gets irritable when he's tired."

"Oh no, he has every reason to be perturbed with me. As I have stated, my behavior was inexcusable, my ignorance on the matter notwithstanding. I hold no delusions of adulatory compensation," Pahres said, "I do, however, possess a rather unique gift."

"The power to give people existential crises?" Spril snarked.

"You've developed a guardian complex with them, haven't you?" Pahres smiled, "That's certainly admirable. But no, I speak of something I have done intentionally. Yrlis, are you still in possession of The Diagram?"

"I'm a doctor. I have a lot of diagrams," Yrlis quipped, "You'll need to be more specific."

"It's a genome map written in the same ancient script as the laboratory signs," Pahres clarified, "Malia took measures to ensure it would fall from the Avatars' hands and toward your own."

Yrlis slapped Spril with her ponytail as she whipped around to face Pahres.

"The one with the extra pair of chromosomes?"

"If you're referring to the one with twenty-four pairs, then yes, that is the one."

"Of course. What else would I …. Y'know what, never mind! What do you know about it?"

"I know how to read it. I could teach you."

"You're fluent in whatever language it's written in?"

"It's called Harkzanian. And yes, I am quite fluent."

"How long would it take you to teach me to read Harkzanian?"

"Inconsequential," Pahres said, "Phonetically, The Diagram is written in Modern Ouristihran. I would need only teach you how to transliterate from Ancient Harkzanian."

"So, it's a cryptograph?"

"Essentially. Am I to assume you accept my offer, then?"

"Yes, thank you," Yrlis elated, "By the way, do you know anything about medicine from the Sisyphus Fir."

"I'm afraid not. Even in the greatest prevalence of belief in its potential, none could bring its fruit to full maturity," Pahres apologized, "Your best hope of building on existing progress would be to work with Gabdur."

Chapter 24

"Our neighborhood is just ahead on the left," Sinkua pointed.

"I remember," Malia noted, "It's been a while, but I've been here before."

"Come to think of it, I don't think I've ever seen the house you grew up in," Galo pondered.

"You have, actually. Grandpa Gijin brought you here when you were a baby," Sinkua corrected, "But, I don't remember much besides CreSam scaring you guys away."

"The real Gijin wouldn't have backed down," Gabdur sighed, "The ancestor who possessed him was too much of a pushover sometimes."

"As far as we're concerned, he was the real Gijin," Galo scathed, "Maybe he wasn't your father, but he was my grandfather. He taught us more than the other could ever have hoped to."

"Much as I'd like you two to air your grievances and move the hell on," MalVek grumbled, "we need to stay focused."

"I am confident that Yahsek is incapable of reading the manuscripts," Nikasu said, "Of course, that is a moot point if he cannot open them either."

"Well, we still don't know if the Avatars actually want to know what's in those books or if they just don't want us to know it" Sinkua countered, "But, didn't Yahsek say Ozzera is fluent in the ancient language, anyway?"

"Who's Ozzera?" MalVek asked.

"She's his chimera companion. Big creature with a lion head and a goat head and a snake for a tail. The lion and goat heads can talk. She said Gabdur can explain more about what she is."

"I'm familiar with chimeras, but it isn't as though I'm the only one," Gabdur said.

"Right, well with Yahsek being a Faux-Hybrid, I think she just wanted to send us on a blind hunt."

"Probably," Gabdur agreed, "But if the Avatars have a chimera, it may take all five of you coming down on her in full force to stop her."

"What about Leviathan?" Galo asked, "If I can summon Leviathan, would that help?"

"Not in a landlocked region," Gabdur said, "Leviathan's power is directly proportionate to his proximity to water and the abundance of it. But I'm guessing you expected that, what with his being a sea serpent."

"We're here," Malia announced, "Let's meet the man who says he's my cousin."

Sinkua hurried out of the car and checked the front of his house. The outside appeared undamaged. As much as he hated to believe Yahsek and Ozzera had deceived them, this small assurance did almost nothing to assuage his worry.

Sinkua didn't find the idea of Yahsek going turn coat to be particularly worrying. His knowledge of The Geneticist had been suspicious, as was his steadfast reluctance to let Nikasu cultivate her milystic powers. Yahsek was a mole, not a traitor. This was a revelation of an enemy, not the loss of an ally.

The idea of functional Faux-Hybrids was more alarming, especially ones with powers such as his.

A torrent of childhood fears rushed from the catacombs of Sinkua's memories as he neared the front door. His chest trembled behind the glow of his necklace. He had endeavored to convert this repository of adolescent pain into a comfortable home but had unwittingly built it around an impostor. Now, this charlatan had found an opportunity to ruin it all, to revert it to a place of suffering, and to slay Sinkua's mother a second time.

Sinkua unlocked the door and slowly turned the knob, hesitating. He closed his eyes and inhaled deeply. They radiated their masking green glow as he opened them and exhaled.

"I want you to teach me how to do that later," Nikasu peeped.

Sinkua flashed her a grin. Returning his attention to the door, he threw it open in hopes of startling Yahsek in the act of sabotage. His heart collapsed into his abdomen as he found a spectacle he failed to anticipate.

"That sick son of a bitch," he muttered, entering only deep enough to let the others inside, "Look what he did."

He hadn't broken anything. Everything he could see from the foyer was accounted for. The walls remained unmarred and the windows intact. And yet, Yahsek had destroyed the home built atop a psychological burial ground and awakened the ghosts waiting to haunt it.

"He moved the furniture?" Nikasu puzzled, "I'm not sure what's weirder, how he did all this in one night or what's sick about it."

"It looks just like when I was a child," Sinkua snarled, averting his eyes, "I can't be down here. Nikasu, you and MalVek look for signs of him. Malia and Galo, rearrange the furniture, please. Any way but this is fine. Just don't let me come down while anything is where it is now. Gabdur, you're with me. We're going upstairs to check on the books."

Nikasu led MalVek out the back door, suspecting Yahsek would have gone that way rather than leave an obvious trail across the front lawn. To her chagrin however, a blanket of nocturnal snow covered any footprints he might have left in the wet grass.

"He left before it snowed," Nikasu deduced, "There are no footprints out here or in the front yard."

"Looks like someone has been at this door," MalVek said, "Whoever it was forgot to wipe their hands."

Nikasu's nose wrinkled as she leaned in for a closer look. A layer of oily dust coated the doorknob, leaving a partial handprint.

"Let's check the fence," MalVek continued, "See if this Ozzera came here."

"Actually if you don't mind," Nikasu piped up, stopping MalVek before he stepped into the snowy grass, "I'd like to try something else."

"Eh? Well, go right ahead," MalVek accepted somewhat begrudgingly.

Nikasu kicked a path through the snow, shuffling to the edge of the patio, and knelt before the first icy blades of grass. Careful not to lay an impression, she gently set her bare hands atop the snow and closed her eyes.

Her thoughts rushed back to those infinite moments in the collapsing elevator. The desperation of necessity and her brother's words had awakened something inside her. Even in reflexive outbursts of her power, she had never accomplished such magnitude, such mastery.

Her arms trembled with milystic coursings, violet shimmers piercing her clenched eyelids. Analytical naggings of their struggle in the elevator accumulated as she obsessively relived it in excruciating slow motion. While Sinkua encouraged her cultivation of her gravimancy from the time they met, Yahsek denied her from behind a mask of concern for her health.

The snow sank under its own amplified weight, pressing more tightly against the soil. Brittle blades of grass buckled and cracked, sinking into the mud. Bent grass flattened, the snow covering it pulled closer to the soil than the rest.

"So, this is the power of the gravimancer," MalVek marveled, "I didn't think you'd have this kind of range."

"What kind of range?" Nikasu panted, opening her shimmering eyes, "Did it work?"

"Hell yeah. Reached almost to the fence."

"Heh. I wasn't sure I could do it. I never got to practice when I was held captive."

"Yahsek discouraged it, I suppose?"

"Of course," Nikasu spat, "And it looks like he left with Ozzera."

"Those are some damn big paw prints," MalVek agreed, "Not much detail, but I can't think why any other creature that big would be in your back yard."

"Or why Yahsek would leave with it," Nikasu growled, "I can't believe I trusted that creepy old man!"

"Hey, don't beat yourself up over it," MalVek consoled, awkwardly patting her shoulder, "Well, unless it helps you do what you just did. In that case, go ahead and beat yourself up. But... not so much that it gets to be a problem."

"You're not really one for comforting people, are you?" Nikasu said, her face an odd combination of grin and grimace.

"Never really have been," MalVek shrugged, "Too much time cut off from the public, I guess."

"Me neither," Nikasu admitted, cracking a shy smile, "I'm terrible with people."

"Yeah well, there's been a lot of that going around lately."

Malia lined the chairs along the wall, and Galo rotated the dining room table. He pulled the candlesticks from the centerpiece and pitched them in the garbage. He tucked the candelabra in a cupboard while Malia returned the chairs in a different arrangement.

"You said you've been here before," Galo recalled, "Did you know Sinkua's parents?"

"I guess he hasn't had a chance to tell you, has he?" Malia noted, "I knew CreSam, but that was back when Sinkua still went by MeiLom with most people."

"Is that why you got involved with these people? Because of what happened to CreSam?"

"Actually, I was in contact with CreSam because of The Coalition, but we lost touch with him shortly after he murdered BeiLou," she explained as they repositioned the sofa, "By the time I was able to reach him again, he was beyond my saving him."

"Saving him?" Galo asked, stopping suddenly, "You were trying to integrate him into The Coalition, then?"

"Reintegrate him, yes. The Omnimath was working him into the fold, but The Harvester took him from us. Unfortunate end to a delicate operation."

"What was so special about him that you would still try to convert him?" Galo puzzled, "If he was too far gone, why not just stop him by force?"

"Obviously, the man was a Carrier," Malia smirked, "He sired a Hybrid son. The Omnimath saw the same potential in Gabdur and BeiLou."

"What about Kabehl and Elemeno? Or Zheal? Or do Hybrid births only require one Carrier parent?"

"Just takes one. Kabehl wasn't a Carrier. Neither was Zheal. Nor is Phylus."

"That means Sinkua is the only one of us born from two Carriers, correct?" Galo asked, "Wait, no. Unless..."

Malia paused, waiting as Galo navigated the tangled family trees. She had been waiting in the car when he learned of it, but she had overheard Vielle and MarLys mention it in passing. She watched him mull over the congested events of the day, a look of epiphany crawling over his face.

"Nikasu shares a father with Sinkua and a mother with Vielle," Galo realized, "Since Phylus isn't a Carrier, you must be one. Ergo, Sinkua and Nikasu both have two Carrier parents."

"Exactly. That's what I was doing the last time I came here."

"Bedding a man who'd just slain his wife? Rather uncouth, don't you think?"

"Hah! That certainly would be," Malia snickered as she checked the glare on the television, "No, I came a few months before he went that far. Good thing, too. He would have been too far gone if I came later, and we might be short a Hybrid."

"The Avatars of Fate might also be short a few organic weapons," Galo quipped.

"We could spend all day debating the morals of eventualities, but you are never to preach to me about what became of my daughter's imprisonment," Malia scathed, "I spent fifteen years entrenched in the Avatars to keep her alive, and I live every day with the regret of letting them take her. My only solace is watching her siblings rehabilitate her."

"I'm... sorry I said it," Galo retracted, "I didn't mean to point any fingers. It's just with all this talk of behavioral analysis and foreseeing outcomes, I have to wonder how The Omnimath decided that was the best course of action."

"Well, he isn't always correct. You can play the odds all day and still come out losing, especially when you're dealing with dependent sequences of events. Going down a run of three-in-four odds ends with a six percent chance after ten steps."

"I hadn't considered that. I apologize for being so presumptive. I suppose you must adjust your methods as new possibilities arise."

"We do, but even having partial foresight two or three steps ahead helps us stay abreast of the Avatars," Malia explained, "But I'm surprised you haven't asked the question that's obviously on your mind."

"I've many questions on my mind," Galo countered, "Which one do you suppose my face is betraying?"

"You want to know why I came here to be impregnated by CreSam while BeiLou was still alive."

"To be honest, I assumed The Omnimath knew BeiLou didn't have long to live. I've more been wondering why nobody intervened."

"We actually didn't know he was about to kill her. My visit was a matter of assuring an outcome," she explained, "We needed our fourth Hybrid, though I suppose she turned out to be our fifth. As you'd expect, coupling two Carriers increases the odds."

"Raising two Hybrid children in the same home would pose an abundance of risks, I'm sure," Galo noted, "The Avatars would be quick to descend on a home such as that."

"MalVek said you were sharp," Malia smiled, "Yes, that was the other reason. The child wouldn't have been safe here, especially during CreSam's indoctrination. We meant for Gijin to take her in and find a safe home for her. We never conceived of the possibility that he would entrust her to Ebralgi. Like I said, Mortvill isn't always right."

"At this point, I suppose there's nothing you can do but reassess the circumstances and work to make amends with her," Galo consoled, "But why were no measures taken to find safer homes for Sinkua and Eytea?"

"It's a concept that I'm not at all fond of," Malia explained, sneering at the very thought, "but The Omnimath refers to it as necessary abuses."

Sinkua raced up the stairs, holding the wall as he whipped around the corner, and rushed down the hall. In his mind, at that moment, their possible value to the Avatars paled against the fact that those books were his last tangible memento of his mother. With reckless haste, he flung open his bedroom door.

That choking lump flared in his throat, reminding him that it had never left. Just like downstairs, Yahsek had rearranged the furniture exactly as it had been in his youth.

Sinkua stared into his father's bedroom from his childhood, as though a gateway through time had been constructed in the doorframe. Yahsek had even incorporated slight changes that CreSam had made shortly after BeiLou's death. Yet, that was far from the worst of Sinkua's troubles.

Yahsek had emptied the cache under the bureau, leaving the antique tomes scattered about the room. Sinkua hurled himself into the room, scrambling to the nearest book. Holding it with his fingertips, he flipped and turned it, checking it for damage.

"My goodness!" Gabdur exclaimed as he caught up, "Are any of them damaged? Are they all here?"

"This one looks okay. There's some fresh scratches along the edge. He was trying to pry it open," Sinkua exhaled, "Check the one on top of the bureau."

"Can do, friend. Sorry I fell behind. I don't like to eavesdrop, but I heard Malia mention Zheal and hesitated," Gabdur explained, blowing dust from the brittle cover, "They discussed your parents as well."

"I'm sure they did. She had CreSam knock her up on purpose," Sinkua dismissed, examining another book, "Look, I'm sure there's a lot I need to know about him that I haven't figured out already, but right now, I'm just concerned with my mother and her books."

"They're the only part of her you have left," Gabdur consoled, moving on to another book, "aren't they?"

"I can't believe that son of a bitch did this," Sinkua snarled, "That's two members of my family he's abused now. When I find him, I'm gonna strangle him until his fucking ears bleed."

"Ease up, friend. No good letting your temper get the best of you right now," Gabdur insisted, "Save it for Yahsek. Besides, it looks like he didn't damage the books much."

"No, I guess he didn't. Just a few shallow scratches."

"Let's pack them away, then. Do you remember how your mother had arranged them?"

"Yes. I never rearranged them, and I just saw them yesterday morning," Sinkua said, squatting next to the emptied cache, "Bring them here, and I'll put them away."

Sinkua studied the spine of the first book as Gabdur gingerly handed it to him. He stood it in the middle of the hole, holding it upright while Gabdur fetched the next book. The cycle repeated over several minutes.

"Okay. Last one," Sinkua sighed, letting a moment of relief settle in.

"Um, are you sure they weren't, perhaps, farther apart? Bit of breathing room, maybe?" Gabdur suggested, his stomach churning with self-doubt.

"Yes. Why? What happened?" Sinkua smoldered.

"Well, I've searched quite thoroughly, and it would appear that, well," Gabdur hesitated, "that was the last one."

"Son of a bitch!"

Sinkua exploded out of the room and stomped to the stairs. He overheard Malia saying something about necessary abuses but thought little of it. Before Galo could respond, Sinkua shouted an interruption.

"Galo! Malia! One of the books is missing!" he called down, "Stop what you're doing and search for it."

Back in the bedroom, he found Gabdur moving the dresser to the opposite wall, thus undoing that much of Yahsek's handiwork. Sinkua opened the window and leaned out, snarling an expletive at the sight of the massive pawprints in the snow.

"Nikasu!" he called down, "Can you tell which way they went after they left?"

"I'll need to move farther out," Nikasu called back, "Would you like me to?"

"Please do. He made off with one of my mother's books."

Nikasu gasped and ran across the lawn, scattering prints in the freshly tightened snow. She dropped to her knees at the edge of the yard and squeezed her hands through the openings in the chain-link fence. She closed her eyes and set her hands on the snow, milystis pulsating in her palms.

"They walked west-northwest across the lawn," MalVek called up to Sinkua, "I suspect they did so deliberately."

"They kept going in the same direction after they left," Nikasu confirmed.

"Okay. Great job, Nikasu. Come back inside," Sinkua invited.

Sinkua rushed down the stairs with Gabdur close behind. The furniture was still in something of disarray, but Galo and Malia had rearranged the larger pieces. As MalVek locked the door behind himself and Nikasu, Sinkua began bringing everyone up to speed on the circumstances.

"In case you two didn't overhear," he began, nodding to Malia and Galo, "Yahsek and Ozzera went west-northwest when they ran off with one of my mother's books."

"I'll notify the others and get someone to track them down," Malia offered.

"NalSet and I will be researching the Mechanical Crypt," MalVek said, "Leave us off this matter."

"Exactly how much of a priority are these books to you?" Sinkua snapped, "Nothing is going to happen in the Mechanical Crypt as long as they don't have the Serpent Bracer and one of the Berininite Chieftains."

"As far as we know. And we know comparably little about the content of the book they stole. Which puts the two roughly on even ground," MalVek quipped, "But if it'll calm you down, I'll ask The Omnimath if this book should take priority."

"No. Forget it," Sinkua barked, shouldering past MalVek on his path to the back door, "I'm up to the fucks with you people. This is the best you can do with your analysis-and-prediction bullshit? Then. You. Suck!

"Galo, stay here with Nikasu until Eytea gets home. Malia, you can stay and get better acquainted with your daughter if you want."

"Brother, you can't be thinking of…" Galo protested.

"Not thinking. Doing. I'm going after Yahsek and Ozzera," Sinkua asserted as he threw open the back door, "I'm going to get that book back, and if they're lucky, I'll keep them alive long enough to beat some answers out of them. Don't follow me."

Sinkua slammed the door and stormed across the lawn, melting snow with milystic heat. He threw himself over the chain-link fence and paused to study the trails of prints. Gaining his bearings, he stalked along the frozen landscape, his eyes fixed on the horizon.

"What are we going to do?" Nikasu panicked, "I can't leave! Who's going to protect the books?"

"Any of the rest of us can stay here," MalVek offered, "And another of us can escort you to follow him at a safe distance."

"You didn't see how he reacted to those books," Gabdur cautioned, "If we don't leave them in the care of Galo and Nikasu like he said, we risk permanently losing his trust."

"Family is too important to him to take lightly," Galo added, "If his little sister sets out in search of him with any of us but me, we'll never live it down."

"Fine then, I'll just give up my work on the Mechanical Crypt to chase after the stray," MalVek barked, "This is just great. I don't know who I want to wallop harder right now."

"Keep hold of yourself," Malia dismissively urged as she dialed her phone, "Wait until I'm done here before you go storming off, too."

"Going to dispatch Pahres and EshCal?" MalVek asked, "Pahres is the better choice for urgency. EshCal for range."

"No, I'm calling Phylus and Vielle, like I promised Nikasu," Malia countered, "They can help with our situation. But call Pahres anyway. EshCal won't be able to help soon enough."

"I'll report back to The Omnimath for signs of The Geneticist," Gabdur announced, "Galo, I'll see you around. Hopefully in better circumstances. It was a pleasure meeting you outside of the fetters of captivity, Nikasu. You two will give my regards to the others, won't you?"

"Madam Brigadier!" a panicked soldier shouted, "Madam Brigadier!"

EshCal paused in the hall, a river of personnel flowing around her. Hurried footsteps approached as someone called to her by a past title. Disoriented by fatigue, her hand moved across her hip, toward the hilt of her epee.

"Brigadier EshCal!" the soldier called.

"That's Brigadier General Elite EshCal," she corrected, turning to halt him, "Or High Minister of Defense EshCal. What do you need?"

"Apologies, madam. That's a mouthful, and I'm in a hurry."

"Then out with it," EshCal spat, continuing down the hall, "I spent all night on a rescue mission, and I'm in no mood to beat around the bush."

"We've been receiving aggressive communications from Tanelen since yesterday evening," the soldier stammered, following EshCal to her office, "Accusations include criminal espionage, unwarranted investigations, and manipulation of private records."

"Forward the transmission records to me," EshCal ordered while she poured herself a cup of coffee, "Do you have any further particulars?"

"Only that it's a fiscal matter. According to their records, someone's been interfering with some pretty valuable accounts."

"Forward the records to the Ministries of Foreign Affairs and Treasury as well. Comply with all subsequent requests for additional intel," she ordered, "Well done, soldier. Dismissed."

EshCal swigged her scalding black coffee as the soldier left her office. She pushed a button under her desk, locking the door. She suspected the accusations pertained to Biroe and KalChi's research, but their efforts hardly amounted to criminal espionage. Nothing for Tanelen to aggress over, unless she had been mistaken or deliberately misinformed. She dialed her phone.

"Prime Minister of Treasury Biroe?" she opened.

"Good morning, High Minister of Defense EshCal," Biroe breezily answered, "What brings you on the line?"

"We have a situation with Tanelen. Details coming shortly."

"What kind of situation?

"Criminal financial espionage. Know anything about it?"

"That was our doing, but nothing we've done has been criminal. We were researching the scandal behind IlcBei's and JalRov's investment accounts."

"What have you discovered?"

"It leads to a bank in Tanelen," Biroe explained, "The Commissioner of the Radial Axiom Arena also banks there. Exclusively, in Tanelen."

"What does that mean for us?"

"The coincidence alone would mean nothing, but he has several personal and business accounts in every country in the Ouristihran Union except Tanelen. Over the past two months, he's closed all but one."

"And you suppose he's done this to raise alarm?"

"Yes, it's largely circumstantial, but the evidence points to the Avatars of Fate."

"Why would Tanelen get knickers in a tangle over this?" EshCal puzzled, "Have you been siphoning the money?"

"We've considered it," Biroe admitted, quietly beaming at her presumption that he could do so, "For now, we're blockading the transfers. They're rerouting to a dummy account I established under an anonymous handle. We'll need more time to remit the funds to their rightful beneficiaries."

"You're a serious piece of work, Biroe," EshCal complimented, "How successful has your system been?"

"We stopped five of the last eight deposits. Four reached the dummy account. The fifth is floating around somewhere."

"Are the Avatars paying taxes on the deposits?"

"Taxes are automatically applied to final deposits, and they're making no evident measures to circumvent them."

"Does that money go to Tanelen or ArcNos?"

"Tanelen. International tax code is rather convoluted. When money is invested in a company in one country via an account hosted in another country, the equity payments are taxed by the country hosting the account."

"I don't have time for an economics lesson. I'll leave that…"

"Corporate officers and directors are the most common exceptions," Biroe added, the words coming so fast, they almost sounded singular, "Sorry. You were saying?"

"If Tanelen doesn't know the story behind that money, they'd assume what you're doing is criminal," EshCal explained, "As far as they're concerned, you're stealing tax revenue."

"Revenue that's rightfully ours," Biroe qualified, "but we can't go at this like they're stealing from us."

"In that case, we need to clear the air with them. Gather up all relevant documentation, scribble in some footnotes, some fiscalese-to-normal-people translations, and forward it to the Ministry of Foreign Affairs. I'll touch base with Phylus."

Phylus nodded to an employee as they passed each other in the hall, smiling with a mouthful of cinnamon bun from a vending machine. He coughed on a partially chewed bite, startled by his phone ringing in his pocket.

"Hello?" he mumbled, chipmunking the bite.

"Phylus? It's Malia. How are you?"

"Been a pretty quiet morning. So, eh, not too shabby, all things considered," Phylus mused, "Ran into Yrlis. Spril's girlfriend. She's back in ArcNos. What's new with you?"

"Yes, I saw her earlier with some others. Listen, we've got a situation," Malia urged.

"Any news on Galo?"

"He's out and safe. We'll catch you up when you get here."

"Nice to hear it. And his captor?" Phylus asked

"The Prophet has reverted to Pahres," Malia spat, hoping SenRas or EshCal had told Phylus about him as she was suddenly unsure if she had mentioned him, "Phylus. Please. Listen to me."

"What does he remember from his time as The Prophet?"

"I don't know. Blurry fragments probably."

"If he can access those memories without changing back, we can get some deep intel on the Avatars," Phylus suggested, diverting the conversation further, "I have no clue how you'd go about doing something like that, but it might be worth asking around."

"Yes, but we'll deal with that later!" Malia barked, "We have a situation with Yahsek and Sinkua."

"Why? What's wrong? What happened to them?" Phylus asked.

"Everything about Yahsek is wrong," Malia grumbled, "But Sinkua is the same guy as always, which is exactly the problem."

"What did Yahsek do? Did he hurt Nikasu?"

"Yes, psychologically, but she has support. He sabotaged the books and made off with one last night during our rescue mission. Sinkua went after him on foot."

"I'll ask to have recon crews dispatched. Do you know their bearings?"

"No crew. We need to travel light," Malia insisted, "Yahsek will be looking out for anyone following him. So will Sinkua. He no longer trusts The Coalition."

"I should think not," Phylus scoffed, "I assume this mission was a Coalition operation."

"I can't say we're not at fault," she sighed, "Look, just get over here as quickly as you can. Nikasu and I are at their house with Galo and Vielle. We'll bring you up to speed on everything."

"I'll take a sick day," he offered, "See you in two hours."

"Thank you, Phylus. And while you're here, I'm ready to come clean about the night I disappeared," Malia asserted, "No more putting it off."

Chapter 25

Malia paced the kitchen as sheets of nocturnal rain slashed at the windowpane. A radio broadcast spoke of seismic activity detected to the west. She felt phantom floor tremblings at their every mention, her efforts to attribute them to unfounded worry falling flat.

"Phylus," she sighed, collapsing into a dining room chair, "You'd better not be driving into that."

Phylus had left earlier in the evening for an overnight assignment, as had become common. Malia and sleep had a troubled relationship on such nights, but tonight, the thunderstorm and talk of earthquakes left her utterly restless.

She opened the refrigerator, pushed aside a pair of medical canisters, and grabbed a can of Diet Popken. She thought better than to caffeinate her already frazzled nerves. A knock at the door proved her right as she nearly dropped the soda can. Catching her breath, she hurried to answer.

"What can I do for you?" she asked, "Besides offering an umbrella."

"Are you Malia?" the stout visitor shouted over the rain.

"Yeah. Do I know you?"

"You might. I'm MalVek. From Veracious Staffing," he introduced.

"Maybe we had an assignment together," Malia pondered, her thoughts straying from her worries.

"Maybe. I've been on several," MalVek agreed. After a pause, he nodded toward the kitchen.

"Oh! Right. Sorry. Come in and get cleaned up," Malia offered, stepping aside, "What brings you out here in the middle of the night?"

"An assignment, of course," he announced, giving a puzzled look.

"Suppose you heard about the quake out west," she guessed, "Do you need to call and cancel? Maybe wait out the storm? I wouldn't mind the company while I wait for my boyfriend to get home."

"Ah no, I'm here to pick you up," MalVek corrected, "Did you not get the call?"

"Nope. I have an assignment tonight?"

"Yes, we're updating and backing up the inventory database at a plant out east."

"No one told me," Malia shrugged.

"Hydraulic component manufacturer? Converting their inventory management system?" he grasped, "None of this rings a bell?"

"I haven't heard from Veracious in three weeks," she guffawed.

"Lazy sons of bitches. Guess it's a good thing I offered to pick you up," MalVek muttered, fishing in his pockets, "Course, that might be why they didn't call you."

"How long is the assignment?"

"They're projecting and paying out for a week, but we can probably take it down in two nights and pocket the last three days' pay," he explained, pulling a damp sheet of paper from his pocket and unfolding it, "Here we are. Paperwork with all the details."

Malia accepted the paper and looked it over. Everything fit MalVek's story. They even went ahead and confirmed her acceptance, which was correct but presumptive nonetheless. It came off suspicious, but such poor communications were common with

Veracious Staffing, perhaps ironically, given their name.

"Okay," she nodded, giving the paper back to him, "Let me get dressed and leave a note for Phylus."

Malia excused herself to the bedroom to find a proper change of clothes. Even if the facility was to be sparsely occupied, working in sweatpants and an oversized t-shirt wouldn't do at all. Startling her in her state of semi-nudity, MalVek called to her from the kitchen.

"We've got over an hour to drive," he announced, "Mind if I take a drink?"

"Go ahead," she offered, wriggling into a blouse, "But not a Strawberry Popken. Phylus is pretty particular about those."

"I get that," MalVek said, "Don't care for fruits and whatnot sullying my cola, anyhow."

Malia returned to the kitchen more appropriately attired. She swapped out her decaffeinated drink for a Blackberry Popken, noticing the medical canisters now sat in the front. Obviously, MalVek only moved them to reach a regular cola, but she shuddered at the thought of a stranger handling those containers.

She scribbled a note to Phylus, threw on her jacket, and grabbed her umbrella. She and MalVek squeezed awkwardly under the umbrella and rushed out into the storm. MalVek got in his car and slammed the door, unlocking the passenger's side while Malia fought to close her umbrella. Drenched in those few seconds of exposure, Malia scrambled into the car.

"Sorry about your seat," she said, tucking her umbrella in a pocket on the door.

"Don't sweat it," MalVek smiled, pulling out of the driveway, "So, have you ever been out east?"

"I'm from the east, actually."

"Ah, you're lucky. This is only my third time. Nice scenery out that way. Makes it worth the commute."

"Oh, I know. The lakes look amazing on clear nights," Malia beamed, buddying up to her co-worker for the long night ahead, "Have you ever gone fishing out there?"

"Haven't had the chance. Heard it's great though."

"My father used to take me when I was little. He'd catch trout that I swear were half as long as my arm is now."

"Sounds like great eating," he mused, "What about Eprilen? Ever been that far east?"

"Poravit's more directly east of here, isn't it? Eprilen's more to the south, right?"

"Is it? Eh, geography was never my best subject. Well, in that case, you been to Poravit?"

"No, I've actually never left the country," Malia sighed, "We've been saving up to move out of Ivaria. Trying to, anyway. We wanna live in Ierodhes. But I think he's getting distracted by this kid Spril who he babysits sometimes. That boy can't stop talking about going to ArcNos and enlisting."

"Malia, I need to ask you something," MalVek cut in, his voice suddenly stern.

"What's up?"

"What would you say if I told you we're not going to a hydraulic component factory?"

"I'd wonder why you lied about where the assignment is. Why? Do we need some kind of special clearance?"

"I guess you could say that."

"O...kay..." Malia worried, squirming in her seat, "Who are you really, and what's going on?"

"I'm exactly who I said I am. My name is MalVek, and I work for Veracious

Staffing," he reiterated, "If you want, we can find a payphone so you can call them and check."

"Fine, I believe you," she huffed, "But where are we going? What kind of clearance are we going to need?"

"Don't worry about that. I've got it covered," MalVek explained, "We're going to Eprilen. You're going to help us fix something."

"I don't know what you've heard, but I'm no good with machines."

"Why do you assume I'm talking about a machine? This is a matter of politics."

"I'm even worse with that!" Malia exclaimed, "Trust me, you've got the wrong girl."

"No, you definitely have the potential we're looking for. You'll have enough time to develop the necessary skill set."

"Okay. MalVek. You're creeping me out. Who do you really work for?"

"Like I said, I work for Veracious Staffing. But as far as this business goes, let's just say our name is currently above your clearance. We deal in predictive analysis and preemptive corrections."

"You mean you try to see the future and stop bad things from happening?"

"Rather reductive, but I suppose it works for layman's terms," MalVek glowered, "We study people and circumstances and calculate potential outcomes. If an outcome that will hurt too many people is too probable, we work to reduce the odds or eliminate the possibility."

"That's impossible, "Malia impugned, "Nobody can know the future that accurately."

"It's a volatile line of work, circumstances changing as they do. For one, anyone whose course we're trying to change can't know what we're doing."

"Well, of course. That would change the possibilities."

"You catch on quick. The boss'll like that," MalVek grinned, "Anyway, are you familiar with a woman named Olsa? I'd say she's a couple of years older than you."

"Never heard of her. Is she behind whatever you want me to fix?" Malia guessed.

"Yep. She's only a junior attorney, but she's already making local headlines," MalVek explained, "Our analysis shows that she's highly likely to run for office. Trouble is, her undefeated track record is making a narcissist of her, which may become sociopathy if she breezes through elections like she's been doing with her cases."

"And you want me to run against her?"

"Not in her first election. You won't be ready by then."

"Probably not, but the higher the office, the higher the stakes," Malia argued, "The sooner I go up against her, the less you have to lose if I fall short."

"We're going to help you work up the rank and file in a different district," MalVek clarified, "When she goes federal, we'll pit our protégé against her."

"So, you want me to be a political puppet for some shadow organization?" Malia grimaced, "I don't like the sound of that."

"Truthfully, she probably will be, too."

"Well, I guess you could say the same about most politicians."

"No, this is worse than your typical foul play. There's another group that'll probably have their eyes on her soon. Assuming they don't already," he explained, "We've been wrong about this sort of thing before, but with them, it's better to be cautious to a fault."

"I'm not necessarily agreeing to this," Malia prefaced, "but I wanna hear more. Unless I can't back out once you fill me in on the details."

"We wouldn't trap you like that, but we would need to keep you away from those other people," MalVek reassured, "Nice to know we've got your attention though. What it comes down to is that we're trying to prevent a distortion of history."

"Protecting the Historical Guild?"

"If Olsa makes federal office, there's a high probability of unfounded revisions or even purgings of records. If she times her run for Prime Duchess right, she could oversee the Ouristihran Union Parliament by the end of her first year in office. That part's mostly speculation for now, but her screwing with historical accounts is pretty damn likely."

"Right, history is written by the winners," Malia agreed, "This wouldn't be the first time someone skewed things to play up their side of it, though."

"We're not talking about different phrasings in school books, like how ArcNosian and Kirtsian ones talk about their trade conflict," MalVek corrected, "We'd be looking at a full-blown overhaul. Facts completely rewritten. Entire events wiped from all but word of mouth."

"Would she really have the authority to do that?"

"She might, and if she does, odds are that she will. Far as we're concerned, that's enough reason to take action against her."

"So, what's your plan if the odds change, and you're wrong about her?"

"If we're completely off base about her, we'll reassign you. Between the rumors around Berinin and suspicious activity in the Northlands, there'll be no shortage of work for you."

"Okay, well I need to let Phylus know where I've gone. He'll worry if I haven't come home by tomorrow afternoon," Malia insisted, "But you need to understand that I'm still not agreeing to this just yet. I'll meet with your boss and get more details from him, but I'm reserving the right to walk away."

"That'll be fine," MalVek accepted, "You've got until tomorrow night to decide. If you work with us, your loved ones will be notified accordingly. If you don't, we'll part ways with no hard feelings and provide you with a cover story for your extended absence."

Phylus stared at the floor, struggling to digest the story. Something about the sequence of events didn't add up. He couldn't pinpoint a fault with any sense of certainty, but Malia's account of that night didn't feel quite right.

Learning that Aleepo was Gabdur, that the man had been hiding out in the open all this time, had been a lot to take in. Even though Spril had done something similar, surviving his own death and taking on a conditional alias. That was much shorter term though. The whole thing, with Gabdur as well as the truth behind Malia's disappearance, made him wonder what other decades-old secrets The Coalition was harboring.

"Let me get this straight. This guy drives off with you in the middle of the night and starts talking about controlling the future or whatever," Vielle snarked, cutting into her father's introspection, "and you just bought it and ran off with him?"

"What? No!" Malia defended, "I told him I'd hear more about their business. I sat down with a few of their agents and talked it over until the sun came up. Then we talked for a few more hours after I slept on it. That's when they had me convinced."

"Whatever. You ran off to work with a bunch of weirdos and left Dad alone with an orphan. Maybe if you hadn't bailed, Spril wouldn't have gotten shot, and we wouldn't have wound up on the street."

"I feel like I'm repeating myself here," Malia quipped, "You owe your existence to the fact that I ran off."

"Oh, well in that case, thank you so much for running away so I could be born. Is that what you want to hear?" Vielle snipped.

"Malia, what did you write in the note?" Phylus cut in, looking up from the floor.

"Come again?"

"You said you left a note. There was one on the kitchen table that said you were leaving me. It went on about how you couldn't take being apart so much and how we were becoming strangers in the same house."

"I don't remember it verbatim, but it wasn't anything like that," Malia protested, "When they said they'd notify my loved ones, I didn't think they meant like that."

"Like what?" Vielle asked, "Did someone forge the letter?"

"It sounds like it. One of their founding agents, Chekov, excels at correspondence mimicry," Malia recalled, "She offered to write a new note, but I thought I should call or send a letter. They eventually talked me into letting her do it, but I didn't know she was going to have me dump you.

"I'm sorry. You probably thought I was a bitch when you read that."

"Chekov as in Doctor Chekov?" Phylus asked.

"Yes, she worked at a genetics facility. Why?"

"She handled Vielle. That is so strange," he remarked, "How many more have we come across without knowing it?"

"Not surprising. She worked there to look for the fourth Hybrid," Malia explained, "Carriers such as myself weren't as rare back then."

"Carriers?" Phylus asked.

"People with the genetic potential to have Hybrid children. The Avatars of Fate have been hunting Carriers since before the Hybrids or even their parents were born. Part of the reason The Coalition was established was to protect the Carriers from extinction."

"MalVek moved the canisters to manipulate an outcome," Nikasu deduced, "Knowing you were a Carrier, he meant to coax Phylus toward artificial conception and incubation."

"You got all that out of that one detail?" Malia asked in proud disbelief, "I only mentioned it because I was weirded out by this stranger handling our stuff like that."

"Well, it makes sense," Nikasu insisted, "So, when do I come into this?"

"That was seven years later, but I want to wait until Sinkua is with you to go into that."

"Speaking of which," Galo interjected as he came into the living room, "Not to impede on your dysfunctional family reunion, but we have someone important whom we need to find."

"Of course," Phylus agreed, "What's become of our curmudgeonly friend?"

"Eytea went to Ferya, so he hasn't been keeping up with his medicine," Nikasu explained, "He thought no one would notice, but his pill bottles never looked right. And he'd been a lot jumpier. Like he was stressed out all the time."

"That's about what I'd expect of him without her around. Humor the tangent, but why did she go to Ferya?"

"Farim came for her in the middle of the night. The Avatars are hunting people connected to the destruction of The Scout's nanochip. Farim figured that meant Eytea's mom was in danger."

"Smart move, then. Okay now, fast forward to this morning."

"Last night, we went to rescue Galo. Yahsek stayed here by himself. On the way home, we found out Yahsek wasn't an authentic Hybrid."

"There were four Coalition agents on site. None of us had heard of him," Malia added, "The bastard even claimed he was my cousin so Nikasu would think he was family."

"I can see teenagers pretending they're Hybrids because they think it makes them look cool," Phylus said, "But someone his age honestly trying to fool people? What kind of person does that?"

"The kind who's doing reconnaissance on the real ones," Galo reasoned, "The kind who's out to steal valuable assets. The kind who wants to psychologically bitchslap us."

"I heard about him stealing one of those books, but what's this about psychological bitchslaps?"

"He redecorated the house to look like it did when Sinkua was an adolescent, shortly after his mother died. Honestly, I don't know which is more disturbing, his effort or his knowledge."

"How could Yahsek have even known what this house looked like back then?"

"My theory is that he used Eytea's drawings. I'm sure she has more than just that one of the shooting," Galo suggested, "But we can address that later. For now, we need a plan to find Sinkua and ensure his safety."

"I'd also like to track down Yahsek and get some intel on him," Malia added, "We need to take that book back, too."

"Do we have any pictures of it? Nikasu, do you think you could give a detailed description?" Phylus proposed, "If we know what we're looking for, I can reach out to Prime Duke Norum to help us track down a second copy."

"I don't think a second copy exists," Malia argued, "I've been under the impression that these are the only printing of each manuscript."

"I'm going to focus on finding Sinkua first. The Coalition can do whatever they want about Yahsek and the book, but our friend is my first priority," Galo insisted, "We don't know who else Yahsek and Ozzera might have joined up with, what they're capable of, or what they'll do if we catch them. He needs to be with us just as much as we need to be with him before we pursue them."

"In that case, I suppose I should be on my way," Malia said, excusing herself, "I'll consult with the available Coalition agents to get a position and trajectory on Yahsek. It may be tricky without a behavioral record though."

The lot of them lost themselves in contemplation as Malia left the house. The circumstances surrounding Sinkua's disappearance had created a volatile situation.

Phylus considered dispatching plain-clothes officers to search for him. He played out scenarios in his mind, but they always ended the same way, Sinkua discovering the officers and reacting, at a minimum, unpleasantly.

Nikasu wrestled with feelings of inadequacy as she begrudgingly accepted that she could not effectively track him the same way she had found Yahsek and Ozzera's trail. A stranger had traveled across the continent and braved the bowels of Facility 3891 to find her, just because they were both Hybrids. Related or not, he would have come for her. Yet, to save him, she could only fixate on an idea both inefficient and beyond her ken.

Vielle faced similar troubles. She had once saved Sinkua's life once in a grand and theatrical manner, but he had since helped her numerous times. He had directed her to Galo for assistance with her arbormancy. He gleaned her sexuality but had kept it to himself. When she learned about Malia and Nikasu, he offered his assistance. Despite all she wanted to do for him though, she had no idea how to track him beyond going west-northwest.

Galo reflected on the bitter thoughts and words he'd had for his brother since leaving Berinin in Chairman LenSom's custody. For so long, he had accused him of selfishness, obstruction, and even honestly issuing his warrant. If Sinkua had been ignorant of this rage when he set out to rescue Galo, he certainly learned about it upon finding his chamber. If he had known, well, he came nonetheless. Now, Galo found himself trapped between two options, each paradoxically proving and disproving his loyalty.

Something needed to change.

"I guess," Vielle began, breaking the long silence, "we need to wait for Eytea."

"That sounds like the best idea," Galo agreed with a slow nod, still deep in thought, "I don't think he has much patience for me right now. If anyone finds him before he gets where he's going, Eytea would be the best one to approach him."

"But he doesn't have anything against me," Nikasu countered, "Maybe he'd like it if his little sister came to find him, like he did for me."

"He doesn't have anything against me right now either, but that's not the point," Vielle argued, "He's unstable, and at best, you and I are only on neutral ground with him. And Eytea's absence only makes things worse for him. He doesn't realize it, but he's going out there for her. It's not about the book as much as holding on to the people he's loved and lost."

"You mean Eytea is a stand-in for his mother?" Nikasu sneered.

"No, that's pop-psych pseudoscience bullshit. I mean that Eytea's absence amplifies every reminder of his losses," Vielle explained, "Ergo, she needs to be the one to find him."

"I'll write a letter," Galo offered, "Do you have her tracking scent?"

"No need," Nikasu insisted, rising from her seat with newfound urgency, "We have her mother's phone number."

Nikasu scooped a pile of scrap paper, cardstock, and coupons from a drawer under the telephone in the kitchen. She slapped the pile on the counter and sifted out the scrap paper, rifling through it until she found Elemeno's number.

"Here you are," she offered, handing Galo the paper and the cordless phone.

Galo mashed the digits on the keypad, drawing out the keytones as though he was playing lo-fi classical music. He pressed the receiver against his ear, only to jerk it away at the horrid shrieking that followed.

"Ahh! What is that noise?" he snapped, slowly bringing the phone back to his ear.

He listened a moment longer and, shaking his head, passed the phone to Vielle.

"No answer?" Phylus asked.

"Her line is disconnected," Vielle said, hanging up.

"I'll write that letter, then," Galo said.

MarLys hopped off the motorcycle and mounted her helmet on the back of the seat. Nervously eyeing the car in the driveway, she waved farewell to Vielle. MarLys smiled all the while, trying to quiet the radial pulse on her neck as it betrayed her masked anxiety.

Vielle could never know of her apprehension about going home. She problems enough, both in general and today, what with her father calling about Sinkua's disappearance and her biological mother promising to come clean.

MarLys hesitated on the doorstep, keys in hand, watching Vielle drive out of sight. Accepting the inevitable, MarLys shoved the key into the deadbolt.

The door flew open and out lunged a handful of jagged knuckles. It grabbed her by the collar of her shirt, a sharp yelp escaping her lips, and dragged her into the house. Another hand clutched her shoulder and used her back to slam the door.

"Who were you with?" the bitter man hissed.

"N... No... Nobody," MarLys lied.

"Don't sass me, you carpetmuncher!" he snarled, knocking the back of her head against the door, "Who was that?"

"It was nobody, Uncle. You don't know her," she insisted, shielding her face.

"Her?!" he shouted, "I don't know her?!"

"Him! I meant him!"

"The hell you did, you bloody dyke," Uncle sneered, drawing his hand across his shoulder.

"It was just a slip of the tongue, I swear," MarLys retracted.

"I bet she's all about those, isn't she, you fucking queer?"

He grabbed both her spindly wrists in one comparatively meaty hand and lifted her upright. His pupils dilated with rage, he plowed the back of his hand across her temple. He repeatedly battered the side of her head as she cried out in anguished protest. MarLys gradually quieted, eventually falling silent. Uncle punctuated the assault with his elbow in her eye socket.

"Fine," MarLys muttered, hocking reddened mucus on the carpet with a teary-eyed glare of grim determination, "You wanna know who I was with? Vielle. My girlfriend."

"Your what?" Uncle grumbled.

"Girl... Friend..." MarLys reiterated, tauntingly drawing out each syllable, "And you can do fuck-all about it."

He threw her to the floor with a contemptuous grunt. He looked her over, waiting for her to roll over and fight back or at least sass him. Muttering another sexual slur, he kicked her side. She turned and looked up at him with bloodshot eyes, her gaze steely and unyielding.

"What?" she challenged, "Do you really think you can change me?"

"Get up."

"You can't keep treating me like this. When Mom and Dad..."

"Go get cleaned up," he ordered, "You have fifteen minutes to start making lunch."

MarLys lifted herself to her hands and knees, scrambling further into the house before standing upright. She watched over her shoulder as she hurried to the stairs and down to the basement.

Her door stood in the corner among building scraps, broken furniture, and spare parts for the furnace. It fit its frame so poorly, she banged her elbow against a busted foosball table when she finally yanked it opened.

To call her bedroom minimal would have been a kindness. She slept on a cot riddled with moth bites and cigarette burns. A Frigid coat doubled as her pillow, and a patchwork quilt of musty old shirts completed the ensemble. A matrix of milk crates turned on their sides served as her dresser. An old mirror stood atop it, permeated with the stench of the junkyard she had salvaged it from. A photograph of Vielle and herself hid behind it.

MarLys sat on a large wooden spool and pulled a rag that had once been underwear from one of the crates. She spat on it a few times and rubbed an area of the mirror, removing the day's dust and fading the perhaps indelible grime from the ageworn glass.

She took a clock radio from its hiding place among the crates and turned on the tape deck, keeping the volume low like always. From another crate, she pulled a makeup kit and began dabbing concealer around her freshly swollen eye. It grew increasingly discolored, taking on sickly shades of purple and yellow. Makeup could hide that much, but the swelling soon became problematic.

MarLys leaned in closer to the mirror, examining each eye. The asymmetry had become too apparent. For her own good, nobody could know of her suffering. Not yet. If Uncle found out, he would only make things worse.

Even after all of Vielle's talk about no longer living lies, MarLys continued to hide her horrible truth behind an excuse of inevitability. The face Vielle adored lied to her, its true features sleeker than the beady eyes and high soft cheekbones suggested. MarLys even deceived her with her complexion, claiming Ierodhesan ancestry to account for her light year-round tan.

MarLys crouched beside her makeshift dresser, aligning her undamaged eye with the corner. White-knuckling the crate, she clenched her eyes, tightened her lips, and reared back.

Uncle returned his attention to the television. He swigged at his bottle of Schauzen's Premier as he dug for the remote in the arm of the recliner. Finding his drink empty, he dropped the bottle and turned to shout toward the basement. His phone cut him off.

"Hello?"

"Status?"

"She's in."

"Has she gained their trust?"

"Yes."

"And you hers?"

"Negative."

"As intended. Tap her room."

"Equipment procured. Awaiting opportunity to install."

"Well done. You've performed as expected."

"Of course. Will that be all, Politician?"

"For now. Keep me informed, Chairman."

Chapter 26

Nikasu stirred under a panel of sunlight stretching across the room. She rolled over and opened her eyes to fabric draped over a firm ridged surface. She pawed at the fabric, groggily rationalizing it as a curtain. Rather than the expected window, she found dark abdominal flesh.

Her face reddening, her eyes trailed upward to find Galo looking down at her. He smiled breezily and chuckled as she stared up at him with confused embarrassment.

"Good morning," he greeted, "It would seem we fell asleep on the couch."

"Huh? Oh, right," Nikasu agreed, hastily sitting up, "We were waiting up for Eytea."

"Well, unless she slipped upstairs to let us sleep, I suppose she hasn't arrived yet," Galo said, "No matter. The pigeon probably just reached Ferya night before last."

"So that's how long it takes," Nikasu noted, defragmenting memories of last night, "Wasn't the television on?"

"I turned it off when it woke me up, but you looked too comfortable to move. You stirred every time I tried to get out from under you."

"How did…" Nikasu puzzled, interrupted by a jostling at the door, "Oh! It's the door. Over there. There's a door. Over there. Someone's doing something. Something to the door. I should go do something about that."

Nikasu hustled to the door, Galo chuckling all the while. She stopped as the doorknob turned, fingers twitching anxiously. Sinkua hadn't struck her as the type to give up a pursuit, never that easily and especially not so soon. Eytea couldn't have been coming home yet. This left only one person who could feasibly be trying to unlock the door. Nikasu backed up to the bottom of the stairs, ready to flee for her scythes and defend the remaining books.

An older female voice slipped through the crack as the door began to open, giving pause to Nikasu's retreat. Her shoulders relaxed with curiosity for this unfamiliar yet pleasant voice. The door swung wide, and there stood Eytea, her back turned as she addressed a woman considerably her elder.

"I'm telling you," the woman insisted, "This place looks so familiar. I feel like I've been here before. And this foyer. I know this foyer."

"Mom. Seriously," Eytea countered, "You know it because of my drawings of it. Remember? The one with Sinkua and…"

"Eytea!" Nikasu exclaimed, "You're home!"

"Of course I am," Eytea coolly smiled as she hung her coat, "You didn't think I was gone for good, did you?"

"No, it's just that you got here so fast. Galo said you probably only got the letter a couple of nights ago," Nikasu fumbled, flabbergasted at Eytea's very presence, "Is this woman your mother?"

"Yeah. Mom, this is Nikasu. Nikasu, this is Mom," Eytea hastily introduced, "Now, what's this about a letter?"

"Did you miss us, or did her home become unsafe?" Galo cut in.

"Both. Nice to see you're back, by the way," Eytea answered, "So this letter?"

"It never got to you?" Nikasu puzzled.

"If it did, would I be asking about it?" Eytea snarked, "We spent most the ride below deck. The bird might have given up on finding us."

"The weather was dreadful," Elemeno commented, "Galo, you would have loved it!"

"I'm sure of it. Nice to see you again, Elemeno. Wonderful to know you're safe," Galo laughed, "Anyway, we wrote to tell you about Sinkua."

"Oh, I wouldn't go so far as to say we're safe. We were attacked by your uncle. We had to leave in such a hurry," Elemeno regaled, "Sestak chased him off the property, but Seschnel… Well, Seschnel didn't fare so well. We had to bury her before we left."

"That is terrible. I'm so sorry things happened that way," Galo consoled, losing himself in the tangential conversation.

"Nikasu," Eytea beckoned, taking her aside, "What happened to Sinkua?"

"A lot happened while you were gone, but I'll give you the quick version," Nikasu said, "We went out to rescue Galo. Things ended alright, but we found out Yahsek might not be on the level or however you say it. We got home, and the furniture was arranged just like it was when Sinkua was a kid."

"That's pretty messed up," Eytea sneered, "What happened next?"

"We realized Yahsek was gone, so we paired off for different tasks," Nikasu continued, "MalVek and I figured out which way he went. Galo and Malia rearranged the furniture. And Sinkua and Gabdur went to check on the books."

"Gabdur?"

"We knew him as Aleepo. He's Galo's biological father. We'll get back to that."

"Yeah, we'd better!" Eytea agreed, "Hey Mom, did you hear that?"

"Something about Aleepo?" Elemeno called back, "We hadn't seen a parcel from him in so long. I do hope he's well."

"He's fine. He was here a few days ago," Eytea assured, "He's Galo's father."

Elemeno immersed herself in a new conversation with Galo, demanding he regale her with the story of meeting his presumed-dead father. Galo complied, albeit uncomfortably, while Eytea returned to her conversation with Nikasu.

"There we go," Eytea smiled, "She'll catch me up on that later. Now, did anything happen to the books?"

"They were scattered all over the room, and one of them was missing," Nikasu said, "The rest just had some scuff marks on the covers."

"Yahsek ran off with one of the books? Why would he do that?"

"He's a Faux-Hybrid. I think they put him with me so he could be a mole if you guys ever broke me out. I don't know if this was exactly their plan all along, but he must have run off to deliver it to the Avatars. He probably works for The Geneticist."

"I'm not sure what troubles me more, that they could have planned something like this or that they created a Faux-Hybrid and a chimera," Eytea puzzled, "The Geneticist was in Ferya three days ago. If you're right about Yahsek working for him, he probably went to meet up with him."

"Of course!" Nikasu exclaimed, "That's where he went. Why didn't I think of that?"

"Think of what?"

"Yahsek and Ozzera went to meet The Geneticist and The Engineer at Laboratory 1341," Nikasu clarified, pacing alongside of the dining table, "If I'm right to believe their labs share a surveillance network, they already know what we did with Galo and Pahres."

"Where is Laboratory 1341? Is it far from here?" Eytea urged.

"It's about a two-hour drive at this time of day," Nikasu said, "But don't you want to know what's become of Sinkua?"

"He went after Yahsek. Right?"

"Yes. How did you know?"

"We've been together long enough," Eytea smiled, digging in a pocket of her hanging coat, "Now, which direction is it from here?"

"Northwestish," Nikasu said, "You're not thinking of going there yourself, are you?"

"Nope. I've got better things to do than chase after some poser Hybrid without much of a clue as to what I'm up against. Besides, I have a faster way to find Sinkua than rendezvousing once he finds where he's going."

From her coat pocket, Eytea pulled a small vial with Sinkua's name written on a strip of tape wrapped around it.

"I'll get you some paper and ribbon," Nikasu offered excitedly, "What should we write?"

"We don't need to write anything," Eytea insisted, "Hey Mom, I need to go find Sinkua. Wanna help me put together a care package?"

Biroe sat among strangers and colleagues in the cramped lobby, anxiously tapping his foot on sound-dampening carpet. He distracted himself reading placards and framed legal notices along the walls. Most were old news, outdated even. Such had become typical of Parliament lately, it seemed, broadcasting as little information as they could get away with.

People trickled into the next room as they were summoned, but the crowd never appeared to diminish. Biroe stared at the clock for several minutes, contemplating the purpose behind his summons. The paperwork indicated little more than that it regarded Tanelen, but he hadn't heard back from Foreign Affairs since he forwarded those messages to Phylus.

"Biroe, Prime Minister of Treasury," the court clerk called.

Biroe followed the clerk into a vast and foreboding courtroom, its vaulted ceiling perhaps higher than that of the Brigadier General Elite's office in the Platinum Hall. The elevated bench placed Parliament discomfortingly higher than everyone else. LenSom sat in the center, slightly but noticeably more elevated than the rest.

A few weeks hadn't been enough time for Biroe to grasp the reasoning behind appointing LenSom as Chairman of Parliament. They handled such affairs internally, so to wit, LenSom had been democratically promoted by his fellow Representatives.

Biroe seethed in silence as charges were leveled against him. Common belief still dictated that he had embezzled federal tax money from Tanelen, his efforts to spread intelligence to the contrary going unnoticed.

"How do you plead to your charges?" LenSom challenged.

"I plead bullshit," Biroe snarked, "Yes, I accessed private accounts. However, I only have access to holding institutions, account holder names, and general ledgers. No account numbers. No identifying figures. All measures were well within accordance with financial investigative statutes."

"So, what you're saying, Mister Prime Minister," LenSom countered, "is that you have special privileges. You have access to the peoples' private finances."

"Hardly. I'd trade my office for a maximum security prison cell if I dicked around in someone's account without evident cause. Only knowing where a person banks won't get you jack, anyhow."

"Then what do you have to say in defense of your rerouting money bound for a high-asset account in Tanelen?"

"You're welcome. That wasn't their money."

"So, now you're playing vigilante over disagreeable corporate policies? I suppose your resolve is respectable, but your methods are unorthodox and, more importantly, illegal. As you should expect, Tanelen is not taking kindly to the tax revenue you've cost them.

Word down the pipeline is that…"

"That was not their money!" Biroe protested, drawling out his syllables, "It was equity from ArcNosian corporations, to be paid to two high-profile ArcNosian investors."

"So, you were just reclaiming what was ours? And who devised such an elaborate scheme to embezzle this money in the first place? I see a lot of intelligent people in this room. Seen a lot more throughout the federal campus. But if you ask me, none of them are capable of such a feat. None but you, that is."

"All evidence points to the Avatars of Fate."

"And you know this how?"

"They're the only people with the resources and motive. The targeted citizens are icons of philanthropy. Essential citizen support programs are at risk of collapsing without their private contributions," Biroe explained, "Furthermore, the Commissioner of the Radial Axiom Arena, an active dissenter of the Avatars, recently closed all of his accounts in Tanelen with the exception of one at this same financial institution. He continues to hold multiple accounts in all other countries."

"And you assume this to mean what? That he's sending you a message?"

"It's too big of a coincidence to disregard it."

"This is all circumstantial evidence. You of all people should realize that," LenSom scolded, "If the Avatars of Fate are stealing from ArcNosians, recourse must follow legal channels."

"Given the weight of the matter, I determined that it was imperative I cut your stupid red tape, rather than wait for the arbitrary mucking to clear."

"Did you bring documentation to corroborate your arguments, Prime Minister?" LenSom sneered.

"Had you not neglected to communicate the specific nature of my summons, I would have," Biroe hissed, "If you would summon him, I sent copies of my paperwork to Prime Minister of Foreign Affairs Phylus. He was to speak with Tanelenese officials and clear the air of this fiasco."

"Yes, well, we spoke with Phylus earlier this morning," LenSom reported with lazy disinterest, "He refused to divulge any such information. His insubordination was equated to acceptance of his charges of serving as your accomplice. As such, he was summarily placed under probation."

"Probation? Did it ever occur to you that he may not have received the information?"

"Prime Minister, you said yourself that he was given the paperwork. Was he or was he not informed of the nature of your operation?"

"I said I sent him the paperwork. I have no knowledge as to its reception. All Prime Ministers and High Ministers know about the turmoil with Tanelen. Had he not yet received the papers, Phylus would have sought my counsel before meeting with a representative of Noble Doyen Joren."

"That will be taken into consideration at his next hearing in ten weeks, but for now, what's done is done."

"How exactly did you come to bring Phylus into this in the first place?"

"This is a matter of foreign relations."

"Yes, but it's a financial issue first. He was your first contact?"

"Actually, Parliament first met with the Ministry of Defense to discuss the likelihood of a martial response from Tanelen," LenSom explained, "High Minister of Defense EshCal suggested we send Phylus to speak with them first. She spoke of your investigation and rather vigilante handling of the situation. We spoke with Phylus thereafter, but not before determining EshCal to have been an accomplice to your operation. She too has been placed on a ten-week probationary sentence."

"Hold on. Your first action is to prepare for militant retaliation? Not to understand the situation? Not to clear the air before the guns come out?" Biroe challenged, "Chairman LenSom, are you deliberately trying to start a war with our technological superiors?"

"At times such as this, our first priority is to order our military to stand by in anticipation of aggressive measures. This is the policy set forth by Parliament and agreed to by the Ministry of Defense."

"Chairman, you are forcing our soldiers into a war that not only can they not win, but that they should not be fighting in the first place. If we can show Tanelen …"

"Well, we'll just have to trust someone else to that, considering…"

"I know. Our Prime Minister of Foreign Affairs is on probation. I formally request to be sent in his stead. I understand the situation better than anyone. You said yourself that I'm the only person around here who could do what the Avatars have done."

"Of course you do," LenSom sneered, his lip twitching at Biroe's mention of the Avatars, "However, given your vigilante methods and the danger it has befallen upon ArcNos, your position is hereby terminated."

"What?! I'm trying to cover everyone's asses, and you have the audacity to fire me? What the fuck kind of Parliament are you running?"

"Your actions are the reason anyone's ass needs covering. You eschewed your responsibility to…"

"It was the Avatars of Fate!" Biroe roared, "Had I not taken immediate action, they would have destroyed our lower class infrastructure and initialized operations in…"

"Interrupt me once more, and you will be held in contempt! Do you understand?" LenSom bellowed, standing to further emphasize his authority, "Your behavior has been irrational, irresponsible, and illegal. Your evidence to implicate the Avatars of Fate is entirely circumstantial. Given that my circumstantial evidence indicates you elaborated the entire scandal, you're lucky I haven't had you arrested."

"You? Since when do you decide the will of Parliament?" Biroe challenged, "Your job is to speak their will, not to …"

"Officers!" LenSom interrupted, "Remove this man from my courthouse."

Biroe sneered at the officers closing in around him as he spun to face the door. He wheeled himself toward the exit, but they grabbed at his chair anyway. With a defiant grunt, Biroe smashed an officer's hand between his elbow and one of the back handles of his wheelchair.

"Don't. Touch. My chair," Biroe snarled, "Eel-pissing traitor."

The officer raised his tonfa and clocked Biroe across the jaw. Blood dripping from the corner of his mouth, Biroe dropped his head and smirked with twisted triumph as another officer escorted him out of the courtroom. Regardless of Parliament's decision and LenSom's execution of such, hundreds of people had witnessed the Chairman's handling of a volatile international affair.

Everyone invited to speak on Biroe's behalf had been deemed and sentenced as criminal accomplices, all through evidence far more circumstantial than his grounds for action. Biroe knew such a scandal could never be quarantined in those walls, not for long. At a minimum, he could launch a private investigation and had already begun plotting such before he reached the building's exit.

A familiar voice called his name, giving him pause. He looked back to find KalChi shoving through the crowd.

"Biroe, wait up," she urged, catching up to him.

"KalChi?" he smiled, "When did you get here?"

"I was in there along the mezzanine. Didn't you see me?"

"Sorry, no. But, you already know what happened then. I want you to take over on this case," Biroe insisted, "Find people you can trust but who LenSom won't be suspicious of in the Ministry of Foreign Affairs. Phylus or Sinkua will help you."

"That's going to be a problem," KalChi confessed, "I've also been discharged."

"Dammit. Did they find out you were working with me?"

"Several members of the Ministry of Treasury were called in to speak on the economic ramifications of the scandal."

"And nobody was invited to speak in my defense while I was present."

"Suspicious, isn't it? We made our cases before your trial. Evidently, LenSom saw no need to have us speak further during your trial."

"Of course not," Biroe sneered as they headed down the access ramp, "He saw a threat to his real allegiance and took measures to remove us. I assume you were dismissed from duty after I left, then?"

"Of course. He obviously made his decision during pretrial. He only kept me in there long enough to flaunt his authority and make an example of you."

"Obviously. Overcompensating traitor."

"You really think he's an Avatar of Fate?" KalChi asked.

"I don't think he's ranked that high, but I do think he works for one," Biroe explained, "Of course, it's largely circumstantial right now. And we both know how much he hates circumstantial evidence."

"He would need to be able to communicate with them clandestinely. He's too smart to use any of his government-issue equipment."

"Home phone? Cellular?"

"Too easy to trace," KalChi argued, maneuvering Biroe along the congested sidewalk.

"Do you have something else in mind?"

"His niece works for a courier company. She's his only family in the area. He could be using her to send correspondence, and nobody would ever know. Not even her."

"Sounds like a good place to start. We'll ask SenRas what he can dig up, as well," Biroe agreed, unlocking his car, "What's his niece's name, and where does she work?"

"Her name is MarLys. She works for Black Tie Delivery."

Yrlis sipped her coffee, her focus waning as she tried to recall how many mugs she had drunk. She slid the cup behind her desk lamp, hiding its shadow from her work. Spril rolled and grunted in their bed behind her, interrupting the choir of crickets from beyond the moonlit curtains.

Yrlis checked off a listing in the decryption legend Pahres had given to her. She scanned The Diagram, searching for completed character strings. These she copied to another sheet, gradually creating her own copy of The Diagram in modern script.

In a moment of weakened resolve, she looked at the clock. Three hours until sunrise. Four and a half until Spril would awaken. She yawned at the thought of her sleeplessness and the day to come of it. Trying to rein in her conviction, she focused on the progress of her decryption.

Yrlis had formed numerous hypotheses about The Diagram, up until the acceptance of futility set it aside. Nearly four years had passed since she last worked on it. But she never forgot it. Never forgot the intrigue. Her hypotheses. Her failure.

Now, every term she decrypted scraped away at the endless list of postulations chiseled into her memories. One in particular stood especially prominent, but by all sensibilities, it should have been impossible.

Minutes marched along, gathering into hours. Yrlis depleted a second pot of coffee, finishing the last mug as avian melodies replaced the chirping of crickets. The decrypted Diagram neared completion as dawn sunbeams filtered through the curtains. Her strongest hypothesis took commanding prominence as she neared the end of Pahres's legend. The others died in the back of her mind, priority going to justifications for the inconceivability of the surviving hypothesis.

Ten minutes before Spril's alarm would go off, Yrlis marked off the last entry. Her eyes scanned for errors while she transcribed the last strings, her mind in civil war between denial and pride. She leaned back to view it as a whole. Complete.

Channeling her elation into her restlessly tapping foot, she examined her findings against her surviving hypothesis. Awash in fatigue and the daze of insurmountable accomplishment, she knew she had no hope of discovering a scientific law here. But a theory seemed possible, even if distant.

Yrlis jumped at the sound of Spril's alarm, banging her knee against the underside of her desk. Startled by the noise, Spril rolled over and hoisted himself up by the headboard. He rubbed his goatee and blinked a few times, his mind and body acclimating to each other.

"You're up early," he grimaced, denying his worry behind a plastic smile.

"We're out of coffee," Yrlis answered as she turned her chair, seeing through to his concern before his face even came into focus, "Sorry. In my head, that sounded like a nicer way to tell you I polished off the can."

"I don't like it when you push yourself this hard," Spril consoled, hobbling to her side, "It's like you're punishing yourself."

"Hm? Never thought of it that way. Guess maybe I could be. Somehow."

"What do you mean? You're not responsible for …"

"I know… Just… Never mind. Okay?" Yrlis insisted, "Come look what I did last night."

"And this morning?"

"Yes. And this morning. Just come look."

Spril leaned over her shoulder, studying the three papers. He recognized the first two, but this third sheet was ne. It looked like The Diagram, but as his vision came into focus, he realized he could read the small writing.

"You've…" he gasped, "You've translated it?!"

"Uh-huh. Well, not so much translated as deciphered," she corrected, "Do you know what this means? We now have a complete and thus far comprehensive human genome map in modern script."

"Thus far?"

"It'll need to be updated for genetic susceptibilities as diseases and our knowledge of them evolve. How often depends on the pedantry of our needs."

"Are you saying that, for instance, you could run susceptibility levels for multiple strains of the common cold?"

"Yeah, but I can throw a rock and hit five better ideas to spend the effort on," Yrlis chuckled, "Anyway, I also figured out that anomaly."

"The twenty-fourth pair?" Spril checked as he dressed himself for work.

"Uh-huh," she nodded, swallowing in a feeble attempt to contain her excitement, "It's the Hybrid Chromosomes."

"This is a genome map for the Hybrids, then? Not for humans?" Spril puzzled, stopping with his pants around his ankles, "Makes sense, I guess, given the work the Avatars of Fate have done with it."

"No, this is a map for both."

"But, humans have twenty-three pairs, don't they?"

"We do, but…"

"Then how does a couple with twenty-three pairs produce a child with twenty-four?"

"Genetic mutation."

"Five in one generation, manifesting as superpowers and inhuman body parts.

How likely is that?"

"I don't know. Just listen. Okay?" Yrlis urged, "We know life began with a handful of single-celled organisms. Now, we have millions of species with more variety in the number of chromosomes than there were species born from the primordial ooze."

"So, parents whose children have a different number of chromosomes are evolution in action?" Spril deduced.

"Sometimes. Rarely. Most times, it's a birth defect. When the anomaly becomes a fixture of the species, the first few generations will usually struggle to acclimate to it. Think of it as species-wide growing pains."

"I'd wager that the Hybrids are a step in evolution. But for the most part, they've had an easy time adapting to their extra pair."

"I thought the same thing until I finished the decryption. There's actually a perfectly sound explanation for how they're so well-adjusted to their extra chromosomes," Yrlis explained, "They're not a step in evolution. They're a manifestation of a preexisting condition."

"You mean everyone's a Hybrid?"

"No, but we all have twenty-four pairs of chromosomes. There's a pair we didn't know about because it's only active in extremely specific pairings. All others neutralize each other, and when that happens, even the most advanced DNA tests will only detect twenty-three pairs. In the rare instances when that pair is activated, and we get a Hybrid with forty-eight detectable chromosomes."

"Besides the obvious, how else does the activated pair set the Hybrids apart? Would it make donor matching more difficult?"

"Maybe. But then again, we've successfully transplanted pig organs into humans, and pigs only have nineteen pairs."

"You mean twenty," Spril snickered.

"Why yes, I would like a side of hybrid bacon with my toast and eggs. Thank you for asking," Yrlis joked, fatigue drawing out her laughter to inappropriate lengths. She forced a stern expression as she continued, "But seriously, this has incredible medical potential."

"I'd imagine so. Theoretically, could you make someone insusceptible to disease?"

"I wouldn't go that far. No immune system will ever be impenetrable. But we could come to understand the Avatars' work and maybe figure out a way to stop it."

"You're talking about reversing their genetic enhancements, right? The Hunter's reinforced bone structure and, from what I've been told, The Criminal's superhuman strength?"

"Yes, but that isn't the whole of it."

"Could you make your own enhancements?"

"It's possible, but I'm not too keen on the ethical implications," Yrlis sneered.

"We wouldn't augment anyone without giving full disclosure and getting their consent," Spril assured, "Besides, I wouldn't condone anything irreversible."

"Well, it would give us an advantage over the Avatars. Or at least less of a disadvantage. I can't promise results, but I'll look into it," Yrlis vowed, "But before I do anything else, I'm going to need several blood and marrow samples from Sinkua. I'll teach you some basic phlebotomy, but I'll need to take the marrow samples myself."

"Does it need to be him, or do you just need a Hybrid to map?" Spril asked.

"Has to be him. If I map his genome, I should be able to use gene therapy to essentially teach his body to fight off his infection. So, the sooner I can get my hands on those samples, the better."

"You could change his genetic structure to cure him?"

"That's a pretty crude way to put it, but I guess you're not completely wrong. It's obviously a designer disease, so I doubt there's any particular genes suited to it. I might be able to synthesize an artificial sirtuin though."

"Would it get rid of the current infection? I thought it had gotten embedded in his bone marrow."

"That's what his doctor said, but if we can tap into the Sisyphus Fir's medicinal potential, we may be able to use it as a delivery system," Yrlis pondered, her mind beginning to wander, "Perhaps, I could synthesize a benign retrovirus. But I would need to accelerate the replication process. Or I could administer a dosage of barbituates to slow his molecular function long enough for the therapeutic retrovirus to take effect."

"You're rambling again," Spril called as he poured himself a glass of orange juice, having drifted to the kitchen.

"Sorry. Thinking out loud," Yrlis excused, "I didn't know you could hear me."

"It's fine. You know I love when you get going like that."

"You're about to have a lot to love, then."

"Oh yeah? Too bad you'll be too tired for me to act on it," Spril snarked, immediately wishing he could swallow his words.

"Well, if that's how you feel," Yrlis teased, sneaking up behind him and sliding her hands up the front of his shirt to explore his chest, "I'll just have to make time."

"I'm going to hold you to that," Spril warned, "Hell, I can think of plenty of things I wanna hold you to. But I need to get going."

"EshCal's suspension starts today, doesn't it?"

"Yeah. We're all meeting up to investigate this whole scandal this evening."

"Sorry, but you'll have to count me out of the first meeting," Yrlis apologized, "With any luck, I'll be asleep."

"You're already doing so much. Probably too much for one person. I'm not gonna drag you to these meetings," Spril insisted, kissing her softly, "Not unless we need your medical insight."

"Oh. Okay then," Yrlis accepted, feeling ironically rejected, "Well, thank you."

"It's no trouble. You've got your job in this, and I've got mine. Anyway, I'll get those samples from Sinkua next time I see him," Spril promised, "How long do you think it will take you to synthesize a cure?"

"Too soon to tell. Could be a few weeks. Could be years," Yrlis explained.

"Fair enough," Spril said, kissing Yrlis goodbye in the open doorway, "One more thing. I don't expect an answer right away, but I'd like to know your thoughts on it when you have a chance." He paused to gather his thoughts into something coherent and, after a couple of seconds, which he could easily have mistaken for minutes, asked, "Would it be possible to activate a human's twenty-fourth pair?"

Chapter 27

Ozzera walked alongside Yahsek on a leash, a black sheet draped over all but her lion head. The night crowd of the highrise district averted their eyes in a sort of disregarding reverence, respecting them by pretending not to see them. A few late-night stragglers overcame fatigue and intoxication long enough to rubberneck. Every one of them quickly lowered their heads and shuffled away fearfully.

So, Yahsek found it especially disconcerting when something gave Ozzera pause.

"What is it?" he urged.

"Someone follows."

"What do you hear?"

"Footsteps. Speaking," Ozzera answered, "Too faint for numbers."

Yahsek drew out his breathing and closed his eyes. His ears stretched upward into points, their concave deepening. The inner surface became leathery and ridged, tiny hairs coating the outside. He normalized his breathing and cocked a morphed ear.

"One person," he reported, "Talking to himself."

"What does he say?"

"It isn't him," Yahsek assured, his ears reverting to their natural form, "He caught our trail once. It won't happen again."

"He is the most persistent of them," Ozzera warned, "'Twould be folly to discount him so easily."

"I'm well aware of who he is."

As they arrived at Laboratory 1341, Yahsek pressed his thumb to the middle of a zero in the phone number on the front door. His thumbprint illuminated neon red, a network of angular lines spawning from it. The door shifted back from the frame, sliding behind and affixing to the adjoining window panel. The conjoined panels shifted, slid, and locked to a third, the three then moving behind a fourth. Ozzera entered first, and Yahsek thumbed the glass again as he followed.

"He awaits you," the receptionist called to them as the door and windows shifted shut.

"Top floor?" Yahsek asked.

"Yes, sir. He expects an explanation for your tardiness."

"Of course he does."

While Yahsek rode the passenger elevator, Ozzera continued to a freight elevator. Secure inside the car, Yahsek pulled the antique book from his pack. The symbols held traces of familiarity, but though he could pronounce a few words, he knew nothing of their modern translations. Somehow though, these were the key to winning the war. Or perhaps simply not losing it.

Ozzera and Yahsek reunited in the round nearly-perimeter corridor on the top level. The office occupied the entire floor, save for this hall and the elevators. Finding the door built to accommodate the bulky chimera, they entered the massive skyward chamber. Ozzera stalked across the vast office and proceeded through a second door, steam hissing from the darkness beyond.

"You're later than we anticipated," The Geneticist greeted, his arm in a sling.

"We encountered unanticipated complications," Yahsek explained, "Our travels became necessarily erratic."

"Did you acquire a specimen?"

"Yes, but I was rushed and could only get one."

Yahsek presented the musty tome to The Geneticist, who looked it over with disdainful curiosity. The Geneticist waved him away, pointing to a nearby desk.

"We lost The Prophet to them nigh four days prior," The Geneticist reported, "According to our surveillance data, that loss is most likely permanent."

"Understood, sir. Would you like to designate him as our next target?"

"I want an account of your absence for the past ninety hours."

"As I told you, we were traveling erratically."

"You were followed."

"Briefly. He never saw us," Yahsek confessed, "I don't have any theories as to how he picked up our trail. He'll not find it again."

"If he found it once, you've already underestimated him," The Geneticist warned, "Such errors will be your downfall."

"As formidable as you credit him to be, we have stymied the threat he poses for a time. Long enough for us to achieve full functionality in preparation for Phase Three."

"You made the designated arrangements?"

"Yes, but I couldn't stay to witness what followed."

"No matter. We have the means to find this ourselves," The Geneticist excused, "But you regard his true threat too lightly. Perhaps incorrectly."

"I concede he's formidable in combat," Yahsek noted, "He also seems to have greater cognitive retention during his outbreaks than we assumed to be possible."

"All of them present the threat of lethal force. His true threat lies in his learning the truth of himself."

"The truth of himself?"

"He must always be denied knowledge of his lineage and origins. This and his condition are our greatest security on Lord Harvester's investment in him. Should these fail, the beast will give way to the warrior, and all we take from him will serve only to make him stronger."

"His and Nikasu's lineage are one in the same, are they not?" Yahsek asked, "They bear the same mark."

"Partially, though his is considerably more complicated."

"I suppose these books explain his lineage, then?"

"Those books hold truths long forgotten by society, annals of the world that was, reduced now to fairytales and campfire stories. They speak of what became of that world and those who remained," The Geneticist explained, "They speak of Sinkua and Nikasu's ancestry and inheritances and, should the legends hold true, the very origins of the Hybrids and the fate which befell them."

"What about this one we brought you? What does it speak of?"

"That I cannot know until The Engineer returns. Only she has the means to open them. We will then need Ozzera to translate."

"Does Lord Harvester know the contents of the books?"

"Not entirely. Much was written even before his time."

"So then," Yahsek pondered, "this is just as much a matter of procuring information as withholding it."

"More so the latter. He knows the threat Sinkua poses as well as the role he is to play. That is enough for him."

"And exactly what is his role in all of this?"

"The Epimetheus Trial essentially begins with him," The Geneticist asserted, "In a manner of speaking, so too must it end with him."

Spril found his desk covered in heaps of letters and memoranda, EshCal's workload having been passed up to him as of her suspension. He snarled at the mass of paperwork and punched the door shut. The whole ordeal stunk of Parliamentary abuse. To think EshCal had this much untended work was absurd. Where others had been deprived of the authority and privilege of their positions, Spril had been thrown to the red tape wolves.

Pacing his office, he snatched the first sheet his hand touched. This one detailed EshCal's court hearing, perhaps deliberately scheduled on his day off. He slapped it atop the filing cabinet and paced back to his desk.

The next sheet prescribed a counterassault in the event of a Tanelenese invasion. Beneath it was a letter from Parliament warning of the imminence of such an attack. In fact, much of the paperwork related to the Tanelenese Financial Scandal and its alleged perpetuation by the Prime Minister and High Minister of Treasury.

Deeper down, Spril found copies of Tanelenese propaganda vilifying both and portraying KalChi as several manners of whore. Their reputable outlets never sank to ad hominem sensationalism, such talk strictly being the realm of gossip rags. Spril tossed a few copies onto the filing cabinet and dropped the rest in the shredder.

While nothing he found from official government channels explicitly spoke of an impending attack, military aggression had become their media's prescription for a misdiagnosed infection. A few pieces of government correspondence suggested taking their case before the Ouristihran Union, others of settling matters privately. Their language, however, quickly escalated from peaceful discourse to hostility.

"Son of a bitch!" he growled, slamming a sample of such correspondence on top of the filing cabinet, "How am I supposed to work like this?"

Only Biroe and KalChi's notes could peacefully resolve the Tanelenese Financial Scandal, but everybody with connections to them had been systematically removed. The only people who knew enough to help either couldn't testify or would no longer to be trusted.

The stench of an inside job hung thickly over the whole affair. Somebody sought to manufacture conflict by exploiting a misunderstanding and escalating it to military aggression. They cut out those who knew otherwise by painting them as traitors and agitators.

Spril braced against the filing cabinet, his eyes darting over stacks of paperwork and propaganda. Tanelen had misunderstood their actions, and Chairman LenSom endeavored to maintain this misunderstanding. With the truth kept suppressed, a diplomatic resolution grew more unlikely every hour.

If Spril let matters continue as they had, war would perhaps be inevitable, and the Avatars of Fate could subsequently reestablish their hold on ArcNos. He could stymy offensive measures for a time, hopefully long enough for Treasury and Foreign Affairs to achieve a peaceful resolution. Of course, Chairman LenSom could invoke his own authority and declare lethal force to be the will of Parliament.

If Spril suspended his own authority, he would be free to take countermeasures without the fetters of red tape and formality. Essentially, he could once again avoid his assassination by faking his own death. This time, metaphorically.

They had clearly learned from their error in timing though, this time casting him into this conundrum on the brink of hostility instead of in the infancy of the scandal. Should he resign, he might not have enough time to alter the course of events.

He pulled his mobile phone from his coat and dialed the one person who could help. The phone rang several times, Spril nervously tapping his foot all the while.

"SenRas?" Spril asked when someone finally answered.

"Yes, what is it, Spril?" SenRas responded.

"We've got a situation here. You might need to get involved."

"Yes," SenRas muttered, sounding distant, "Excuse me. What's troubling you, young man?"

"I assume you're aware of what's going on with Tanelen."

"That depends on what you mean by what's going on. Who is stealing from whom, and who intends to invade whom?"

"I mean what's actually going on versus Parliament's cover-up. What's the prevailing conception?"

"We're stealing from them, and they're threatening to attack us."

"What do you know to the contrary?"

"LenSom is a suspected agent of the Avatars of Fate, most likely under The Politician."

"I suspected he and Olsa were behind this. Have you spoken to Biroe?"

"It was Biroe who brought this theory to my attention."

"In that case, I can skip the backstory and cut to my point," Spril concluded, "I suspect their endgame is a war between Tanelen and ArcNos."

"They still need to cut off your authority, then."

"Not necessarily. He could go over my head or simply distract me. My office has been inundated with paperwork, probably to keep me busy while he launches an offensive."

"So, they're reestablishing a presence in ArcNos."

"That's what it looks like. Our best measure against this war is to deliver Biroe and KalChi's records on the Tanelenese Financial Scandal to Tanelen," Spril explained, "But they've both been discharged, and Phylus and EshCal have been suspended for the next ten weeks."

"That won't necessarily be a problem," SenRas assured, his voice trailing off.

"Nobody who knows the full story has the necessary authority to be taken on their word or as an emissary for anyone who would."

"Perhaps not, but the documentation alone proves our case. It sounds to me like you're worrying more than you ought."

"Strange words coming from you. Suppose they've infiltrated Tanelen as well."

"And if they have?"

"Any attempt at prosecution will bring a more violent response, one that we are not equipped to counter or even endure."

"They'll be forced to expose themselves, and we'll prove they've infiltrated the two most militantly powerful federal governments in the Ouristihran Union."

"And unite ArcNos and Tanelen against them."

"Exactly. My son-in-law's vision will finally come to pass," SenRas prophesized, "If we send emissaries to Tanelen, we'll either correct the misunderstanding or expose denizens of the Avatars in Tanelen. Either way, it ends poorly for the Avatars."

"But after how much unnecessary bloodshed?"

"That I cannot know," SenRas sighed, "We'll discuss this further this evening."

SenRas hung up and shoved his phone in his pocket, staring at the envelope on his desk all the while. It beared XalRut's return address, penned in her handwriting, but its postmark was dated more than a week after she died.

It couldn't have been from her, not unless the coroner had found it among her belongings. Had that been the case, it would have been marked as posthumous. If XalRut had an unmailed letter to him, AinZun had no reason to mail it in her stead.

Of course, AinZun could have been employing a psychological gambit. Given Yahsek's interior design work at Sinkua's house, this sort of psychological assassination fit their methods. Their every move sought to turn allies against each another or cripple a threat from within.

Fed up with the worry and suspense, SenRas pointed the envelope away from himself and ripped it open. He pinched the corners and shook it. Nothing fell out. He flicked the base, thinking the paper might be stuck.

Two bullets dropped out. One settled where it landed. One rolled to his coffee mug.

His jawbone trembled under the stress of clenched teeth, trying to suppress the lump in his throat. He picked up the dented and bloodied bullet, the one that had landed and settled, with trembling fingers. Tracer round. XalRut's name had been written around the base in red ink.

Swallowing, he picked up the unfired bullet from beside his mug. Same model of incendiary round as the first, but this one beared his name.

The little girl he had orphaned was coming to make good on her promise.

"Entering biogenesis chamber," a staticked voice spoke in The Geneticist's ear.

"Status confirmed, Ozzera," he answered, "Initiating monitoring systems."

The Geneticist pushed his chair away from the console and rose to his feet. He raised his hands and waggled his fingers, their tips tingling with electrical sensation, and pressed his palms together. As he parted his hands, an electronic screen hovered before the wall, spanning forty-five degrees.

The screen erupted to life with diagnostic displays. Flicking his fingers, The Geneticist scrolled through graphs, charts, and infrared images of Ozzera's genetic structure, neural activity, and metabolic data. As her mind shifted into a meditative state, her insight and upper level rationale continued to rise.

"Looking good," The Geneticist complimented, "The Engineer will have no trouble activating the swarm with these vitals."

"Connect me to the satellite monitoring entities," Ozzera requested, "I will report her proximity."

With an upward swipe of his index finger, a map of ArcNos appeared with landscapes and artificial structures rendered in perfect proportions. He aligned his thumb and forefinger with a tab in the corner, pulled it down, and aerially tapped his selection. An electronic constellation appeared on the screen. Lights changed color to denote their activation as he tapped them. By grabbing the activated lights and pulling them into the diagnostics home screen, he linked the selected entities to the biogenesis chamber.

"Connection successful," he reported.

"Connection confirmed."

Ozzera's closed eyes flickered as three remote images faded into clarity on the backs of her eyelids. She rolled each pair of eyes, panning the viewable radius of the security monitors. She opened one eye in each pair to switch to the next security monitor. Eventually, she found The Engineer near a monitor a few kilometers from the highrise district.

"Engineer located," Ozzera reported, "Requesting communications relay patch in District 05. Surveillance Monitoring Entity D4E8D5. Access Code D3E0E4."

"Communications relay patch initiated," Ebralgi answered, "Connection established. Communications relay patch online."

"Engineer. Do you copy?" Ozzera called.

From the corner of her remote view, Ozzera saw AinZun stop and cringe at her words. AinZun plugged one ear, and Ozzera called again. The Engineer approached the console, connected a set of headphones, and began typing.

"Blown earpiece. Quarun."

"You rated their auditory resilience at one hundred fifty-five decibels. Your sidearm registers an average output of one hundred sixty," Ozzera reminded, "You and Yahsek shall address this flaw later. What is your estimated time of arrival?"

"Fourteen kilometers. Bus stop, three blocks. Next stop, seventeen minutes. Less than one hour."

"Excellent. The Geneticist has uploaded my data into the biogenesis chamber."

"Infiltration status?"

"Yahsek retrieved one of the books."

"What of the others?"

"Scattered about the Would-Be General's old bedroom," Ozzera answered, "Between redecorating and trying to open the books, he ran short on time."

"Lost The Prophet," AinZun furiously typed, "Can translate for them."

"Understood," Ozzera said, "Where do we stand on Phase One?"

"Close. Treasury and Foreign Affairs down. Defense falling. One leg."

"What is the delay on Defense?"

"One more scrupulous than expected."

"The Politician's protégé has performed below his advertised proficiency."

"Quick study. Proven crucial. Five of six. Enough to initiate Phase Two."

"Agreed. This is a minor setback. A manageable one."

"Will activate patrol drones when I arrive," The Engineer promised, "Vitals?"

"The Geneticist is pleased with my diagnostics. Neural activity is performing at near optimum levels. We also need you to open this book."

"I know. After patrol drone link."

"Understood. I shall update Yahsek and The Geneticist."

"Bus approaching."

They both disconnected the call, and with a few keystrokes, The Engineer purged all records of their conversation from the console. She then walked away, dodging through the crowd as she headed to the bus stop.

This tar patch felt so familiar. Or at least relevant. Sinkua stood among oil stains tinged red in the middle of the damaged street, trying to rein in what this place could have meant to him. A sharp pang flared in his stomach. Clutching his abdomen, he staggered to the sidewalk and continued along.

He'd put aside his pursuit of Yahsek, but the back of his mind stubbornly obsessed over reclaiming that book. Food and rest dominated his conscious efforts. Days melted together. Meals ran scarce. The city had all but been abandoned, and he had forgotten his wallet anyhow.

He collapsed shoulder-first against a brick wall, abrading flesh as he slid down. Hunger pains manifested as a dry throaty belch. Malnourished and disoriented, distorted images culminated into migrainous aggravation. He emptied his pockets, but his trembling hands turned up only lint. Even with his warped sense of time, he knew too much had passed since his last dosage.

Sinkua curled up on the frozen concrete, his gullet conducting a sickly chorus of hacking, dry heaving, and belching. He spat blood and wiped a smear of sweat from his forehead as the sting of crystallization set in. He rolled over and looked to the sky, a sliver of survival instinct thinking to regain his bearings.

The sky was overcast, too much so for him to pick out the sun. Perhaps, Nikasu could have helped, but his eyes proved ineffective against such a shroud. Sneering with self-loathing, he looked to his sides.

"Nothing's left," he groaned, "Everyone's gone. No people. No commerce. Nothing to forage. Nothing to hunt. Nothing to scavenge."

He cleared his throat with a guttural cough and swallowed his bloodied phlegm. He sat up unsteadily and surveyed the broken cityscape, his loathing externalizing into contempt. This place he once called home had taken him back only to make waste of him.

Nothing grew here anymore.

Nothing survived.

They had ruined it. Salted the earth. In his furious hubris, he braved terrain none dared tread, and this urban wasteland ingested him as tribute to those who created it. He shut his eyes and hammered the brick wall with his fist until abrading flesh gave way to blood.

Red particulate penetrated the wound, raking freshly exposed skin. It had been years since he last felt pangs like these, those of his poverty in Ferya having been dulled by Eytea's companionship. He ground his teeth and trembled as a paralytic tightening climbed his spine. Welcoming the chaos, his consciousness braved the dark clouds of its own obstruction.

"This city wants to give up on me? Again? After all I've done? Wasn't it enough? Why not?" he snarled, "Why the fuck wasn't it enough!?"

Launching to his feet on naught but adrenaline, Sinkua whipped around and plowed his white-knuckle fist through the wall. Blood and red dust scattered as knuckles cracked and bricks shattered. He groaned gutturally, overwhelmed by the sensation of empowerment as he manipulated his pain and wounded his tomb. His fists came ablaze as he battered the wall, his necklace shimmering against their fiery glow. The dying flesh of fresh wounds curled into the flames.

Dirty blood oozing between his fingers, he leaned his forehead against the wall as he struggled to catch his breath. His left eyelids twitched feverishly, the bioluminescence of his eyes flickering like flames clinging to the last fibers for candlewicks. Gasping against his swelling throat swelled, he stamped the wall with bloody handprints.

A small shadow swept by, giving him pause as something like solace interrupted his collapse. Bracing himself on his forearm, he turned to look for who else dared to brave the fallen metropolis. He found it flitting about and reached out to it. Zeroing in on his scent, a tracking pigeon descended and perched on his outstretched hand.

Sinkua stared at it desperately, its message at best a secondary priority. He looked over its lean form, sighing and forcing gratitude for its meager offering. Transfixing the pigeon's stare in his own, he grabbed it by the neck and ripped away the scroll.

The bird flapped and scrambled, clawing at the air and cooing pleadingly. Sinkua squeezed tighter, tears welling under his eyelids.

"I'm sorry," he choked, "But I don't think I've eaten in days."

"Put down that bird," called an approaching voice, "Don't you even care who sent it?"

"Eytea?" Sinkua answered, dropping the bird and looking about frantically.

She lit upon the pavement with her wings spread to their full span, smiling radiantly at the sight of him. They locked eyes with each another, his drawn southward by the emphasized swiveling of her hips.

"See something you like?" Eytea teased.

"Yeah," Sinkua coughed, throwing his arms around her, "Yeah, I do."

"It's good to see you too, hon," she whispered, pressing herself against him as she futilely fought back tears of elation and relief, "Real good to see you're alive."

"How did you find me?"

"The bird, you doof," Eytea laughed, pulling back to see his face and planting a kiss on his bloodstained lips, "Nikasu told me you ran off. So, I sent a tracker pigeon after you and followed it."

"Of course, you'd think of something like that," Sinkua smiled.

"To be fair, I probably wouldn't be this resourceful if it wasn't for you. If anyone else was out here, you would've come up with it first."

"I'd thank you, but I'm sure you're buttering me up to tell me we need to figure a way out of here."

"Well, I was gonna use the bird, but you just had to go and scare him off."

"Sorry about that. I just…" Sinkua fumbled.

"Don't sweat it, love. We'll figure something out. Let's just sit down and rest."

Leaning on each other, they returned to the sidewalk and lowered themselves to the concrete. Eytea unclipped the satchel on her hip, Sinkua watching curiously as she opened it.

"When I heard what a hurry you left in, I thought I should bring you a few things," she explained, reaching into the bag.

"Yeah, I realized I forgot my wallet after I got here," he confessed, "Between trying to find my way back and trying to find my way through, I guess I lost my bearings."

"I've got that," she said, presenting his wallet, "But it doesn't look like it'll do you any good. I wish I'd thought to bring you something to eat."

"It's okay," he smiled, "Like you said, we'll figure something out. Besides, now…"

"Oh, come on!" Eytea laughed, pulling a thermos from her bag, "You left nearly five days ago. Do you seriously think I'd only bring you your wallet?"

"Heh, I suppose that's thinking too little of you," Sinkua snickered, taking a long pull from the thermos.

"Damn right it is," Eytea boasted, smiling as he drenched his palate.

"Wow," he gasped as it ran down his throat, "I'm so famished, even tap water tastes amazing."

"Probably because it isn't tap water. It's milystic."

"I'm surprised Galo stuck around after I stormed out like that."

"He said it was his way of saying 'No hard feelings,'" Eytea explained, "My mom made something for you, too, but I'm sorry if it tastes strange."

"Oh, your mom is staying with us, too?" Sinkua asked as he watched her withdraw a third offering, "Who came after her?"

"The Geneticist. All four of us had to fight him off. Sestak is staying with her neighbors while she's here. Seschnel didn't survive the battle though. We had to bury her before we left."

"Sorry to hear that," he consoled, kissing her temple.

"Don't worry. She had a full life. And she died protecting us," she said, "Now here, eat this. And don't complain, because I already apologized."

"You'd have a hard time finding food I'd complain about right now," he laughed, "What is it?"

"Peanut butter and bacon sandwich."

"You're right. That is strange. Your mom's idea?"

"Yeah, she said it's probably just what you need right now," Eytea explained as Sinkua stuffed a quarter of it into his mouth.

"I don't know if you've ever had one of these," he mumbled with stuffed cheeks, "but it tastes as weird as it sounds."

"Well, lucky you. That one's all yours," she teased, "Have you had any episodes?"

"I was about to have my first," he said between bites, "Do you think that's what she was talking about? Tending to my protein withdrawals?"

"I'm sure it crossed her mind, but she didn't say anything about it. Are you starting to feel better?"

"Definitely. Thank you," he professed, chewing the last bite of the sandwich, "Looks like he landed some good hits on you."

"Oh, these bruises? These are nothing. Mom had to get stitches."

"I was about to ask how you paid him back, but let's talk about that instead. Elemeno got in on the action?"

"Yeah, but he never touched her. Her injury was her own doing," Eytea explained, "See, she got a revolver after I told her she was on their hit list."

"Smart."

"Right, well he was saying some real nasty stuff to me. The kind of stuff that would've made you put your fist inside his chest cavity. All of a sudden, she goes all badass and puts her gun to the back of his head. He's trying to be cool about it, but his body goes completely rigid. Then, she turns and unloads it at the broad side of the stable."

"To scare the horses out and after him?"

"Exactly. The bullets ricocheted, and one of them clipped her shoulder and tore down to the collar bone."

"Damn! Your mom's pretty hardcore."

"Well yeah. She did help me snap Kabehl's neck, after all," she boasted, "Anyway, Sestak crushed his shoulder, like how that giant did to me at Radial Axiom. He and Seschnel took turns knocking him around until he drove his bladed tonfa into Seschnel's chest. Sestak knocked the fence down chasing him off the property."

"Again, sorry to hear you lost Seschnel like that," Sinkua reiterated, rising to his feet and offering his hand, "But at least she went down fighting."

"Sestak has always been protective of the girls in his life. Sometimes, you remind me of him," Eytea smiled, "Seschnel was just returning the favor."

"If you're saying this is your way of returning some favor, you're too late. You did that a long time ago."

"Oh, come on. You know that's not why I do stuff like this. I do it because it's the right thing to do," Eytea insisted, "And because I love you."

"I love you, too," Sinkua grinned, "Now let's find another tracker pigeon while we can. Feels like it might start raining soon."

From a nearby alley came the sound of bricks cracking. Fragments of red stone shattered against the concrete, a masonic cacophony echoing between the walls. They stopped and listened as the sound compounded upon itself.

"I think someone's back there," Eytea said, "Let's go check on them."

Sinkua followed Eytea into the alley. Chunks of brick dropped from the wall, broken away by internal forces. As the holes widened, their creators came more clearly into view. Absurd tangles of metallic appendages clung to the infrastructure, strangling the rebar and cracking the masonry to free themselves.

"Shit. Run!" Sinkua gasped, backpedaling and trying to pull Eytea along.

Enraptured by fear, Eytea's eyes fixated on a writhing mass of appendages. Her body became deadweight. Her cold sweaty hand fell from Sinkua's grasp. Sinew spawned from the metallic joints, sweeping away brick dust as it spread over the writhing limbs. Eytea's heart jackhammered her rib cage. Her breathing grew ragged and panicked as she became aware of her psychological paralysis

Raw tissue pulsating, the creature burst from its urban structural nest with a horrific shriek and outstretched claws gnashing.

Chapter 28

The Omnimath leaned back in his ornate throne, intricate patterns adorning its towering backrest. He propped his foot on his opposite knee and locked his fingers, resting his chin atop his steepled index fingers. Three of his associates stood before him, the blue serpentine trails in the floor glowing more brightly around their feet.

"Chekov."

"Sir?" Chekov answered with shaking conviction.

"I have been given to understand that your decision to not speak of Vielle was not a conscious effort of disloyalty. Is that correct?"

"It is, sir. I did not know she was a Hybrid, nor did I suspect she could have been bound to Yggdrasil."

"Of course not. You and I had not spoken of such matters," The Omnimath agreed, "Many are familiar with Yggdrasil as a concept. Legends and fairytales speak robustly of the Great Tree. But the true nature of its existence is truly privileged knowledge in this age. As is the mark of the Yggdrasil Hybrid."

"I had heard stories of her exploits in ArcNos," Chekov confessed, "I recognized her name and thought to check my records. But I had no contact with MalVek and NalSet during that time."

"That was as intended. Once they made position, Malia was the next of us to make contact," The Omnimath said, "She bade NalSet deliver a message, reminding me of the promise I had made to her."

"Of course, sir. Excuse me for leading this meeting along a tangent," Chekov apologized, "As I was saying, I found her name in my incubation records. I had noted her ears in the margin."

"Do you recall what you wrote?"

"I wondered if she was a Hybrid we hadn't accounted for or something we had failed to consider. An incomplete manifestation, perhaps."

"What conclusion did you draw upon learning of her abilities?"

"I her to be a Dryad left over after the death of Yggdrasil. Of course, I thought it was impossible for her to be the Yggdrasil Hybrid," Chekov explained, "But even knowing that, I confess that I chose not to discuss my findings with you."

"And why might that be?" The Omnimath asked, leaning forward in his levitating chair, "Fear, perhaps?"

"Sir, I..." Chekov stammered, "Whoever she was, she was unaccounted for. I knew talking about her could put her at risk."

"She placed herself at risk by public demonstration of her arbormancy. Had it not been for the assassinations of The Scout and The Hunter, my brother would undoubtedly have learned of her. Though he possesses not the same knowledge as I, he would soon have gleaned the relevance of her existence."

"Sir..."

"Why did you fight to save that which had already died?"

"I... I remembered him," Chekov swallowed, "How happy he was to have her. How hard he worked for her. That kind of love is rare. If he were to lose her because of who she is, I couldn't live with myself knowing I had abetted such a tragedy."

"You stood guard over nothing to preserve a concept…"

"Pahres has spoken with Vielle," MalVek interrupted, "He explained the anomaly in as much detail as he was comfortable discussing. She's at ease about it for the time being."

"As she ought to be. I have neither the intention nor the need to take her from the ones she loves," The Omnimath assured, eyeing Chekov.

"That being the case, we formally withdraw our opposition," NalSet added, "Her death, come when it may, will serve a greater purpose. A privilege afforded to few."

"Seconded," MalVek agreed, "We only opposed your ending her life too soon. But even hers cannot be prolonged indefinitely. Everyone passes from this world."

"It certainly is a convenience for your kind," The Omnimath sighed with cryptic cadence, "Yet so many fear it. So many shun those who love them most dearly as their end draws near. In all my centuries, I have yet to comprehend their handling of such matters. But I have long understood the desire to prolong one's time with another."

"Then you understand why we couldn't let you know about her?" NalSet asked.

"I understand why you believed you could not. You knew something of her potential, but you erroneously divined my intentions. Given that you could only presume from my nature, I am thus at fault for having not been more forthright."

"We're sorry, sir," Chekov said, "We thought you were too disconnected from death."

"Life, death, and love are not as foreign of concepts to me as you might think, but I understand how you could perceive such," The Omnimath excused, "Love stands strong in the face of death. Never have I harbored motives of impeding it of doing thus."

"Is that why you've afforded Malia her time with them?" NalSet asked.

"In part, I suppose so. Malia lost much because of us. More than even I had anticipated," The Omnimath said, "Furthermore, our involvement in these affairs has compounded matters perhaps beyond my foresight. We may soon find necessity in changing our role until such time as we might bring clarity to the paths."

"What do you mean? Are we to break contact with them?" MalVek asked.

"Vielle is still an anomaly. Pahres's psyche is dependent upon the potential of Yggdrasil coming into this world," The Omnimath said, "Our presence has precipitated violations in causality and created catalysts for such. Continue as we have, and even I cannot know what we might bring about next."

"Could Vielle's link to Yggdrasil be a matter of violated causality?" Chekov asked.

"In a manner of speaking, perhaps. Though from another perspective, it is not. As is the case with all such violations. Had the catalyst occurred in her lifetime, she would indeed have previously been a Dryad, as you theorized. Possessed of arbormancy yet with diminished potential and greater troubles in managing it."

"She struggled considerably during the war," MalVek interjected, "She learned quite a bit, but it was a grueling process."

"Interesting," The Omnimath pondered, "As it were, these violations will continue to proliferate even if we wholly withdraw our involvement. Our actions, our decisions put these events into motion, but not by removing ourselves might we halt or hinder the machinations of violated causality."

"What do you suggest, then?" NalSet asked, "Are we to try to take control of these machinations?"

"We cannot control them, but we can come to understand them. In order to do so, our allies must come to understand us."

"You wish to tell them…?" Chekov began to ask.

"I wish to guide them to knowledge, beginning within The Coalition," the Omnimath explained, "Upon this dawn, I have dispatched a message to Malia. That is my other reason for leaving her with them."

"So she can pass along the message?" MalVek asked.

"So they can come to understand it together," The Omnimath clarified, "When they help her find the truth within my words, we shall amass a greater force toward reining in what our involvement has wrought."

Vielle leaned back on the counter while Phylus confirmed their orders. She watched the window, though her attention jumped to the door at every sign of movement. Behind her, the clerk made small talk with her father. She recalled he took their order last time. Judging by how she felt his eyes on her, he recognized her as well.

A few weeks ago, she might have found it refreshing. To be remembered by a stranger may have offered a measure of validation. Now, she found it unnerving, grinding against her pensive introspection. Her father elbowed her.

"Snap out of it, cookieface," her father teased, "Grab a tray."

"Sorry," Vielle blushed, "I'm just... distracted."

"Nervous?"

"Would you blame me?"

"Not really. There's a lot going down. Heavier stuff than we dealt with back then, maybe," Phylus mused, "Or maybe it's just our positions and how much more we know."

"Plus who and what's on the line."

"Speaking of who's on the line, I thought your girlfriend was joining us."

"She is. That's what's distracting me," Vielle explained as she set the tray on the table.

"Afraid she got lost down here?"

"Afraid who got lost?" SenRas cut in.

"My girlfriend is meeting us here," Vielle answered, "She was on a delivery, but I thought she'd be here by now."

"I'm sure she'll turn up just fine," SenRas smiled, "We'll save a seat for her."

"Did you say she's on a delivery?" Biroe asked, to which Vielle nodded.

KalChi nudged Biroe with her elbow. He looked to her with urgency in his eyes, but she shook her head. They mumbled to each other, their conversation inaudible beyond the air between them but apparent nonetheless.

"Why, what's up?" Vielle butted in.

"I was just..." Biroe answered.

"It's nothing, dear. Don't worry about it," KalChi interrupted, "He thought she might have delivered to his office a few days before he was discharged."

"Right," Biroe absently agreed, "Whoever she was, she left something in my office."

"Anyway," Spril grunted, "Can we cut the small talk and get to business?"

"Of course," Phylus said, "Biroe, start us off."

"Well, we've all but proven that the Avatars of Fate are behind the Tanelenese Financial Scandal," Biroe reported, "We followed the intercepted equity payments through scores of accounts in dozens of banks until they stopped at one of particular interest in Tanelen."

"The Commissioner of the Radial Axiom Arena closed all of his accounts in Tanelen except one at the same bank. We think he did this to send a message," KalChi provided.

"I could start a deeper investigation to build a more solid case against them," Malia offered, "After all, I only know of one other group of people who could pull off a scandal on that scale. No offense to you."

"None taken, but we've investigated deeply enough," Biroe smirked, "After the final deposit in Tanelen, the money is being invested at 1341 West Heniokhos Boulevard."

"Laboratory 1341," Spril nodded, "That explains the empty subterranean levels. They're still in the financing stage of some of their operations."

"We've rerouted the transactions on a comparably convoluted path, ending in an account held under a manufactured identity. We've hit some delays, but we're in the process of returning the money to its rightful owners," Biroe boasted, "Hence no offense taken."

"I'd like to think that means they haven't completed the Mechanical Crypt," Galo said, "but I doubt they would have taken me down there if they weren't ready to have me activate it."

"Perhaps or perhaps not. It's possible they only took you when they did as retaliation for having lost me," Nikasu suggested, "They may have planned to hold you while they finished building the Mechanical Crypt. Besides, with Yahsek and Ozzera taking one of the books there, they may be looking into other ventures."

"These people don't just abandon an operation when someone interferes," EshCal reasoned, "They'll eventually circle back to funding Laboratory 1341 at the expense of whoever they deem inferior or contrary."

"Actually," Spril pondered, "Perhaps not."

"They're trying to take down ArcNos again after we thwarted that five years ago."

"I mean they may have had their fill. You guys said that money was coming out of a bank in Tanelen, right?" Spril asked.

"Yeah," Biroe nodded, "And that was where we concluded the Avatars were working out of during the ArcNosian Civil War."

"Right, and when you two took back that money, LenSom got you out of the way, along with EshCal and Phylus. Prime Minister and High Minister of Treasury, High Minister of Defense, and Prime Minister of Foreign Affairs, gone in a single scandal," Spril summarized, "He also played on Sinkua's temper for an excuse to fire him. Phylus kept him on as a civilian consultant, but since that position only existed between the two of them, removing Phylus cut Sinkua out as well. That leaves me as the only Subtransit Resistance veteran in a Ministry position, but I can't do nearly as much alone as the five of us could together."

"I guess that means I'm safe since I'm not in a Ministry," Vielle added.

"Your job is safe, but being the Yggdrasil Hybrid puts you at substantial risk by itself," Malia countered, "They won't take losing The Prophet lightly, either."

"In any case," Spril continued, "The only reason I've dodged the axe is because I've kept my mouth shut no matter how much I've wanted to shoot off at it. Now, there are rumors of an impending Tanelenese invasion."

"LenSom said the first order of business was discussing countermeasures with the Ministry of Defense," Biroe supplied, "He said that was standard protocol."

"Common sense protocol for volatile foreign relationships is to dispatch the Ministry of Foreign Affairs. We don't have a standard protocol for unsubstantiated rumors because we don't deal in gossip rags," Spril snipped, "And if those discussions took place, I was not a part of them. That means Chairman LenSom is addressing these rumors by mobilizing a military response team of his own accord by way of eliminating Subtransit Resistance veterans who might influence matters otherwise."

"You think they're using LenSom start a war between ArcNos and Tanelen, wherein they control both sides, with Laboratory 1341 serving as their central dispatch point," Nikasu suggested, "Their endgame being a full-blown occupation of both nations, correct?"

"Exactly! I love this kid!" Spril beamed, "Whatever they're hiding at 1341, a fabricated invasion is the perfect cover to launch it."

"That would mean the timing of Yahsek and Ozzera's betrayal was a matter of necessity, not opportunity," EshCal said, "They knew LenSom would soon have the opportunity to eliminate most of us and were getting in position for the coming war."

"I had been thinking the same thing since Biroe said they were working out of

Tanelen during the war," Nikasu said, "But I didn't want to interrupt before I knew if that's what you guys were thinking, too."

"Someone as clever as you should never feel like they have to keep quiet," Phylus insisted, Malia watching them both, "especially at times like this."

"Thanks, Dad," Nikasu grinned, sampling split seconds of eye contact.

"Nikasu, he isn't actually your…" Malia reminded as her hands curled over Phylus's forearm.

"I know. But Sinkua said he wouldn't mind if I called him that," Nikasu shrugged, "So I've been working up the courage to do it, because I thought it might be nice. It was."

"Of course you can call me Dad," Phylus said, "You're family as far as I'm concerned. All of you guys are, really."

"As much as I love seeing our bonds tightening, we need to develop our plan for Tanelen, LenSom, and 1341," Spril redirected.

"I offered to go to Tanelen to mitigate the scandal," Biroe said, "I stand by that offer, whether on official Ministry business or not."

"I'll accompany you," KalChi offered.

"I should go as well," Phylus said, "This is likely to require a fine diplomatic touch."

"I can testify that the Ministry of Defense hasn't sanctioned any displays of aggression," EshCal reminded, "I'll come along as a guard escort, as we can reasonably expect resistance against gaining the necessary audience."

"Okay, so EshCal, Phylus, Biroe, and KalChi will go to Tanelen to mitigate the financial scandal and dispel rumors of pending military action," Spril reiterated, "Does anybody have any suggestions as to what to do about LenSom?"

"Well, it used to be that folks like you hired folks like me to take care of folks like him when they stepped too far out of line," SenRas recalled, "Now, we have to go through all this procedural bullshit and smear him politically first. Given how quickly he's building his corruption rap sheet though, I'd say we're well on our way."

"Once we clear up matters in Tanelen, we'll have him nailed if signs of aggression continue," Phylus said, "I'll work to get a statement of truce from Noble Doyen Joren, thus disproving any rumors of an impending invasion."

"Meanwhile, SenRas and I will draw up whatever other damning intel we can find on him," Malia offered.

"We'll need to prove that you, Spril, were absent from his discussion with the Ministry of Defense," SenRas said, "More to the point, we'd like to prove that you were deliberately excluded."

"Excellent," Spril nodded, "Moving to other orders, Yrlis has deciphered The Diagram and is now undergoing further research."

"Has she figured out what the two additional chromosomes are?" Phylus asked.

"They're the Hybrid Chromosomes, but everyone actually has them. Typically, the two chromosomes nullify each other so entirely that no DNA test can detect them. Meaning the idea that humans have forty-six chromosomes is actually a misconception," Spril explained, "Yrlis theorizes that the Hybrid Chromosomes are the key to the Avatars' biological weapons."

"Kabehl was powered by an intravenous nanochip," SenRas reminded, recalling XalRut's immeasurable assistance.

"True, but it may have operated based on a bond to his neutralized Hybrid Chromosomes," Spril answered, "And that doesn't exempt Amirione or what we learned about Masfaru. But even if it isn't directly tied in with all of them, Yrlis contends that understanding the Hybrid Chromosomes could be the key to disabling that facet of their operations."

"Does she intend to develop an antiserum to The Geneticist's enhancements?" Galo asked.

"Something to that effect."

"If she wants to deactivate the manually activated Hybrid Chromosome, she should expect complications based on how long the subject has been active," Galo explained.

"I'll pass your advice on to her tonight," Spril said, "She's on the fence as to whether it's possible to artificially activate the Hybrid Chromosome though. Which reminds me, she needs blood and marrow samples from Sinkua."

"She wants to cure him," Nikasu gleaned, "Like I told EshCal, I'll help however I can. They probably used my blood as the base for his infection. So maybe Yrlis can synthesize a cure from it."

"You have no reason to feel guilty," Galo assured, his hand on her shoulder, "The infection was most likely engineered specifically to his genome. They would need to derive it directly from his genetic matter. Your half-sibling relationship shouldn't be close enough."

"That's, um, nice to know I suppose," Nikasu nodded, absently rubbing his hand, "But if there's any way I can help him through this, I at least owe him that much."

"Have you had any luck finding him?" Vielle asked, glaring at Galo.

"Eytea went searching of him behind a tracker pigeon this morning," Galo said, withdrawing his hand, "We've yet to hear from either of them. Spril, could you also tell Yrlis that I'd like to help with her research once Sinkua and Eytea come home?"

"She would be better off working with Gabdur," Malia countered, "Not to say you couldn't help, but you have responsibilities in Berinin."

"Nenbard can manage affairs in my absence, perhaps better than I can. But Gabdur's expatriation from Masnethegean culture has given him the intellectual edge. I'll concede him that," Galo admitted, "And if a war comes between ArcNos and Tanelen, I'm better suited to the front lines than he."

"Malia, didn't you also tell us Chekov is a member of The Coalition?" Phylus recalled, "Spril, you remember her, right? We met her when we picked up Vielle."

"Picked me up from where?" Vielle cut in.

"Yrlis's mother?" Spril asked.

"Yes, she worked at the fertility clinic," Phylus confirmed, nodding to Vielle.

"Well, son of a mother. Yrlis'll be interested to know that."

"Just say the word, and I'll ask The Omnimath to arrange for Gabdur and Chekov to collaborate with Yrlis," Malia offered.

"Thanks. I'll let her know."

"I'll keep myself available, should my input be needed," Galo said, "I'll be staying with Nikasu and Elemeno, safeguarding the remaining books."

"Vielle, if Sinkua and Eytea haven't come home by the time I leave for Tanelen, I want you to go stay with them," Phylus implored, "They need you just as much as you need them."

"Once they're back, we'll split up between the two homes," Galo ordered, "Just as during the war, we're less vulnerable if we spread out in clusters."

"My home is open as well," Spril offered, "We can expect it to be targeted if they learn of Yrlis's research. Our home will need protection, and I offer mine in return."

"So we're all clear on our assignments?" Phylus checked.

"Vielle's girlfriend hasn't turned up, but aside from that, we've addressed everything," Biroe confirmed.

"Excellent. In that case, come up front with me, Vielle. Business and dinner are done," Phylus said, "Now, on to the cocktails!"

"Dad, we're at a fast food restaurant," Vielle laughed, briefly distracted from her worry over MarLys.

"What?" Phylus remarked, feigning surprise, "Oh. Right. They don't serve those here, do they?"

"I hope you've always been this good at staying positive," Malia said with an apologetic smirk.

"A clever girl taught me you have hold tighter to hope when optimism no longer makes sense," Phylus answered, cocking his head toward Vielle.

All eyes turned to the door as it swung open by the hand of a fidgeting young woman. Noticing her uniform, Biroe nudged KalChi urgingly. The girl's eyes darted about the room until her eventual eye contact with Vielle subdued her nervous tics. Biroe and KalChi whispered harshly to each other. Vielle excused herself from her father's side and broke away to greet her.

"MarLys," Vielle beamed, pulling her into a hug, "I was starting to worry you got lost down here."

"Maybe a little," MarLys laughed, watching Biroe watching her, "I'm not that late, am I?"

"No, you're fine. It's just that there's a lot of shady dealings going on, and I'd hate for something to happen to you because of me."

"Actually, um, something has been happening to me," MarLys confessed, struggling to hold eye contact, "I don't think it's your fault, but it is because we're together."

"Somebody has a problem with you dating a Hybrid?" Vielle scolded, withholding suspicion of a more common social epidemic.

MarLys stepped to the booth and reached in to pat Galo's hand. Galo tilted his head with curious sympathy as he turned to her. From deeper in the booth, Nikasu looked knowingly into her eyes. Artificial symmetry couldn't hide the scars from another who'd borne them.

"You're Galo, right?" MarLys asked.

"Yes. Sorry I was such an ass when we met."

"I never held it against you. Anyway, could you wet a napkin for me?"

"Of course," Galo smiled, saturating a napkin in his hand, "Vielle told you of my hydromancy, did she?"

"She told me about all of you," MarLys said as she accepted the napkin, "Thanks."

She returned to Vielle, the two of them standing in the open, surrounded by friends, family, and strangers. They stared at one another, Vielle's unease growing as MarLys tried to suppress her own. Drawing on inspiration from Vielle's café revelations, MarLys lifted the napkin and smeared it across her eyes.

MarLys rubbed vigorously for a few seconds, caking the napkin with damp makeup. She swallowed nervously as she lowered her paper mask, her bruises laid bare. Vielle's nerves tightened into sympathetic resolve. Galo's mouth fell open in shock and pity, while Nikasu nodded in solemn empathy. Vielle pulled MarLys into a stronger embrace, a teardrop from MarLys splashing silently on her shoulder.

"This was because of us?" she asked.

"Uh-huh. It was…"

"I knew people would disapprove. For more reasons than you knew about. It's none of their damn business, but I knew. I should've warned you," Vielle apologized, "I should've told you who I am. I should never have kept that from you."

"It's okay. I'm not sure this has anything to do with you being a Hybrid."

"Who did this to you?"

"My uncle. He's staying at my parents' house while they're away on business."

"Honey, just say the word, and we'll get you out of there," Vielle promised, "If you want, we'll even send SenRas after him to scare him straight."

"Thanks, but I don't want to be a burden on your home."

"Well, maybe we could look for an apartment together."

"If I heard your name correctly, we need to get you away from your uncle and under protection immediately," Biroe cut in, "You're MarLys, right?"

"I am," MarLys nodded, approaching the booth as Vielle rejoined her father at the counter, "Do you know my uncle?"

"Yes, that bastard is running a scandal to defame the Subtransit Resistance and orchestrate a war with Tanelen. Sinkua, KalChi, and I lost our jobs, and Phylus and EshCal got suspended because of him."

"I didn't know the Chairman of Parliament had that much authority," MarLys puzzled, "Can he seriously do that?"

"Until a Representative publicly challenges him, he's officially acting on their behalf," Spril said, "The fact that he's gone unchallenged doesn't necessarily mean they agree with him though. He specializes in coercion and usually non-physical intimidation. But obviously, he has no problem crossing that line with people smaller than him. Or with no leverage over him."

"I should've come forward sooner," MarLys apologized, "I didn't know he was hurting anyone else. I thought he was taking all his anger out on me. That's why I never said anything."

"We're researching a theory that he works for the Avatars of Fate," SenRas said, "We suspect he works for the one they call The Politician. Her real name is Olsa."

"The former Prime Duchess was one of them?" MarLys gasped.

"Still is," Malia qualified, "I was charged with stopping her from reaching that office. Failing that, I orchestrated her impeachment while working as her Judge. Now, it would appear she's set her sights on ArcNos, with LenSom serving as her proxy."

"MarLys, has he ever had you deliver any parcels for him?" Biroe asked.

"He's hired me a few times, yeah. But he never went through Black Tie. Just went straight through me. Never to the same place twice, either," MarLys answered, trailing off as horrid realization crept in, "Oh shit! Do you think he's been using me as a runner?"

"Sounds like it. He's probably having you deliver non-urgent correspondence," Biroe nodded, "Not to put any blame on you. You didn't know he was hurting anyone else."

"What's this about non-urgent correspondences?" Vielle asked, returning with Phylus, each with a tray of desserts.

"LenSom might have used me to communicate with his boss," MarLys explained, "SenRas just told me my uncle probably works for an Avatar of Fate called The Politician."

"In that case, you're definitely coming to stay with me," Vielle asserted, "We're going to rework our living arrangements to weather the fallout from these scandals."

A bloody scream from outside shattered the pensively settling sense of security. Pastry crumbs scattered and drinks sloshed as heads shot up and turned toward the window. Biroe shoved away from the table to let everyone else out of the booth.

"It came from the top of the stairs," Spril pointed out, "I'll go check it out."

Cries of agony followed, perforated by the harsh grinding of alloy joints and metal scratching concrete. A man limped frantically across the window, his flesh and clothes smeared with a sickly concoction of grease and blood. He glimpsed the congregation of Subtransit Resistance veterans and reached for the door with trembling arms.

A pair of alloy claws skewered his back, spraying bloody mist from the exit wounds in his chest. His assailant faced his body to the window and withdrew the blades. Blood spattered on the glass as the knifelike appendages plunged again through the wounds. Serrated claws punctured the bloodstained glass, and the man's body slammed against the window, shattering it and collapsing through.

"What the hell is that thing?!" KalChi shouted at the sadistic amalgamation of metal and sinew, "Is it one of theirs?"

"It must be," Nikasu agreed, fixating on it, "Look how it's just sitting there. Watching us."

"So, this is what they've replaced the sentinels with?" Spril sneered, swaggering to the middle of the dining room to face it.

The creature launched itself at Spril with a deafening shriek, outstretched claws flailing wildly. Standing in stoic defiance, Spril rapidly analyzed the erratic lashings of its bloodied appendages. Suffering not a scratch, he raised his hand into the mess of blades and grabbed the creature by what could only be called its face.

Within the split second before collision, its red sensor light flickered out. Spril's knuckles popped as his fingertips pressed against the fleshy alloy, his eyes widening with nearly maddening levels of aggression. Its body fell limp in his grasp. In a swift flowing motion, Spril released the creature and plowed his other fist through the crimson beacon, shattering the biomechanical visage his with bare knuckles. Sinew and circuitry spewed from the impact point as the flesh and alloy corpse tumbled back out the window.

"Okay. What... was that thing?" KalChi gasped, everyone in the room staring bewilderedly at Spril, "And what did he just do?"

"I must have tripped a circuit when I grabbed it," Spril said, "Lucky break."

The noise of metal on concrete returned, compounding into a cacophony and drawing nearer.

"More are coming," Spril announced, "We need an escape plan."

"It was watching us," Nikasu shuddered.

"We need to find Sinkua and Eytea," Galo insisted.

Spril sidled to the counter, keeping one eye on the door and one on the window.

"Do you need something, sir?" the cashier asked, trembling behind his forced mask of professionalism.

"Do you have a gun in the safe?"

"Yeah. Why? Do you need it? I can't shoot worth a damn."

"It's for Phylus. The guy who ordered our food," Spril explained, "Bring it to me, okay? Move slowly and don't turn your back."

The cashier nodded vigorously, wide eyes reddening with his refusal to blink. He took long calculated strides backward into the kitchen and slipped behind a wall. Moments later, he emerged with a pistol, his trembling waning slightly as he passed the gun to Spril.

"What should we do?" he asked, straining to keep his fear out of his voice.

"Phylus's daughter, the Berininite, and the girl with purple eyes are going to run. That should draw them away."

"Should?"

"I think they're after them."

"You think!?" the cashier panicked.

"This is the first I've seen of them. Phylus and I will stay here and stand guard in case we're wrong. Take everyone else to the back," Spril ordered, "Don't come out before I say so."

Spril returned to the table and thrust the pistol into Phylus's hand.

"You've got intel to deliver to Tanelen, but first they need to get topside," Spril ordered, pointing to Galo, Vielle, and Nikasu, "Me and you are gonna cover their escape and hold this position while they draw off the heat."

"Aim for the face, then?" Phylus confirmed as he checked the clip.

"That'll work. Remember, one shot..."

"One kill. Don't have to tell me."

"I'll stay behind as well," SenRas offered, "I'll only need a moment in the kitchen to arm myself."

"All right," Spril nodded, digging in his pocket, "On my mark, you three rush the door, break right, and head topside. Vielle, here's the keys to my car. The glaive and scythes are in the back seat. Don't forget, we also have the books.

"KalChi, take Biroe and break left. EshCal, cover them. Take the first eastbound train you come to. MarLys and Malia, wait in the back with everyone else. Everyone ready?"

Metallic claws plunged through the door, serrated appendages shredding away at the wood. Two creatures tore their way inside through the fibrous wounds while three more scuttled through the shattered window. Spril pulled his quarterstaff out of the crossbeams on the underside of the table.

"Go!" Spril shouted, sweeping his staff toward the guarded exits.

Galo rushed to the front, keeping his stride as he shoulder-checked a leaping biomech, and bounded through the open window. Vielle and Nikasu followed through the cleared path, Nikasu clutching Vielle's hand and easing the pull of gravity on both of them. Phylus popped off two shots, spraying scarlet from the two at the door. SenRas guided MarLys and Malia to the back of the restaurant.

EshCal rushed to the door and kicked it open without breaking her stride. She surveyed the maddened Epsilon Boarding Dock as she drew her epee. Biroe unlocked his wheels, joints popping as he white-knuckled his leather-wrapped armrests. KalChi took hold of the handles and, drawing on adrenaline reserves she had never fathomed, bolted to the open door.

Abominant creatures flooded into the boarding dock from the street, leaving a wake of screams and ravaged corpses. Biroe ground his teeth smooth, his heart jackhammering his ribs as KalChi accelerated to an eastward sprint. Adrenaline surging, she all but kept pace with EshCal's unhindered stride. Hearing an ambitious predator closing in, EshCal whipped about and dispatched an airborne creature with a swift impaling thrust.

The quick and the lucky boarded open trains, shoving oblivious offboarding passengers back into the cars. Those less fortunate or opportunistic came to grisly ends, biomechs dragging and scattering their entrails as they skittered away in search of their next prey.

EshCal fell back to cover KalChi and Biroe while they waited to board a train. KalChi tried over and over to perch Biroe's front wheels on the unfolding handicap ramp. Though she succeeded at last after several failures, she soon realized that, no matter her exertion, she hadn't the strength to lift the rest of him. People bounded over the ramp to lay claim to a piece of the diminishing vacancy.

Two strangers emerged from the train car, braving the din beyond their mobile refuge. They each grabbed one of Biroe's wheels and hoisted him into the car, shouting for KalChi and EshCal to follow. KalChi leapt over the still unfolding ramp and hammered the abort button. EshCal sliced open a biomech and fled for the train, ducking under the top of the doorframe as she bounded over the retracting ramp.

Chapter 29

Galo, Vielle, and Nikasu rushed to the stairs, wretched creatures banking in pursuit at the sight of them. Thorny vines sprouted from Vielle's wrists, serving as substitutes for her cat-o'-nine-tails. Fortified by the Serpent Bracer, Galo pulverized any biomechs that came within reach with his crystal fists. Nikasu eased the burden of gravity with her fingers upon each of their backs, enabling strides so long they more bounded than ran up the stairs.

At the top of the stairs, they found only a fraction of the forces had poured into the Epsilon Boarding Dock. Scores, perhaps hundreds, more biomechs scrambled about topside, hurtling pedestrians and drivers into madness. The parking lot, and in it Spril's car and Vielle's motorcycle, lay on the other side of the road. To both the relief and apprehension of onlookers paralyzed in horror, the bizarre beings converged upon the three emerging from the Subtransit.

"Vielle, Nikasu, get our weapons," Galo ordered as water flowed silkenly from his neck, rippling and freezing over his body to encase him in prismatic armor, "I'll draw them off."

Galo charged deeper into the converging onslaught, stretching the space between himself and the girls. He deftly pivoted and wove through the swarm of biomechs, raw sinew rippling as their alloy claws chiseled at his armor. Water pooled in the chinks and froze hastily, forming smoky crystal scabs.

Focusing on drawing the swarm away from the girls and the Subtransit entrance, Galo carved a path largely on the defensive. Those who engaged him directly, he dispatched with unreluctant lethality. Only those eager to avoid him did he truly prey upon, chaotic yet preternaturally focused frozen appendages lashing out from his armor.

"What do we do about the books?" Nikasu shouted over the din as she and Vialled hurried through the parking lot.

"Don't know yet," Vielle admitted, struggling to think louder than the mausolean clamor, "These things can't keep coming forever. We'll hold them back until the others can join us."

Vielle unlocked Spril's car and ran for her motorcycle. Nikasu threw open the door and grabbed the weapons from the floorboard, her scythes in her off hand and Galo's glaive in the other. She sought out Galo's crystalline yet agile form among the chaos of alloy and bare sinew, lightening his glaive with her milystic flow.

"Galo! Catch!" she shouted, the urgency of her voice sweeping it over the cacophony.

Seeing him cast a slight glance toward his shoulder in acknowledgement, she hurled the weapon like a beastly javelin. The blade carved through the air, roaring toward him on a strange trajectory as the milystic enhancement gradually depleted.

Galo danced back on the balls of his feet, baiting abominant beings and drawing their ire. He whipped around and snatched his glaive out of the air, coupling its momentum with his brute force to cleave a nearby airborne biomech in two. He ejected his encasing as the creature split apart upon his blade, crystalline armor exploding from his body.

"Do we have a plan, or are we fighting until we come up with one?" Galo called from the momentary clearing.

"Spread out and push 'em west until the others can join us," Vielle called back,

"We'll ask Spril to take us to find Sinkua and Eytea."

"Solid plan," Galo said, "Don't let this point fall behind the horizon."

Galo pounded out meters between himself and the Subtransit entrance in loping westward strides. He swerved and pivoted around the creatures as they converged around him, carving through biomechs with furious grace. Flesh and shrapnel trailed from the tip of his glaive with every swipe as he slashed through the pack with lethal efficiency.

Her heart pummeling her ribcage, Nikasu quieted her fearful trembling as the biomechanical fiends swarmed her. With freshly tapped potential, she slashed at them two by two as they leapt at her with serrated appendages lashing madly. Her raw strength not quite sufficient to slay them by the blade, swellings of g-force channeled through her scythes buckled and collapsed their joints. The locked and weighted beasts cracked apart as they crashed violently into the pavement, spewing fragments of black stone from their burial craters.

Vielle struggled with the storage compartment on the back of her motorcycle. She frantically jerked at the latch as the din of metal raking asphalt closed in. The scraping swelled to a crescendo and abruptly stopped, an atrophying shadow looming over her. The latch snapped open, and Vielle swiped her cat o' nine tails from the compartment. She ducked under her assailant as it barreled over her head and jumped back as she righted herself. With nine tails bound together, she cracked the beast with a battlecry ill-fitted to her stature. Her sneakers struck pavement, and she sprinted westward, passing the decommissioned biomech before it landed.

Hindered by asymmetry, Galo sheathed his glaive and stormed the pack bareknuckle, again only engaging those who directly attacked or tried to avoid him. Those who came within arm's reach ricocheted violently off his frozen fist, the cyan glow of the Serpent Bracer pulsating with every strike. Once he was satisfied with the distance he had created, he stopped and turned to face the swarm he had plowed through.

He leapt high and back, aiming his glaive downward in a double-fisted grip. His feet pounded the pavement, his body dropping into a crouch as he wedged his blade into a crack. Shimmering ice snaked along the asphalt throughout the pack. The ice fractured against the pavement and erupted through the swarm like shrapnel, impaling and scattering a mess of them.

"Nikasu, break for it!" Galo bellowed, "Vielle, cover her!"

Nikasu forced an opening through the circling pack and pushed westward. An enraged abomination sprang at her side with a vicious shriek. Inspired by Spril's defense of Epsilon Burger, she turned and raised her empty hand, holding both scythes in the other.

She caught it by the face, the impact forcing her arm back. Its claws clamped around her forearm, boring into her flesh. Stifling a scream as blood tiger-striped her pale skin, she unleashed a torrent of milystis into her grappling predator. The surge of g-force collapsed the biomech into itself, crushing it under its own weight.

The slain creature hanging from her forearm, she whipped around and bludgeoned another with it. The collision knocked the crushed beast from her forearm, gaping her wounds. She cried out shrilly as aerial trails of scarlet coiled from the gashes.

Delirious from the sudden and rapid blood loss, Nikasu dropped her scythes and clutched her ruined forearm, fingers staining crimson as she failed to stem the flow. The pain throbbed up her arm, her stomach threatening to expel partially digested chicken strips. In ephemeral focus, she heard her name called again. Leaving her weapons where they landed, she staggered westward with a seemingly inebriated gait.

Hearing her sister's agonized cry, Vielle constricted an attacking biomech in the tails of her whip and hurled away its alloy carcass. In her moment's reprieve, she watched in horror as, unarmed and bleeding profusely, Nikasu hobbled deeper into the swarm. The Platinum Orchid pulsated in her pocket as an array of thorny vines erupted from her shoulder blades.

The vines snapped about an almost sentient manner, fiercely protecting Vielle as she rushed to Nikasu's aid. Like fibrous tentacles, they lashed and coiled around predatory drones, reacting to her subconscious instincts.

Vielle stumbled as she shouted Nikasu's name, sacrificing equilibrium for command of her weaponized arbormantic armor. A fistful of vines penetrated cracks in the pavement, anchoring her upright, as several more shot forth and enveloped Nikasu. They bandaged her wound, stanching the blood loss, and shielded her from biomechs circling her. Nikasu relaxed her legs and collapsed to her knees as Vielle devoured the distance between them.

Vielle unwrapped the vines from Nikasu, save for those bandaging her arm. She wrapped her arm around her sister's shoulders and lifted her to her feet. Nikasu leaned on Vielle, lightening both of their bodies. Vielle bounded west in loping strides, carrying Nikasu with a combined weight of less than her usual self.

The last of the biomechs approaching the Subtransit turned to give chase.

Their boots pounding through fetid puddles, Eytea and Sinkua ran from a swelling cacophony of metal on asphalt. Alloy joints shrieked as bladed limbs folded and stretched. Brick dust rained on the sidewalk as mechanical nightmares burst out of their nests, encasing themselves in raw muscle tissue as they flew.

Morningstar scorching, Sinkua turned and swung at the approaching sound. A stream of fire bared a glimpse of their growing numbers. He twisted his weapon and swung downward, driving spikes into a biomech as it hurled itself at him. A ferocious bellow erupted from the nether reaches of his lungs as he pulverized the creature against the pavement. The impact point vomited searing strips of flesh and smoldering metal shrapnel.

Bounding backward, he snapped his morningstar upward at the next to strike. Stunned but operational, it tumbled back and landed belly up. With a lift of his arm, a pillar of flame engulfed it and hurled it deeper into the swarm. It crashed and bounced off its ilk, bruising and denting them. Sinkua turned about to face them in earnest as they closed in.

Eytea whipped around and slashed the growing darkness, her axe blade cleaving an airborne biomech. She batted one half with the flat side of her spearhead and booted the other into the agitated horde. Two more pounced at her, flesh pulsating around their hungry claws. She impaled one, setting it thrashing with a voltaic torrent, and bludgeoned the other with the jolting mechanical corpse.

Fists tightly clenched, she pumped a steady current into the skewered abomination. The deadened biomech sparking violently, the alloy skeleton shrieked along the spearhead as Eytea whipped it off her weapon and into the swarm. She opened her hand, and the pent-up charge exploded from the creature, a frenzying orb of lightning surging through its surrounding ilk.

"Take the air!" Sinkua barked, "Find higher ground!"

"Not 'til you can get there, too!" Eytea argued.

"You'll cover more ground up there," he shouted over the shrill scraping of metal joints.

"I'm only doing this to cover you," she insisted, hovering above the tainted pavement, "Run! Ignore them and just run!"

They nodded to each other, and Eytea watched Sinkua pound out steadily harder and longer strides. He appeared reluctant to hit a full sprint and leave her behind, predictably incapable of shaking his worry over her safety among their numbers.

From securely above, Eytea blasted a forked lightning bolt from her axe blade and into the raging swarm. Abominant beasts seized violently, tumbling over each other and sending the current arcing to their predatory brethren. Eytea watched with a sly grin as

Sinkua sheathed his morningstar and hit an urgent sprint.

Sinkua wove along the broken street, tripping up and stymying the fiends as they trailed his erratic movements. Muddy water splashed his legs as he veered into an alley, braving a labyrinth of urban passageways. The predatory abominations gave chase, crumbling bricks announcing new births as he passed. They climbed and clawed over one another, throwing themselves and each other at him.

At the end of a straightaway, he spotted a fire escape with the bottommost ladder partly dropped. It appeared low enough that he could jump to it, but he knew that might also have put it within their reach. With a surge of adrenaline and a fiery burst from under his boots, he exploded into a loping sprint well beyond his presumed limits. His footfalls sent faint tremors up the walls, the stomping of steel-toed combat boots on dank pavement echoing throughout the brick chamber.

As he neared the fire escape, he realized the ladder was higher than it had looked from afar. With no room to slow down or change course, he tightened his fists and ran harder, bounding straight at the wall. Desperation overcoming fear, he took five strides up the wall from atop a heap of garbage and wedged his fingers through the underside of the wrought iron balcony. The pile of garbage collapsed and scattered beneath him. He scrambled to the middle of the balcony's underside, legs tense and atremble as he braced himself by the toes of his boots.

They gathered and bustled beneath him, jumping and snapping ferociously. A few blocks away, he could hear Eytea blasting those she'd kept behind. Too much distance and noise separated them for him to expect any more direct help.

They piled atop themselves and launched each other at the balcony, claws biting and clapping at the hanging pyromancer. Sinkua thrust upward, pressing himself against the iron. Still they lashed at his unguarded back, shredding fabric and stinging flesh.

Hands and feet trembling with the strain of his awkward position, he crawled to the edge of the balcony. The thunder of Eytea's assault drew closer, inspiring a glimmer of hope. They piled themselves higher, his warm blood dripping on them as their claws cut deeper into his back. He gritted his teeth to suppress the screams they craved. Each tensing of his muscles pushed more blood from the wounds, thick drops spattering on their sinewy bodies.

Reaching the edge of the balcony, he grabbed the bars and frantically shuffled his feet out to the edge. The biomechs piled higher still, springing and slashing at his hanging buttocks. He hoisted himself up over the railing and into the balcony. One of the abominations latched onto the bottom rung just as he pulled the ladder up. It sprang into his haven with claws flailing, but he jabbed it with a fiery fist and sent it collapsing into the darkness below.

Safe from the enraged swarm, he hurled a ball of flame skyward and burst it above the building with a sweep of his arm. He paused, seconds dragging eternally as he heard nothing over the furious cacophony below. With a thunderous crackle, a bolt of lightning shot skyward from just above the rooftops. Finally able to catch his breath, he dropped upon the mildewy doormat.

He flung an additional fireball every few seconds, relaying his position. Eytea's shadow cast over him in the fading light of his last beacon, shrinking she descended along the side of the apartment building. They both exhaled in relief as she lit upon the railing and hopped down into the balcony.

"I knew you'd find shelter if you could focus on it," Eytea panted, "Thank you."

"I should be thanking you," Sinkua smiled, "For covering me, I mean."

"Honestly, I don't know how much longer I could have kept that up. My wings haven't been this sore since, well you know."

"Since you rescued me after I faced CreSam's firing squad?"

"Uh-huh. Just thinking about it cramps up my shoulder blades."

"Sometimes I don't think I've thanked you enough for that," he confessed.

"You have," she assured, kissing his cheek, "You've kept us both well. The horses when they were under our care, too. All I've ever wanted is for you to stay alive."

"Speaking of staying alive, did you bring any more sandwiches? My stomach is tying itself in knots."

"So's mine," she sympathized, "But I only brought the one. The thermos is still half-full. Wanna split it?"

"Keep it. I've had my share."

"Honey, I brought that stuff for you."

"I know and thank you. But that was when you thought you'd use the pigeon to lead us home," he argued, "If I knew we'd both be stuck here, I would've saved half the sandwich for you, too."

"And I would've shoved it right down your handsome little throat," Eytea countered, patting his belly with a smile, "I ate more on the ferry yesterday than you've eaten in the past five days, and I only had six iolas for the food carts."

"Just drink the water," Sinkua insisted as he stood and faced the door, "Besides, I have a plan."

"What do you have in mind?" she asked, reluctantly sipping the still-crisp water, "I don't think anyone lives here."

"Yeah, but they used to. And judging by the balcony furniture, they abandoned it," he reasoned, drawing his morningstar and unbinding the chain, "Or maybe the sentinels got 'em. I don't know. Either way, their stuff is still here."

"You mean we're gonna break in and rummage for whatever's still edible after five and a half years?"

"You got it. We'll probably just find stale cereal and crackers. Maybe if we're lucky, we'll find some jerky," he said, "But we'll have something in our stomachs at least."

"So, you wouldn't break into abandoned stores to take food, even though you had no idea when or where you might get your next meal," she recalled, "But now that we've been run up here, you're totally nonchalant about breaking into an apartment and acting like we live here?"

"First of all, those windows were barred. Sure, normally I could heat them and bend them. But by the time I was desperate enough to try, I'd let myself get too malnourished to pull it off," he protested, pausing to shatter the glass with his morningstar, "Second off, I was still moving, so I had a reason to think I'd find my way out soon. We, on the other hand, are stuck here until we muster up the strength to fight our way through those things."

"Or someone finds us," she added.

"Right, but in either case, we're stuck here. And even if I can keep ignoring my own stomach, I'm not about to lie out here and let you go hungry," he countered, stepping through the frame and habitually groping for a light switch.

"In that case, I'm saving this water."

"I really don't need it. This is me thanking you."

"No, I mean in case we find some rice or pasta," Eytea justified, "But as much as I love your selective altruism, I really wish you could've tossed it sooner and gotten yourself something to eat before I found you."

"My nightmare was about this city. I know there's nobody left, nobody to stop me from taking what I need. But the thought of stealing from them makes me sick, like I'm robbing their graves," Sinkua sneered, using his hand as a torch as he explored the apartment, "I know its hopeless, but I keep telling myself that maybe someone got out alive."

"Things finally got bad enough that you stopped worrying about it?"

"Not really. Once we find some food, I'm gonna leave some money on the counter."

"In case they come home?" Eytea smiled.

"Yeah," Sinkua solemnly nodded, "Just in case."

"You folks alright?" one of the men asked as the doors shut.

"Getting there," KalChi heaved, "Just need to… catch… my breath."

"Buddy, that is a world class woman you got there," the other complimented, "You'd best be treating her right."

"Yeah," Biroe panted, his head swimming with an adrenaline high, "KalChi's really something."

"KalChi, eh? Pleasure to meet you," the second said, offering a handshake.

"Truly," the first agreed, "Always an honor to meet a hero. Isn't that right, General EshCal?"

"You should know it's Brigadier General Elite EshCal now. Or High Minister if you'd rather," EshCal scoffed with a sly grin, "I knew I recognized you. You served in my platoon during our defection to Parliamentary ArcNos."

"Retired Sergeant Elite ZeiTun at your service," ZeiTun bowed, "This gentleman is my cousin Pircean."

"Honored to make your acquaintance, Madam High Minister," Pircean professed, "ZeiTun has spoken of you at length."

"How have you fared since the war?" EshCal asked, forcing nonchalance toward Pircean's adulation.

"Picking up. Moved to Haprian to be closer to my paternal family. Fucked up my spine something fierce on our last counteroffensive. Spent the fence-crashing ceremony filing discharge papers. Lovely day, really," ZeiTun recounted, "Think I may've aggravated it a smidge just now."

"Sorry about that," Biroe said, patting the small of his back as he added, "Obviously, I can sympathize."

"Don't sweat it. It'll loosen up," ZeiTun shrugged.

"You always have been quick to heal," Pircean complimented.

"Guess so," ZeiTun shrugged, "By the way, this bloke here's another bigshot from the Subtransit Resistance."

"Me?" Biroe guffawed, "I was just an accountant who got dragged kicking and screaming into the whole bloody mess."

"That was you leading their cavalry into our ambush, wasn't it?" ZeiTun baited.

"Hah! Yeah, I guess I was," Biroe smiled, feigning humility, "I guess you took part in the ambush, then?"

"Just shy of it, actually. Was docking a lance launcher when I threw out my back. Couldn't stand up. Had to fall back."

"Sounds like you saw as much of the battle as I did," Biroe snickered, "Once I parked the car, I curled up under the dash and closed my eyes, hoping the whole thing would be over quickly."

"Have you two been working together since the war?" Pircean asked.

"Some. More directly since we established the Ministries," EshCal explained.

"What brought you two down here together?" Pircean pried, "Or is that classified?"

"I'm sure someone would say it is, but my commanding officer would disagree," EshCal said, rubbing her chin thoughtfully, "So, that someone can bite me."

Without further acknowledgement, EshCal walked away, shouldering her way to the front of the car. Pircean and ZeiTun watched in confusion, while Biroe and KalChi nodded knowingly.

"I suppose that's a no, then?" Pircean puzzled, turning to ZeiTun, "Did I offend her?"

"No, you gave her an idea," Biroe answered, "At least I think that's what just happened. Hard to tell with her. Hell, for the longest time, we thought she was working for the Avatars of Fate."

"So did we," ZeiTun admitted, "She had everyone fooled."

"Well, as for your question, Pircean, several of us met down here to discuss how we lost our jobs," KalChi chimed in, "Biroe and I were discharged because of the Tanelenese Financial Scandal, which we were working to fix. Sinkua, the pyromancer with glowing green eyes, was fired over a diplomatic scandal with Berinin."

"Damn. What about EshCal?" Pircean asked.

"Suspended for ten weeks," Biroe said, "So's Phylus, Prime Minister of Foreign Affairs."

"How did that happen?"

"Short version, some stuff went down following the Tanelenese Financial Scandal, and they didn't agree with a certain Chairman's handling of it," Biroe sneered, "Rather than negotiate, he thought it would be simpler to just hang them out for a while."

"I guess that's the someone who can bite her, then," ZeiTun gleaned.

The intercom beeped, drawing everyone's attention. The rumble of intermeshed conversations dwindled to a muted roar. Speakers in the ceiling crackled and hummed.

"Attention, passengers of Subtransit eastbound train five-two-nine," EshCal announced, "This is High Minister of Defense EshCal. I assume everyone noticed the unusual creatures storming the Epsilon Boarding Dock. Some of you might have engaged them. If you did, the Ministry of Defense hopes you're well and thanks you for your assistance.

"Moving on, I'm sure everyone is curious as to the meaning of their arrival. I honestly can't say what they were or where they came from. Not because it's classified, but because we don't know. Not yet, at least. I can, however, warn you against the lies you're going to hear.

"Anonymous account holders in Tanelen have continuously stolen equity payments from two high-profile ArcNosian philanthropists, IlcBei and JalRov. They're the reason maintenance and repairs have fallen behind in a certain apartment complex. They're the reason a certain staffing agency has been forced to significantly reduce its benefit policies. They're the reason the Subtransit has started charging and has experienced a marked decline in general maintenance. If, during your ride, you happen across a one-legged man in a wheelchair and a woman with strawberry blonde hair, thank them. Thoroughly. They have worked tirelessly to return that money to its rightful beneficiaries.

"Chairman LenSom has led people to believe that Tanelen thinks we have embezzled from them. Furthermore, he has perpetuated rumors that Tanelen speaks of aggression should our silence on the matter continue. Silence which he has forced. Know that the Ministry of Defense has received no such missive from any representative of Noble Doyen Joren.

"Bearing all of this in mind, I'll bet iolas to ickers that Chairman LenSom will proclaim those creatures to be products of Tanelenese technology. He'll use this belief to build support for an invasion of our northward neighbors. Do not trust him. He failed to turn us against Berinin, and now he aims to turn us against Tanelen. We cannot let that happen. Tanelen has not threatened us.

"Ladies and gentlemen, this was an inside job."

Spril batted a leaping biomech with a backhanded swing of his quarterstaff, buckling its joints. As it flew, SenRas plunged a knife sharpener through its red sensor.

Hearing another launch at his back, SenRas spun about and dropped to a crouch as he bisected it with a meat cleaver.

They poured through the window in pairs. Phylus popped off two shots as they crested the frame and sent them tumbling backward onto the next to come.

"They're on board!" Phylus announced.

"These things keep coming!" Spril grunted, sweeping his quarterstaff through a pack of them, "Why aren't they following the Hybrids?"

"Do that magic trick with your hand again," SenRas joked, sundering one in midair, "Maybe that'll get rid of them."

"That was just lucky," Spril refuted as he stomped one, scattering metal chaff, "Phylus, how are you doing over there?"

"Six shots left," Phylus called from behind the bench, "I'll have to fall back if they don't clear out soon."

"Cover me," SenRas ordered as he dashed to the counter.

"Where are you going?" Phylus shouted as he spent a bullet on a biomech in pursuit of SenRas.

"Getting you more ammo."

In the back of the kitchen, employees and patrons huddled against the walls and under the counters. Malia and MarLys leaned against the door to the walk-in freezer, the latter unaware of the former's connection to her girlfriend. Eye contact was fleeting and awkward, each suspecting a judgmental glance from the other.

"Sounds like they're having trouble out there," Malia said, immediately regretting how coldly she had broken the silence, "But I'm sure they can handle it."

"Me too," MarLys nodded, staring at a strip of dirty grout between her feet, "Two of them fought in the war, right?"

"Yes, Spril and Phylus," Malia confirmed, her heart jackhammering, "SenRas helped assassinate one of the Avatars responsible for creating the imperial regime."

"Then I'm sure they'll be fine," MarLys nodded, her throat swelling as her eyes trailed upward.

"You're worried about her, aren't you?" Malia asked, glancing aside at SenRas rummaging in the cutlery, "Vielle, I mean."

"If Spril was right about those things hunting the Hybrids, I'm worried about all of them. But I know those guys will go help once they're done here," MarLys explained, "But Vielle? I mean, what can I even do for someone who goes through this sort of thing? All I can do is sit here, and I hate it."

"I probably haven't known her as long as you have, but I think you're doing all you need to do," Malia consoled, "You believe in her, but you're still worried about her. All she needs is someone like you to be there for her. Someone who's not afraid to stay with her."

"I could never betray her. Not after all that anomaly talk. Nobody deserves to be alone after hearing such things."

"You're a good person, MarLys."

"Thank you. You seem pretty decent yourself."

"Been a long time since anyone said that about me."

"Why's that?"

"I'd rather not talk about it. So, how did you and Vielle meet?"

SenRas rushed out of the kitchen and ducked into the booth. He handed Phylus a box.

"They keep this much spare ammo?" Phylus asked, peering over the backrest just long enough to unload his last two shots.

"No, just the one clip," SenRas said, opening the box, "All they have is knives. Dozens and dozens of knives."

"What the hell am I supposed to do with these?" Phylus shouted as SenRas hurried back to the fray, "I can't get close enough to stab them!"

"Throw them," SenRas bluntly argued, "If you can aim a gun and throw a baseball, you can figure out how to throw knives."

Phylus gripped a knife by the blade, pinching it between his thumb and forefinger. Centering it in his field of vision, he watched the biomechs pouring in through the window. He studied their timing, counting seconds between each.

Gritting his teeth, he threw the first knife. It stuck in the window frame, just behind one of the sinewy drones. He snatched another knife and whipped it off purely on instinct, spattering blood and oil as he skewered the biomech. He threw the next two with the same haste and abandon, staking another two invaders. Deliberating over his fifth shot, he struck short of his target.

"Guess I choke if I overthink it," Phylus mumbled to himself, eyeing SenRas, "Gotta calm down."

Spril plowed his fist through the face of an airborne fiend, suffering cuts along his forearm as the sensor stayed alight until he shattered it. He jerked his arm back, elbowing another as it hovered above his shoulder, and whacked a third with his quarterstaff.

An ephemeral spark flickered in the corner of his eye, odd seeing as Phylus had spent the clip. The scent of butane filled his nostrils as though the chemical enveloped him, abruptly diminishing to a more distant proximity. That of tobacco followed, briefly drawing his eyes toward the booth.

Phylus rose from behind the seat, standing with one foot propped atop the backrest. He held an open box of kitchen cutlery under his arm, their blades gleaming under the fluorescent lights. His lips held a cigarette, the cherry running nearly a quarter of its length.

Lips curling into a contemptuous sneer, he snapped out knives in rapid succession, the next one taking flight before the current one had landed. Each skewered a different predatory biomech, often staking their targets to the floor or the wall.

"They're thinning," Spril announced, "We just need to hold out a bit longer."

"Don't get sloppy now," SenRas encouraged, "They still need our help upstairs."

"I'll cover that," Spril insisted, "You take Malia and MarLys to safety. Phylus, catch up with EshCal, Biroe, and KalChi when we're done."

"I'm not leaving until Vielle is safe!" Phylus barked, his eyes darting between targets.

"Dammit, Phylus! She won't be safe until you get to Tanelen. None of us will be!" Spril shouted, "Once it's clear, get in your car and go to the docks."

"We need you in Tanelen," SenRas added, "You can do more there than any of us."

"Biroe and KalChi can fix it on their own," Phylus argued, "I can still help here."

"And when they do, LenSom won't be able to blame these bastards on Tanelen," SenRas said, "But we need you to negotiate an active alliance with them."

"I thought that was your plan all along," Spril said, "Ally with Tanelen to hunt the Avatars of Fate and expel their influence."

"Fine!" Phylus begrudgingly gave in, skewering a drone to the wall, "Hold them off until I'm in my car."

Silence fell over the restaurant. No more crawled through the window. Nothing scurried through the door.

"We're done," SenRas flatly announced, "I'll get Malia and MarLys. You gentlemen go topside and handle your business."

"Take the Subtransit," Phylus ordered, "Get them as far from the action as possible before you even talk about surfacing."

"As Malia's comrade and your friend, I'll protect them both with my life," SenRas swore, "Good luck to both of you."

SenRas went to the back of the restaurant to announce their safety and retrieve Malia and MarLys. Phylus pulled the last drag off his cigarette and flicked it into the ashtray at the back of the table. Spril headed for the door, waving for Phylus to follow.

Bodies both human and biomechanical laid strewn about the Epsilon Boarding Dock, most deceased but a few clutching impotently to evanescent glimmers of life. Phylus and Spril had no time for either and thus pressed on toward their obligations above.

The cacophony of carnage swelled as they bounded up the stairs. On the surface, they found the swarm concentrated a few blocks to the west. Vielle, Galo, and Nikasu stood in the thick of it, theirs backs to one another as they fended off the surrounding assault.

"I'm trusting you with them," Phylus reminded, "Don't forget about the books."

"I know. I'll take care of things here. You just get on that boat and handle the rest," Spril encouraged, "They'll be fine."

"Right. Just one more thing to do. Wait here."

Phylus sprinted to his car, threw open the door, and thrust himself into his seat. He peeled out of the parking lot, blaring the horn as he whipped onto the road. The biomechs scattered at the decibel blast, voraciously closing in on the Hybrids again as the sound faded. Phylus hammered the horn to keep them off Vielle, Nikasu, and Galo, but they became less responsive with each blaring.

Near the edge of the swarm, he slammed the brakes and jerked the steering wheel to the left, fishtailing and crashing through a pack of abominations. Fragments of sinewy metal ricocheted off his car as the drones shattered against the body panels. He rolled down the passenger's side window as he came to a stop.

"Vielle!" Phylus shouted, "Give me Spril's keys. He's gonna get you three out of here."

"Catch!" Vielle called back, pitching the keys through the open window, "How are things downstairs?"

"All clear on Epsilon. SenRas and Malia are taking MarLys somewhere safe. I'm going to meet Biroe, KalChi, and EshCal at the docks," Phylus reported, "You kids fight hard. Take care of each other."

"You too, Dad. Good luck in Tanelen."

Salty humidity filled the air as SenRas, Malia, and MarLys climbed the stairs out of the Subtransit station. Cars passed without disruption. Pedestrians walked without fear. Whatever had become of the outbreak, it clearly hadn't reached this far east.

"Looks like we're safe," MarLys pointed out, "Thank you, Mister SenRas."

"Please, call me SenRas, young lady," SenRas insisted, "The Hybrids are like family to me, one of them literally. As long as you and Vielle are together, I'd rather dispense with formality."

"You're a lot different than you were during the war," Malia noted.

"The same could be said of you, but I'd say much has changed for both of us since then."

"So, you two fought in the war together?" MarLys asked, "Were you in the Subtransit Resistance like Vielle?"

"Not exactly," Malia dodged, "Officially, we worked for Imperial ArcNos, but we were both plotting against the empire. Trouble was, neither of us knew the other was a mole, so we ended up fighting each other instead."

As though to save her from another uncomfortable conversation, an avian shadow settled over the three of them. A tracker pigeon descended amongst them, hovering before

Malia with wings aflutter. Malia offered her hand, and the bird lit upon it. Puzzled, she untied the note from its leg and dismissed the messenger bird.

Malia unrolled the note and read it. Bewilderment consuming her expression, she read it a second and third time. It was brief and ambiguous, which was typical if she was right to think it had come from The Omnimath.

"Is something wrong?" MarLys asked.

"I don't know. I don't even know what this letter is supposed to mean," Malia puzzled, "SenRas, I think it's from Mortvill."

"What does it say?" SenRas asked.

"He is not perfect, Malia. – Mr. Mor."

Chapter 30

"I think we lost them," Vielle noted, watching out the back of the car.

"Do we have any idea what those things were?" Galo asked, "I'd venture it's obvious enough who's responsible for them."

"Painfully obvious," Spril said, "I suspect their deployment is linked to the rumors of a Tanelenese invasion."

"Do you think Tanelen has allied with them?" Galo pondered, "Or that they've planted operatives?"

"No, I mean…" Spril stumbled, realizing the danger he might have sent the others into, "EshCal is part of The Coalition now. If the Avatars have assimilated Tanelen, she can get the dirt and get the four of them home alive.

"But what I meant is that LenSom may use this to justify declaring war against Tanelen. He and The Politician likely orchestrated the outbreak for that exact purpose."

"And once ArcNos attacks Tanelen, those who would sooner strike back will outnumber those open to respectful discourse," Galo somberly nodded.

"People respond to violence with more violence. It's our nature," Vielle added apologetically, "The best way to end a war is to never let it start."

"Our plan is for Phylus to draw up an alliance with Tanelen against the Avatars of Fate," Spril reported, "Once Biroe and KalChi have settled the financial damages, it should be an easy sell for him."

"This is what that building was for," Nikasu mumbled, staring out the window, "1341 West Heniokhos Boulevard. Laboratory 1341."

"What's that?" Spril asked, "Those things came from there?"

"Yes. They manufactured this invasion while they created the opportunity to release it."

"Maybe that's why they took me hostage," Galo suggested.

"Possibly," Nikasu agreed, "You may have been meant to power those units. Although given that the Mechanical Crypt is suited specifically to the Chieftain Bloodline, I believe they held more ambitious pursuits for you."

"I hadn't considered that," Galo admitted, "I still have the Serpent Bracer…"

"Meaning they were linked to a different power source," Vielle said.

"That's why Yahsek and Ozzera left!" Nikasu gasped, her amethyst eyes widening.

"Do you think that's what was in that book?" Spril asked, "Another way to activate the Mechanical Crypt?"

"One of them is responsible for the power source. It's not being done from that same room, but one of them must be controlling the drones."

"Okay, now how can we use that knowledge against them?" Spril spitballed, "Could we use one to send a signal back to the command module?"

"That means Elemeno is in danger," Galo sidetracked, "Yahsek and Ozzera worked for The Geneticist, and he obviously had a hand in designing those wretches. Elemeno and Eytea bested him before they came to ArcNos."

"Probably a joint effort between The Geneticist and The Engineer," Vielle added, "But seeing as she broke The Scout's neck, that just puts her in even more danger."

"In that case, SenRas is also in trouble," Spril said, "But these drones seem like they're more interested in you Hybrids than anyone else."

"SenRas can handle himself. He and Malia are part of The Coalition," Galo assured, "Get Elemeno and go back to Sinkua's house."

"They may return there for the rest of the books," Nikasu warned, "Once he's retrieved Elemeno, it would be advisable to keep moving."

"When they find the house vacant and the books missing, they'll tear apart the house and scatter to find us and the books."

"I'm with Galo on this one. If they want the remaining books, we know where they'll look first. We can run now and chase them later, or we can stand and face them," Spril reasoned, "The old town is just off this exit. Are we sure Sinkua and Eytea are in there?"

"We know this is where they went," Nikasu confirmed.

"As soon as we find them, drop us off and hurry out of here," Galo urged, "Find Elemeno and escort her to their house. Should our theory pan out, the five of us together will so satiate them that they'll have no appetite for the rest of you."

Nikasu rolled down her window, letting the Frigid night air whip harshly throughout the car. She breathed deeply, bathing her airways in the scent. She licked her lips feverishly, her tongue darting in and out of her mouth. Worried, she cocked an ear.

"They're here," she announced.

"What, do you smell them?" Spril asked facetiously.

"Yes. This place smells like them."

"Wait. You can smell Sinkua and Eytea?" Galo puzzled.

"Don't be absurd. I smell the drones. The wind stinks of their grease," Nikasu clarified, "I can hear them, as well. Scraping. Scratching. Clawing. We're getting close."

"How do you plan to find Eytea and Sinkua?" Spril asked, "Find the drones and follow them?"

"Yes. The attack will be centered around them," Galo said, "But Sinkua has barely eaten in days, so they may have sought shelter."

"If so, they'll be on higher ground," Vielle noted.

The stench of oil grew to overwhelm the inside of the car. Nikasu rolled up her window, but it failed to shut out the grating of jagged blades along ruined pavement. Spril turned on the high beams, only to slam the brakes at the spectacle before them.

Scores of biomechs scrambled over each other with frantic voracity. They poured down an alley and out of sight, while others flooded out from around the corner and circled back. They stacked themselves and launched each other up the walls, clawing furiously at the bricks.

"I... uh... think they're in there," Vielle swallowed.

"I'll circle the perimeter. You three stay down," Spril ordered, "We're going to use Sinkua and Eytea's position to surround the drones."

He switched off the headlights, turned on the fog lights, and crept past the alley. Around the first corner, he found the biomechs in an utter frenzy. Strips of tissue peeled from their alloy skeletons as they clawed unavailingly at timeworn masonry. They built ever greater piles of themselves, those at the bottom being sacrificed under the weight of their fellow brood. Metallic limbs raked across each other in such mass as to create an aggravating cacophony of shrieks, giving the illusion of sentience.

The frenzy swelled as they neared a dilapidated apartment complex. Under the light of the nearly full triad of moons, Spril saw rain-mildewed furniture on several balconies. The once residents of this urban wasteland had either abandoned it or died in the sentinel raid. No warning. No chance to fight. Nor to flee. Now, a raging swarm of biomechanical predators clawed at the barred doors and hurled each other at the windows. If not for the absence of ground floor windows, they would have long since taken this emaciated structure.

"I found them," Spril announced, stopping the car, "Still figuring out how to get you guys inside."

"Is it safe to come up?" Galo asked.

"Might as well. They're too busy to notice you."

Galo sat upright and gasped in horror at the carnage. Curiously, Vielle sat up only to recoil regretfully. She urged Nikasu to stay down until they were ready to enter the building, fearing the sight of the frenzying drones could hurl her into a dysfunctional panic.

"If you can drive up to the front entrance, that should create a large enough clearing that we can get inside and shut them out before any follow," Galo suggested, his eyes darting about and sizing up the infestation.

"Eh, I don't think so. That whole plan hinges on the door being unlocked," Spril refuted, "We need to get you onto a balcony."

"If we circle the building, maybe we can figure out how Sinkua and Eytea got inside," Nikasu said.

"Alleys're too tight," Spril argued.

"She has a good point though," Vielle noted, "They must have gotten inside without letting the drones in with them."

"No more than they could handle, anyway," Galo added.

"Right, but the point is, they got in safely somehow," Vielle concluded.

"Well, they didn't break the door in. The frame is intact," Galo observed.

"Does the building have fire escapes?" Nikasu called from her hiding place.

"Yes, but all the second floor ladders are up on this side," Spril said, "I doubt she could have flown him up there fast enough. Maybe, they found one on another side."

"But how do we get up there from this side?" Galo asked.

"I can pull myself up with my vines and drop the ladder," Vielle suggested, "But we'll have to jump from the roof of the car."

"You did shoot off the back of Biroe's car rather quickly," Galo recalled, "But you'll be working against gravity this time."

"I guess this is where I come in, then," Nikasu asserted, sitting up to take stock of the infestation despite Vielle's wishes, "Galo and I will give you a boost. Just spring off our hands and we'll take care of the rest."

"Can you reduce the pull of gravity on me fast enough?"

"I can cut it in half in the time it'll take to throw you," Nikasu boasted, "But doing it that fast might make you throw up."

"All right, everyone on the roof. Galo, brace yourself and Nikasu. You know how. Vielle, stay low and hold the doors. I'll keep the windows cracked," Spril ordered, "Drop the ladder as soon as you're up there. Once we're under the balcony, you'll only have a few seconds to get the job done."

Sinkua paced the living room, his body crisscrossing candlelight shadows across the floor. The biomechs had tried for hours to breach their shelter, and it sounded like the entire swarm now surrounded the building. Even if they couldn't reach the balcony, with such great numbers, they would eventually break through the bricks and infrastructure.

"Any ideas?" Eytea asked, biting a stale cracker.

"Short of having you fly out for help, no," Sinkua admitted, waggling a strip of old jerky, "But I know you wouldn't go for that, and I don't think this place'll hold up long enough anyway."

"Definitely not and probably not."

"We could go up on the roof."

"And send up a beacon," Eytea nodded, "Our friends must be searching for us by now."

"Not what I had in mind," Sinkua said, "If we can hold out until sunrise, we can figure out which way is southeast. Then, you can fly us along the rooftops until we're out of the city."

"Sounds risky," Eytea worried, "I don't know how far I can carry you before my wings give out."

"In that case, you'd better get your strength up," Sinkua said, pitching a strip of jerky to her, "We'll rest when we can, but we might not always have time."

Eytea caught the jerky and snapped off a bite. As much as she tried to deny it, she knew they had run out of more desirable options. The swarm had grown too dense to fight through, and their shelter wouldn't hold but a few more hours. Escape required they find a way around the surrounding biomechs. Unless this apartment complex had sewer or Subtransit access, that left the rooftops as their only path, and underground travel denied them the guidance of sunlight anyway.

Even as cornered as they were, she fretted over the thought of carrying him such a distance. It would be an accumulation of short flights, but the only time she had managed to fly with him, she had been high on the adrenaline of desperation. These were undeniably mortal circumstances, but her failure didn't necessarily equal death.

She leaned against the wall as she chewed, candlelight flickering over her face. She closed her eyes and imagined the building aflame and collapsing. Her imagination feeding on the ruckus outside, she thought of the abominant predators breaching the walls and pouring into her and Sinkua's last refuge. Her imagination conjured earthquakes, tornadoes, and that enigmatic giant from the Radial Axiom Arena. No matter the summoned crisis though, her pulse never quickened beyond what the actual circumstances elicited.

Her eyes shot open to the sound of a shutting door and muffled voices. Her heart jackhammered with her anxiety over this new unknown. She could sooner believe The Engineer and The Geneticist had found them than any of their friends having tracked them down and breached the swarm.

The anonymous intruders came near enough that she could pick out three different voices but no identifying qualities or distinct words. Maybe they brought Yahsek. Maybe they sent three of The Geneticist's test subjects. Or three subordinate operatives. No matter, they were closing in, and Sinkua looked to be none the wiser.

Awash in internalized panic, Eytea looked about for a means of escape. They could climb the fire escapes to the roof, but she doubted they could outrun their pursuers for long.

Contemplating how they could have been tracked further compounded her worries. Her eyes widened with grievous epiphany as she noticed candlelight glinting off the doorjamb and sill at the edge of the kitchen.

She hastily doused the nearest candle, despite knowing they had already been found. Panic took precedence over reason. Sinkua furrowed his brow and cocked his head at the sight of Eytea flitted about, snuffing candles.

"What's going on?" he asked.

Someone pounded on the front door, more as though to break it down than beckon invitation. Sinkua and Eytea both jumped and spat an expletive, backing up and reaching for their weapons. The intruder pounded again, cracking the timeworn doorframe. A blade penetrated between the door and the frame, prying and cracking the two. The deadbolt snapped free, and the door swung unencumbered.

"How did you get in here?" Sinkua blurted.

"How did we get in here?" Galo recoiled, "How did you get in here?!"

"You assholes! I thought the Avatars found us!" Eytea shouted, expelling her tension.

"Sorry. We couldn't exactly announce ourselves," Vielle excused, her bangs sweaty and her breath smelling acidic, "But seriously, how did you get in here?"

"Did Eytea fly you up to the fire escape?" Nikasu asked, "That's sort of how we got in. Galo and I threw Vielle up to the fire escape from on top of Spril's car, and she dropped the ladder for us."

"I found one in back that was down part of the way. I thought I could jump to it, but instead, I ran up the wall and grabbed the underside of the balcony," Sinkua recounted, "Don't ask how because I wouldn't believe it if I wasn't there when it happened."

"Sounds just like you, brother," Galo laughed, "I wish I could have seen that."

"Where's Spril now?" Eytea asked.

"He went to find your mother," Vielle reported, "We had a meeting at Epsilon Burger, and he sent her out sightseeing instead of leaving her alone at your house."

"And the books?" Sinkua pried, fighting to suppress his fury at the thought of their being left unguarded.

"Spril has them in his car," Nikasu assured, seeing the tension drain from her brother's posture as she spoke.

"Those biomechs crashed the meeting. We all managed to get out safely," Vielle added.

"What have you guys figured out about them?" Galo asked.

"I suspect they're connected to Yahsek and Ozzera's disappearance," Sinkua theorized, "What happened to everyone else?"

"We had the same thought. SenRas, Malia, and MarLys escaped once the way was clear. We don't know exactly where they went, but I'm sure they're safe," Galo answered.

"EshCal, Biroe, and KalChi went to the docks. They're going to Tanelen to clear up the confusion before things get worse," Nikasu added.

"And my dad went to catch up with them before they disembark," Vielle concluded.

"Wait. What confusion?" Sinkua asked, "Tanelen is behind this?"

"No, but that's what people are going to think," Vielle explained, "It's a long story. Chairman LenSom is using the Tanelenese Financial Scandal to start a war between ArcNos and Tanelen. So we suspect anyway."

"And he's gonna pass those things off as the first wave from Tanelen. Got it," Sinkua affirmed, "So, while those four are out dispelling rumors, we're stuck here on cleanup duty. What's The Coalition doing about all this? Fuck-all, I take it?"

"We don't know, so we shouldn't expect them to come to our rescue here," Nikasu shrugged, "I'm through with waiting around to be rescued anyway."

"We've got all five Hybrids armed and backed into a corner," Eytea observed, her lips curling into a vicious smile, "Ever since Sinkua and I moved back to ArcNos, they've kept us separated and turned against each other. This is exactly what they've been trying to avoid."

"Are you thinking we can fight our way out?" Galo asked.

"I'm thinking we can wipe out the infestation," Eytea asserted, "Let's show those sons of bitches they were right to fear us."

"We'll go out the back," Sinkua ordered, "We can bottleneck them in the narrow alleys."

"Vielle and I will go just outside of the alleys," Eytea added, "We'll force them to split up and surround them. And give the rest of you more room to fight."

Sinkua nodded firmly and grabbed his morningstar from against the wall. Stuffing a strip of jerky in his cheek, he swaggered to the shattered back door. He stood in the frame, his searing gaze casting beyond the balcony to survey the carnage. Biomechanical drones scrambled over each other, clawing at the deteriorating walls.

"Eytea," he called back over his shoulder, "You brought my pills, right?"

"Yeah," she said, "Do you need one?"

Despite having baited it, he paused to consider the question, assessing the swarm more consciously now. Succumbing to an episode would give him the strength to destroy any drones that came his way while enduring their lacerations. But it would come at the price of his cognizance and eventually his consciousness. This battle required a careful balance between the two states of fury and finesse. He couldn't approach it the same way he had gone into his last confrontation with VanSen. Spril was right.

"Better make it two."

Eytea brought two pills to him. She smiled warmly, a stark contrast to the cold madness below, as he popped the pills and swallowed them with a mouthful of saliva. She followed him onto the balcony, and Galo, Vielle, and Nikasu joined them shortly.

Sinkua balanced atop the rail, white-knuckling his morningstar. His ruby medallion pulsated radiantly, spreading its empowering warmth throughout his body. He flicked open the bindings of his weapon, letting the chain unravel. The ball struck the wet wrought iron rail with a resonating clang.

Scores of drones halted at the sound, skittering about to face the source. They scrambled and piled under the balcony at the sight of their five marks gathered above. They threw each other at the balcony, clawing at the air with diminishing futility.

Sinkua bounded from the rail, launching himself into the biomechanical maelstrom. He churned the air with his morningstar, milystis surging so powerfully, it set the ball and chain aglow in scarlet. The spin of his weapon accelerated as he plummeted, spiraling into a furious blur of heated steel.

Combat boots scattered muck and gravel as they crashed into the pavement. Pent-up milystis exploded from his morningstar in a spectacular array of flames as he shattered a drone, mechanical entrails spewing over its unliving comrades. He whipped about as he righted himself and bludgeoned another biomech in flight, sending it soaring toward the balcony and bleeding flaming oil.

"Vielle, grab hold of me," Eytea urged, "We're covering the perimeter."

Vielle tightened the binding on her cat-o'-nine-tails . She wrapped her legs around Eytea's waist and hooked her arms under her shoulders. Behind her, Sinkua mounted the railing.

"You're sure you can carry me?" Vielle asked, "Nikasu would be easier."

"She needs those two more than you do. No offense, Nikasu."

"None taken," Nikasu shrugged, "Just go, Vielle. You can help her than I could."

"Don't worry about her," Galo assured, sensing Vielle's unease, "You know how Sinkua is about family."

Vielle nodded and forced a smile.

Gripping her halberd, Eytea spread her wings and flew the two of them from the balcony. Dozens of predators separated from the fray to trail them, exactly as Eytea had predicted. Eytea fired potshots of lightning into the splinter swarms, struggling to aim and fire while staying aloft. They dipped nauseatingly with each bolt she called forth.

A block from the rear of the apartment, she swooped low over the maddened creatures. Vielle hung from Eytea's bent knees, Eytea dipping lower still as Vielle unbound her cat-o'-nine-tails from her hip. Abominations leapt at them, their claws slashing voraciously.

Vielle lashed furiously as she dropped, reinforced tails raking through hungry claws and ripping through glowing crimson cores. She slammed her palm against the wet pavement, enduring embedded detritus as she sent milystis coursing through the asphalt. Thorny plumes erupted from the cracks, impaling a mess of biomechs.

Eytea swooped down and hooked a drone on the inner curve of her axe, arcing upward with it. She stopped abruptly, high above the pandemonium, and hurled the biomech upward. Holding her halberd above her head, she impaled the drone as it fell past her. She folded her wings back and shot straight down, setting the creature's body aglow and crackling with milystis of barely retained purity. Spreading her wings just before landing, she slammed the spearhead of her halberd into the pavement. The pressurized milystis exploded violently from her staked victim, a massive web of electricity arcing throughout the swarm.

Nikasu watched in amazement, her mouth agape as her brother leapt from the balcony with utter nonchalance for the height. Galo patted her shoulder and snickered. Such spectacles had grown so familiar as to be normal for him. He climbed atop the railing as a biomech pounced at Sinkua from behind.

"You'll be fine, Nikasu," Galo assured, his words punctuated by spiked metal striking alloy and flesh, "Just use their weight against them. Well, here's my ride."

Galo jumped from the rail, plunging his glaive through the uppercutted biomech at the zenith of its arc. He encased its body in jagged ice, gripped it with his calloused feet, and rode it into the thick of the melee. Thrusting his legs straight, he shattered the drone against the pavement, spraying crystalline shrapnel into its swarming brethren.

He whipped the impaled core from his glaive, hurling it with frayed wires crackling as the ice melted. It crashed hard into another drone, electrocuting it with drenched wiring. He carved an arc in the pavement with the tip of his glaive, a wall of water rising in its wake and surging against the swarm.

Nikasu's eyes darted frantically along the fray below. She analyzed biomech predators individually and in groups. She studied Sinkua's techniques and tracked Galo's movements. All the while, she muttered to herself, struggling to make sense of the chaos below.

Her amethyst eyes widened with realization as Galo scattered the drones with a rushing hydromantic wall. Surging milystis throughout herself, she lightened her body and bounded over the railing. Scythes drawn, she lit upon the murky pavement as her gravity steadily normalized.

A biomech sprang through the dying hydromantic barricade as Nikasu's shoes struck pavement, its claws gnashing ferociously. Nikasu ducked and plunged her scythe into its underbelly, hooking it on the blade. Her arm trembled as she flooded the writhing body with gravimantic milystis.

She pitched the dying beast from her scythe, lobbing it over the swarm. With a swipe of her other blade, a purplish-blue light erupted from the writhing body in chaotic tendrils. The biomech collapsed atop its brethren with rapidly magnified weight, pulverizing them into a swelling asphalt crater.

Flames glinting off puddles of stale oil and rain, Sinkua plowed his morningstar through a crowd of biomechs knocked toward him by Galo's landlocked tidal wave. Their scorched claws ripped through one another as fire penetrated wounds on trails of bleeding oil.

Sinkua jumped back as Nikasu threw her victim into the furious pack. Hearing another biomech leap at him from behind, he twisted in midair and plowed his enflamed fist through its core, striking with such velocity that he came away unscathed. As Nikasu's gravity bomb landed, Sinkua ignited the mechanical entrails with a sweep of his arm.

Vielle bobbed and spun through the crowd, lashing at biomechs with her cat-o'-nine-tails reinforced with thorns and braided vines. One by one, she corralled them, encasing each in a prison of woven foliage.

Vielle looked skyward and fled down an alley. She slashed fiercely at the swarming creatures, individually controlling each tail of her whip more through milystic manipulation than sheer dexterity. Narrow trickles of blood ran down her arms, wisping along behind her as biomechs raked at her as she powered through the swarm.

Eytea hovered low, just within reach of the pack. She dodged and wove gracefully, baiting them to spring at her and sidestepping on the air. Her halberd crackling with electricity, she sliced through biomechs at the peak of their jump. Those still twitching upon landing, she silenced with a jolt of lightning.

The Frigid night air hummed around Eytea as she swooped over Vielle's corralled swarm. Eytea launched herself high above the rooftops as Vielle dashed into an alley. Bracing her halberd on her shoulder, Eytea aligned the speartip with the center of the pack. Her blades glowed yellow with electromantic milystis, flowing into and condensing in the spearhead. The glow bled out of the tip and coalesced into a spherical whorl of crackling energy.

As though shedding a husk, the milystic orb exploded into a ball of lightning as Eytea fired it into the swarm. Imprisoned biomechs writhed and snapped panickedly, fighting to free themselves. The ball of lightning erupted in a spectacular array of lightning bolts, scorching the vines and shredding through the tangled masses and beyond.

More biomechs poured into the brick and pavement labyrinth, migrating from farther reaches of the fallen metropolis. Eytea maintained her vantage point above the rooftops, surveying the perimeter and firing lightning bolts at each entrance with deadly precision. Vielle shredded biomechs as she dashed through the labyrinth, eliminating most that she faced and forcing the rest into clusters for Eytea.

Keeping Nikasu in the corner of his eye, Galo danced through biomechs with fatal grace, gliding along the ruinous pavement on the balls of his feet. He struck with deadly efficiency, facing each opponent only long enough to deliver a swift killing blow. He lacerated them with crystalline blades whipped from the edge of his glaive and impaled them with icicle spires shot from the Serpent Bracer.

Galo pivoted and glimpsed a biomech within a split second of gouging his torso. He jumped back and swung with the flat of his blade, batting the creature into a wall. Another pounced from just beyond his peripheral vision, ripping a horrific scream from the Berininite Hybrid's lungs as it plunged its claws between the coils of the Serpent Bracer.

Nikasu rushed about and bounded over drones, herding them into agitated clusters as they scrambled over each other in pursuit of the gravimantic Hybrid. She whipped around and skewered one as it leapt from atop a mounded horde, her blade crackling purplish-blue. Amplified deadweight plummeted onto the others as she withdrew her scythe, turning their sinewy metallic talons into shrapnel.

Nikasu jumped as Galo's scream rattled her eardrums. Fragments of her last assault still settling, she dashed away to his aid. Enraged by her demolition of their kin, dozens of biomechs set upon her, forcing her back. Nikasu yelled out to Sinkua, announcing Galo's peril.

Sinkua incinerated airborne drones, spiraling them into a rapid panic. Their enflamed talons flailing madly, he bludgeoned scorched biomechs with his morningstar. Scraps of metal and sinew ripped and snapped from their bodies as he sent them careening. He slumped over in a fleeting moment of reprieve, his breath short, throat swelling, and temples throbbing.

Sinkua clutched his chest, his pulse hastening painfully. He swung his morningstar recklessly as his vision blurred. In a blink of lucidity, he shoved his weapon into its holster, absentmindedly leaving the chain unbound, and hurled whorls of flame into the ravenous pack. He distantly heard something like Galo crying out, but he dismissed it as matters Galo could handle. Nikasu's shouting to him breached the shrieking chaos within, but failing equilibrium and a raging swarm of talons rendered him useless to help.

Galo punched at the creature latched to his forearm. Blood churned out of the gashes as the beast yanked his arm wildly, rendering a solid blow all but impossible. His head grew light and his body heavy. To the horror of his fading cognition, the drone hooked its claws under the coils of the Serpent Bracer, wriggling and twisting it loose. The wretched beast leapt from Galo's shredded limb, robbing him of the Serpent Bracer.

Galo called out in belligerent protest as the thieving creature escaped into the horde, the Serpent Bracer being passed among them erratically. His surroundings warping and blurring, Galo collapsed to his knees as more biomechs closed in around him.

"Sinkua!" Nikasu screamed, swarmed and helpless, "Galo's down! They got the Serpent Bracer!"

"Get Eytea on that!" Sinkua shouted back, gaining a moment of clarity as he learned of his friend's distress, "Don't let them leave the city with it!"

Toeing the edge of a breakdown, Sinkua blazed a brutal path to Galo. He found his brother on his knees, his arm and leg soaked in blood. Predatory drones circled him, gnashing their claws tauntingly. Galo swung weakly as they lashed at his Chieftain Sage robe. Sinkua crashed the gathering, scattering them with his fiery morningstar.

"Where's Eytea?" Sinkua called to anyone who might hear.

"Perimeter duty!" Vielle shouted back, sprinting at him with scores of abominations in pursuit, "What happened?"

"Drop!"

Sinkua's medallion shone as it only had in that old recurring nightmare. The light flowed down his arms and gathered in his hands, palms throbbing and aglow with subdermal heat. As Vielle fell to her knees, Sinkua thrust his hands forth with his fingers curled and palms forward. A furious inferno erupted from his hands, roaring through the pack of voracious predators. Metal and sinew fused under the intense heat, smoke spewing from their torched bodies.

As she looked up, Vielle found Galo behind Sinkua, blood-soaked and down on all fours.

"Oh no, Galo!" she cried out, running past Sinkua, "What happened to him?"

"One got his arm. Dug in deep," Sinkua answered in short bursts, panting from the exertion, "Got Serpent Bracer. Ran off."

"We need to get out of here. We don't have time to fight them off."

"We need to get the Serpent Bracer back."

"I'll get Eytea," Nikasu asserted.

Weathering the scratches, Nikasu broke through the pack surrounding her. Lightening her body to the extent of her ability, she sprang and grabbed the bars around the lowest balcony. She pulled herself atop the rail with gymnastic agility and leapt up to the next balcony.

"Hold them off," Vielle urged as she dialed her phone.

"What are you doing?" Sinkua protested, "This isn't..."

"Spril!" Vielle exclaimed, disregarding Sinkua.

"What's wrong?" Spril answered.

"We need to get out. Galo's bleeding badly."

"Just got Elemeno. Be right there. How bad otherwise?"

"Thinning," Vielle assured, "But they got the Serpent Bracer."

"Stole or destroyed?"

"Stole. Nikasu and Eytea are tracking it."

Nikasu flailed her arms and called out from the rooftop of the apartment building.

Eytea looked around as though she heard something, but she shrugged it off as her attention shifted back to perimeter control. Nikasu drew in a deep breath and deafeningly shouted her name.

"Nikasu!" Eytea yelled back, startled by the outburst, "How did you get up here?"

"Balconies. We've got trouble."

"What's going on?" Eytea asked, lighting upon the edge of the rooftop.

"Galo's bleeding severely. A drone tore up his arm."

"Shit! I'll be come down to help cover him."

"Wait!" Nikasu urged, grabbing Eytea's arm before she could jump, "It ran off with the Serpent Bracer."

"I'll find it."

Eytea circled the perimeter, scouting for the greened relic. Nikasu bounded strategically across rooftops, her head growing light from the milystic exertion, searching within the alleyway labyrinth. On the ground, Vielle tended to Galo's injuries, wrapping his forearm in vines and vocally fending off the clutches of unconsciousness. Sinkua guarded them ardently, turning predators to prey as they dared to hunt the falling.

Minutes marched by with conditions below straining to hold steady and those above becoming ever more hopeless.

Its driver navigating the tight fit with adrenalized instinct, a familiar vehicle plowed through the alleys. It barreled through hordes of biomechs, suffering dents and scratches as it crushed the writhing beasts. Sinkua stepped aside as the car stopped in front of them and helped Vielle bring Galo upright.

"Where are Eytea and Nikasu?" Spril asked as he rolled down his window.

"Searching," Sinkua said, tipping his chin up as he and Vielle walked Galo to the car.

"Oh goodness!" Elemeno cried out, "What in the world happened to that poor boy?"

"One of those things got him," Vielle grunted, bracing her knees under her share of Galo's weight, "He's alive, but he's about to pass out."

"Hurry along. Get him in here," Elemeno urged, "Get Nikasu and my daughter back down here so we can take this young man to a hospital."

Vielle and Sinkua laid Galo across the back seat. Vielle scooted in next to Galo, sitting him up and leaning him against the door.

Sinkua shot three fireballs skyward. He waited pensively for a moment and repeated. Eytea descended shortly, her arms wrapped under Nikasu's shoulders. Sinkua got in the car and waved urgingly for them to follow.

"We haven't found the Serpent Bracer," Eytea refused, "They must have left with it."

"Young lady, get your tokus in this car," Elemeno commanded, "Your friend needs a hospital and all the love we can fit in this car along the way."

"Mom! What are you doing here?"

"Spril was picking me up from sightseeing when your friend Vielle called him. Now, get in this car."

"But we haven't found the Serpent Bracer!"

"I don't care. His health is more important."

"It's bait," Nikasu interjected, "They want us to chase them."

"They want to keep us scrambling," Sinkua added, "It's like you said, Eytea. They've been splitting us up and turning us on each other."

"You're right," Eytea sighed, "I'm sorry."

Eytea scooted in beside Sinkua, squeezing his thigh and smiling apologetically. Nikasu climbed over the back seat to sit up front between Elemeno and Spril. Eytea shut the door, and Spril threw the car into reverse. He backed out of the brick and pavement labyrinth and gunned it to the edge of the urban wasteland.

Chapter 31

Vielle stumbled out to the hall, choking back a catch in her throat. Suppressing tears behind sunken eyes, she pulled her phone from her pocket. Personnel and other guests walked by with little more than a passing glance. She dialed with shaky fingers.

Nobody answered. She hung up without leaving a message, white-knuckling her phone in blind frustration. No matter the hour, it wasn't like her to ignore her calls, especially after the evening they'd had.

Her phone rang. She answered in spite of the unfamiliar number.

"Who is this?" she opened, her nerves frazzled.

"Vielle?"

"I asked you first."

"It's me," the other person vaguely explained, "MarLys."

"Oh. I'm sorry. You sound weird."

"I'm on a landline."

"Why didn't you answer your cellular?"

"In case LenSom bugged it. SenRas said his and Malia's might be, too."

"That wouldn't surprise me," Vielle sighed, "Listen, um… Where are you guys now?"

"SenRas checked us into a hotel," MarLys answered, "He paid cash and used aliases for all of us."

"That's good. Real good. I'm glad you're safe."

"What about you? Did you find Sinkua and Eytea?"

"Uh-huh. But…"

"Great! How are they?"

"Better now. They went home. But Galo…"

"Well, that's wonderful news."

"Yes. It's great for them. Her mom's cooking a big dinner for all of them," Vielle huffed, "Look, can you come out here? I really need you tonight."

"Um, I guess I could get a cab. I don't know how much time we'll have. It's pretty late," MarLys puzzled, "Are you at home?"

"West Bend General Hospital," Vielle said, her throat catching at the mention.

"Why? What happened?"

"It's… It's Galo."

"What happened to him?" MarLys fretted, "Is he okay?"

"No, he um… Damn," Vielle spat, grasping at her last shreds of composure, "One of those things got hold of him. Tore his forearm up real bad. He lost a lot of blood. We had to wait for Spril to come get us, and um…"

"Oh no," MarLys gasped, "Is he um… You know… Did he…?"

"He went into shock. He's in a coma," Vielle whimpered, "But they don't know when or even if he'll recover."

"I am so sorry, Vielle," MarLys professed, "Did they try a blood donation?"

"No. They were going to, but Spril told them about his extra chromosomes. It's a, um, Hybrid thing. I'll explain later. Anyway, the doctor said that in his state, he'll be safer on a saline and potassium drip," Vielle explained, still confused herself, "I guess a bad donation is worse than no donation. I don't know how this stuff works."

"It's good that you're staying with him, then," MarLys said, "I'm looking up taxi services now."

"Thank you. I offered to take the first night's vigil, but I can't do this alone."

"I understand, honey. You don't have to be so strong all the time. It was nice of you to let the others go home and rest."

"They really needed it. Sinkua had hardly eaten in days. Eytea just got back from Ferya this morning. And Nikasu doesn't need this kind of stress."

"Can any of you donate to Galo?"

"No, Sinkua is the only match."

"So, why can't he?" MarLys puzzled, "Was it because he's malnourished?"

"It's um… Well partly, but that's not the main problem," Vielle muddled, "It's complicated. His blood is sort of toxic. There's also something wrong with his bone marrow, but I can't really explain it right now."

"That's okay. I'm sure he'd do it if there was a way."

"He argued with Galo's doctor for over an hour."

"Stubborn as always," MarLys chuckled, "Hey, I found an all-hours taxi service in the area. Expect me in a couple of hours, okay?"

"Thank you, MarLys."

"Get some rest until then. What room are you in?"

"4077."

"Okay, I'll be there as soon as I can. I love you."

"I love you, too."

Elemeno scraped a pile of diced onions into a bowl, plucking strays from crevices in the cutting board. She hacked off the stem off a bell pepper with swiftness and precision indicative of years of experience. As she scooped out the seeds, she stopped and breathed deeply of the piquancy surrounding her.

"Spril, be a dear and baste the roast, would you?" she beckoned.

"Okay, but then I really need to…" Spril insisted as he opened the oven.

"And when you're done with that, stir the pasta, please" Elemeno continued.

"Of course, but after that I really must get going."

"Nonsense! You haven't eaten yet."

"It's the middle of the night. Yrlis must be worried sick."

"Then call her."

"I can't. She's either sleeping or working. In either case, I don't want to interrupt her."

"Well, there you go. All the more reason to stay," Elemeno smiled, "How upset will she be if you come home this late and empty-handed?"

"Well, I suppose that would be bad," Spril mumbled, rubbing the back of his head, "I think it'd be just as bad if I showed up that much later, even if I brought dinner."

"Not the dinners I make," Elemeno said, winking, "Besides, everyone knows the best way to anyone's heart is through their stomach. Sure, they only say that about men, but we all know it's true for women, too."

"Fine, I'll stay!" Spril laughed, patting her shoulders, "I guess I did work up an appetite tonight."

"That's the spirit! Now, go sit with your friends. I'll call you when it's ready."

Spril shuffled to the living room, perturbed yet humored. Top brass of a military force renowned and respected across all of Ouristihra, and a rural woman he'd just met that morning bent him to her will. She certainly had a way of driving people, much like her late husband yet quite the opposite. It was no wonder she had been able to stand up to Kabehl.

"You might as well give up," Sinkua advised, "Once she's set on mothering you, there's no stopping her. Best to just ride it out and enjoy the meals."

"Our mother-daughter time was always spent worrying about Kabehl dropping in," Eytea explained, "So, she never really got it out of her system."

"I resent that!" Elemeno teasingly retorted.

"That's okay. We still love you," Eytea answered.

"Just the way you are," Sinkua added.

"Inside joke?" Spril asked, to which Eytea nodded.

"You guys are adorable," Nikasu laughed, "I wish I could've met you sooner. Maybe I could've seen Yahsek for who he really is."

"It's not your fault. He had all of us fooled," Sinkua said.

"They both did," Eytea agreed, "But NalSet wasn't even suspicious of Ozzera. You'd think in his position, he'd know something was amiss."

"Maybe," Spril nodded, "But he's a mechanical and electrical scientist and engineer. Not a geneticist or a spy."

"I guess recon is more Malia's forte," Eytea conceded, "If she went in with us, she probably could've warned us."

"Or Gabdur," Sinkua added, "He'd know if it was plausible for the Avatars of Fate to create and control a chimera."

"Oh yeah! She told you to find him to learn more about who she is," Nikasu recalled, "I remember because I was staring at your boots when she said it. They had blood on them."

"But why would she lead us to her enemy?" Eytea asked.

"So she could find him," Spril said.

"More to the point, so she could bring him to The Geneticist," Sinkua added, "Those guys have two and a half decades of unfinished business."

"Gabdur did call himself The Geneticist's antithesis," Eytea recalled, "So, Ozzera sent us looking for him to help her master win a rivalry?"

"This is far more than just a rivalry," Sinkua cautioned.

"Pahres was most likely in flux at the time," Spril said, "The Avatars had one of their own going turncoat on them. And they'd just outed Malia as a double agent. Ozzera may have been out to uncover whoever was taking their operatives."

Sinkua's eyes grew wide with horrified epiphany. This wasn't about a rivalry, revenge, or compensating for a failed assassination. She wasn't out to discover and execute one of the only people who could match wits with her master. Ozzera knew exactly who he was, and she wanted him alive.

"No," he exhaled, shaking his head, "It's all wrong."

"Eh? You have an idea?" Spril asked.

"The answer," Sinkua corrected, "It's the Mechanical Crypt. She wanted Gabdur as the power source."

"But it needs the Serpent Bracer to work," Nikasu said.

"Which they have now!" Eytea exclaimed.

"I know that, but I mean just getting him wouldn't have done them any good."

"She wanted him so they could kill Galo to get the Serpent Bracer," Spril clarified.

"Okay, now that makes sense," Nikasu nodded, "So, this infestation was all about getting the Serpent Bracer, then?"

"And killing Galo," Sinkua added, his lips curling into a disgusted sneer, "Still don't know if they succeeded there, but they managed to panic and scatter us again in the meantime."

"That reminds me," Spril said, "Yrlis wants blood and marrow samples from you. I have a phlebotomy kit under the driver's seat of my car."

"Okay, but why?"

"I guess I never got around to telling you," Spril said, "She translated The Diagram. It's a genome map for humans and Hybrids."

"But I thought it showed an extra pair of chromosomes," Eytea said.

"That's the Hybrid Chromosome. Everyone has it, but I guess it neutralizes itself in nearly everyone," Spril muddled, "Yrlis can explain it better anyway."

"So, she needs some Hybrid samples to map?" Sinkua gleaned.

"In that case, I'll give samples, too. It sounds fascinating," Eytea said.

"Me too," Nikasu piped up, "I mean, I have been before, but I want it done by someone who will actually do some good with it."

"You two will have to wait," Spril refused, returning his attention to Sinkua, "She's trying to synthesize a cure for your condition. Something to teach your body to fight it at a genetic level, I think."

"Tell her we need a way to clean my blood before she gets into that," Sinkua insisted, "That way, I can donate to Galo."

"I plan to. Hence why talking about him reminded me to ask you."

"She should call Doctor Ophalin in Ferya," Eytea suggested, "He has all of Sinkua's medical records and blood samples from the past five and a half years."

"Would he still have samples from that far back?" Spril asked.

"It's been almost a year since I saw him, but he still had samples from my first visit in cold storage," Sinkua said, "I don't know about ones from visits since then."

"The only reason he would save them would be so he can track the progression of the disease against your medication," Nikasu reasoned, "So he should have at least one sample from every visit."

"How would you even know that?" Sinkua asked.

"Eavesdropping on The Geneticist's lab techs," she explained, "Someone left behind a copy of the genome map when we left Ferya, and for a while after that, they saved more blood samples."

"Just so you know," Elemeno called from the kitchen, a plethora of aromas carrying her words, "I won't have all this talk of murder and disease at my dinner table."

"Do you need any help?" Sinkua offered.

"Nope. Everything's ready. You kids come eat," Elemeno said, "And no worrying over Galo, either. He's in the best hands he can possibly be in."

Throughout the meal, their conversation drifted into more casual affairs, though pensive tension still clung to them in spite of the pleasantries. Elemeno spoke at length about her sightseeing and window shopping. Nikasu laughed softly at Elemeno's excitement, hearing a reflection of herself from her first days out in the world.

By the end of dinner, crickets had begun to lose soundscape territory to the earliest predawn birds. A tinge of ruddy orange brushed the eastern horizon, seeping upward into the dying night sky. Their plates empty and bellies full, they each dismissed themselves from the table.

"Nikasu and I will clean up," Eytea offered, "Go get some rest, Mom."

"Oh, are you sure?" Elemeno asked, fighting back a yawn, "You girls have had such a long day."

"Yeah. And now we're fine. Go sit down."

"I'll get the kit from my car," Spril said, "Sinkua, wait for me in your room."

Sinkua nodded and headed upstairs, a fragment of anxiety losing its stranglehold on his mind. After nearly six years with nothing but suppressants, he spared little faith in Yrlis's approach panning out any better. If his body could learn how to fight the infection, it should have figured it out on its own by now. Instead, it had become a part of him, as though his body had assimilated the disease into itself. Nonetheless, he did trust that she could make it possible for him to donate to Galo.

Reflecting on Galo's condition brought about a whole different manner of worry. The Avatars needed the Serpent Bracer to power the Mechanical Crypt. But they also needed a member of the Chieftain Bloodline. Judging by Gabdur's story, Ebralgi had no reason to think his brother-in-law survived that night. Yet, that biomech assaulted Galo with fatal intent. It should have been under orders to take him alive, but it was perfectly content with bleeding him out to get the Serpent Bracer.

"Something wrong?" Spril asked, pulling him out of his contemplation.

"Why do you ask?"

"You've got that look you get when something's bothering you. It's more or less how you always look, but right now it's, well, more."

"What happened tonight bothers me," Sinkua opened, "Not just Galo being in a coma, but how that drone was so willing to kill him. Eager even."

"Well, I wasn't there to see it," Spril said, wrapping a length of fabric around Sinkua's arm, "But from how Galo looked and how I know you, I'll take you on your word."

"Okay well, if we're right about this being about the Mechanical Crypt, then…" Sinkua began while Spril smeared iodine on his inner elbow, "By the way, have you done this before?"

"Twice," Spril said, showing two puncture marks on his arm, "Anyway, about the Mechanical Crypt?"

"Right, they would need Galo alive to get in the room and to…"

"Say no more. I've already had the same thought."

"Do you think they know who Aleepo really is?" Sinkua asked, watching the needle disappear into his arm .

"Yes, but how?" Spril added, attaching the first vial.

"The Geneticist shouldn't have any reason to think Gabdur is alive. As far as he's concerned, Gabdur went into the woods and died alone, grieving over Zheal."

"I'll have EshCal reach out to The Coalition tomorrow. If the Avatars know about Gabdur, one of them should know how."

"I'll ask Grandpa what he can find."

"I also need to speak with NalSet," Spril said, more reminding himself, "I know what I said, but I'm not comfortable with how accepting he was of Yahsek and Ozzera."

"You really didn't seem convinced of it yourself. But really, with all their talk about there only being four Hybrids, you'd think he would be more skeptical. Yet, here comes a sixth with some weirdass beast, and NalSet just shrugs them off?"

"Yeah, it's awfully suspicious. Don't get the wrong idea. I don't expect to find out he's a turncoat."

"Although, it would explain how the Avatars knew about Gabdur," Sinkua sidetracked.

"There's a disturbing thought, someone feeding Coalition intel to the Avatars," Spril sneered, "In any case, I need to know what he chalked those two up to. Because if someone who's devoted their whole life to subverting the Avatars of Fate gleans the same wrong answers as us, what chance do we have against them?"

"It's scary as hell, but we'll just have to figure it out without them. Just like we used to do," Sinkua said, "Besides, weren't you the one who said we should assume…"

"Operate under the assumption that nobody is coming to our rescue," Spril grinned.

"So you get what I'm saying? Just because they got one over on NalSet doesn't mean we're boned," Sinkua assured, "But I do still want to know what he thought, too. If we're going to work with them, we need to know what they don't know."

"Of course," Spril agreed, plugging the last vial, "I'll give these to Yrlis and tell her about the situation with Galo when I get home."

"What about the marrow samples?"

"Yrlis will get those herself. She'll call you when she needs them."

"All right," Sinkua said, "By the way, um... thanks for, you know, saving our asses tonight."

Spril nodded solemnly and said, "That's what I'm here for."

EshCal's gaze systematically paced the eastbound Subtransit car, assessing the other passengers. Most paid her no bother. A few eyed her shrewdly. She watched them in the corner of her eye, scrutinizing their demeanor for justifications for their nosiness. But the multiplicity of circumstances surrounding her rendered passing glances of body language all but useless.

News of her suspension had gone public, agitating debate and social splintering. Explanations varied across demographics, most holding at least a shred of truth. Talk of her involvement in the Tanelenese Financial Scandal was entirely speculative though.

The train stopped, and the conductor announced their location. EshCal stood abruptly.

"Come on. This is our stop."

Biroe unlocked his wheels, and KalChi followed EshCal with him, confused but compliant. They eyed her scrutinously, wondering if her suspicion had advanced into paranoia.

"Three times enough for you?" Biroe challenged, "Honestly, I don't even think we were in danger on the first train."

"We were," EshCal insisted, walking to a bench, "The longer we spent on that train, the more likely someone could give us away."

"Wouldn't we have been safe after the first switch?" KalChi asked.

"No, they'd expect that."

"So, what now? Wait for the next train and ride it out to the docks?" Biroe guessed.

"No, they'll expect that, too. Human behavior tends to work in threes. That means they'll assume we either stayed on the third train or made three transfers," EshCal explained, "When they find out we got off the third train, they'll look for us on the next train to stop here. And that's where they'll lose the trail."

"Where will we be? Up there in a cab, or down here on a different train?" KalChi asked.

"Topside biding our time. We may still be ahead of Phylus. We can rendezvous here and finish our commute with him."

The three headed up into the night, EshCal on the stairs and KalChi and Biroe in a nearby elevator. Traffic was sparse, cars passing in broad intervals. The streets had gone dark, street lamps a rarity and the lights of commerce doused for the evening. Only an all-hours diner and a convenience store remained open.

KalChi suggested they wait near the convenience store, offering to buy snacks and drinks for everyone. Biroe insisted they'd save money and get better food from the diner, but KalChi argued that they could watch for Phylus from the curbside bench. So, EshCal and Biroe waited at the bench while KalChi sauntered across the convenience store parking lot.

"There's something I've been wanting to ask you," Biroe said, "It's about your new line of work."

"You can ask all the questions you want," EshCal welcomed, "Just know that I'm not obligated to answer them."

"Of course," he accepted, "But, well, was this your goal all along? Were you always out to bring down the Avatars?"

"I hate to admit it, but no. That's where I stand apart from Malia and SenRas. I guess it's because they had someone else to fight for. All I had was ambition."

"Hmm. I only had myself to worry about back then, too."

"If you're thinking to judge me, I'd advise you…"

"Oh no. It isn't that," Biroe insisted, "I'm just wondering, if I was as much of an asset to them as you were, if I would've done the same thing."

"I heard what you did after those soldiers killed your co-worker. I forgot her name, but I know what you did about it."

"But they had to kill someone I worked with before I even thought about doing something about it. Until then, I just put up with their crap and assumed either I'd get used to it or someone else would stand up to them."

"They hurt lots of people I worked with. Marched several hundred to their death, even," EshCal countered, 'But I still followed them because it seemed like the best idea. They helped CreSam move up the rank and file so quickly. I thought that if I worked with them, I could become the first female Brigadier General Elite."

"I'm in no position to judge. I'm sure I would have done the same thing if I thought I could make history with them. But they thought I was weak and expendable. So…"

"Well, I wouldn't exactly…"

"Can you shut up long enough for me to say I forgive you?" Biroe barked, "I'm trying to tell you I don't hold what you did against you!"

"And there it is!" EshCal laughed.

"There what is?"

"The strength you act like you don't have. You just stood up to the Brigadier General Elite, the High Minister of Defense, and a member of The Coalition, even though you can't actually stand up," she exclaimed, "Don't think you're weak just because you can't fight on the front lines. You saw the Avatars of Fate for what they really were, and you kept your head down until you could do something about it. And as soon as you saw a chance to push back, you took it and still haven't let up. If you ask me, that makes you stronger than me."

"Um, thanks," Biroe blushed, "So, what made you finally switch sides?"

"A mission at sea. Following CreSam's orders to the letter would have meant firing on a cruise liner that had drifted into international waters. I ordered my fleet to stand down, but a few ships ignored my orders and stuck to the original mission parameters. They broke formation and attacked the cruise liner."

"They shot at vacationing civilians?"

"Yes. That's when I realized what had become of ArcNos under the Avatars' control. What I would become if I stayed on the path I was on," EshCal recollected, "Most of my fleet went mutinous. I managed to rally enough support to strike them down though."

A westbound car stopped just beyond the parking lot entrance. It backed up, the silhouette of its driver looking back at Biroe and EshCal. The driver pulled into the parking lot and stepped out.

"Where's KalChi?" Phylus called.

"Getting snacks and drinks," Biroe answered, tilting his head toward the store, "Where have you been?"

"At the docks," Phylus said, joining EshCal on the bench, "Have you guys been waiting here long?"

"Just a few minutes," EshCal said, "How are things at Epsilon?"

"We held Epsilon Burger without any casualties. Can't say the same of the boarding dock. Vielle, Nikasu, and Galo pushed them away from the Subtransit entrance. Spril took them to find Sinkua and Eytea and sent me to catch up with you guys," Phylus recapped, "When I didn't see you at the docks, I realized I must have passed you."

"That was my fault," EshCal said, "I suspected someone might trail us."

314

"So you train-hopped to shake them," Phylus nodded, more confirming than asking, "I thought that may have been the case."

KalChi returned, handing out drinks as well as chips for Biroe and roasted peanuts for EshCal. Phylus furrowed his brow at his poor timing and excused himself. KalChi placed her hand against his chest to stop him.

"I saw you pull in," KalChi laughed, bringing a second bag from behind her back, "Beef sticks and Strawberry Popken."

"I see you've been talking to Malia," Phylus smirked.

"Maybe. Got you a pack of cigarettes, too."

"Always the people-pleaser," Biroe mused, shaking his head.

"I prefer to be called an overachiever."

"So Phylus, how are things on the coast?" EshCal asked.

"Not good," Phylus warned, taking a swig of his Strawberry Popken, "Chairman LenSom has declared a state of emergency. Only authorized federal personnel can leave the country. Civilian and district government docks are on lockdown."

"And for all intents and purposes, we're currently civilians," Biroe muttered.

"Exactly. So, we need a way to slip out undetected."

"I can get us there," EshCal offered, "But I need all of you need to swear to silence before I can say anything more about it."

"You had another way to get us there, but you're just now bringing it up?" KalChi accused, "Maybe I should've kept your peanuts for myself."

"That's a bit harsh," Biroe teased, "Maybe she has a private boat."

"I do, but it's at a lake down south," EshCal said, briefly sidetracking, "No, this is a piece of Coalition tech. I'm under orders not to use it with non-personnel, but I think this warrants an exception."

"What does it do?" Phylus asked.

"It'll allow us to enter The Coalition's headquarters through any door," she explained, "It can also let us leave HQ through any doors that have previously been used as an entry point. I don't understand how it works, but they have a networked memory of the doors they've been used on."

"So you could walk into that diner, come back out of it later, but the whole time you were at The Coalition's headquarters?" KalChi reasoned, trying to wrap her mind around the concept.

"Exactly, or I could walk out of any other building the tech has been used on," EshCal affirmed, "But I wouldn't use it at the diner. Too many witnesses."

"Well, if you need to scout ahead and announce us, we'll wait here," Phylus said, "I'm sure he has plenty of secrets he'd still like to keep."

"Thank you. I'll head into town and find a suitable deployment point."

SenRas and Malia trekked the dim corridor, umbral scissors splitting and crossing under the incremental sconces. They stopped at the edge of darkness, a pair of rough hands reaching out from beyond the cusp.

"Follow me," he ordered.

"Good morning, NalSet," SenRas answered as they complied, "Staying out of trouble?"

"You know the answer to that perfectly well," NalSet grumbled, guiding them through the dark, "The Omnimath is right this way."

NalSet laid his hand on the door, and an outline of blue light in the otherwise pitch black passageway granted them entrance.

Having only visited once before, SenRas took pause at the meeting chamber. His mouth slightly agape, he marveled at the intricate track lighting along the floor, the insignia on the backs of the seats, and the levitating chair at their center.

"Ah, Malia and SenRas. Welcome," Mortvill warmly greeted, leaning forward in his floating throne, "Am I to assume you received my letter?"

"Yes, but I must admit, all the only sense I've been able to make of it is that it came from you," Malia confessed.

"Ah-hm. That is most unfortunate. You just missed your friends, by the way. They left a few hours ago," he said, "They would have been much obliged to aid you, I am certain."

"Who was here?" SenRas asked, "And on what business?"

"EshCal," Mortvill answered, "She escorted three others. Non-Coalition. They required entry to Tanelen. Equal parts necessity and urgency brought them here via gate strip. It would seem someone has declared a state of emergency in ArcNos."

"What's becoming of you, sir? Are you dialing back your sense of secrecy?" Malia pried.

"I suppose I'm endeavoring to trust more willingly. They tread not beyond the sconces, nonetheless," Mortvill assured, "Now then, what business do you bring before us? I understand The Diagram has been successfully transliterated from Ancient Harkzanian to Modern Ouristihran script."

"Yes, Pahres served integral in teaching Yrlis the Harkzanian alphabet," Malia confirmed, flashing a smile to Pahres, "I believe he has compensated for any transgressions he committed as The Prophet since he joined The Coalition."

"Seeing as The Prophet failed to activate the Mechanical Crypt, I am inclined to agree," Mortvill nodded, his tone grave, "With the Platinum Orchid securely in Vielle's possession, Pahres is no longer at risk and has, as you can plainly see, been welcomed back into the fold."

"I owe both your children a debt of gratitude for freeing me of his bindings," Pahres professed, "I shudder to ponder what may have come about otherwise."

"Speaking of which, is Vielle well now?" Chekov interjected, "I understand she had something of an existential crisis."

"She's better," Malia said, "But she's still struggling to comprehend everything."

"We told her she was not meant to be and that my dichotomous existence hinges on her decisions," Pahres recollected, "And we gave her a flower which we told her will grow into an eldritch tree that spans existence. I would dare say that to be overmuch for anyone to swallow."

"I am pleased to know she is well. Should you find the opportunity, do assure her that the answers she seeks will come in due time," Mortvill implored, "What of the search for the pilfered tome?"

"We're confident it was taken to Laboratory 1341," SenRas asserted, "Sinkua set off in pursuit, but the last we heard, he was unaccounted for."

"Yes, I understand he and MalVek came to a bit of a spat. Quite unfortunate, I must say. I spoke with him on the matter, reasoning that he mustn't tempt the young man's anger."

"Speaking of which, Yrlis is trying to use The Diagram to develop a cure for him," Malia cut in, "Spril has asked to enlist help for her."

"She would be regarded as a legend were she to do it alone," Chekov reminded.

"If she wanted that, she would've gone public about her work on Spril. Instead, only her closest colleagues know the details of it," Malia argued, "You know perfectly well that she's not out for fame."

"Of course not," Chekov smiled.

"Her endeavors require she mature the Sisyphus Fir," Mortvill said, "Without its organic bonding agents, no cure will take hold. Now, what sort of help does Spril seek for her?"

"Understood," Malia nodded, "He wants to know if we can spare Gabdur and Chekov. We're also calling on Sinkua's physician, Doctor Ophalin of Ferya."

"Am I right to conclude my daughter's boyfriend knows of my work?" Chekov worried.

"Phylus deserved an explanation for my disappearance. Seeing as you forged a breakup note in my name, you were relevant to my story," Malia snipped, "So yes, he knows you and I work together. Will you help or not?"

"I will, but I can't have Yrlis knowing who I work for," Chekov insisted, "Not yet, mind you."

"If Spril already told her, I can't do anything about that," Malia shrugged, "What about Gabdur?"

"He has been under protective custody since returning from his mission on Heniokhos Boulevard," Mortvill answered, "Should Galo prove impossible to apprehend alive, they will require him to activate the Mechanical Crypt."

"Have you determined what it does?" SenRas interjected.

"I am afraid not. I must concede that it may be beyond my ken. The brothers and I have endeavored to understand it from MalVek's observations and photographs, but both have proven insufficient."

"I see. Could it have anything to do with an army of organic robots?"

"From what we know, I cannot fathom so. Why do you ask?"

"We were attacked by a swarm of biomechanical creatures yesterday evening."

"It would be a reasonable assumption to say they originated in Laboratory 1341," Mortvill said, "It is, however, theoretically impossible that the apparatus relates to them. What we know of its structure is not suited to such functionality, and both living Chieftains are, in some manner, accounted for. Had something become of Galo, you would have opened with such."

"We actually don't know what happened to any of the Hybrids. We split up during the chaos," SenRas clarified, "But I'm sure I would have been notified had anything untoward happened to…"

SenRas's phone interrupted him. Mortvill leaned back in his seat, his hairline wrinkling above an arched eyebrow behind his mask. He swept his hand forth nonchalantly, signaling for SenRas to answer.

"We believe Chairman LenSom of the ArcNosian Parliament seeks to start a war between ArcNos and Tanelen," Malia explained while SenRas took his call, "He perpetuated the financial unrest surrounding the funding of Laboratory 1341 into an economic scandal. Furthermore, he's tainted popular conceptions on both sides and is using this mutual hatred to escalate matters to a military scandal."

"Yes, I have witnessed evidence of what you speak of here. It is truly unfortunate, reopening forgotten wounds after centuries of coexistence. And through such a place as that," Mortvill sighed disdainfully, his words trailing off as though his mind wandered. His attention and his voice snapped back as he concluded, "Surely, he works for one of theirs."

"Undoubtedly. We suspect he works for The Politician."

"I agree with your deduction. We will dispatch reconnaissance to study the fallen Prime Duchess. I am also now more certain these biomechanical entities originated in Laboratory 1341. I would need to see one to speak conclusively, but I have a theory as to what they may be."

"Really? Because I couldn't tell what the hell they were supposed to be."

"I speak from an engineering perspective, not an aesthetic one. If I am correct, Ozzera was connected to a machine which used her neurological impulses and biometric activity to power and control the creatures."

"Could she really maintain all of them at once?" Malia gasped.

"She would be virtually unconscious during the process, but..."

"Sinkua is on the phone," SenRas announced, unaware he had interrupted his superior, "He's demanding answers."

"On what matters?" Mortvill asked, his forehead tightening above furrowed brows.

"He wants to know how Gabdur's cover was blown."

"What has become of Gabdur?" Mortvill pried, leaning forward.

"Nothing that we know of. Galo was maimed by one of those creatures. It took the Serpent Bracer," SenRas reported, "Sinkua said it seemed unconcerned with keeping him alive."

"I understand his logic," Mortvill nodded, "It would only slay Galo to obtain the Serpent Bracer were it aware of Gabdur's continued survival."

"Precisely. So, Sinkua wants to know how the Avatars knew."

"It could have malfunctioned," Malia suggested, "With Ozzera controlling so many of them, it's bound to happen with at least a few."

"Possibly, but it is considerably more probable that she knew it safe to slaughter the Chieftain Sage."

"He says Gabdur visited Nikasu and met Ozzera and Yahsek," SenRas said, "Could Gabdur have accidentally revealed his identity to them?"

"As I explained to your colleagues, none of us suspected their true allegiance. Even I regarded them as unforeseen allies. It is therefore plausible that his identity was revealed in that meeting," Mortvill reasoned, "At this time, however, inquiring such of him would compromise his position."

"I have another theory to pursue," Malia offered, "If Sinkua will have me as a guest again, he and I can research it together."

"He's currently visiting Galo at West Bend General Hospital. The Chieftain Sage suffered shock due to his injury and slipped into a coma," SenRas said, "I'll have him make time for you."

"Does this pertain to your tenure with them?" Mortvill asked of Malia.

"It does, sir," Malia answered, "Though I never spoke of Aleepo or Gabdur."

"Very well. Having set that particular worry to rest, I permit you the use of any equipment and sundries necessary to your research," Mortvill said, "We will also deploy surveillance and guard units to Galo's location."

Chapter 32

Sinkua shoved his phone in his pocket, sighing disdainfully. While he couldn't confirm his hunch about Gabdur, Mortvill certainly hadn't discounted it. Compounding his troubles, he couldn't fathom what alternative theory Malia would need his help to research. He had come to them for answers, and hers was to come to him.

He moved to the other side of the bed and watched the monitor. The machine beeped in a slow rhythm, accompanied by a pulsating green light. Uncountable minutes passed in eternal ephemera, vital numbers floating in tight clusters to an unchanging rhythm. Sinkua closed his eyes, inhaling deeply through his nose and licking his lips, and turned to face Galo as he opened his eyes.

"I don't know how to say this," he began, wondering if Galo could hear him, "but I think Gabdur outed himself when he visited Nikasu. Mortvill, the guy in charge of The Coalition, said they didn't know Ozzera and Yahsek were Avatar plants. I don't see how they couldn't. Isn't it their job to know?

"It's like I told MalVek. Remember? They must suck at their job is this is the best they can do. How can they say it's their job to fend off the Avatars of Fate when they're giving them this much ground? It's sickening!

"Anyway, that thing that took the Serpent Bracer seemed to be okay with killing you to get it. So, we figure whoever was responsible for them must have known about Gabdur. Spril and I think it happened when he visited Nikasu in one of their labs. Mortvill says it's plausible.

"Problem is, we can't ask Gabdur. He's under protective custody. Has been since we rescued you. Not even The Coalition knows where he is. They've broken all contact. I guess it's so nobody can trace them to each other. But I don't know how they're supposed to tell him when it's safe to return. Or keep tabs on his guard detail.

"Honestly, I don't get how those people think. Some of their ideas are so ass-backwards, it's like they ripped up pages from the Avatar codex and had a drunken gibbon staple them back together."

Grumbling in his throat as he sighed, Sinkua dropped into his chair at Galo's bedside. With the dagger gifted to him from Gijin, he chopped a tail off his bandana and set it aside on the bedsheets. He untied the bandana and evened the tails, fighting to stuff his shaggy hair under its diminished cover.

"Looks like I'll need a haircut," he mused.

Sinkua laid the swatch of fabric on his leg and rubbed his palm heel over it until it lay reasonably flat. He took off his necklace, a sharp chill piercing his sternum, and held it with the back turned upward. Bracing his elbow on his inner thigh, he dragged the blade along the rim of the medallion. Silver filings rained onto his lap as he circled the perimeter. To his annoyance, a scant few landed on the red cloth.

"I'm sorry about what happened," he said as he peeled away at the heat-softened metal, "I mean… about everything. If I told you I was going to Lenguardia, maybe you wouldn't have believed I had you arrested for war crimes. But I thought it'd be better for all of us if you didn't know. It wasn't to shut you out. We just needed a Hybrid on the outside in case something went wrong. And if that someone didn't know where the rest of us were, they couldn't accidentally lead the Avatars to us.

"And I'm sorry we took so long to find you after The Prophet got you. I feel like The Coalition wasn't really all that concerned about you. Mortvill's league of fuck-ups were all bent on getting Pahres back. You and Vielle were just a means to an end. Made me sick.

"And well, I'm sorry for letting this happen to you. I tried to help you. I really did. I don't know if you saw, but all I could do for you was hold off the drones. Vielle tended to your wounds while Nikasu and Eytea chased down the Serpent Bracer."

Sinkua collected the silver filings onto the fabric swatch, tapping them into a single mound in the middle. He plucked tiny shavings from the denim stitching of his jeans, taking particular care not to leave anything larger than an eyelash. Angling the medallion, he swiped the blade across the back of the gem, hacking away a trail of ruby dust.

This wasn't the first damage it had suffered, the sight of those old scratches conjuring memories of the end of the war. He briefly considered that this may have been the same hospital Spril and EshCal had taken him to, but he dismissed the idea as he remembered that had been a temporary Subtransit hospital. Still, thoughts of that day fortified his confidence in his task, and this seemed like the best setting for it for a number of reasons.

"They never found it, by the way. I guess that means the Avatars have it now, probably at Laboratory 1341. So now, they've got something I got from my mother and something you got from your grandfather. They know Gabdur is alive, and it's only a matter of time until they figure out you're laid up in a hospital bed.

"There's no other way to say it. This sucks. They've taken every advantage right out from under us. Now, don't get me wrong. I am damn happy we got you back, rescued Nikasu, and got Vielle over her existential crisis. But we are severely outgunned here. And whatever the Mechanical Crypt does, I'd rather read about it than see it for myself. But if they get you or Gabdur, we're not gonna have a choice in the matter."

A visitor knocked on the door, slowly turning the handle.

"We have company. Strange. I said I wanted to come alone," he told Galo, then turned his attention to the door and called, "Who is it?"

"Farim," she answered, "Can I come in? Or is this a bad time?"

"I wasn't expecting you, so it's not any sort of time," he shrugged, "Come on in."

"Hey," Farim whispered, slowly closing the door, "How's he doing?"

"Stable," Sinkua nodded, returning to his work, "You don't have to whisper. He's in a coma, not taking a nap."

"I know. It's just that, um…"

"Farim came to visit. She looks pensive," Sinkua told Galo, then turned to Farim and asked, "So, what brings you here?"

"Someone matching the description of one of the Avatars who murdered Uulan was seen in Ferya," she began, more setting the stage than informing.

"I know. The Geneticist," he cut in, "His real name is Ebralgi."

"Right. Eytea told me about him," Farim said, "I went to Elemeno's house to check on them, and her neighbor told me what happened."

"Real pity about Seschnel," Sinkua frowned, "I don't know how I'd take dying like that. Protecting someone I love. Depends what kind of closure I die with. However and whenever it happens though, I think we both know I'll go down fighting."

"I know how you feel," Farim solemnly nodded, "Anyway, I was passing by ArcNos, so I stopped over to find them and make sure they were okay."

"That was nice of you. And then you came here to check on Galo?"

"Partly. I also wanted to talk to you."

"How do I factor into this?"

"I wanted to, um…" Farim trailed off, distracted by his whittling, "Can I ask what you're doing?"

"Collecting silver shavings and ruby dust," Sinkua flatly answered, "Obviously."

"Are you, well...?" she wondered, eyes widening with sudden realization, "Is this for...?"

"Yeah. Keep it quiet. Now. You were saying?"

"My lips are sealed," Farim promised, "Anyway, I want to apologize to you."

"You didn't do anything wrong," Sinkua shrugged, "If it wasn't for you, Elemeno would be dead."

"I know. But I took Eytea away in the middle of the night. I didn't even let her wake you up to tell you. I can't imagine how much we worried you."

"Well yes. But it helped me realize what she means to me. Maybe I should be thanking you."

"I'm not about to take credit for that," Farim refused, "And I heard you got a little too distressed while she was gone. Skipping your medication? Lashing out at your friends?"

"I'm not about to blame you for the stupid things I did," Sinkua countered, "But I would have blown up at MalVek even if Eytea was home. Asshole had it coming."

"I'm sure you had your reasons," she snickered, "In any case, I'm sorry I couldn't tell you I was taking Eytea away. I knew you wouldn't be happy about it, but I'm sorry it put you in such a bad way."

"It's okay. Really. I don't think I was ever angry at you about it," he assured, "But thanks for being concerned about me."

"It's good to see you're doing better, given the circumstances."

"You should have been here a few minutes ago. I was venting to Galo about everything that's been going wrong," Sinkua said, "By the way, you said you were passing by ArcNos. You got business in the area I should know about?"

"Not in the area," Farim answered, "I'm, well, following up on a lead in Tanelen."

"Last time someone told me they were going to Tanelen and left it at that, it didn't end well," he sneered, "What sort of business do you have up there?"

"It's more personal than business, really. Too personal to go any further into it."

"More personal than a marriage proposal?"

"A different sort of personal," Farim said, "There's a reason I never talked about my past with any of the Subtransit Resistance. It's too dangerous."

"Farim. You do know who I really am, don't you? You're talking to the poster child of checkered pasts and dangerous histories," Sinkua chided, "Whatever skeletons you're dragging around, I can't be any worse off for knowing about them."

"I... don't mean it would be too dangerous for you," she corrected, eyeing him urgingly, "Understand?"

"We've gone into battle together, but you can't tell me about your past?"

"It isn't anything personal, Sinkua," Farim insisted, "I like you well enough and trust you about as much as I can trust anyone. But I can't risk information reaching the wrong ears. Even by accident. Common bloodshed doesn't always make for an airtight bond."

"Fine," Sinkua conceded, "I'll drop it for now. But whenever you've resolved whatever it is you're on about, I expect you to fill me in on it."

"I'll tell you what I can when I can," she said, "So that stuff you were saying about venting to Galo. Does it have to do with why he doesn't have the Serpent Bracer?"

"It does. Should I start there and work backward, or start when Eytea left and work forward?"

"Second one."

"By the way," Sinkua said, lifting the blade from the gemstone, "Does this make you uncomfortable?"

"Does what make me uncomfortable? Galo's injuries?" Farim asked, "I investigate strange murders. Trust me, I've seen worse."

"Not that. I mean watching me do this."

"Why would it?"

"Eytea told me I remind you of your ex-husband. She also told me how it ended," Sinkua said, "Not to prod about your past, but I thought watching me do this might stir up memories you'd rather not think about."

"Oh no, not at all. You sort of have a passing resemblance to him, but you only really reminded me of him when you and I first met. You guys act nothing alike," Farim assured, "Now then, on with your story."

MarLys and Vielle headed down the sidewalk, hand in hand. Vielle squeezed her hand, and MarLys turned her eyes toward her, her gratitude shining through in her smile.

MarLys's uncle had had her living in perpetual fear since her parents left the country. But through this fascinating woman, she had found solace from his abuses and the strength to stand up to him. Avatar, Chairman, or just another drunken bully, it no longer mattered. No measure of persecution from that spit of a man could cripple her as it once had. Not with Vielle by her side.

Vielle watched her in the corner of her eye, comparably grateful for her presence. While she had fretted over her existential crisis, rife with invalid existences and conditional identities, MarLys had anchored her with purpose. Even for all Vielle's instability, MarLys saw strength enough to lean on her shoulder and offered hers in return. Vielle silently wondered if the woman by her side knew how much she had done for her.

"How do you think they're doing?" MarLys asked, "Everyone was so..."

"Galo's in capable hands," Vielle interrupted, not hearing anything MarLys said after her question, "I'm sure he'll be okay, as long as we keep a constant vigil."

"Of course. We can't leave him unguarded," MarLys nodded.

"And with Sinkua there, he's the safest he can be," Vielle asserted.

"Of course," MarLys passively agreed, "By the way, Sinkua said he wants to talk to me when we go to visit Galo tonight."

"Really? But he barely knows you," Vielle puzzled, "Did he say why?"

"No, just that he wants to talk to me in private. In fact, he was very particular that we be alone," MarLys said, pondering his possible intentions, "But I have no idea what he might have on his mind."

"I could guess," Vielle said, "He wants to give you that talk. You know. The 'hell to pay if you hurt her' talk."

"Hm. I suppose that could be it," MarLys said, thumbing through a newsstand, "I saw how he looked at you. You're definitely spot on about his big brother complex."

Vielle flipped through an adjacent newsstand, taking passive notice of headlines as they jumped from her thumb to her fingers. Only the morning after, and already they spoke of the infestation. She contemplated if such media haste came more from ambition or recklessness.

"Here it is," MarLys announced, pulling a bundle from the rack.

"Grab us that bench, and I'll . . ." Vielle said, trailing off as she paused over a headline.

"You'll... What?" MarLys asked, puzzling as Vielle's expression turned from worry to horror.

Vielle's eyes reddened as she stared unblinkingly at the headline, the very print burning itself into her retinas. Fretting over what chaos this news would surely portend, she read down to the fold. With an anxious lump lodged in her throat, she yanked the page from its confines, recklessly fanning the rest of the newspaper.

"No way," she muttered, legs trembling as she eased down onto the cold concrete,

"No way. You have got to be kidding me. This can't have happened."

"Vielle," MarLys urged, crouching beside her, "What's wrong? What can't have happened?"

"That attack last night."

"We were there. I know we…"

"It wasn't isolated. Not how we thought," Vielle choked, "We thought they wanted the Hybrids. And the Serpent Bracer. There were two others. Didn't think of them. Oh no no no!"

"Oh geez, no. Did they get some old friends from the Subtransit Resistance?"

"One of them. Yes. They found IlcBei and JalRov among last night's victims."

"The two investors in the Tanelenese Financial Scandal?" MarLys gaped, snatching the newspaper from Vielle.

"The two being used in it, yeah," Vielle specified as MarLys scanned the article, "Rumors are gonna fly by day's end, and if the Avatars have one hand in Parliament, they've got the other in the media. They're gonna rally the people of ArcNos against Tanelen before the week is out."

"Honey, did you…"

"Hold that thought. I need to call my Dad and warn him," Vielle dismissed.

"You're right," MarLys announced, reclaiming Vielle's attention, "But they were faster about it than you thought."

"What?" Vielle blinked, "They're… already blaming Tanelen?"

"Just short of it. Says here that authorities suspect the attack was either the result of poorly managed Tanelenese military testing or their response to the financial scandal," MarLys said, "One thing they got right is that ArcNos has been working to return the money to its rightful owners. But this reads like Tanelen stole it deliberately."

"No mention of the Avatars of Fate?"

"Of course not."

"Alright," Vielle said, snatching back the newspaper, "Let's grab a bench. I'll call my Dad. You find us a good apartment."

Sprawled unceremoniously across the bed, Yrlis's eyes hesitantly flickered open. Feeling body heat radiating with hers, she reached back and groped around. A warm smile crept over her face as an arm wrapped around her shoulders. She closed her eyes and curled back against him.

"You're home," she sighed sleepily.

"Meeting ran late," Spril yawned, somewhat lying, "Did you wait up long?"

"Mm-mm. When did you get in?"

"Around three. Maybe four."

"What kept you out so…"

"I brought home leftovers," Spril interrupted, "We can warm it up for lunch."

"You're not gonna weasel your way out with some microwaved Epsilon Burger," Yrlis snipped, sheets flowing down her body as she propped herself up on her elbow.

"Roast beef, pasta primavera, and sourdough rolls," Spril countered, mirroring her posture with mock sass, "Elemeno cooked supper for us after we brought Sinkua and Eytea home."

"Well, a homecooked meal might help you," she conceded, "But I'd be more impressed if you cooked it. You still have to explain yourself."

"Let's hear about your night first," Spril insisted as he dressed himself, "Have you made any headway on understanding the Hybrid Chromosomes?"

"I stayed up late studying the genome map. I'm getting a vague working knowledge of how the Hybrid Chromosomes work into our knowledge of the human genome, but the finer points of it are still beyond me."

"I'm sure you'll get it eventually."

"I don't think you understand how much you're expecting of me. This changes everything we thought we knew about our genetics. Decades of gene theory research will have to be scrapped and reworked around this new information."

"Have you come up with any ideas about what it does?" Spril asked, "In non-Hybrids, I mean."

"Obvious answer would be that it does nothing, right? I mean, it only presents itself in Hybrids. If it did anything for everyone else, we would have seen signs of it by now. Must be inert, right? Junk code."

"Makes sense. But you're going to tell me I'm wrong, aren't you?"

"Turns out this thing isn't just tacked onto the end like a carbon signature."

"I have no idea what that is."

"It's where... Never mind," Yrlis brushed off, "Anyway, the Hybrid Chromosomes are an integral component in the human genome. It fills in gaps that we didn't even know were there."

"How can we not know they're there?" Spril puzzled, "Wouldn't they have been apparent from the eighty percent that had already been mapped. Or was that too soon to tell?"

"We had actually done just over eighty-five percent, but the general consensus was that the rest would cover all the holes. And if you didn't know any better, you'd think it was complete with the observable chromosomes."

"It looks complete, but it's not?"

"Something like that. The Hybrid Chromosomes reinforce our genetic structure. Without them, our genome would be incredibly unstable."

"Then, what is it? Our genome is stable, so we make sense of it with the genes we can observe?"

"I'm not a psychologist, but it's probably something like that. We have no reason to suspect there's more to it, so we use what we know to justify the outcome."

"Okay. So. If we look at the human genome without the Hybrid Chromosomes, it looks complete and stable," Spril recapped, "Right?"

"Only because we don't know something is missing," Yrlis reiterated, "Probably."

"But if we look at it with the Hybrid Chromosome, it looks better? Then if we remove it, we notice gaps that we didn't see before?"

"That's the layman's gist of it, yes. It makes us as sturdy as we think we are," Yrlis nodded, "So, were you able to get blood samples from Sinkua?"

"Yes, but he's not ready to give marrow samples yet," Spril answered, "Last night..."

"Why not?" she asked, lowering her brows, "I told you I need both as soon as possible."

"I know, but Galo was assaulted last night," Spril said, "He lost a lot of blood and fell into a coma."

"Shit. I swear, that man has been having the worst luck ever since we agreed to work together," Yrlis lamented, "So, you suppose we need some special method of hemodialysis to allow Sinkua to donate enough blood to bring Galo out of his coma. Is that right?"

"Yes, but Galo's doctor won't chance it with Sinkua's condition."

"Well, Galo's liver ought to be able to filter out the toxicity of any blood he receives from Sinkua," Yrlis argued, "Should be especially easy, seeing as he's never had a drop of liquor."

"Believe me, Sinkua pushed all these arguments. But the doctor still refused."

"This doctor. Did anyone mention the Hybrid Chromosome to him?"

"We did. As a precaution."

"He thinks Hybrids can only take transfusions from each other, doesn't he?"

Spril nodded sheepishly, realizing he had been wrong to trust the doctor's overly cautious judgment. Then again, none of them had known that the Hybrid Chromosome served as a clandestine stabilizer in the human genome. Just like Yrlis said, they had assumed it was inert in everyone else.

"What if you told him what we just discussed?" Spril suggested, "About the Hybrid Chromosome stabilizing the human genome? Do you think you could change his mind about using a non-Hybrid donor?"

"I can give you my writings to take to him. I'll speak to him myself if it comes to that, but I'm swamped as it is," Yrlis said, "But yes, if he comes to understand that it serves a function in non-Hybrids, he ought to let up."

"Then, let's hope your research doesn't go over his head," Spril smiled.

Yrlis swiped a Popken Lime from the refrigerator, taking note of the blood samples. She grabbed the eggs and bacon, releasing the aroma of Elemeno's leftovers from the box under them. Her stomach grumbled with equal parts hunger and anticipation. As she closed the fridge, Spril snatched the bacon and eggs out of her hand.

"I'll make breakfast," he insisted, "Go sit down. You've got a lot of work to do."

"Are you sure?"

"No. You're just revolutionizing human gene theory. No big deal."

"I... um... You know that's not what I meant," she snickered, "But I get your point."

"Besides," Spril said as Yrlis headed to the couch, "menial tasks give me time to think."

Spril turned on the stove eye and put the skillet on it. He stared at the black coil as it reddened, reflecting on the night before. Absently going through the motions of making breakfast, he thought back on the behavior of the drones and the pattern of the infestation.

When they invaded the Subtransit, they behaved with structured chaos. Patterns emerged within the bedlam. Deadly efficient predators, single units or pairs diverged only long enough to clear the fringes along their path. But as a whole, they continued eastward, only expending resources on Epsilon Burger because of the threat found there by their scouts. Spril had made them a target.

He had ascribed their panic around the apartment building to their inability to infiltrate it. Surely an impassable obstacle to their directives would set them haywire. Given their patterns in the Subtransit however, that sounded unlikely. With such efficiency as they showed at the Epsilon Boarding Dock, they would have better coordinated their efforts in the alleyway labyrinth. Instead, their behavior reminded him of what he had been told about the imperial sentinels after NalSet hijacked them.

Perhaps, he considered, their erratic behavior was better attributed to conflicting directives. They might have been trapped in a programming loop between reworking their infiltration strategy and hunting a secondary target. In fact, that explained the persistent divergence of some of the biomechs in the Subtransit.

They weren't clearing a path. They were searching for a secondary target, someone without an active Hybrid Chromosome to zero in on.

Gabdur was the most obvious answer. The biomechs hadn't been particularly given to taking prisoners, but perhaps the effort spent on a few taking him alive had rendered the rest of them unruly. But Gabdur had been in protective custody at the time, probably several kilometers from any biomech hunting grounds, somewhat thankfully. The Mechanical Crypt would remain dormant, but countless bystanders had died to see to this, unknowing of their sacrifice.

"Breakfast is ready," Spril called, mentally running down chains of association.

"Smells great," Yrlis complimented, returning to the kitchen with her half-empty Popken Lime.

"Thanks," he smiled as he handed her a plate and followed her to the table, "By the way, on the drive to the hospital, Eytea told me about their encounter with Ebralgi. You know, The Geneticist of the Avatars of Fate."

"I'm familiar. What about the old ass?"

"Well, she said his body had a pretty strange defense mechanism. It would contort and actually split open to avoid harm. But it only worked if he was aware of the threat."

"So, you need a way to sneak up on him?"

"Elemeno landed a kick to his back, but I suspect it was only because he didn't perceive her as a threat. I think the less of a threat he perceives, the less effective his defense mechanism," Spril reasoned, "But I can't exactly pit Biroe against him in hand-to-hand combat."

"Sounds like a dangerous theory to test," Yrlis agreed, "Did Eytea try to hit him from behind, too?"

"Yeah. She said his back split open just before she stabbed him. But to be fair, she did announce herself."

"Hmm. So your theory is inconclusive, but getting more data points may not be worth the risk. Quite the conundrum you've gotten yourself into, babe," Yrlis mulled, then raised her glass and said, "Welcome to the scientific community."

"That's why I'm working on another approach," Spril said, "But I need to run something by you. See if you think it's feasible."

"I don't know how much help I can be. I'm swamped as it is."

"Malia and I are recruiting help for you."

"I, um… I didn't ask…" Yrlis fumbled, "You really didn't have to."

"It was supposed to be a surprise, so I won't say who we're calling in," Spril insisted, "In any case, Eytea said she aimed for his spine, meaning his backbone split apart and mended itself."

"Shifting state bone structure?"

"Something like that, I suppose. His bones are solid, but the threatened area apparently behaves like a liquid to avoid harm. So that got me thinking…"

"The enzymes must be linked to his central nervous system, perhaps directly into visual and auditory processing," Yrlis mumbled, ensconcing herself in contemplation, "This is an incredibly ambitious and even more dangerous development."

"As I was saying," Spril cut back in, "After the war, The Scout's and The Hunter's bodies were exsanguinated and cremated. Their blood was destroyed. Their ashes were dumped in international waters. And their bone fragments were placed in high-security cold storage under the capitol building."

"For what reason?"

"Protecting the remaining organic material, so the Avatars or any sympathizers can't extract their tech from it. We also thought The Hunter's could be used to treat bone deficiencies, but the research funds have yet to become available."

"Okay, reasonable enough. But why didn't I hear about any of this?"

"It's highly classified. You're only the fourth person to know the whole story, but officially, you know nothing about it. Only the Prime Minister of Healthcare, EshCal, and myself have official clearance to this information, and we can only share it if all three of us agree to do so. The Ministry of Research and Development doesn't even know what they're hiding for us," he explained, "But if we can get The Hunter's bone fragments out of storage, do you think it would be possible to extract the reinforcing agents?"

"Possible? Yes. Plausible? No. The calcification process has most likely contaminated the enzymes," she cautioned, "But it might be possible to fill in the gaps on a partial extraction. Why? Do you think it might counteract The Geneticist's defensive enhancement?"

"I'm hoping so," Spril nodded, "If we can dope him with whatever was in The Hunter's bones, I figure one of three things will happen. One, his bones go back to normal. Two, they still shift, but it's too slow to give him a significant advantage. Three, his bones become brittle, like quenched metal."

"I suppose any of those sound plausible."

"My money is on the second, but I'm hoping for the third."

"So, do you have a plan to get the fragments?" Yrlis asked, "You can't ask the Prime Minister of Healthcare without revealing that you talked to someone else about it. EshCal can't enter the capitol building without drawing suspicion. And I'm sure Parliament has you under a microscope, looking for a case against you."

"I know they do," Spril agreed, "But I have a couple of people in mind for the job."

Sinkua slid down the armchair and propped his outstretched legs on the footrest, lying down as best as he could manage. The lights dimmed and his eyes dimmer, he clicked aimlessly through television channels. Every news station flashed cinematic portrayals of the biomech infestation, all but glorifying the carnage.

He sneered as he muted the set. Still watching the screen in the corner of his eye, he turned his attention to the door. It didn't move. Hadn't for hours. Not since the last check-in. He looked at the clock. They were running late.

"Can you believe this?" he asked, "They're covering the attack from last night on the news, right? Well, every time they update the death count, they sound like they're bragging about it. Or they're proud of it. Of course, nobody mentions the Avatars of Fate. Or the Chieftain Sage getting laid up in a hospital. Guess I shouldn't be surprised though. The media hasn't tried to visit you that I know of.

"Newspapers might have better details. They usually do, you know. There's so many of them, that's where the leaks always crop up when there's a cover-up. Vielle said she was going to look for an apartment with MarLys today. Maybe they noticed something.

"Honestly, I don't even know what I want to see. A sign that they're paying attention? That they care? Something that doesn't glorify the killing? That might be it. I guess everyone loves a winner. Even if the winner is a monster."

The television still silenced, he stopped on a medical drama. Too lost in thought to notice the lack of dialogue, he watched the cast lip-sync their roles for a few minutes. Finally noticing the silence as the show broke to commercial, he unmuted the set.

"I wonder how Yrlis is doing," he continued, "I don't know what you think of her these days, but I really think she's our best shot at getting you out of your coma. Maybe Gabdur could help, but I don't think it's safe for him to come here.

"In any case, you'd better wake up soon. I've got something big planned, and I need you to be awake for it. Farim's the only other person who knows about it, and that was an accident. MarLys is going to help, but I'll only tell her if she figures it out."

The handle clacked and turned, and the door creaked open. Someone peeked inside.

"Speaking of which," Sinkua grinned.

"Can I come in?"

"Are you alone?"

"Yeah. She's at the vending machines."

"Come in."

MarLys stepped inside and shut the door. She turned up the lights, Sinkua shielding his eyes, and frowned at the sight of Galo. Her soft features tightened into hard lines of bitter sympathy. He hadn't moved since that morning, and that morning, he hadn't moved since the night before.

"I've been thinking," she said, keeping her eyes on Galo, "Trying to figure out why you would want to talk to me alone."

"I'm sorry if I made you nervous," he said, sipping his Cherry Popken, "That wasn't my intention."

"It's okay. I understand what she means to you."

"...You do?"

"Yes, and you don't have to worry. I'm not going to hurt her," MarLys assured, compounding his confusion, "I know we haven't been together long, but I feel like we have long-term potential."

"What are you talking about?"

"Oh, come on! Sometimes, you just know these things," MarLys said, mustering the courage to make eye contact, "I'm sure you and Eytea knew it from the day you met. I bet nobody had to give you that talk."

"What are you...? Oh, I know what it is," Sinkua said, "You think I asked you here to give you the 'hurt her and I'll break you in half' talk, don't you?"

"Vielle called it the 'hell to pay if you hurt her' talk, but yes," MarLys snickered, "Well! Now that I've thoroughly embarrassed myself."

"No, you haven't. You had a good reason to think that's what this was about," he shrugged, "But you girls look happy together. Genuinely happy. I know you won't hurt her."

"Thank you. She really is something, huh?"

"Someone else here thinks so. Did she tell you Galo had a crush on her during the war?"

"Yeah," MarLys laughed, "But she also told me I don't have to worry about him trying to snake on her."

"No, he isn't like that," Sinkua confirmed, "And just so you know, it took Eytea and me a long time to feel that way about each other. But now that we've been there for a few years, I need your help."

"Relationship advice?" MarLys asked, "I guess a lesbian would be the best choice. I mean, if you want to know what a woman wants in a relationship, who better to ask than a woman in a relationship with another woman?"

"Hah! Well, that's a good point," he said as he took the bundle of red fabric from the windowsill, "But, you're still wrong. I need you to deliver something. Privately."

"This isn't anything, y'know," MarLys sneered as he tossed the bundle to her, "unpleasant?"

"What?" Sinkua recoiled, "Why would you think that?"

"My uncle was having me make deliveries off the books," she explained, "I recently found out he's in cahoots with the Avatars of Fate."

"This is nothing like that. Who's your uncle, anyway?"

"LenSom. You know him from Parliament."

"Yeah, I've met the bastard. I wouldn't want to live with him either," he said, "But back to my request, I just want this handled by as few people as possible. No strangers manhandling it and losing it in a sorting facility."

"Am I allowed to know what it is?" she asked with a mischievous smile.

"Only if you can figure it out from this," he challenged, handing her a sealed envelope.

MarLys read the address and crookedly pursed her lips. Her eyes bounced between the envelope, the red bundle, and Sinkua's face. He tried to keep his expression neutral, but a smile cracked through his defenses as her eyes trailed down his neck. In a fit of epiphany, she grabbed the medallion and turned it over.

"Oh no way!" she squealed, "Did you seriously?"

"Took a while, but yes," he grinned, "But it's not like I've had much else to do in here."

"And you're really going to?"

"I'd be stupid not to."

"Oh wow. This is just…" she stammered, "This is so romantic! I never thought a man could think this way!"

"I'm not sure how to take that."

"It's a compliment, I promise."

"If you say so. Anyway, keep this a secret, okay?"

"Of course. Of course! Does anybody else know?"

"Just Farim, but she walked in on me and figured it out. Damn detectives," he said, shaking his fist in mock discontent, "But she promised to keep it a secret, too."

"Aw, now I feel special!" she beamed, "How soon do you need it done?"

"No rush. My biggest concern is that Galo is conscious when I do it," Sinkua said, "The specs are in the envelope, along with a signed blank check and a letter giving you permission to write in the amount up to a specified limit. I asked one of the doctors to notarize it for me."

"You've certainly thought of everything."

"I've tried to be thorough. I don't know how much to pay you though."

"For this? Oh, you don't have to pay me, sweetie," she insisted, "I'm just honored to be a part of this."

"Honor doesn't pay the rent," he asserted, "Do you get paid per hour, per delivery, distance, weight, what?"

"It's a combination of a lot of factors. I don't know the formula, but I'd ballpark this at about fifteen iolas both ways."

"Fifteen? That's all?"

"I ride a bicycle, so I get less for vehicle maintenance and no recharge comp," she explained, "But if you opted for value-of-package insurance, you'd pay more, so I'd get more in my commission."

"Oh, okay. Well, I can't afford that value-of-package business, but I'll pay you sixty iolas for the whole job," he offered, "Thirty on confirmation of delivery. Thirty when you bring back the finished product."

"That's awfully generous of you," she remarked, "Not that I'm complaining."

"Well, this is important to me. And you have Uncle Bitchboy to get away from," Sinkua reasoned, "Anyway, I'm going home. You and Vielle have fun."

"Thanks. I'll see you later," MarLys smiled, "Say goodnight to your fiancée for me."

Chapter 33

Yrlis tucked the knot of Spril's necktie behind his collar. She adjusted his coat, symmetrically framing his navy blue tie. Meticulous well beyond necessity, she plucked at strands of dust between the stitches.

Spril pulled her hand away and kissed it.

"I'm going to be fine," he said, patting his breast pocket.

"You don't know people in the scientific community like I do," she argued.

"I know the one I need to know well enough."

"No. Seriously," Yrlis said, "We hate to be told we're wrong. Everybody does, but we're expected to take everything objectively. That just makes it harder not to get attached to our theories. A lot of us take them very personally."

"Honey," Spril beckoned, squeezing her hand, "What you just said really didn't make any sense. I know you think it did, but..."

"Hey, don't patronize me," she snipped, stifling a laugh, "You know what I mean. Forbidden things are more tempting."

"That I understand. So, I need to ease him into it?"

"Definitely. But most importantly, remember that you're just the messenger. Don't let him think you had any part in this. Not even with collecting the samples."

"Are your colleagues really that defensive?"

"It's not about that. If he thinks any part of this came from someone without a medical or otherwise scientific background, he won't listen. It's just how we are."

Spril nodded with partial understanding. From one perspective, he empathized with the tendency to offer less credence to outsiders. Someone of lesser acumen shouldn't be able to prove him wrong or outperform him. Looking from another angle, that kind of stubborn myopia sometimes blinded specialists from considering alternative outlooks.

Absent any military background, Sinkua and Galo had led multiple successful assaults against the imperial war machine. They demonstrated that acumen need not come from formal training. Then again, Spril knew he had a unique perspective afforded to few. He had enlisted in ArcNos's military with no official relevant extracurricular activities to his name. Yet he had ascended the ranks so meteorically as to all but outrun formality and rigor.

Sitting in the car with the radio turned low, he pulled the papers from his pocket and unfolded them. On first sight, his jaw slacked and pupils dilated. After all their discussions, he fathomed himself to have a conversational grasp on the material. Just from the first paragraph of Yrlis's report, he realized that saying she dumbed it down for him was a kindness.

Of course, her ability to express these principles in layman's terms only further proved her grasp of them. Nonetheless, Spril felt lost in the incomprehensible jargon, doubting his pronunciations only slightly more often than he doubted if they were words at all. Unaware of the escaping minutes, he read deeper into the report, trying to find the conversational grasp he had always assumed he had.

He noticed the clock as he scratched the back of his neck. If he spent much longer in the driveway, he would miss the gap in morning traffic. Huffing with bewilderment and awe, he returned the papers to his pocket and backed out of the driveway.

He clicked through radio stations as he drove, looking for something tolerable. On any other commute, music served little more purpose than to occupy the silence. His swamped mind and frazzled nerves, however, made the tiniest nuisance insufferable.

As he pulled onto the highway, he stopped on a news station, probably a bad idea on any day. Though he had no interest in listening to polarizing drivel, at least the anchor spoke with a mellow cadence, absent the manufactured outrage typical of his colleagues. Once he had a free hand again, Spril reached to change the station, only to turn up the volume as something caught his ear.

The anchor's voice becoming unsettled, he recapped the abrupt appearance of bizarre murderous creatures two nights prior. Another day had afforded emergency responders and investigators time for more thorough assessments and concise explanations. More importantly to the media machine, it had also afforded sensationalists and crackpots time for more scare tactics and conspiratorial waxings about shapes, colors, and numbers that may or may not have been relevant.

The reporter proclaimed, with a heavier grain of authority than he should have been allowed, that anonymous analysts had all but confirmed Tanelen's involvement. His connecting it to the Tanelenese Financial Scandal held a sense of likely inadvertent truth, but it fell apart with his misunderstanding of the affair. He, like most ArcNosians, believed Tanelen's tax money embezzlement to have been deliberate. That combined with their advanced technology made blaming Tanelen for the deaths of IlcBei and JalRov, thousands of collateral fatalities, and several million iolas in property damage became easy. In fact, it sounded downright sensible.

Spril jabbed the radio, switching to a white noise frequency and turning it off with his knuckles. Five years dormant, and Ouristihra had all but forgotten about the Avatars of Fate. To many people, they had only ever been an urban legend back then, but several press releases had since confirmed both their existence and their hand in Imperial ArcNos.

Reluctant as he was to admit it, he had also grown complacent in the half decade of peace. As weeks passed with no sign of the Avatars, the new administration had come to believe their victory had wrecked the machine and ruined the beast. With the chaos they had wrought in a few weeks' time though, he knew they had spent that time silently orchestrating further sabotage.

The new administration had worked to rebuild after the war in ArcNos and beyond. Phylus and Calhosin, the High Minister of Foreign Affairs, had mended relations with their neighbors, achieving peace initially tenuous but fortifying with time. Spril and EshCal had restructured the military to prevent a relapse of regrettable history. Biroe and KalChi had reworked the budget to guide the receding economy away from catastrophe. Some immersed themselves more deeply in their prior lifestyles while others found entirely new purposes. But all of these efforts at restoration had played into the Avatars' machinations.

While peace had bred complacency, the Avatars of Fate had regrouped their forces and reassessed their methods. Just as they had done to create Imperial ArcNos, they had nudged the levers and greased the gears to engender circumstances suited to their agenda. And as ArcNos stood on the cusp of instability and recovery, they set their masterpiece into motion.

Spril realized they had only achieved as much of a semblance of security as the Avatars permitted. Enough to maximize the damage when they collapsed the floor, dropping everyone into their chaotic designs before anyone of consequence could scramble for footing.

Disgruntled and sweaty, he tore into the parking lot and hunted for an open space. Once he claimed one, he thrust himself from his car and stormed up the lot. He loosened his necktie as he walked, his gait rumpling the pleats in his slacks and wrinkling his coat.

Inside the hospital, he moved with such purpose that nobody thought to hinder him, not even to offer help. His memory of the layout still vivid, he bypassed the directory and quickly found the elevator to the trauma ward. Tapping his foot on the elevator floor, he slapped the fourth floor button and jabbed the door close button.

On the fourth floor, he shouldered unrelentingly past medical personnel, orderlies, and administrative staff. As far as he cared, every one of them blamed Tanelen for the attack and wrote off the Avatars of Fate as a fictional scapegoat. To hear some tell it, Galo's hospitalization had been a Tanelenese plot to agitate virtually nonexistent unrest between Berinin and ArcNos.

Spril opened the door to Room 4077 and peered inside. Galo lay as he last saw him, his forearm heavily bandaged. Machines beeped and hummed in steady rhythms, the absence of disconcerting noise boding about as well as could be hoped for. A visitor maintained the vigil, but there were no medical personnel in the room.

"Oh hey, Spril!" Nikasu called out, "I didn't know you were coming today."

"Hey, Nikasu," Spril answered, "Where's Doctor Macal?"

"Nurse said he spends too much time in the lounge," she said, Spril shaking his head with disgust, "Oh, Eytea's here, too. She's in the bathroom. You know, in case you want to wait and..."

"Didn't come to visit," he interrupted, his patience running a deficit, "Here on business."

"Okay, well... Maybe when... You know..." Nikasu trailed off, dejection consuming her voice.

"I'll stop by when I'm done," Spril said, forcing a smile and stymying his anger since she'd had no part in it.

Spril continued up the hall, moving with such purpose that others swerved around him without any apparent thought. Room numbers and names passively filed themselves into his memory through the corners of his eyes. He stopped beside the door to the lounge before consciously realizing he had found it.

An angry stranger threw the door open and stormed into the lounge, briefly drawing the ire of the resting staff within. Their ire was drawn only briefly however as they shrugged him off as a disillusioned next of kin. He had come to the wrong place. Human resources had programs for his sort.

"I'm looking for Doctor Macal," Spril announced. Finding his presence ignored, he shouted, "Macal!"

"Y-Yes?" someone answered.

"You're Doctor Macal?" Spril asked with an accusatory cadence as he approached the back of the couch.

"Present," the squat Haprianite confirmed, "What can I do for you, sir?"

"You're Galo's doctor, right?"

"I'm sorry, but I have several patients right now. You'll need to..."

"Two nights ago. Lacerations. Coma."

"Sorry, but that describes many of my..."

"4077!"

"Ah yes, the Berininite coma patient," Doctor Macal answered, unsettlingly indifferent and ignorant of Galo's standing, "I have his file here on the table."

"This one here?" Spril baited, moving to the front of the couch, "This one on top?"

"Yes, that's the one. I was about to look it over, just as soon as the next commercial break comes along."

Spril swiped the manila folder from the table. Doctor Macal lunged to his feet in protest.

"Not anymore," Spril asserted, swatting the top of Macal's head with the file.

"That is classified information, sir!" Macal huffed, "As Galo's doctor, I must forbid you to read or tamper with it."

"You're not his doctor. Thirty seconds ago, you didn't even know his name."

"If you want a different doctor for him, you will need to prove kinship or otherwise authorizing affiliation and file a formal request with human resources."

"How about I file a formal back of my hand across your face?"

"Sir, I understand your concern," Macal asserted, "Just know that I am doing everything in my power to help your... brother?"

"He's not my... Do I look like a Southlander?" Spril snapped, their argument drawing an audience, "But besides that, no you're not."

"I'm sure there's plenty you think I can do, but I promise I'm..."

"Denying him a blood transfusion?"

"Ah yes," Macal nodded, "I understand you disagree with my decision. I know it's difficult to be objective when the patient is close to you. I try not to get attached to my patients, but..."

"Cut the canned empathy. Just tell me one thing," Spril said, "How many pairs of chromosomes does a pig have?"

"Nine...teen," Macal answered, shrinking back toward the couch.

"Right. Now, by a show of hands, who here has saved a patient's life with a pig organ?"

Roughly a dozen doctors raised their hands.

"I see your point," Macal conceded, "Even though he possesses an anomalous twenty-four pairs of chromosomes, the patient can accept a transfusion from a donor with the human standard of twenty-three. I will assign a nurse to search the donor database."

"No. You won't. His new doctor will," Spril asserted, "By a show of hands, who already thought Doctor Macal was a jackass before now?"

More people than before raised their hands. Doctor Macal sank deeper into the couch. Spril made his way to the doctor who appeared to agree the most eagerly and handed him the folder.

"What's your name?" Spril asked.

"Tiban, sir," the doctor answered, offering a solid handshake.

"Nice to meet you, Doctor Tiban. My name is Spril."

"I know," Doctor Tiban nodded, "I recognize you."

"It's about time somebody did," Spril laughed, presenting Yrlis's report, "Well seeing as you're Galo's doctor now, I was asked to deliver these papers to you."

"Something pertaining to his case, I presume?"

"Yes and well beyond that. It pertains to that twenty-fourth pair of chromosomes."

"I'm sure it's a fascinating read," Tiban smirked, waggling the papers, "I'll start on it over the rest of my lunch."

"Well, I hope it makes more sense to you than it did me," Spril said, piquing Doctor Tiban's curiosity.

"Don't trouble yourself if it's beyond you. Genetics is a pretty complex topic, and this promises to be all the more so," Tiban said as he skimmed the first page. He thumbed back to Galo's file, glanced it over, and added, "But I should warn you, we've hit a shortage of compatible donor blood."

"Well, the doctor who wrote this has been working with a potential donor who also has a visible and active twenty-fourth pair."

"I believe you mean present and active?"

"Actually... You know what? Just read her report."

"I know what this is about," Macal cut in, "This is about that contaminated donor with the unkempt hair and the costume contact lenses."

"Those were his real eyes, and no, this report isn't about him," Spril countered, then tauntingly added, "But her next one might be."

"You're trying to bring a bag of his blood in here!"

"Shut up, Macal," Tiban flatly objected, "As Chieftain Sage Galo's doctor, I forbid you to interfere with his case."

"Chieftain…?" Macal puzzled, his manner becoming bitter, "Well, this guy doesn't have the authority to reassign his doctor. He needs to file with human resources just like everyone else. But if you want to toss in that heap of conspiracy drivel, you'd better lawyer up while you're at it. Because his…"

Tiban's eyes widened as he noticed the name on the letterhead. Not only had the subject famed among neurologists and geneticists come to him. The missive he delivered came from the very doctor who had revolutionized stem cell reconstructive surgery.

"Macal!" Tiban interrupted, shutting down the squat Haprianite's protest, "Do you have any idea who these people are?"

KalChi sat on the foot of the bed, resting her chin on her crossed forearms behind Biroe's shoulders. Biroe clicked through the television channels, hastily passing daytime soaps and syndicated dramas. He stopped on a local news station, curious about Tanelen's perspective on the events in ArcNos.

EshCal stepped out of the bathroom with her hair wrapped in a towel, a cloud of steam wafting with her movements. She tightened the complimentary robe and leaned against the wall.

"Have they said anything about the biomechs yet?" she asked, nodding to the television.

"We just got to this channel," Biroe answered.

"Hmm? What about the biomechs?" Phylus grumbled, sitting up on the couch.

"Hey, you're awake," KalChi teased, "Good morning."

"Okay, everybody shut up," Biroe hissed, "The international segment is coming up."

Phylus propped himself somewhat upright and leaned on the armrest. He blinked away fatigue as his eyes acclimated to the light from the television.

EshCal shed the robe, her slender physique framed by boyshorts and a tanktop, and dressed herself. With Phylus half-asleep and Biroe's unwavering fidelity to KalChi, she found no discomfort in her state of partial undress.

The international segment opened with news about ArcNos. They recounted the outbreak of creatures made of flesh, masonry, and machinery, using borrowed footage to confirm yesterday's rumors. Dynamic death toll estimates ranged from the upper hundreds to the lower thousands and climbing.

"They might not know about IlcBei and JalRov yet," Phylus noted, recalling his phone call from Vielle.

"Depends how entrenched their investigators are down there," KalChi noted, "They're recycling clips from ArcNos's broadcasts, so they can't be that deep."

Biroe pressed his finger to her lips, urging her not to encourage Phylus's disruptive ponderings. KalChi stopped and shrank back, mildly embarrassed.

The anchor segued into a discussion with a local robotics engineer. He asserted that, despite assumptions from their southerly neighbors, Tanelen could not have been involved in the attack. Extrapolated from collected remains, exploded structural diagrams of the biomechs showed their design did not match any of the styles of any of the top robotics firms in Tanelen. None of the lesser firms would have had the resources to dispatch so large a supply in one night.

That much showed promise. If they could introduce this information in ArcNos, Tanelen would be absolved of suspicion of involvement. Their greatest trouble would be finding a politically neutral ArcNosian scientist to endorse the information. Someone the people would trust not to be speaking out of partisan favor.

Hopes of preserving coexistence deteriorated as the anchor proceeded to a report from a political analyst. She correctly interpreted the event as an inside job, but she misrepresented it as an affront against Tanelen.

The political analyst based her assertion on IlcBei and JalRov having been among the victims, both evidently hunted quite aggressively. Biroe turned up the volume as she recapped the financial scandal. Local knowledge dictated the tax money from those equity payments to be the rightful property of Tanelen. Neither incriminating nor absolving the embezzlers, the information had been distorted to claim that IlcBei and JalRov held offshore accounts in Tanelen.

This meant two highly affluent ArcNosians had been paying taxes to another country, a decision that might offend their unstable homeland government. Also, by rerouting the funds to IlcBei's and JalRov's ArcNosian accounts, ArcNos's Ministry of Treasury had stolen tax revenue from Tanelen. Circling back to the biomech blitzkrieg, the anchor and political analyst concluded that ArcNos had killed their own citizens to silence them and prevent Tanelen from reclaiming the tax revenue.

"How did they even…?" KalChi stammered, "How did they come up with those two having accounts here?"

"Bullshitting," Biroe muttered, turning off the television.

"This is going to complicate our meeting with Noble Doyen Joren," EshCal warned, "But if we can prove IlcBei and JalRov weren't connected to the account, we should be in the clear."

"The account is held anonymously," Biroe reminded, "But we have a paper trail beginning at JalRov's and IlcBei's accounts in ArcNos."

"We need to approach this with needle-threading diplomacy," Phylus cautioned, "If they suspect even the slightest accusation, any chance of peaceful resolution will likely fall off the table."

"Biroe and I will emphasize that we've found the scandal to have been the work of independent agents not acting on behalf of any government," KalChi said.

"Good, but avoid all mention of the Avatars of Fate until we've secured their cooperation," EshCal said.

"Why?" KalChi puzzled, "I thought the purpose of this trip was to enlist their support against the Avatars."

"In part, but circumstances have necessitated changes to our approach," EshCal countered, "Since the Avatars are said to operate out of Tanelen, they're a very sensitive topic here. Relations being as dicey as they are right now, if we mention them prematurely, Noble Doyen Joren may accuse us of implicating a black ops branch of his government."

"After you prove that the money started in ArcNos, just let me take over the conversation," Phylus insisted, "This is what I came here to do."

"Well, you have an hour to prepare your report," EshCal said, nodding to the clock.

They immersed themselves in various tasks, squeezing final preparations into their last hour. Biroe and KalChi arranged their papers for optimal presentation, their quiet discussion occasionally elevating to brief arguments. Phylus scrawled on a notepad, bringing order among the two nations' conflicting accounts and the actual events. True to her guard escort charade, EshCal cleaned her epee and pistol. Despite multiple polishings since then, traces of the assault on Epsilon still lined her blade.

Precisely as scheduled, a knock came at the door at noon. EshCal opened it to a bespectacled gentleman in a black suit. He silently motioned for them to follow him and turned away with no more acknowledgement than Phylus beginning to rise from the couch. Sensing the silent messenger's absence of patience, KalChi pushed Biroe's wheelchair.

They rode the elevator to the ground floor in discomforting silence. KalChi and Biroe kept their eyes cast downward, avoiding eye contact via the reflections in the door. EshCal and Phylus surreptitiously studied the messenger's demeanor. The messenger disregarded the lot of them, simply staring straight ahead as though fascinated by his reflection.

The messenger led them into a private conference room behind an unmarked door and left without announcement or salutation. Tanelen's Noble Doyen waited at the head of the table, flanked by two suited guards. A cordial yet plastic smile spread over his face at the sight of his guests.

"Well well, this certainly is a curious development," he greeted, standing and approaching them.

"It's an honor to meet with you again, Noble Doyen Joren," Phylus professed, slightly bowing his head.

"Likewise, sir," Joren answered, offering a handshake, "I'll need to speak with my personal assistant once we've concluded affairs here. Well-meaning as he may be, the fool only said I was to receive representatives from ArcNos. He failed to mention that my guests would be of such caliber."

"That may be because we're not here in any official capacity," KalChi explained, "We came of our own volition. Independently."

"Yes, I'm familiar with the recent cullings of your administration. Hence why this meeting is so curious," Joren said, "Though, I must admit, I am not familiar with you, young miss."

"My name is KalChi. It's a pleasure to meet you, Noble Doyen Joren, sir."

"Ah, of course. Your name is familiar, but I hadn't a face to place with it," Joren clarified, "I must apologize for the guards. Necessary precautions of ambiguous arrangements."

"No need to apologize," EshCal excused, "I've come primarily as a guard escort, should diplomacy fail."

"The four of you have been chastised and expelled by a government we have found to be corrupt," Joren reminded, "Only by one of us pledging allegiance to the state of that administration may diplomacy fail at this juncture."

"My allegiance is still to that administration. We all endeavored to build it following the ArcNosian Civil War," EshCal said, "Our qualms are with individuals and what they have wrought within it."

"I'm afraid I require further insight before I might weigh in on the matter," Joren insisted, his brow wrinkling, "Be that as it may, what have you come to discuss with me?"

"I assume you're familiar with the nature of the ongoing economic scandal between our nations," Biroe asserted, "You are also familiar with famed philanthropists IlcBei and JalRov, correct?"

"Yes, they've generated considerable buzz among the citizenry," the Noble Doyen nodded, returning to his seat as Phylus, EshCal, and KalChi took theirs, "My sources inform me that one of them was a co-signator on a domestic account."

"I'm aware of the rumors concerning their patronage with certain Tanelenese banks, Mister Noble Doyen. I also understand your discontent over losing the tax revenue generated by those accounts," Biroe said. He presented the paperwork to Joren and continued, "However, our research shows that the monies were originally to be deposited in accounts held in ArcNosian financial institutions."

"We have not concretely determined who has been intercepting the transactions," Phylus added, "but we are confident that they were acting without the endorsement of either of our nations."

Joren accepted the papers and thumbed through them, waving one of his guards over to read them over his shoulder. They mumbled to one another for a few moments until the Noble Doyen dismissed the guard and returned his attention to his guests.

"Very well. I concede this as proof of ArcNos's entitlement to the disputed tax monies," Joren agreed, "Be that as it may, our records indicate JalRov as a co-signator on the domestic account ultimately receiving the disputed funds. I believe this paperwork should prove as sufficient evidence to our assertion."

On Joren's signal, the second of his flanking guards produced a file from a briefcase and handed it Biroe. The incriminatory account number etched into his memory, Biroe found them identical. His eyes darted about the page, searching for evidence of forgery but finding none.

"I must confess our ignorance of JalRov's involvement," Biroe said, "We'll need time to study this information before we can discuss his actions further."

"Despite multiple attempts to reach JalRov, we only succeeded in speaking with IlcBei. In fact, she contacted us during the initial stages of our investigation," KalChi added, "But if JalRov was an insider, that would account for our inability to reach him."

"Indeed it would," Joren nodded, "It would also, however, entitle Tanelen to approximately half of the generated tax revenue."

"Whether Biroe and KalChi or their as yet undetermined replacements, our Prime Minister and High Minister of Treasury will determine Tanelen's share with the utmost priority," Phylus offered, "I should implore you to assign representatives of your Treasury Department to run calculations for verification purposes. Compensation will be disbursed upon our two Treasuries reaching an agreement."

"As much as I appreciate the sentiment, I'm afraid it will prove insufficient," Joren sighed, "More to the point, it comes too late."

"How do you suppose?" Phylus calmly asked, his eyes darting aside as he glimpsed EshCal bringing her hand to her hip, "I apologize for any impact the misplaced tax revenue has had on your economy, but you must understand that this has been the result of an error which we are endeavoring to correct."

"As you saw, our research showed the account to have been held anonymously," Biroe added, drawing a sharp glare from Phylus.

"JalRov's silence notwithstanding, we had no evidence to suggest either of them had their name on that account," Phylus said, "If he wished his income to contribute to the further advancement of Tanelen, he could and should have done so in a less contrived manner. The chosen methodology created disorder unbecoming of the analysis drawn from his background report."

"Murderers rarely seem capable of such atrocities before they have their first victim," Joren sharply mused, "I did not know this JalRov nor this IlcBei. Not personally. Most would find suspicion in ones so grandly philanthropic. To say malice would be readily ascribed may go beyond rationalization, but many would speculate their generosity to have been a façade."

"Having personally worked with IlcBei as representatives of Parliamentary ArcNos, I can attest that she truly was as charitable as she appears on paper," Phylus said.

"Yes, I'm familiar with her work within the Subtransit Resistance, as well as your own and this gentleman's. Biroe, correct?" Joren said, a tinge of derision lacing his voice, "I'm also familiar with EshCal's tenure with Imperial ArcNos and the coup she staged against them upon the eleventh hour. Or rather, when it best suited her agenda."

"What are you implying?" EshCal asked, her eyes betraying the scowl she suppressed.

"You are an ambitious lass. Always have been. Just as then, you've shown yourself as a turncoat upon the precipice of political unrest. It causes wonder as to your aspirations and, more pertinently, true allegiances."

"I have never turned against my government. Then just as now, I acted against corruption wrought by individuals within it."

"Of course, of course. You wouldn't think to stoke both sides of a conflict, no matter your potential gains," Joren dismissed, "I apologize for inciting this tangent as well as for so debasing your character. I intended no such implications as to draw your ire."

"You were asserting how some might find IlcBei's and JalRov's philanthropy to be suspect," Phylus reminded, "From what you know, what is your take on them?"

"With your endorsement, I trust IlcBei as she appears on paper. JalRov, however, is rather an enigma, given his duplicitous involvement," Joren reasoned, eyeing EshCal, "Our greatest trouble, however, is with ArcNos's treatment of them."

"No doubt, you speak of the recent dispatching of biomechanical drones," Phylus deduced, "Research is ongoing as to the party responsible for this tragedy."

"According to our reports, it was an inside job."

"May I ask where these reports originated?"

"Why, with your ever-ambitious High Minister of Defense, of course," Joren said, sweeping his hand toward EshCal in mock reverence, "It would seem the irrevocable title of ArcNos's first female Brigadier General Elite has proven too lowly an aspiration for her mark on your nation's history."

"EshCal, is this true?" Phylus asked with a practiced calmness.

"Yes, but the report has been decontextualized," EshCal defended, addressing Joren, "I clearly indicated that Chairman LenSom has been exploiting circumstances and creating scandals to advance what would be an otherwise unendorsed agenda. I also predicted he would wrongly implicate Tanelen in the outbreak, thus absolving Tanelen to those present."

"Meaning this was the work of ArcNosian representatives. LenSom is Chairman of your Parliament, correct?" Joren baited, drawing EshCal's calculating glare as he fixed eye contact with Phylus, "Thus, this was an inside job."

"From that perspective, I suppose it might be taken as such," Phylus conceded, "But I must inform you that we are working to correct this lapse in judgment and restore order."

"Thousands of people have died, and you refer to it as a lapse in judgment?"

"I do not regard their deaths so lightly. I speak of trusting LenSom with such authority. He had proven disagreeable, but our initial assessment bore out a comparatively immaterial threat. We believed the debate engendered by his contrary nature would encourage growth. Had we reason to suspect such a tragedy as an eventuality of his appointment, he would never have been permitted a seat in Parliament."

"I see," Joren noted, furrowing his brow, "Be that as it may, he has come to be an uncontested authority in ArcNos for the time being. My understanding is that you have yet another nine weeks of suspension to fulfill."

"That is correct," Phylus said, "In the meantime, we're working independently to mitigate the damages perpetuated by his actions."

"Were circumstances comparable to those preluding the ArcNosian Civil War, I may have cause to trust you. But you lack the resources to effectively revolt at this hour."

"If we can reach our associates within our respective Ministries, we can launch an internal coup. Most of them are loyal more to their Prime Ministers and High Ministers than to the Chairman of Parliament."

"No, I'm afraid this has progressed too far with no material counteractive measures," Joren refused, "We can forgive ArcNos for its misappropriation of our share of the tax monies, just as Tanelen had, to your detriment, calculated wholly in our own favor. However, we cannot turn blindly to your handling of these matters."

"Let me remind you that this was an isolated transgression by a single corrupt individual," Phylus steadfastly argued.

"Yes, one who holds largely uncontested power for the next nine weeks and whose transgressions you have failed to prevent," Joren countered, "Tanelen as little tolerance for governments executing their citizenry, none whatsoever with such sentences issued without trial. To furthermore have them hunted like wild game is inexcusably dehumanizing."

"Chairman LenSom will be forced to account for such," Phylus asserted, mirroring the Noble Doyen's impassioned demeanor, "We will see to that by whatever means justifiable."

"In what time? How many more will die in the meanwhile?" Joren snapped, "Moreover, you must stop interrupting me."

"My apologies, Noble Doyen, sir."

"Of course. Now furthermore, Tanelen has never tolerated being used as a scapegoat. Our civilization being so advanced as it is, you must understand we draw a large amount of inconsiderate suspicion."

"I presume this is the reason for your isolation," Phylus inferred, "Best to remain neutral if people are so quick to suspect you of wrongdoing."

"You understand perfectly, I see," Joren said, "But I'm afraid that there's nothing you can do to change my mind at this juncture."

"In that case, in what direction do you see these matters progressing from here?"

"For the time being, we shall wait to see what resolution you and your associates might effect. But know that I lack confidence in your ability to do so."

"Yes, you've made that abundantly clear."

"Should your administration continue with such dishonorable pursuits, Tanelen will be forced into direct counteractive measures," Joren asserted, "Should matters escalate such as to necessitate lethal force, we cannot promise discrimination on basis of expressed allegiances."

"Of course. You couldn't possibly know the philosophies of every soldier," Phylus agreed, a plastic smile masking his derision, "But as little stock as you take in my promises, I can assure you we will not let it escalate that far."

"Of course. You couldn't possibly have them stand trial before you execute them," KalChi mocked under her breath.

"We'll not hold our breath," Joren countered, darting a glare at KalChi, "If any representative of ArcNos continues to force our hand, whether by will or by order, by knowledge or by ignorance, that hand shall come down upon the entirety of ArcNos."

Noble Doyen Joren thrust himself out of his seat and made for the coat rack in the back corner of the conference room. EshCal subtly scrutinized his movements as well as those of his guards. They surrounded him as he reached for his coat, their mesomorphic frames easily encompassing him. EshCal considered that they may have only been shielding him in this moment of vulnerability. Between their shoulders, however, a ripple in his shirt sleeve caught her attention. She saw a tapering darker line in the shadow of the fold, symmetrical and unchanging with the motions of the fabric.

"If you'll have me," EshCal announced, standing as well, "I would remain here as a liaison until matters have been settled."

"That won't be necessary," Joren refused, smiling as buttoned his coat and stepped beyond his guards, "We have all the information we need from your organization."

Malia set the metallic case on the coffee table and opened it, laying out an array of intricate wiring an complex circuitry. Sinkua watched in bewilderment, crouching beside the coffee table.

"What exactly does this do?" he asked.

Malia raised her finger and flipped a switch. The apparatus emitted a low buzz, accompanied shortly by a pulsating hum.

"There," she nodded, "Now, we can speak freely."

"Great. So what does this thing do?" Sinkua reiterated.

"The part I just turned on blocks wireless transmissions," Malia explained.

"In case of eavesdropping?"

"Exactly. The rest is a specialized video data converter," she continued, "The Engineer created an exclusive video format for their recon and security jobs. Your house being one of them. This converts it to a format readable by virtually any television or personal computer."

"Hmm. I guess The Coalition can be pretty clever when they want to be," Sinkua begrudgingly complimented, "Is this stolen, or did The Omnimath design it?"

"Somewhere in between," Malia said as she connected the wiring, "The brothers made it using video transmitters I stole from The Engineer."

"I think I remember they did something similar during the ArcNosian Civil War," Sinkua mused, "Anyway, how sure are you of your theory?"

"Ninety percentish. It's not the only way, but it would account for Gabdur's cover being blown and how Yahsek got the intel he needed for his redecorating job," Malia explained, "But I didn't think it would still be active after all this time. I installed the system, but my briefing on it was, well, brief. With The Engineer, everything is on a strict need-to-know basis."

"And you didn't need to know," Sinkua said, "It sounds like they suspected you of ulterior allegiances for longer than you thought."

"I know. CreSam as well."

Malia walked the perimeter of the living room, running her fingertips along the wall. She traced her memories back through the years, picturing the living room as it had been decorated some two decades prior. Her index finger paused on an imperfection, malleable with a roughened texture.

"Did you find something?" Sinkua asked.

"This spot's been tampered with," Malia said, her forehead wrinkling, "Someone drilled a hole and filled it with quick-drying plaster. Cheap stuff."

"Did you install a camera there?"

Malia nodded as she chipped away the plaster with her pen knife. To her chagrin, she only found the perhaps permanent impression of a tap in the back of the hole.

"It's gone."

"Yahsek took it," Sinkua concluded, "Between outing you as a turncoat and redecorating my house, he must have figured I'd learn about the cameras."

"The walls were decorated differently when I installed the taps. It's possible he overlooked one."

"Or counted on a false sense of security and left one on purpose."

Malia waggled her pen knife in his direction and nodded as she scanned the room. Picturing the old decor, she traced the edges of windows and past portraits beyond their corners. She pointed across the room, focusing on a particular invisible intersection.

"Right there," she asserted, crossing the room, "I planted one behind this picture."

"Could it have seen through the picture like they do with the walls?" Sinkua asked as he lifted the framed painting from its nails.

"No, but technically they don't see through the walls. They're covered with a special polymer which is opaque from one side and translucent from the other," Malia explained, scratching the wall with her pen knife, "The taps amplify the light they absorb, though not enough to see through near-opacities."

"Ah, so they work like Nikasu's eyes."

"More or less. Where is she, by the way?"

"Visiting Galo with Eytea."

"SenRas told me what happened to him. How is he holding up?"

"About as well as we can expect right now," Sinkua said, fighting back his anxiety over the duality of Galo's unchanging condition, "Did you find one?"

"Yes!" Malia announced, plucking the tap from its decades-old nest, "Screw the red coaxial cable into the back of the television and turn it to channel five."

Sinkua hooked up the converter while Malia checked the tap for signs of tampering or disrepair. Finding it untouched since she installed it, she plugged it into the apparatus.

Malia held one button for a few seconds, then pressed another. Silent blackness replaced the dead air static and eventually crumbled away, followed by Malia plucking the bug while Sinkua watched from the couch. She paused the playback.

"It's been recording all this time," Sinkua sneered.

"I'm afraid so," Malia frowned, "Let me show you how to work this thing, and we'll see how far back the recording goes."

Sinkua sat beside her and listened as she explained how to operate the device. Consciously, he heard only the basics, being distracted by his ulterior agenda of curiosity and longing. He rewound through weeks of blackness, slowing through hours of movers setting out furniture, and paused as the décor abruptly rearranged and CreSam moved across the screen. Motion sensors in the taps had bypassed the vacant years.

"We have what we need. I'll check for the rest of the taps, and we'll destroy them," Malia asserted, "They already know about Gabdur, but we can't have your house going on as a security risk."

"Not yet."

Faded memories taking on traces of lucidity, Sinkua lapsed backward through the aftermath of his youth. He paused at the sight of himself ten years younger, intrigued by the distantly familiar teenager on the screen. Continuing back through years he thought irrevocably lost, he watched his childhood play out in reverse.

Chapter 34

CreSam exhaled heavily, wiping the sweat from his forehead. He leaned on his elbows and rested his face in his hands. He tangled his fingers in his thick black hair and nervously cleared his throat. Wincing, he pulled his fingers out of his hair and clasped the ridge of his right hand.

A slim arm reached down from behind his shoulder and wrapped his hand in a warm damp washcloth. CreSam looked back and smiled sorrowfully at his wife. BeiLou grazed the back of her fingers along his cheek, reciprocating the apologetic smile. CreSam grasped her fingers, his meaty mitt swallowing her petite hand.

"I had to kill a man," he grumbled.

"Sorry to hear that," she consoled, "Did you encounter some resistance?"

"Wasn't that. Had to kill my partner," CreSam clarified, drawing a pistol of unusual design and setting it on the coffee table, "We didn't work well together, but that's no reason for me to kill him."

"So, this is it, then? You're one of… them now?"

"Just in the fold. Me and a few others."

"I guess we're past the point of no return, then," BeiLou sighed.

"I guess so," CreSam nodded, "I can't believe I did that. I just pulled the trigger and watched him die. Dumped him in the Northland Sea. Even acted like I enjoyed it."

"What matters are your intentions. You and I know how you felt about it and where you see this going."

"History might never know my intentions."

"Besides us and them, nobody knows what happened, right?"

"I guess not," he conceded, "I almost convinced myself that I enjoyed watching him die… watching his body float away…"

"Just don't lose sight of yourself," BeiLou consoled, kissing his hand, "Never forget who you are."

"I knew this was coming. They've been watching me since I enlisted," he mumbled almost inaudibly, "I don't know how long I can keep doing this."

"You said yourself that Gijin will get over it," BeiLou reminded, "But I don't like what this is doing to MeiLom."

"If the old man would join them, he'd understand," CreSam grumbled, "And maybe he could get through to MeiLom."

"Why don't you try?"

"His own son couldn't get him to join. What makes you think I'd fare any better?"

"That isn't. . ."

"My forté is making enemies," CreSam continued, interrupting her, "No matter how much I hate it and wish otherwise, he has to be one of them."

"Why don't you try getting through to MeiLom?" BeiLou clarified.

CreSam hefted himself to his feet with a throaty sigh. He paced the living room, seeming to consider the suggestion. On its face, it sounded simple enough, conceivable even, but his shoulders slumped as though the very thought manifested as a physical burden. At this point, nothing could be trusted to be so simple. His affiliations complicated matters too greatly.

"You know I can't do that. It would never work out."

"MeiLom is stronger than you think," BeiLou argued, "Smarter, too."

"I know. He's a clever kid. Tough as he is sharp," CreSam agreed, "But I can't get him involved."

BeiLou grabbed his arm and turned him around, craning her neck to meet his eyes. She swallowed, steadying herself to speak, as though her words burdened her throat.

"He's one of them," she said, "The people they told you about. MeiLom is one of them."

"I've suspected he was for a while," he said, "They told me the boy is important. That he must be protected. That's why I can't get him involved. Not the way you want."

"But they can protect him better than we could," she grasped, "Couldn't you two work together?"

"No. If he learns about them, so do they. Then everything falls apart. This family. Them. Our plans," he refused, "Everything."

"Maybe there's another way."

"Listen, honey. I know this upsets you. I hate that I'll have to tear apart our family. I hate watching my son grow away from me," CreSam bemoaned, "But he and I can never be on the same side at the same time. That's just how it has to be. Enemies in life. Allies in death."

"Why? Because your boss says so?" BeiLou challenged, "CreSam, that man won't even show you his face. The only people who wear masks are people with something to hide."

"Everyone has their secrets, and he has just as much a right to his own as anyone else," CreSam said, "You and I have plenty."

"I suppose you're right," BeiLou conceded, "But I'm sorry, I just can't accept that you two can never be on the same side. He's one of them. I think he'd make a good ally when he's old enough."

"I know he would. But he has to find them on his own. Without me. If I introduce him to them, I'll ruin everything."

"Would you, now?" BeiLou challenged, "How would it ruin everything to take your son, a child they said must live, into the fold?"

"It goes against the operation," CreSam vaguely dismissed.

"What if there's another way?"

"We've spent the past year developing this plan, myself and some of the greatest minds of this age. Mostly them. But if you have a better idea, I'm sure they'd love to entertain it."

"Don't get snarky with me," BeiLou sneered, "What if you make amends with MeiLom and get him to convince Gijin to join them?"

"Even as close as they are, I doubt MeiLom could change his mind," CreSam said, "But out of curiosity, to what end?"

"Teach Gijin about your plan. Gain his cooperation."

"He won't cooperate if he knows what we're planning."

"I don't mean your methods," BeiLou said, "I mean your endgame."

"Our methods won't work if he knows our endgame," CreSam argued, "He needs to truly believe that I'm his enemy."

"So, that's how it has to be, then?" BeiLou muttered, plopping down on the couch.

"I'm afraid so," CreSam sighed, sitting beside her, "They both need to. It's the only way things can turn out the way we need them to."

"But if everything is staged, shouldn't everyone who's involved know the score?" BeiLou grasped.

"You make it sound this is all a show."

"Isn't that what it is? Put on a puppet show and make them think they're pulling the strings?"

"It's more of an experiment," CreSam insisted, "But no matter what analogy you use, certain people will be better suited for their job if they don't know what their job is."

"But if all of you work together, you can protect each other. Instead, you're willing to give up your family for a chance . . ."

"Do you have any idea what this is doing to me?" he snarled, "I have to forsake everyone I respect and care about to become this generation's greatest enemy. HarEin has to condemn me. Gijin has to fear me. And MeiLom has to hate me. Can you even begin to comprehend that? My duty is to raise my son, my own flesh and blood, to hate me."

"Is it really worth that much?" BeiLou gasped, tears welling in her eyes.

"Time will answer that question," he sighed, "Let's be grateful we still have each other."

"I wish I could do more for you. I'm getting nowhere on the one job I was trusted with."

"They're in a safe place. That's all that matters for now."

"But imagine the difference it would make if I could open even just one of them."

"Those were given to you before I started working with them," CreSam reminded, "If they needed it done faster, they would have reached out to you by now. For now, you just need to keep them safe."

"What am I supposed to do, then?" BeiLou pleaded, rubbing the back of her neck, "Idle along while everything else falls apart? I can only pretend to stand aside for so long before I'm actually letting this happen."

"Stay the course," he said, "Stay close to our son. Keep him close to the old man. When the time comes, they'll both be better suited to their jobs."

BeiLou looked to him with eyes consumed by sorrow and regret. She wiped anxious beads of sweat from her forehead, her bangs rippling along the salty smears.

"What if he wasn't one of them?" she asked, "Would it have to be like this? Would you need to push him away?"

"I don't know. If MeiLom wasn't one of them, we might not even be involved. Maybe he's the whole reason any of them had any interest in us."

"He can never know that. He can't think this is his fault."

"I know. He's not to blame. But I know," CreSam agreed, "But if he wasn't one of them, and we were still in this place, I think it would still have to be this way. I don't like the methods. In fact, I hate them. But I trust that they'll work. But even knowing that, I have to take solace in knowing that a worthy patriarch is taking my place."

"I understand," BeiLou said, "And I'm glad Gijin has taken a liking to him, too. But I suppose you would need to push them toward each other even if MeiLom wasn't one of them. It'll make it more personal."

"The greatest sacrifices always are."

CreSam leaned back on the couch, propping his foot on his knee. Splayed over his leg was a manila folder with a stack of papers, the letterhead obstructed. Two emblems adorned the inside of the folder. On the left inner face was the coat of arms of the ArcNosian Military Guild superimposed over the ArcNosian flag. On the tab on the right was the symbol of his rank beside his title and name.

He thumbed through the stack, skimming each page. His face screwed up into a look of bewildered discontent as the stack shallowed. As he reached the end, he went back to the start and began reading each page in earnest.

"Papa!" a small voice called.

Loud footfalls, unbefitting to so small a voice, tramped toward him. CreSam closed his eyes and exhaled a shadow of an apology. His concentration broken, he ground his teeth and turned with a snarl. Atop the steps into the sunken living room stood the son he'd been ordered to push away.

"What do you want, boy?" CreSam snapped, hiding his sorrow behind a mask of anger.

"I, um… wanna give you this," MeiLom said, struggling to make eye contact, "A lady brought you this box. But you were asleep."

CreSam snatched the box, nearly toppling the boy with how aggressively he yanked it from his grasp. He examined the parcel, trying to ignore his son's prying eyes. CreSam gave him a moment's eye contact, the discontent in his expression giving way to concern.

"Who gave you this?" he asked.

"Some lady in a uniform," MeiLom shrugged.

"The mail carrier?"

"Nuh-uh. She had different clothes. They said, um…"

"What did she look like?"

"Tall and pretty. She had black hair, and…"

"Did she tell you her name?" CreSam barked.

"Nuh-uh. I think she had a name tag, but maybe I forgot it," MeiLom shrank back, "Her shirt said Black Tea Driver."

"Black Tie Delivery?"

"No! Black. Tea. Driver."

"Fine! Whatever!" CreSam snarled, "Just go play in your room."

"Okay," MeiLom nodded, wiping his nose on his sleeve, "Did someone send you a present, Papa?"

"That's none of your business. I said go play in your room."

CreSam set aside the package, feigning indifference, and returned to his work. With forcedly stern eyebrows, he watched MeiLom's reflection in the surface of the coffee table. As the image of the child moved off of the glass, CreSam dropped his head into his hands and sighed.

He grabbed the package and set it on his lap. The only marking it bore was a short alphanumeric sequence along the edge. His shoulders slumping with eventual acceptance, he opened the parcel.

He rooted through a heap of tissue paper and packing peanuts and drew out a small portable phone. Within moments of his finding the power button and turning it on, the device rang. CreSam looked over his shoulder and, finding himself alone, answered the phone.

"C151?" he asked.

"Good. It has arrived," came a hoarse voice through the earpiece.

"What does this mean?"

"You are not in a place to question us."

"I do not doubt, my lord. I only wish to know why I've been labeled this way."

"C151 is a code designation. Nothing more than a serial number."

"I understand. Is this how I'm to stay in contact with you, then?"

"For the time being, Subject C151."

"Would it be possible for you to call me by my name?"

"You have no name," the voice hissed, "We shall call you by the name we grant you, should you earn one."

"Understood," CreSam swallowed, "What would you have me do?"

"Are you to deserve consideration for christening, we mandate you accomplish a particular task."

"Anything, my liege."

"Your unwavering fealty amuses us."

"What do you ask of me?"

"A single demonstration of your loyalty. A sacrifice."

"A sacrifice? Wasn't he enough?"

"Beyond your common service, you possessed no bond to so paltry a man as he. You wished him perished absent our encouragement."

"Of course. It is as The Scout spoke. For most, the line between hatred and murder is drawn by fear of arbitrary laws."

"Therefore, his death constituted not a sacrifice and thus was not a demonstration of your loyalty and resolve."

"Who is my target, then?"

"Never have we invested in you as poetic, yet we have found poignant truth resonant in your words," the voice rasped, "The greatest sacrifices are always more personal."

"Do you mean to say…?"

"Yes. Our eyes and ears are upon you. Of course, we'll not speak to the nameless of our methods. Suffice it to say, Subject M237 has proven herself as quite the opportunist. At this rate, she is liable to surpass you in reaping a name."

"That miserable bitch?" CreSam snarled, "She'll need to work harder than that to surpass me. Who's my target?"

"It is at this point that we have come to an impasse. Being incapable of deciding whose sacrifice would serve as the greater tribute, we thought to bestow upon you the burden of decision."

"Who are my options?"

"The woman or the boy. You will inform us of your decision by acting upon it," the voice ordered, "Decide at your leisure but beware the risk inherent in hesitation. We promise not that none more suited will supplant you. Naught shall be done, in fact, to protect you from obsolescence. In the meanwhile, we shall be watching and waiting."

BeiLou paced the living room, holding a small book by the base of its spine. She looked up every time she turned the page, seeming discomforted by her surroundings. Now and then, she glanced at the walls. She swallowed and leaned nearer to her book, as though hiding her face from an unseen eavesdropper.

She gasped herself breathless as the front door banged open, the paperback falling shut as it clapped against the floor. Clutching her chest and panting heavily, BeiLou knelt to recover the book. As she stood, she looked up to find CreSam looming over her.

"What business do you have with this?" he growled, snatching the book.

"I ought to ask you the same thing," BeiLou said, trembling, "Why are you studying this? What does it have to do with your service?"

"My service?" CreSam asked, exhaling an apology between breaths, "Who are you to question my service?"

"Of course. I… I'm sorry," she said, mouthing her acceptance, "I don't mean to stand in your way."

"You'd better not. Another move like that, and I'll have you watch as I demonstrate my loyalty."

"Please, no! Anything but that!" BeiLou sobbed. She turned as she whispered, "Too far."

"Sorry. Had to," CreSam exhaled. He then snarled, "I haven't decided, but you should count yourself lucky I even told you about it."

"I consider myself lucky to be with you as you prepare to make so grand a mark on

346

history," she professed, grazing her fingernails down his chest, "It's an honor to have you put me in such a position."

"Is that why you stay? To become a martyr?"

"I'd have it no other way. If this is how I must prove my loyalty, then I'll proudly accept that fate," BeiLou professed. Under her breath, she asked, "Do you get this stuff?"

"In that case, would you rather die swiftly or in prolonged agony?" CreSam asked, then whispered, "Getting better."

"My death will mark the start of a new era. There's no use in dwelling on the remains of the old one," she said. She ran her hand through her hair as she mouthed, "I'm here to help."

"Of course. Your death should be swift. That's why I'm studying this. So I know how best to sacrifice whomever I choose, you or the boy."

"Why wouldn't you choose me? How better to show my loyalty than by giving my life for their vision?" she pleaded. In a nigh silent whisper, she said, "Stop doing that."

"Anyone so loyal might serve a better purpose alive," CreSam explained, then muttered, "I'm sorry. I have to."

"Their cause means nothing to him," BeiLou argued, "He doesn't deserve the honor of dying for it. Better he should live with the shame of his ignorance."

"That's for me to decide," he reminded, whispering, "How much do you understand?"

"Of course. Don't let me stand in your way," she conceded, bowing her head and lowering herself onto the couch as she mouthed, "Enough to know my chances."

CreSam sat beside her with the paperback she had dropped. He drew a pen from his shirt pocket and marked passages as he read.

His glare darted to BeiLou on occasion. From the corner of his eye, he watched seethingly as she fidgeted. Catching his cast iron gaze, she contained her tics and shrank back into the corner of the couch. His attention returned to his book.

BeiLou pulled a notepad from under the coffee table and began scribbling down the page. At times, she paused and glanced over at CreSam, then resumed her feverish scrawling in earnest.

"Are the trains still running today?" CreSam asked, looking up from his work.

"There should be one or two left tonight," BeiLou said, "Why?"

"I just remembered I have a debt to pay. The trains are my best shot at doing it today."

"Oh right, the loan you took out last month. I thought you still had a few days on it."

"My loan is due in three days. We shouldn't put it off to the last day."

BeiLou sat on the edge of the armchair with a pair of CreSam's pants draped over the arm. She thumbed through a stack of papers, her lips faintly moving as she read. When she finished the last page, she scribbled in the air with her fingertip, nodding thoughtfully. She lingered on the last page a moment longer and, her focus shifting as she cocked her ear, straightened the papers on her lap.

Exhaling a long sigh, BeiLou slid the document under the coffee table. She drew a pistol from the pocket of CreSam's pants, fixating on it for a few moments. As the door unlocked, she knelt in front of the chair and shoved the gun between the arm and the cushion. Disheveling herself, she rose to her feet and looked to the front door.

"We need to talk," she announced, mouthing, "Everything is set."

"I have enough problems to deal with aside from you," CreSam grumbled, slamming the door.

"What problems do you have? Working as a soldier? The man I married was man enough to handle a soldier's life and a family life. What happened to him?"

"Who are you to judge me?" he barked, "I'm out every day trying to better myself as a soldier, and you have the gall to speak like that to me?"

"Better yourself? CreSam, I know about your crutch," BeiLou challenged, "You're not bettering yourself. You're out for power."

"What? What did you say?" he snarled as he descended into the living room, whispering, "Are you ready?"

"I know of your dealings with foreign agents. Weapon agents," she asserted, exhaling, "I trust you."

"Who told you this?"

"It doesn't matter, but I'm going to expose you. I'm sorry, but this can't go unnoticed. Your disloyalty needs to be known before it becomes a serious threat."

"Who are you to stop me from my mission? What do you think you can do?" he challenged, whispering, "I am so sorry."

"I can do plenty, CreSam. Whatever you're up to with them, it can't be good for the country. I can't let history take that road. I'll do everything I can to keep it from happening, even if it means turning against my husband," she professed, mouthing, "Keep a steady hand."

CreSam drew his handgun and aimed it at her. Crocodile tears flooding her eyes and rolling down her cheeks, BeiLou collapsed to her knees. His gun arm steady, he approached in long deliberate strides as she rummaged in the armchair. In rehearsed unison, he pressed the barrel of his pistol to her forehead as she withdrew the gun she had hidden in the char and pressed it to his chest with trembling arms.

"They're waiting for us," he whispered, then shouted, "Pull the trigger, and we both die. See the mess you've gotten yourself into? If only you had stayed out of the way and let me do my job. I have big plans involving these agents, you see, and I don't need anybody getting in the way. History be damned."

"What's happened to you, CreSam? It didn't used to be like this," BeiLou pleaded, murmuring, "They'll protect me, right?"

"What's happened? The truth happened. I must rise to claim my rightful title. It is for them, for all they've given me," CreSam professed, mouthing, "We all will. I love you."

The doorknob rattled. BeiLou's eyes widened as the reality of the interruption sank in. Panicking, she dropped the gun on the chair. CreSam looked to her urgingly, arching an eyebrow.

"You're breaking script," he mouthed, speaking so rapidly, it came out as a single word.

"We didn't plan for this," she hissed through her teeth.

"What do we do?"

"Line up the shot and take it."

"What if it's…?"

"Not until tomorrow."

CreSam angled the barrel against her forehead. BeiLou clenched her teeth and squeezed her eyes shut, clutching the upholstery of the armchair. CreSam swallowed and exhaled one last apology.

BeiLou opened her eyes and looked up at him, whispering her trust in him. Her attention shifted to the front door, genuine shock overcoming her rehearsed forced composure.

"MeiLom! No!" BeiLou called out, lunging forth.

"What?!" CreSam shouted, his arm jerking as his head whipped around.

His finger pulled back on the trigger. BeiLou collapsed into a heap of herself, smoke and blood streaming from her throat. Teary-eyed and flush with insurmountable anguish,

CreSam knelt over her, cradling her dying body and cursing himself.

Chapter 35

A linoleum cacophony of footsteps clattered throughout the congested waiting room. Several conversations coalesced into a dense cloud of gray noise. Papers rustled in hands. Clipboards clapped against tables and countertops.

None of this quelled the noise in Sinkua's head. He sat among friends and strangers with his head in his hands and his fingers tangled in his hair. Cluttered decibels failing to drown out his turmoil, he turned inward to navigate his anxiety. Yet, that same noise made it impossible to face his troubles. Too quiet to silence the worry. Too loud to sort it out.

Eytea rubbed his upper back, crookedly pursing her lips as she looked him over. Ever since she and Nikasu returned from visiting Galo without him, he had been increasingly wont to self-consuming introspection. Troublingly so. He had spoken less each day since, becoming much as she imagined he had been as a child.

"Big brother," Nikasu beckoned, crouching in front of him, "I got you some cashews. You like cashews, right? I think I've seen you eat them before."

"They're good," Sinkua mumbled, accepting the bag with brief eye contact, "Thanks."

"I got four," Nikasu teased, nudging Eytea.

"My perky white butt, you got four!" Eytea said, "Contractions only count as one."

"Uh-huh. You're just jealous 'cause I got him to eat something."

Sinkua glared at them out of the corner of his eye. He grunted his disapproval and popped a cashew in his mouth. Nikasu and Eytea looked away.

"Maybe we shouldn't do this in front of him," Eytea suggested.

"Probably not. But seriously, Sinkua," Nikasu said, "What's bothering you? You're talking even less than I did when you guys found me. Remember?"

"Are you worried about the procedure?" Eytea asked, "No, that can't be it. That just came up yesterday."

"Not that," Sinkua mumbled, partially lying.

"Good. Because I don't think I have to tell you, it could be much worse," Nikasu backhandedly reassured, inconsiderate of the faded memories she could have agitated.

"Not a good time!" Eytea exclaimed, reaching across Sinkua to slap Nikasu's arm.

"I mean how they treated me and the other hostages in their labs. It's not like he..." Nikasu trailed off, "Oh! Oh geez! I am so sorry. I didn't even think about... you know..."

"It's okay," Sinkua muttered.

"It's just, well... You saw how bad it was when you came for me. So at least you know you'll be better off than them, right?," Nikasu said, eloquence crumbling in her fluster, "But I sorta forgot you'd been, you know, um..."

"... in one, too."

"I'll shut up now."

"Not bothering me."

"My talking doesn't bother you? Not even when I'm talking about that?"

Sinkua sighed in disdain over her pushiness. Annoying as she was, her effort somehow comforted him, even if it confused him. He had spent months putting the same effort into her, but somehow he doubted he deserved her reciprocation. In spite of his doubt though, he wondered if the moments of coherent empathy were worth her tendency to prod at old scars.

"No, I mean my time down there isn't bothering me. Not right now," he explained, Nikasu and Eytea staring agape, "I don't remember it, and that's pretty nice. Not that I credit The Geneticist with being at all sympathetic, but I have to give him credit for his intelligence. Not for knowing how to do it, but for knowing how good it would be for his long-term survival if I forgot what he had done to me."

"I, um… Okay. That… narrows it down," Eytea said, flustered by the flood of monologue, "Don't even start counting, Nikasu. We all know you won."

"Seventy," Nikasu said.

"I thought I told you to stop that."

"I wish you two wouldn't make a game out of this," Sinkua said.

"Eleven," Eytea joked, nudging him, "Okay, we're done now. Seriously. But I wish you'd tell me what's bothering you."

"Got a lot going on right now. Just having trouble calming down," Sinkua shrugged, "You know how I get."

"Better than anyone. You lock everyone out and bottle up your problems until you snap," she said with a trace of scolding in her voice, "You insist on dealing with everything yourself instead of opening up and letting us help."

"I'll tell you if I need it."

A slender arm stretched above the standing crowd. Sinkua lifted his head, craning his neck to see over the crowd from his seat. A head popped up, shoulder-length hair bouncing. Sinkua waved her over, and MarLys maneuvered through the crowd to join them.

"This came for you today," MarLys announced, grinning smugly as she handed him an envelope.

"What's going on?" Eytea asked.

"I hired her to bring us our mail while we're here," Sinkua said, stuffing the envelope in his pocket, "In case we have to stay a while."

"Hired her, or asked her as a favor?"

"Hired. Just like I said."

"Can we afford that right now?"

"She's trying to get away from Uncle Bitchboy," Sinkua reminded, "She needs the money more than we do."

"I told him I'd do it for free," MarLys said, throwing up her hands in deflection of the argument, "He insisted on paying me."

"Sounds just like my man," Eytea teased, rubbing his back.

"Vielle is upstairs with Galo," Nikasu said, "She's keeping him company while they get ready."

"I know. She told me she was going ahead," MarLys said, "Who else is up there?"

"His new doctor, a surgical resident, and two interns. Chekov also came down to help Yrlis, so they're both up there, too. And Ophalin came in from Ferya. He's helping them set up," Nikasu rattled off, "And Spril is standing guard."

"Sounds like a lot of important people in one room," MarLys remarked, "Sinkua, are you excited?"

"Excited?" Sinkua puzzled, "Most people would ask if I'm nervous."

"I'm not most people," MarLys shrugged, "Some of the best minds in medicine are up there, getting ready to help you get your best friend out of a coma. That's gotta be cool. The dude who developed your medication even came out here from the other end of the Northlands to help."

"Hm? Yeah, I guess it is kinda cool when you put it that way."

"Right? You're giving him a part of yourself, and everyone in there is focused on making sure both of you get through it okay."

"Heh. Thanks," Sinkua smirked, "I needed that."

Minutes passed with idle conversation. Eventually, an announcement over the intercom summoned Sinkua upstairs. He poured the last few cashews into his mouth and waved for Eytea to follow him.

"I'm not allowed in the operating room with you," she said, "I'll be watching from the observation deck."

"Just to the fourth floor," he clarified, chipmunking the half-chewed nuts, "Need to talk somewhere a little less public."

Both their minds scattered and rushed as they rode the elevator in shared silence. Eytea contemplated why he pulled her aside, her thoughts escalating to both more dire and more optimistic matters. Sinkua, meanwhile, endeavored to distract himself from the matter, keeping his body language from betraying his secret.

From the elevator hub, he led her into a mostly unoccupied hall. Sinkua stopped and stretched, feigning nonchalance, and leaned against the wall. Eytea breathed deeply in vain hopes of calming her pulse as she joined him.

"What's up, sweets?" she asked.

"MarLys was right, you know. This whole thing is pretty damn cool. What I get to do. Who's making it happen."

"Yeah. It was nice of her to put it that way."

"But I'd be lying if I said I'm not nervous."

"I know. And it's okay," Eytea said, cupping her hand over his stubbly jawline, "I'm just glad you're talking about it. I know that's hard for you."

"I don't know what they did to me in that lab, but this is the first time I've been operated on since then," Sinkua said, cupping his hand over hers, "Ophalin has run a lot of tests on me, but they've mostly been noninvasive. Nothing like what they've told me about this procedure."

"I know. It's kinda scary," Eytea agreed, swallowing her nervousness, "But it's like MarLys said, you're gonna be surrounded by people who just want to help."

"Regardless, I don't know how well I'm going to hold up," he argued, "My mind has been turned labyrinthine, and nobody I can trust knows what they did to my body."

"Sinkua," she urged, "If you're worried you won't make it, you need to say something. Tell the doctors. Please."

"No. No. It's not that. I'm sure I'll survive. I trust them to keep me alive," he said, "But I might not come out of it the same person I am now. Who I've become is just as much a product of the memories I've lost as the ones we've created."

"No matter what happens, we'll all be there for you," Eytea said, "And I'll always love you."

"At least part of me will always love you as well. That much of me is intrinsic," Sinkua smiled, pulling the envelope from his pocket, "So, I wanted to give you something before I go in. Close your eyes."

Sinkua opened the envelope and dropped the ring into his hand. He marveled at the brilliant craftsmanship and intricate detail. It looked precisely as ordered and better than he had imagined. With a smile and a swallow, his first tell of anxiety since he found the courage to pull her aside, he opened Eytea's hand, placed the ring on her palm, and closed her fist around it.

"Okay," he said, kissing her knuckles, "Open your eyes."

Eytea's pupils dilated in disbelieving elation as she opened her hand. It had felt so obvious against her palm, yet it seemed so unlikely. Irrational even. She knew it might eventually happen, but she had never expected it so soon. Not even in the near future. Her heart raced as she gazed upon it, elegant in its simple brilliance.

"Sinkua," she gasped, "Is this...?"

"Yeah," he nodded, flipping his necklace over, "Did it when I came here alone."

"So it's…? Do you mean to…?" Eytea stammered.

"You don't have to answer right away," Sinkua insisted.

"Okay… Ah…"

"I've gotta get going. They're waiting for me," he said, turning toward the main hall, "And our friends are waiting for you downstairs."

Eytea watched him walk away, his gait exuding the confidence she had come to adore. As her heart settled into a brisk jog, she admired the ring more closely, marveling at the seamless structure of the gemstone. Thrilled and nervous, she slipped it over her finger. It fit comfortably, the ruby radiating a pleasant warmth. Swallowing her apprehension, she rushed out to the main hall.

"Sinkua!" she called out.

"What is it?" he asked as he stopped and turned around.

Visions of their future bombarded her mind. Her heart nearly bruised itself, it drummed against her ribcage so fiercely. She fidgeted pensively, abandoning any hope of keeping her composure.

Almost breathlessly, Eytea exhaled a single word.

A black dress shoe stamped the metallic stile, throwing the door ajar. The handle banged against the adjoining wall, glass panes reverberating deafeningly. In swaggered a gentleman of dark complexion, nattily enrobed in a grey suit. He circled the brim of his fedora with his thumbs and forefingers, straightening it as the door clapped shut behind him.

"Sir!" the receptionist shouted, launching to his feet within his circular desk, "What business do you…?"

The intruder silently drew a pistol from his inner breast pocket, interrupting the receptionist's protest with an unhesitant gunshot. The bullet zipped through his forehead, spiraling a stream of blood and neural matter out of the back of his skull.

Gabdur pocketed the gun and burst into a furious sprint, a holster at his hip bouncing and knocking against his thigh. He bounded onto the massive stone planter, trampled the indoor flora, and leapt off the other side. His steely gaze seared through the receptionist's collapsing form.

Grasping the tail of his mortal coil, the receptionist reached for the underside of the desk. Gabdur produced the gun once more and blew out the man's shoulder with a second shot. The receptionist collapsed upon himself, expelling his last breath in dysphonic agony.

Gabdur threw himself over the desk and landed standing on the freshly slain receptionist. He ripped the security badge from the receptionist's belt loop with a derisive sneer. He vaulted back over the desk and headed for the stairs to the balcony over the lobby.

Up on the balcony, he took a segmented metal ball from his pocket, impressed a panel, and lobbed it into the circular desk below. The device swelled and burst into dull shrapnel as Gabdur walked away, leaving its red core gyrating and spewing sallow smoke.

Gabdur swiped the badge and shouldered the door open. Nearby workers threw themselves to their feet, alarmed by his explosive entrance. Some struck buttons on their desks and fled deeper into the facility. Others armed themselves and swarmed the entrance.

"Get to the lobby!" one commanded, "Intercept his backup!"

Gabdur drew a half-meter gleaming black metal pole from his hip holster. He squeezed the center, opening holes in the ends. Concentrated beams of black light shone from the chambers, adopting a silvery hue and curving slightly some half a meter out. The luminescence dulled to a shimmer and tightened into opacity, shaping into a double-headed fauchard.

The self-appointed commander charged as Gabdur's weapon coalesced, his butterfly knife snapping into position. Gabdur caught a sharp breeze across his throat as he leaned back to dodge the slashing blade. His double-headed fauchard wholly formed, he leaned back on the door, pushing it shut, and launched himself at his attacker. The forward blade parted sinew and bone with little resistance, amputating his assailant's knife-arm. Spinning the pole around his wrist, he brought forth the rear blade and sliced through his attacker's neck.

Those who had followed their now-decapitated commander stumbled over each other as they scrambled out of the foyer. Gabdur charged the withdrawing force, gracefully carving through flesh with his photonic fauchard. At the end of the hall, he leapt and kicked off one wall, then the opposite, and bounded over the stumbling crowd.

Gabdur carved into an operative as he came down, bisecting him from scalp through sternum. He dropped to a crouch as he landed and whipped the shimmering polearm in a circle above his head, ripping through all within its radius.

"I've come only for that which is rightfully mine," Gabdur boomed as he came upright, "Stand aside, and I'll permit you to live. Should you stand to hinder me, I'll not hesitate to force you aside."

"The alarms have already been sounded," an operative challenged, "It's too late for you. Nobody's coming to save you."

Gabdur swiftly leveled his pistol at the man's head, his eye twitching. His lips curled into a derisive sneer as his finger curled around the trigger. Screams emanated from beyond the balcony in the lobby, and he turned and put a bullet through the window in the door at the end of the hall instead.

Sallow smoke and agonized shrieks seeped through the hole, causing further panic in the communal office. Gabdur holstered his pistol and strode calmly past them as they scrambled over each other. Tendrils of the sickly yellow smoke coiled around the limbs of the fallen, ravaging flesh with oozing welts and festering boils.

Gabdur swiped the badge at the back of the communal office and passed through to the next hall. Wisps of smoke licked the underside of the door as he mule-kicked it shut. Behind him, they cried out in agony as the yellow smoke coiled around their bodies. Stoic and steadfast, he pressed on to a stairwell down the hall.

The blaring of alarm klaxons swelled into a ubiquitous clangor. Gabdur dematerialized his photonic fauchard and returned the pole to its holster. He drew his pistol again and reached into his pocket as he kicked open the push-bar door.

Gabdur looked up the geometric arrangement of staircases, stretching up through countless floors. He grimaced as guards poured in above, the stairwell becoming a gauntlet. Clutching a metallic ball, he stared through the lot of them as they leveled their firearms over the rails. He pressed a button in its surface and hurled the ball into their midst. Steadying his pistol on his forearm, he fired at the ball as it reached its apex.

The orb exploded as the bullet struck, transferring the bullet's momentum into a spherical pressure wave. Staircases and banisters bent and buckled under the mounting impact. Firearms and body armor crumpled like aluminum foil. Bodies slammed against the wall. Banisters and landings shattered. Rebar snapped and plunged through concrete and compressed bone.

Concrete and metal chaff rained from the spherical crater. Gabdur hurried up the stairs while loosened banisters creaked and groaned above. Three floors up, he left the stairwell as crinkled wrought iron bars broke away. Metal and stone crashed clamorously, the racket echoing throughout the stairwell.

Gabdur headed down the hall and entered an elevator. He swiped the badge and hit the top floor button. The button blinked and buzzed, the elevator refusing the command. A scrolling marquee over the door notified him of the badge's insufficient clearance. He pushed the next button down, yielding the same results.

He continued down the matrix of buttons, each one failing. Though he hadn't expected to ride to the top with the receptionist's badge, he had thought he could at least make it halfway. His chagrin grew with every failure in the lower half of the matrix. When he pressed the sixth floor button though, the top floor button lit up, and the doors closed. The marquee notified him of an external override.

Gabdur drew the obsidian pole and manifested his photonic fauchard. Dozens of floors up, the elevator stopped and opened to a long curving passageway. Across the hall, a metal door hissed and slid open.

"You clearly have some grievances to air with me," a sonorous voice called from within, "Please. Come in. Let us tend to these qualms."

Gabdur swaggered into the room, surveying the vast command center laboratory. Ebralgi stood in the center of the room, steady and dispassionate, holding his tonfa down at his side. Their gazes fixed on each other. Gabdur flinched as he failed to draw the bewilderment he had anticipated from his homicidal brother-in-law.

"I had been told you yet lived," Ebralgi snickered, "Honestly, I could hardly believe it. Never had I credited you with more than a shred of vitality."

"You'd be surprised what a person can do when you take everything from them," Gabdur spat, holding stares with Ebralgi as they circled each other.

"Regardless of my misassessment of you, I'm surprised you've come here. Your aberrant behavior continues to elude me. Perhaps, your mind is too irrational for me to map," Ebralgi mused, "The Engineer did foretell you would come here, however, should we allow Ozzera to lay waste to your bastard."

"I gather the last revocable fragments of the life you stole from me, and you needed convincing that I would give chase when you tried to rob me those as well?" Gabdur derided, "You either assume me to be a coward or a fool."

"Stole from you? In your entire pathetic existence, you have done naught to deserve your life of nepotistic status and luxury!" Ebralgi roared, "Neither you, your father, nor your bastard son proved worthy of the mantle. I'd sooner put my faith in an ape to be the guiding light of the Sacred City!"

"And you think yourself more fit to lead? You hide in this tower while we bleed for our principles."

"You think this makes a hero of you? Rats bleeds for crumbs if the shortest path draws it."

"If you think me a rat, my vitality shouldn't come as a surprise."

"I suppose not," Ebralgi conceded, "Though I don't think you a rat. You're more an insect."

"And I suppose you think yourself a spider," Gabdur sneered, "I'm only here for the Serpent Bracer. No matter your judgment of my family, it is not yours to hold."

"Nor do I intend to hold it," Ebralgi assured, holding up his hands in acquiescence, "It is your birthright to wield it, and I harbor no intent of hindering you from such."

"Then tell me what you have done with it!" Gabdur bared.

"Though I must correct you," Ebralgi continued, ignoring the command, "This room is indeed a spider web, but I am not the spider."

Gabdur opened his mouth to spit a retort, but the words crumbled in his lungs as long jagged mandibles clamped around his torso. They ripped his suit and choked off his ability to speak. The black jaws lifted him high and slammed his body against the silvery tile floor. Bruised and disoriented, he rolled over to face his assailant.

A horrible figure crouched over him. Compound eyes occupied most of his scraggly visage. A set of oversized mandibles stretched forth from his fanged mouth. His long gnarled fingers curled and tapered into points. Coarse prickly fibers lined his arms.

"What in the names of the gods have you done to this man?" Gabdur recoiled, scrambling backward on his buttocks.

"Yahsek is, perhaps, my greatest success," The Geneticist boasted, "That is, at least, among my human subjects."

"This is what you've endeavored to create?"

"He is one of many possible ends for the means I pursue. This is but a sampling of his manifestation of the artificial milystis that few can generate and fewer still and endure and harness."

"For people who think so ill of the Hybrids, you've certainly devoted a bounty of resources to creating your own."

"Do not mistake Yahsek for some cheap facsimile. Nor our ambition for envy," The Geneticist insisted, "We act only as our hands have been forced."

"You fabricate discord and think your hands forced?" Gabdur scathed.

"We set out on this path to level the field," The Geneticist barked, "We are creating soldiers to restore the numbers taken from our Goddess. But as you people have continuously impeded the uprising, we have been forced to tilt the field to our advantage."

"It's as we thought, then. You strive to awaken her," Gabdur sighed, rising to his feet, "She no longer exists in this realm. The veil you seek is a myth."

"Do you really think I would squander my intelligence on chasing fairytales?" The Geneticist sneered, "The legend of the barrier is rooted in truth, and our Goddess awaits just beyond it."

"And you think your artificial milystis will light the way?" Gabdur asked, "The Trifecta would not have erected so flimsy a seal."

"Perish the thought. We'll not sacrifice our greatest creations for the uprising."

"We wouldn't expect it to work anyhow," Yahsek added, his face reverting to its human state, "The minutiae and nuances of natural milystis is beyond the ken of even our Lord Harvester, never mind The Geneticist. We couldn't even break the seal in the underground temple. Hence why we had taken Galo."

"Which returns us to the Serpent Bracer," The Geneticist concluded, "You came here for it, and as your reward for reaching us, so shall you have it. Yahsek, escort our esteemed guest downstairs. I have other preparations to address. We may have lost The Prophet, but The Engineer will elate to learn of our acquisition upon her victorious return."

SenRas stared up the towering capitol building, large nearly frozen raindrops crashing intermittently. He snickered as he recalled the story of his grandson's infiltration, only now truly appreciating the weight of the undertaking. He looked down and shook his head, pausing as a banded pebble caught his eye.

He sparked a cigarette as he walked to the front of the capitol building. He leaned on the wall and took a few deep drags, leaving the long cherry hanging precariously. Spying movement in the vestibule, he shoved off of the wall and headed from the front door.

He flicked his cigarette toward the butt can, feigning ignorance as it landed near the dead grass. The man exiting the building rushed over and stamped out the smoldering cherry.

As the man bent over to pick up the smoking butt, SenRas swiped his wallet from his back pocket. He sifted through it, ignoring his cash and bank cards, and took his security pass. Pocketing the card, he cleared his throat urgingly.

"Excuse me," SenRas called out.

"You got something to say?" the man spat.

"I believe you dropped this in there, sir," SenRas said, gesturing toward to the vestibule as he offered the wallet.

"Oh. Thanks," he shrank back, "I guess that makes us even."

"Call it as you must."

SenRas entered the capitol building with no further acknowledgement of the stranger and strode through the lobby to the stairwell.

Despite the numerous suspensions, terminations, and scandals propagated by Chairman LenSom, SenRas had succeeded in keeping his job. Getting inside the capitol building was no obstacle, but the extent of his security clearance came from people who had been deposed. He thus presumed his clearance had been largely revoked, much of it being unnecessary for the Prime Minister of Human Resources. Assuming Spril had been honest with him though, even his former clearance wouldn't have gained him access to his target.

SenRas ran down the stairs, his dress shoes clapping against the tiled steps. At the end of six split flights, he reached a door absent of handle, keyhole, and window. A bolted placard denoted its restricted access but said nothing of how those so privileged might enter.

He held his hand in front of each bolt in succession. At one, a pale red light flickered on his palm. He waved the card over this bolt, and the door clicked open with a muffled beep.

A long bland corridor stretched onward to incredible depths. Unmarked doors lined the walls at regular intervals, leaving those unprivileged wholly ignorant to the contents of each chamber.

As he walked, he gradually came to hear the faint sounds of movement, presumably from one of the rooms ahead. Worrying he may have tripped some unknown security measure, he slowed his gait and softened his footfalls. The hidden noise continued, sounding more pronounced as he moved more quietly.

SenRas slowed as the sound grew more distinct, trying to zero in on its source. He paused before each door, shallowing his breathing to keep his position all but undetectable. He focused on the noise, but rather to his chagrin, he realized it fell all but silent with him.

Considering the noises may have been born from echoes and paranoia, SenRas resumed his natural stride. His eyes darted side to side, checking each door for even the slightest anomaly. On one, he noticed tool marks across the frame and bolting panel.

He leaned in to inspect the scratches, running his fingertip over the,. It looked like someone had tried to jimmy a flathead screwdriver behind the panel, but the durable construct had held up and dulled the tool instead. Hearing no signs of presence inside the room, SenRas assumed the intruder's resolve had been dulled along with it.

With a resonating clomp, the door flew open and crashed against SenRas's head. Spewing an expletive, he collapsed onto his haunches. Blackness rippling in his peripheral vision, he rubbed his forehead and checked his hand for blood.

A figure donning boots coated in alloy out of the storage chamber, cold fog roiling around her. SenRas's eyes trailed up the domineering form. Since the day he lost XalRut, he had known this encounter would eventually come.

"Hello, old man," The Engineer hissed, bending down to lift his head by the chin, "I'll assume you got my message."

Malia pulled a crumpled scrap of paper from her pocket as she stepped off of the elevator, moving aside for those entering but offering no further acknowledgment. Nodding to herself, she pivoted sharply and headed down the hall.

She stopped by a placard as she rounded the first corner, checking the paper one last time. Having committed the numeric string to memory, she ripped up the paper and dropped the scraps down the rubbish chute. As the chute clanged shut, Malia entered the Ministry of Research and Development.

An announcement over the intercom told of unauthorized access to a high-security storage chamber. The unnamed intruder had caused something of a fracas, but officers on site had contained the threat. Malia flashed a smirk and exhaled a relieved sigh.

Hearing movement in branching halls, she stopped at the water cooler for a drink.

She sipped her water in feigned nonchalance as Ministers passed with little mind for the stranger. Given the anonymity inherent in so vast a Ministry, her presence caused no suspicion. She refilled her drink and continued on, treading softly down a vacant branching hall.

Ascertaining her solitude, she stopped before an obsidian plate glass door. A silver box with a keyhole protruded from the wall beside it. Malia withdrew a pin from her pocket and jimmied it into a hole on the underside of the box. With a hollow clack, the front of the box swung open to reveal a numeric keypad. She entered the first half of the recently memorized string, and the door slid open with a sighing hiss.

A long wall-mounted tabletop ran the length of the opposite wall. It was lined with two parallel rows of keyholes and panels. She pulled an apparently nondescript key from her pocket, holding it close to see the tiny etching in its teeth. Finding the corresponding panel, she inserted the key and pressed down.

The adjoining panel turned over, revealing another numeric keypad, and she entered the second half of the string. The keypad beeped twice, and the panel turned back over. The keyhole sank, becoming flush with the tabletop.

As Malia left the room, she brushed shoulders with an especially fidgety Research and Development Minister. He gave an awkward sidelong glance.

"Just checking that security breach on our end," Malia explained, nodding with a confident smirk as they fell into stride alongside each other.

"Of course," he sighed, "Business as usual around here, eh?"

"What's your clearance?" Malia asked, arching an eyebrow.

"Third Tier, but I didn't mean, ah, you know," he fumbled, "I don't know anything, if that's what you mean."

"I don't know what you mean," Malia shrugged, "What don't you know?"

"Anything about the security breach."

"Then why did you bring it up?"

"I… Um… I don't…"

"ArcNos has no shortage of enemies," she warned, her cadence abruptly turning authoritative, "Never take that lightly, young man."

"Right. That's what I meant," the Minister agreed, nodding a bit too enthusiastically, "I bet there's dozens of threats we never hear about because they never get that far."

"Who told you that?" Malia scolded with a captivating steely glare.

"Oh, um, just guessing," he shrugged, "By the way, I've never seen you in here before."

"I would think not."

"Did you transfer in from a satellite office?"

"Something like that."

"So, you're new here?"

"No, you're just not supposed to see me."

"Oh! I didn't mean to say that I've seen you now," he stammered, "Did I learn too much, and now you have to kill me? Are you some kind of secret agent who has to kill anyone who finds out who you are?"

"Now you're just being ridiculous," Malia chided, "If you were right, you would've just gotten yourself killed. I just have a higher security clearance than you. That's all."

"Well then, what's your clearance?"

"You don't have the clearance to know that."

Distracted by their conversation, Malia bumped into a third person as they exited the Ministry of Research and Development. She squealed with alarm at the man standing before them, his arms folded and expression disdainfully flat. The anxious employee shrank back into the Ministry and shut the door.

"Ch-Chairman LenSom!" Malia gasped, moving back.

"Who are you?" LenSom demanded.

"I'm just, you know," Malia stammered, her back pressed to the wall, "That is to say..."

"Do you have clearance to be here?"

"In a manner of speaking, but not exactly."

"Show me your identification," he ordered, "Otherwise, I'll have you detained and forced from the premises."

"I... don't... exactly have that," she fumbled, "You see, I, ah..."

"Oh. I see. I know exactly what you are," he seethed, snatching her by the wrist, "What manner of fools does the Noble Doyen presume us to be, sending the likes of you? Is this an insult or his idea of a joke?"

"What are you talking about?" she yelped, "I don't know the Noble Doyen!"

"That son of a bitch can send all the spies he wants, but he should damn well respect us enough to send someone worth my time," LenSom barked, dragging Malia to the elevator, "Come on! I'll teach that bastard not to trifle with me."

"What are you going to do?" Malia choked.

"This building is going on full lockdown. If any of your less pathetic associates are found on the premises, we'll be forced to issue an ultimatum of war," LenSom snarled, "How does that sit with your allegiances?"

Klaxons blaring ubiquitously throughout the capitol building, Representative TolRou exited through a subbasement door and entered the Subtransit. She carried a wooden box under one arm. A banded pebble dropped from her other hand, getting kicked down the boarding dock as she walked.

Chapter 36

Finding the door slightly open, Sinkua peeked into Room 4077. The people he didn't recognize, he assumed to be Chekov, Galo's new doctor, the surgeon, and the interns. He knocked on the door, nudging it the rest of the way open.

"I heard someone up here needs a blood donor," he announced.

"Sinkua," Spril greeted, standing nearest to the door, "Glad you made it."

"Wouldn't miss it for anything," Sinkua shrugged with a grin.

"Right," Spril nodded, "Step out in the hall with me."

Spril shouldered past him, his eyes fixed straight ahead. He grabbed Sinkua by the wrist, physically beckoning him to follow.

"Close the door," Spril ordered.

"What's going on?" Sinkua asked, complying.

"Are you prepared for this?" Spril asked.

"I wouldn't have come if I wasn't," Sinkua said, "What's wrong?"

"It's just..." Spril said, "This is an intense procedure. I've read about torture devices that sounded more sensible than what they've prepared for you."

"I'm sure I've seen worse, even if I don't remember it," Sinkua said, "Besides, I'll be under when it happens."

"Localized anesthesia," Spril said, "You'll be conscious the whole time. Do you still want to go through with this?"

"Of course. I have to and I choose to. Why are you trying to talk me out of it?"

"I'm not. It's... about your medication."

"My protein inhibitors?"

"Yeah, I..."

"Galo's body will flush those out. He'll be fine."

"That's not the issue. The machine is going to keep those out of his bloodstream."

"I thought ..."

"The doctors will explain it. But I should have been clearer. It's about the conversation we had about your medication."

"Oh. That," Sinkua muttered, tipping back against the wall and folding his arms, "What is it, then? I can't do it because I didn't stick to my regimen?"

"Not that," Spril sighed, "I actually just wanted to apologize to you."

"Wait. Apologize for what?"

"I made some pretty harsh accusations. But you were right. I'm no better."

"Well, I don't know how much of it I meant, but me and you are both pretty lacking in self-preservation," Sinkua chided, "So, are you saying you're done pointing fingers when guilty, too?"

"Hypocrite or not, it doesn't make me wrong," Spril refuted.

"Let's not get into this right now," Sinkua groaned, rubbing the back of his head, "Five minutes ago, I was having the best day of my life."

"I was wrong to bring it up when and how I did," Spril said, "Eytea was away. Galo was in danger. And your sister was preparing to go into battle for the first time."

"That was a shitty time to throw that at me."

"Right, well... Most of all, I was wrong to treat you like you don't care."

"You should know better than to mistake my failures for apathy."

"I know. Most people wouldn't go through with this. Not even for their best friend."

"I'd be an asshole if I didn't."

"You're a good man, Sinkua," Spril said, "Don't listen to anyone who tells you otherwise. Not even me."

"I don't know how much that means coming from you."

"Now what's that supposed to mean?" Spril scoffed.

"Just joking with you," Sinkua grinned, patting his shoulder, "Come on. I've got a life to save."

"Of course," Spril nodded, "By the way, what was that about having the best day of your life?"

"Oh that?" Sinkua asked, "I proposed to Eytea."

"No shit? How'd that go?"

"I gave her the ring. Told her she didn't have to answer right away."

"She answered anyway, didn't she?"

"Yeah. How'd you know?"

"How she's been acting around you. A look on her face. A cadence in her voice. She's been hoping you'd ask."

"Yrlis is giving off the same signs, isn't she?"

"What do you say we go wake Galo up?"

Back in the hospital room, Sinkua became encompassed by largely unfamiliar medical professionals. With Spril flanking his left shoulder, he panned the room, taking stock of new faces and curious equipment.

"Sinkua," one of the doctors called, pushing to the front and offering a solid handshake, "It's good to see you again."

"Doctor Ophalin," Sinkua greeted, "Thanks for coming out here for this."

"Well, you know, I've gotten a few publishing deals out of working with you," Ophalin boasted, "So, I'd be an asshole if I didn't."

"You heard our conversation, huh?" Sinkua laughed.

"Every word of it," Ophalin smirked, "Congratulations, by the way."

"Thank you. Not everyone can get Spril to admit that he was wrong, and it is not an achievement I take lightly."

"We're going to talk," Yrlis muttered to Spril.

"In due time," he whispered back.

"Wonderful to see you're in such high spirits," another doctor cut in, "Truly wonderful. I'm Doctor Tiban, Galo's attending physician."

"I'm Sinkua, Galo's attending donor."

"I know. It is such a privilege to finally meet you. I've studied your file as well as Doctor Yrlis's writings on your kind. You, young sir, are quite the fascinating specimen."

"I don't know about that," Sinkua said, "There are four others just like me, plus one that came out of a lab. But he's an Avatar bitch, so he can piss on an eel."

"Oh now, it's not merely your being a Hybrid that I speak of. That twenty-fourth chromosome is infinitely intriguing, don't take me wrong," Tiban said, "I mean what they've done to you and what's become of you in spite of it."

"Don't get suckered in, Tiban," Sinkua scowled, "Those bastards are as rotten as they come, and the one who did this to me isn't worthy of any respectable person's praise. I'd kill him myself, but I have friends he deserves it from more than me."

"I harbor no intentions of praising any of them. Their goals redefine the very concept of inhumanity. But I can't deny that the science they've harnessed is phenomenal. If we can get our hands on their notes, we could revolutionize the treatment of chronic ailments," Tiban explained, "Smart medicine could become a reality, targeting malignant foreign bodies on a cellular level and using nutrients in the body to replicate."

"Pseudoscience journals talk about curing cancer with specific diets. Tumors are allergic to cucumbers, and that sort of bunk," Ophalin added, "If we master this technology, we can bring a grain of truth to those claims. Subjective to the patient, ailment, and treatment regimen, mind you."

"We'll need to tightly monitor the information to avoid distortion in publication," Yrlis insisted, recalling her spat with Galo around the time of the ArcNosian Civil War, "But essentially, he's right. If we were to develop a treatment specifically targeted to bone cancer cells, we can have it replicate via, say…"

"Calcium in the bones," Sinkua interrupted, nodding in comprehension, "Then, the patient could keep the treatment active with a high-calcium diet."

"More or less, yes. The patient would require follow-up treatments, but those ought to become less frequent as the technology matures," Tiban qualified, "But as much I love such an impassioned discussion, I'm afraid we're taking the conversation astray."

"That's not the point you were trying to make?"

"In part, yes, but I also wish to discuss what's become of you as a result, or perhaps in spite of, what was done to you. Your body's reaction has been nothing short of phenomenal."

"Don't give The Geneticist credit for that. You know what they say about broken clocks."

"This has nothing to do with his work," Tiban assured, "In fact, I would say he failed."

"How do you figure? He successfully infected me. He successfully disjointed my mind. He successfully turned me into a time bomb. So, how do you figure he failed?"

"Because you are alive. And sane."

"I've got some good people watching my back."

"Sinkua, we have pored over your records extensively, and our research bears out that this infection should have killed you years ago," Tiban sternly explained, "Even with medication and your friends helping you keep your outbreaks under control, we would have given you one year tops from the day of your diagnosis."

"Besides losing control during an outbreak, how else would it kill me?" Sinkua asked.

"There are numerous possibilities, the most likely being brain hemorrhaging. The fact that you are neurologically functional is nothing short of a medical marvel," Ophalin interjected, "The microtumors should have become malignant and proliferated. The substance in your marrow should have caused it to become cancerous. The infection to your blood protein should have destroyed your liver long ago, your heart more recently. And we've yet to determine within an acceptable margin of error how long it had lain dormant before you exhibited symptoms. But according to your blood work, everything has been rather stable since I initially diagnosed you."

"What does that mean exactly?" Sinkua asked, "My body is fighting it off? Could I be cured of it in a few years?"

"I wouldn't count on that. Essentially, your body and the infection have been in a stalemate for the better part of six years," Ophalin clarified, "The infection is running its course, but your long-term health has remained stable, at least since you recovered from the incident that brought you into my care."

"What about before I recovered?"

"That's where matters get, well, particularly curious," Ophalin sighed, struggling to find the right words.

"According to your initial blood work, your outbreaks appear to be a catalyst for the maladies which Doctor Ophalin has described," a middle-aged woman explained, "I'm Doctor Chekov, by the way."

"Yrlis's mother," Sinkua noted, "Nice to meet you."

"Likewise," Chekov nodded, "As I was saying, blood samples from during and immediately after your incidents are scarce, but chronic liver damage has proven apparent. Our currently prevailing theory is that your body becomes more susceptible to the aforementioned detriments during this time."

"But when I come out of it, everything looks fine?" Sinkua asked, to which Chekov nodded, "So this means what? My body is fixing itself?"

"In a manner of speaking, at least on an internal level. However, we're at a loss as to how or why this is occurring. None of our findings indicate it to be a natural response," Chekov said, "In fact, the only explanation for this phenomenon is, at this time, the irrefutable fact of its occurrence. It must happen because it is already happening."

"Maybe I got doped with something like The Scout's nanochip?" Sinkua grasped.

"No signs of that either. At this point, I would contend that our only hope of a logical explanation lies in your Hybrid Chromosomes," Yrlis offered, "But with our knowledge of that being in its infancy, that's yet to pan out."

"The fact of the matter," Ophalin added, reinserting himself in the discussion, "is that somehow, something is teaching and directing your body to repair itself after your outbreaks. Possibly on a more advanced level than The Scout's nanochip, judging by what I've learned about it."

"And you were worried this operation might hurt me," Sinkua snarked, elbowing Spril.

They all shared a brief laugh, settling as Chekov asked, "Now then, are you ready to move forward with the procedure?"

"Yeah, enough talk about me," Sinkua insisted, "Let's talk about how we're going to get Galo back in the action."

"We've modified a hemodialysis machine based on multiple biometrics drawn from your blood work. I won't bore you with the finer machinations of the device, but I will say that these modifications, as well as the circumstances necessitating them, have called for a few key changes to the standard treatment process," Tiban began.

"What sort of changes?" Sinkua asked, "Is Galo going to be at risk?"

"No more than usual," Tiban said, "But we'll need to draw blood from multiple points, and the more quickly your blood is moving, the more conducive it is to our needs."

"You're going to shove a tube into my heart."

"Into your aorta, more specifically. But I prefer to say that we're going to inject a phlebotomy needle. It sounds, ah, not quite so reckless. We'll also be drawing from a few of your radial pulse points. Still on board so far?"

"Spril said I'd get anesthetic," Sinkua shrugged, "I'm not worried."

"Ah, not for those," Tiban refuted, "Dulling your nerve response at those points would decelerate your circulation below the critical point. The anesthetic is for the surgery."

"There's surgery?"

"Yes, we'll need to bypass your liver," Ophalin said, taking the conversational reins, "Between your condition and your internal healing response, your liver is in constant flux between infection and health. As blood exits your liver, it carries brief traces of that infection."

"And you're afraid it could infect Galo, because my blood might not clean itself in his body."

"Precisely," Ophalin said, "So, we have to reroute your circulatory system around your liver."

"Sounds intense," Sinkua said "How dangerous is that? Cutting off my liver, I

"For the liver, actually quite minimal," Ophalin assured, "For you in general, a bit more but still not so much. Granted, there are risks to any surgery, but bypassing your liver is actually among the lesser of them in this case."

"Once we get started, how long do you think it will take for Galo to come out of it?"

"Hard to say. Our estimates range from thirty minutes to six hours," Yrlis answered, "But even after he wakes up, it may take several hours for both of you to fully recover. Spril will guard the room the entire time."

"Damn right," Spril asserted, acknowledging Sinkua with a firm nod.

"Well then, let's get to it," Sinkua said, "I've got a wedding to plan, and my best man doesn't even know about it yet."

An announcement over the intercom called Spril to the lobby. The others looked to him inquisitively, but Spril just signaled that he would return shortly and left the room. Sinkua shrugged and assumed Spril's position at the door, refusing to continue with the operation until he returned.

"Uncle Spril!" someone called out, "Spril, over here!"

"Vielle!" Spril called back, weaving through the crowd to find her, "Did you have me paged? What's going on?"

"There's some old lady here to see you," Vielle explained, "She won't say who she is, but she insists you're expecting her."

"I am. You mean you don't recognize her?"

"Nope."

"Good."

Leaving Vielle no less confused, Spril move to the next row of seats. There, he found an old lady holding a wooden box. He sat beside her and laid his hand on her shoulder.

"Always a pleasure to see you, madam," he greeted.

"Thank you for upholding my anonymity," TolRou said, "This is good. Nobody here seems to recognize me."

"Are you wearing a disguise? You don't look any different."

"I haven't trusted him since the inception of the Ministries. Hence, I've maintained a low profile since then."

"In case you had to do something like this?"

"Anything I needed to keep off his radar, yes," TolRou explained, "By the way, your plan worked in as much as I acquired the parcel and escaped."

"Excellent job," Spril remarked, "What of the others?"

"Both taken captive. Building is on lockdown. That's the part that didn't work."

"That actually was part of the plan."

"Why wasn't I told about this?" TolRou objected.

"That's why," Spril said, noting her discomposure, "Knowing that would have unnerved you to the point that you may not have been able to uphold your role in the operation."

"Will they be okay?" TolRou worried, "His authority is virtually uncontested, and we know almost nothing about his liaison. Is this box really worth giving them those two as hostages?"

"It is, but truthfully, they've only succeeded in taking themselves hostage," Spril countered, "Our agents orchestrated their own capture."

EshCal sat in the window frame with one foot on the floor and the other propped on the sill. Ice crystals coated the other side of the glass, patches withering against her body heat. Her expression contrastingly stoic, her foot drummed on the floor as she channeled her anxiety down her leg.

Phylus sat atop the back of the couch, too engrossed in his work to pay mind to the shoeprints he left on the cushions. On his lap sat a pad of paper riddled with notes encrypted in his own style of shorthand. He waggled his pen between his fingers as he mulled over his writings, marking passages as he gleaned further insights.

Biroe and KalChi sat before a spread of paperwork covering the top of the bureau. Analyzing a vast array of figures, they hunted for connections between the late JalRov and the anonymously held Tanelenese account. While nothing suggested his ability or motive to mastermind such a scandal, even less indicated falsehood in Joren's claims.

"Out of curiosity," KalChi blurted out, "Just thinking out loud here, but do we know when we're going back to ArcNos?"

"This isn't the right time to…" EshCal grumbled.

"I know. But It's never the right time to bring it up," KalChi snipped, "Phylus is trying to make sense his observations. Biroe and I are investigating what Joren said about JalRov. And you're… doing whatever it is that you do all day. But are we just gonna stay here until this all blows over?"

"We've contacted our most trusted associates within our respective Ministries," Phylus added in fragmented delivery, frequently trailing off and pausing to tend to his notes.

"They know our whereabouts," Biroe assured, his eyes never straying from their paperwork, "More importantly, they know what we learned from Joren, and they're all working to mitigate the damage on our side."

"This isn't the right time to make our move," EshCal cut in, scowling at the continuous interruption.

"How do you suppose?" KalChi asked, "Like Biroe said, our people know where we are and what's happening. Wouldn't it be easier to keep in touch with them if we went home?"

"It would also be easier for Joren to accuse us of foul play if we go home to collaborate with people who, on paper, still work for Chairman LenSom," Phylus explained, "Too much diplomatic risk."

"Well, they can't force us to stay. It's not like we're hostages here."

"That's where you're wrong," EshCal said, "Noble Doyen Joren knows where we're staying, and we should assume we're being monitored to some extent. If we pack up and leave, he can justifiably construe that as abandonment of negotiations and a perceived threat of aggression."

"I hadn't thought of it like that," Biroe admitted, pushing away from their work to join the conversation in earnest, "By that logic, we are hostages here. So, the question is just as much how do we make our move as when?"

"He may eventually tire of waiting and break the stalemate," Phylus suggested.

"So we're waiting until they attack?" KalChi gasped, "Do you realize how many lives we may be risking?"

"That's a worst-case scenario," EshCal said, "But our poorly timed departure could result in even more casualties than if we wait for Tanelen to draw first blood. You need to understand the gravity of the situation we're in. Ouristihra's two most powerful militaries are on the brink of war with each other."

"I know it's frustrating to be stuck here," Biroe empathized, "But our isolation may be the only thing preserving the stalemate."

"Beyond that, if we move now, we'll specifically endanger two of our associates and spoil their operation," EshCal added.

"I think you lost us there," Phylus said, "What have you heard?"

"NalSet relayed a report to me last night. Malia and SenRas orchestrated a heist on the capitol building. They were captured by LenSom and The Engineer. The building is now on lockdown."

"Not much of a heist if they got captured," Biroe snarked, "Shouldn't we help them?"

"They set out to be captured, and we've already helped them by getting people in our Ministries working to clear up the scandal," EshCal clarified, "Any further intervention on our part is liable to get them killed."

"But Joren holds a poor opinion of the ArcNosian administration," KalChi argued, "Given LenSom's abuse of authority and excessive domestic force, shouldn't we take this opportunity to prove we're not loyal to him?"

"Malia isn't one of his people. She hasn't worked for ArcNos in any official capacity since the end of the ArcNosian Civil War."

"Do you think LenSom might claim Tanelen sent her and use that to justify attacking them?" KalChi asked, "That would get us marked as traitors if we try to help her."

"She's a tad dark to be Tanelenese," Phylus mused, "And we have insiders who can contest that claim if he makes it. The body count may still be high, but the conflict will end much faster if he starts it that way. We can prove none of us work for Tanelen and absolve them of any wrongdoing. The ArcNosian administration may become divided again, but the fighting would be easier to contain."

"So we'd have another civil war?" KalChi sneered.

"If we can gain Joren's trust, we stand a chance of settling this without bloodshed," Biroe suggested, "We need to show him that the problem is LenSom. Not ArcNos at large."

"We have a more imminent threat than LenSom on our hands," EshCal cut in, "If we make our move before SenRas and Malia make theirs, we can expect The Engineer to signal Joren to pull the trigger on his ultimatum. His trust is out of the question."

"Hold on," KalChi said, "I thought the Avatars didn't work for Tanelen. Or vice versa."

"Right. We know beyond reasonable doubt that their base of operations is here," Phylus added, "But they don't have any government affiliations here... Do they?"

"Not in any joint official capacity," EshCal partially conceded, "Did any of you notice the Noble Doyen's arm when he was reaching for his coat?"

"No, but I hadn't given it any thought," Phylus shrugged, "I assumed his guards were just surrounding him while he was vulnerable."

"Well, it would seem Malia put Olsa out of two jobs when she masterminded her impeachment. And The Harvester was decidedly ambitious in replacing her."

"Wait," Biroe stammered, "Do you mean to say...?"

"Yes. Noble Doyen Joren is The Politician. And now, the double agent who ruined his predecessor and leaked their research and a saboteur who held back the ArcNosian invasion from the inside and destroyed The Scout's nanochip are locked up with The Engineer and their new ArcNosian proxy."

"Sounds like a risky combination," KalChi said.

"Yes, but given their deeply seated vendettas, LenSom and The Engineer won't leave until they've ruined or killed Malia and SenRas," EshCal said, "Even though LenSom initiated the lockdown, he only succeeded in taking The Engineer and himself hostage."

Phylus snickered under his breath, his chest and folded arms bouncing. Ten years ago, he would never have expected that sort of reasoning from EshCal. It sounded like the sort of scheme Sinkua or Spril would devise, walking into a trap and set it off on their assailant. Clearly, one of them was behind this operation, probably Spril. Whether EshCal's sentiment was genuine or parroted, he couldn't quite tell.

Everyone returned their tasks, the weight of the conversation bearing down subjectively.

Knowing Joren's alternate identity complicated Phylus's assessment. While it explained much of his behavior at the meeting, his persona didn't reflect any sort of transition. He seemed to be the same man that he had been before the ArcNosian Civil War.

Biroe and KalChi suspected more strongly now that the Noble Doyen had lied about JalRov's involvement. Unfortunately, nothing on hand disproved his claim. Standard court proceedings would place the onus on Joren, but a person of his influence would have no trouble deflecting that burden. Given what became of Mikalan when he defied the last Politician, they knew better than to hope for another iconoclast in the Union Parliament. The only way they could exonerate JalRov and destroy the Avatars' scapegoat would be with hard evidence.

The mark on Joren's arm had etched itself into EshCal's memory. In the days since, she had tried to reject the truth, denying how perfectly it rationalized his behavior. For that, as well as fear of creating bias, she had kept this terrible secret to herself.

Sharing her knowledge had given rise to new outlooks on recent events, but their endgame remained unclear. From Tanelen, forcibly assimilating ArcNos was the most tactically rational next step. Granted, the Avatars of Fate had never been rational in any traditional sense, but her work with The Hunter had granted EshCal a measure of insight. It would fit their methodology to start a war between the Northland powers to serve their endgame. Whatever that may have been.

The thought processes behind each scheme and every event, individually and collectively, coalesced into a swelling epiphany.

Hiding the Platinum Orchid ensnared Pahres in labyrinthine duality and drew Galo toward ruin. Hunting the destroyers of The Scout's nanochip removed Eytea from ArcNos, diverted Farim's focus, and put SenRas on paranoid alert. Stealing one of the ancient tomes sent cracks through Sinkua's psychological fortitude, which led to unrest in The Coalition. Yahsek and Ozzera's treachery proliferated into distrust among the Hybrids and destabilized Nikasu. The biomech assault scattered them throughout Tanelen and ArcNos. And Joren's ultimatum and dual status kept the four of them from leaving.

"Son of a bitch!" EshCal shouted, lunging off of the windowsill.

"What happened?" Phylus spat, nearly throwing his papers she startled him so.

"I know what they're after."

"You figured out why they're putting ArcNos and Tanelen at war with each other?"

"Not that. That might not even be their actual goal."

"You think the threat of war could just be a red herring?" KalChi asked, "Seems a tad extreme, no matter what they're out to do."

"You obviously haven't been dealing with them that long," EshCal derided.

"My last employer was contracted in developing and financing the Triad Titan project."

"Fine, then, you obviously haven't been paying attention that long. Collateral damage isn't an issue for these people, and they don't care if clandestinity takes ten times the effort of a direct approach."

"She's right," Biroe said, "That's how they operate. How they stay in control. Lay out multiple paths. Plant different lines of groupthink for each one. It's all to hide their true agenda and stay ahead of their enemies."

"Precisely. And this war is just one more means to their ends," EshCal continued, "And those ends are where we need to start. Both to understand them and to fight them."

"Cut off their goal instead of trying to stop them from reaching it," Phylus said, "So, where are they going with all of this?"

"Everything they've done has served two key purposes. The first has been to keep the Hybrids, the Subtransit Resistance, and The Coalition splintered. Succeeding there, they've been able to mastermind their second agenda," EshCal explained, "While we've been scrambling, they've been preparing to assimilate ArcNos into their dominion over Tanelen. Two Northland titans controlled by the Avatars of Fate."

"I don't know. It might sound more feasible if they began with ArcNos and went after Tanelen," Phylus mulled, "Tanelen outclasses us across the board, save for the scope of our Ministry of Defense."

"That may have been what they were trying to do when they had CreSam," Biroe suggested.

"Most likely, but the Subtransit Resistance ruined that by the mere fact of existing," EshCal said, "The Avatars tried to take ArcNos, and ArcNos fought back harder than anticipated. Clearly, they learned from their mistakes when they took hold of Tanelen."

"Well, how do they have Tanelen assimilate ArcNos without revealing themselves? Despite the press releases, a lot of people still write the off as an urban legend, because they arrange a cover-up for everything they do," Phylus challenged, "If we don't move from here while negotiations are pending, they have no justifiable reason to attack. And with Tanelen outclassing ArcNos in everything but our Ministry of Defense, they have no conceivable reason to seek an alliance."

"You're exactly right," EshCal said, "Something has to bring them to seek either war or alliance."

"LenSom is preoccupied, and we're preserving the stalemate by staying here," KalChi said, "What else is there?"

"The catalyst is in Laboratory 1341," EshCal asserted, "Whether by war or alliance, activating the Mechanical Crypt is going to set the stage for the assimilation."

"Whatever activating it actually does," KalChi added.

"I'd rather not wait to find out," Biroe insisted, "But do the Avatars of Fate even know what it does?"

"Well, The Omnimath doesn't know, and he's the only person who can outmaneuver The Harvester," EshCal said, "So, it's safe to assume that they don't know either. But you're right. We can't afford to wait and see. Not what the Mechanical Crypt does nor how they'll use it to usher in their assimilation."

"I guess MalVek and NalSet haven't had any luck with it," Phylus noted.

"Nothing yet, and it being beyond them says plenty."

"Well, we know the Avatars have the Serpent Bracer. They need that to activate it, right?" KalChi asked, to which Phylus nodded, "Well, Galo is in the hospital, and Gabdur is under protective custody."

"Yes, but consider what happened," Phylus said.

"You think he went after the Serpent Bracer? How would he know they had it?" KalChi puzzled, "More to the point, why would he walk into that place, knowing full well that they're looking for him?"

"If he's anywhere in the Northlands, he knows about the outbreak," EshCal reasoned.

"From there, it's easy enough to find out what became of Galo," Phylus continued, "Chieftain Sage turned falsely accused war criminal ends up hospitalized in ArcNos? Even if West Bend keeps the press out, that won't stay silent."

"Okay, so he knows Galo is in trouble and could assume they took the Serpent Bracer. But would he really go in there by himself?" KalChi grasped.

"Honey," Biroe urged, "We're talking about his son. He had more than enough reason when he learned they put him in the hospital. If he suspects they also took the Serpent Bracer, he couldn't justify not doing it."

"Also consider the role The Geneticist played in the biomech outbreak and in

Gabdur's past," Phylus said, "This is the man who killed his wife and father and drove him out of Berinin. Every provocation between them is extremely personal, and he just tried to kill his son and made off with an heirloom of the Chieftain Bloodline."

"Disciplined soldiers have rushed in blind and furious over less," EshCal noted, "Hell, I'm surprised Gabdur didn't snap his neck years ago."

"What's our plan, then?" KalChi asked, "Do we reach out to our friends in ArcNos and have them check out Laboratory 1341? Or do we slip out of here and do it ourselves?"

"Sort of, but not exactly," EshCal muddled, digging in her pack, "We're leaving here, but ArcNos isn't our next move. We're going back to the base first."

"To mobilize?"

"Now you're catching on," EshCal said with a wink as she withdrew her portal strip, "Let's see if those sons of bitches can survive the full force of The Coalition bearing down on them."

MalVek crept down the dimly lit hall, his shadows scissoring over the tiles. A dull blue light flickered and crackled through the space between the door and the frame. He squinted at the interference, his lips curling in discontentment. The light faded out, and he opened the door.

The Frigid storm raged on as it had for days. Ephemeral glimpses of a displaced image interrupted the whited-out cityscape. With each flicker, he glimpsed another room through a fractalized electric blue screen. Warped fragments of conversation bled through the barricade, something about malfunctions and traveling by other means. MalVek squeezed the communicator in his earlobe.

"Hello, MalVek," Mortvill answered, "Are we receiving guests?"

"Not quite," MalVek said, "We've got a situation out here."

"Analyze the threat and report accordingly," Mortvill ordered, a stern tone replacing his cordial cadence.

"EshCal and her companions are trying to come to us via portal strip, but the gateway won't fully materialize."

"They are still in Tanelen, are they not?"

"Correct."

"Does it appear to a matter of malfunctioning hardware?" Mortvill suggested, "Might you go to them and escort them here with yours?"

"Doubt it. Looks like external interference."

"Impossible. The technology is beyond him. He can't have developed the means to disrupt the dynamic frequencies with any notable consistency."

"It isn't that finely tuned. I'm catching broken glimpses here and there. I think they see me, too," MalVek explained, "This looks more like variable EMP tech. Multiple or mobile transmitters. Possibly both."

"They've outfitted their biomechanical units with EMP transmitters. The Politician means to enact the next phase between ArcNos and Tanelen," Mortvill deduced, "We haven't the means, however, to determine their numbers, their distance, or their range. We know only that they are near enough to interfere yet presumably far enough to not be heard."

"Too many variables, not enough constants," MalVek said, "What would you have us do?"

"I am familiar with Biroe's capacity for automotive maneuvering as well as Phylus's acumen for projectile martial arts. Between those and EshCal's battlefield talents, they might escape the blackout field long enough to activate her portal strip."

"That's assuming they can get their hands on a functioning car," MalVek warned, "Plus KalChi complicates matters."

"She is a bit of a deadweight in this matter, is she not?"

"Yeah, but we can't ask them to leave her behind."

"I wouldn't think to suggest it. To ask such a sacrifice would destabilize Biroe well beyond what would come of losing her in combat."

"You're getting quite the grasp on your sense of humanity."

"I am not wholly devoid of empathy."

"Are we to intercept the assault and give them a chance to escape?"

"They intend to usher in a war. It is more than I intend for you and NalSet to endure unassisted," Mortvill refused, "The two of you will go to them by car, as near as the EMP transmitters will permit, and collaborate on counteroffensive measures. Make use of one of our portal garages."

"Understood," MalVek said, "What about Pahres?"

"I'm sending him to ArcNos."

"For what reason?"

"EshCal means to enlist our aid. Given her multiple attempts to use her portal strip, she is ignorant of the interference and thus the cause of it as well. She has already informed us of the Noble Doyen's treachery. Further developments regarding Malia and SenRas would only come from their termination of radio silence," Mortvill explained, "The only plausibilities are complications with Gabdur or at West Bend General Hospital."

370

Chapter 37

From the darkness came a dull hum, reverberating upon unseen walls. Faint blips accompanied the growling in a slow rhythm. Indistinguishable mutterings slipped through the white noise.

A hand settling upon his shoulder disrupted the calmness of the dull noise. The shook him, drawing his mind into consciousness. Sinkua opened his eyes and took stock of his surroundings as they came into focus.

"What time is it?" he mumbled, puzzling at the night sky outside the window.

"Bit after one in the morning."

"Damn. I didn't think it would take this long."

"It didn't. They finished nearly ten hours ago."

"Huh. Why didn't anyone wake me up?"

"I told them to let you sleep."

"Oh. Thanks," Sinkua yawned, "How's Galo?"

"Quite well, thanks for asking," Galo smiled, rolling his chair to the foot of the bed, "You're really not yourself when you first wake up, you know."

"You!" Sinkua exclaimed, "You're awake! And... And moving. And... How long have you been sitting here?"

"I don't know. A few hours perhaps," Galo shrugged, "After what you did, I felt I owed you as much."

"Everyone held a vigil," Sinkua brushed off, "Vielle and MarLys took the first night. I went home with Eytea and had dinner."

"If I knew you tried to stay on the first night, I would have sent you home myself," Galo said, "But I'm referring to the procedure."

"They told you about that, huh?"

"Of course. And well, I don't think I ever got to say this to you, but I'm sorry."

"For what? What happened to you wasn't your fault."

"I mean for how I spoke of you when I was with The Prophet."

"You weren't yourself. Neither was he," Sinkua said, "If The Coalition can welcome him back, I can forgive our spat."

"Yes, well I painted you as the asshole of assholes," Galo said, "But the truth is, I remember everything you've ever done for me, for our friends, for Berinin, and for ArcNos."

"I failed to save Grandpa Gijin and ran away from CreSam until he couldn't be helped."

"No one blames you for either of those. Did you blame Eytea when she couldn't fly you down into that abandoned laboratory in Ferya?"

"I guess not, but..."

"There you go!" Galo exclaimed, "So, how can I blame you for what happened to Grandpa when you were the only one who tried to save him? I was too busy attacking the Triad Titan. If anyone should feel they let him down, it's me."

"If I attacked the Triad Titan in your place, I would have caused more collateral damage," Sinkua argued, "But Gijin may have survived if you had tried to save him in my place."

"Sinkua," Galo urged, rolling his chair to the head of the bed, "What happened to you?"

"What are you talking about?"

"They told me you were upbeat and wisecracking before the operation. Doctor Ophalin said you had some news to share with me, in fact."

"I've… Well… A lot happened while you were out."

"But nothing has happened to you since I woke up," Galo countered, "I know how you cope when something is upsetting you. You either curl up in some mental corner or start throwing punches. But I've never seen you take to your worries with overblown optimism."

"Then why would my happiness mean anything's wrong?" Sinkua asked.

"You went into surgery exceedingly happy, but you woke up acting like you discovered you kick puppies in your sleep," Galo snarked, "Ergo, something bad happened, but you were pretending nothing was wrong. Was it what happened with the biomechs?"

"Maybe a little," Sinkua shrugged, "But I wasn't exactly pretending. I did have a reason to be in high spirits."

"Yeah? Well, let's talk about that, then," Galo insisted, "You ought to have reason to be in a better mood than this."

"On my way up here for pre-op, I, um…" Sinkua fumbled, oddly more nervous to tell him than he had been to ask her, "I proposed to Eytea."

"Well congratulations, brother!" Galo exclaimed, "What sort of ring did you get her?"

"That's your first question?" Sinkua smirked.

"You'd have been miserable had she said no. So as I was saying, what sort of ring?"

"Silver with milystic ruby."

"You mean you," Galo said, gesturing to the medallion, "cut pieces from that and had it custom crafted?"

"Yeah," Sinkua coolly smiled, "I shaved off the pieces while I was sitting with you. MarLys handled the deliveries. All off the books."

"Well, I'm the farthest thing from an expert on romance, but even I know a good move when I see it. Damn well played, brother!"

"Hah! Thanks. You should've seen MarLys when she figured it out. If I put any stock in that sexual conversion tripe, I would've thought she was about to switch teams."

"But are you sure about this?" Galo challenged, "Getting married, I mean."

"Why shouldn't I be?" Sinkua argued, "I know life with me won't be safe, but she was already involved before we met. It's not like I'm marrying someone who has nothing to do with the Avatars, The Coalition, or the Hybrids."

"Well no, but are you sure it's what you truly want right now?" Galo clarified, "The moment we bring it up, you're chipper again. Could you have proposed to cover up whatever has been eating at you?"

"That… might have something to do with it," Sinkua shrugged, rubbing the back of his head, "But I started making the ring before I got the news."

"Finally," Galo sighed, "We're about to hear some answers out of you."

"You know I don't like to bother people with my problems," Sinkua said, "Especially if I know they can't help me."

"That's not it. This is about you blaming yourself for what happened to Grandpa and CreSam. You obsess over your failures so much that you think we all judge you as harshly as you judge yourself."

"I don't expect anyone to follow my train of thought, much less to think like me. Not since I started having my episodes."

"I understand you a lot better than you think, Sinkua. You shut everyone out because you don't think you deserve our help or even our sympathy."

"And what good is sympathy?" Sinkua spat, "It can't change the past. It can't bring back the dead."

"No, it can't. But it can bind us. Make us stronger. Show us we don't have to face the world alone," Galo said, "Look, you have dozens of people watching out for you. We all have our own lives, and maybe we can't relate to all of each other's problems. But we all count on each other, and we expect the same of you. None among us would ignore you in your time of despair."

"You really wanna know what happened?" Sinkua asked, "You think it's gonna make everything better if I tell you?"

"I don't think it will solve anything, but I still want to know," Galo said, "Speaking your problems won't fix them, but it will ease your burden to share them with a friend."

"Fine. You know how I thought what happened to CreSam happened because I ran away?"

"Yes, but SenRas said it was the drugs the Avatars gave him. You couldn't have done anything about that."

"Turns out it was worse than I thought. When I was a child, CreSam was involved with The Coalition."

"Your father was also an Avatar hunter?"

"Was until I got in the way. He enlisted with the Avatars of Fate as a mole, but my stupid ass ruined it. Because of me, he lost everything."

"You did what was right with the situation you were given. The secrets he kept from you aren't your fault. He should have shared his intentions with you."

"I think he planned to when he returned from Tanelen. But I was gone when he came home. Hard to say though. By then, he had been slipping for five years because of me."

"Do you mean…?"

"Yes. She's dead because of me," Sinkua spat, "Got some sympathetic words for that? A little lip-service bandage? By extension of my ignorance, I killed my mother, drove my father mad, sent ArcNos to war with itself, and ruined an operation to destroy the Avatars of Fate. My father became the most hated man in ArcNos, possibly Ouristihra, because of me."

"What happened between your parents was between them. You interfered by accident, if at all, and I doubt CreSam blamed you for it. The Avatars of Fate drove him mad. ArcNos was already fractured when we got here. We all agreed to declare war for tactical purposes. And you helped stop the Avatars from advancing their agenda in the Northlands."

"I can't see it that way. If I hadn't walked in when I did, none of that would have happened."

"He pulled the trigger, Sinkua!" Galo yelled, fighting back the urge to shake him by his hospital gown, "Not. You."

"You didn't see what happened."

"Neither did you!"

"Yes, I did!" Sinkua barked, "They staged the whole thing. CreSam had to sacrifice one of us to prove his loyalty to the Avatars. He and my mother spent years developing a plan to fake her execution. They had everything set up perfectly, but I came home early and ruined everything!"

"Sinkua," Galo urged, forcing his voice steady, "The only people who were in your house when you came home are dead. How could you possibly know any of this?"

"The same way they knew your father was still alive."

The door creaked open as Spril rapped upon it. He abruptly turned up the dimmer switch, flooding the room with fluorescent light. Sinkua winced and sneered at the intrusion.

"Get dressed," Spril flatly ordered, "We have company."

"Hold on. We're not done," Galo dismissed, "What do you mean? They tapped your house?"

"Tiny cameras in the living room walls," Sinkua said, taking his shirt from the coat rack, "They installed them when I was a kid. YahSek took them when he left, but a few days ago, Malia found one he'd left behind. Still worked."

"After that long?" Galo wondered aloud as he pulled his Chieftain Robe from the same rack, "I would have thought they'd given up on that house once it had been abandoned."

"It's a puzzler," Sinkua agreed. A folded sheet of paper fell from his coat as he slung it around his shoulders. "But whatever their reason for continuing to watch my house, there's no telling what we've given away."

"Sinkua," Spril cut in, snatching the paper off the floor, "Why do you have a letter to Malia?"

"She gave it to me when she visited. Said she couldn't make sense of it and thought I might see something she didn't," Sinkua explained, "Honestly, I think she was just looking for someone to pawn it off on so she didn't have to think about it anymore."

"Was she right?"

"I figured out as much as she did, which wasn't much. Just that there must be a hidden meaning and probably who it's from. You can read it if you want. She just wants to know what it means. She doesn't really care who figures it out."

Spril unfolded the note and read, "He is not perfect, Malia. – Mr. Mor."

"Does that sound like anything to you?"

"Sounds like relationship advice. But who's Mr. Mor?"

"We think it's Mortvill. So, it probably isn't relationship advice."

"Probably not. I'm gonna keep this, okay?" Spril said, more insisting than asking, "If Yrlis and I can't figure it out, maybe the Ministry of Research and Development can get something out of it. Now, come on. Pahres and the others are waiting for us in the lobby."

Galo followed Sinkua and Spril to the elevator, wondering what development had brought Pahres to them. The man had put great effort into brainwashing and sacrificing him, and now he sought his counsel. Yet, their history did not unsettle him quite as much as their positions in matters. To wit, Pahres could only have come for two reasons. Either something happened at the Mechanical Crypt, or he had news for Vielle.

Galo furrowed his brow as he shuffled along the hall to the lobby. If Pahres needed to tell Vielle something about the Platinum Orchid, he scarcely needed them to congregate over it. Any such news could be shared privately. Had something untoward become of Gabdur, surely Pahres wouldn't have idled away in the lobby. Besides, Gabdur was smarter than to storm Laboratory 1341 expecting to take back the Serpent Bracer.

"Galo," Pahres greeted, "It's a pleasure to see you in a more agreeable condition."

"I'm still a tad out of sorts, but thank you," Galo said, "What brings you here?"

"I spoke of myself, actually. But I'm here because of your father," Pahres sighed, using his scepter as a walking stick as he approached the Berininite Hybrid.

"He thinks The Geneticist took Gabdur," Nikasu interjected, "Actually, he thinks Gabdur got captured, but not like Malia and SenRas."

"Hold on," Galo insisted, "What happened to Malia and SenRas?"

"They pulled a heist on the capitol building and let themselves be taken hostage," Spril explained, "They're going to deal with LenSom and The Engineer."

"Thanks," Galo said, his lips rigid at having been kept in the dark, "Now Pahres, what has become of Gabdur?"

"We suspect he was captured trying to reclaim the Serpent Bracer," Pahres said, "We have yet to discern the function of the Mechanical Crypt, but if those creatures serve as any indication, ArcNos cannot endure whatever might come of it."

"And we know what it will do to him," Galo said, cringing, "How certain are we that he went in there?"

"Does it matter?" Eytea challenged, "Gabdur and the Serpent Bracer are both missing. We know where one is. If the other is also there, it saves us the trip."

"Yes, but how quickly we move in, where we go once we're inside, and how much attention we can afford to draw to ourselves all depend on whether they have him. Congratulations, by the way," Galo said, patting her upper back as he paced behind her, "So Pahres, what proof of his capture do you offer?"

"I have not so much proof as circumstance. Given the developments between ArcNos and Tanelen, it would seem the next logical step is to activate the Mechanical Crypt. The Avatars have already claimed Tanelen, and they've gained substantial ground in ArcNos via Chairman LenSom."

"They're going to lay waste to both sides and merge the two countries under their control," Sinkua gleaned, "Design the chaos and enforce their own sense of order."

"That's one theory, yes," Pahres agreed, "And seeing as Galo stands before us…"

"…Nobody came after me," Galo concluded, "The only reason they wouldn't have tried is if they already have what they need."

"If powering up the Mechanical Crypt is the next move, something must have happened in Tanelen," Vielle insisted, "What is it? Is my Dad alright?"

"He's with EshCal," MarLys consoled, "And you've told me about his sharpshooting. They'll be fine."

"So too are they accompanied by MalVek and NalSet. As I understand, they are confronted with biomechanical beasts outfitted with electromagnetic pulse transmitters. The portal strips malfunction within their field. The brothers should be aiding them in escaping their range as we speak, but I hoped to request your assistance in this matter, Eytea," Pahres said, "You and I can gate to a nearby location, whereby you might disrupt the interference and allow them a hastier retreat."

"If you think I can help, I'm willing to try," Eytea said, "But it could backfire horribly. I've never dealt with EMPs. They might interfere with my electromancy."

"That's true. You are an electrical power source, so to speak," Spril said, "It would be reasonable to expect an EMP field to disrupt your powers."

"Technically, everyone is an electrical power source," Nikasu argued, "But if the pulse beacons interfered with neuro- or cardioelectrical activity, they could not have attempted to activate the portal strips."

"You're doing that robot thing again," Sinkua muttered.

"Sorry."

"If Eytea can, well, tune herself to counter the frequency before she enters the EMP field, she might be able to stop it," Spril suggested, then asked, "Does that sound like something you could do?"

"Maybe. I don't know. But even if I can't, I can at least help them fight their way out. Unless the EMPs shut down my powers," Eytea muddled, "So, I don't know. Maybe I can help, but I might just make things worse."

"Then it's your call, Sinkua," Spril said, "What's your take on all of this?"

"Why is it my call?" Sinkua argued, "I don't make her decisions."

"No, but I defer to your judgment on Hybrid tactics."

"You're today's hero," Eytea smiled, kissing her fiancé's cheek, "I'll go where you ask me to."

"I think you should stay here," Sinkua said, returning her smile as he looked into her eyes, "We need you here more than they do."

"You sure you're thinking with the right head?" Vielle teased.

"Yeah. Yeah, of course," Sinkua insisted, closing his eyes and nodding rapidly, "Like she said, the EMPs might disable her. And she's the only one of us who can fly. That may prove useful once we're inside the lab."

"Very well then," Pahres nodded, "What of the rest of you? I have come in a large van, should the lot of you choose to accompany us."

"Everyone here is staying in ArcNos. No more splitting up. We're going to rescue Gabdur and take back the Serpent Bracer," Sinkua ordered, "Together."

"The doctors are still examining The Hunter's bone fragments," Spril reminded, "As much as I hate to capitulate to their divide-and-conquer tactics, I need to stay here to deliver the Hunter Formula once they've isolated it."

"Let me deal with that," MarLys insisted, "I can't fight with you guys, but we all know I'm the best one for this job."

"If we all leave, there won't be anyone here to protect you," Spril worried , "Then again, anyone who might come after you will be preoccupied."

"Exactly! I'll be fine," MarLys smiled, "Just trust me, okay. I know it isn't much, but if this is how I can help, I'm gonna do it."

"I can respect that," Spril grinned, "Okay. Stay back and deliver the extract when it's ready. The rest of us will go to Laboratory 1341."

"But if it starts looking too dangerous, get out while you can," Vielle insisted, holding MarLys's shoulders, "It isn't worth risking your life over. This can't be the only way to take down The Geneticist. But you're the only you we've got."

MalVek shuddered in a paradoxical fit of agoric claustrophobia, clutching the steering wheel with knuckles as white as the landscape. Shards of ice sprayed up the side of the car, chewed and regurgitated by the tire treads.

NalSet scribbled furiously in a notepad, his elbow crumpling the heap of parchment papers on his lap. His eyes darted erratically, assessing relationships between calculations and diagrams. His hand shaking, he snapped his pencil between his thumb and forefinger.

"I've looked at this thing from every possible angle, and there's only one sensible outcome," NalSet asserted, straining to steady his voice.

"What thing?" MalVek asked, "The interference?"

"Not that. I don't have enough data points," NalSet countered, his gaze fixated both on and through the mound of papers, "The Mechanical Crypt."

"What have you discovered?"

"You won't like it."

"A means to awaken their Goddess and her Hybrid? I suspected their performance at Radial Axiom was something of a warning."

"Nothing so metaphysical, but that may be their endgame with it, given The Omnimath and The Harvester's common condition."

"I assume we need to go to ArcNos once we've dispatched the interference here," MalVek deduced, "Find the means to stop it or, failing that, fight back."

"There is no fighting it!" NalSet barked, frustrated by his brother's hubris, "Despite what we presumed, the arrangement of the pipelines isn't random. They're positioned for optimum hydrogeological efficacy."

"You mean it's going to...?"

"Yes. Nothing to fight back against. Nowhere to take shelter."

"Call Pahres," MalVek said, "Brief him on the situation. Arrange for a mass evacuation."

"What of our interests there?" NalSet asked, pulling his phone from his coat pocket.

"As long as the Mechanical Crypt is dormant, they'll stay behind until the Serpent Bracer and the Chieftain Bloodline have been secured. Should that prove impossible, Pahres will remain to escort the survivors."

NalSet pounded the buttons on his phone, but his chagrin grew with each failed call.

"I can't call out. The storm is blocking the signal."

"I... don't... think it's... the storm," MalVek stammered, slowing the car to a stop.

"Are we in range of..." NalSet began to ask, trailing off in a stupor as he looked up, "... Son of a bitch."

Chaotically flickering red lights disrupted the frozen cityscape. The horizon birthed swarms of biomechanical beasts, their bodies like bizarre arachnids. The dashboard display flickered and blackened. The engine struggled and eventually surrendered to the wave of interference.

NalSet and MalVek stepped out of the defunct vehicle and watched the obstructed skyline. Gnarled screams perforated the howl of the storm as the plague of red lights poured from the horizon like freshly spilled blood. In fraternally instinctive unison, they tightened their belts, checked their holsters, and patted their coat pockets.

"Got everything you need?" NalSet asked.

"Yeah," MalVek grumbled, "Let's go."

KalChi rushed along the battered asphalt, throwing up ice shrapnel with the wheels of Biroe's chair. A shrieking cacophony of metal scraping ice and pavement surrounded them, permeated by agonized shrieks born from flesh rended from bone.

Trembling fearfully, KalChi whipped around as a shadow stretched over them. An airborne biomech loomed overhead with sinewy claws lashing.

Prefaced by a warning shout, a shotgun blast rang out and echoed between the towers. The creature's midsection burst open, shattering the red light and breaking the electromagnetic pulse beacon in its exoskeleton.

"Keep running!" Phylus barked as KalChi looked back with dumbfounded gratitude, "Get out of range!"

"Don't make me carry you!" EshCal added, skewering a drone on her epee.

"There has to be a way we can help," KalChi pleaded.

"Help by getting out of the way," EshCal shouted, "The portal strip won't work here."

"So we're just supposed to leave you behind?"

"I don't think that's what they mean, honey," Biroe said, forcing steadiness in his voice.

"Yes, we do," Phylus said, picking off another biomech, "We can't keep watching your backs, and you've got other work to do."

"Do you really expect us to just..." KalChi protested.

"Dammit KalChi!" EshCal roared, "Run the fuck away! Use the portal strip! Send backup!"

"KalChi," Biroe urged, "Go. Don't look back. Just run. They'll be fine."

"Cover yourselves," a voice called from ahead, "We'll help out here."

A shotgun soared forth through the plague of ice and fog. Biroe caught it and checked the clip, finding it full.

"Drop!" a second voice bellowed from behind.

A shimmering sledgehammer roared through the storm, pulverizing falling sleet. Biomechs leapt at it, barely altering its trajectory as it fragmented their bodies. Phylus and EshCal fell to their knees, tissue and metal raining on them as the hammer passed. Biroe threw his weight to one side, toppling his wheelchair and pulling KalChi down with him. The luminous hammer vanished into the storm, the pulsation of its spin stopping with a clap.

"Do as she says," NalSet said, spinning the hammer around his forearm as he stepped into view.

"We'll get this under control," MalVek added, emerging from the opposite side with his hand outstretched, "Go to ArcNos and start evacuating."

"What region?" KalChi asked, pulling herself and Biroe upright, "And how wide a radius?"

"All of it," NalSet said, throwing the sledgehammer back to MalVek.

"No time for details, but the Mechanical Crypt is gonna fuck up everyone's day," MalVek said, "Once it's activated, there's no stopping or escaping it."

"That's how we can help," Biroe said, curling his hand over KalChi's.

"Right," KalChi nodded, "Let's get going."

"Our car is six kilometers due west of here," NalSet said, pitching the keys to Biroe, "The portal strip will work just past it."

"We'll contain the fighting here," MalVek added.

KalChi and Biroe fled westward, never looking back.

NalSet drew a length of pipe from his belt holster. He pressed a panel the center, and a hole opened in the end. A straight beam of light shone out of the hole, fanning out a meter and a half from end of the pipe.

"What is that thing?" Phylus asked, glancing back as he picked off another creature.

"Something like my hammer," MalVek said, "but more his style."

MalVek pounded the bizarre beasts in a berserker fury, spraying sinew and alloy with every pulverizing blow. Oil and blood ran down the handle and soaked his hands, but his weapon remained immaculate. He caught one in flight, pressing it to the ground and smashing it against the frozen pavement. The point of impact vomited a sickly stew of frostbitten stone mixed with flesh and metal in a broth of blood and oil.

EshCal baited the biomechs into leaping at her. As they took to the air, she plunged her epee through their red beacon light. She wove and dodged through the swarm with almost unnatural celerity. She dropped to her side as one pounced from her blind spot. She caught herself on her hand and thrust her blade upward and through her assailant.

Hearing another lunge from behind, she bent backward and snagged it on the end of her epee. She whipped it forth as she erected herself and grabbed it by a leg. The creature writhed and thrashed in her grasp as she held it dangling at arm's length. She sliced off the leg and punted the body into the swarm with a guttural grunt. Mechanical shrieks resonating stereophonically, she slashed her epee and the severed leg out to either side. Each blade ripped through an aerial abomination, stopping their pincer strike.

Phylus shuffled back, distancing himself from the worst of the swarm. His eyes darted about, tracking several biomechs simultaneously. He kept his shotgun down at his side, raising it only when he was sure of a killing shot.

Leaving a shimmering trail in its wake, an axe blade streaked down beside him. It bisected a drone without any noticeable resistance. Phylus had seen neither the drone nor the axe approaching.

"That's what this thing is," NalSet said. Ice and oil fell from the luminous blade as he hoisted his battleaxe back to his shoulder. "I might be violating protocol here, but I brought you a prototype."

NalSet handed Phylus a metal pipe.

"How do I use it?" Phylus asked.

"Squeeze the panel in the middle," NalSet said, "Hang back. I'll cover you while it warms up."

Both ends of the pipe opened as Phylus thumbed the panel. From one end shone a long straight beam of light, and from the other, a shorter ray hooked at a forty-five degree angle. The light condensed upon itself, concentrating and molding.

"Your battleaxe and his hammer are…?" Phylus asked, trailing off as he came to a loss for words.

"Hyperconcentrated photonic emissions," NalSet nodded, "They're made of light waves so dense that they mimic certain properties of solid matter."

"That's um… Damn," Phylus remarked, too fascinated to take much notice of his surroundings.

"I know," NalSet grinned, cleaving a scurrying creature, "Call for me when it's done. I've got one more present for you."

NalSet barreled into the thick of the pack, joining EshCal and MalVek in the onslaught. His battleaxe ripped through airborne abominations, easily splitting them in half. Now and again, he armed his off hand with half of a cleaved biomech and violently disposed of it as it became mangled beyond use.

Phylus marveled at the flawless glimmering form in his hand, ignorant of the scurrying drawing nearer from behind. He opened the clip and found it shimmering with nearly blinding luminescence. He propped the butt against his shoulder and fired into the swarm. A luminous bullet erupted forth and shattered the sound barrier, leaving a trail of ambient photons suspended in its wake. Pulsating with every impact, the bullet bored through abominations until it dissipated in the fog.

Smirking wickedly, he fired off a barrage of photonic shots. Perforated trails of light punctuated with radiant bullets burned through the pack. Keeping the others within his peripheral vision, he picked off biomechs as they closed in around them.

"NalSet!" Phylus shouted, a series of well-placed shots affording the curmudgeonly scientist ample elbow room.

"Catch!" NalSet called back, turning around only long enough to pitch a metallic ball, "Hit the button and lob it at one of these little shits."

Phylus snatched the ball, pushed the button, and whipped it back into the crowd with a vicious bellow. Figuring it for some manner of grenade, he aimed for the heaviest concentration of drones. A testament perhaps more to his luck than his aim, it settled on the back of a creature in the densest part of the swarm.

"Now what?" Phylus shouted, to which NalSet signaled for him to wait.

"Both of you get back," NalSet bellowed to EshCal and MalVek, working the perimeter of the biomechanical plague, "We never calculated the blast radius but…"

"We never thought we'd need to," MalVek cut in, "I know."

"Blast radius?" EshCal yelled as she carved a path out of the chaos, "What blast radius?"

"Just get back!" NalSet barked, "Both of you. You're not safe here."

"Neither are you," MalVek countered, "Come on!"

"Shut up and run!" NalSet shouted, "I have to hold them."

Snarling apprehensively, MalVek grabbed EshCal's free hand and ran with her. As they separated upon escaping the pack, he slapped a fourth metallic rod against her palm. He instructed her to activate it once they had stopped running. She shoved it into her empty epee holster.

Deeming them adequately corralled, NalSet abruptly turned and rushed away from the crowd. Those who fled the swarm, he cleaved with his shimmering battleaxe. As he caught up with EshCal and MalVek, safely distanced from the clattering masses, he called back to Phylus.

"Fire!" NalSet bellowed, his voice resonating between a pair of skyscrapers.

Phylus aligned the metallic ball in his sights, finding NalSet had kept the one carrying it near the center of the pack. Spitting an expletive insult, Phylus fired a single shot. The radiant bullet zipped through the air, obliterating the sound barrier and vaporizing blood-dusted sleet. The ball swelled as the bullet plunged into it, light rays shining through irregular cracks in its surface.

All four of them fell to their elbows and knees. The device burst open, the initial impact annihilating the biomech it sat upon and shattering those nearest to it. A spherical wave emanated from the exploding orb, crushing and discarding biomechs and altering the very shape of the street. The wave stretched beyond the sidewalk, driving through the pavement and into the firmament below. Underground utility lines bent and snapped. Hollowed foundations caved in and crumbled. Walls bowed inward. Destructive reverberations spread throughout the city block.

The ball of light dissipated, leaving a spherical crater expanding deep beneath the street and well into the surrounding buildings. Scraps of biomechs rained into the pit, twitching as they stubbornly clinging to functionality. Errant jolts arced among them, converging them toward the center of the pit.

Slabs of wall sloughed off of the surrounding towers. Steel and glass fell like hail upon the fragmented abominations. Infrastructure snapped, further bowing the warped skyscrapers.

The pit overflowed as increasingly larger pieces dropped from the bent towers. Buildings collapsed into and plunged through each other, compounding their destructive force. In a single coalesced mass, they buried the convulsing remains of the swarm.

His mouth agape, Phylus rose to his feet with the photonic shotgun hanging from his deadweight hand. He pushed his mouth shut, only to have it fall open again. A crackling sound drifted over the horizon, compounding upon itself on the fringes of audibility.

"That worked better than I expected," NalSet snickered.

The sound grew louder, merging with the noise of the storm and the aftershocks.

"Phylus, you son of a bitch!" MalVek laughed, "No way that shot could've been better. Where'd you learn to handle a shotgun like that?"

The crackling swelled into a pulsating cacophony.

"That was incredible!" EshCal exclaimed, trembling from the shockwaves, "First thing when we get back, I'm putting you in charge of an infantry class."

Fusing metal and melding flesh joined the cacophony, becoming all but impossible to brush off as the sounds of residual destruction.

"My marksmanship? That's you're all going on about?" Phylus laughed, his upper body trembling with the awe of incomprehension, "How did that even...?"

An appendage of tissue and alloy grabbed his ankles and jerked his feet out from under him, pulling a string of violent expletives from his throat. The photonic shotgun fell from his hand and reverted to its dormant state as his face smashed and bounced on the gnarled pavement. His blood smeared along the icy pavement as the appendage dragged his unconscious body.

The appendage curled upward, formed of biomech scraps bound with flickering arcs of electromagnetism. The plaguing mass had become a collective entity, their scattered hive mind coalescing into a singular beast of chaos.

MalVek drew back his sledgehammer. The patchwork abomination reared back and tightened its hold on Phylus's leg. MalVek lowered his weapon and sighed in frustrated dissent. The creature eased its grip and ran away, Phylus's body flailing.

"What... the hell... just happened?" EshCal stammered.

"Their biomech drones are more advanced than we gave them credit for," NalSet confessed, "It appears they're capable of emulating the properties of nanobots, though on a macroscopic scale."

"Programmable matter?" MalVek asked, "I was unaware they had mastered that technology. Even macroscopically."

"For the love of crap, would you two talk like normal people!?" EshCal screamed, "What was that, and what are we going to do about it?"

"The biomechs we destroyed reassembled themselves into some sort of collective beast," MalVek explained, "Either it'd be a lot bigger or there'd be more like it if Phylus hadn't buried most of them in that crater."

"Won't do us any of us any good to chase it," NalSet added, "If we try to attack it while it has Phylus, we're sure to get him killed."

"Well, we can't just let it take him," EshCal argued, "We'll regroup with Biroe and KalChi and return with reinforcements."

"That thing was perfectly content to take him alive as long as we didn't intervene," NalSet said, "We need to fall back."

"He's right. Once it had him, it didn't try to hurt him further until I threatened it," MalVek added, "We can't go at it with brute force."

"Of course," EshCal sighed, "I'm sorry"

"No need to apologize," MalVek shrugged.

"We'll return to ArcNos and assemble a search and rescue team," EshCal ordered.

"It needs him for something," NalSet said, "Hence it taking him alive."

"He could just be bait," MalVek macabrely suggested.

"Then we'll plan for an infiltration as well," EshCal insisted.

Chapter 38

SenRas assessed his environs through blurred and narrowed vision. His neck popped as he lifted his head. A pattering on his shoulder brought his attention to a stinging sensation in his ear. He dabbed his earlobe, finding it sliced open and dripping blood.

"Interesting piece of tech you've got here," The Engineer chided, waggling his communicator disc between her fingers, "Looks an awful lot like one of our older models."

"You have no right to take it," SenRas snarled, managing to sit upright.

"Take it? This primitive junk?" The Engineer scoffed, "We're beyond this tech, old man. You couldn't even reach the rest of your organization in Tanelen with it. Not with what we've set loose there."

"What have you done to them?" SenRas gasped, "And what do you know about them?"

"We've suspected their existence for years. Unearthing scrapped prototypes and poorly discarded blueprints and such," the Engineer explained, "Finding a first-gen bug in the Subtransit shortly after the war cemented it. Looked a lot like this one, except they even went so far as to mark it as one of ours."

"That's how you…"

"Yes. That's how we learned of Malia's treachery," she cut off, "It's also how LenSom came into our fold. He brought it to us in exchange for power."

"You've gained far less than you think," SenRas chided, unsteadily rising to his feet, "Our capabilities are well beyond your comprehension. Whatever you've set loose on Tanelen will be nary an obstacle."

"Don't be so sure, old man, but I didn't dispatch it," The Engineer sneered, "This was LenSom's doing. His own style of revenge."

"Revenge," SenRas sighed, "That manner of thinking is exactly why the Avatars of Fate can never amount to The Coalition. Your rage and hubris blind you. Murderers, liars, and cheaters driven by petty notions of vengeance on behalf of other murderers, liars, and cheaters. I used to be so much like you, but I've come to regret every day of it."

"My vengeance is against another murderer, liar, and cheater," The Engineer barked, pounding her fist against his sternum.

SenRas gasped hoarsely and staggered back. The Engineer circled him, snickering at the frailty of this once assassin.

"I have devoted my life to atoning for what I did that day," SenRas sighed, "But you of all people have no right to chastise me. Not after what you've done to avenge that poor man."

Rolling his shoulder as he righted himself, SenRas plowed his fist into The Engineer's abdomen. She doubled over, holding her stomach and staggering.

"Atoning? You took pleasure in his death."

"I ran when I learned what I had been made to do," SenRas scolded, "I fled the guild, abandoned my family, and surrendered my bounty to you."

"Oh, I see what's happening here. You and I speak of different murders," The Engineer snickered, though no authentic jocularity touched her features, "I'm sure losing my father deeply troubled the child I once was. But his was a small life, inconsequential in the shadows of the Avatars of Fate."

"Then you speak of…" SenRas said, recoiling in sickened epiphany.

"The Scout. We spent years developing his nanochip, and you and that meddlesome woman destroyed it."

"To think I thought you had a care for your father's death. Your son followed you into the Avatars of Fate, and you encouraged both his indoctrination and his inoculation."

"Indoctrination, yes, but his enhancement was of his choosing," The Engineer countered, "He even suggested The Geneticist dose your grandson with a derivative treatment."

"I was trying to get him out," SenRas snarled, "Seeing as I killed your father, I thought I might at least save your son."

"We knew you were trying to take CreSam from us. The Criminal only thought it fitting we take Sinkua from you," The Engineer boasted, "I suppose what I felt for him was something akin to maternal pride."

Those words battered SenRas's composure, his thoughts bombarded with memories of his solitary agony. For years, he had pulled against CreSam and Sinkua as they spiraled into madness, alone in his conviction that they could still be saved.

Now this woman, grown from the girl he thought he owed his life to, thought his son-in-law, whom she had ruined, to be her possession. Years of hardship. Years of atonement. And she blasphemed it in so few words. He lowered his head, unable to stomach the sight of her.

"Take him from you?" he growled, "You took him from his son, a fate I contended because it was my fault his wife grew up without her father. It's the same reason I fought to save Masfaru."

"You fought to deny them greatness. Nothing more," she said, taking one step back and pressing her pistol barrel against the top of his forehead, "But you're done getting in our way."

"You had my daughter murdered," SenRas began, straightening his back, "Trapped my son-in-law in his own mind. And made my grandson self-destructive."

"A means to an end, each one of them," The Engineer insisted, her iris shimmering as she kept the barrel aligned with his forehead, "You've become more than a nuisance, old man. I'll take pleasure in my intimate vantage point as I watch your skull split open."

"You took everything from me!" SenRas bellowed. He snatched her pistol in the split second of her shaken composure. "And when I made amends with the wife I left behind, you stole her from me as well."

"You don't have the balls to pull the trigger," she derided as SenRas aimed at her chest, "Not after your lecture about anger and vengeance."

"You don't know me as well as you think," SenRas countered, cocking the gun, "You may be right though. I've long outgrown such petty matters."

"Do you seriously think you stand to gain anything from showing me compassion?"

"I never said anything about compassion."

SenRas aimed the barrel at The Engineer's shimmering iris. For all her taunting, she had forgotten to deactivate the scope link in her contact lens. She stared down an abyssal loop of the gun barrel and her own eye. Layers of imagery multiplied endlessly, smearing through and spiraling into each another.

The Engineer's head snapped back as the contact lens ruptured against her eyeball. She clutched her eye socket, blood seeping between her fingers. SenRas lowered his arm and dropped the gun.

"I also never said anything about vengeance without anger," he continued, "You've caused immeasurable suffering. But you'll not have the privilege of my expending any more emotion on you for it. Instead, you will suffer alone. And for you, I will feel nothing."

She bent down to grab the gun as he turned his back to her. She stopped at the sight of her hand, appalled by the grotesque state of her fingers. Blood slowly worked down a network of sickly crevices. A strip of flesh sloughed off as she traced one of the cracks with her fingernail, exposing muscle tissue and nerve endings. Shrieking in horrified agony, she dabbed the area around her wounded eye. Bits of flesh stuck to her finger, anchored to her face by strands of bloody endodermis.

"What have you done to me?" she hissed.

"You're not the first Avatar to ask me that."

SenRas took off his polyester overshirt and pitched it at her. A cloud of white dust burst from the fabric as the shirt collided with her face. The necrotoxin began working into her freshly exposed flesh.

SenRas pulled a packet of alcohol wipes from his pocket as he left the room and locked the door.

Malia sat fidgeting in the corner of the vast office, surrounded by shelves of leather-bound books and trophy cases of medals and commendation plaques. She contemplated her surroundings, along with his reasoning, to the sound of arrhythmic tapping.

"Why did you bring me here?" she seethed.

"Come now. I would have thought that much to be obvious enough," Chairman LenSom drolled, peering from behind the monitor, "I intend to keep an eye on you."

"I meant to the Prime Minister of Defense's office in particular."

"It's... complicated," he dismissed, returning to his work.

"Do you mean to make the High Minister's suspension permanent, in a manner of speaking?"

"No. Not in any manner of speaking."

"And keeping me as a witness?" Malia pried, "Is this hubris, or do you mean to execute me when you're finished here?"

"Neither."

"Neither?"

"Neither," he droned, "I'm simply following orders."

"Right," she derided, "We all know you work for The Politician."

"Of course, I do," LenSom boasted, rolling Spril's chair out from behind the desk, "And I'm under orders to bait you."

"Bait me? How is having me watch you start a war baiting me?"

"No surprise you knew about that. They told me you were clever."

"But you weren't trying to be subtle," Malia gleaned, feigning enthrallment as she rose from her seat.

"And that is exactly how this is baiting you," LenSom said, also standing, "You thrive on scandal. You crave it. For without it, you are irrelevant. Dare I say, obsolete."

"Thrive on it?" Malia scoffed, pacing the floor, "My job is to restore political order."

"Of course it is," LenSom chided, "But chaos necessitates you. The truth is, you've so long yearned for unrest that you're reveling in this. You've been becoming less the asset since you sabotaged Former Prime Duchess Olsa."

"So that's what this is about," Malia said, "You're under orders to get revenge."

"See there? One glimpse under the platter dome, and you're all but frothing at the mouth," LenSom remarked, "Your every thought is consumed with gorging yourself on it, rivaled only by your desire to share it with the world."

"Is it now?" Malia taunted, swerving nearer to the desk, "And what do you suppose would come of that?"

"Your ruin," LenSom hissed, "When you reveal what you've witnessed here, the consequent deaths will be on your hands. And the splintered authorities of the ArcNosian

Ministries will be helpless to mitigate the damage you caused."

"And you just assume I'll still go through with it?" Malia puzzled, "Even after you've told me your plan?"

"Of course. It's in your nature. The Chairman of the ArcNosian Parliament collaborates with an Avatar of Fate, the once Prime Duchess of Eprilen, to fabricate a war between ArcNos and Tanelen. The very mention of it sends your mind reeling," he smirked, "Tell the world, and Eprilen will be drawn into the war as well."

"Actually, if Eprilen gets involved, it will be of their own volition. But given Prime Duke Norum's pacifistic foreign policy, I wouldn't count on any martial intervention on their part," she countered, "You see, I know who you really work for. Noble Doyen Joren is The Politician."

"How could you possibly know that?" he stammered, backing behind the desk as though it might shield him from her prying insight.

"I have eyes on the inside," she said, "Not that it matters. I could still ruin both of you with the intel you've given me."

"Of course. The Prophet," he muttered, his voice dripping contempt on the alias, "But you can never hope to prove your story with nobody to corroborate it."

"Too bad for you, that's not why I'm here."

"If not that, then for what?"

"Just like you, I was sent as a red herring," Malia said, "I had my own reasons for agreeing to the assignment though."

"And now here you are, rich with knowledge of scandal and dying to share it with the world," LenSom taunted, "But without a paper trail, everything will trace back to Prime Ministers Spril, Phylus, and Biroe."

"Actually, I already had a paper trail before I came here. MarLys told me everything," Malia countered, "We have enough evidence to book you in maximum security lockdown for the next five administrations."

"Why was she talking to you?" he snarled, "She was only supposed to leak on about Vielle."

"I'm Vielle's mother," she said, ambling to his side of the desk.

"So you're the mother of that Hybrid harlot who's been corrupting my sister's bastard offspring."

"See now, that sort of talk doesn't sit well with me. It's also my reason for coming here."

In a smooth swift motion, Malia drew Spril's emergency pistol from the top drawer of his desk. LenSom stumbled back and dropped into the chair as she aimed the gun at his chest. He shoved away from her frantically, but she matched his retreat with slow deliberate strides.

"After everything you just learned, you're going to execute me over homophobia?" LenSom sputtered, "You're even more deceptive than they told me. Crazier, too."

"Not just homophobia. Homophobia against my daughter's girlfriend. You see, I've grown quite fond of both of them. So knowing that you beat your niece doesn't sit well with me. In fact, it sickens me. You sicken me," Malia sibilated, her voice falling to a breath above a whisper as she crouched to eye level, her nose a hair's breadth from his, "Which is why I'm not going to execute you. I'm going to murder you. Slowly. Painfully. Garishly."

Malia pressed the barrel against his chin and cocked the hammer. LenSom white-knuckled the arms of the chair, his entire body trembling. Malia glared into his eyes, watching hungrily as they overflowed with fear.

She stood and unloaded the clip into the plate glass window behind him. He lunged at her, but she stomp-kicked him in the sternum, forcing him back into the chair. She smacked him across his face with the butt of the empty pistol, blood and tooth chips spewing from his distorted mouth.

Overcome with fury, LenSom grabbed her wrist and twisted until she dropped the gun. Malia deftly reversed the hold and drew agonized screams as she plowed her elbow into his wrist and folded his hand back against his forearm. His vision clouding and stomach churning, she pinned his other arm under her foot and unlaced her shoe.

"In case nobody filled you in," Malia seethed, staring coldly into his wavering eyes as she tied his good arm to the chair, "I have something of an aversion to child abuse."

Malia turned the chair around and bashed it against the window. LenSom cried out as his hands and knees pummeled the plate glass. Spider web cracks formed around the bullet holes. Over and over, she reared back and slammed the chair into the window, the cracks gradually reaching toward each other. LenSom's screams waned with each strike, consciousness slipping too far to mount any further protest.

After some dozen strikes, the window gave way. Reinforced glass fragments burst outward, inviting the updraft into the office. Malia leaned the chair forward, and LenSom tumbled out of it, his mangled hand bouncing against his leg. LenSom dangled through the busted window, his restrained arm scraping and burning against its nylon bindings.

Malia tipped the base of the chair higher. LenSom's hanging weight pulled it through the window frame. Tied to the office chair of the Prime Minister of Defense, the treacherous Chairman of Parliament fell from the highest window of the capitol building.

Vielle rolled the Platinum Orchid in her hand, the frozen landscape zipping past in the corner of her eye. Her flesh seemed to pulsate at the very touch of it, as though it reached for the milystis coursing through her.

She shot a sidewise glance to Galo, reflecting on what he had been made to endure. She wondered what nefarious plans the Avatars of Fate might hatch for her and her relic, assuming they had learned about either from The Prophet. As she thought on it, her introspection gave her the insight to peer through Galo's façade of stoicism.

Her memories fixated on the times she had ignored him to focus on her own affairs. While others had worked to protect her, she had fled in search of an unattainable normalcy. Even though she held the first bedside vigil, their common relics and inherent struggles consumed her thoughts with guilt of the distance she had put between them. Both bound to an eldritch entity. Both manipulated by the Avatars of Fate. Yet she had pushed away from him.

"What's our entrance plan?" Nikasu blurted out, giving Vielle a knowing glance.

"If they've not yet taken Gabdur to the Mechanical Crypt, they will soon," Pahres answered from the driver's seat.

"I'll search for him in the shrine, then," Galo said, "He and I are the only people who can open that door."

"Eytea and I will go with you," Sinkua said, "Gabdur won't go down there willingly, so we can count two things. He'll be injured, and the shrine will be guarded. We'll cover you while you get him out."

"And I can fly him out if he needs me to," Eytea added.

"Won't be necessary," Sinkua said, nodding toward Vielle and their common half-sister, "That's where Nikasu and Vielle come in."

"Of course," Spril said, "Between their powers, the two of them can hoist any of you out of there with relative ease."

"You'll be there to cover us, right?" Vielle asked.

"The whole time."

The towering forest of glass and steel tapered off. Skyscrapers atrophied into modest office buildings, factories, and apartments. Snow blanketed the landscape more thickly, given a more survivable environment absent of artificial urban heat. Galo's hand

386

twitched as he fixated on it. The snow faintly appeared to sink, perhaps at his unconscious will, but it ebbed so sluggishly that it could have been an illusion.

Pahres squeezed his earlobe, activating his communicator implant.

"Pahres speaking."

"MalVek. What's the status down there?"

"I'm accompanying Spril and the Hybrids to Laboratory 1341 where we intend to rescue Gabdur and reclaim the Serpent Bracer. What of the infestation?"

"No longer an issue, but we've suffered losses."

"What manner of losses?"

"Is that MalVek?" Spril interjected, catching errant traces of his voice, "Ask him to check on SenRas and Malia. We can't risk a phone trace."

"MalVek," Pahres said, "Spril needs you to check on SenRas and Malia."

"The heist was a success, but I need to know if they're okay."

"He says the…"

"I heard him," MalVek interrupted, "Hold on."

MalVek cut the connection, leaving them in disconcerting silence. Several drawn-out minutes later, Spril's portable phone rang.

"Hello?"

"Spril," MalVek urged, "Put me on speaker."

"Malia and I are on conference," SenRas added, announcing himself.

"Right," Spril said, complying with MalVek's order, "Was the operation a success?"

"For the most part," SenRas answered, "LenSom and The Engineer are out of the way."

"That was the plan, right?" Galo asked, "So, what's this about 'for the most part'?"

"My communicator implant was destroyed," SenRas reported and facetiously added, "And I lost my favorite shirt."

"I also kinda broke your office, Spril," Malia added, "Oh, and your chair is on the sidewalk."

"We can fix the collateral damage," Spril laughed, "Well done pulling this off. I mean that."

"What happened with the EMP biomechs in Tanelen?" Eytea cut in.

"No longer a problem," MalVek said, "When did you two eliminate The Engineer and LenSom?"

"Roughly two hours ago," SenRas said.

"I left Tanelen at The Omnimath's behest approximately eight hours ago," Pahres said.

"So we can still attribute this outbreak to Chairman LenSom," Spril noted.

"MalVek, what about that giant from the tournament?" Sinkua asked, "Any chance we might…?"

"Highly improbable," MalVek spat, audibly discomforted by the memory, "The titan himself can't exist, and the Avatars lack the resources to have created two generator discs."

"But we saw the disc slide away," Eytea reminded, "Can we expect another interruption like that?"

"I wouldn't think so," Malia assured, "The apparatus was piloted by The Engineer. She was probably the only one of them who knew how to operate it."

"Perhaps with the exception of The Harvester," Pahres reminded, "Though I doubt him willing to relegate himself to such a task."

"So, once we take down Yahsek, Ozzera, and The Geneticist, we're in the clear, right?" Vielle chimed in, "At least for now, I mean. The war will be averted, and the Avatars will be cut off from ArcNos again."

"Joren will still be a problem," Malia said, "But thanks to your girlfriend, I have ten kilometers of paper trails for an impeachment trial."

"We have, however, run into complications with your father," MalVek added, his stern voice growing unstable, "He's currently unaccounted for."

"What happened to him?" Vielle and Nikasu called out in unison.

"I'm not sure how to explain it to those not educated in biomechanics or macroscopic applications of nanotechnology, but something or some things took him," MalVek answered, "He had just wrecked most of the infestation, and a big collective of them grabbed him and ran off."

"From what we've seen, that doesn't sound like them," Eytea said, "The Avatars must have something to gain from taking him hostage. Bait, maybe?"

"I had the same thought," MalVek said, "Which is why you all need to stay away for now. We suspect Vielle is their ultimate target."

"I don't care," Vielle protested, "I won't let them take him and do nothing about it."

"Vielle, that's exactly what they want you to do," Sinkua argued, "He just said they're probably baiting you."

"Sometimes, you have to walk into a trap to catch your hunter," Vielle countered, "You and Uncle Spril have both done and would both do the same thing."

"Sis, I want to go almost as much as you do," Nikasu said, "I know how they treat their prisoners. But if they're using him to get to you, they'll lock him up and wait. Truthfully, he's safer if we stay out of this than if we rush in after him."

"We need both of you at Lab 1341," Spril reminded, "Your roles in this are crucial."

"Even if you figure out where they've taken him and infiltrate it," Sinkua added, "they'd most likely execute him once they know you're inside."

"Then what are we supposed to do?" Vielle pleaded.

"Unallocated Coalition resources are going into determining Phylus's location," MalVek assured, "You folks concentrate on stopping the Mechanical Crypt."

"Have you figured out its function?" Galo asked, his voice wavering with dreadful anticipation.

"Yeah, and it ain't pleasant," MalVek muttered, "Can't say how far the pipes run, though, except the northbound lines. Those go well into the Northland Sea. Possibly clear to Tanelen."

"What does it do?" Galo barked.

"It's gonna use the energy from the Serpent Bracer to carve off the top seventy or so meters of crust. Maybe all of ArcNos. Maybe just the northwestern quadrant," MalVek explained, "Leviathan will be sacrificed to accomplish this."

"Is that really possible?" Galo gasped

"On paper, yes. We don't if the Avatars developed this technology, because it isn't ours," MalVek said, "Not that it matters right now. Just keep it from happening, and we can ask who and how later."

"We need to start evacuating on both sides," Spril ordered, "MalVek, relay to EshCal that she's to remain in Tanelen to assist with evac efforts. I understand that it will take some effort to express the coming crisis to them. But nobody needs to leave the country as of yet. Start from the southern coast and move them northward, prioritizing urban and densely populated areas."

"I'm on it. NalSet and I will assist, as well."

"Good to hear. How are Biroe and KalChi?"

"Alive. We've sent them to one of our safehouses."

"Like the bed and breakfast in Ferya?" Sinkua asked knowingly.

"SenRas and I will assemble evac teams to deploy from the capitol building," Malia said.

"We have multiple interests to protect at West Bend General Hospital," Spril advised.

"Doctors Yrlis, Chekov, and Ophalin are there developing a secret weapon to take down The Geneticist," Vielle clarified, "MarLys is waiting to deliver it."

"We'll make it a priority," SenRas assured.

"I don't think that's what they had in mind," Malia said.

"It's not," Spril confirmed, "SenRas, you stay and organize the teams. Malia, go to West Bend and oversee the evac effort directly. Clear out everyone you can who's not working on the project and take over for MarLys."

"All due respect, sir, I am better suited to work in her stead, given what we're facing," SenRas argued, "Malia and I will assemble the evac teams together, but once they've been deployed, I would advise you to send me to West Bend in her stead."

"I can't allow that," Malia insisted, "Someone my daughter loves is in danger. I refuse to do nothing about it but run and hide."

"You're taking her to safety," SenRas said, "But that manner of thinking is exactly why you cannot be trusted with this job. You're too emotionally invested, while I can remain pragmatic."

"Listen to me, old man!" Malia snapped, "I have spent my entire adult life hiding while my daughters and their fathers suffered. My emotional investment is exactly why I'm the best one for this job. And pragmatism can fuck off if it means giving up on the delivery just because things get sketchy."

"Enough!" Spril barked, "Once you've deployed the evac teams from the capitol building, both of you are to direct evac efforts at West Bend General Hospital. Malia will stay behind to relieve MarLys."

"Once your job is complete, SenRas, contact MalVek or myself for further directives," Pahres added, "Malia, you will receive yours when you rendezvous with us."

"As you wish, sirs," SenRas complied.

"We've nearly arrived," Spril said, "You all have your assignments. Cutting the line."

Highrises speckled the skyline as they crested the horizon. Frosted windows mottled the city lights with swift snowfall giving the illusion of flickering. Shorter buildings emerged as the horizon's firstborn reached higher. Ice crystals reflected and refracted lights both natural and municipal, setting the nocturnal cityscape aglow.

A cluster of buildings centered around Heniokhos Boulevard appeared to shimmer. Refracted glares flashed and warped as melting ice smeared down their faces. The luminary tremor expanded, larger sheets of ice sloughing off of glass and metal to the tune of the vibrating lights.

Pedestrians on Heniokhos scrambled along the snowy concrete in search of shelter. Vehicles spun and skittered over the trembling frozen pavement. Pahres contended with a spinout, ultimately colliding the back end of the van with a lamp post. He cut the engine, and they unloaded into the vicious storm.

"We've got eight blocks between us and the thirteen hundred block!" Spril shouted over the municipal bedlam, "Keep your feet flat and your faces…"

At the heart of the geological storm, a clutch of trembling skyscrapers came to an unprefaced standstill. A circular wave of stability rippled outward from the quieted epicenter. Pedestrians steadied themselves and looked to each other in confusion as the once volatile ground fell silent.

Exploiting the calm, Galo broke away in full sprint. Cracked windows zipped past as he consumed the distance in long pounding strides. Thoughts of Gabdur, the father he only recently knew, left to die in the shrine adrenalized him.

He rushed through intersections with no regard for traffic signals, weaving around and bounding across the hoods of cars slowed by the weather. Hearing footsteps nearing from behind, he glanced back to find his friends closing in. He skidded to a halt at the end of the one thousand block, a dull rumbling permeating the fringes of audibility.

Snow and ice dropped through deep gashes in the pavement on the thirteen hundred block. The cracks stretched and branched, pulling the precipitation underground and leaving the streets dry. The hydrogeological feeding grounds radiated outward, leaving a wake of ravaged asphalt.

"The pipelines are drawing in water from outside," Galo announced as the snow collapsed beneath them, "We need to hurry."

"What do you think that means?" Sinkua asked between breaths, struggling to match Galo's resumed stride.

"It means ArcNos is about to get leveled."

"No, I mean that it has to take in water. MalVek said they'd use Leviathan to power the Mechanical Crypt."

"Maybe they need more energy than they can get out of Leviathan," Nikasu suggested, "They're still using Leviathan to activate it, but they need a way to generate more power output to fulfill their purposes."

"You think they repurposed the Mechanical Crypt?" Vielle asked.

"It's just a hunch, but yes."

"That would explain the additional funding," Sinkua said.

"And why they've held off on this for so long," Eytea added.

"If you're right, that could work to our advantage," Galo said.

"And if I'm wrong?" Nikasu asked.

"Then we may have an even greater enemy on our hands," Galo forewarned, "Once The Coalition figures out who built it."

Ozzera prowled the subterranean labyrinth, her claws raking the antique ceramic floor. She stopped to breathe deeply into her lion nose, her snakehead tail tasting the air. The familiar scent of that Southlander filled the crypt.

"I see we have succeeded in our preparations for Phase Three," Ozzera said as she approached the entrance to the central chamber.

"As she advised him we would," Yahsek quipped, holding Gabdur's unconscious body by the back of his shirt, "I assume we've successfully enacted Phase Two."

"The ultimatum and the declaration have been issued. The Politician and his protégé have executed their roles satisfactorily," Ozzera reported, "This came not without setbacks however. On both fronts."

"We know The Engineer's location and trust she will make short work of the traitor and the assassin," Yahsek assured, "What of the northern assault squadron?"

"We lost several drones, but the bloodshed has been attributed to ArcNos."

"As was expected. They were created to be sacrificed."

"Those destroyed are scarcely my concern," Ozzera argued, "I lost command of a material fraction of them during of the fray."

"This doesn't come as a surprise," Yahsek sneered, "Prototypes are notoriously fraught with complications. The Criminal learned this all too well."

"The link did not simply short out, Yahsek," Ozzera seethed, "Though they doubtlessly held the reins but ephemerally, somebody interrupted the biogenesis network and wrested control of the errant drones."

"They are a tenacious lot, but these years of peace have made them complacent and weak," Yahsek somewhat conceded, "Onward with Phase Three."

Yahsek lifted Gabdur by his underarm, digging his claws into soft flesh as he yanked him upright. Looking him over disdainfully, he shoved the Serpent Bracer over the fallen Chieftain's forearm. Yahsek lifted Gabdur's hand by the wrist and slapped it against the ivory door handle.

Gabdur jolted violently as his fingers wrapped around the handle, repelling Yahsek from his side. In flux between dichotomous states of consciousness, his mind's eye flickered maddeningly. A chorus of voices shouted into the depths of his mind, screaming in his ears from afar in some impossible tongue. Blood seeped from fresh wounds around his shoulder, though he only became aware of it as it dripped on the Serpent Bracer.

In evanescent glimpses of consciousness, he pieced together a nasal voice reciting a monologue in Modern Ouristihran while a guttural voice chanted in one of the dead languages. From the maddened chorus inside his mind, a glimmer of order began to emerge. They spoke along with the guttural voice, hastening beyond it and shouting from the darkness in unstably unified thought.

The inscription aglow in cerulean, Yahsek gripped the handle over Gabdur's hand and pulled the massive door open. Gabdur's mind settled into a state of faded consciousness.

"Do you have the slightest notion of what this wretched device will bring about?" he muttered, "The destruction born from this place will be inescapable."

"Yes," Yahsek sibilated as he dragged Gabdur inside with Ozzera following, "A veritable feast for our Master."

"From this crypt shall a garden of chaos take root," Ozzera's goat head recited, her lion head keeping pace in an ancient tongue, "At the center of this grove of madness shall our Goddess emerge replenished. So must it all come to pass for the arising."

"Even if she still existed, this machine was not designed to bring her across the veil," Gabdur argued, "The arising you seek will not come from here."

"This is but a preparation in Her service," Yahsek countered, hauling him to the top of the ziggurat, "Our methods are beyond such lesser minds as yours."

"Do you truly believe she will take you under her wing in exchange for your offerings? That she would smile on your oblations and bestow compassion upon you?" Gabdur challenged, perched atop the ziggurat, "Nothing of gain becomes of loyalty to that pandemonious harbinger. She is the iconoclast of such human notions as love and mercy. None but her proxy are exempt from her wrath. Not even your Lord Harvester."

"You talk too much!" Yahsek snarled, bashing Gabdur across the back of the head.

Gabdur stumbled, his legs failing, and collapsed atop the circular ziggurat. Yahsek grabbed a fistful of his hair and pounded his face against the helicoid chamber. Gabdur writhed and flailed as Yahsek reared back, but the serpentine abyss screamed forth again. Over and over, that wretched Faux-Hybrid slammed his face against the chamber until blood dripped from a ring of welts.

Yahsek pulled Gabdur's upper half upright and delivered a cloven hoof kick to his chest. Gabdur spat up blood as he swayed from the peak of the sacrificial shrine. Yahsek caught him by the arm and shoved his fist into the chamber.

A cerulean glow exploded from the Serpent Bracer. The light pulsated and flickered chaotically. The chorus of voices returned, screaming ever louder from places unspeakable and directions indescribable. The altar twisted his arm as it drew in the Serpent Bracer to feed upon its eldritch energy.

Sweat coated his face, mingling with bloody discharge from his welts, as he fought the unrelenting pull of the shrine. In a glimmer of lucidity, he anchored his thoughts to the Serpent Bracer. Aligning his mind with the power within it, he channeled the frenetic glow into a cohesive milystic shimmer. The voices screamed in unison, as though occupied of a single mind.

Gabdur unleashed the torrent of energy into the altar, his body backfiring violently. The blue light streamed along the pipelines, dimming as it spread down the ziggurat, along the floor, and upward into the darkness. His body exhausted, he slumped over in capitulation to the irresistible draw of the Mechanical Crypt.

He writhed in agony as the apparatus twisted his arm another rotation. His flesh stretched and ripped around the edges of the puncture wounds inflicted by Yahsek. The Serpent Bracer coiled deeper into the chamber, the azure glow pulsating ever more brightly along the pipelines. Blood spewed from his shoulder and underarm as the wounds melded into a single laceration encircling his arm.

Nerves and tendons snapped, shredded asunder by the winding pull of the chamber. The pipelines radiated with a pulsating sapphire shimmer. Exploding through split seconds of grayed consciousness, Gabdur's screams filled the room to the internal accompaniment of agonized voices screaming in his mind.

Blood streamed down the dais, creating patches of macabre amethyst glow where it ran across the pipelines. Cartilage stretched as his elbow neared the top of the hole. He cried out deafeningly, the voices joining him in sympathetic chorus.

The last strips of sinew broke. Failing cartilage snapped. The gaping wound vomited plasmatic as his arm ripped away from his torso. The voices screamed as one, joining his tortured cries, and faded into an unknowable abyss as he collapsed from atop the ziggurat.

From the floor of the altar, Gabdur watched helplessly as his severed arm turned the final revolutions into the sacrificial chamber. Surrounded by ominous pulsations of sapphire tinged with amethyst, his vision withered into blackness.

Chapter 39

A black shoe slammed against the metallic stile, launching the door open. The handle banged against the adjoining wall, spreading spider web cracks throughout the weakened plated glass. In swaggered Galo with newfallen snow clinging to his Chieftain Sage Robe. He stepped aside and held the door with his foot, surveying the lobby while the others followed.

He had expected, even hoped for, an aggressive response to such a brazen entrance. Instead, he was met with an awkward resonating silence. His nostrils curled as he circled the stone fountain, a foul yet vaguely familiar stench steadily growing. Halfway around, he came across a leaving of fresh corpses, their flesh riddled with boils. A harsh odor beyond that of death emanated perhaps from the abscesses.

"It would appear Gabdur entered willingly," Pahres noted, "Precisely as we suspected."

"At least he put up a fight before they got him," Spril said.

"What's this other smell?" Sinkua puzzled.

"It may be what killed them," Pahres suggested.

"Or some leftover stink from it," Eytea added, "I would think we'd feel sick by now if it were some kind of poisonous gas."

"The smell is strongest over there," Nikasu said, pointing to the receptionist's desk.

"Of course!" Pahres exclaimed, clapping once, "A necrotizing gas bomb. Gabdur must have pilfered one from his guards before he fled protective custody."

"We should assume the boils are contagious," Spril asserted, looking to Galo and receiving an agreeing nod, "Vielle, can you take one of their security badges?"

Nodding affirmatively, Vielle curled a thin vine several times around a belt loop of one of the dead operatives. She retracted the vine until it was taut and yanked back, popping the stitching. The belt loop ripped away with a few more tugs, the security badge falling from it. Vielle released the strip of fabric and retracted her milystic vine, while Spril dragged the badge to himself with his quarterstaff.

"Are we sure the elevators are safe?" Eytea challenged.

"We're taking the stairs," Spril said, "The badge is for the stairwells."

"Wise gambit, sir," Pahres nodded, "Judging by my glimpses into The Prophet's thoughts, The Geneticist has most assuredly taken autonomy over the elevators. Provided the tremors have not disabled them."

"You can remember your time here as The Prophet?" Vielle asked, her voice stern with worry.

"Only elusive fragments, I'm afraid," Pahres dismissed, leading the entourage up the swooping lobby stairs.

"I thought your memories were mutually exclusive," Vielle protested, "As long as I have the Platinum Orchid, you're supposed to be stable."

"The memories do not alter my persona," Pahres insisted, pushing a welted corpse aside as he opened the door above the lobby, "They are better analogous to another's photo album."

"That isn't exactly what worries me," she corrected, tilting her head at the bullet hole in the window as she pieced together Gabdur's tactic.

"His identity is tied to how likely you are to plant Yggdrasil, isn't it?" Galo asked, pausing to commit the horrid boils to memory as he dodged corpses, "That's why Gabdur wanted me to deliver the Platinum Orchid to you. He was preserving Yggdrasil and saving both Pahres and me."

"The stability of my nature is a paltry matter next to its true relevance," Pahres said, "You are, however, quite right on all counts."

"That's what worries me," Vielle said, weaving through the scattering of corpses, "I've made up my mind, so the only way…"

"At your disposal is a gauge for the likelihood of your survival," Pahres interrupted, opening the door to the stairwell, "Regard this as an advantage."

"Any of us could die tonight," Sinkua asserted, trailing off as he craned his neck to gaze at the spherical crater overhead, "Everything else we've ever dealt with pales next to what we're up against. And what's at stake."

"We all knew we might die when we set out to come here, especially knowing they could activate the Mechanical Crypt," Nikasu added, shouting over footfalls echoing in cacophonous accompaniment with the tremors below, "But you have the privilege of knowing when your death is approaching."

"Yeah," Vielle flippantly agreed, "But that doesn't mean I wanna be reminded about it all the time."

In uncomfortable vocal silence, they spiraled deeper down the stairwell. The tremors grew as they descended, crescendoing into a ubiquitous rattling. At the end of the stairs, Galo shoved open the door with the butt of his glaive.

"The Omega cell is a decoy," Pahres advised, "A cover for a service elevator."

"But is it in service?" Sinkua asked.

"Likely not, thus you will need these," Pahres said, opening his coat to show a clutch of spider mines fastened to its liner, "The legs have been reinforced with an alloy recently developed by NalSet and MalVek."

"Galo, Eytea, Sinkua, go down to the Mechanical Crypt," Spril ordered, "Vielle and Nikasu, follow them at a distance and wait in the Omega cell. Pahres and I will stand guard out here."

"I'll come and let you know when they start pulling the boys up," Eytea said as they each took a pair of spider mines, hiding her anxiety behind a plastic smile, "We'll be back soon. All of us."

"We look forward to it," Spril said, saying nothing of her obvious façade, "Good luck."

"Luck has no place here," Galo insisted, his forearm feeling awkward in its nudity, "Gabdur may not have been much of a father, but I won't let him die here after he saved me from this very fate."

"Just as we'd all expect from you," Spril nodded, "By the way, when you find him alive, tell him I said, 'It's nice to see you're doing well, sir.' He'll know what it means."

With that last order, Galo, Sinkua, and Eytea hurried to the Omega cell with Vielle and Nikasu trailing at a less urgent pace.

Galo snapped out the prongs of a spider mine with a flick of his wrist. He mounted it at the center of the ship's wheel lock and punched it with the butt of his glaive . A conic blast reduced the locking mechanism to a smoldering hole, and Galo pulled the bolt and threw open the door.

"Take the floor, brother," he ordered, Sinkua nodding compliantly.

"Whoever took him down there came back up," Eytea observed as Sinkua opened his first spider mine, "Odd we didn't see anyone."

"Must be hiding," Sinkua said, heating the floor with his hand, "Waiting for a chance to ambush us."

"Should we warn Spril and Pahres?"

"They'll be fine," Galo said, "Hurry up."

Sinkua jammed the prongs through the softened concrete and stomped on the button. The floor vomited fragmented stone and snapped rebar into the hidden elevator shaft.

Eytea fanned away the smoky particulate with her duster and leapt into the hole. She spread her wings as her shoulders cleared the opening, gliding down to the bottom of the shaft.

The doors at the bottom looked like common service elevator doors, suggesting the architects found no need for secrecy at this level. Eytea straddled her first spider mine across the crack and jabbed it with the heel of her palm. The blast destroyed the locking mechanism, and she parted the doors with little resistance.

Galo lowered himself into the hole, hanging from the smoldering edge. Eytea flew up to him and glided down with him as best as she could manage. After she took a brief respite, she did the same with Sinkua.

"These tremors should be setting off the motion sensors," Galo said, the ubiquitous trembling vibrating his voice, "Finding the shrine will be the easy part."

Weapons drawn and coursing with milystis, they ran through the quaking labyrinth. Galo led the search with Eytea and Sinkua at his flanks.

A blue shimmer from around a curve lured them. As they neared the bend, a purplish tinge drew Galo's attention to the floor. A trail of blood trickled along the tiles, shimmering against the faint cyan glow.

Galo rushed around the turn, stomping through a puddle of blood growing from beneath the doors. The runic text glowed brilliantly, the cerulean light glinting violet off the sanguinary outpouring. Galo gripped the ivory handle, his arm quaking with an involuntary spike of milystis. The massive door groaned as he pulled it open, Sinkua and Eytea assisting as they reached him. Either it recognized him even without the Serpent Bracer, or that security measure had been removed when the Mechanical Crypt had been activated.

The wretched ziggurat rumbled ferociously inside the towering bastion. Serpentine trails of blue light traced the pipes, pulsing in a cardiac rhythm. Blood ran from the top of the device, an outcropping of bone and coiled flesh visible from against the wall. A hollow pillar of cerulean light shone from the helictic chamber, piercing the inky abyss above. A voice groaned from behind the machine, audible perhaps only because of the compounding of echoes.

"Who..." it moaned, "H-.... Help."

Galo rushed around the machine, bounding over the tangle of illuminated pipelines. Gabdur lay sprawled out behind the device, groaning and coughing likely as his only means of retaining consciousness. Blood trickled from a gnarled wound where his arm had been ripped away by the infernal mechanism.

Galo dropped to his knees, staining the Chieftain Sage Robe with his father's blood. He propped Gabdur's head on his forearm, tilting him slightly upright. Galo turned Gabdur's head, pried his mouth open, and pounded his chest. Gabdur hacked painfully, expelling blood from his roughened throat.

"Gabdur!" Galo shouted, shaking him, "Gabdur, can you hear me?"

"Galo... Son," Gabdur gasped, his eyelids fluttering.

"Yes, it's me. Your son," Galo choked, "Hold on. Sinkua and Eytea are here."

"I... tried to... help," Gabdur muttered, "Didn't... quite work."

"They're going to help you," Galo said, "Just hang on. Don't die on us."

"They spoke to me," Gabdur hoarsely whispered, cracking a brief smile, "I heard them."

"Who did?"

"Leviathan. Spoke inside... Many voices... Old language."

"You heard him in your mind?" Galo asked, to which Gabdur nodded, "Could you understand him?"

"Her. She said... this... not... purpose. Machine... not meant..." Gabdur choked, unintelligible mumblings filling the gaps, "... sacrificing. Not ori-.... original design."

"Someone altered the machine?" Galo urged, eliciting another wobbling nod, "Who? Why was it built?"

"I don't..." Gabdur whispered, his eyes widening as they crossed his son's, "She screamed for you."

"We'll take it from here, brother," Sinkua offered, holding Galo's shoulder, "You know what you need to do."

Galo kissed Gabdur's forehead and, entrusting him to Eytea and Sinkua, scaled the monolithic ziggurat.

"Hold on to this," Eytea said, laying her halberd across Gabdur's chest, "You're going to need it."

"For... For what?"

"To bite down on," Sinkua answered, pressing his red-hot palm against the wound.

Gabdur writhed as his flesh and sinew melted together under Sinkua's fiery grasp. Eytea knelt atop his chest, bracing herself on the floor almost uselessly against his thrashing. In a flash of lucidity, Gabdur pulled the handle to his mouth and buried his teeth in it.

"By the way," Sinkua said, pressing harder as he further heated his hand, "Spril said to tell you, 'It's nice to see you're doing well, sir.' He'll feel like an ass if you make him wrong."

"You know how those authority types hate to be wrong," Eytea added, checking that his pulse was stable enough.

"We can't... have that," Gabdur winced, cracking a grin.

Galo stood atop the heart of the Mechanical Crypt, the conversation below floating on the edge of audibility. Gabdur's severed arm jutted from the helictic port, a ring of cerulean light rising through the slit between flesh and machine. The limb nigh exsanguinated, a drop of blood squeezed through the shredded sinew and ruptured cartilage.

Galo turned the severed limb counterclockwise. Being so emaciated, however, the Serpent Bracer no longer had any hold on it. Dreading and thus refusing the inevitable, he pushed the arm against one side and tried again, but the ruined arm still failed to grip the relic.

He pulled his father's violently severed arm from the port, the ring of blue light filling into a radiant beam. His hand trembling, he curled his fingers over the edge of the hole, touching his fingertips to the Serpent Bracer. His head snapped back as a chaotic chorus of voices screamed into his mind in unfamiliar tongues.

"Galo!" a warped and reverberating scream burst through the madness, "Get me.... out... You must... Help!"

"Leviathan?!"

"Yes, child!" the voice within echoed, the tumultuous ensemble coalescing, "Reclaim your relic. Withdraw me from this wretched mechanism."

"How?!" Galo panicked, "The machine will feed on both of us!"

"Wrong!" Leviathan cried out, "Your milystis empowers you to overcome this monstrosity!"

"The milystis coming out of here feels just like mine."

"My body is your milystis made flesh, but I cannot resist the machine in this incorporeal state," the disembodied serpent explained, "Possessing not the milystis, nor could your father overcome it. But you! You are stronger than this infernal mechanism! Dare not let this bastardized use of it come to fruition!"

"What would you have me do?" Galo called back.

"Place your arm inside the conduit and draw back our energy. Circle the pedestal to withdraw your Serpent Bracer."

With a resonating bellow, Galo plunged his forearm into the helicoid port. The copper scales radiated with a comforting familiarity as they brushed his goose-pimpled flesh. Milystis surged up his forearm, throwing back his upper body.

Galo trembled intensely, sweat beading in his bangs and running down his face. The conduit's hunger for his milystis manifested as physical strain. His knees surrendered, and he collapsed atop the dais, bashing his face against the platform.

"I have anchored myself to you," Leviathan exclaimed, "Quickly! While I still have strength to offer."

Galo wiped his bloody nose on his shoulder and pushed his upper body erect. Conviction mounting through grinding teeth, he hefted himself up to a crouch. Wincing with each step, he sidled counterclockwise around the pedestal.

"They have taken too much of me," Leviathan fretted, "We must hasten!"

"If you can talk," Galo snarled, his voice erratically shifting register, "you can be saved. Hold on!"

"Not for that," she said, "They have taken enough for their purposes."

The sound of gears locking into place filled the room.

"What!? How?!" he protested, shuffling more quickly around the dais, "I thought you had to die for this thing to activate!"

Galo's body relaxed. The conduit no longer pulled against him.

"They must have drawn from an external source."

The bastion dimmed as the cerulean glow of the pipelines faded and died.

"Of course. The snow," Galo said, "When this is over, I have a lot of questions for you."

Steam hissed as the shell split, separating the tiers of the ziggurat.

"And I will answer all that I know."

The lowest ring began to rise, splitting around and enveloping the pipelines. As it leveled with the next layer, the casings fused and merged the two rings. The conjoined rings rose as one toward the next tier.

"Sinkua! Eytea!" Galo shouted.

"We're getting him!" Sinkua called back, draping Gabdur's arm across his shoulders.

Three rings ascended together, milystically charged pipelines stretching as the machine lifted them. Galo shuffled frantically around the platform, the tail of the Serpent Bracer nearing the top of the conduit. The ascension of the rings hastened.

Galo pulled the end of the Serpent Bracer from the conduit as the last ring began to lift him to the top of the ziggurat. He withdrew his arm, grabbed the copper tail, and unscrewed it by hand. The podium tremored and, with a piercing hiss, ascended toward the abyss. Still unwinding the Serpent Bracer, Galo looked down the side of the column. The others had fled, but the floor had begun to rise with the machine.

In fact, it appeared to outpace the machine, as though to converge with the column at the top of the shaft. Galo's forearm twitched and throbbed as he twisted the copper serpent more quickly. Halfway up the towering double doors, the floor continued to close in on the podium. Galo liberated the Serpent Bracer and shoved it victoriously onto his forearm, with Leviathan flooding his thoughts with expressions of gratitude and urgency.

Galo checked the fastenings on his glaive and, with only the top third of the doors left exposed, leapt from the ascending column. He kicked off the wall, the side of the pillar, then the wall once more. He landed in a crouch and, bellowing ferociously, rammed the door and tumbled out into the labyrinth.

Sinkua stopped and cocked his ear. Nodding confidently, he patted Gabdur on the back.

"Your boy made it out," he boasted, "Eytea, you two keep going."

"You're going back, aren't you?" Eytea grimaced.

"Wouldn't be me if I didn't," Sinkua smiled, "Don't worry. We'll catch up."

"He may be injured," Gabdur added, his voice faint.

"Okay, go ahead. Galo needs you," Eytea said, "I'll tell Vielle and Nikasu you went back to help him."

Eytea slowly flapped her wings to ease the burden of supporting Gabdur alone. After the torture he had suffered, he could only stagger in a rather belligerent manner. The grinding of the machine reverberated throughout the temple, joining the ubiquitous tremors in reminding them of the probable futility of their haste.

Eytea sprinted as she found the open elevator doors, mostly dragging Gabdur though he endeavored to match her pace. Guiding him by his forearm and the small of his back, Eytea shoved him into the elevator shaft and kept running. Her sprint abruptly disencumbered, she slapped her palms against the back wall of the elevator shaft to stop herself.

"Wait here," she said.

Gabdur compliantly sat against the wall, his head lolling with his flickering consciousness. Eytea flew through the hole in the ceiling and into the decoy Omega cell, panting with the stress of urgency.

"Did you rescue Gabdur?" Nikasu asked, fidgeting impatiently, "Where are Sinkua and Galo? Are they okay?"

"Gabdur is down there," Eytea said, nodding toward the hole, "Galo ran into some trouble. Sinkua went back to help."

"And you let him!?" Nikasu protested, pounding on Eytea's chest.

"He doesn't need my permission to do what's necessary," Eytea countered, grabbing Nikasu's wrist, "Look, I know how stressful this is for you, but you need to focus."

"Come on, sis," Vielle said, "Gabdur needs us, and our boys will be back any minute."

Vielle knelt beside the hole and extended a pair of vines from the backs of her wrists. One milystic vine coiled around Gabdur's outstretched arm, while the other encircled his torso. His body secured, Vielle broke off one of the vines and handed it to Nikasu.

Nikasu's eyes flared amethyst as she sent pulsations of milystis down the vine. Gabdur swayed upward as she eased the burden of gravity, his body dangling like a marionette. Pulling hand over hand, she and Vielle hoisted him up the elevator shaft and into the Omega cell.

"Thank you both," Gabdur professed as he emerged though the charred hole, "I must be going. The apparatus will soon be in position."

"You would leave knowing the danger your son is in?" Vielle challenged.

"I entrust his safety to Sinkua," Gabdur countered, "Besides, I am of no use to you here."

"Let him go," Eytea insisted, "Spril will decide what he'll do."

"What about you?" Nikasu asked.

"I'll stay here and wait for our boys."

"When you see them, tell them I couldn't be prouder," Gabdur implored, "Nor more grateful."

"I'm sure they know," Eytea smiled, "Now hurry out of here."

Gabdur shambled up the corridor, clutching his hastily sealed wound. Traces of distant conversation permeated audibility, words not quite distinguishable. The voices grew more distinct as they loudened, their familiarity encouraging him.

The tremors abruptly stopped. A loud burst echoed deeply. The floor trembled as it shifted, slabs of broken stone scraping across each other below. Gabdur braced himself on the wall as the floor dropped a few centimeters.

"Everything alright back there?" one of the voices called out.

"Spril!" Gabdur shouted back, "We need to hurry. The building is moving."

"I know, but it's not just the building. Where are the Hybrids?"

"Sinkua went back to help Galo. The girls are waiting to pull them up."

A vast shadow loomed over Gabdur as he emerged from the corridor. The stench of malevolent breath filled his lungs. Too weak to defend himself, he looked up and caught only a glimpse of Yahsek's beastly form before a pair of arms wrapped around him.

Spril tackled Gabdur in a sprint, rolling across the floor with him. Pahres bashed Yahsek with his ceremonial staff, concentric rings jangling, and sent Yahsek tumbling across the shifting floor.

Yahsek rose to a crouch, the fur on his arms rippling and arachnid mandibles gnashing. Pahres pitched his staff and split his bangs away from his forehead.

"You two begin evacuating the area. Refuge is becoming a scarce commodity," Pahres ordered, "I will tend to matters here."

"Fine, but only for his sake," Spril begrudgingly agreed, nodding toward Gabdur, "Come on. Let's head topside."

Pahres pressed the ridges of his hands together, connecting the two halves of his insignia tattoo. It resembled that of the Avatars of Fate but with forks and curls stylizing the vertical lines. Inhaling deeply and holding it, he pressed his palms to his forehead. Pale golden light seeped between his fingers. He lowered his hands with a prolonged exhale, revealing the stylized insignia on his forehead.

The black mark radiating an outline of golden glow, Pahres gripped the hilt of his weapon. From the bulky sheath, he drew a tangle of chains and obtuse triangular metallic panels. His insignia flickering and shimmering, the length of chain connected to the hilt unraveled. At its end, a bladed panel hung aloft. The next length of chain untangled, extending at an angle. This repeated along seven lengths of chain, seven bladed triangular panels hovering ominously at their ends.

Pahres brandished the hilt. The chains retracted beginning with the outermost, assembling the panels into a single blade and locking that into the hilt. Pahres swirled the katana around his wrist tauntingly.

"Come now, you foul wretch," he challenged.

"Pahres!" Spril shouted from the stairwell door with Gabdur bracing on his shoulder, "If this is all a ruse, it won't do you any good to get rid of me."

Yahsek snarled as he stomped about, slapping the floor with his rugged palms. His arachnid mandibles retracted as his mouth stretched to accommodate a row of canine teeth. Hooked claws curled over his leathery fingertips. A thick tail sprouted from the base of his spine. He burst into an infuriated charge, swerving maddeningly. Insignia ablaze, Pahres reared back and sliced the putrid air.

Yahsek thrashed and spat as he closed in on his prey. Pahres's blade snapped loose from the hilt, the chain uncoiling out of the chamber. Yahsek crouched and slid under the blade. Pahres's jaw twitched as the seven segments split apart. Yahsek snarled what Pahres could only assume to be a threat, his voice dissipating against a wall of air. Pahres winced and tightened one side of his jaw as he positioned each section of his sword. Yahsek pounced.

The sound of Yahsek's snarling exploded into audibility, abruptly shifting from incomprehensibly muffled to deafeningly loud. Pahres yanked the hilt back, jaws clenched and insignia outlined in brilliant glow. Yahsek descended upon him, his gaping maw frothing. Blades and chains encircled the Faux-Hybrid, slashing his armor of leathery flesh. Yahsek yelped and writhed, limbs flailing at the lashing blades.

Pahres brandished the hilt, the blades further lacerating his beastly enemy as they snapped back together. He clutched a fistful of his own hair, pressing his palm heel against his ear. As Yahsek regained his composure, Pahres lowered his hand and snuck a glance, finding it stained red. Plagued by a disorienting throbbing on the side of his head, he sliced half-blindly to meet Yahsek's slashing claws.

"Galo!" Sinkua shouted, his voice echoing throughout the trembling labyrinth.

"Sinkua!" Galo called back, coming to face him as he rounded the bend, "What are you still doing down here?"

"Making sure you get out alive, you putz," Sinkua snarked.

"Of course," Galo snickered, "Wouldn't be you if you didn't."

"We left you alone with a giant machine that wants to eat your energy," Sinkua quipped, "Believe it or not, that didn't sit well with me."

"Thank you, but we need to hurry," Galo insisted, running alongside him, "The building has begun to move, and we're below the shift line."

"Fuck. I had a bad feeling that's what that sound was," Sinkua muttered, watching the ceiling apprehensively.

"That and about half the country. Leviathan filled me in on some details about the Mechanical Crypt."

"So, he's still alive, then?"

"She. And yes," Galo nodded, "She says everything on this side of the northeastern and southwestern fault lines is being carved off just below sea level."

Yahsek ripped into Pahres's sword-arm, wisps of blood and endodermis streaming from his claws. Pahres slashed Yahsek's exposed underarm before the first drop of blood hit the floor, a ribbon of Faux-Hybrid blood rippling from the tip of his katana. Pahres jerked back and squeezed his bloodied forearm as the pain suddenly registered, his insignia flickering like a candle drowning in its own melted wax.

Held erect purely by stubborn grit, Pahres switched his sword arm and sliced the air. Yahsek swiped at Pahres's chest, his claws dripping plasmatic and yearning to bathe deeper. Insignia flaring erratically, Pahres's katana snapped apart with diminishing coordination. Five keratin knives burrowed along his chest, mangling muscle fibers and notching his ribcage. A drop of blood fell from each of Pahres's ears as the chained blades surrounded Yahsek.

Adrenalized by the prospect of escape, Galo burst into a sprint as he sighted the charred and parted elevator doors. Sinkua followed a few strides behind, incapable of matching his brethren's pace. Galo ran several steps up the back wall of the elevator shaft and grabbed a pair of vines that Vielle had lowered into the chasm.

Eytea and Nikasu caught Vielle as she tumbled forth from the sudden weight. Nikasu steadily amplified the pull of gravity on Vielle's body, making her a more effective counterweight. Eytea grabbed one of the vines and cut it loose, further easing Vielle's burden.

Yahsek snatched Pahres's forearm in his beastly jaws, serrated teeth grinding through the tender sinew. Pahres screamed in anguish, his insignia flickering desperately. Trusting his already wounded yet unhindered arm, he tossed the hilt back to his dominant hand. He jerked the sword back, and the triangular knives further lacerated Yahsek's leathery flesh.

Halfway up the elevator shaft, Galo looked down to find Sinkua urging him on, impatiently punching his own palm. The hole nearing the edge of the shaft, Galo planted his feet and ran up the wall while Eytea and Vielle pulled. When the vines became too slack, he released the ends and grabbed higher as they uncurled and dropped.

Rage consuming his pain, Yahsek chomped off a mouthful of muscle and fat from Pahres's arm. Pahres cried out as fibrous tendons snapped apart. Yahsek swiped across his face with a furious howl. Pahres writhed and dropped his katana as a claw dug into his cornea. Pahres's eyeball uprooted from its socket with a nauseating pop, and the optic nerve snapped in a plasmatic outburst as Yahsek claimed his trophy.

"We don't have time. Nikasu! Take the line!" Eytea ordered, thrusting the vine at her.

Eytea dove into the hole as Nikasu took the vine, wings spreading as her shoulders passed under the floor. Upon landing, she pulled Sinkua into a full nelson and wrapped her legs around his waist. She pulled them both airborne with a powerful push of her wings, climbing higher up the chasm with each beat.

Yahsek hoisted Pahres by the throat, craning his neck as he gave his victim a disdainful once over. Pahres's insignia flickered and reluctantly faded to black.

"Filthy traitor," Yahsek sibilated, "You don't deserve the mercy of an execution. Instead, you'll waste away here, rotting and buried in the wreckage. Honored by nobody. Remembered only by those you've betrayed."

"To value the honor of so destructive a people is folly," Pahres choked out, "I have taken pleasure in forsaking your master. Thus it shall be that I die without regret, an experience perhaps solitary in signifying true greatness."

Nikasu and Vielle lifted Galo with rapid hand over hand pulls. Galo burst triumphantly into the Omega cell, running up the wall as the hole crept over the edge of the shaft.

Eytea flapped harder and faster, rushing up the elevator shaft with her fiancée enveloped in four limbs. Nikasu anxiously peered into the pit and found they had only made half the trip. Her body trembling with adrenaline and milystis, she jumped into the elevator shaft.

Sinkua caught Nikasu in his partially outstretched arms and pulled her against himself. She embraced his neck and wrapped her legs over Eytea's. The weight of the trio lightened drastically and Nikasu flooded their bodies with gravitational milystis.

Eytea flew as though encumbered by no more than the weight of her halberd and clothes. Her back scraped the hole, and Nikasu's the wall, as they emerged into the Omega cell. They released one another, Nikasu and Eytea panting as everyone's weight normalized. Hardy greetings of survival and reunion exchanged all around, the five Hybrids rushed up the corridor toward the central hub.

Yahsek tightened his grip, cracking Pahres's trachea. He tossed the body aside unceremoniously, sending it sliding along a smearing of its own blood. Snickering victoriously, he sauntered to the stairwell as his body reverted to its human form.

A lashing across his tenderized back disrupted his strut. He whipped about angrily, finding the Hybrids he had assumed buried emerging from the Omega corridor. The augmented whips of Vielle's cat-o'-nine-tails retracted, the lot of them standing in defiance of what we thought to have been certain death.

"Hold it," Vielle ordered.

"Our sister wishes to speak with you," Sinkua warned, "Eytea, go upstairs with Galo. Find The Geneticist."

"Three versus one?" Yahsek growled, his back hunching as his limbs swelled and transformed, "This hardly seems fair."

"I'm not afraid anymore, Yahsek. I no longer fear the outside world. Hardships. Trust. Struggles. Commitment. Pain. Love. These things don't scare me anymore," Nikasu asserted, boldly striding toward him, "I no longer fear myself. Nor the power I've inherited. And I no longer fear you. Nor Ozzera. You see, I understand now why the two of you went to such lengths to hinder me."

"You are still just a pathetic child," Yahsek spat, his fingers melding into a point, "Just as weak and helpless as the day we planted ourselves as your cellmates."

"You've always feared me!" Nikasu shouted, pointing at him with one of her scythes as her eyes radiated violet, "Only by projecting your fear onto me could you restrain my potential. Suppress me to compensate for your impotence. Sinkua was right. I am what you feared."

Yahsek wriggled his tentacular arms, acclimating himself to their new form. With a guttural snarl, he swiped at Nikasu with an extended appendage. Nikasu drew back her arm and brought forth the other, plunging a curved blade through the serpentine limb. Yahsek cracked his other tentacle like a whip. Nikasu winced at the stinging suckers lashing along her abdomen. Through squinting eyes, she slashed at the assailing appendage, piercing it in a clumsier manner than the first.

Nikasu braced her legs and tightened her grip on her scythes, her amethyst stare threatening to burn holes through Yahsek. He jerked back, thinking to disarm her and pull her off her feet. Instead, her scythes gashed further along his tentacles, the spattering of blood on tile echoing in the vast empty basement.

Nikasu released her weapons and firmly yanked Yahsek's tentacles. He barreled forward helplessly, lightened by the milystis she had pumped through his body. Just before he came within her reach, he braced himself on cloven hooves, slipped his appendages from her grasp and pivoted to put his back to her.

Sinkua's morningstar arced overhead as Yahsek unexpectedly came face to face with the curmudgeonly Hybrid. Yahsek lashed at him but, hindered by the scythe still hanging from it, landed his tentacle in Sinkua's grasp. Flames burst into existence along the ball and chain of the morningstar as Sinkua cracked it down, ravaging scaly flesh with fiery spikes. Yahsek writhed feverishly as Sinkua jerked down on his morningstar and pulled back on the tentacle.

Yahsek reared back with his free tentacle. Nikasu gripped her scythe, still dangling from the serpentine appendage, and braced her knees as she weighted herself. Yahsek grunted and snarled, pulling futilely against the diminutive deadweight.

A pair of vines coiled around his neck, aborting his resistance. Vielle strangled off all but the faintest wisps of breath and bent his torso back.

Sinkua wrapped the end of the tentacle around his hand, pulling harder on his morningstar as the spikes broke through the underside of Yahsek's arm. He twisted and jerked the handle, gouging and shredding through the serpentine limb. With a screaming crimson geyser, the boneless appendage snapped free, the edges of the sever wound set ablaze. Yahsek tried to scream out in protest, but his voice died in his constricted throat.

Sinkua removed Nikasu's scythe and pitched aside the severed limb. It reverted to its human form as it bounced and writhed across the floor. Sinkua tossed the scythe to Nikasu, lobbing it high over Yahsek's head.

Yahsek completed his interrupted counterattack as Nikasu looked up to catch her other weapon. The very ability to breathe burst forth from her throat as a cloven hoof crashed into her chest. She pulled her scythe from his tentacle as she dropped to her knees and doubled over.

Yahsek intercepted the other scythe, the end of his tentacle splitting into opposable digits. Vines grinding into his throat, he whipped around and hacked through the milystic growths. He mule-kicked Sinkua before he could exploit his turned back, the snap of cracking ribs echoing in the vast room. Sinkua collapsed to his hands and knees, gasping hoarsely.

With Nikasu and Sinkua incapacitated, Yahsek charged at Vielle, hooves clattering cacophonously against the tiles. Blood dripped faster from his sever wound. Vielle poised herself and drew back, stretching the tails of her whip and lining them with thorns. Coarse hair rippled along Yahsek's arm as his muscles bulged. He hurled the scythe at Vielle as his thumb retracted.

Vielle bobbed to the side, the pilfered weapon screaming over her shoulder. A meaty paw with thick claws swept before her face as she lifted her head. Yelping with broken conviction, she shrank back from the ursine assault. The claws grazed flesh despite her effort to parry, leaving four thin trails of blood along ridged skin.

In the split second between his claws leaving her face and returning to his side, Vielle lashed all nine thorny tails across Yahsek's unguarded abdomen. The wounds he gave her, she returned twofold with one to spare. She followed through with an upward snap, then cracked down upon his collarbone and shoulders.

Yahsek roared ferociously, raising his ursine paw over his head. As he came down, he wailed in infuriation as a curved blade slashed up his spine.

"Face me like a man, you miserable bitch!" Nikasu screamed.

Yahsek spun about and swiped at Nikasu. She leaned back, letting the claws pass within a finger's breadth of her face, and sliced along the underside of his arm. A trail of blood rippled from the tip of her blade as it carved through sinew.

Hearing Vielle poising to strike from behind, Yahsek delivered a solid mule-kick to her chest. He pawed at Nikasu again, but she ducked the attack and swiped at his midsection.

The rumbling paused for a split second, and the floor jostled and dropped. Yahsek pounded the side of Nikasu's head as she stumbled, boring his claws into her scalp. With a guttural roar, he threw her to the floor, blood trickling from the holes he had gouged.

"All that talk for this?" Yahsek scoffed.

"I'm not done yet," Sinkua rasped, erecting himself, "Neither are they."

Yahsek snickered as Sinkua staggered toward him, sanguinary phlegm dribbling over his chapped lips. Sinkua cleared his throat and popped his neck, one eye twitching beside a throbbing vein in his temple

"I know your secret. How you endure these episodes," Yahsek taunted, "With these two incapacitated, you'll lose control in a matter of seconds. Deny it all you want. You're finished."

"You don't know half my secrets," Sinkua snarled.

"Oh, but I'm just itching to learn them," Yahsek hissed, "See, the irony of it all is that we had planned to unleash the two of you against each other. Let the two of you sort each other out and keep the stronger in our service."

"We'd never…" Sinkua choked out.

"But somehow, you've resisted the infection. Even turned it to your advantage at times. Not only that, you've helped her adjust to the outside world. Made a functional humanoid of her," Yahsek continued, ignoring Sinkua's mounting opposition, "Infuriating as the ends are, your means are a matter of interest. You've eschewed your role as a weapon for one of preservation."

"No," Sinkua asserted, his voice churning with blood and phlegm, "The irony is that you don't know the first thing about fighting like an animal."

A gob of sanguinary mucus burst from his lips with a sickening smack. It splattered against the bridge of Yahsek's nose, splashing over his eyes with a stinging burn. Sinkua pulled his second spider mine from his pocket and slammed the prongs into Yahsek's chest.

Debris rained from the ceiling, stealing his attention. While Yahsek pawed at his coated eyes, Sinkua quickly assessed the circumstances.

"Nikasu! Vielle!" he called out, "Get out! I'll finish things here!"

Bracing on each other, Vielle and Nikasu reluctantly scrambled to the door. They shut themselves in the stairwell and waited at the bottom, despite Sinkua's command.

Sinkua threw a jab at the spider mine, but, his sight restored, Yahsek gouged his forearm and jerked him aside. Yahsek shredded the puncture wounds as he withdrew his claws and slashed down Sinkua's torso, slicing from shoulder to opposite hip.

With a guttural bellow, Sinkua plowed his fist into Yahsek's face. The beastly Faux-Hybrid's nose collapsed, and shattered teeth nicked his throat. Sinkua bashed the side of Yahsek's head with his morningstar, firelight glinting off the blood spewing from the smoldering wounds.

Sinkua dropped to his knees, his episode unchecked for too long. Thickened blood dribbled over his lips and caked his beard as he strained to breath between coughs. Yahsek positioned his hoof over the back of Sinkua's head.

A tangle of blades and chains flew from a direction long disregarded, falling clumsily against his back and hitting the floor unceremoniously. Puzzled and frustrated, Yahsek left Sinkua to fall deeper into his episode and turned to address the interruption.

Nikasu and Vielle hurried out of the stairwell and to Sinkua's side.

Pahres shambled in the general direction of Yahsek, scarcely able to stand upright, much less walk, in his battered state. Blood trickled from his festering eye socket, a steady rhythm dripping from the severed vein.

"I won't... let... you stop them," Pahres gasped, "Yggdrasil... will... take root."

"Yggdrasil was destroyed thousands of years ago," Yahsek chortled, swaggering toward Pahres as his limbs reverted to their human form.

"Only as... you know it."

Yahsek plowed his knee into Pahres's stomach and hammered his temple. Pahres winced and stumbled but, with defiance transcendent of pain, erected himself once more. Grunting with each blow, Yahsek clobbered Pahres's already battered upper body.

"Beat me... all you wish. Someone like... you... can never... hurt me," Pahres huffed, "I have... redemption. Nothing... can change... that. Not even... you."

In an ephemeral flicker of lucidity, Pahres palmed Yahsek's fist, intercepting it in front of his throat. His muscles quaked as he strained against the infuriated Faux-Hybrid, the very thought of standing upright heavily taxing his body. Driven by a surge of adrenaline, Pahres twisted Yahsek's arm into a hammerlock and pressed his other arm across his neck, pulling him back into a chokehold.

"But I still refuse to die on anyone's terms but my own."

Pahres released Yahsek's wrist and pounded the button on the spider mine. The device exploded through both their bodies, vomiting smoldering entrails out of their backs. They collapsed together, smoke streaming from gaping holes in their torsos. Their lifeless bodies collapsed upon the tiles, Pahres wearing an expression of serenity with his arm still clutching Yahsek's throat.

"He... He just..." Nikasu stammered, "He killed himself! Why? Why would he do that!?"

"He sacrificed himself so we could escape," Sinkua corrected, his voice still hoarse with blood and phlegm, "For Vielle. So she could plant Yggdrasil."

"But... But he could have..." Nikasu grasped, struggling to come to grips with this man she barely knew giving his life to destroy her nemesis.

"That man chose to die to protect what was important to him. He stood up for something, and he only fell when and where he allowed himself to," Sinkua asserted, holding Nikasu's shoulders and looking firmly into her eyes, "We cannot take that for granted."

"Right," Vielle absently nodded, her eyes locked on the macabre spectacle, "Come on. We still have work to do."

The elevator doors groaned open, the floor restless as Galo and Eytea stepped off into the round corridor. Feeling the floor shift, Galo braced his knees and craned his neck to peer around the bends. The door directly across from the elevator seemed too obvious to not be a trap, but there were no others as far as he could see.

"This isn't the time for cold feet," Eytea scolded, misreading his apprehension.

"It isn't that," Galo dismissed, grabbing the door handle, "Watch your step."

Inside the monolithic penthouse, machinery and terminals far beyond either of their kens lined the silvery walls. Seemingly alien technology hummed and pulsated, each in its own rhythm, the composite flirting with chaos. Layers of digital meter melded in a sort of inverse synergy, coalescing into less than the sum of its parts.

A series of plated window panels spanned a quarter of the perimeter, indicating that the round corridor tapered off just beyond the vantage point from the elevator. Masonry fragments quaked loose by the Mechanical Crypt plinked against the glass as they fell from the overhang. The highrise across the boulevard leaned toward Laboratory 1341. Larger fragments broke away from the southern faces of the buildings and shattered against the pavement.

Light pierced through as steam hissed from a wall panel, drawing Galo's and Eytea's attention. The panel slid inside the wall, opening to brilliant cerulean luminescence. A silhouette donning a trench coat emerged, his features assuming definition as the wall shut itself behind him.

"You're not who I expected," The Geneticist grimaced, snapping his tonfa from its strappings, "But if I can't save either of you for The Engineer, it's her own damn fault for running late. Victims of consequence and all."

"Victims of consequence, indeed," Eytea derided, "The Engineer is dead. Killed by SenRas. You know. The same man who broke Kabehl's little toy."

"I can't say I'm surprised. Nor can I grieve her death. Only her failure. She had become obsessed with vengeance. Just as I'm sure the two of you are," The Geneticist goaded, "Why else would you come here on the eve of such a cataclysm? To deliver an empty threat? Perhaps an ultimatum?"

"No ultimatums. No threats. Not even vengeance," Galo flatly countered, drawing his glaive, "Such petty words will never amount to adequate punishment for your atrocities. No. I'm only here to do what's necessary."

"Then, get on with it!" The Geneticist snapped, pointing at Galo with his tonfa as the blades jutted from the ends.

Galo carved the air in three intersecting arcs, his glaive streaming with a milystic shimmer. Three arcs of ice traced its path, ripping forth at the end of each swing.

The Geneticist leaned back to dodge the first, his spine bending implausibly. His torso flowed upright, rippling as he erected himself. The second blade of ice sliced through the side of his coat, threatening to split and dislodge a kidney. His skin parted and folded in on itself, stretching inward from hip to navel. He turned his back to the third blade as the second crashed into a terminal. The milystic ice sank into the tanned hide, melting into an array of blue light that rippled and dissipated along the surface.

"Son of a bitch," Eytea muttered, clutching her halberd.

"After the humiliation I suffered, I decided to upgrade," The Geneticist boasted, "But what of you? Same as always, I suppose?"

"This sounds just like you, Ebralgi," Galo sneered, his voice stinging as he spoke his birth name, "Destroying others to advance yourself. Tell me, how well did you sleep after you poisoned your sister?"

"Don't you dare lecture me on matters of conscience!" Ebralgi roared, "I destroy only what is necessary. The Chieftain Bloodline has long impeded the Avatars of Fate. Lord Harvester decreed it to be severed."

"My mother was not of the Chieftain Bloodline!" Galo bellowed.

"No, but she proved instrumental to it," The Geneticist drolled, "Thus we made of her an instrument at our disposal."

"Enough talking!" Eytea snapped.

Shielding her face with one wing, she rushed forth with her halberd drawn back. The spearhead crackled as it carved the floor, and she sliced upward between The Geneticist's legs.

His torso gullied up its center, stretching away from the sparking blades. He wedged his tonfa between the blades, stopping the halberd just short of his chin.

Eytea's arms trembled as she strained to move her halberd. A rippling of flesh flowed down The Geneticist's arms and into his hands as he shoved the weapon back. The handle slid through Eytea's grip, lurching nearer to her abdomen.

Galo swept in from the side, beyond The Geneticist's peripheral vision, and stabbed through the gash in his coat. The Geneticist's attention never straying from Eytea, his torso split open to Galo's growing bewilderment. Overwhelmed with frustration, Galo slashed and stabbed furiously. Yet no matter how quickly or deeply he struck, the flesh parted and thus rendered his assault impotent. A passive glimmer in the corner of The Geneticist's eye taunted Galo's constant failure.

The Geneticist jabbed Eytea's stomach with the butt of her halberd and dislodged his tonfa. Bored with Galo's impotent rage, he slashed at the hydromantic Hybrid. Eytea fired a jolt of electricity from her spearhead, only for the energy to dissipate along the grains of his coat.

Galo leaned back from the bladed tonfa, grabbed it by the grip, and shoved it back. With the abrupt reversal of momentum, he ripped the weapon from The Geneticist's hand. The nigh untouchable Avatar's composure briefly shaken, Galo clocked him across the side of his head.

The cracking of carbon steel against bone resonated along the curved walls. Galo followed with a blow to the opposite temple, The Geneticist grinding his teeth in pain and aggravation. Galo grabbed him by the lower jaw and thrust his tonfa at his face.

As Galo stabbed at him, Eytea fired another jolt of milystic lightning, this one aimed at his seemingly vulnerable head. The Geneticist grabbed the tonfa, stopping it short of gouging his skull. A surge of electricity enveloped his head, quaking it violently. The bombarding current arced down his arms, passing under his trench coat, and into the carbon steel rod. His palms singed by the electrocution, Galo blurted an expletive as he released the tonfa.

Eytea dashed forth, gliding just above the floor. The Geneticist slashed as she closed in, but she swiftly pivoted and flew back out of his reach, positioning herself across from Galo. She slashed and stabbed at The Geneticist's torso, triggering its now predictable contortions.

As The Geneticist's body warped and stretched away from Eytea, Galo pummeled the mounds of flesh cropping out from his back. His skin rippled with each landed blow, their impact dissipating throughout his body. Galo grabbed an outcropping, working his fingers into it as it tried to retract and normalize.

The Geneticist tried to turn to face him, but Galo held fast and moved with him. He reached behind his shoulder with his tonfa, only for Eytea to take to being disregarded with a stomping kick to the stomach. Aligning the blow with the fistful of flesh in Galo's grasp, her strike knocked The Geneticist deeper into his clutches.

The Serpent Bracer pulsated with a swelling cerulean glow, the sound of Leviathan's breath echoing within Galo's mind. Crystalline patterns spread along The Geneticist's flesh. The Berininite Avatar writhed and grumbled, his groan crescendoing into a labored cry of pain.

The fistful of iced flesh broke loose, vomiting a spectacular array of crystalline blood. Leviathan's breath and the glow of the Serpent Bracer faded in tandem. The spider web crystal pattern dissipated from The Geneticist's back. Galo clocked the back of his head with the organic trophy. Beyond the window, police helicopters navigated the raining debris. Galo discarded his prize against the window with a vicious grunt, denting the glass.

Teeth clenched in fury, The Geneticist grabbed Eytea by the neck, clamping her throat. Pain shot down her arms, and she dropped her halberd. He tossed her aside dismissively. As she slid along the silvery tiles, he whipped around and sliced with his modified tonfa.

Galo took the slash across his chest and plunged his glaive into The Geneticist's abdomen. Blood dripped from the blade as the tip poked through his back. The Geneticist's face contorted into a look of shock, the blow to his ego perhaps wounding him more than that to his body. Galo stepped forward, walking him toward the window. An isolated sound of rapidly buffeting air closed in from above.

Galo ripped his glaive out of The Geneticist's abdomen, flinging a trail of blood over his shoulder. The Geneticist doubled over, clutching his gaping wound. Blood gurgled in his throat. A helicopter emblazoned with the logo of West Bend General Hospital descended hovered near the window.

"You brat," The Geneticist snarled, "Both of you. Such brats. Do you have any idea what you're meddling with?"

"Do you?" Galo challenged, "You've spent years trying to copy and obsolete us. Yet even with your supposed upgrades, you've all but failed."

"You are blinded by power you neither deserved nor earned," The Geneticist goaded, pulling his bloody hands away to show the wound fusing shut, "I am far from finished."

"That's not what he meant," Eytea smirked.

The side door of the helicopter opened. Malia braced herself and leveled the shotgun, aligning The Geneticist in its scope. Her brows knitted tight as the stream of blood down his back tapered off, the once gaping wound rippling shut.

Three gunshots rang out, three bullets wedging into the plated glass in rapid succession. The Geneticist snickered at the predictable failure of the aerial cavalry.

Malia opened the chamber and reloaded the shotgun with a single modified bullet. She tightened the straps of her emergency parachute as they began to slip off her shoulders. With painstaking effort, she aligned the tight cluster of bullet holes in the scope.

"That was it?" The Geneticist challenged, breaking the stretch of apprehensive silence.

A fourth bullet punctured the damaged window. His sealing wound reopened at the sound of glass breaking. The altered bullet zipped through him harmlessly, boring into Galo's midsection instead.

Malia recoiled in shock and contrition. Not only had she failed at her mission, the mission she had wrested from SenRas, she had put a bullet in one of the Hybrids. She dropped her shotgun, her hands trembling. The emptied firearm bounced and tumbled out of the helicopter.

Galo doubled over and fell to his knees, clutching his stomach. Diluted blood seeped between his fingers as he soaked the wound in boiling water. His face screwed up and body trembled in agony, the stabbing pain of the bullet hole and the searing of melting the wound shut both paling next to the strain of his every joint hardening. His very bones seemed to petrify from within.

Eytea watched in horror, struggling to collect herself long enough to protect him. As she managed to level her halberd and steady her legs, The Geneticist pitched his tonfa at her with a dismissive grunt. She dropped to her knees to parry the bladed carbon steel rod.

The Geneticist pulled Galo to his feet by his bottom jaw. Galo struggled to clench his fist, ultimately failing as the Hunter Formula grafted to his marrow. His glaive remained in his grasp only by the butt of the blade nestling in the crook of his thumb and index finger. The Geneticist grabbed the back of his shirt collar, spun around, and bashed his head against the damaged glass.

Cracks spread from the bullet holes in a spider web pattern. The Geneticist pounded him against the plated glass again, further stretching the cracks. Movement becoming slightly less labored, Galo folded his arms over the top of his head. The glass gave way on the next blow.

An entire window panel burst outward in a spectacular array of glass fragments tinged red at the center. Shards became embedded in Galo's arms and scalp. More stung his chest and legs as he tumbled through the spray, adorning his clothes with wisps of blood.

A voice cried out through the tumult and deafening pain, muffled but calling his name. Glass shards ripped along his exposed face as he looked up.

Malia stood in the open side door of the West Bend helicopter, her arm drawn back with a backpack hanging from her hand. She hurled the parachute pack at Galo in a final desperate effort to save him from her failure.

Recognizing the telltale loop and string, Galo reached out with his glaive. A strap hooked on the blade, threatening to either disarm him or split against the edge. Freefalling from the leaning highrise, Galo slung the pack from his glaive to his shoulder. He hastily secured the other strap and pulled the string, deploying the parachute. Shaken by the abruptly altered momentum, his weapon dropped from his grip and tumbled toward the quaking ground.

A blow to the back disrupted what had become a smooth descent, jostling his briefly calmed mind back into a panic. The northern face of Laboratory 1341 crashed against his back as the city shifted below. He scraped down the wall, his parachute raking along the framed glass and rough masonry. He kicked off in an effort to gain some distance on the northwardly creeping structure.

Snagged on cracks and outcroppings, the parachute ripped as Galo kicked away. His fall now unencumbered, he tumbled and bounced down the face of the tower. Between the aggravating jostling of each collision, he noticed the pain gradually subsiding. Realizing he could move freely again, he slid out of the now useless parachute pack.

Galo braced his feet against the wall, laying on his side with his arm stretched upward. Blood and debris caked in his palm as he slid down the face of the highrise. He closed his eyes and balled his free hand into a white-knuckle fist, the Serpent Bracer glowing brilliantly.

Galo sprang out from a fifth story window. The cerulean glow of the Serpent Bracer swallowed his arm. The greened copper heirloom pulsated with its hunger to envelop his body in its milystic light. He drew back his fist as he plummeted, releasing a war bellow from the depths of his lungs.

He landed on three points, two feet and a palm heel cracking the pavement. His backdrawn fist barreled downward with the coupled momentum of gravity and adrenalized strength. Asphalt shattered under the impact of his reinforced knuckles, spewing from the quaking boulevard.

The shape of the Serpent Bracer, formed only as blue light now, coiled down his arm and into the hole. Cracks spread from the point of impact, traced in cerulean glow, their reach marked by concentric rings. Brilliant milystis exploded upward, discarding and obliterating the fragmented asphalt.

A familiar yet unfathomable warmth surrounded him. The milystic column lifted him into itself, his body ascending it with his glaive floating by his side. Below, the light condensed and faded into duller but more varied shades of turquoise and bronze, the edges forming into colossal scales. At the zenith of the pillar of light, an enormous head lined with intricate horns took shape. The incorporeal warmth released him, setting him atop the head of the towering serpent.

"Le-Leviathan?" he asked, more out of disbelief than uncertainty.

"'Tis I, friend. It is an honor to finally meet you," Leviathan professed, speaking aloud now, "and a privilege to once again be free."

"And I you," Galo said, reclaiming his glaive from the last traces of sapphire light, "Can you see if my friends have made it out?"

"All have safely departed the building."

"Perfect. Now, let's end this."

Leviathan stretched her mouth wide, baring scores of serrated teeth in her abyssal maw. With her bonded Hybrid mounted atop her, she roared down upon the tower wherein he had saved her from apocalyptic sacrifice. Her teeth shredded masonry and structural beams, stripping away the roof and baring The Geneticist's penthouse operations. Eytea flew through the hole where the roof had been, leaving The Geneticist hypnotized in terror.

"Come on!" Galo bellowed, fixing his steely glare upon and pointing his glaive at The Geneticist.

Leviathan descended upon the tower once more, her jaw gaping. Her teeth rended concrete and rebar with ease, flesh and bone all the more so. The Geneticist's remains lay shredded along her incisors.

Leviathan spat the carcass into the cold dusk wind, slunk down, and coiled around the tower. Support beams warped, buckled, and snapped as she constricted. Chunks of masonry broke away, bouncing off her scales and raining onto the ravaged boulevard. Tiled concrete and rebar snapped and shattered. Elevator shafts twisted and collapsed on themselves.

Leviathan unwrapped herself, the terranean remains of Laboratory 1341 rolling off of her body. The debris overflowed the exposed basement levels, collapsing their internal structures into a cavern of rubble.

"It is finished," Leviathan proclaimed.

"Not yet," Galo worried, "Why hasn't the Mechanical Crypt stopped?"

"Once activated, continued function does not require the power core."

"Of course it doesn't," he grumbled, "Okay, I have an idea. How quickly can you get to the northern border."

"I will return to my metallic state. Drop me in the sewer, and I can reach my destination within one of your hours."

"Will you be able to...?"

"Now that you have freed me, yes. Until the end of your generation, I can convert states at will, yours or mine," Leviathan explained as her body shrank, "Being that I exist beyond your perceived dimensions, so too may I manipulate the measure of my presence. What would you have me do?"

"Go to the Northland Sea and hold back the island," Galo ordered, resisting the urge to prod for more answers.

"What you ask of me is likely impossible," Leviathan cautioned.

"Slow it as best you can."

"As you wish, but I implore you to neither expect nor rely upon miracles."

"I… don't even know that word."

With a look of curiosity frozen in her eyes, Leviathan's flesh converted to greened copper, her body resuming the shape of the Serpent Bracer. Galo slipped her over his forearm and ran to the nearest sewer lid.

"Galo!" someone called through the tectonic discord.

"Sinkua?" Galo shouted back.

"Galo!" Sinkua exclaimed, emerging through the choking dust, "Was that Leviathan? How did you do that?"

"Yes, but I'm… not entirely sure," Galo half-fibbed, "We still have a lot of work to do."

Another figure burst through the dust and smoke, trailed by three more silhouettes. Nikasu rushed to Galo's side, crashing her body into his. Choking back tears, she clutched his shirt with one hand and impotently thumped his chest with the other.

"You big idiot!" Nikasu screamed, "Don't scare me like that! Jumping out of windows, and… and… whatever that was!"

"Nikasu! Nikasu," Galo urged, holding her hands, "I'm sorry. I was thrown. And the rest, well… I'm sorry I scared you. But I'm fine now. Truly. And you?"

"Yahsek is dead," Vielle reported, emerging from behind Nikasu.

"But we lost Pahres," Nikasu added, "He, um… He sacrificed himself to kill Yahsek. And to protect us."

"All that's left is to stop the Mechanical Crypt," Spril added, "No way Ozzera could have survived the demolition."

"I'm working on that," Galo said, "Sinkua, help me with this sewer access."

"I suppose you and Leviathan have a plan?" Gabdur asked, hobbling alongside Spril, "Yet again, I cannot thank you enough."

"I'm sending her to the northern coast. She's going to try to hold the severed land in place," Galo explained, "Vielle, once she's stopped the ground from shifting, we need you to plant Yggdrasil."

"I'll do what I can," Vielle promised.

"I know you will," Galo nodded, "Pahres said it spans reality, so I'm assuming it can anchor half a country."

He jammed the butt of his glaive into a hole in the sewer lid. Sinkua took the lower half of the shaft, and together they pried the lid out of the hole. Galo kissed the head of the Serpent Bracer and dropped it into the sewer.

Eytea swooped down among them as Galo and Sinkua replaced the sewer cover. With the southern faces of neighboring highrises looming ever closer, she threw her arms around Sinkua's neck. The gemstone in her ring shimmered warmly at his touch.

"You're still alive," she smiled, "Once we stop the island, it's over, right?"

"Sure, but first we have to survive long enough to stop it," Sinkua countered, "Leviathan is going to try to push it back, and then Vielle will plant Yggdrasil."

"The closer she plants it to the Mechanical Crypt, the better," Gabdur added, shouting over the noise of shattering wreckage.

"We'll help with the evac efforts in the meantime," Spril ordered, "Let's move!"

Walls sloughed off of their infrastructure, baring fractured support beams. Reinforced masonry rained upon the streets, battering both upon impact. Piercing screams rang out through the tumult, punctuating people's final moments.

They hurried along the boulevard in search of survivors. Eytea soared a few meters above, guiding lost refugees to nearby rescue helicopters along relatively safe routes.

A West Bend helicopter landed in the intersection at the end of the block. Malia jumped out and beckoned them along, offering a means of escape. Nikasu slowed as Malia came more clearly into view though, unwittingly mirroring her expression as it transformed from hopeful urgency to bewildered panic.

A cacophony of stone and metal permeated the thundering of collapsing architecture. The noise compounded, drawing nearer and crescendoing into undeniable dissonance. Nikasu white-knuckled her scythes, her hands trembling.

Vielle turned to call for her, but her voice caught as she discovered the source of the cacophony, an incarnation of madness compiled from blocks of urban ruins.

"Nikasu!" Vielle screamed, her voice exploding through the constriction of fear.

Nikasu jerked about, coming to face a plague of chaotically structured biomechs stretching toward the horizon. She drew back a scythe with a shriek of desperate anger, the blade crackling with gravimantic milystis. Numerous abominations erupted from the wreckage as others assembled from the churning detritus.

A bolt of lightning shot from behind Nikasu, forking to obliterate three of the airborne beasts. Nikasu leapt back and slashed another as it dropped upon her, shredding flesh and collapsing the stone skeleton under its own amplified weight. She bisected the next with a slash of her second blade.

"Malia!" Spril called, "Take Gabdur and get out of here! The rest of us will stay and contain these things."

"I won't leave my son like this!" Gabdur protested.

"You're in no shape to help," Spril countered, "Get in."

"Where should we go?" Malia asked.

"Help evacuate Sinkua's neighborhood. Elemeno is still there."

"You got it. Tell my girls I'll come back to see them when this is over," Malia requested, "Come on, Gabdur. Let's go save some more lives."

Vielle cracked her thorny cat-o'-nine-tails into the swarm, rending strips of flesh from multiple drones. Galo carved through the growing crowd of abominations, curved blades of ice flying from the edge of his glaive. Sinkua rushed into the assault with his morningstar flailing wildly, drawing their offenses and obliterating them as they attacked. Eytea swooped in and out of the massacre, skewering creatures on her halberd and arcing lightning throughout clusters of them. Nikasu scissored and impaled airborne abominations with her twin scythes, flooding their amorphic bodies with devastating g-force. Spril pulverized biomechs with alternating ends of his quarterstaff, deflecting the beasts of chaos as they launched themselves at him.

"What the fuck is going on!?" Spril barked.

"Ozzera must still be alive," Nikasu called back.

"Leviathan destroyed the building," Spril protested, "Nobody could have survived that."

"She's either deeper down," Sinkua grunted, scorching the remains of a biomech as they fell from it shattered core, "or hooked up off-site."

"Either way, we need to go back so Vielle can plant Yggdrasil," Galo reminded, sweeping a sheet of ice through a cluster of biomechs, "Come on!"

They hurried back down the thirteen hundred block, maneuvering over the quickening ruins of the north side of Heniokhos Boulevard. Sinkua, Vielle, and Nikasu forced a path through the swarm. Galo and Spril brought up the rear, running backward and fending off drones newly born out of the wreckage behind them. Eytea circled above, picking off biomechs closing in from the periphery.

Highrises swayed and crumbled. Sirens wailed throughout the tumultuous carnage. Rescue helicopters navigated columns of smoke and choking aerial detritus. Towers collapsed upon vehicles packed with evacuees, trucks and helicopters alike. Crooked propellers snapped off of their mounts, flailing madly and annihilating biomechs as they crashed into the living wreckage.

Galo arched an eyebrow, his jaw tightening and teeth grinding, as he noticed a frightful curiosity developing. A swelling of flickering red lights swept toward them in the wake of devitalized wreckage, the sensors of felled biomechs renewed. The ruins of the highrise district came ablaze with hundreds upon hundreds of crimson oculi. Biomech drones reassembled and compiled into new larger chaotic forms, enveloping their bodies in raw sinew.

Swarms of renascent abominations launched themselves at Galo and Spril. Eytea electrocuted the biomechs from above, milystic lightning arcing throughout the pack. Spril aimed for the sensors, shattering the red power cores with the end of his quarterstaff. Galo bisected drones with his crystalline glaive, splitting their cores and freezing the circuitry within.

The pursuing creatures consumed and assimilated the remains of their fallen ilk, individuals growing larger and stronger as their numbers diminished. Biomechs dwarfing sedans barreled through the wreckage with appendages of architecture and sinew flailing wildly. They gorged themselves on the rubble as they ravaged the highrise district, insatiably building upon themselves.

"Brother!" Galo desperately called over his shoulder.

"I know!" Sinkua called back, "We've got the same problem!"

Overgrown biomechs swarmed in from all sides, their footfalls shattering debris and feeding scraps to their maddening forms. Vielle manipulated her cat-o'-nine-tails around their limbs, grinding through flesh with curved jagged thorns. Nikasu threw herself atop them, plunging her blades into their backs and overwhelming their bodies with destructive g-force. Galo carved through fleshy layers of masonry and steel with his icy glaive, parrying their slashing claws as he dug for their power cores. Sinkua sundered appendages with his blazing morningstar, incinerating the amputation wounds and stunting their reassembly. Eytea swooped down in a streak of amethyst, impaling biomechs on her halberd and overloading their bodies with electrified milystis. Spril cracked his quarterstaff across appendages in rapidly formulating patterns, shattering cores through openings of his own forging.

Their efforts, however, proved largely ineffective. With several blocks of urban ruins to gorge themselves on, the growth of each creature far outpaced the depletion of their numbers.

A single coherent structure emerged from the remnants of the thirteen hundred block, a cylinder radiating an ominous red glow. Power cores shone more brightly in its vicinity, shimmering and flickering blindingly as though their proximity threatened to overload their circuitry.

Sinkua's eyes flared with tsavorite glow, peering through the crimson glare enveloping the cylinder. Ensconced within it was that wretched chimera, her body anchored to the luminous walls by a mad tangle of tubes and wires. With such power at her control, Gabdur's premonition rang all the more deeply. Surely, it would take all five of them to bring her down.

"It's Ozzera!" Sinkua bellowed.

He charged viciously, his morningstar flailing to the sides and scorching holes in flanking biomechs. Those who blocked his path, he shouldered at full sprint, challenging the durability of their hectically formed bodies. His bones screamed with every impact, his chest quaking with increasingly ragged breath.

A ferocious war bellow began erupting from his lungs at he reentered the thirteen hundred block. The roar rolled from his throat as he stormed into the epicenter of the disaster, reverberating through plasmatic phlegm in the back of his throat. He spun his morningstar with increasing ferocity, its fiery head streaking against the backdrop of the approaching dawn.

Sinkua punctuated his warcry with the crash of his morningstar against the biogenesis chamber. A brilliant spray of fire and crimson light exploded from a luminous barricade surrounding the capsule, ricocheting his weapon and yanking him back by his arm.

Ozzera grimaced wickedly, all three pairs of eyes fixing their cold stare upon him. They called out in unified fury, a chaotic chorus of roaring, bleating, and hissing.

A spike in the wreckage rippled to life, churning the ruins as it rushed down Heniokhos Boulevard. It swelled into a living wave, rending biomechs and consuming their scraps. Sinkua holstered his morningstar and rushed after it, weaving around the few drones to have survived the cannibalistic wave.

The tsunami of wreckage cast aside his friends with little regard, their bodies bouncing along the municipal ruins in dwindling consciousness. It assimilated even the largest of the biomechs, growing incontestably massive. The trail of living ruins coalesced under Eytea, churning as fragments of shattered power cores assembled into a monolithic oculus.

Sinkua pounded out the last meters of churning wake in long loping strides. Eytea swooped and bobbed erratically, desperately trying to shake the stalking roil of coalescing wreckage.

Galo struggled to his feet, looking toward the northern horizon. He patted Vielle's shoulder and pointed to the skyline. Vielle hobbled into the thirteen hundred block, crescendoing toward a limping run.

A spire of sinew and razed architecture erupted from the churning ruins. Sinkua holstered his morningstar and leapt from the wreckage, reaching for the growing column of sentient rubble. He caught it high and climbed to the peak, riding it as it roared skyward.

Eytea darted about in a panic. Her halberd dropped from her trembling hands. The spire closed in on her, corralling her.

Sinkua launched himself from the top of the column, arms outstretched to pull her from its path. Eytea reached for him, so failing in her efforts to escape that she poured the entirety of her trust into his desperately hatched gambit.

The sentient pillar bludgeoned Sinkua, sending him tumbling to the ground. He rolled over as he fell and reached for Eytea helplessly, screaming in agonized protest. Blood churned in his throat, eyes welling with tears as the inevitable transpired beyond his reach.

The renascent rubble spiraled into a point and drilled into Eytea's abdomen. It shredded her entrails, her body quaking with devastating agony as she reached down for Sinkua. Her wings grew rigid, her body held aloft by the sinewy wreckage. Her spine shattered, paralyzing her in her final seconds. Her wings ripped from her back as the appendage carved out of her epidermis, reddened plumage exploding into the cold howling wind. The resonant call of Sinkua's name burst of her lungs, riding into the bloodstained wind on her final breath.

Sinkua crashed onto the ruins, his eyes flooding with tears. His chest bounced with feverish breath. His eyes fixated on the macabre spectacle, his fingers grinding into the rubble under his back. Bloody feathers rained upon him, her wings landing on either side of him. A guttural outcry erupted from the greatest depths of his lungs.

Sinkua lurched to his feet, his entire body trembling. Eytea's lifeless body landed beside him, crushing one of her own severed wings. He turned to see her face once more, his eyes twitching with incomprehensible madness. A hardened expression of fear and agony had chiseled itself into her face, indelibly burning his failure into his memories.

He unraveled his morningstar and set it ablaze with a blinding milystic inferno, his every thought consumed by vengeance. The fire churned angrily, his turbulent thoughts incapable of controlling it. Flames swept over his body, extinguishing and reigniting chaotically.

The biomechanical appendage curled downward. Sinkua swung at the beastly spire, but with his vision distorted by tears, the creature bludgeoned him onto his back. He rose in defiance of death, but it knocked him aside yet again. Over and over, he tried to stand against the wretched amorphic beast, only to be effortlessly cast off.

The reality of his impotence sank in quickly. It could have slaughtered him several times over, but it, or rather Ozzera, made sport of him. She had slain Eytea to set an example and now exerted her dominance by repeatedly demonstrating his inferiority, carving it into every facet of his mind.

Sinkua forced himself to his hands and knees purely on decaying resolve, the paralysis of capitulation setting in. The spire of living wreckage loomed above, curling down toward him. The tip split in four, spreading like some horrible alien mouth. A deafening shriek erupted from the monolithic scarlet power core in its throat. Sinkua covered his head and huddled atop the rubble.

Spril intercepted the assault as though he spontaneously manifested from the choking air between Sinkua and the abomination. He raised his hand to the creature, aligning his palm with the center of the core. The appendages enveloped both of them. Spril dug his boots into the wreckage, staring defiantly into the cold crimson oculus.

His arm jolted with a surge of indescribable energy. The massive power core shattered in the throat of the beast in a shower of glinting red particulate. The cocooning appendages snapped back, ricocheting off the force of the explosion. The biomechanical spire collapsed into a heap of its own remains.

Power cores shattered in brilliant crimson display all along Heniokhos Boulevard. The lights in the biogenesis chamber burst, circuitry exploding and scorching Ozzera's flesh. Her heads dropped, consciousness expelled from her body by the invasive power surge.

The Platinum Orchid shimmered jade in Vielle's grasp as she ran. Vines sprouted from her arms like hairs standing with anticipation. Thousands of voices screamed inside her mind, their words incomprehensible in both their numbers and their tongues.

With a snap of her elbow and a flick of her wrist, she flung the artifact at the defunct chamber and the stunned chimera within. Ozzera lifted her lion head groggily, choking out a defiant roar as the Platinum Orchid sailed toward her. The relic bounced and settled under the biogenesis chamber. Vielle exhaled, the vines along her arms retracting.

A brilliant column of emerald light erupted from the ground, shining through the chamber and stretching skyward. Ozzera seized violently, overwhelmed by the bombardment of concentrated arbormantic milystis. A narrow tree trunk manifested up the center of the column, impaling Ozzera as it gained opacity. The trunk spread to fill the milystic pillar, pulverizing the biogenesis chamber and obliterating the chimera.

Radiant milystic roots bored through the rubble and deep into the ground, snaking far beyond the ruinous highrise district. Limbs rich with foliage erupted from the trunk, stretching toward every horizon. The trunk expanded beyond the pillar of light, effortlessly hurling wreckage from the path of its growth.

Each of them held fast to the base of a root, riding the trunk as it stretched across the highrise district. Sinkua reached for Eytea, but an outcropping root snatched her body and carried it beyond his reach. Galo pinned him to the trunk as he lunged for her, his face tightening with the pain of saving his brother by denying him the solace of his deceased fiancée's hand.

Now expanded across several ruinous city blocks, the growth of the trunk gradually tapered off. Branches abundant with flora lined the monolithic trunk from base to peak, the highest limbs taking residence among the clouds and reaching toward all horizons.

The quaking stopped as the growth halted.

    Yggdrasil had taken root once more.

    Listless days and restless nights blurred together, dilating and contracting into an indeterminate warping of time. Vielle and Nikasu accompanied Malia to Tanelen to investigate Phylus's disappearance. Spril and EshCal poured themselves into restoration and relief efforts. Elemeno returned home to Ferya, distraught over the demise of her last remaining kin. Galo returned to his duties in Berinin, inviting Gabdur to visit the annexed island. SenRas, Biroe, and KalChi investigated Noble Doyen Joren, focusing on his communications with the late Chairman LenSom and once Prime Duchess Olsa. MarLys assisted with their research as an informer and third party advisor. Ophalin returned to his medical practice in Ferya and Yrlis to her research of the Sisyphus Fir, the two comparing notes on genomic studies when their schedules allowed it.

    Sinkua sat alone in his time of greatest despair. Galo's words rang hollow in his memory. Counterfeit friends abandoned him, disregarding his pain and leaving him to stew in solitary mourning.

    In the depths of a nearly moonless night, he grabbed a screwdriver from a kitchen drawer and hobbled upstairs. His hands steady for the first time in countless days, he removed their bedroom door. With two lengths of rope from the garage, he strapped the door to his back with the engraving facing outward.

    Sinkua walked along the roots of Yggdrasil, his head low and his focus singular. He hiked across numerous days and nights, stopping for rest and food only when the lack of either threatened to cast him into a coma or the embrace of death. He fed on fallen leaves and strips of root bark, refusing to stray from his path in the delirium of his bereavement.

    He arrived in the northwest highrise district, teetering on the precipice of death. He circled the trunk in search of Eytea's body. Beneath the base, the roots stretched beyond sight into an inky chasm. A tiny glimmer caught his eye, sparkling within a tangle of roots near the trunk.

    Energized by the discovery, he rushed to it as best as his ailing body permitted. Indeed, an emaciated fingertip lay against a root, adorned with her engagement ring. He fell to his knees, tears of relief trickling down his sallow and sunken cheeks. His elation dissolved as he clutched her hand however, finding it severed at the middle of her forearm.

    He staggered backward, clutching her hand to his chest but fearful of the state of the rest of her body. His back crashed against the trunk. He gazed up its imposing height, stretching into the night sky, and down the chasm of roots, reaching into absolute darkness.

    He propped the door against the trunk of Yggdrasil. With tearful eyes his plunged his dagger into it, just above the word he had carved for her all those years ago. He hung his necklace from the dagger, a sharp chill flooding his veins. He kissed her fingers and pressed her hand to his chest. Perched on a root, he pulled his bandana down over his eyes.

    Sinkua leaned forth and surrendered himself to the abyss.

Epilogue

"Another has come?"

"Where are we?"

"Beyond. I suppose."

"How long have you been here?"

"Time is irrelevant. How did you come here?"

"I don't remember. Do you remember how you ended up here?"

"I got in over my head. They learned of my work."

"Your work?"

"Eyes of the Dragon bring meals, yet still even I cannot find an exit. "

"Eyes of the Dragon? Who are you?"

"Is it her? Could she have sent you?"

"Could who have sent me?"

"My young lady was always so brilliant. Is she well?"

About the Author

Meticulous to the point of obsession and ambitious to the point of anxiety, E. A. Setser is a career author and publisher trapped in a day jobber's body. He holds a degree in accounting, which has nothing to do with his job in the commercial graphics industry, but it probably helps with being the founder of Social Detriment Publishing. Maybe.

Originally from Tennessee, E. A. and his wife Celia and son Tavin have been working to escape The Bible Belt. They have now made it to Lawrenceburg, IN.

Merch: https://www.zazzle.com/social_detriment
Twitter: https://twitter.com/EASetser
Facebook: www.facebook.com/SocialDetriment
Amazon: www.amazon.com/author/easetser